To all my wonderful friends and readers:

Happy tenth anniversary! It's hard to believe it's been so long since this all first got started. And yet, my little babies have turned into giant teenagers, so I can't escape the truth.

Thank you for ten years of adventure beyond my wildest expectations for my life. I am a very prosaic kind of person, but my experience with this community of readers has made me believe—just a little bit—in magic.

To celebrate this milestone, I've created some new bonus material to add to your enjoyment of the world of *Twilight*. (In typical Stephenie Meyer form, the bonus material is actually longer than *Twilight*.) You can find *Life and Death* by flipping this book over and starting from the back. I enjoyed revisiting Forks so very much, and I hope you have the same experience I did.

You are fantastic and I love you.

Thank you!
Stephenie

twilight

THE TENTH ANNIVERSARY EDITION

STEPHENIE MEYER

Megan Tingley Books

LITTLE, BROWN AND COMPANY

New York   Boston

Little, Brown and Company

Hachette Book Group
1290 Avenue of the Americas, New York, NY 10104
Visit us at lb-teens.com

Little, Brown and Company is a division of Hachette Book Group, Inc.
The Little, Brown name and logo are trademarks of Hachette Book Group, Inc.

The publisher is not responsible for websites (or their content)
that are not owned by the publisher.

Tenth Anniversary Edition: October 2015

ISBN: 978-0-316-26839-4

10 9 8 7 6 5 4 3 2 1

RRD-C

Printed in the United States of America

Zephyr Typeface used in *Twilight*. Software © P22 Type Foundry, Inc.

For my big sister, Emily,
without whose enthusiasm this story might still be unfinished.

➤➤ ◄◄

B ut of the tree of the knowledge of good and evil,
thou shalt not eat of it:
for in the day that thou eatest thereof
thou shalt surely die.

Genesis 2:17

PREFACE

I'D NEVER GIVEN MUCH THOUGHT TO HOW I WOULD DIE—THOUGH I'D had reason enough in the last few months—but even if I had, I would not have imagined it like this.

I stared without breathing across the long room, into the dark eyes of the hunter, and he looked pleasantly back at me.

Surely it was a good way to die, in the place of someone else, someone I loved. Noble, even. That ought to count for something.

I knew that if I'd never gone to Forks, I wouldn't be facing death now. But, terrified as I was, I couldn't bring myself to regret the decision. When life offers you a dream so far beyond any of your expectations, it's not reasonable to grieve when it comes to an end.

The hunter smiled in a friendly way as he sauntered forward to kill me.

1. FIRST SIGHT

My mother drove me to the airport with the windows rolled down. It was seventy-five degrees in Phoenix, the sky a perfect, cloudless blue. I was wearing my favorite shirt—sleeveless, white eyelet lace; I was wearing it as a farewell gesture. My carry-on item was a parka.

In the Olympic Peninsula of northwest Washington State, a small town named Forks exists under a near-constant cover of clouds. It rains on this inconsequential town more than any other place in the United States of America. It was from this town and its gloomy, omnipresent shade that my mother escaped with me when I was only a few months old. It was in this town that I'd been compelled to spend a month every summer until I was fourteen. That was the year I finally put my foot down; these past three summers, my dad, Charlie, vacationed with me in California for two weeks instead.

It was to Forks that I now exiled myself—an action that I took with great horror. I detested Forks.

I loved Phoenix. I loved the sun and the blistering heat. I loved the vigorous, sprawling city.

"Bella," my mom said to me—the last of a thousand times—before I got on the plane. "You don't have to do this."

My mom looks like me, except with short hair and laugh lines. I felt a spasm of panic as I stared at her wide, childlike eyes. How could I leave my loving, erratic, harebrained mother to fend for herself? Of course she had

Phil now, so the bills would probably get paid, there would be food in the refrigerator, gas in her car, and someone to call when she got lost, but still . . .

"I *want* to go," I lied. I'd always been a bad liar, but I'd been saying this lie so frequently lately that it sounded almost convincing now.

"Tell Charlie I said hi."

"I will."

"I'll see you soon," she insisted. "You can come home whenever you want—I'll come right back as soon as you need me."

But I could see the sacrifice in her eyes behind the promise.

"Don't worry about me," I urged. "It'll be great. I love you, Mom."

She hugged me tightly for a minute, and then I got on the plane, and she was gone.

It's a four-hour flight from Phoenix to Seattle, another hour in a small plane up to Port Angeles, and then an hour drive back down to Forks. Flying doesn't bother me; the hour in the car with Charlie, though, I was a little worried about.

Charlie had really been fairly nice about the whole thing. He seemed genuinely pleased that I was coming to live with him for the first time with any degree of permanence. He'd already gotten me registered for high school and was going to help me get a car.

But it was sure to be awkward with Charlie. Neither of us was what anyone would call verbose, and I didn't know what there was to say regardless. I knew he was more than a little confused by my decision—like my mother before me, I hadn't made a secret of my distaste for Forks.

When I landed in Port Angeles, it was raining. I didn't see it as an omen— just unavoidable. I'd already said my goodbyes to the sun.

Charlie was waiting for me with the cruiser. This I was expecting, too. Charlie is Police Chief Swan to the good people of Forks. My primary motivation behind buying a car, despite the scarcity of my funds, was that I refused to be driven around town in a car with red and blue lights on top. Nothing slows down traffic like a cop.

Charlie gave me an awkward, one-armed hug when I stumbled my way off the plane.

"It's good to see you, Bells," he said, smiling as he automatically caught and steadied me. "You haven't changed much. How's Renée?"

"Mom's fine. It's good to see you, too, Dad." I wasn't allowed to call him Charlie to his face.

I had only a few bags. Most of my Arizona clothes were too permeable for Washington. My mom and I had pooled our resources to supplement my winter wardrobe, but it was still scanty. It all fit easily into the trunk of the cruiser.

"I found a good car for you, really cheap," he announced when we were strapped in.

"What kind of car?" I was suspicious of the way he said "good car for *you*" as opposed to just "good car."

"Well, it's a truck actually, a Chevy."

"Where did you find it?"

"Do you remember Billy Black down at La Push?" La Push is the tiny Indian reservation on the coast.

"No."

"He used to go fishing with us during the summer," Charlie prompted.

That would explain why I didn't remember him. I do a good job of blocking painful, unnecessary things from my memory.

"He's in a wheelchair now," Charlie continued when I didn't respond, "so he can't drive anymore, and he offered to sell me his truck cheap."

"What year is it?" I could see from his change of expression that this was the question he was hoping I wouldn't ask.

"Well, Billy's done a lot of work on the engine—it's only a few years old, really."

I hoped he didn't think so little of me as to believe I would give up that easily. "When did he buy it?"

"He bought it in 1984, I think."

"Did he buy it new?"

"Well, no. I think it was new in the early sixties—or late fifties at the earliest," he admitted sheepishly.

"Ch—Dad, I don't really know anything about cars. I wouldn't be able to fix it if anything went wrong, and I couldn't afford a mechanic...."

"Really, Bella, the thing runs great. They don't build them like that anymore."

The thing, I thought to myself... it had possibilities—as a nickname, at the very least.

"How cheap is cheap?" After all, that was the part I couldn't compromise on.

"Well, honey, I kind of already bought it for you. As a homecoming gift." Charlie peeked sideways at me with a hopeful expression.

Wow. Free.

"You didn't need to do that, Dad. I was going to buy myself a car."

"I don't mind. I want you to be happy here." He was looking ahead at the road when he said this. Charlie wasn't comfortable with expressing his emotions out loud. I inherited that from him. So I was looking straight ahead as I responded.

"That's really nice, Dad. Thanks. I really appreciate it." No need to add that my being happy in Forks is an impossibility. He didn't need to suffer along with me. And I never looked a free truck in the mouth—or engine.

"Well, now, you're welcome," he mumbled, embarrassed by my thanks.

We exchanged a few more comments on the weather, which was wet, and that was pretty much it for conversation. We stared out the windows in silence.

It was beautiful, of course; I couldn't deny that. Everything was green: the trees, their trunks covered with moss, their branches hanging with a canopy of it, the ground covered with ferns. Even the air filtered down greenly through the leaves.

It was too green—an alien planet.

Eventually we made it to Charlie's. He still lived in the small, two-bedroom house that he'd bought with my mother in the early days of their marriage. Those were the only kind of days their marriage had—the early ones. There, parked on the street in front of the house that never changed, was my new—well, new to me—truck. It was a faded red color, with big, rounded fenders and a bulbous cab. To my intense surprise, I loved it. I didn't know if it would run, but I could see myself in it. Plus, it was one of those solid iron affairs that never gets damaged—the kind you see at the scene of an accident, paint unscratched, surrounded by the pieces of the foreign car it had destroyed.

"Wow, Dad, I love it! Thanks!" Now my horrific day tomorrow would be just that much less dreadful. I wouldn't be faced with the choice of either walking two miles in the rain to school or accepting a ride in the Chief's cruiser.

"I'm glad you like it," Charlie said gruffly, embarrassed again.

It took only one trip to get all my stuff upstairs. I got the west bedroom that faced out over the front yard. The room was familiar; it had belonged to me since I was born. The wooden floor, the light blue walls, the peaked ceiling, the yellowed lace curtains around the window—these were all a part of my childhood. The only changes Charlie had ever made were switching the crib for a bed and adding a desk as I grew. The desk now held a secondhand computer, with the phone line for the modem stapled along the floor to the nearest phone jack. This was a stipulation from my mother, so that we could stay in touch easily. The rocking chair from my baby days was still in the corner.

There was only one small bathroom at the top of the stairs, which I would have to share with Charlie. I was trying not to dwell too much on that fact.

One of the best things about Charlie is he doesn't hover. He left me alone to unpack and get settled, a feat that would have been altogether impossible for my mother. It was nice to be alone, not to have to smile and look pleased; a relief to stare dejectedly out the window at the sheeting rain and let just a few tears escape. I wasn't in the mood to go on a real crying jag. I would save that for bedtime, when I would have to think about the coming morning.

Forks High School had a frightening total of only three hundred and fifty-seven—now fifty-eight—students; there were more than seven hundred people in my junior class alone back home. All of the kids here had grown up together—their grandparents had been toddlers together. I would be the new girl from the big city, a curiosity, a freak.

Maybe, if I looked like a girl from Phoenix should, I could work this to my advantage. But physically, I'd never fit in anywhere. I *should* be tan, sporty, blond—a volleyball player, or a cheerleader, perhaps—all the things that go with living in the valley of the sun.

Instead, I was ivory-skinned, without even the excuse of blue eyes or red hair, despite the constant sunshine. I had always been slender, but soft somehow, obviously not an athlete; I didn't have the necessary hand-eye coordination to play sports without humiliating myself—and harming both myself and anyone else who stood too close.

When I finished putting my clothes in the old pine dresser, I took my bag of bathroom necessities and went to the communal bathroom to clean myself up after the day of travel. I looked at my face in the mirror as I brushed through my tangled, damp hair. Maybe it was the light, but already I looked sallower, unhealthy. My skin could be pretty—it was very clear, almost translucent-looking—but it all depended on color. I had no color here.

Facing my pallid reflection in the mirror, I was forced to admit that I was lying to myself. It wasn't just physically that I'd never fit in. And if I couldn't find a niche in a school with three thousand people, what were my chances here?

I didn't relate well to people my age. Maybe the truth was that I didn't relate well to people, period. Even my mother, who I was closer to than anyone else on the planet, was never in harmony with me, never on exactly the same page. Sometimes I wondered if I was seeing the same things through my eyes that the rest of the world was seeing through theirs. Maybe there was a glitch in my brain.

But the cause didn't matter. All that mattered was the effect. And tomorrow would be just the beginning.

I didn't sleep well that night, even after I was done crying. The constant *whoosh*ing of the rain and wind across the roof wouldn't fade into the background. I pulled the faded old quilt over my head, and later added the pillow, too. But I couldn't fall asleep until after midnight, when the rain finally settled into a quieter drizzle.

Thick fog was all I could see out my window in the morning, and I could feel the claustrophobia creeping up on me. You could never see the sky here; it was like a cage.

Breakfast with Charlie was a quiet event. He wished me good luck at school. I thanked him, knowing his hope was wasted. Good luck tended to avoid me. Charlie left first, off to the police station that was his wife and family. After he left, I sat at the old square oak table in one of the three unmatching chairs and examined his small kitchen, with its dark paneled walls, bright yellow cabinets, and white linoleum floor. Nothing was changed. My mother had painted the cabinets eighteen years ago in an attempt to bring some sunshine into the house. Over the small fireplace in the adjoining handkerchief-sized family room was a row of pictures. First a wedding picture of Charlie and my mom in Las Vegas, then one of the three of us in the hospital after I was born, taken by a helpful nurse, followed by the procession of my school pictures up to last year's. Those were embarrassing to look at—I would have to see what I could do to get Charlie to put them somewhere else, at least while I was living here.

It was impossible, being in this house, not to realize that Charlie had never gotten over my mom. It made me uncomfortable.

I didn't want to be too early to school, but I couldn't stay in the house anymore. I donned my jacket—which had the feel of a biohazard suit—and headed out into the rain.

It was just drizzling still, not enough to soak me through immediately as I reached for the house key that was always hidden under the eaves by the door, and locked up. The sloshing of my new waterproof boots was unnerving. I missed the normal crunch of gravel as I walked. I couldn't pause and admire my truck again as I wanted; I was in a hurry to get out of the misty wet that swirled around my head and clung to my hair under my hood.

Inside the truck, it was nice and dry. Either Billy or Charlie had obviously cleaned it up, but the tan upholstered seats still smelled faintly of tobacco, gasoline, and peppermint. The engine started quickly, to my relief, but loudly, roaring to life and then idling at top volume. Well, a truck this old was bound to have a flaw. The antique radio worked, a plus that I hadn't expected.

Finding the school wasn't difficult, though I'd never been there before. The school was, like most other things, just off the highway. It was not obvious that it was a school; only the sign, which declared it to be the Forks High School, made me stop. It looked like a collection of matching houses, built with maroon-colored bricks. There were so many trees and shrubs I couldn't see its size at first. Where was the feel of the institution? I wondered nostalgically. Where were the chain-link fences, the metal detectors?

I parked in front of the first building, which had a small sign over the door reading FRONT OFFICE. No one else was parked there, so I was sure it was off limits, but I decided I would get directions inside instead of circling around in the rain like an idiot. I stepped unwillingly out of the toasty truck cab and walked down a little stone path lined with dark hedges. I took a deep breath before opening the door.

Inside, it was brightly lit, and warmer than I'd hoped. The office was small; a little waiting area with padded folding chairs, orange-flecked commercial carpet, notices and awards cluttering the walls, a big clock ticking loudly. Plants grew everywhere in large plastic pots, as if there wasn't enough greenery outside. The room was cut in half by a long counter, cluttered with wire baskets full of papers and brightly colored flyers taped to its front. There were three desks behind the counter, one of which was manned by a large, red-haired woman wearing glasses. She was wearing a purple t-shirt, which immediately made me feel overdressed.

The red-haired woman looked up. "Can I help you?"

"I'm Isabella Swan," I informed her, and saw the immediate awareness light her eyes. I was expected, a topic of gossip no doubt. Daughter of the Chief's flighty ex-wife, come home at last.

"Of course," she said. She dug through a precariously stacked pile of documents on her desk till she found the ones she was looking for. "I have your schedule right here, and a map of the school." She brought several sheets to the counter to show me.

She went through my classes for me, highlighting the best route to each on the map, and gave me a slip to have each teacher sign, which I was to bring back at the end of the day. She smiled at me and hoped, like Charlie, that I would like it here in Forks. I smiled back as convincingly as I could.

When I went back out to my truck, other students were starting to arrive. I drove around the school, following the line of traffic. I was glad to see that most of the cars were older like mine, nothing flashy. At home I'd lived in one of the few lower-income neighborhoods that were included in the Paradise Valley District. It was a common thing to see a new Mercedes or Porsche in the student lot. The nicest car here was a shiny Volvo, and it stood out. Still, I cut the engine as soon as I was in a spot, so that the thunderous volume wouldn't draw attention to me.

I looked at the map in the truck, trying to memorize it now; hopefully I wouldn't have to walk around with it stuck in front of my nose all day. I stuffed everything in my bag, slung the strap over my shoulder, and sucked in a huge breath. I can do this, I lied to myself feebly. No one was going to bite me. I finally exhaled and stepped out of the truck.

I kept my face pulled back into my hood as I walked to the sidewalk, crowded with teenagers. My plain black jacket didn't stand out, I noticed with relief.

Once I got around the cafeteria, building three was easy to spot. A large black "3" was painted on a white square on the east corner. I felt my breathing gradually creeping toward hyperventilation as I approached the door. I tried holding my breath as I followed two unisex raincoats through the door.

The classroom was small. The people in front of me stopped just inside the door to hang up their coats on a long row of hooks. I copied them. They were two girls, one a porcelain-colored blonde, the other also pale, with light brown hair. At least my skin wouldn't be a standout here.

I took the slip up to the teacher, a tall, balding man whose desk had a nameplate identifying him as Mr. Mason. He gawked at me when he saw my name—not an encouraging response—and of course I flushed tomato red. But at least he sent me to an empty desk at the back without introducing me to the class. It was harder for my new classmates to stare at me in the back, but somehow, they managed. I kept my eyes down on the reading list the teacher had given me. It was fairly basic: Brontë, Shakespeare, Chaucer, Faulkner. I'd already read everything. That was comforting . . . and boring. I wondered if my mom would send me my folder of old essays, or if she would think that was cheating. I went through different arguments with her in my head while the teacher droned on.

When the bell rang, a nasal buzzing sound, a gangly boy with skin problems and hair black as an oil slick leaned across the aisle to talk to me.

"You're Isabella Swan, aren't you?" He looked like the overly helpful, chess club type.

"Bella," I corrected. Everyone within a three-seat radius turned to look at me.

"Where's your next class?" he asked.

I had to check in my bag. "Um, Government, with Jefferson, in building six."

There was nowhere to look without meeting curious eyes.

"I'm headed toward building four, I could show you the way. . . ." Definitely over-helpful. "I'm Eric," he added.

I smiled tentatively. "Thanks."

We got our jackets and headed out into the rain, which had picked up.

I could have sworn several people behind us were walking close enough to eavesdrop. I hoped I wasn't getting paranoid.

"So, this is a lot different than Phoenix, huh?" he asked.

"Very."

"It doesn't rain much there, does it?"

"Three or four times a year."

"Wow, what must that be like?" he wondered.

"Sunny," I told him.

"You don't look very tan."

"My mother is part albino."

He studied my face apprehensively, and I sighed. It looked like clouds and a sense of humor didn't mix. A few months of this and I'd forget how to use sarcasm.

We walked back around the cafeteria, to the south buildings by the gym. Eric walked me right to the door, though it was clearly marked.

"Well, good luck," he said as I touched the handle. "Maybe we'll have some other classes together." He sounded hopeful.

I smiled at him vaguely and went inside.

The rest of the morning passed in about the same fashion. My Trigonometry teacher, Mr. Varner, who I would have hated anyway just because of the subject he taught, was the only one who made me stand in front of the class and introduce myself. I stammered, blushed, and tripped over my own boots on the way to my seat.

After two classes, I started to recognize several of the faces in each class. There was always someone braver than the others who would introduce themselves and ask me questions about how I was liking Forks. I tried to be diplomatic, but mostly I just lied a lot. At least I never needed the map.

One girl sat next to me in both Trig and Spanish, and she walked with me to the cafeteria for lunch. She was tiny, several inches shorter than my five feet four inches, but her wildly curly dark hair made up a lot of the difference between our heights. I couldn't remember her name, so I smiled and nodded as she prattled about teachers and classes. I didn't try to keep up.

We sat at the end of a full table with several of her friends, who she introduced to me. I forgot all their names as soon as she spoke them. They seemed impressed by her bravery in speaking to me. The boy from English, Eric, waved at me from across the room.

It was there, sitting in the lunchroom, trying to make conversation with seven curious strangers, that I first saw them.

They were sitting in the corner of the cafeteria, as far away from where I sat as possible in the long room. There were five of them. They weren't talking, and they weren't eating, though they each had a tray of untouched food in front of them. They weren't gawking at me, unlike most of the other students, so it was safe to stare at them without fear of meeting an excessively interested pair of eyes. But it was none of these things that caught, and held, my attention.

They didn't look anything alike. Of the three boys, one was big—muscled like a serious weight lifter, with dark, curly hair. Another was taller, leaner, but still muscular, and honey blond. The last was lanky, less bulky, with untidy, bronze-colored hair. He was more boyish than the others, who looked like they could be in college, or even teachers here rather than students.

The girls were opposites. The tall one was statuesque. She had a beautiful figure, the kind you saw on the cover of the *Sports Illustrated* swimsuit issue, the kind that made every girl around her take a hit on her self-esteem just by being in the same room. Her hair was golden, gently waving to the middle of her back. The short girl was pixielike, thin in the extreme, with small features. Her hair was a deep black, cropped short and pointing in every direction.

And yet, they were all exactly alike. Every one of them was chalky pale, the palest of all the students living in this sunless town. Paler than me, the albino. They all had very dark eyes despite the range in hair tones. They also had dark shadows under those eyes—purplish, bruiselike shadows. As if they were all suffering from a sleepless night, or almost done recovering from a broken nose. Though their noses, all their features, were straight, perfect, angular.

But all this is not why I couldn't look away.

I stared because their faces, so different, so similar, were all devastatingly, inhumanly beautiful. They were faces you never expected to see except perhaps on the airbrushed pages of a fashion magazine. Or painted by an old master as the face of an angel. It was hard to decide who was the most beautiful—maybe the perfect blond girl, or the bronze-haired boy.

They were all looking away—away from each other, away from the other students, away from anything in particular as far as I could tell. As I watched, the small girl rose with her tray—unopened soda, unbitten apple—and walked away with a quick, graceful lope that belonged on a runway. I watched, amazed at her lithe dancer's step, till she dumped her tray and glided through the back door, faster than I would have thought possible. My eyes darted back to the others, who sat unchanging.

"Who are *they*?" I asked the girl from my Spanish class, whose name I'd forgotten.

As she looked up to see who I meant—though already knowing, probably, from my tone—suddenly he looked at her, the thinner one, the boyish one, the youngest, perhaps. He looked at my neighbor for just a fraction of a second, and then his dark eyes flickered to mine.

He looked away quickly, more quickly than I could, though in a flush of embarrassment I dropped my eyes at once. In that brief flash of a glance, his face held nothing of interest—it was as if she had called his name, and he'd looked up in involuntary response, already having decided not to answer.

My neighbor giggled in embarrassment, looking at the table like I did.

"That's Edward and Emmett Cullen, and Rosalie and Jasper Hale. The one who left was Alice Cullen; they all live together with Dr. Cullen and his wife." She said this under her breath.

I glanced sideways at the beautiful boy, who was looking at his tray now, picking a bagel to pieces with long, pale fingers. His mouth was moving very quickly, his perfect lips barely opening. The other three still looked away, and yet I felt he was speaking quietly to them.

Strange, unpopular names, I thought. The kinds of names grandparents had. But maybe that was in vogue here—small-town names? I finally remembered that my neighbor was called Jessica, a perfectly common name. There were two girls named Jessica in my History class back home.

"They are . . . very nice-looking." I struggled with the conspicuous understatement.

"Yes!" Jessica agreed with another giggle. "They're all *together* though—Emmett and Rosalie, and Jasper and Alice, I mean. And they *live* together."

Her voice held all the shock and condemnation of the small town, I thought critically. But, if I was being honest, I had to admit that even in Phoenix, it would cause gossip.

"Which ones are the Cullens?" I asked. "They don't look related. . . ."

"Oh, they're not. Dr. Cullen is really young, in his twenties or early thirties. They're all adopted. The Hales *are* brother and sister, twins—the blondes—and they're foster children."

"They look a little old for foster children."

"They are now, Jasper and Rosalie are both eighteen, but they've been with Mrs. Cullen since they were eight. She's their aunt or something like that."

"That's really kind of nice—for them to take care of all those kids like that, when they're so young and everything."

"I guess so," Jessica admitted reluctantly, and I got the impression that she didn't like the doctor and his wife for some reason. With the glances she was throwing at their adopted children, I would presume the reason was jealousy. "I think that Mrs. Cullen can't have any kids, though," she added, as if that lessened their kindness.

Throughout all this conversation, my eyes flickered again and again to the table where the strange family sat. They continued to look at the walls and not eat.

"Have they always lived in Forks?" I asked. Surely I would have noticed them on one of my summers here.

"No," she said in a voice that implied it should be obvious, even to a new arrival like me. "They just moved down two years ago from somewhere in Alaska."

I felt a surge of pity, and relief. Pity because, as beautiful as they were, they were outsiders, clearly not accepted. Relief that I wasn't the only newcomer here, and certainly not the most interesting by any standard.

As I examined them, the youngest, one of the Cullens, looked up and met my gaze, this time with evident curiosity in his expression. As I looked swiftly away, it seemed to me that his glance held some kind of unmet expectation.

"Which one is the boy with the reddish brown hair?" I asked. I peeked at him from the corner of my eye, and he was still staring at me, but not gawking like the other students had today—he had a slightly frustrated expression. I looked down again.

"That's Edward. He's gorgeous, of course, but don't waste your time. He doesn't date. Apparently none of the girls here are good-looking enough for him." She sniffed, a clear case of sour grapes. I wondered when he'd turned her down.

I bit my lip to hide my smile. Then I glanced at him again. His face was turned away, but I thought his cheek appeared lifted, as if he were smiling, too.

After a few more minutes, the four of them left the table together. They all were noticeably graceful—even the big, brawny one. It was unsettling to watch. The one named Edward didn't look at me again.

I sat at the table with Jessica and her friends longer than I would have if I'd been sitting alone. I was anxious not to be late for class on my first day. One of my new acquaintances, who considerately reminded me that her name was Angela, had Biology II with me the next hour. We walked to class together in silence. She was shy, too.

When we entered the classroom, Angela went to sit at a black-topped lab table exactly like the ones I was used to. She already had a neighbor. In fact, all the tables were filled but one. Next to the center aisle, I recognized Edward Cullen by his unusual hair, sitting next to that single open seat.

As I walked down the aisle to introduce myself to the teacher and get my slip signed, I was watching him surreptitiously. Just as I passed, he suddenly went rigid in his seat. He stared at me again, meeting my eyes with the strangest expression on his face—it was hostile, furious. I looked away quickly, shocked, going red again. I stumbled over a book in the walkway and had to catch myself on the edge of a table. The girl sitting there giggled.

I'd noticed that his eyes were black—coal black.

Mr. Banner signed my slip and handed me a book with no nonsense about introductions. I could tell we were going to get along. Of course, he had no choice but to send me to the one open seat in the middle of the room. I kept my eyes down as I went to sit by *him*, bewildered by the antagonistic stare he'd given me.

I didn't look up as I set my book on the table and took my seat, but I saw his posture change from the corner of my eye. He was leaning away from me, sitting on the extreme edge of his chair and averting his face like he smelled something bad. Inconspicuously, I sniffed my hair. It smelled like strawberries, the scent of my favorite shampoo. It seemed an innocent enough odor. I let my hair fall over my right shoulder, making a dark curtain between us, and tried to pay attention to the teacher.

Unfortunately the lecture was on cellular anatomy, something I'd already studied. I took notes carefully anyway, always looking down.

I couldn't stop myself from peeking occasionally through the screen of my hair at the strange boy next to me. During the whole class, he never relaxed his stiff position on the edge of his chair, sitting as far from me as possible. I could see his hand on his left leg was clenched into a fist, tendons standing out under his pale skin. This, too, he never relaxed. He had the long sleeves of his white shirt pushed up to his elbows, and his forearm was surprisingly hard and muscular beneath his light skin. He wasn't nearly as slight as he'd looked next to his burly brother.

The class seemed to drag on longer than the others. Was it because the day was finally coming to a close, or because I was waiting for his tight fist to loosen? It never did; he continued to sit so still it looked like he wasn't breathing. What was wrong with him? Was this his normal behavior? I questioned my judgment on Jessica's bitterness at lunch today. Maybe she was not as resentful as I'd thought.

It couldn't have anything to do with me. He didn't know me from Eve.

I peeked up at him one more time, and regretted it. He was glaring down at me again, his black eyes full of revulsion. As I flinched away from him, shrinking against my chair, the phrase *if looks could kill* suddenly ran through my mind.

At that moment, the bell rang loudly, making me jump, and Edward Cullen was out of his seat. Fluidly he rose—he was much taller than I'd thought—his back to me, and he was out the door before anyone else was out of their seat.

I sat frozen in my seat, staring blankly after him. He was so mean. It wasn't fair. I began gathering up my things slowly, trying to block the anger that filled me, for fear my eyes would tear up. For some reason, my temper was hardwired to my tear ducts. I usually cried when I was angry, a humiliating tendency.

"Aren't you Isabella Swan?" a male voice asked.

I looked up to see a cute, baby-faced boy, his pale blond hair carefully gelled into orderly spikes, smiling at me in a friendly way. He obviously didn't think I smelled bad.

"Bella," I corrected him, with a smile.

"I'm Mike."

"Hi, Mike."

"Do you need any help finding your next class?"

"I'm headed to the gym, actually. I think I can find it."

"That's my next class, too." He seemed thrilled, though it wasn't that big of a coincidence in a school this small.

We walked to class together; he was a chatterer—he supplied most of the conversation, which made it easy for me. He'd lived in California till he was ten, so he knew how I felt about the sun. It turned out he was in my English class also. He was the nicest person I'd met today.

But as we were entering the gym, he asked, "So, did you stab Edward Cullen with a pencil or what? I've never seen him act like that."

I cringed. So I wasn't the only one who had noticed. And, apparently, that *wasn't* Edward Cullen's usual behavior. I decided to play dumb.

"Was that the boy I sat next to in Biology?" I asked artlessly.

"Yes," he said. "He looked like he was in pain or something."

"I don't know," I responded. "I never spoke to him."

"He's a weird guy." Mike lingered by me instead of heading to the dressing room. "If I were lucky enough to sit by you, I would have talked to you."

I smiled at him before walking through the girls' locker room door. He was friendly and clearly admiring. But it wasn't enough to ease my irritation.

The Gym teacher, Coach Clapp, found me a uniform but didn't make me dress down for today's class. At home, only two years of P.E. were required. Here, P.E. was mandatory all four years. Forks was literally my personal hell on Earth.

I watched four volleyball games running simultaneously. Remembering how many injuries I had sustained—and inflicted—playing volleyball, I felt faintly nauseated.

The final bell rang at last. I walked slowly to the office to return my paperwork. The rain had drifted away, but the wind was strong, and colder. I wrapped my arms around myself.

When I walked into the warm office, I almost turned around and walked back out.

Edward Cullen stood at the desk in front of me. I recognized again that tousled bronze hair. He didn't appear to notice the sound of my entrance. I stood pressed against the back wall, waiting for the receptionist to be free.

He was arguing with her in a low, attractive voice. I quickly picked up the gist of the argument. He was trying to trade from sixth-hour Biology to another time—any other time.

I just couldn't believe that this was about me. It had to be something else, something that happened before I entered the Biology room. The look on his face must have been about another aggravation entirely. It was impossible that this stranger could take such a sudden, intense dislike to me.

The door opened again, and the cold wind suddenly gusted through the room, rustling the papers on the desk, swirling my hair around my face. The girl who came in merely stepped to the desk, placed a note in the wire basket, and walked out again. But Edward Cullen's back stiffened, and he turned slowly to glare at me—his face was absurdly handsome—with piercing, hate-filled eyes. For an instant, I felt a thrill of genuine fear, raising the hair on my arms. The look only lasted a second, but it chilled me more than the freezing wind. He turned back to the receptionist.

"Never mind, then," he said hastily in a voice like velvet. "I can see that it's impossible. Thank you so much for your help." And he turned on his heel without another look at me, and disappeared out the door.

I went meekly to the desk, my face white for once instead of red, and handed her the signed slip.

"How did your first day go, dear?" the receptionist asked maternally.

"Fine," I lied, my voice weak. She didn't look convinced.

When I got to the truck, it was almost the last car in the lot. It seemed like a haven, already the closest thing to home I had in this damp green hole. I sat inside for a while, just staring out the windshield blankly. But soon I was cold enough to need the heater, so I turned the key and the engine roared to life. I headed back to Charlie's house, fighting tears the whole way there.

2. OPEN BOOK

THE NEXT DAY WAS BETTER...AND WORSE.

It was better because it wasn't raining yet, though the clouds were dense and opaque. It was easier because I knew what to expect of my day. Mike came to sit by me in English, and walked me to my next class, with Chess Club Eric glaring at him all the while; that was flattering. People didn't look at me quite as much as they had yesterday. I sat with a big group at lunch that included Mike, Eric, Jessica, and several other people whose names and faces I now remembered. I began to feel like I was treading water, instead of drowning in it.

It was worse because I was tired; I still couldn't sleep with the wind echoing around the house. It was worse because Mr. Varner called on me in Trig when my hand wasn't raised and I had the wrong answer. It was miserable because I had to play volleyball, and the one time I didn't cringe out of the way of the ball, I hit my teammate in the head with it. And it was worse because Edward Cullen wasn't in school at all.

All morning I was dreading lunch, fearing his bizarre glares. Part of me wanted to confront him and demand to know what his problem was. While I was lying sleepless in my bed, I even imagined what I would say. But I knew myself too well to think I would really have the guts to do it. I made the Cowardly Lion look like the Terminator.

But when I walked into the cafeteria with Jessica—trying to keep my eyes from sweeping the place for him, and failing entirely—I saw that his four siblings of sorts were sitting together at the same table, and he was not with them.

Mike intercepted us and steered us to his table. Jessica seemed elated by the attention, and her friends quickly joined us. But as I tried to listen to their easy chatter, I was terribly uncomfortable, waiting nervously for the moment he would arrive. I hoped that he would simply ignore me when he came, and prove my suspicions false.

He didn't come, and as time passed I grew more and more tense.

I walked to Biology with more confidence when, by the end of lunch, he still hadn't showed. Mike, who was taking on the qualities of a golden retriever, walked faithfully by my side to class. I held my breath at the door, but Edward Cullen wasn't there, either. I exhaled and went to my seat. Mike followed, talking about an upcoming trip to the beach. He lingered by my desk till the bell rang. Then he smiled at me wistfully and went to sit by a girl with braces and a bad perm. It looked like I was going to have to do something about Mike, and it wouldn't be easy. In a town like this, where everyone lived on top of everyone else, diplomacy was essential. I had never been enormously tactful; I had no practice dealing with overly friendly boys.

I was relieved that I had the desk to myself, that Edward was absent. I told myself that repeatedly. But I couldn't get rid of the nagging suspicion that I was the reason he wasn't there. It was ridiculous, and egotistical, to think that I could affect anyone that strongly. It was impossible. And yet I couldn't stop worrying that it was true.

When the school day was finally done, and the blush was fading out of my cheeks from the volleyball incident, I changed quickly back into my jeans and navy blue sweater. I hurried from the girls' locker room, pleased to find that I had successfully evaded my retriever friend for the moment. I walked swiftly out to the parking lot. It was crowded now with fleeing students. I got in my truck and dug through my bag to make sure I had what I needed.

Last night I'd discovered that Charlie couldn't cook much besides fried eggs and bacon. So I requested that I be assigned kitchen detail for the duration of my stay. He was willing enough to hand over the keys to the banquet hall. I also found out that he had no food in the house. So I had my shopping list and the cash from the jar in the cupboard labeled FOOD MONEY, and I was on my way to the Thriftway.

I gunned my deafening engine to life, ignoring the heads that turned in my direction, and backed carefully into a place in the line of cars that were waiting to exit the parking lot. As I waited, trying to pretend that the earsplitting rumble was coming from someone else's car, I saw the two Cullens and the Hale twins getting into their car. It was the shiny new Volvo. Of course. I hadn't noticed their clothes before—I'd been too mesmerized by their faces. Now that I looked, it was obvious that they were all dressed exceptionally well; simply, but in clothes that subtly hinted at designer origins. With their remarkable good looks, the style with which they carried themselves, they could have worn dishrags and pulled it off. It seemed excessive for them to have both looks and money. But as far as I could tell, life worked that way most of the time. It didn't look as if it bought them any acceptance here.

No, I didn't fully believe that. The isolation must be their desire; I couldn't imagine any door that wouldn't be opened by that degree of beauty.

They looked at my noisy truck as I passed them, just like everyone else. I kept my eyes straight forward and was relieved when I finally was free of the school grounds.

The Thriftway was not far from the school, just a few streets south, off the highway. It was nice to be inside the supermarket; it felt normal. I did the shopping at home, and I fell into the pattern of the familiar task gladly. The store was big enough inside that I couldn't hear the tapping of the rain on the roof to remind me where I was.

When I got home, I unloaded all the groceries, stuffing them in wherever I could find an open space. I hoped Charlie wouldn't mind. I wrapped potatoes in foil and stuck them in the oven to bake, covered a steak in marinade and balanced it on top of a carton of eggs in the fridge.

When I was finished with that, I took my book bag upstairs. Before starting my homework, I changed into a pair of dry sweats, pulled my damp hair up into a ponytail, and checked my e-mail for the first time. I had three messages.

"Bella," my mom wrote...

Write me as soon as you get in. Tell me how your flight was. Is it raining? I miss you already. I'm almost finished packing for Florida, but I can't find my pink blouse. Do you know where I put it? Phil says hi. Mom.

I sighed and went to the next. It was sent eight hours after the first. "Bella," she wrote . . .

Why haven't you e-mailed me yet? What are you waiting for? Mom.

The last was from this morning.

Isabella,
If I haven't heard from you by 5:30 p.m. today I'm call-ing Charlie.

I checked the clock. I still had an hour, but my mom was well known for jumping the gun.

Mom,
Calm down. I'm writing right now. Don't do anything rash.
  Bella.

I sent that, and began again.

Mom,
   Everything is great. Of course it's raining. I was waiting for something to write about. School isn't bad, just a little repetitive. I met some nice kids who sit by me at lunch.
   Your blouse is at the dry cleaners—you were supposed to pick it up Friday.
   Charlie bought me a truck, can you believe it? I love it. It's old, but really sturdy, which is good, you know, for me.

I miss you, too. I'll write again soon, but I'm not going to check my e-mail every five minutes. Relax, breathe. I love you.

Bella.

I had decided to read *Wuthering Heights*—the novel we were currently studying in English—yet again for the fun of it, and that's what I was doing when Charlie came home. I'd lost track of the time, and I hurried downstairs to take the potatoes out and put the steak in to broil.

"Bella?" my father called out when he heard me on the stairs.

Who else? I thought to myself.

"Hey, Dad, welcome home."

"Thanks." He hung up his gun belt and stepped out of his boots as I bustled about the kitchen. As far as I was aware, he'd never shot the gun on the job. But he kept it ready. When I came here as a child, he would always remove the bullets as soon as he walked in the door. I guess he considered me old enough now not to shoot myself by accident, and not depressed enough to shoot myself on purpose.

"What's for dinner?" he asked warily. My mother was an imaginative cook, and her experiments weren't always edible. I was surprised, and sad, that he seemed to remember that far back.

"Steak and potatoes," I answered, and he looked relieved.

He seemed to feel awkward standing in the kitchen doing nothing; he lumbered into the living room to watch TV while I worked. We were both more comfortable that way. I made a salad while the steaks cooked, and set the table.

I called him in when dinner was ready, and he sniffed appreciatively as he walked into the room.

"Smells good, Bell."

"Thanks."

We ate in silence for a few minutes. It wasn't uncomfortable. Neither of us was bothered by the quiet. In some ways, we were well suited for living together.

"So, how did you like school? Have you made any friends?" he asked as he was taking seconds.

"Well, I have a few classes with a girl named Jessica. I sit with her friends at lunch. And there's this boy, Mike, who's very friendly. Everybody seems pretty nice." With one outstanding exception.

"That must be Mike Newton. Nice kid—nice family. His dad owns the sporting goods store just outside of town. He makes a good living off all the backpackers who come through here."

"Do you know the Cullen family?" I asked hesitantly.

"Dr. Cullen's family? Sure. Dr. Cullen's a great man."

"They . . . the kids . . . are a little different. They don't seem to fit in very well at school."

Charlie surprised me by looking angry.

"People in this town," he muttered. "Dr. Cullen is a brilliant surgeon who could probably work in any hospital in the world, make ten times the salary he gets here," he continued, getting louder. "We're lucky to have him— lucky that his wife wanted to live in a small town. He's an asset to the community, and all of those kids are well behaved and polite. I had my doubts, when they first moved in, with all those adopted teenagers. I thought we might have some problems with them. But they're all very mature—I haven't had one speck of trouble from any of them. That's more than I can say for the children of some folks who have lived in this town for generations. And they stick together the way a family should—camping trips every other weekend. . . . Just because they're newcomers, people have to talk."

It was the longest speech I'd ever heard Charlie make. He must feel strongly about whatever people were saying.

I backpedaled. "They seemed nice enough to me. I just noticed they kept to themselves. They're all very attractive," I added, trying to be more complimentary.

"You should see the doctor," Charlie said, laughing. "It's a good thing he's happily married. A lot of the nurses at the hospital have a hard time concentrating on their work with him around."

We lapsed back into silence as we finished eating. He cleared the table while I started on the dishes. He went back to the TV, and after I finished washing the dishes by hand—no dishwasher—I went upstairs unwillingly to work on my math homework. I could feel a tradition in the making.

That night it was finally quiet. I fell asleep quickly, exhausted.

The rest of the week was uneventful. I got used to the routine of my classes. By Friday I was able to recognize, if not name, almost all the students at school. In Gym, the kids on my team learned not to pass me the ball and to step quickly in front of me if the other team tried to take advantage of my weakness. I happily stayed out of their way.

Edward Cullen didn't come back to school.

Every day, I watched anxiously until the rest of the Cullens entered the cafeteria without him. Then I could relax and join in the lunchtime conversation. Mostly it centered around a trip to the La Push Ocean Park in two weeks that Mike was putting together. I was invited, and I had agreed to go, more out of politeness than desire. Beaches should be hot and dry.

By Friday I was perfectly comfortable entering my Biology class, no longer worried that Edward would be there. For all I knew, he had dropped out of school. I tried not to think about him, but I couldn't totally suppress the worry that I was responsible for his continued absence, ridiculous as it seemed.

My first weekend in Forks passed without incident. Charlie, unused to spending time in the usually empty house, worked most of the weekend. I cleaned the house, got ahead on my homework, and wrote my mom more bogusly cheerful e-mail. I did drive to the library Saturday, but it was so poorly stocked that I didn't bother to get a card; I would have to make a date to visit Olympia or Seattle soon and find a good bookstore. I wondered idly what kind of gas mileage the truck got...and shuddered at the thought.

The rain stayed soft over the weekend, quiet, so I was able to sleep well.

People greeted me in the parking lot Monday morning. I didn't know all their names, but I waved back and smiled at everyone. It was colder this morning, but happily not raining. In English, Mike took his accustomed seat by my side. We had a pop quiz on *Wuthering Heights*. It was straightforward, very easy.

All in all, I was feeling a lot more comfortable than I had thought I would feel by this point. More comfortable than I had ever expected to feel here.

When we walked out of class, the air was full of swirling bits of white. I could hear people shouting excitedly to each other. The wind bit at my cheeks, my nose.

"Wow," Mike said. "It's snowing."

I looked at the little cotton fluffs that were building up along the sidewalk and swirling erratically past my face.

"Ew." Snow. There went my good day.

He looked surprised. "Don't you like snow?"

"No. That means it's too cold for rain." Obviously. "Besides, I thought it was supposed to come down in flakes—you know, each one unique and all that. These just look like the ends of Q-tips."

"Haven't you ever seen snow fall before?" he asked incredulously.

"Sure I have." I paused. "On TV."

Mike laughed. And then a big, squishy ball of dripping snow smacked into the back of his head. We both turned to see where it came from. I had my suspicions about Eric, who was walking away, his back toward us—in the wrong direction for his next class. Mike apparently had the same notion. He bent over and began scraping together a pile of the white mush.

"I'll see you at lunch, okay?" I kept walking as I spoke. "Once people start throwing wet stuff, I go inside."

He just nodded, his eyes on Eric's retreating figure.

Throughout the morning, everyone chattered excitedly about the snow; apparently it was the first snowfall of the new year. I kept my mouth shut. Sure, it was drier than rain—until it melted in your socks.

I walked alertly to the cafeteria with Jessica after Spanish. Mush balls were flying everywhere. I kept a binder in my hands, ready to use it as a shield if necessary. Jessica thought I was hilarious, but something in my expression kept her from lobbing a snowball at me herself.

Mike caught up to us as we walked in the doors, laughing, with ice melting the spikes in his hair. He and Jessica were talking animatedly about the snow fight as we got in line to buy food. I glanced toward that table in the corner out of habit. And then I froze where I stood. There were five people at the table.

Jessica pulled on my arm.

"Hello? Bella? What do you want?"

I looked down; my ears were hot. I had no reason to feel self-conscious, I reminded myself. I hadn't done anything wrong.

"What's with Bella?" Mike asked Jessica.

"Nothing," I answered. "I'll just get a soda today." I caught up to the end of the line.

"Aren't you hungry?" Jessica asked.

"Actually, I feel a little sick," I said, my eyes still on the floor.

I waited for them to get their food, and then followed them to a table, my eyes on my feet.

I sipped my soda slowly, my stomach churning. Twice Mike asked, with unnecessary concern, how I was feeling. I told him it was nothing, but I was wondering if I *should* play it up and escape to the nurse's office for the next hour.

Ridiculous. I shouldn't have to run away.

I decided to permit myself one glance at the Cullen family's table. If he was glaring at me, I would skip Biology, like the coward I was.

I kept my head down and glanced up under my lashes. None of them were looking this way. I lifted my head a little.

They were laughing. Edward, Jasper, and Emmett all had their hair entirely saturated with melting snow. Alice and Rosalie were leaning away as Emmett shook his dripping hair toward them. They were enjoying the snowy day, just like everyone else—only they looked more like a scene from a movie than the rest of us.

But, aside from the laughter and playfulness, there was something different, and I couldn't quite pinpoint what that difference was. I examined Edward the most carefully. His skin was less pale, I decided—flushed from the snow fight maybe—the circles under his eyes much less noticeable. But there was something more. I pondered, staring, trying to isolate the change.

"Bella, what are you staring at?" Jessica intruded, her eyes following my stare.

At that precise moment, his eyes flashed over to meet mine.

I dropped my head, letting my hair fall to conceal my face. I was sure, though, in the instant our eyes met, that he didn't look harsh or unfriendly as he had the last time I'd seen him. He looked merely curious again, unsatisfied in some way.

"Edward Cullen is staring at you," Jessica giggled in my ear.

"He doesn't look angry, does he?" I couldn't help asking.

"No," she said, sounding confused by my question. "Should he be?"

"I don't think he likes me," I confided. I still felt queasy. I put my head down on my arm.

"The Cullens don't like anybody...well, they don't notice anybody enough to like them. But he's still staring at you."

"Stop looking at him," I hissed.

She snickered, but she looked away. I raised my head enough to make sure that she did, contemplating violence if she resisted.

Mike interrupted us then—he was planning an epic battle of the blizzard in the parking lot after school and wanted us to join. Jessica agreed enthusiastically. The way she looked at Mike left little doubt that she would be up for anything he suggested. I kept silent. I would have to hide in the gym until the parking lot cleared.

For the rest of the lunch hour I very carefully kept my eyes at my own table. I decided to honor the bargain I'd made with myself. Since he didn't look angry, I would go to Biology. My stomach did frightened little flips at the thought of sitting next to him again.

I didn't really want to walk to class with Mike as usual—he seemed to be a popular target for the snowball snipers—but when we went to the door, everyone besides me groaned in unison. It was raining, washing all traces of the snow away in clear, icy ribbons down the side of the walkway. I pulled my hood up, secretly pleased. I would be free to go straight home after Gym.

Mike kept up a string of complaints on the way to building four.

Once inside the classroom, I saw with relief that my table was still empty. Mr. Banner was walking around the room, distributing one microscope and box of slides to each table. Class didn't start for a few minutes, and the room buzzed with conversation. I kept my eyes away from the door, doodling idly on the cover of my notebook.

I heard very clearly when the chair next to me moved, but my eyes stayed carefully focused on the pattern I was drawing.

"Hello," said a quiet, musical voice.

I looked up, stunned that he was speaking to me. He was sitting as far away from me as the desk allowed, but his chair was angled toward me. His hair was dripping wet, disheveled—even so, he looked like he'd just finished shooting a commercial for hair gel. His dazzling face was friendly, open, a slight smile on his flawless lips. But his eyes were careful.

"My name is Edward Cullen," he continued. "I didn't have a chance to introduce myself last week. You must be Bella Swan."

My mind was spinning with confusion. Had I made up the whole thing? He was perfectly polite now. I had to speak; he was waiting. But I couldn't think of anything conventional to say.

"H-how do you know my name?" I stammered.

He laughed a soft, enchanting laugh.

"Oh, I think everyone knows your name. The whole town's been waiting for you to arrive."

I grimaced. I knew it was something like that.

"No," I persisted stupidly. "I meant, why did you call me Bella?"

He seemed confused. "Do you prefer Isabella?"

"No, I like Bella," I said. "But I think Charlie—I mean my dad—must call me Isabella behind my back—that's what everyone here seems to know me as," I tried to explain, feeling like an utter moron.

"Oh." He let it drop. I looked away awkwardly.

Thankfully, Mr. Banner started class at that moment. I tried to concentrate as he explained the lab we would be doing today. The slides in the box were out of order. Working as lab partners, we had to separate the slides of onion root tip cells into the phases of mitosis they represented and label them accordingly. We weren't supposed to use our books. In twenty minutes, he would be coming around to see who had it right.

"Get started," he commanded.

"Ladies first, partner?" Edward asked. I looked up to see him smiling a crooked smile so beautiful that I could only stare at him like an idiot.

"Or I could start, if you wish." The smile faded; he was obviously wondering if I was mentally competent.

"No," I said, flushing. "I'll go ahead."

I was showing off, just a little. I'd already done this lab, and I knew what I was looking for. It should be easy. I snapped the first slide into place under the microscope and adjusted it quickly to the 40X objective. I studied the slide briefly.

My assessment was confident. "Prophase."

"Do you mind if I look?" he asked as I began to remove the slide. His hand caught mine, to stop me, as he asked. His fingers were ice cold, like he'd been holding them in a snowdrift before class. But that wasn't why I jerked my hand away so quickly. When he touched me, it stung my hand as if an electric current had passed through us.

"I'm sorry," he muttered, pulling his hand back immediately. However, he continued to reach for the microscope. I watched him, still staggered, as he examined the slide for an even shorter time than I had.

"Prophase," he agreed, writing it neatly in the first space on our worksheet. He swiftly switched out the first slide for the second, and then glanced at it cursorily.

"Anaphase," he murmured, writing it down as he spoke.

I kept my voice indifferent. "May I?"

He smirked and pushed the microscope to me.

I looked through the eyepiece eagerly, only to be disappointed. Dang it, he was right.

"Slide three?" I held out my hand without looking at him.

He handed it to me; it seemed like he was being careful not to touch my skin again.

I took the most fleeting look I could manage.

"Interphase." I passed him the microscope before he could ask for it. He took a swift peek, and then wrote it down. I would have written it while he looked, but his clear, elegant script intimidated me. I didn't want to spoil the page with my clumsy scrawl.

We were finished before anyone else was close. I could see Mike and his partner comparing two slides again and again, and another group had their book open under the table.

Which left me with nothing to do but try to not look at him...unsuccessfully. I glanced up, and he was staring at me, that same inexplicable look of frustration in his eyes. Suddenly I identified that subtle difference in his face.

"Did you get contacts?" I blurted out unthinkingly.

He seemed puzzled by my unexpected question. "No."

"Oh," I mumbled. "I thought there was something different about your eyes."

He shrugged, and looked away.

In fact, I was sure there was something different. I vividly remembered the flat black color of his eyes the last time he'd glared at me—the color was striking against the background of his pale skin and his auburn hair. Today, his eyes were a completely different color: a strange ocher, darker than butterscotch, but with the same golden tone. I didn't understand how that could be, unless he was lying for some reason about the contacts. Or maybe Forks was making me crazy in the literal sense of the word.

I looked down. His hands were clenched into hard fists again.

Mr. Banner came to our table then, to see why we weren't working. He looked over our shoulders to glance at the completed lab, and then stared more intently to check the answers.

"So, Edward, didn't you think Isabella should get a chance with the microscope?" Mr. Banner asked.

"Bella," Edward corrected automatically. "Actually, she identified three of the five."

Mr. Banner looked at me now; his expression was skeptical.

"Have you done this lab before?" he asked.

I smiled sheepishly. "Not with onion root."

"Whitefish blastula?"

"Yeah."

Mr. Banner nodded. "Were you in an advanced placement program in Phoenix?"

"Yes."

"Well," he said after a moment, "I guess it's good you two are lab partners." He mumbled something else as he walked away. After he left, I began doodling on my notebook again.

"It's too bad about the snow, isn't it?" Edward asked. I had the feeling that he was forcing himself to make small talk with me. Paranoia swept over me again. It was like he had heard my conversation with Jessica at lunch and was trying to prove me wrong.

"Not really," I answered honestly, instead of pretending to be normal like everyone else. I was still trying to dislodge the stupid feeling of suspicion, and I couldn't concentrate.

"You don't like the cold." It wasn't a question.

"Or the wet."

"Forks must be a difficult place for you to live," he mused.

"You have no idea," I muttered darkly.

He looked fascinated by what I said, for some reason I couldn't imagine. His face was such a distraction that I tried not to look at it any more than courtesy absolutely demanded.

"Why did you come here, then?"

No one had asked me that—not straight out like he did, demanding.

"It's ... complicated."

"I think I can keep up," he pressed.

I paused for a long moment, and then made the mistake of meeting his gaze. His dark gold eyes confused me, and I answered without thinking.

"My mother got remarried," I said.

"That doesn't sound so complex," he disagreed, but he was suddenly sympathetic. "When did that happen?"

"Last September." My voice sounded sad, even to me.

"And you don't like him," Edward surmised, his tone still kind.

"No, Phil is fine. Too young, maybe, but nice enough."

"Why didn't you stay with them?"

I couldn't fathom his interest, but he continued to stare at me with penetrating eyes, as if my dull life's story was somehow vitally important.

"Phil travels a lot. He plays ball for a living." I half-smiled.

"Have I heard of him?" he asked, smiling in response.

"Probably not. He doesn't play *well*. Strictly minor league. He moves around a lot."

"And your mother sent you here so that she could travel with him." He said it as an assumption again, not a question.

My chin raised a fraction. "No, she did not send me here. I sent myself."

His eyebrows knit together. "I don't understand," he admitted, and he seemed unnecessarily frustrated by that fact.

I sighed. Why was I explaining this to him? He continued to stare at me with obvious curiosity.

"She stayed with me at first, but she missed him. It made her unhappy ... so I decided it was time to spend some quality time with Charlie." My voice was glum by the time I finished.

"But now you're unhappy," he pointed out.

"And?" I challenged.

"That doesn't seem fair." He shrugged, but his eyes were still intense.

I laughed without humor. "Hasn't anyone ever told you? Life isn't fair."

"I believe I *have* heard that somewhere before," he agreed dryly.

"So that's all," I insisted, wondering why he was still staring at me that way.

His gaze became appraising. "You put on a good show," he said slowly. "But I'd be willing to bet that you're suffering more than you let anyone see."

I grimaced at him, resisting the impulse to stick out my tongue like a five-year-old, and looked away.

"Am I wrong?"

I tried to ignore him.

"I didn't think so," he murmured smugly.

"Why does it matter to *you*?" I asked, irritated. I kept my eyes away, watching the teacher make his rounds.

"That's a very good question," he muttered, so quietly that I wondered if he was talking to himself. However, after a few seconds of silence, I decided that was the only answer I was going to get.

I sighed, scowling at the blackboard.

"Am I annoying you?" he asked. He sounded amused.

I glanced at him without thinking...and told the truth again. "Not exactly. I'm more annoyed at myself. My face is so easy to read—my mother always calls me her open book." I frowned.

"On the contrary, I find you very difficult to read." Despite everything that I'd said and he'd guessed, he sounded like he meant it.

"You must be a good reader then," I replied.

"Usually." He smiled widely, flashing a set of perfect, ultrawhite teeth.

Mr. Banner called the class to order then, and I turned with relief to listen. I was in disbelief that I'd just explained my dreary life to this bizarre, beautiful boy who may or may not despise me. He'd seemed engrossed in our conversation, but now I could see, from the corner of my eye, that he was leaning away from me again, his hands gripping the edge of the table with unmistakable tension.

I tried to appear attentive as Mr. Banner illustrated, with transparencies on the overhead projector, what I had seen without difficulty through the microscope. But my thoughts were unmanageable.

When the bell finally rang, Edward rushed as swiftly and as gracefully from the room as he had last Monday. And, like last Monday, I stared after him in amazement.

Mike skipped quickly to my side and picked up my books for me. I imagined him with a wagging tail.

"That was awful," he groaned. "They all looked exactly the same. You're lucky you had Cullen for a partner."

"I didn't have any trouble with it," I said, stung by his assumption. I regretted the snub instantly. "I've done the lab before, though," I added before he could get his feelings hurt.

"Cullen seemed friendly enough today," he commented as we shrugged into our raincoats. He didn't seem pleased about it.

I tried to sound indifferent. "I wonder what was with him last Monday."

I couldn't concentrate on Mike's chatter as we walked to Gym, and P.E. didn't do much to hold my attention, either. Mike was on my team today. He chivalrously covered my position as well as his own, so my woolgathering was only interrupted when it was my turn to serve; my team ducked warily out of the way every time I was up.

The rain was just a mist as I walked to the parking lot, but I was happier when I was in the dry cab. I got the heater running, for once not caring about the mind-numbing roar of the engine. I unzipped my jacket, put the hood down, and fluffed my damp hair out so the heater could dry it on the way home.

I looked around me to make sure it was clear. That's when I noticed the still, white figure. Edward Cullen was leaning against the front door of the Volvo, three cars down from me, and staring intently in my direction. I swiftly looked away and threw the truck into reverse, almost hitting a rusty Toyota Corolla in my haste. Lucky for the Toyota, I stomped on the brake in time. It was just the sort of car that my truck would make scrap metal of. I took a deep breath, still looking out the other side of my car, and cautiously pulled out again, with greater success. I stared straight ahead as I passed the Volvo, but from a peripheral peek, I would swear I saw him laughing.

3. PHENOMENON

WHEN I OPENED MY EYES IN THE MORNING, SOMETHING WAS DIFFERENT.

It was the light. It was still the gray-green light of a cloudy day in the forest, but it was clearer somehow. I realized there was no fog veiling my window.

I jumped up to look outside, and then groaned in horror.

A fine layer of snow covered the yard, dusted the top of my truck, and whitened the road. But that wasn't the worst part. All the rain from yesterday had frozen solid—coating the needles on the trees in fantastic, gorgeous patterns, and making the driveway a deadly ice slick. I had enough trouble not falling down when the ground was dry; it might be safer for me to go back to bed now.

Charlie had left for work before I got downstairs. In a lot of ways, living with Charlie was like having my own place, and I found myself reveling in the aloneness instead of being lonely.

I threw down a quick bowl of cereal and some orange juice from the carton. I felt excited to go to school, and that scared me. I knew it wasn't the stimulating learning environment I was anticipating, or seeing my new set of friends. If I was being honest with myself, I knew I was eager to get to school because I would see Edward Cullen. And that was very, very stupid.

I should be avoiding him entirely after my brainless and embarrassing babbling yesterday. And I was suspicious of him; why should he lie about his eyes? I was still frightened of the hostility I sometimes felt emanating from him, and I was still tongue-tied whenever I pictured his perfect face. I was well aware that my league and his league were spheres that did not touch. So I shouldn't be at all anxious to see him today.

It took every ounce of my concentration to make it down the icy brick driveway alive. I almost lost my balance when I finally got to the truck, but I managed to cling to the side mirror and save myself. Clearly, today was going to be nightmarish.

Driving to school, I distracted myself from my fear of falling and my unwanted speculations about Edward Cullen by thinking about Mike and Eric, and the obvious difference in how teenage boys responded to me here. I was sure I looked exactly the same as I had in Phoenix. Maybe it was just that the boys back home had watched me pass slowly through all the awkward phases of adolescence and still thought of me that way. Perhaps it was because I was a novelty here, where novelties were few and far between. Possibly my crippling clumsiness was seen as endearing rather than pathetic, casting me as a damsel in distress. Whatever the reason, Mike's puppy dog behavior and Eric's apparent rivalry with him were disconcerting. I wasn't sure if I didn't prefer being ignored.

My truck seemed to have no problem with the black ice that covered the roads. I drove very slowly, though, not wanting to carve a path of destruction through Main Street.

When I got out of my truck at school, I saw why I'd had so little trouble. Something silver caught my eye, and I walked to the back of the truck—carefully holding the side for support—to examine my tires. There were thin chains crisscrossed in diamond shapes around them. Charlie had gotten up who knows how early to put snow chains on my truck. My throat suddenly felt tight. I wasn't used to being taken care of, and Charlie's unspoken concern caught me by surprise.

I was standing by the back corner of the truck, struggling to fight back the sudden wave of emotion the snow chains had brought on, when I heard an odd sound.

It was a high-pitched screech, and it was fast becoming painfully loud. I looked up, startled.

I saw several things simultaneously. Nothing was moving in slow motion, the way it does in the movies. Instead, the adrenaline rush seemed to make my brain work much faster, and I was able to absorb in clear detail several things at once.

Edward Cullen was standing four cars down from me, staring at me in horror. His face stood out from a sea of faces, all frozen in the same mask of shock. But of more immediate importance was the dark blue van that was skidding, tires locked and squealing against the brakes, spinning wildly across the ice of the parking lot. It was going to hit the back corner of my truck, and I was standing between them. I didn't even have time to close my eyes.

Just before I heard the shattering crunch of the van folding around the truck bed, something hit me, hard, but not from the direction I was expecting. My head cracked against the icy blacktop, and I felt something solid and cold pinning me to the ground. I was lying on the pavement behind the tan car I'd parked next to. But I didn't have a chance to notice anything else, because the van was still coming. It had curled gratingly around the end of the truck and, still spinning and sliding, was about to collide with me *again.*

A low oath made me aware that someone was with me, and the voice was impossible not to recognize. Two long, white hands shot out protectively in front of me, and the van shuddered to a stop a foot from my face, the large hands fitting providentially into a deep dent in the side of the van's body.

Then his hands moved so fast they blurred. One was suddenly gripping under the body of the van, and something was dragging me, swinging my legs around like a rag doll's, till they hit the tire of the tan car. A groaning metallic thud hurt my ears, and the van settled, glass popping, onto the asphalt—exactly where, a second ago, my legs had been.

It was absolutely silent for one long second before the screaming began. In the abrupt bedlam, I could hear more than one person shouting my name. But more clearly than all the yelling, I could hear Edward Cullen's low, frantic voice in my ear.

"Bella? Are you all right?"

"I'm fine." My voice sounded strange. I tried to sit up, and realized he was holding me against the side of his body in an iron grasp.

"Be careful," he warned as I struggled. "I think you hit your head pretty hard."

I became aware of a throbbing ache centered above my left ear.

"Ow," I said, surprised.

"That's what I thought." His voice, amazingly, sounded like he was suppressing laughter.

"How in the..." I trailed off, trying to clear my head, get my bearings. "How did you get over here so fast?"

"I was standing right next to you, Bella," he said, his tone serious again.

I turned to sit up, and this time he let me, releasing his hold around my waist and sliding as far from me as he could in the limited space. I looked at his concerned, innocent expression and was disoriented again by the force of his gold-colored eyes. What was I asking him?

And then they found us, a crowd of people with tears streaming down their faces, shouting at each other, shouting at us.

"Don't move," someone instructed.

"Get Tyler out of the van!" someone else shouted. There was a flurry of activity around us. I tried to get up, but Edward's cold hand pushed my shoulder down.

"Just stay put for now."

"But it's cold," I complained. It surprised me when he chuckled under his breath. There was an edge to the sound.

"You were over there," I suddenly remembered, and his chuckle stopped short. "You were by your car."

His expression turned hard. "No, I wasn't."

"I saw you." All around us was chaos. I could hear the gruffer voices of adults arriving on the scene. But I obstinately held on to our argument; I was right, and he was going to admit it.

"Bella, I was standing with you, and I pulled you out of the way." He unleashed the full, devastating power of his eyes on me, as if trying to communicate something crucial.

"No." I set my jaw.

The gold in his eyes blazed. "Please, Bella."

"Why?" I demanded.

"Trust me," he pleaded, his soft voice overwhelming.

I could hear the sirens now. "Will you promise to explain everything to me later?"

"Fine," he snapped, abruptly exasperated.

"Fine," I repeated angrily.

It took six EMTs and two teachers—Mr. Varner and Coach Clapp—to shift the van far enough away from us to bring the stretchers in. Edward vehemently refused his, and I tried to do the same, but the traitor told them I'd hit my head and probably had a concussion. I almost died of humiliation when they put on the neck brace. It looked like the entire school was there, watching soberly as they loaded me in the back of the ambulance. Edward got to ride in the front. It was maddening.

To make matters worse, Chief Swan arrived before they could get me safely away.

"Bella!" he yelled in panic when he recognized me on the stretcher.

"I'm completely fine, Char—Dad," I sighed. "There's nothing wrong with me."

He turned to the closest EMT for a second opinion. I tuned him out to consider the jumble of inexplicable images churning chaotically in my head. When they'd lifted me away from the car, I had seen the deep dent in the tan car's bumper—a very distinct dent that fit the contours of Edward's shoulders . . . as if he had braced himself against the car with enough force to damage the metal frame. . . .

And then there was his family, looking on from the distance, with expressions that ranged from disapproval to fury but held no hint of concern for their brother's safety.

I tried to think of a logical solution that could explain what I had just seen—a solution that excluded the assumption that I was insane.

Naturally, the ambulance got a police escort to the county hospital. I felt ridiculous the whole time they were unloading me. What made it worse was that Edward simply glided through the hospital doors under his own power. I ground my teeth together.

They put me in the emergency room, a long room with a line of beds separated by pastel-patterned curtains. A nurse put a pressure cuff on my arm and a thermometer under my tongue. Since no one bothered pulling the curtain around to give me some privacy, I decided I wasn't obligated to wear the stupid-looking neck brace anymore. When the nurse walked away, I quickly unfastened the Velcro and threw it under the bed.

There was another flurry of hospital personnel, another stretcher brought to the bed next to me. I recognized Tyler Crowley from my Government class beneath the bloodstained bandages wrapped tightly around his head. Tyler looked a hundred times worse than I felt. But he was staring anxiously at me.

"Bella, I'm so sorry!"

"I'm fine, Tyler—you look awful, are you all right?" As we spoke, nurses began unwinding his soiled bandages, exposing a myriad of shallow slices all over his forehead and left cheek.

He ignored me. "I thought I was going to kill you! I was going too fast, and I hit the ice wrong. . . ." He winced as one nurse started dabbing at his face.

"Don't worry about it; you missed me."

"How did you get out of the way so fast? You were there, and then you were gone. . . ."

"Umm . . . Edward pulled me out of the way."

He looked confused. "Who?"

"Edward Cullen—he was standing next to me." I'd always been a terrible liar; I didn't sound convincing at all.

"Cullen? I didn't see him . . . wow, it was all so fast, I guess. Is he okay?"

"I think so. He's here somewhere, but they didn't make him use a stretcher."

I knew I wasn't crazy. What had happened? There was no way to explain away what I'd seen.

They wheeled me away then, to X-ray my head. I told them there was nothing wrong, and I was right. Not even a concussion. I asked if I could leave, but the nurse said I had to talk to a doctor first. So I was trapped in the ER, waiting, harassed by Tyler's constant apologies and promises to make it up to me. No matter how many times I tried to convince him I was fine, he continued to torment himself. Finally, I closed my eyes and ignored him. He kept up a remorseful mumbling.

"Is she sleeping?" a musical voice asked. My eyes flew open.

Edward was standing at the foot of my bed, smirking. I glared at him. It wasn't easy—it would have been more natural to ogle.

"Hey, Edward, I'm really sorry—" Tyler began.

Edward lifted a hand to stop him.

"No blood, no foul," he said, flashing his brilliant teeth. He moved to sit on the edge of Tyler's bed, facing me. He smirked again.

"So, what's the verdict?" he asked me.

"There's nothing wrong with me at all, but they won't let me go," I complained. "How come you aren't strapped to a gurney like the rest of us?"

"It's all about who you know," he answered. "But don't worry, I came to spring you."

Then a doctor walked around the corner, and my mouth fell open. He was young, he was blond...and he was handsomer than any movie star I'd ever seen. He was pale, though, and tired-looking, with circles under his eyes. From Charlie's description, this had to be Edward's father.

"So, Miss Swan," Dr. Cullen said in a remarkably appealing voice, "how are you feeling?"

"I'm fine," I said, for the last time, I hoped.

He walked to the lightboard on the wall over my head, and turned it on.

"Your X-rays look good," he said. "Does your head hurt? Edward said you hit it pretty hard."

"It's fine," I repeated with a sigh, throwing a quick scowl toward Edward.

The doctor's cool fingers probed lightly along my skull. He noticed when I winced.

"Tender?" he asked.

"Not really." I'd had worse.

I heard a chuckle, and looked over to see Edward's patronizing smile. My eyes narrowed.

"Well, your father is in the waiting room—you can go home with him now. But come back if you feel dizzy or have trouble with your eyesight at all."

"Can't I go back to school?" I asked, imagining Charlie trying to be attentive.

"Maybe you should take it easy today."

I glanced at Edward. "Does *he* get to go to school?"

"Someone has to spread the good news that we survived," Edward said smugly.

"Actually," Dr. Cullen corrected, "most of the school seems to be in the waiting room."

"Oh no," I moaned, covering my face with my hands.

Dr. Cullen raised his eyebrows. "Do you want to stay?"

"No, no!" I insisted, throwing my legs over the side of the bed and hopping down quickly. Too quickly—I staggered, and Dr. Cullen caught me. He looked concerned.

"I'm fine," I assured him again. No need to tell him my balance problems had nothing to do with hitting my head.

"Take some Tylenol for the pain," he suggested as he steadied me.

"It doesn't hurt that bad," I insisted.

"It sounds like you were extremely lucky," Dr. Cullen said, smiling as he signed my chart with a flourish.

"Lucky Edward happened to be standing next to me," I amended with a hard glance at the subject of my statement.

"Oh, well, yes," Dr. Cullen agreed, suddenly occupied with the papers in front of him. Then he looked away, at Tyler, and walked to the next bed. My intuition flickered; the doctor was in on it.

"I'm afraid that *you'll* have to stay with us just a little bit longer," he said to Tyler, and began checking his cuts.

As soon as the doctor's back was turned, I moved to Edward's side.

"Can I talk to you for a minute?" I hissed under my breath. He took a step back from me, his jaw suddenly clenched.

"Your father is waiting for you," he said through his teeth.

I glanced at Dr. Cullen and Tyler.

"I'd like to speak with you alone, if you don't mind," I pressed.

He glared, and then turned his back and strode down the long room. I nearly had to run to keep up. As soon as we turned the corner into a short hallway, he spun around to face me.

"What do you want?" he asked, sounding annoyed. His eyes were cold.

His unfriendliness intimidated me. My words came out with less severity than I'd intended. "You owe me an explanation," I reminded him.

"I saved your life—I don't owe you anything."

I flinched back from the resentment in his voice. "You promised."

"Bella, you hit your head, you don't know what you're talking about." His tone was cutting.

My temper flared now, and I glared defiantly at him. "There's nothing wrong with my head."

He glared back. "What do you want from me, Bella?"

"I want to know the truth," I said. "I want to know why I'm lying for you."

"What do you *think* happened?" he snapped.

It came out in a rush.

"All I know is that you weren't anywhere near me—Tyler didn't see you, either, so don't tell me I hit my head too hard. That van was going to crush us both—and it didn't, and your hands left dents in the side of it—and you left a dent in the other car, and you're not hurt at all—and the van should have smashed my legs, but you were holding it up. . . ." I could hear how crazy it sounded, and I couldn't continue. I was so mad I could feel the tears coming; I tried to force them back by grinding my teeth together.

He was staring at me incredulously. But his face was tense, defensive.

"You think I lifted a van off you?" His tone questioned my sanity, but it only made me more suspicious. It was like a perfectly delivered line by a skilled actor.

I merely nodded once, jaw tight.

"Nobody will believe that, you know." His voice held an edge of derision now.

"I'm not going to tell anybody." I said each word slowly, carefully controlling my anger.

Surprise flitted across his face. "Then why does it matter?"

"It matters to me," I insisted. "I don't like to lie—so there'd better be a good reason why I'm doing it."

"Can't you just thank me and get over it?"

"Thank you." I waited, fuming and expectant.

"You're not going to let it go, are you?"

"No."

"In that case . . . I hope you enjoy disappointment."

We scowled at each other in silence. I was the first to speak, trying to keep myself focused. I was in danger of being distracted by his livid, glorious face. It was like trying to stare down a destroying angel.

"Why did you even bother?" I asked frigidly.

He paused, and for a brief moment his stunning face was unexpectedly vulnerable.

"I don't know," he whispered.

And then he turned his back on me and walked away.

I was so angry, it took me a few minutes until I could move. When I could walk, I made my way slowly to the exit at the end of the hallway.

The waiting room was more unpleasant than I'd feared. It seemed like every face I knew in Forks was there, staring at me. Charlie rushed to my side; I put up my hands.

"There's nothing wrong with me," I assured him sullenly. I was still aggravated, not in the mood for chitchat.

"What did the doctor say?"

"Dr. Cullen saw me, and he said I was fine and I could go home." I sighed. Mike and Jessica and Eric were all there, beginning to converge on us. "Let's go," I urged.

Charlie put one arm behind my back, not quite touching me, and led me to the glass doors of the exit. I waved sheepishly at my friends, hoping to convey that they didn't need to worry anymore. It was a huge relief—the first time I'd ever felt that way—to get into the cruiser.

We drove in silence. I was so wrapped up in my thoughts that I barely knew Charlie was there. I was positive that Edward's defensive behavior in the hall was a confirmation of the bizarre things I still could hardly believe I'd witnessed.

When we got to the house, Charlie finally spoke.

"Um . . . you'll need to call Renée." He hung his head, guilty.

I was appalled. "You told Mom!"

"Sorry."

I slammed the cruiser's door a little harder than necessary on my way out.

My mom was in hysterics, of course. I had to tell her I felt fine at least thirty times before she would calm down. She begged me to come home—forgetting the fact that home was empty at the moment—but her pleas were easier to resist than I would have thought. I was consumed by the mystery Edward presented. And more than a little obsessed by Edward himself. Stupid, stupid, stupid. I wasn't as eager to escape Forks as I should be, as any normal, sane person would be.

I decided I might as well go to bed early that night. Charlie continued to watch me anxiously, and it was getting on my nerves. I stopped on my way to grab three Tylenol from the bathroom. They did help, and, as the pain eased, I drifted to sleep.

That was the first night I dreamed of Edward Cullen.

4. INVITATIONS

In my dream it was very dark, and what dim light there was seemed to be radiating from Edward's skin. I couldn't see his face, just his back as he walked away from me, leaving me in the blackness. No matter how fast I ran, I couldn't catch up to him; no matter how loud I called, he never turned. Troubled, I woke in the middle of the night and couldn't sleep again for what seemed like a very long time. After that, he was in my dreams nearly every night, but always on the periphery, never within reach.

The month that followed the accident was uneasy, tense, and, at first, embarrassing.

To my dismay, I found myself the center of attention for the rest of that week. Tyler Crowley was impossible, following me around, obsessed with making amends to me somehow. I tried to convince him what I wanted more than anything else was for him to forget all about it—especially since nothing had actually happened to me—but he remained insistent. He followed me between classes and sat at our now-crowded lunch table. Mike and Eric were even less friendly toward him than they were to each other, which made me worry that I'd gained another unwelcome fan.

No one seemed concerned about Edward, though I explained over and over that he was the hero—how he had pulled me out of the way and had nearly been crushed, too. I tried to be convincing. Jessica, Mike, Eric, and everyone else always commented that they hadn't even seen him there till the van was pulled away.

I wondered to myself why no one else had seen him standing so far away, before he was suddenly, impossibly saving my life. With chagrin, I realized the probable cause—no one else was as aware of Edward as I always was. No one else watched him the way I did. How pitiful.

Edward was never surrounded by crowds of curious bystanders eager for his firsthand account. People avoided him as usual. The Cullens and the Hales sat at the same table as always, not eating, talking only among themselves. None of them, especially Edward, glanced my way anymore.

When he sat next to me in class, as far from me as the table would allow, he seemed totally unaware of my presence. Only now and then, when his fists would suddenly ball up—skin stretched even whiter over the bones—did I wonder if he wasn't quite as oblivious as he appeared.

He wished he hadn't pulled me from the path of Tyler's van—there was no other conclusion I could come to.

I wanted very much to talk to him, and the day after the accident I tried. The last time I'd seen him, outside the ER, we'd both been so furious. I still was angry that he wouldn't trust me with the truth, even though I was keeping my part of the bargain flawlessly. But he had in fact saved my life, no matter how he'd done it. And, overnight, the heat of my anger faded into awed gratitude.

He was already seated when I got to Biology, looking straight ahead. I sat down, expecting him to turn toward me. He showed no sign that he realized I was there.

"Hello, Edward," I said pleasantly, to show him I was going to behave myself.

He turned his head a fraction toward me without meeting my gaze, nodded once, and then looked the other way.

And that was the last contact I'd had with him, though he was there, a foot away from me, every day. I watched him sometimes, unable to stop myself—from a distance, though, in the cafeteria or parking lot. I watched as his golden eyes grew perceptibly darker day by day. But in class I gave no more notice that he existed than he showed toward me. I was miserable. And the dreams continued.

Despite my outright lies, the tenor of my e-mails alerted Renée to my depression, and she called a few times, worried. I tried to convince her it was just the weather that had me down.

Mike, at least, was pleased by the obvious coolness between me and my lab partner. I could see he'd been worried that Edward's daring rescue might have impressed me, and he was relieved that it seemed to have the opposite effect. He grew more confident, sitting on the edge of my table to talk before Biology class started, ignoring Edward as completely as he ignored us.

The snow washed away for good after that one dangerously icy day. Mike was disappointed he'd never gotten to stage his snowball fight, but pleased that the beach trip would soon be possible. The rain continued heavily, though, and the weeks passed.

Jessica made me aware of another event looming on the horizon—she called the first Tuesday of March to ask my permission to invite Mike to the girls' choice spring dance in two weeks.

"Are you sure you don't mind . . . you weren't planning to ask him?" she persisted when I told her I didn't mind in the least.

"No, Jess, I'm not going," I assured her. Dancing was glaringly outside my range of abilities.

"It will be really fun." Her attempt to convince me was halfhearted. I suspected that Jessica enjoyed my inexplicable popularity more than my actual company.

"You have fun with Mike," I encouraged.

The next day, I was surprised that Jessica wasn't her usual gushing self in Trig and Spanish. She was silent as she walked by my side between classes, and I was afraid to ask her why. If Mike had turned her down, I was the last person she would want to tell.

My fears were strengthened during lunch when Jessica sat as far from Mike as possible, chatting animatedly with Eric. Mike was unusually quiet.

Mike was still quiet as he walked me to class, the uncomfortable look on his face a bad sign. But he didn't broach the subject until I was in my seat and he was perched on my desk. As always, I was electrically aware of Edward sitting close enough to touch, as distant as if he were merely an invention of my imagination.

"So," Mike said, looking at the floor, "Jessica asked me to the spring dance."

"That's great." I made my voice bright and enthusiastic. "You'll have a lot of fun with Jessica."

"Well . . ." He floundered as he examined my smile, clearly not happy with my response. "I told her I had to think about it."

"Why would you do that?" I let disapproval color my tone, though I was relieved he hadn't given her an absolute no.

His face was bright red as he looked down again. Pity shook my resolve.

"I was wondering if . . . well, if you might be planning to ask me."

I paused for a moment, hating the wave of guilt that swept through me. But I saw, from the corner of my eye, Edward's head tilt reflexively in my direction.

"Mike, I think you should tell her yes," I said.

"Did you already ask someone?" Did Edward notice how Mike's eyes flickered in his direction?

"No," I assured him. "I'm not going to the dance at all."

"Why not?" Mike demanded.

I didn't want to get into the safety hazards that dancing presented, so I quickly made new plans.

"I'm going to Seattle that Saturday," I explained. I needed to get out of town anyway—it was suddenly the perfect time to go.

"Can't you go some other weekend?"

"Sorry, no," I said. "So you shouldn't make Jess wait any longer—it's rude."

"Yeah, you're right," he mumbled, and turned, dejected, to walk back to his seat. I closed my eyes and pressed my fingers to my temples, trying to push the guilt and sympathy out of my head. Mr. Banner began talking. I sighed and opened my eyes.

And Edward was staring at me curiously, that same, familiar edge of frustration even more distinct now in his black eyes.

I stared back, surprised, expecting him to look quickly away. But instead he continued to gaze with probing intensity into my eyes. There was no question of me looking away. My hands started to shake.

"Mr. Cullen?" the teacher called, seeking the answer to a question that I hadn't heard.

"The Krebs Cycle," Edward answered, seeming reluctant as he turned to look at Mr. Banner.

I looked down at my book as soon as his eyes released me, trying to find my place. Cowardly as ever, I shifted my hair over my right shoulder to hide my face. I couldn't believe the rush of emotion pulsing through me—just because he'd happened to look at me for the first time in a half-dozen weeks. I couldn't allow him to have this level of influence over me. It was pathetic. More than pathetic, it was unhealthy.

I tried very hard not to be aware of him for the rest of the hour, and, since that was impossible, at least not to let him know that I was aware of him. When the bell rang at last, I turned my back to him to gather my things, expecting him to leave immediately as usual.

"Bella?" His voice shouldn't have been so familiar to me, as if I'd known the sound of it all my life rather than for just a few short weeks.

I turned slowly, unwillingly. I didn't want to feel what I knew I *would* feel when I looked at his too-perfect face. My expression was wary when I finally turned to him; his expression was unreadable. He didn't say anything.

"What? Are you speaking to me again?" I finally asked, an unintentional note of petulance in my voice.

His lips twitched, fighting a smile. "No, not really," he admitted.

I closed my eyes and inhaled slowly through my nose, aware that I was gritting my teeth. He waited.

"Then what do you want, Edward?" I asked, keeping my eyes closed; it was easier to talk to him coherently that way.

"I'm sorry." He sounded sincere. "I'm being very rude, I know. But it's better this way, really."

I opened my eyes. His face was very serious.

"I don't know what you mean," I said, my voice guarded.

"It's better if we're not friends," he explained. "Trust me."

My eyes narrowed. I'd heard *that* before.

"It's too bad you didn't figure that out earlier," I hissed through my teeth. "You could have saved yourself all this regret."

"Regret?" The word, and my tone, obviously caught him off guard. "Regret for what?"

"For not just letting that stupid van squish me."

He was astonished. He stared at me in disbelief.

When he finally spoke, he almost sounded mad. "You think I regret saving your life?"

"I *know* you do," I snapped.

"You don't know anything." He was definitely mad.

I turned my head sharply away from him, clenching my jaw against all the wild accusations I wanted to hurl at him. I gathered my books together, then stood and walked to the door. I meant to sweep dramatically out of the room, but of course I caught the toe of my boot on the doorjamb and dropped my books. I stood there for a moment, thinking about leaving them. Then I sighed and bent to pick them up. He was there; he'd already stacked them into a pile. He handed them to me, his face hard.

"Thank you," I said icily.

His eyes narrowed.

"You're welcome," he retorted.

I straightened up swiftly, turned away from him again, and stalked off to Gym without looking back.

Gym was brutal. We'd moved on to basketball. My team never passed me the ball, so that was good, but I fell down a lot. Sometimes I took people with me. Today I was worse than usual because my head was so filled with Edward. I tried to concentrate on my feet, but he kept creeping back into my thoughts just when I really needed my balance.

It was a relief, as always, to leave. I almost ran to the truck; there were just so many people I wanted to avoid. The truck had suffered only minimal damage in the accident. I'd had to replace the taillights, and if I'd had a real paint job, I would have touched that up. Tyler's parents had to sell their van for parts.

I almost had a stroke when I rounded the corner and saw a tall, dark figure leaning against the side of my truck. Then I realized it was just Eric. I started walking again.

"Hey, Eric," I called.

"Hi, Bella."

"What's up?" I said as I was unlocking the door. I wasn't paying attention to the uncomfortable edge in his voice, so his next words took me by surprise.

"Uh, I was just wondering ... if you would go to the spring dance with me?" His voice broke on the last word.

"I thought it was girls' choice," I said, too startled to be diplomatic.

"Well, yeah," he admitted, shamefaced.

I recovered my composure and tried to make my smile warm. "Thank you for asking me, but I'm going to be in Seattle that day."

"Oh," he said. "Well, maybe next time."

"Sure," I agreed, and then bit my lip. I wouldn't want him to take that too literally.

He slouched off, back toward the school. I heard a low chuckle.

Edward was walking past the front of my truck, looking straight forward, his lips pressed together. I yanked the door open and jumped inside, slamming it loudly behind me. I revved the engine deafeningly and reversed out into the aisle. Edward was in his car already, two spaces down, sliding out smoothly in front of me, cutting me off. He stopped there—to wait for his family; I could see the four of them walking this way, but still by the cafeteria. I considered taking out the rear of his shiny Volvo, but there were too many witnesses. I looked in my rearview mirror. A line was beginning to form. Directly behind me, Tyler Crowley was in his recently acquired used Sentra, waving. I was too aggravated to acknowledge him.

While I was sitting there, looking everywhere but at the car in front of me, I heard a knock on my passenger side window. I looked over; it was Tyler. I glanced back in my rearview mirror, confused. His car was still running, the door left open. I leaned across the cab to crank the window down. It was stiff. I got it halfway down, then gave up.

"I'm sorry, Tyler, I'm stuck behind Cullen." I was annoyed—obviously the holdup wasn't my fault.

"Oh, I know—I just wanted to ask you something while we're trapped here." He grinned.

This could not be happening.

"Will you ask me to the spring dance?" he continued.

"I'm not going to be in town, Tyler." My voice sounded a little sharp. I had to remember it wasn't his fault that Mike and Eric had already used up my quota of patience for the day.

"Yeah, Mike said that," he admitted.

"Then why—"

He shrugged. "I was hoping you were just letting him down easy."

Okay, it was completely his fault.

"Sorry, Tyler," I said, working to hide my irritation. "I really am going out of town."

"That's cool. We still have prom."

And before I could respond, he was walking back to his car. I could feel the shock on my face. I looked forward to see Alice, Rosalie, Emmett, and Jasper all sliding into the Volvo. In his rearview mirror, Edward's eyes were on me. He was unquestionably shaking with laughter, as if he'd heard every word Tyler had said. My foot itched toward the gas pedal . . . one little bump wouldn't hurt any of them, just that glossy silver paint job. I revved the engine.

But they were all in, and Edward was speeding away. I drove home slowly, carefully, muttering to myself the whole way.

When I got home, I decided to make chicken enchiladas for dinner. It was a long process, and it would keep me busy. While I was simmering the onions and chilies, the phone rang. I was almost afraid to answer it, but it might be Charlie or my mom.

It was Jessica, and she was jubilant; Mike had caught her after school to accept her invitation. I celebrated with her briefly while I stirred. She had to go, she wanted to call Angela and Lauren to tell them. I suggested—with casual innocence—that maybe Angela, the shy girl who had Biology with me, could ask Eric. And Lauren, a standoffish girl who had always ignored me at the lunch table, could ask Tyler; I'd heard he was still available. Jess thought that was a great idea. Now that she was sure of Mike, she actually sounded sincere when she said she wished I would go to the dance. I gave her my Seattle excuse.

After I hung up, I tried to concentrate on dinner—dicing the chicken especially; I didn't want to take another trip to the emergency room. But my head was spinning, trying to analyze every word Edward had spoken today. What did he mean, it was better if we weren't friends?

My stomach twisted as I realized what he must have meant. He must see how absorbed I was by him; he must not want to lead me on . . . so we couldn't even be friends . . . because he wasn't interested in me at all.

Of course he wasn't interested in me, I thought angrily, my eyes stinging—a delayed reaction to the onions. I wasn't *interesting*. And he was. Interesting...and brilliant...and mysterious...and perfect...and beautiful...and possibly able to lift full-sized vans with one hand.

Well, that was fine. I could leave him alone. I *would* leave him alone. I would get through my self-imposed sentence here in purgatory, and then hopefully some school in the Southwest, or possibly Hawaii, would offer me a scholarship. I focused my thoughts on sunny beaches and palm trees as I finished the enchiladas and put them in the oven.

Charlie seemed suspicious when he came home and smelled the green peppers. I couldn't blame him—the closest edible Mexican food was probably in southern California. But he was a cop, even if just a small-town cop, so he was brave enough to take the first bite. He seemed to like it. It was fun to watch as he slowly began trusting me in the kitchen.

"Dad?" I asked when he was almost done.

"Yeah, Bella?"

"Um, I just wanted to let you know that I'm going to Seattle for the day a week from Saturday...if that's okay?" I didn't want to ask permission—it set a bad precedent—but I felt rude, so I tacked it on at the end.

"Why?" He sounded surprised, as if he were unable to imagine something that Forks couldn't offer.

"Well, I wanted to get a few books—the library here is pretty limited—and maybe look at some clothes." I had more money than I was used to having, since, thanks to Charlie, I hadn't had to pay for a car. Not that the truck didn't cost me quite a bit in the gas department.

"That truck probably doesn't get very good gas mileage," he said, echoing my thoughts.

"I know, I'll stop in Montesano and Olympia—and Tacoma if I have to."

"Are you going all by yourself?" he asked, and I couldn't tell if he was suspicious I had a secret boyfriend or just worried about car trouble.

"Yes."

"Seattle is a big city—you could get lost," he fretted.

"Dad, Phoenix is five times the size of Seattle—and I can read a map, don't worry about it."

"Do you want me to come with you?"

I tried to be crafty as I hid my horror.

"That's all right, Dad, I'll probably just be in dressing rooms all day— very boring."

"Oh, okay." The thought of sitting in women's clothing stores for any period of time immediately put him off.

"Thanks." I smiled at him.

"Will you be back in time for the dance?"

Grrr. Only in a town this small would a *father* know when the high school dances were.

"No—I don't dance, Dad." He, of all people, should understand that—I didn't get my balance problems from my mother.

He did understand. "Oh, that's right," he realized.

The next morning, when I pulled into the parking lot, I deliberately parked as far as possible from the silver Volvo. I didn't want to put myself in the path of too much temptation and end up owing him a new car. Getting out of the cab, I fumbled with my key and it fell into a puddle at my feet. As I bent to get it, a white hand flashed out and grabbed it before I could. I jerked upright. Edward Cullen was right next to me, leaning casually against my truck.

"How do you *do* that?" I asked in amazed irritation.

"Do what?" He held my key out as he spoke. As I reached for it, he dropped it into my palm.

"Appear out of thin air."

"Bella, it's not my fault if you are exceptionally unobservant." His voice was quiet as usual—velvet, muted.

I scowled at his perfect face. His eyes were light again today, a deep, golden honey color. Then I had to look down, to reassemble my now-tangled thoughts.

"Why the traffic jam last night?" I demanded, still looking away. "I thought you were supposed to be pretending I don't exist, not irritating me to death."

"That was for Tyler's sake, not mine. I had to give him his chance." He snickered.

"You . . ." I gasped. I couldn't think of a bad enough word. It felt like the heat of my anger should physically burn him, but he only seemed more amused.

"And I'm not pretending you don't exist," he continued.

"So you *are* trying to irritate me to death? Since Tyler's van didn't do the job?"

Anger flashed in his tawny eyes. His lips pressed into a hard line, all signs of humor gone.

"Bella, you are utterly absurd," he said, his low voice cold.

My palms tingled—I wanted so badly to hit something. I was surprised at myself. I was usually a nonviolent person. I turned my back and started to walk away.

"Wait," he called. I kept walking, sloshing angrily through the rain. But he was next to me, easily keeping pace.

"I'm sorry, that was rude," he said as we walked. I ignored him. "I'm not saying it isn't true," he continued, "but it was rude to say it, anyway."

"Why won't you leave me alone?" I grumbled.

"I wanted to ask you something, but you sidetracked me," he chuckled. He seemed to have recovered his good humor.

"Do you have a multiple personality disorder?" I asked severely.

"You're doing it again."

I sighed. "Fine then. What do you want to ask?"

"I was wondering if, a week from Saturday—you know, the day of the spring dance—"

"Are you trying to be *funny*?" I interrupted him, wheeling toward him. My face got drenched as I looked up at his expression.

His eyes were wickedly amused. "Will you please allow me to finish?"

I bit my lip and clasped my hands together, interlocking my fingers, so I couldn't do anything rash.

"I heard you say you were going to Seattle that day, and I was wondering if you wanted a ride."

That was unexpected.

"What?" I wasn't sure what he was getting at.

"Do you want a ride to Seattle?"

"With who?" I asked, mystified.

"Myself, obviously." He enunciated every syllable, as if he were talking to someone mentally handicapped.

I was still stunned. *"Why?"*

"Well, I was planning to go to Seattle in the next few weeks, and, to be honest, I'm not sure if your truck can make it."

"My truck works just fine, thank you very much for your concern." I started to walk again, but I was too surprised to maintain the same level of anger.

"But can your truck make it there on one tank of gas?" He matched my pace again.

"I don't see how that is any of your business." Stupid, shiny Volvo owner.

"The wasting of finite resources is everyone's business."

"Honestly, Edward." I felt a thrill go through me as I said his name, and I hated it. "I can't keep up with you. I thought you didn't want to be my friend."

"I said it would be better if we weren't friends, not that I didn't want to be."

"Oh, thanks, now that's *all* cleared up." Heavy sarcasm. I realized I had stopped walking again. We were under the shelter of the cafeteria roof now, so I could more easily look at his face. Which certainly didn't help my clarity of thought.

"It would be more...*prudent* for you not to be my friend," he explained. "But I'm tired of trying to stay away from you, Bella."

His eyes were gloriously intense as he uttered that last sentence, his voice smoldering. I couldn't remember how to breathe.

"Will you go with me to Seattle?" he asked, still intense.

I couldn't speak yet, so I just nodded.

He smiled briefly, and then his face became serious.

"You really *should* stay away from me," he warned. "I'll see you in class."

He turned abruptly and walked back the way we'd come.

5. BLOOD TYPE

I MADE MY WAY TO ENGLISH IN A DAZE. I DIDN'T EVEN REALIZE WHEN I first walked in that class had already started.

"Thank you for joining us, Miss Swan," Mr. Mason said in a disparaging tone.

I flushed and hurried to my seat.

It wasn't till class ended that I realized Mike wasn't sitting in his usual seat next to me. I felt a twinge of guilt. But he and Eric both met me at the door as usual, so I figured I wasn't totally unforgiven. Mike seemed to become more himself as we walked, gaining enthusiasm as he talked about the weather report for this weekend. The rain was supposed to take a minor break, and so maybe his beach trip would be possible. I tried to sound eager, to make up for disappointing him yesterday. It was hard; rain or no rain, it would still only be in the high forties, if we were lucky.

The rest of the morning passed in a blur. It was difficult to believe that I hadn't just imagined what Edward had said, and the way his eyes had looked. Maybe it was just a very convincing dream that I'd confused with reality. That seemed more probable than that I really appealed to him on any level.

So I was impatient and frightened as Jessica and I entered the cafeteria. I wanted to see his face, to see if he'd gone back to the cold, indifferent person I'd known for the last several weeks. Or if, by some miracle, I'd really heard what I thought I'd heard this morning. Jessica babbled on and on about her dance plans—Lauren and Angela had asked the other boys and they were all going together—completely unaware of my inattention.

Disappointment flooded through me as my eyes unerringly focused on his table. The other four were there, but he was absent. Had he gone home? I followed the still-babbling Jessica through the line, crushed. I'd lost my appetite—I bought nothing but a bottle of lemonade. I just wanted to go sit down and sulk.

"Edward Cullen is staring at you again," Jessica said, finally breaking through my abstraction with his name. "I wonder why he's sitting alone today."

My head snapped up. I followed her gaze to see Edward, smiling crookedly, staring at me from an empty table across the cafeteria from where he usually sat. Once he'd caught my eye, he raised one hand and motioned with his index finger for me to join him. As I stared in disbelief, he winked.

"Does he mean *you*?" Jessica asked with insulting astonishment in her voice.

"Maybe he needs help with his Biology homework," I muttered for her benefit. "Um, I'd better go see what he wants."

I could feel her staring after me as I walked away.

When I reached his table, I stood behind the chair across from him, unsure.

"Why don't you sit with me today?" he asked, smiling.

I sat down automatically, watching him with caution. He was still smiling. It was hard to believe that someone so beautiful could be real. I was afraid that he might disappear in a sudden puff of smoke, and I would wake up.

He seemed to be waiting for me to say something.

"This is different," I finally managed.

"Well . . ." He paused, and then the rest of the words followed in a rush. "I decided as long as I was going to hell, I might as well do it thoroughly."

I waited for him to say something that made sense. The seconds ticked by.

"You know I don't have any idea what you mean," I eventually pointed out.

"I know." He smiled again, and then he changed the subject. "I think your friends are angry with me for stealing you."

"They'll survive." I could feel their stares boring into my back.

"I may not give you back, though," he said with a wicked glint in his eyes. I gulped.

He laughed. "You look worried."

"No," I said, but, ridiculously, my voice broke. "Surprised, actually... what brought all this on?"

"I told you—I got tired of trying to stay away from you. So I'm giving up." He was still smiling, but his ocher eyes were serious.

"Giving up?" I repeated in confusion.

"Yes—giving up trying to be good. I'm just going to do what I want now, and let the chips fall where they may." His smile faded as he explained, and a hard edge crept into his voice.

"You lost me again."

The breathtaking crooked smile reappeared.

"I always say too much when I'm talking to you—that's one of the problems."

"Don't worry—I don't understand any of it," I said wryly.

"I'm counting on that."

"So, in plain English, are we friends now?"

"Friends...," he mused, dubious.

"Or not," I muttered.

He grinned. "Well, we can try, I suppose. But I'm warning you now that I'm not a good friend for you." Behind his smile, the warning was real.

"You say that a lot," I noted, trying to ignore the sudden trembling in my stomach and keep my voice even.

"Yes, because you're not listening to me. I'm still waiting for you to believe it. If you're smart, you'll avoid me."

"I think you've made your opinion on the subject of my intellect clear, too." My eyes narrowed.

He smiled apologetically.

"So, as long as I'm being... not smart, we'll try to be friends?" I struggled to sum up the confusing exchange.

"That sounds about right."

I looked down at my hands wrapped around the lemonade bottle, not sure what to do now.

"What are you thinking?" he asked curiously.

I looked up into his deep gold eyes, became befuddled, and, as usual, blurted out the truth.

"I'm trying to figure out what you are."

His jaw tightened, but he kept his smile in place with some effort.

"Are you having any luck with that?" he asked in an offhand tone.

"Not too much," I admitted.

He chuckled. "What are your theories?"

I blushed. I had been vacillating during the last month between Bruce Wayne and Peter Parker. There was no way I was going to own up to that.

"Won't you tell me?" he asked, tilting his head to one side with a shockingly tempting smile.

I shook my head. "Too embarrassing."

"That's *really* frustrating, you know," he complained.

"No," I disagreed quickly, my eyes narrowing, "I can't *imagine* why that would be frustrating at all—just because someone refuses to tell you what they're thinking, even if all the while they're making cryptic little remarks specifically designed to keep you up at night wondering what they could possibly mean . . . now, why would that be frustrating?"

He grimaced.

"Or better," I continued, the pent-up annoyance flowing freely now, "say that person also did a wide range of bizarre things—from saving your life under impossible circumstances one day to treating you like a pariah the next, and he never explained any of that, either, even after he promised. That, also, would be *very* non-frustrating."

"You've got a bit of a temper, don't you?"

"I don't like double standards."

We stared at each other, unsmiling.

He glanced over my shoulder, and then, unexpectedly, he snickered.

"What?"

"Your boyfriend seems to think I'm being unpleasant to you—he's debating whether or not to come break up our fight." He snickered again.

"I don't know who you're talking about," I said frostily. "But I'm sure you're wrong, anyway."

"I'm not. I told you, most people are easy to read."

"Except me, of course."

"Yes. Except for you." His mood shifted suddenly; his eyes turned brooding. "I wonder why that is."

I had to look away from the intensity of his stare. I concentrated on unscrewing the lid of my lemonade. I took a swig, staring at the table without seeing it.

"Aren't you hungry?" he asked, distracted.

"No." I didn't feel like mentioning that my stomach was already full—of butterflies. "You?" I looked at the empty table in front of him.

"No, I'm not hungry." I didn't understand his expression—it looked like he was enjoying some private joke.

"Can you do me a favor?" I asked after a second of hesitation.

He was suddenly wary. "That depends on what you want."

"It's not much," I assured him.

He waited, guarded but curious.

"I just wondered . . . if you could warn me beforehand the next time you decide to ignore me for my own good. Just so I'm prepared." I looked at the lemonade bottle as I spoke, tracing the circle of the opening with my pinkie finger.

"That sounds fair." He was pressing his lips together to keep from laughing when I looked up.

"Thanks."

"Then can I have one answer in return?" he demanded.

"One."

"Tell me *one* theory."

Whoops. "Not that one."

"You didn't qualify, you just promised one answer," he reminded me.

"And you've broken promises yourself," I reminded him back.

"Just one theory—I won't laugh."

"Yes, you will." I was positive about that.

He looked down, and then glanced up at me through his long black lashes, his ocher eyes scorching.

"Please?" he breathed, leaning toward me.

I blinked, my mind going blank. Holy crow, how did he *do* that?

"Er, what?" I asked, dazed.

"Please tell me just one little theory." His eyes still smoldered at me.

"Um, well, bitten by a radioactive spider?" Was he a hypnotist, too? Or was I just a hopeless pushover?

"That's not very creative," he scoffed.

"I'm sorry, that's all I've got," I said, miffed.

"You're not even close," he teased.

"No spiders?"

"Nope."

"And no radioactivity?"

"None."

"Dang," I sighed.

"Kryptonite doesn't bother me, either," he chuckled.

"You're not supposed to laugh, remember?"

He struggled to compose his face.

"I'll figure it out eventually," I warned him.

"I wish you wouldn't try." He was serious again.

"Because...?"

"What if I'm not a superhero? What if I'm the bad guy?" He smiled playfully, but his eyes were impenetrable.

"Oh," I said, as several things he'd hinted fell suddenly into place. "I see."

"Do you?" His face was abruptly severe, as if he were afraid that he'd accidentally said too much.

"You're dangerous?" I guessed, my pulse quickening as I intuitively realized the truth of my own words. He *was* dangerous. He'd been trying to tell me that all along.

He just looked at me, eyes full of some emotion I couldn't comprehend.

"But not bad," I whispered, shaking my head. "No, I don't believe that you're bad."

"You're wrong." His voice was almost inaudible. He looked down, stealing my bottle lid and then spinning it on its side between his fingers. I stared at him, wondering why I didn't feel afraid. He meant what he was saying—that was obvious. But I just felt anxious, on edge...and, more than anything else, fascinated. The same way I always felt when I was near him.

The silence lasted until I noticed that the cafeteria was almost empty.

I jumped to my feet. "We're going to be late."

"I'm not going to class today," he said, twirling the lid so fast it was just a blur.

"Why not?"

"It's healthy to ditch class now and then." He smiled up at me, but his eyes were still troubled.

"Well, I'm going," I told him. I was far too big a coward to risk getting caught.

He turned his attention back to his makeshift top. "I'll see you later, then."

I hesitated, torn, but then the first bell sent me hurrying out the door—with a last glance confirming that he hadn't moved a centimeter.

As I half-ran to class, my head was spinning faster than the bottle cap. So few questions had been answered in comparison to how many new questions had been raised. At least the rain had stopped.

I was lucky; Mr. Banner wasn't in the room yet when I arrived. I settled quickly into my seat, aware that both Mike and Angela were staring at me. Mike looked resentful; Angela looked surprised, and slightly awed.

Mr. Banner came in the room then, calling the class to order. He was juggling a few small cardboard boxes in his arms. He put them down on Mike's table, telling him to start passing them around the class.

"Okay, guys, I want you all to take one piece from each box," he said as he produced a pair of rubber gloves from the pocket of his lab jacket and pulled them on. The sharp sound as the gloves snapped into place against his wrists seemed ominous to me. "The first should be an indicator card," he went on, grabbing a white card with four squares marked on it and displaying it. "The second is a four-pronged applicator—" he held up something that looked like a nearly toothless hair pick "—and the third is a sterile micro-lancet." He held up a small piece of blue plastic and split it open. The barb was invisible from this distance, but my stomach flipped.

"I'll be coming around with a dropper of water to prepare your cards, so please don't start until I get to you." He began at Mike's table again, carefully putting one drop of water in each of the four squares. "Then I want you to carefully prick your finger with the lancet. . . ." He grabbed Mike's hand and jabbed the spike into the tip of Mike's middle finger. Oh no. Clammy moisture broke out across my forehead.

"Put a small drop of blood on each of the prongs." He demonstrated, squeezing Mike's finger till the blood flowed. I swallowed convulsively, my stomach heaving.

"And then apply it to the card," he finished, holding up the dripping red card for us to see. I closed my eyes, trying to hear through the ringing in my ears.

"The Red Cross is having a blood drive in Port Angeles next weekend, so I thought you should all know your blood type." He sounded proud of himself. "Those of you who aren't eighteen yet will need a parent's permission— I have slips at my desk."

He continued through the room with his water drops. I put my cheek against the cool black tabletop and tried to hold on to my consciousness. All around me I could hear squeals, complaints, and giggles as my classmates skewered their fingers. I breathed slowly in and out through my mouth.

"Bella, are you all right?" Mr. Banner asked. His voice was close to my head, and it sounded alarmed.

"I already know my blood type, Mr. Banner," I said in a weak voice. I was afraid to raise my head.

"Are you feeling faint?"

"Yes, sir," I muttered, internally kicking myself for not ditching when I had the chance.

"Can someone take Bella to the nurse, please?" he called.

I didn't have to look up to know that it would be Mike who volunteered.

"Can you walk?" Mr. Banner asked.

"Yes," I whispered. Just let me get out of here, I thought. I'll crawl.

Mike seemed eager as he put his arm around my waist and pulled my arm over his shoulder. I leaned against him heavily on the way out of the classroom.

Mike towed me slowly across campus. When we were around the edge of the cafeteria, out of sight of building four in case Mr. Banner was watching, I stopped.

"Just let me sit for a minute, please?" I begged.

He helped me sit on the edge of the walk.

"And whatever you do, keep your hand in your pocket," I warned. I was still so dizzy. I slumped over on my side, putting my cheek against the freezing, damp cement of the sidewalk, closing my eyes. That seemed to help a little.

"Wow, you're green, Bella," Mike said nervously.

"Bella?" a different voice called from the distance.

No! Please let me be imagining that horribly familiar voice.

"What's wrong—is she hurt?" His voice was closer now, and he sounded upset. I wasn't imagining it. I squeezed my eyes shut, hoping to die. Or, at the very least, not to throw up.

Mike seemed stressed. "I think she's fainted. I don't know what happened, she didn't even stick her finger."

"Bella." Edward's voice was right beside me, relieved now. "Can you hear me?"

"No," I groaned. "Go away."

He chuckled.

"I was taking her to the nurse," Mike explained in a defensive tone, "but she wouldn't go any farther."

"I'll take her," Edward said. I could hear the smile still in his voice. "You can go back to class."

"No," Mike protested. "I'm supposed to do it."

Suddenly the sidewalk disappeared from beneath me. My eyes flew open in shock. Edward had scooped me up in his arms, as easily as if I weighed ten pounds instead of a hundred and ten.

"Put me down!" Please, please let me not vomit on him. He was walking before I was finished talking.

"Hey!" Mike called, already ten paces behind us.

Edward ignored him. "You look awful," he told me, grinning.

"Put me back on the sidewalk," I moaned. The rocking movement of his walk was not helping. He held me away from his body, gingerly, supporting all my weight with just his arms—it didn't seem to bother him.

"So you faint at the sight of blood?" he asked. This seemed to entertain him.

I didn't answer. I closed my eyes again and fought the nausea with all my strength, clamping my lips together.

"And not even your own blood," he continued, enjoying himself.

I don't know how he opened the door while carrying me, but it was suddenly warm, so I knew we were inside.

"Oh my," I heard a female voice gasp.

"She fainted in Biology," Edward explained.

I opened my eyes. I was in the office, and Edward was striding past the front counter toward the nurse's door. Ms. Cope, the redheaded front office receptionist, ran ahead of him to hold it open. The grandmotherly nurse looked up from a novel, astonished, as Edward swung me into the room and placed me gently on the crackly paper that covered the brown vinyl mattress on the one cot. Then he moved to stand against the wall as far across the narrow room as possible. His eyes were bright, excited.

"She's just a little faint," he reassured the startled nurse. "They're blood typing in Biology."

The nurse nodded sagely. "There's always one."

He muffled a snicker.

"Just lie down for a minute, honey; it'll pass."

"I know," I sighed. The nausea was already fading.

"Does this happen a lot?" she asked.

"Sometimes," I admitted. Edward coughed to hide another laugh.

"You can go back to class now," she told him.

"I'm supposed to stay with her." He said this with such assured authority that—even though she pursed her lips—the nurse didn't argue it further.

"I'll go get you some ice for your forehead, dear," she said to me, and then bustled out of the room.

"You were right," I moaned, letting my eyes close.

"I usually am—but about what in particular this time?"

"Ditching *is* healthy." I practiced breathing evenly.

"You scared me for a minute there," he admitted after a pause. His tone made it sound like he was confessing a humiliating weakness. "I thought Newton was dragging your dead body off to bury it in the woods."

"Ha ha." I still had my eyes closed, but I was feeling more normal every minute.

"Honestly—I've seen corpses with better color. I was concerned that I might have to avenge your murder."

"Poor Mike. I'll bet he's mad."

"He absolutely loathes me," Edward said cheerfully.

"You can't know that," I argued, but then I wondered suddenly if he could.

"I saw his face—I could tell."

"How did you see me? I thought you were ditching." I was almost fine now, though the queasiness would probably pass faster if I'd eaten something for lunch. On the other hand, maybe it was lucky my stomach was empty.

"I was in my car, listening to a CD." Such a normal response—it surprised me.

I heard the door and opened my eyes to see the nurse with a cold compress in her hand.

"Here you go, dear." She laid it across my forehead. "You're looking better," she added.

"I think I'm fine," I said, sitting up. Just a little ringing in my ears, no spinning. The mint green walls stayed where they should.

I could see she was about to make me lie back down, but the door opened just then, and Ms. Cope stuck her head in.

"We've got another one," she warned.

I hopped down to free up the cot for the next invalid.

I handed the compress back to the nurse. "Here, I don't need this."

And then Mike staggered through the door, now supporting a sallow-looking Lee Stephens, another boy in our Biology class. Edward and I drew back against the wall to give them room.

"Oh no," Edward muttered. "Go out to the office, Bella."

I looked up at him, bewildered.

"Trust me—go."

I spun and caught the door before it closed, darting out of the infirmary. I could feel Edward right behind me.

"You actually listened to me." He was stunned.

"I smelled the blood," I said, wrinkling my nose. Lee wasn't sick from watching other people, like me.

"People can't smell blood," he contradicted.

"Well, I can—that's what makes me sick. It smells like rust . . . and salt."

He was staring at me with an unfathomable expression.

"What?" I asked.

"It's nothing."

Mike came through the door then, glancing from me to Edward. The look he gave Edward confirmed what Edward had said about loathing. He looked back at me, his eyes glum.

"*You* look better," he accused.

"Just keep your hand in your pocket," I warned him again.

"It's not bleeding anymore," he muttered. "Are you going back to class?"

"Are you kidding? I'd just have to turn around and come back."

"Yeah, I guess. . . . So are you going this weekend? To the beach?" While he spoke, he flashed another glare toward Edward, who was standing against the cluttered counter, motionless as a sculpture, staring off into space.

I tried to sound as friendly as possible. "Sure, I said I was in."

"We're meeting at my dad's store, at ten." His eyes flickered to Edward again, wondering if he was giving out too much information. His body language made it clear that it wasn't an open invitation.

"I'll be there," I promised.

"I'll see you in Gym, then," he said, moving uncertainly toward the door.

"See you," I replied. He looked at me once more, his round face slightly pouting, and then as he walked slowly through the door, his shoulders slumped. A swell of sympathy washed over me. I pondered seeing his disappointed face again . . . in Gym.

"Gym," I groaned.

"I can take care of that." I hadn't noticed Edward moving to my side, but he spoke now in my ear. "Go sit down and look pale," he muttered.

That wasn't a challenge; I was always pale, and my recent swoon had left a light sheen of sweat on my face. I sat in one of the creaky folding chairs and rested my head against the wall with my eyes closed. Fainting spells always exhausted me.

I heard Edward speaking softly at the counter.

"Ms. Cope?"

"Yes?" I hadn't heard her return to her desk.

"Bella has Gym next hour, and I don't think she feels well enough. Actually, I was thinking I should take her home now. Do you think you could excuse her from class?" His voice was like melting honey. I could imagine how much more overwhelming his eyes would be.

"Do you need to be excused, too, Edward?" Ms. Cope fluttered. Why couldn't I do that?

"No, I have Mrs. Goff, she won't mind."

"Okay, it's all taken care of. You feel better, Bella," she called to me. I nodded weakly, hamming it up just a bit.

"Can you walk, or do you want me to carry you again?" With his back to the receptionist, his expression became sarcastic.

"I'll walk."

I stood carefully, and I was still fine. He held the door for me, his smile polite but his eyes mocking. I walked out into the cold, fine mist that had just begun to fall. It felt nice—the first time I'd enjoyed the constant moisture falling out of the sky—as it washed my face clean of the sticky perspiration.

"Thanks," I said as he followed me out. "It's almost worth getting sick to miss Gym."

"Anytime." He was staring straight forward, squinting into the rain.

"So are you going? This Saturday, I mean?" I was hoping he would, though it seemed unlikely. I couldn't picture him loading up to carpool with the rest of the kids from school; he didn't belong in the same world. But just hoping that he might gave me the first twinge of enthusiasm I'd felt for the outing.

"Where are you all going, exactly?" He was still looking ahead, expressionless.

"Down to La Push, to First Beach." I studied his face, trying to read it. His eyes seemed to narrow infinitesimally.

He glanced down at me from the corner of his eye, smiling wryly. "I really don't think I was invited."

I sighed. "I just invited you."

"Let's you and I not push poor Mike any further this week. We don't want him to snap." His eyes danced; he was enjoying the idea more than he should.

"Mike-schmike," I muttered, preoccupied by the way he'd said "you and I." I liked it more than I should.

We were near the parking lot now. I veered left, toward my truck. Something caught my jacket, yanking me back.

"Where do you think you're going?" he asked, outraged. He was gripping a fistful of my jacket in one hand.

I was confused. "I'm going home."

"Didn't you hear me promise to take you safely home? Do you think I'm going to let you drive in your condition?" His voice was still indignant.

"What condition? And what about my truck?" I complained.

"I'll have Alice drop it off after school." He was towing me toward his car now, pulling me by my jacket. It was all I could do to keep from falling backward. He'd probably just drag me along anyway if I did.

"Let go!" I insisted. He ignored me. I staggered along sideways across the wet sidewalk until we reached the Volvo. Then he finally freed me—I stumbled against the passenger door.

"You are so *pushy*!" I grumbled.

"It's open," was all he responded. He got in the driver's side.

"I am perfectly capable of driving myself home!" I stood by the car, fuming. It was raining harder now, and I'd never put my hood up, so my hair was dripping down my back.

He lowered the automatic window and leaned toward me across the seat. "Get in, Bella."

I didn't answer. I was mentally calculating my chances of reaching the truck before he could catch me. I had to admit, they weren't good.

"I'll just drag you back," he threatened, guessing my plan.

I tried to maintain what dignity I could as I got into his car. I wasn't very successful—I looked like a half-drowned cat and my boots squeaked.

"This is completely unnecessary," I said stiffly.

He didn't answer. He fiddled with the controls, turning the heater up and the music down. As he pulled out of the parking lot, I was preparing to give him the silent treatment—my face in full pout mode—but then I recognized the music playing, and my curiosity got the better of my intentions.

"Clair de Lune?" I asked, surprised.

"You know Debussy?" He sounded surprised, too.

"Not well," I admitted. "My mother plays a lot of classical music around the house—I only know my favorites."

"It's one of my favorites, too." He stared out through the rain, lost in thought.

I listened to the music, relaxing against the light gray leather seat. It was impossible not to respond to the familiar, soothing melody. The rain blurred everything outside the window into gray and green smudges. I began to realize we were driving very fast; the car moved so steadily, so evenly, though, I didn't feel the speed. Only the town flashing by gave it away.

"What is your mother like?" he asked me suddenly.

I glanced over to see him studying me with curious eyes.

"She looks a lot like me, but she's prettier," I said. He raised his eyebrows. "I have too much Charlie in me. She's more outgoing than I am, and braver. She's irresponsible and slightly eccentric, and she's a very unpredictable cook. She's my best friend." I stopped. Talking about her was making me depressed.

"How old are you, Bella?" His voice sounded frustrated for some reason I couldn't imagine. He'd stopped the car, and I realized we were at Charlie's house already. The rain was so heavy that I could barely see the house at all. It was like the car was submerged under a river.

"I'm seventeen," I responded, a little confused.

"You don't seem seventeen."

His tone was reproachful; it made me laugh.

"What?" he asked, curious again.

"My mom always says I was born thirty-five years old and that I get more middle-aged every year." I laughed, and then sighed. "Well, someone has to be the adult." I paused for a second. "You don't seem much like a junior in high school yourself," I noted.

He made a face and changed the subject.

"So why did your mother marry Phil?"

I was surprised he would remember the name; I'd mentioned it just once, almost two months ago. It took me a moment to answer.

"My mother...she's very young for her age. I think Phil makes her feel even younger. At any rate, she's crazy about him." I shook my head. The attraction was a mystery to me.

"Do you approve?" he asked.

"Does it matter?" I countered. "I want her to be happy...and he is who she wants."

"That's very generous.... I wonder," he mused.

"What?"

"Would she extend the same courtesy to you, do you think? No matter who your choice was?" He was suddenly intent, his eyes searching mine.

"I-I think so," I stuttered. "But she's the parent, after all. It's a little bit different."

"No one too scary then," he teased.

I grinned in response. "What do you mean by scary? Multiple facial piercings and extensive tattoos?"

"That's one definition, I suppose."

"What's your definition?"

But he ignored my question and asked me another. "Do you think that *I* could be scary?" He raised one eyebrow, and the faint trace of a smile lightened his face.

I thought for a moment, wondering whether the truth or a lie would go over better. I decided to go with the truth. "Hmmm ... I think you *could* be, if you wanted to."

"Are you frightened of me now?" The smile vanished, and his heavenly face was suddenly serious.

"No." But I answered too quickly. The smile returned.

"So, now are you going to tell me about your family?" I asked to distract him. "It's got to be a much more interesting story than mine."

He was instantly cautious. "What do you want to know?"

"The Cullens adopted you?" I verified.

"Yes."

I hesitated for a moment. "What happened to your parents?"

"They died many years ago." His tone was matter-of-fact.

"I'm sorry," I mumbled.

"I don't really remember them that clearly. Carlisle and Esme have been my parents for a long time now."

"And you love them." It wasn't a question. It was obvious in the way he spoke of them.

"Yes." He smiled. "I couldn't imagine two better people."

"You're very lucky."

"I know I am."

"And your brother and sister?"

He glanced at the clock on the dashboard.

"My brother and sister, and Jasper and Rosalie for that matter, are going to be quite upset if they have to stand in the rain waiting for me."

"Oh, sorry, I guess you have to go." I didn't want to get out of the car.

"And you probably want your truck back before Chief Swan gets home, so you don't have to tell him about the Biology incident." He grinned at me.

"I'm sure he's already heard. There are no secrets in Forks." I sighed.

He laughed, and there was an edge to his laughter.

"Have fun at the beach . . . good weather for sunbathing." He glanced out at the sheeting rain.

"Won't I see you tomorrow?"

"No. Emmett and I are starting the weekend early."

"What are you going to do?" A friend could ask that, right? I hoped the disappointment wasn't too apparent in my voice.

"We're going to be hiking in the Goat Rocks Wilderness, just south of Rainier."

I remembered Charlie had said the Cullens went camping frequently.

"Oh, well, have fun." I tried to sound enthusiastic. I don't think I fooled him, though. A smile was playing around the edges of his lips.

"Will you do something for me this weekend?" He turned to look me straight in the face, utilizing the full power of his burning gold eyes.

I nodded helplessly.

"Don't be offended, but you seem to be one of those people who just attract accidents like a magnet. So . . . try not to fall into the ocean or get run over or anything, all right?" He smiled crookedly.

The helplessness had faded as he spoke. I glared at him.

"I'll see what I can do," I snapped as I jumped out into the rain. I slammed the door behind me with excessive force.

He was still smiling as he drove away.

6. SCARY STORIES

As I sat in my room, trying to concentrate on the third act of *Macbeth,* I was really listening for my truck. I would have thought, even over the pounding rain, I could have heard the engine's roar. But when I went to peek out the curtain—again—it was suddenly there.

I wasn't looking forward to Friday, and it more than lived up to my non-expectations. Of course there were the fainting comments. Jessica especially seemed to get a kick out of that story. Luckily Mike had kept his mouth shut, and no one seemed to know about Edward's involvement. She did have a lot of questions about lunch, though.

"So what did Edward Cullen want yesterday?" Jessica asked in Trig.

"I don't know," I answered truthfully. "He never really got to the point."

"You looked kind of mad," she fished.

"Did I?" I kept my expression blank.

"You know, I've never seen him sit with anyone but his family before. That was weird."

"Weird," I agreed. She seemed annoyed; she flipped her dark curls impatiently—I guessed she'd been hoping to hear something that would make a good story for her to pass on.

The worst part about Friday was that, even though I knew he wasn't going to be there, I still hoped. When I walked into the cafeteria with Jessica and Mike, I couldn't keep from looking at his table, where Rosalie, Alice, and Jasper sat talking, heads close together. And I couldn't stop the gloom that engulfed me as I realized I didn't know how long I would have to wait before I saw him again.

At my usual table, everyone was full of our plans for the next day. Mike was animated again, putting a great deal of trust in the local weatherman who promised sun tomorrow. I'd have to see that before I believed it. But it was warmer today—almost sixty. Maybe the outing wouldn't be completely miserable.

I intercepted a few unfriendly glances from Lauren during lunch, which I didn't understand until we were all walking out of the room together. I was right behind her, just a foot from her slick, silver blond hair, and she was evidently unaware of that.

"...don't know why *Bella*"—she sneered my name—"doesn't just sit with the Cullens from now on," I heard her muttering to Mike. I'd never noticed what an unpleasant, nasal voice she had, and I was surprised by the malice in it. I really didn't know her well at all, certainly not well enough for her to dislike me—or so I'd thought.

"She's my friend; she sits with us," Mike whispered back loyally, but also a bit territorially. I paused to let Jess and Angela pass me. I didn't want to hear any more.

That night at dinner, Charlie seemed enthusiastic about my trip to La Push in the morning. I think he felt guilty for leaving me home alone on the weekends, but he'd spent too many years building his habits to break them now. Of course he knew the names of all the kids going, and their parents, and their great-grandparents, too, probably. He seemed to approve. I wondered if he would approve of my plan to ride to Seattle with Edward Cullen. Not that I was going to tell him.

"Dad, do you know a place called Goat Rocks or something like that? I think it's south of Mount Rainier," I asked casually.

"Yeah—why?"

I shrugged. "Some kids were talking about camping there."

"It's not a very good place for camping." He sounded surprised. "Too many bears. Most people go there during the hunting season."

"Oh," I murmured. "Maybe I got the name wrong."

I meant to sleep in, but an unusual brightness woke me. I opened my eyes to see a clear yellow light streaming through my window. I couldn't believe it. I hurried to the window to check, and sure enough, there was the sun. It was in the wrong place in the sky, too low, and it didn't seem to be as close as it should be, but it was definitely the sun. Clouds ringed the horizon, but a large patch of blue was visible in the middle. I lingered by the window as long as I could, afraid that if I left the blue would disappear again.

The Newtons' Olympic Outfitters store was just north of town. I'd seen the store, but I'd never stopped there—not having much need for any supplies required for being outdoors over an extended period of time. In the parking lot I recognized Mike's Suburban and Tyler's Sentra. As I pulled up next to their vehicles, I could see the group standing around in front of the Suburban. Eric was there, along with two other boys I had class with; I was fairly sure their names were Ben and Conner. Jess was there, flanked by Angela and Lauren. Three other girls stood with them, including one I remembered falling over in Gym on Friday. That one gave me a dirty look as I got out of the truck, and whispered something to Lauren. Lauren shook out her cornsilk hair and eyed me scornfully.

So it was going to be one of *those* days.

At least Mike was happy to see me.

"You came!" he called, delighted. "And I said it would be sunny today, didn't I?"

"I told you I was coming," I reminded him.

"We're just waiting for Lee and Samantha . . . unless you invited someone," Mike added.

"Nope," I lied lightly, hoping I wouldn't get caught in the lie. But also wishing that a miracle would occur, and Edward would appear.

Mike looked satisfied.

"Will you ride in my car? It's that or Lee's mom's minivan."

"Sure."

He smiled blissfully. It was so easy to make Mike happy.

"You can have shotgun," he promised. I hid my chagrin. It wasn't as simple to make Mike and Jessica happy at the same time. I could see Jessica glowering at us now.

The numbers worked out in my favor, though. Lee brought two extra people, and suddenly every seat was necessary. I managed to wedge Jess in between Mike and me in the front seat of the Suburban. Mike could have been more graceful about it, but at least Jess seemed appeased.

It was only fifteen miles to La Push from Forks, with gorgeous, dense green forests edging the road most of the way and the wide Quillayute River snaking beneath it twice. I was glad I had the window seat. We'd rolled the windows down—the Suburban was a bit claustrophobic with nine people in it—and I tried to absorb as much sunlight as possible.

I'd been to the beaches around La Push many times during my Forks summers with Charlie, so the mile-long crescent of First Beach was familiar to me. It was still breathtaking. The water was dark gray, even in the sunlight, white-capped and heaving to the gray, rocky shore. Islands rose out of the steel harbor waters with sheer cliff sides, reaching to uneven summits, and crowned with austere, soaring firs. The beach had only a thin border of actual sand at the water's edge, after which it grew into millions of large, smooth stones that looked uniformly gray from a distance, but close up were every shade a stone could be: terra-cotta, sea green, lavender, blue gray, dull gold. The tide line was strewn with huge driftwood trees, bleached bone white in the salt waves, some piled together against the edge of the forest fringe, some lying solitary, just out of reach of the waves.

There was a brisk wind coming off the waves, cool and briny. Pelicans floated on the swells while seagulls and a lone eagle wheeled above them. The clouds still circled the sky, threatening to invade at any moment, but for now the sun shone bravely in its halo of blue sky.

We picked our way down to the beach, Mike leading the way to a ring of driftwood logs that had obviously been used for parties like ours before. There was a fire circle already in place, filled with black ashes. Eric and the boy I thought was named Ben gathered broken branches of driftwood from the drier piles against the forest edge, and soon had a teepee-shaped construction built atop the old cinders.

"Have you ever seen a driftwood fire?" Mike asked me. I was sitting on one of the bone-colored benches; the other girls clustered, gossiping excitedly, on either side of me. Mike kneeled by the fire, lighting one of the smaller sticks with a cigarette lighter.

"No," I said as he placed the blazing twig carefully against the teepee.

"You'll like this then—watch the colors." He lit another small branch and laid it alongside the first. The flames started to lick quickly up the dry wood.

"It's blue," I said in surprise.

"The salt does it. Pretty, isn't it?" He lit one more piece, placed it where the fire hadn't yet caught, and then came to sit by me. Thankfully, Jess was on his other side. She turned to him and claimed his attention. I watched the strange blue and green flames crackle toward the sky.

After a half hour of chatter, some of the boys wanted to hike to the nearby tidal pools. It was a dilemma. On the one hand, I loved the tide pools. They had fascinated me since I was a child; they were one of the only things I ever looked forward to when I had to come to Forks. On the other hand, I'd also fallen into them a lot. Not a big deal when you're seven and with your dad. It reminded me of Edward's request—that I not fall into the ocean.

Lauren was the one who made my decision for me. She didn't want to hike, and she was definitely wearing the wrong shoes for it. Most of the other girls besides Angela and Jessica decided to stay on the beach as well. I waited until Tyler and Eric had committed to remaining with them before I got up quietly to join the pro-hiking group. Mike gave me a huge smile when he saw that I was coming.

The hike wasn't too long, though I hated to lose the sky in the woods. The green light of the forest was strangely at odds with the adolescent laughter, too murky and ominous to be in harmony with the light banter around me. I had to watch each step I took very carefully, avoiding roots below and branches above, and I soon fell behind. Eventually I broke through the emerald confines of the forest and found the rocky shore again. It was low tide, and a tidal river flowed past us on its way to the sea. Along its pebbled banks, shallow pools that never completely drained were teeming with life.

I was very cautious not to lean too far over the little ocean ponds. The others were fearless, leaping over the rocks, perching precariously on the edges. I found a very stable-looking rock on the fringe of one of the largest pools and sat there cautiously, spellbound by the natural aquarium below me. The bouquets of brilliant anemones undulated ceaselessly in the invisible current, twisted shells scurried about the edges, obscuring the crabs within them, starfish stuck motionless to the rocks and each other, while one small black eel with white racing stripes wove through the bright green weeds, waiting for the sea to return. I was completely absorbed, except for one small part of my mind that wondered what Edward was doing now, and trying to imagine what he would be saying if he were here with me.

Finally the boys were hungry, and I got up stiffly to follow them back. I tried to keep up better this time through the woods, so naturally I fell a few times. I got some shallow scrapes on my palms, and the knees of my jeans were stained green, but it could have been worse.

When we got back to First Beach, the group we'd left behind had multiplied. As we got closer we could see the shining, straight black hair and copper skin of the newcomers, teenagers from the reservation come to socialize. The food was already being passed around, and the boys hurried to claim a share while Eric introduced us as we each entered the driftwood circle. Angela and I were the last to arrive, and, as Eric said our names, I noticed a younger boy sitting on the stones near the fire glance up at me in interest. I sat down next to Angela, and Mike brought us sandwiches and an array of sodas to choose from, while a boy who looked to be the oldest of the visitors rattled off the names of the seven others with him. All I caught was that one of the girls was also named Jessica, and the boy who noticed me was named Jacob.

It was relaxing to sit with Angela; she was a restful kind of person to be around—she didn't feel the need to fill every silence with chatter. She left me free to think undisturbed while we ate. And I was thinking about how disjointedly time seemed to flow in Forks, passing in a blur at times, with single images standing out more clearly than others. And then, at other times, every second was significant, etched in my mind. I knew exactly what caused the difference, and it disturbed me.

During lunch the clouds started to advance, slinking across the blue sky, darting in front of the sun momentarily, casting long shadows across the beach, and blackening the waves. As they finished eating, people started to drift away in twos and threes. Some walked down to the edge of the waves, trying to skip rocks across the choppy surface. Others were gathering a second expedition to the tide pools. Mike—with Jessica shadowing him—headed up to the one shop in the village. Some of the local kids went with them; others went along on the hike. By the time they all had scattered, I was sitting alone on my driftwood log, with Lauren and Tyler occupying themselves by the CD player someone had thought to bring, and three teenagers from the reservation perched around the circle, including the boy named Jacob and the oldest boy who had acted as spokesperson.

A few minutes after Angela left with the hikers, Jacob sauntered over to take her place by my side. He looked fourteen, maybe fifteen, and had long, glossy black hair pulled back with a rubber band at the nape of his neck. His skin was beautiful, silky and russet-colored; his eyes were dark, set deep above the high planes of his cheekbones. He still had just a hint of child-ish roundness left around his chin. Altogether, a very pretty face. However, my positive opinion of his looks was damaged by the first words out of his mouth.

"You're Isabella Swan, aren't you?"

It was like the first day of school all over again.

"Bella," I sighed.

"I'm Jacob Black." He held his hand out in a friendly gesture. "You bought my dad's truck."

"Oh," I said, relieved, shaking his sleek hand. "You're Billy's son. I proba-bly should remember you."

"No, I'm the youngest of the family—you would remember my older sisters."

"Rachel and Rebecca," I suddenly recalled. Charlie and Billy had thrown us together a lot during my visits, to keep us busy while they fished. We were all too shy to make much progress as friends. Of course, I'd kicked up enough tantrums to end the fishing trips by the time I was eleven.

"Are they here?" I examined the girls at the ocean's edge, wondering if I would recognize them now.

"No." Jacob shook his head. "Rachel got a scholarship to Washington State, and Rebecca married a Samoan surfer—she lives in Hawaii now."

"Married. Wow." I was stunned. The twins were only a little over a year older than I was.

"So how do you like the truck?" he asked.

"I love it. It runs great."

"Yeah, but it's really slow," he laughed. "I was so relieved when Charlie bought it. My dad wouldn't let me work on building another car when we had a perfectly good vehicle right there."

"It's not that slow," I objected.

"Have you tried to go over sixty?"

"No," I admitted.

"Good. Don't." He grinned.

I couldn't help grinning back. "It does great in a collision," I offered in my truck's defense.

"I don't think a tank could take out that old monster," he agreed with another laugh.

"So you build cars?" I asked, impressed.

"When I have free time, and parts. You wouldn't happen to know where I could get my hands on a master cylinder for a 1986 Volkswagen Rabbit?" he added jokingly. He had a pleasant, husky voice.

"Sorry," I laughed, "I haven't seen any lately, but I'll keep my eyes open for you." As if I knew what that was. He was very easy to talk with.

He flashed a brilliant smile, looking at me appreciatively in a way I was learning to recognize. I wasn't the only one who noticed.

"You know Bella, Jacob?" Lauren asked—in what I imagined was an insolent tone—from across the fire.

"We've sort of known each other since I was born," he laughed, smiling at me again.

"How nice." She didn't sound like she thought it was nice at all, and her pale, fishy eyes narrowed.

"Bella," she called again, watching my face carefully, "I was just saying to Tyler that it was too bad none of the Cullens could come out today. Didn't anyone think to invite them?" Her expression of concern was unconvincing.

"You mean Dr. Carlisle Cullen's family?" the tall, older boy asked before I could respond, much to Lauren's irritation. He was really closer to a man than a boy, and his voice was very deep.

"Yes, do you know them?" she asked condescendingly, turning halfway toward him.

"The Cullens don't come here," he said in a tone that closed the subject, ignoring her question.

Tyler, trying to win back her attention, asked Lauren's opinion on a CD he held. She was distracted.

I stared at the deep-voiced boy, taken aback, but he was looking away toward the dark forest behind us. He'd said that the Cullens didn't come here, but his tone had implied something more—that they weren't allowed; they were prohibited. His manner left a strange impression on me, and I tried to ignore it without success.

Jacob interrupted my meditation. "So is Forks driving you insane yet?"

"Oh, I'd say that's an understatement." I grimaced. He grinned understandingly.

I was still turning over the brief comment on the Cullens, and I had a sudden inspiration. It was a stupid plan, but I didn't have any better ideas. I hoped that young Jacob was as yet inexperienced around girls, so that he wouldn't see through my sure-to-be-pitiful attempts at flirting.

"Do you want to walk down the beach with me?" I asked, trying to imitate that way Edward had of looking up from underneath his eyelashes. It couldn't have nearly the same effect, I was sure, but Jacob jumped up willingly enough.

As we walked north across the multihued stones toward the driftwood seawall, the clouds finally closed ranks across the sky, causing the sea to darken and the temperature to drop. I shoved my hands deep into the pockets of my jacket.

"So you're, what, sixteen?" I asked, trying not to look like an idiot as I fluttered my eyelids the way I'd seen girls do on TV.

"I just turned fifteen," he confessed, flattered.

"Really?" My face was full of false surprise. "I would have thought you were older."

"I'm tall for my age," he explained.

"Do you come up to Forks much?" I asked archly, as if I was hoping for a yes. I sounded idiotic to myself. I was afraid he would turn on me with disgust and accuse me of my fraud, but he still seemed flattered.

"Not too much," he admitted with a frown. "But when I get my car finished I can go up as much as I want—after I get my license," he amended.

"Who was that other boy Lauren was talking to? He seemed a little old to be hanging out with us." I purposefully lumped myself in with the youngsters, trying to make it clear that I preferred Jacob.

"That's Sam—he's nineteen," he informed me.

"What was that he was saying about the doctor's family?" I asked innocently.

"The Cullens? Oh, they're not supposed to come onto the reservation." He looked away, out toward James Island, as he confirmed what I'd thought I'd heard in Sam's voice.

"Why not?"

He glanced back at me, biting his lip. "Oops. I'm not supposed to say anything about that."

"Oh, I won't tell anyone, I'm just curious." I tried to make my smile alluring, wondering if I was laying it on too thick.

He smiled back, though, looking allured. Then he lifted one eyebrow and his voice was even huskier than before.

"Do you like scary stories?" he asked ominously.

"I *love* them," I enthused, making an effort to smolder at him.

Jacob strolled to a nearby driftwood tree that had its roots sticking out like the attenuated legs of a huge, pale spider. He perched lightly on one of the twisted roots while I sat beneath him on the body of the tree. He stared down at the rocks, a smile hovering around the edges of his broad lips. I could see he was going to try to make this good. I focused on keeping the vital interest I felt out of my eyes.

"Do you know any of our old stories, about where we came from—the Quileutes, I mean?" he began.

"Not really," I admitted.

"Well, there are lots of legends, some of them claiming to date back to the Flood—supposedly, the ancient Quileutes tied their canoes to the tops of the tallest trees on the mountain to survive like Noah and the ark." He smiled, to show me how little stock he put in the histories. "Another legend claims that we descended from wolves—and that the wolves are our brothers still. It's against tribal law to kill them.

"Then there are the stories about the *cold ones.*" His voice dropped a little lower.

"The cold ones?" I asked, not faking my intrigue now.

"Yes. There are stories of the cold ones as old as the wolf legends, and some much more recent. According to legend, my own great-grandfather knew some of them. He was the one who made the treaty that kept them off our land." He rolled his eyes.

"Your great-grandfather?" I encouraged.

"He was a tribal elder, like my father. You see, the cold ones are the natural enemies of the wolf—well, not the wolf, really, but the wolves that turn into men, like our ancestors. You would call them werewolves."

"Werewolves have enemies?"

"Only one."

I stared at him earnestly, hoping to disguise my impatience as admiration.

"So you see," Jacob continued, "the cold ones are traditionally our enemies. But this pack that came to our territory during my great-grandfather's time was different. They didn't hunt the way others of their kind did—they weren't supposed to be dangerous to the tribe. So my great-grandfather made a truce with them. If they would promise to stay off our lands, we wouldn't expose them to the pale-faces." He winked at me.

"If they weren't dangerous, then why...?" I tried to understand, struggling not to let him see how seriously I was considering his ghost story.

"There's always a risk for humans to be around the cold ones, even if they're civilized like this clan was. You never know when they might get too hungry to resist." He deliberately worked a thick edge of menace into his tone.

"What do you mean, 'civilized'?"

"They claimed that they didn't hunt humans. They supposedly were somehow able to prey on animals instead."

I tried to keep my voice casual. "So how does it fit in with the Cullens? Are they like the cold ones your great-grandfather met?"

"No." He paused dramatically. "They are the *same* ones."

He must have thought the expression on my face was fear inspired by his story. He smiled, pleased, and continued.

"There are more of them now, a new female and a new male, but the rest are the same. In my great-grandfather's time they already knew of the leader, Carlisle. He'd been here and gone before *your* people had even arrived." He was fighting a smile.

"And what are they?" I finally asked. "What *are* the cold ones?"

He smiled darkly.

"Blood drinkers," he replied in a chilling voice. "Your people call them vampires."

I stared out at the rough surf after he answered, not sure what my face was exposing.

"You have goose bumps," he laughed delightedly.

"You're a good storyteller," I complimented him, still staring into the waves.

"Pretty crazy stuff, though, isn't it? No wonder my dad doesn't want us to talk about it to anyone."

I couldn't control my expression enough to look at him yet. "Don't worry, I won't give you away."

"I guess I just violated the treaty," he laughed.

"I'll take it to the grave," I promised, and then I shivered.

"Seriously, though, don't say anything to Charlie. He was pretty mad at my dad when he heard that some of us weren't going to the hospital since Dr. Cullen started working there."

"I won't, of course not."

"So do you think we're a bunch of superstitious natives or what?" he asked in a playful tone, but with a hint of worry. I still hadn't looked away from the ocean.

I turned and smiled at him as normally as I could.

"No. I think you're very good at telling scary stories, though. I still have goose bumps, see?" I held up my arm.

"Cool." He smiled.

And then the sound of the beach rocks clattering against each other warned us that someone was approaching. Our heads snapped up at the same time to see Mike and Jessica about fifty yards away, walking toward us.

"There you are, Bella," Mike called in relief, waving his arm over his head.

"Is that your boyfriend?" Jacob asked, alerted by the jealous edge in Mike's voice. I was surprised it was so obvious.

"No, definitely not," I whispered. I was tremendously grateful to Jacob, and eager to make him as happy as possible. I winked at him, carefully turning away from Mike to do so. He smiled, elated by my inept flirting.

"So when I get my license...," he began.

"You should come see me in Forks. We could hang out sometime." I felt guilty as I said this, knowing that I'd used him. But I really did like Jacob. He was someone I could easily be friends with.

Mike had reached us now, with Jessica still a few paces back. I could see his eyes appraising Jacob, and looking satisfied at his obvious youth.

"Where have you been?" he asked, though the answer was right in front of him.

"Jacob was just telling me some local stories," I volunteered. "It was really interesting."

I smiled at Jacob warmly, and he grinned back.

"Well," Mike paused, carefully reassessing the situation as he watched our camaraderie. "We're packing up—it looks like it's going to rain soon."

We all looked up at the glowering sky. It certainly did look like rain.

"Okay." I jumped up. "I'm coming."

"It was nice to see you *again*," Jacob said, and I could tell he was taunting Mike just a bit.

"It really was. Next time Charlie comes down to see Billy, I'll come, too," I promised.

His grin stretched across his face. "That would be cool."

"And thanks," I added earnestly.

I pulled up my hood as we tramped across the rocks toward the parking lot. A few drops were beginning to fall, making black spots on the stones where they landed. When we got to the Suburban the others were already loading everything back in. I crawled into the backseat by Angela and Tyler, announcing that I'd already had my turn in the shotgun position. Angela just stared out the window at the escalating storm, and Lauren twisted around in the middle seat to occupy Tyler's attention, so I could simply lay my head back on the seat and close my eyes and try very hard not to think.

7. NIGHTMARE

I TOLD CHARLIE I HAD A LOT OF HOMEWORK TO DO, AND THAT I DIDN'T want anything to eat. There was a basketball game on that he was excited about, though of course *I* had no idea what was special about it, so he wasn't aware of anything unusual in my face or tone.

Once in my room, I locked the door. I dug through my desk until I found my old headphones, and I plugged them into my little CD player. I picked up a CD that Phil had given to me for Christmas. It was one of his favorite bands, but they used a little too much bass and shrieking for my tastes. I popped it into place and lay down on my bed. I put on the headphones, hit Play, and turned up the volume until it hurt my ears. I closed my eyes, but the light still intruded, so I added a pillow over the top half of my face.

I concentrated very carefully on the music, trying to understand the lyrics, to unravel the complicated drum patterns. By the third time I'd listened through the CD, I knew all the words to the choruses, at least. I was surprised to find that I really did like the band after all, once I got past the blaring noise. I'd have to thank Phil again.

And it worked. The shattering beats made it impossible for me to think— which was the whole purpose of the exercise. I listened to the CD again and again, until I was singing along with all the songs, until, finally, I fell asleep.

I opened my eyes to a familiar place. Aware in some corner of my consciousness that I was dreaming, I recognized the green light of the forest.

I could hear the waves crashing against the rocks somewhere nearby. And I knew that if I found the ocean, I'd be able to see the sun. I was trying to follow the sound, but then Jacob Black was there, tugging on my hand, pulling me back toward the blackest part of the forest.

"Jacob? What's wrong?" I asked. His face was frightened as he yanked with all his strength against my resistance; I didn't want to go into the dark.

"Run, Bella, you have to run!" he whispered, terrified.

"This way, Bella!" I recognized Mike's voice calling out of the gloomy heart of the trees, but I couldn't see him.

"Why?" I asked, still pulling against Jacob's grasp, desperate now to find the sun.

But Jacob let go of my hand and yelped, suddenly shaking, falling to the dim forest floor. He twitched on the ground as I watched in horror.

"Jacob!" I screamed. But he was gone. In his place was a large red-brown wolf with black eyes. The wolf faced away from me, pointing toward the shore, the hair on the back of his shoulders bristling, low growls issuing from between his exposed fangs.

"Bella, run!" Mike cried out again from behind me. But I didn't turn. I was watching a light coming toward me from the beach.

And then Edward stepped out from the trees, his skin faintly glowing, his eyes black and dangerous. He held up one hand and beckoned me to come to him. The wolf growled at my feet.

I took a step forward, toward Edward. He smiled then, and his teeth were sharp, pointed.

"Trust me," he purred.

I took another step.

The wolf launched himself across the space between me and the vampire, fangs aiming for the jugular.

"No!" I screamed, wrenching upright out of my bed.

My sudden movement caused the headphones to pull the CD player off the bedside table, and it clattered to the wooden floor.

My light was still on, and I was sitting fully dressed on the bed, with my shoes on. I glanced, disoriented, at the clock on my dresser. It was five-thirty in the morning.

I groaned, fell back, and rolled over onto my face, kicking off my boots.

I was too uncomfortable to get anywhere near sleep, though. I rolled back over and unbuttoned my jeans, yanking them off awkwardly as I tried to stay horizontal. I could feel the braid in my hair, an uncomfortable ridge along the back of my skull. I turned onto my side and ripped the rubber band out, quickly combing through the plaits with my fingers. I pulled the pillow back over my eyes.

It was all no use, of course. My subconscious had dredged up exactly the images I'd been trying so desperately to avoid. I was going to have to face them now.

I sat up, and my head spun for a minute as the blood flowed downward. First things first, I thought to myself, happy to put it off as long as possible. I grabbed my bathroom bag.

The shower didn't last nearly as long as I hoped it would, though. Even taking the time to blow-dry my hair, I was soon out of things to do in the bathroom. Wrapped in a towel, I crossed back to my room. I couldn't tell if Charlie was still asleep, or if he had already left. I went to look out my window, and the cruiser was gone. Fishing again.

I dressed slowly in my most comfy sweats and then made my bed— something I never did. I couldn't put it off any longer. I went to my desk and switched on my old computer.

I hated using the Internet here. My modem was sadly outdated, my free service substandard; just dialing up took so long that I decided to go get myself a bowl of cereal while I waited.

I ate slowly, chewing each bite with care. When I was done, I washed the bowl and spoon, dried them, and put them away. My feet dragged as I climbed the stairs. I went to my CD player first, picking it up off the floor and placing it precisely in the center of the table. I pulled out the head-phones, and put them away in the desk drawer. Then I turned the same CD on, turning it down to the point where it was background noise.

With another sigh, I turned to my computer. Naturally, the screen was covered in pop-up ads. I sat in my hard folding chair and began closing all the little windows. Eventually I made it to my favorite search engine. I shot down a few more pop-ups and then typed in one word.

Vampire.

It took an infuriatingly long time, of course. When the results came up, there was a lot to sift through—everything from movies and TV shows to role-playing games, underground metal, and gothic cosmetic companies.

Then I found a promising site—Vampires A–Z. I waited impatiently for it to load, quickly clicking closed each ad that flashed across the screen. Finally the screen was finished—simple white background with black text, academic-looking. Two quotes greeted me on the home page:

Throughout the vast shadowy world of ghosts and demons there is no figure so terrible, no figure so dreaded and abhorred, yet dight with such fearful fascination, as the vampire, who is himself neither ghost nor demon, but yet who partakes the dark natures and possesses the mysterious and terrible qualities of both.—Rev. Montague Summers

If there is in this world a well-attested account, it is that of the vampires. Nothing is lacking: official reports, affidavits of well-known people, of surgeons, of priests, of magistrates; the judicial proof is most complete. And with all that, who is there who believes in vampires?—Rousseau

The rest of the site was an alphabetized listing of all the different myths of vampires held throughout the world. The first I clicked on, the *Danag,* was a Filipino vampire supposedly responsible for planting taro on the islands long ago. The myth continued that the *Danag* worked with humans for many years, but the partnership ended one day when a woman cut her finger and a *Danag* sucked her wound, enjoying the taste so much that it drained her body completely of blood.

I read carefully through the descriptions, looking for anything that sounded familiar, let alone plausible. It seemed that most vampire myths centered around beautiful women as demons and children as victims; they also seemed like constructs created to explain away the high mortality rates for young children, and to give men an excuse for infidelity. Many of the stories involved bodiless spirits and warnings against improper burials. There wasn't much that sounded like the movies I'd seen, and only a very few, like the Hebrew *Estrie* and the Polish *Upier,* who were even preoccupied with drinking blood.

Only three entries really caught my attention: the Romanian *Varacolaci,* a powerful undead being who could appear as a beautiful, pale-skinned human, the Slovak *Nelapsi,* a creature so strong and fast it could massacre an entire village in the single hour after midnight, and one other, the *Stregoni benefici.*

About this last there was only one brief sentence.

Stregoni benefici: An Italian vampire, said to be on the side of goodness, and a mortal enemy of all evil vampires.

It was a relief, that one small entry, the one myth among hundreds that claimed the existence of good vampires.

Overall, though, there was little that coincided with Jacob's stories or my own observations. I'd made a little catalogue in my mind as I'd read and carefully compared it with each myth. Speed, strength, beauty, pale skin, eyes that shift color; and then Jacob's criteria: blood drinkers, enemies of the werewolf, cold-skinned, and immortal. There were very few myths that matched even one factor.

And then another problem, one that I'd remembered from the small number of scary movies that I'd seen and was backed up by today's reading— vampires couldn't come out in the daytime, the sun would burn them to a cinder. They slept in coffins all day and came out only at night.

Aggravated, I snapped off the computer's main power switch, not waiting to shut things down properly. Through my irritation, I felt overwhelming embarrassment. It was all so stupid. I was sitting in my room, researching vampires. What was wrong with me? I decided that most of the blame belonged on the doorstep of the town of Forks—and the entire sodden Olympic Peninsula, for that matter.

I had to get out of the house, but there was nowhere I wanted to go that didn't involve a three-day drive. I pulled on my boots anyway, unclear where I was headed, and went downstairs. I shrugged into my raincoat without checking the weather and stomped out the door.

It was overcast, but not raining yet. I ignored my truck and started east on foot, angling across Charlie's yard toward the ever-encroaching forest. It didn't take long till I was deep enough for the house and the road to be invisible, for the only sound to be the squish of the damp earth under my feet and the sudden cries of the jays.

There was a thin ribbon of a trail that led through the forest here, or I wouldn't risk wandering on my own like this. My sense of direction was hopeless; I could get lost in much less helpful surroundings. The trail wound deeper and deeper into the forest, mostly east as far as I could tell. It snaked around the Sitka spruces and the hemlocks, the yews and the maples. I only vaguely knew the names of the trees around me, and all I knew was due to Charlie pointing them out to me from the cruiser window in earlier days. There were many I didn't know, and others I couldn't be sure about because they were so covered in green parasites.

I followed the trail as long as my anger at myself pushed me forward. As that started to ebb, I slowed. A few drops of moisture trickled down from the canopy above me, but I couldn't be certain if it was beginning to rain or if it was simply pools left over from yesterday, held high in the leaves above me, slowly dripping their way back to the earth. A recently fallen tree— I knew it was recent because it wasn't entirely carpeted in moss—rested against the trunk of one of her sisters, creating a sheltered little bench just a few safe feet off the trail. I stepped over the ferns and sat carefully, making sure my jacket was between the damp seat and my clothes wherever they touched, and leaned my hooded head back against the living tree.

This was the wrong place to have come. I should have known, but where else was there to go? The forest was deep green and far too much like the scene in last night's dream to allow for peace of mind. Now that there was no longer the sound of my soggy footsteps, the silence was piercing. The birds were quiet, too, the drops increasing in frequency, so it must be raining above. The ferns stood higher than my head, now that I was seated, and I knew someone could walk by on the path, three feet away, and not see me.

Here in the trees it was much easier to believe the absurdities that embarrassed me indoors. Nothing had changed in this forest for thousands of years, and all the myths and legends of a hundred different lands seemed much more likely in this green haze than they had in my clear-cut bedroom.

I forced myself to focus on the two most vital questions I had to answer, but I did so unwillingly.

First, I had to decide if it was possible that what Jacob had said about the Cullens could be true.

Immediately my mind responded with a resounding negative. It was silly and morbid to entertain such ridiculous notions. But what, then?

I asked myself. There was no rational explanation for how I was alive at this moment. I listed again in my head the things I'd observed myself: the impossible speed and strength, the eye color shifting from black to gold and back again, the inhuman beauty, the pale, frigid skin. And more—small things that registered slowly—how they never seemed to eat, the disturbing grace with which they moved. And the way *he* sometimes spoke, with unfamiliar cadences and phrases that better fit the style of a turn-of-the-century novel than that of a twenty-first-century classroom. He had skipped class the day we'd done blood typing. He hadn't said no to the beach trip till he heard where we were going. He seemed to know what everyone around him was thinking . . . except me. He had told me he was the villain, dangerous. . . .

Could the Cullens be vampires?

Well, they were *something*. Something outside the possibility of rational justification was taking place in front of my incredulous eyes. Whether it be Jacob's *cold ones* or my own superhero theory, Edward Cullen was not . . . human. He was something more.

So then—maybe. That would have to be my answer for now.

And then the most important question of all. What was I going to do if it was true?

If Edward was a vampire—I could hardly make myself think the words— then what should I do? Involving someone else was definitely out. I couldn't even believe myself; anyone I told would have me committed.

Only two options seemed practical. The first was to take his advice: to be smart, to avoid him as much as possible. To cancel our plans, to go back to ignoring him as far as I was able. To pretend there was an impenetrably thick glass wall between us in the one class where we were forced together. To tell him to leave me alone—and mean it this time.

I was gripped in a sudden agony of despair as I considered that alternative. My mind rejected the pain, quickly skipping on to the next option.

I could do nothing different. After all, if he was something . . . sinister, he'd done nothing to hurt me so far. In fact, I would be a dent in Tyler's fender if he hadn't acted so quickly. So quickly, I argued with myself, that it might have been sheer reflexes. But if it was a reflex to save lives, how bad could he be? I retorted. My head spun around in answerless circles.

There was one thing I was sure of, if I was sure of anything. The dark

Edward in my dream last night was a reflection only of my fear of the word Jacob had spoken, and not Edward himself. Even so, when I'd screamed out in terror at the werewolf's lunge, it wasn't fear for the wolf that brought the cry of "no" to my lips. It was fear that *he* would be harmed—even as he called to me with sharp-edged fangs, I feared for *him*.

And I knew in that I had my answer. I didn't know if there ever was a choice, really. I was already in too deep. Now that I knew—*if* I knew—I could do nothing about my frightening secret. Because when I thought of him, of his voice, his hypnotic eyes, the magnetic force of his personality, I wanted nothing more than to be with him right now. Even if...but I couldn't think it. Not here, alone in the darkening forest. Not while the rain made it dim as twilight under the canopy and pattered like footsteps across the matted earthen floor. I shivered and rose quickly from my place of concealment, worried that somehow the path would have disappeared with the rain.

But it was there, safe and clear, winding its way out of the dripping green maze. I followed it hastily, my hood pulled close around my face, becoming surprised, as I nearly ran through the trees, at how far I had come. I started to wonder if I was heading out at all, or following the path farther into the confines of the forest. Before I could get too panicky, though, I began to glimpse some open spaces through the webbed branches. And then I could hear a car passing on the street, and I was free, Charlie's lawn stretched out in front of me, the house beckoning me, promising warmth and dry socks.

It was just noon when I got back inside. I went upstairs and got dressed for the day, jeans and a t-shirt, since I was staying indoors. It didn't take too much effort to concentrate on my task for the day, a paper on *Macbeth* that was due Wednesday. I settled into outlining a rough draft contentedly, more serene than I'd felt since...well, since Thursday afternoon, if I was being honest.

That had always been my way, though. Making decisions was the painful part for me, the part I agonized over. But once the decision was made, I simply followed through—usually with relief that the choice was made. Sometimes the relief was tainted by despair, like my decision to come to Forks. But it was still better than wrestling with the alternatives.

This decision was ridiculously easy to live with. Dangerously easy.

And so the day was quiet, productive—I finished my paper before eight. Charlie came home with a large catch, and I made a mental note to pick up a book of recipes for fish while I was in Seattle next week. The chills that flashed up my spine whenever I thought of that trip were no different than the ones I'd felt before I'd taken my walk with Jacob Black. They should be different, I thought. I should be afraid—I knew I should be, but I couldn't feel the right kind of fear.

I slept dreamlessly that night, exhausted from beginning my day so early, and sleeping so poorly the night before. I woke, for the second time since arriving in Forks, to the bright yellow light of a sunny day. I skipped to the window, stunned to see that there was hardly a cloud in the sky, and those there were just fleecy little white puffs that couldn't possibly be carrying any rain. I opened the window—surprised when it opened silently, without sticking, not having opened it in who knows how many years—and sucked in the relatively dry air. It was nearly warm and hardly windy at all. My blood was electric in my veins.

Charlie was finishing breakfast when I came downstairs, and he picked up on my mood immediately.

"Nice day out," he commented.

"Yes," I agreed with a grin.

He smiled back, his brown eyes crinkling around the edges. When Charlie smiled, it was easier to see why he and my mother had jumped too quickly into an early marriage. Most of the young romantic he'd been in those days had faded before I'd known him, as the curly brown hair—the same color, if not the same texture, as mine—had dwindled, slowly revealing more and more of the shiny skin of his forehead. But when he smiled I could see a little of the man who had run away with Renée when she was just two years older than I was now.

I ate breakfast cheerily, watching the dust motes stirring in the sunlight that streamed in the back window. Charlie called out a goodbye, and I heard the cruiser pull away from the house. I hesitated on my way out the door, hand on my rain jacket. It would be tempting fate to leave it home. With a sigh, I folded it over my arm and stepped out into the brightest light I'd seen in months.

By dint of much elbow grease, I was able to get both windows in the truck almost completely rolled down. I was one of the first ones to school; I hadn't even checked the clock in my hurry to get outside. I parked and headed toward the seldom-used picnic benches on the south side of the cafeteria. The benches were still a little damp, so I sat on my jacket, glad to have a use for it. My homework was done—the product of a slow social life—but there were a few Trig problems I wasn't sure I had right. I took out my book industriously, but halfway through rechecking the first problem I was day-dreaming, watching the sunlight play on the red-barked trees. I sketched inattentively along the margins of my homework. After a few minutes, I suddenly realized I'd drawn five pairs of dark eyes staring out of the page at me. I scrubbed them out with the eraser.

"Bella!" I heard someone call, and it sounded like Mike. I looked around to realize that the school had become populated while I'd been sitting there, absentminded. Everyone was in t-shirts, some even in shorts though the temperature couldn't be over sixty. Mike was coming toward me in khaki shorts and a striped Rugby shirt, waving.

"Hey, Mike," I called, waving back, unable to be halfhearted on a morning like this.

He came to sit by me, the tidy spikes of his hair shining golden in the light, his grin stretching across his face. He was so delighted to see me, I couldn't help but feel gratified.

"I never noticed before—your hair has red in it," he commented, catching between his fingers a strand that was fluttering in the light breeze.

"Only in the sun."

I became just a little uncomfortable as he tucked the lock behind my ear.

"Great day, isn't it?"

"My kind of day," I agreed.

"What did you do yesterday?" His tone was just a bit too proprietary.

"I mostly worked on my essay." I didn't add that I was finished with it—no need to sound smug.

He hit his forehead with the heel of his hand. "Oh yeah—that's due Thursday, right?"

"Um, Wednesday, I think."

"Wednesday?" He frowned. "That's not good.... What are you writing yours on?"

"Whether Shakespeare's treatment of the female characters is misogynistic."

He stared at me like I'd just spoken in pig Latin.

"I guess I'll have to get to work on that tonight," he said, deflated. "I was going to ask if you wanted to go out."

"Oh." I was taken off guard. Why couldn't I ever have a pleasant conversation with Mike anymore without it getting awkward?

"Well, we could go to dinner or something...and I could work on it later." He smiled at me hopefully.

"Mike..." I hated being put on the spot. "I don't think that would be the best idea."

His face fell. "Why?" he asked, his eyes guarded. My thoughts flickered to Edward, wondering if that's where his thoughts were as well.

"I think...and if you ever repeat what I'm saying right now I will cheerfully beat you to death," I threatened, "but I think that would hurt Jessica's feelings."

He was bewildered, obviously not thinking in *that* direction at all. "Jessica?"

"Really, Mike, are you *blind*?"

"Oh," he exhaled—clearly dazed. I took advantage of that to make my escape.

"It's time for class, and I can't be late again." I gathered my books up and stuffed them in my bag.

We walked in silence to building three, and his expression was distracted. I hoped whatever thoughts he was immersed in were leading him in the right direction.

When I saw Jessica in Trig, she was bubbling with enthusiasm. She, Angela, and Lauren were going to Port Angeles tonight to go dress shopping for the dance, and she wanted me to come, too, even though I didn't need one. I was indecisive. It would be nice to get out of town with some girlfriends, but Lauren would be there. And who knew what I could be doing tonight.... But that was definitely the wrong path to let my mind wander down. Of course I was happy about the sunlight. But that wasn't completely responsible for the euphoric mood I was in, not even close.

So I gave her a maybe, telling her I'd have to talk with Charlie first.

She talked of nothing but the dance on the way to Spanish, continuing as if without an interruption when class finally ended, five minutes late, and we were on our way to lunch. I was far too lost in my own frenzy of anticipation to notice much of what she said. I was painfully eager to see not just him but all the Cullens—to compare them with the new suspicions that plagued my mind. As I crossed the threshold of the cafeteria, I felt the first true tingle of fear slither down my spine and settle in my stomach. Would they be able to know what I was thinking? And then a different feeling jolted through me—would Edward be waiting to sit with me again?

As was my routine, I glanced first toward the Cullens' table. A shiver of panic trembled in my stomach as I realized it was empty. With dwindling hope, my eyes scoured the rest of the cafeteria, hoping to find him alone, waiting for me. The place was nearly filled—Spanish had made us late— but there was no sign of Edward or any of his family. Desolation hit me with crippling strength.

I shambled along behind Jessica, not bothering to pretend to listen anymore.

We were late enough that everyone was already at our table. I avoided the empty chair next to Mike in favor of one by Angela. I vaguely noticed that Mike held the chair out politely for Jessica, and that her face lit up in response.

Angela asked a few quiet questions about the *Macbeth* paper, which I answered as naturally as I could while spiraling downward in misery. She, too, invited me to go with them tonight, and I agreed now, grasping at anything to distract myself.

I realized I'd been holding on to a last shred of hope when I entered Biology, saw his empty seat, and felt a new wave of disappointment.

The rest of the day passed slowly, dismally. In Gym, we had a lecture on the rules of badminton, the next torture they had lined up for me. But at least it meant I got to sit and listen instead of stumbling around on the court. The best part was the coach didn't finish, so I got another day off tomorrow. Never mind that the day after they would arm me with a racket before unleashing me on the rest of the class.

I was glad to leave campus, so I would be free to pout and mope before I went out tonight with Jessica and company. But right after I walked in the door of Charlie's house, Jessica called to cancel our plans. I tried to be happy that Mike had asked her out to dinner—I really was relieved that he finally seemed to be catching on—but my enthusiasm sounded false in my own ears. She rescheduled our shopping trip for tomorrow night.

Which left me with little in the way of distractions. I had fish marinating for dinner, with a salad and bread left over from the night before, so there was nothing to do there. I spent a focused half hour on homework, but then I was through with that, too. I checked my e-mail, reading the backlog of letters from my mother, getting snippier as they progressed to the present. I sighed and typed a quick response.

Mom,
Sorry. I've been out. I went to the beach with some friends. And I had to write a paper.

My excuses were fairly pathetic, so I gave up on that.

It's sunny outside today—I know, I'm shocked, too—so I'm going to go outside and soak up as much vitamin D as I can. I love you,
    Bella.

I decided to kill an hour with non-school-related reading. I had a small collection of books that came with me to Forks, the shabbiest volume being a compilation of the works of Jane Austen. I selected that one and headed to the backyard, grabbing a ragged old quilt from the linen cupboard at the top of the stairs on my way down.

Outside in Charlie's small, square yard, I folded the quilt in half and laid it out of the reach of the trees' shadows on the thick lawn that would always be slightly wet, no matter how long the sun shone. I lay on my stomach, crossing my ankles in the air, flipping through the different novels in the book, trying to decide which would occupy my mind the most thoroughly. My favorites were *Pride and Prejudice* and *Sense and Sensibility*. I'd read the first most recently, so I started into *Sense and Sensibility,* only to remember after I began chapter three that the hero of the story happened to be named *Edward*. Angrily, I turned to *Mansfield Park,* but the hero of that piece was named *Edmund,* and that was just too close. Weren't there any other names available in the late eighteenth century? I snapped the book shut, annoyed, and rolled over onto my back. I pushed my sleeves up as high as they would go, and closed my eyes. I would think of nothing but the warmth on my skin, I told myself severely. The breeze was still light, but it blew tendrils of my hair around my face, and that tickled a bit. I pulled all my hair over my head, letting it fan out on the quilt above me, and focused again on the heat that touched my eyelids, my cheekbones, my nose, my lips, my forearms, my neck, soaked through my light shirt. . . .

The next thing I was conscious of was the sound of Charlie's cruiser turning onto the bricks of the driveway. I sat up in surprise, realizing the light was gone, behind the trees, and I had fallen asleep. I looked around, muddled, with the sudden feeling that I wasn't alone.

"Charlie?" I asked. But I could hear his door slamming in front of the house.

I jumped up, foolishly edgy, gathering the now-damp quilt and my book. I ran inside to get some oil heating on the stove, realizing that dinner would be late. Charlie was hanging up his gun belt and stepping out of his boots when I came in.

"Sorry, Dad, dinner's not ready yet—I fell asleep outside." I stifled a yawn.

"Don't worry about it," he said. "I wanted to catch the score on the game, anyway."

I watched TV with Charlie after dinner, for something to do. There wasn't anything on I wanted to watch, but he knew I didn't like baseball, so he turned it to some mindless sitcom that neither of us enjoyed. He seemed happy, though, to be doing something together. And it felt good, despite my depression, to make him happy.

"Dad," I said during a commercial, "Jessica and Angela are going to look at dresses for the dance tomorrow night in Port Angeles, and they wanted me to help them choose . . . do you mind if I go with them?"

"Jessica Stanley?" he asked.

"And Angela Weber." I sighed as I gave him the details.

He was confused. "But you're not going to the dance, right?"

"No, Dad, but I'm helping *them* find dresses—you know, giving them constructive criticism." I wouldn't have to explain this to a woman.

"Well, okay." He seemed to realize that he was out of his depth with the girlie stuff. "It's a school night, though."

"We'll leave right after school, so we can get back early. You'll be okay for dinner, right?"

"Bells, I fed myself for seventeen years before you got here," he reminded me.

"I don't know how you survived," I muttered, then added more clearly, "I'll leave some things for cold-cut sandwiches in the fridge, okay? Right on top."

It was sunny again in the morning. I awakened with renewed hope that I grimly tried to suppress. I dressed for the warmer weather in a deep blue V-neck blouse—something I'd worn in the dead of winter in Phoenix.

I had planned my arrival at school so that I barely had time to make it to class. With a sinking heart, I circled the full lot looking for a space, while also searching for the silver Volvo that was clearly not there. I parked in the last row and hurried to English, arriving breathless, but subdued, before the final bell.

It was the same as yesterday—I just couldn't keep little sprouts of hope from budding in my mind, only to have them squashed painfully as I searched the lunchroom in vain and sat at my empty Biology table.

The Port Angeles scheme was back on again for tonight and made all the more attractive by the fact that Lauren had other obligations. I was anxious to get out of town so I could stop glancing over my shoulder, hoping to see him appearing out of the blue the way he always did. I vowed to myself that I would be in a good mood tonight and not ruin Angela's or Jessica's enjoyment in the dress hunting. Maybe I could do a little clothes shopping as well. I refused to think that I might be shopping alone in Seattle this weekend, no longer interested in the earlier arrangement. Surely he wouldn't cancel without at least telling me.

After school, Jessica followed me home in her old white Mercury so that I could ditch my books and truck. I brushed through my hair quickly when I was inside, feeling a slight lift of excitement as I contemplated getting out of Forks. I left a note for Charlie on the table, explaining again where to find dinner, switched my scruffy wallet from my school bag to a purse I rarely used, and ran out to join Jessica. We went to Angela's house next, and she was waiting for us. My excitement increased exponentially as we actually drove out of the town limits.

8. PORT ANGELES

Jess drove faster than the Chief, so we made it to Port Angeles by four. It had been a while since I'd had a girls' night out, and the estrogen rush was invigorating. We listened to whiny rock songs while Jessica jabbered on about the boys we hung out with. Jessica's dinner with Mike had gone very well, and she was hoping that by Saturday night they would have progressed to the first-kiss stage. I smiled to myself, pleased. Angela was passively happy to be going to the dance, but not really interested in Eric. Jess tried to get her to confess who her type was, but I interrupted with a question about dresses after a bit, to spare her. Angela threw a grateful glance my way.

Port Angeles was a beautiful little tourist trap, much more polished and quaint than Forks. But Jessica and Angela knew it well, so they didn't plan to waste time on the picturesque boardwalk by the bay. Jess drove straight to the one big department store in town, which was a few streets in from the bay area's visitor-friendly face.

The dance was billed as semiformal, and we weren't exactly sure what that meant. Both Jessica and Angela seemed surprised and almost disbelieving when I told them I'd never been to a dance in Phoenix.

"Didn't you ever go with a boyfriend or something?" Jess asked dubiously as we walked through the front doors of the store.

"Really," I tried to convince her, not wanting to confess my dancing problems. "I've never had a boyfriend or anything close. I didn't go out much."

"Why not?" Jessica demanded.

"No one asked me," I answered honestly.

She looked skeptical. "People ask you out here," she reminded me, "and you tell them no." We were in the juniors' section now, scanning the racks for dress-up clothes.

"Well, except for Tyler," Angela amended quietly.

"Excuse me?" I gasped. "What did you say?"

"Tyler told everyone he's taking you to prom," Jessica informed me with suspicious eyes.

"He said *what*?" I sounded like I was choking.

"I told you it wasn't true," Angela murmured to Jessica.

I was silent, still lost in shock that was quickly turning to irritation. But we had found the dress racks, and now we had work to do.

"That's why Lauren doesn't like you," Jessica giggled while we pawed through the clothes.

I ground my teeth. "Do you think that if I ran him over with my truck he would stop feeling guilty about the accident? That he might give up on making amends and call it even?"

"Maybe," Jess snickered. "*If* that's why he's doing this."

The dress selection wasn't large, but both of them found a few things to try on. I sat on a low chair just inside the dressing room, by the three-way mirror, trying to control my fuming.

Jess was torn between two—one a long, strapless, basic black number, the other a knee-length electric blue with spaghetti straps. I encouraged her to go with the blue; why not play up the eyes? Angela chose a pale pink dress that draped around her tall frame nicely and brought out honey tints in her light brown hair. I complimented them both generously and helped by returning the rejects to their racks. The whole process was much shorter and easier than similar trips I'd taken with Renée at home. I guess there was something to be said for limited choices.

We headed over to shoes and accessories. While they tried things on I merely watched and critiqued, not in the mood to shop for myself, though I did need new shoes. The girls'-night high was wearing off in the wake of my annoyance at Tyler, leaving room for the gloom to move back in.

"Angela?" I began, hesitant, while she was trying on a pair of pink strappy heels—she was overjoyed to have a date tall enough that she could wear high heels at all. Jessica had drifted to the jewelry counter and we were alone.

"Yes?" She held her leg out, twisting her ankle to get a better view of the shoe.

I chickened out. "I like those."

"I think I'll get them—though they'll never match anything but the one dress," she mused.

"Oh, go ahead—they're on sale," I encouraged. She smiled, putting the lid back on a box that contained more practical-looking off-white shoes.

I tried again. "Um, Angela . . ." She looked up curiously.

"Is it normal for the . . . Cullens"—I kept my eyes on the shoes—"to be out of school a lot?" I failed miserably in my attempt to sound nonchalant.

"Yes, when the weather is good they go backpacking all the time—even the doctor. They're all real outdoorsy," she told me quietly, examining her shoes, too. She didn't ask one question, let alone the hundreds that Jessica would have unleashed. I was beginning to really like Angela.

"Oh." I let the subject drop as Jessica returned to show us the rhinestone jewelry she'd found to match her silver shoes.

We planned to go to dinner at a little Italian restaurant on the board-walk, but the dress shopping hadn't taken as long as we'd expected. Jess and Angela were going to take their clothes back to the car and then walk down to the bay. I told them I would meet them at the restaurant in an hour—I wanted to look for a bookstore. They were both willing to come with me, but I encouraged them to go have fun—they didn't know how preoccupied I could get when surrounded by books; it was something I preferred to do alone. They walked off to the car chattering happily, and I headed in the direction Jess pointed out.

I had no trouble finding the bookstore, but it wasn't what I was look-ing for. The windows were full of crystals, dream-catchers, and books about spiritual healing. I didn't even go inside. Through the glass I could see a fifty-year-old woman with long, gray hair worn straight down her back, clad in a dress right out of the sixties, smiling welcomingly from behind the counter. I decided that was one conversation I could skip. There had to be a normal bookstore in town.

I meandered through the streets, which were filling up with end-of-the-workday traffic, and hoped I was headed toward downtown. I wasn't paying as much attention as I should to where I was going; I was wrestling with despair. I was trying so hard not to think about him, and what Angela had said . . . and more than anything trying to beat down my hopes for Saturday, fearing a disappointment more painful than the rest, when I looked up to see someone's silver Volvo parked along the street and it all came crashing down on me. Stupid, unreliable vampire, I thought to myself.

I stomped along in a southerly direction, toward some glass-fronted shops that looked promising. But when I got to them, they were just a repair shop and a vacant space. I still had too much time to go looking for Jess and Angela yet, and I definitely needed to get my mood in hand before I met back up with them. I ran my fingers through my hair a couple of times and took some deep breaths before I continued around the corner.

I started to realize, as I crossed another road, that I was going the wrong direction. The little foot traffic I had seen was going north, and it looked like the buildings here were mostly warehouses. I decided to turn east at the next corner, and then loop around after a few blocks and try my luck on a different street on my way back to the boardwalk.

A group of four men turned around the corner I was heading for, dressed too casually to be heading home from the office, but they were too grimy to be tourists. As they approached me, I realized they weren't too many years older than I was. They were joking loudly among themselves, laughing raucously and punching each other's arms. I scooted as far to the inside of the sidewalk as I could to give them room, walking swiftly, looking past them to the corner.

"Hey, there!" one of them called as they passed, and he had to be talking to me since no one else was around. I glanced up automatically. Two of them had paused, the other two were slowing. The closest, a heavyset, dark-haired man in his early twenties, seemed to be the one who had spoken. He was wearing a flannel shirt open over a dirty t-shirt, cut-off jeans, and sandals. He took half a step toward me.

"Hello," I mumbled, a knee-jerk reaction. Then I quickly looked away and walked faster toward the corner. I could hear them laughing at full volume behind me.

"Hey, wait!" one of them called after me again, but I kept my head down and rounded the corner with a sigh of relief. I could still hear them chortling behind me.

I found myself on a sidewalk leading past the backs of several somber-colored warehouses, each with large bay doors for unloading trucks, padlocked for the night. The south side of the street had no sidewalk, only a chain-link fence topped with barbed wire protecting some kind of engine parts storage yard. I'd wandered far past the part of Port Angeles that I, as a guest, was intended to see. It was getting dark, I realized, the clouds finally returning, piling up on the western horizon, creating an early sunset. The eastern sky was still clear, but graying, shot through with streaks of pink and orange. I'd left my jacket in the car, and a sudden shiver made me cross my arms tightly across my chest. A single van passed me, and then the road was empty.

The sky suddenly darkened further, and, as I looked over my shoulder to glare at the offending cloud, I realized with a shock that two men were walking quietly twenty feet behind me.

They were from the same group I'd passed at the corner, though neither was the dark one who'd spoken to me. I turned my head forward at once, quickening my pace. A chill that had nothing to do with the weather made me shiver again. My purse was on a shoulder strap and I had it slung across my body, the way you were supposed to wear it so it wouldn't get snatched. I knew exactly where my pepper spray was—still in my duffel bag under the bed, never unpacked. I didn't have much money with me, just a twenty and some ones, and I thought about "accidentally" dropping my bag and walking away. But a small, frightened voice in the back of my mind warned me that they might be something worse than thieves.

I listened intently to their quiet footsteps, which were much too quiet when compared to the boisterous noise they'd been making earlier, and it didn't sound like they were speeding up, or getting any closer to me. Breathe, I had to remind myself. You don't know they're following you. I continued to walk as quickly as I could without actually running, focusing on the right-hand turn that was only a few yards away from me now. I could hear them, staying as far back as they'd been before. A blue car turned onto the street from the south and drove quickly past me. I thought of jumping out in front of it, but I hesitated, inhibited, unsure that I was really being pursued, and then it was too late.

I reached the corner, but a swift glance revealed that it was only a blind drive to the back of another building. I was half-turned in anticipation; I had to hurriedly correct and dash across the narrow drive, back to the sidewalk. The street ended at the next corner, where there was a stop sign. I concentrated on the faint footsteps behind me, deciding whether or not to run. They sounded farther back, though, and I knew they could outrun me in any case. I was sure to trip and go sprawling if I tried to go any faster. The footfalls were definitely farther back. I risked a quick glance over my shoulder, and they were maybe forty feet back now, I saw with relief. But they were both staring at me.

It seemed to take forever for me to get to the corner. I kept my pace steady, the men behind me falling ever so slightly farther behind with every step. Maybe they realized they had scared me and were sorry. I saw two cars going north pass the intersection I was heading for, and I exhaled in relief. There would be more people around once I got off this deserted street. I skipped around the corner with a grateful sigh.

And skidded to a stop.

The street was lined on both sides by blank, doorless, windowless walls. I could see in the distance, two intersections down, streetlamps, cars, and more pedestrians, but they were all too far away. Because lounging against the western building, midway down the street, were the other two men from the group, both watching with excited smiles as I froze dead on the sidewalk. I realized then that I wasn't being followed.

I was being herded.

I paused for only a second, but it felt like a very long time. I turned then and darted to the other side of the road. I had a sinking feeling that it was a wasted attempt. The footsteps behind me were louder now.

"There you are!" The booming voice of the stocky, dark-haired man shattered the intense quiet and made me jump. In the gathering darkness, it seemed like he was looking past me.

"Yeah," a voice called loudly from behind me, making me jump again as I tried to hurry down the street. "We just took a little detour."

My steps had to slow now. I was closing the distance between myself and the lounging pair too quickly. I had a good loud scream, and I sucked in air, preparing to use it, but my throat was so dry I wasn't sure how much volume I could manage. With a quick movement I slipped my purse over my head, gripping the strap with one hand, ready to surrender it or use it as weapon as need demanded.

The thickset man shrugged away from the wall as I warily came to a stop, and walked slowly into the street.

"Stay away from me," I warned in a voice that was supposed to sound strong and fearless. But I was right about the dry throat—no volume.

"Don't be like that, sugar," he called, and the raucous laughter started again behind me.

I braced myself, feet apart, trying to remember through my panic what little self-defense I knew. Heel of the hand thrust upward, hopefully breaking the nose or shoving it into the brain. Finger through the eye socket—try to hook around and pop the eye out. And the standard knee to the groin, of course. That same pessimistic voice in my mind spoke up then, reminding me that I probably wouldn't have a chance against one of them, and there were four. Shut up! I commanded the voice before terror could incapacitate me. I wasn't going out without taking someone with me. I tried to swallow so I could build up a decent scream.

Headlights suddenly flew around the corner, the car almost hitting the stocky one, forcing him to jump back toward the sidewalk. I dove into the road—*this* car was going to stop, or have to hit me. But the silver car unexpectedly fishtailed around, skidding to a stop with the passenger door open just a few feet from me.

"Get in," a furious voice commanded.

It was amazing how instantaneously the choking fear vanished, amazing how suddenly the feeling of security washed over me—even before I was off the street—as soon as I heard his voice. I jumped into the seat, slamming the door shut behind me.

It was dark in the car, no light had come on with the opening of the door, and I could barely see his face in the glow from the dashboard. The tires squealed as he spun around to face north, accelerating too quickly, swerving toward the stunned men on the street. I caught a glimpse of them diving for the sidewalk as we straightened out and sped toward the harbor.

"Put on your seat belt," he commanded, and I realized I was clutching the seat with both hands. I quickly obeyed; the snap as the belt connected was loud in the darkness. He took a sharp left, racing forward, blowing through several stop signs without a pause.

But I felt utterly safe and, for the moment, totally unconcerned about where we were going. I stared at his face in profound relief, relief that went beyond my sudden deliverance. I studied his flawless features in the limited light, waiting for my breath to return to normal, until it occurred to me that his expression was murderously angry.

"Are you okay?" I asked, surprised at how hoarse my voice sounded.

"No," he said curtly, and his tone was livid.

I sat in silence, watching his face while his blazing eyes stared straight ahead, until the car came to a sudden stop. I glanced around, but it was too dark to see anything beside the vague outline of dark trees crowding the roadside. We weren't in town anymore.

"Bella?" he asked, his voice tight, controlled.

"Yes?" My voice was still rough. I tried to clear my throat quietly.

"Are you all right?" He still didn't look at me, but the fury was plain on his face.

"Yes," I croaked softly.

"Distract me, please," he ordered.

"I'm sorry, what?"

He exhaled sharply.

"Just prattle about something unimportant until I calm down," he clarified, closing his eyes and pinching the bridge of his nose with his thumb and forefinger.

"Um." I wracked my brain for something trivial. "I'm going to run over Tyler Crowley tomorrow before school?"

He was still squeezing his eyes closed, but the corner of his mouth twitched. "Why?"

"He's telling everyone that he's taking me to prom—either he's insane or he's still trying to make up for almost killing me last . . . well, you remember it, and he thinks *prom* is somehow the correct way to do this. So I figure if I endanger his life, then we're even, and he can't keep trying to make amends. I don't need enemies and maybe Lauren would back off if he left me alone. I might have to total his Sentra, though. If he doesn't have a ride he can't take anyone to prom . . . ," I babbled on.

"I heard about that." He sounded a bit more composed.

"*You* did?" I asked in disbelief, my previous irritation flaring. "If he's paralyzed from the neck down, he can't go to the prom, either," I muttered, refining my plan.

Edward sighed, and finally opened his eyes.

"Better?"

"Not really."

I waited, but he didn't speak again. He leaned his head back against the seat, staring at the ceiling of the car. His face was rigid.

"What's wrong?" My voice came out in a whisper.

"Sometimes I have a problem with my temper, Bella." He was whispering, too, and as he stared out the window, his eyes narrowed into slits. "But it *wouldn't* be helpful for me to turn around and hunt down those . . ." He didn't finish his sentence, looking away, struggling for a moment to control his anger again. "At least," he continued, "that's what I'm trying to convince myself."

"Oh." The word seemed inadequate, but I couldn't think of a better response.

We sat in silence again. I glanced at the clock on the dashboard. It was past six-thirty.

"Jessica and Angela will be worried," I murmured. "I was supposed to meet them."

He started the engine without another word, turning around smoothly and speeding back toward town. We were under the streetlights in no time at all, still going too fast, weaving with ease through the cars slowly cruising the boardwalk. He parallel-parked against the curb in a space I would have thought much too small for the Volvo, but he slid in effortlessly in one try. I looked out the window to see the lights of La Bella Italia, and Jess and Angela just leaving, pacing anxiously away from us.

"How did you know where . . . ?" I began, but then I just shook my head. I heard the door open and turned to see him getting out.

"What are you doing?" I asked.

"I'm taking you to dinner." He smiled slightly, but his eyes were hard. He stepped out of the car and slammed the door. I fumbled with my seat belt, and then hurried to get out of the car as well. He was waiting for me on the sidewalk.

He spoke before I could. "Go stop Jessica and Angela before I have to track them down, too. I don't think I could restrain myself if I ran into your other friends again."

I shivered at the threat in his voice.

"Jess! Angela!" I yelled after them, waving when they turned. They rushed back to me, the pronounced relief on both their faces simultaneously changing to surprise as they saw who I was standing next to. They hesitated a few feet from us.

"Where have you been?" Jessica's voice was suspicious.

"I got lost," I admitted sheepishly. "And then I ran into Edward." I gestured toward him.

"Would it be all right if I joined you?" he asked in his silken, irresistible voice. I could see from their staggered expressions that he had never unleashed his talents on them before.

"Er...sure," Jessica breathed.

"Um, actually, Bella, we already ate while we were waiting—sorry," Angela confessed.

"That's fine—I'm not hungry." I shrugged.

"I think you should eat something." Edward's voice was low, but full of authority. He looked up at Jessica and spoke slightly louder. "Do you mind if I drive Bella home tonight? That way you won't have to wait while she eats."

"Uh, no problem, I guess..." She bit her lip, trying to figure out from my expression whether that was what I wanted. I winked at her. I wanted nothing more than to be alone with my perpetual savior. There were so many questions that I couldn't bombard him with till we were by ourselves.

"Okay." Angela was quicker than Jessica. "See you tomorrow, Bella... Edward." She grabbed Jessica's hand and pulled her toward the car, which I could see a little ways away, parked across First Street. As they got in, Jess turned and waved, her face eager with curiosity. I waved back, waiting for them to drive away before I turned to face him.

"Honestly, I'm not hungry," I insisted, looking up to scrutinize his face. His expression was unreadable.

"Humor me."

He walked to the door of the restaurant and held it open with an obstinate expression. Obviously, there would be no further discussion. I walked past him into the restaurant with a resigned sigh.

The restaurant wasn't crowded—it was the off-season in Port Angeles. The host was female, and I understood the look in her eyes as she assessed Edward. She welcomed him a little more warmly than necessary. I was surprised by how much that bothered me. She was several inches taller than I was, and unnaturally blond.

"A table for two?" His voice was alluring, whether he was aiming for that or not. I saw her eyes flicker to me and then away, satisfied by my obvious ordinariness, and by the cautious, no-contact space Edward kept between us. She led us to a table big enough for four in the center of the most crowded area of the dining floor.

I was about to sit, but Edward shook his head at me.

"Perhaps something more private?" he insisted quietly to the host. I wasn't sure, but it looked like he smoothly handed her a tip. I'd never seen anyone refuse a table except in old movies.

"Sure." She sounded as surprised as I was. She turned and led us around a partition to a small ring of booths—all of them empty. "How's this?"

"Perfect." He flashed his gleaming smile, dazing her momentarily.

"Um"—she shook her head, blinking—"your server will be right out." She walked away unsteadily.

"You really shouldn't do that to people," I criticized. "It's hardly fair."

"Do what?"

"Dazzle them like that—she's probably hyperventilating in the kitchen right now."

He seemed confused.

"Oh, come on," I said dubiously. "You *have* to know the effect you have on people."

He tilted his head to one side, and his eyes were curious. "I dazzle people?"

"You haven't noticed? Do you think everybody gets their way so easily?"

He ignored my questions. "Do I dazzle *you*?"

"Frequently," I admitted.

And then our server arrived, her face expectant. The hostess had definitely dished behind the scenes, and this new girl didn't look disappointed. She flipped a strand of short black hair behind one ear and smiled with unnecessary warmth.

"Hello. My name is Amber, and I'll be your server tonight. What can I get you to drink?" I didn't miss that she was speaking only to him.

He looked at me.

"I'll have a Coke." It sounded like a question.

"Two Cokes," he said.

"I'll be right back with that," she assured him with another unnecessary smile. But he didn't see it. He was watching me.

"What?" I asked when she left.

His eyes stayed fixed on my face. "How are you feeling?"

"I'm fine," I replied, surprised by his intensity.

"You don't feel dizzy, sick, cold...?"

"Should I?"

He chuckled at my puzzled tone.

"Well, I'm actually waiting for you to go into shock." His face twisted up into that perfect crooked smile.

"I don't think that will happen," I said after I could breathe again. "I've always been very good at repressing unpleasant things."

"Just the same, I'll feel better when you have some sugar and food in you."

Right on cue, the waitress appeared with our drinks and a basket of breadsticks. She stood with her back to me as she placed them on the table.

"Are you ready to order?" she asked Edward.

"Bella?" he asked. She turned unwillingly toward me.

I picked the first thing I saw on the menu. "Um...I'll have the mushroom ravioli."

"And you?" She turned back to him with a smile.

"Nothing for me," he said. Of course not.

"Let me know if you change your mind." The coy smile was still in place, but he wasn't looking at her, and she left dissatisfied.

"Drink," he ordered.

I sipped at my soda obediently, and then drank more deeply, surprised by how thirsty I was. I realized I had finished the whole thing when he pushed his glass toward me.

"Thanks," I muttered, still thirsty. The cold from the icy soda was radiating through my chest, and I shivered.

"Are you cold?"

"It's just the Coke," I explained, shivering again.

"Don't you have a jacket?" His voice was disapproving.

"Yes." I looked at the empty bench next to me. "Oh—I left it in Jessica's car," I realized.

Edward was shrugging out of his jacket. I suddenly realized that I had never once noticed what he was wearing—not just tonight, but ever. I just couldn't seem to look away from his face. I made myself look now, focusing. He was removing a light beige leather jacket now; underneath he wore an ivory turtleneck sweater. It fit him snugly, emphasizing how muscular his chest was.

He handed me the jacket, interrupting my ogling.

"Thanks," I said again, sliding my arms into his jacket. It was cold—the way my jacket felt when I first picked it up in the morning, hanging in the drafty hallway. I shivered again. It smelled amazing. I inhaled, trying to identify the delicious scent. It didn't smell like cologne. The sleeves were much too long; I shoved them back so I could free my hands.

"That color blue looks lovely with your skin," he said, watching me. I was surprised; I looked down, flushing, of course.

He pushed the bread basket toward me.

"Really, I'm not going into shock," I protested.

"You should be—a *normal* person would be. You don't even look shaken." He seemed unsettled. He stared into my eyes, and I saw how light his eyes were, lighter than I'd ever seen them, golden butterscotch.

"I feel very safe with you," I confessed, mesmerized into telling the truth again.

That displeased him; his alabaster brow furrowed. He shook his head, frowning.

"This is more complicated than I'd planned," he murmured to himself.

I picked up a breadstick and began nibbling on the end, measuring his expression. I wondered when it would be okay to start questioning him.

"Usually you're in a better mood when your eyes are so light," I commented, trying to distract him from whatever thought had left him frowning and somber.

He stared at me, stunned. "What?"

"You're always crabbier when your eyes are black—I expect it then," I went on. "I have a theory about that."

His eyes narrowed. "More theories?"

"Mm-hm." I chewed on a small bite of the bread, trying to look indifferent.

"I hope you were more creative this time . . . or are you still stealing from comic books?" His faint smile was mocking; his eyes were still tight.

"Well, no, I didn't get it from a comic book, but I didn't come up with it on my own, either," I confessed.

"And?" he prompted.

But then the waitress strode around the partition with my food. I realized we'd been unconsciously leaning toward each other across the table, because we both straightened up as she approached. She set the dish in front of me— it looked pretty good—and turned quickly to Edward.

"Did you change your mind?" she asked. "Isn't there anything I can get you?" I may have been imagining the double meaning in her words.

"No, thank you, but some more soda would be nice." He gestured with a long white hand to the empty cups in front of me.

"Sure." She removed the empty glasses and walked away.

"You were saying?" he asked.

"I'll tell you about it in the car. If . . ." I paused.

"There are conditions?" He raised one eyebrow, his voice ominous.

"I do have a few questions, of course."

"Of course."

The waitress was back with two more Cokes. She sat them down without a word this time, and left again.

I took a sip.

"Well, go ahead," he pushed, his voice still hard.

I started with the most undemanding. Or so I thought. "Why are you in Port Angeles?"

He looked down, folding his large hands together slowly on the table. His eyes flickered up at me from under his lashes, the hint of a smirk on his face.

"Next."

"But that's the easiest one," I objected.

"Next," he repeated.

I looked down, frustrated. I unrolled my silverware, picked up my fork, and carefully speared a ravioli. I put it in my mouth slowly, still looking down, chewing while I thought. The mushrooms were good. I swallowed and took another sip of Coke before I looked up.

"Okay, then." I glared at him, and continued slowly. "Let's say, hypothetically of course, that...someone...could know what people are thinking, read minds, you know—with a few exceptions."

"Just *one* exception," he corrected, "hypothetically."

"All right, with one exception, then." I was thrilled that he was playing along, but I tried to seem casual. "How does that work? What are the limitations? How would...that someone...find someone else at exactly the right time? How would he know she was in trouble?" I wondered if my convoluted questions even made sense.

"Hypothetically?" he asked.

"Sure."

"Well, if...that someone..."

"Let's call him 'Joe,'" I suggested.

He smiled wryly. "Joe, then. If Joe had been paying attention, the timing wouldn't have needed to be quite so exact." He shook his head, rolling his eyes. "Only *you* could get into trouble in a town this small. You would have devastated their crime rate statistics for a decade, you know."

"We were speaking of a hypothetical case," I reminded him frostily.

He laughed at me, his eyes warm.

"Yes, we were," he agreed. "Shall we call you 'Jane'?"

"How did you know?" I asked, unable to curb my intensity. I realized I was leaning toward him again.

He seemed to be wavering, torn by some internal dilemma. His eyes locked with mine, and I guessed he was making the decision right then whether or not to simply tell me the truth.

"You can trust me, you know," I murmured. I reached forward, without thinking, to touch his folded hands, but he slid them away minutely, and I pulled my hand back.

"I don't know if I have a choice anymore." His voice was almost a whisper. "I was wrong—you're much more observant than I gave you credit for."

"I thought you were always right."

"I used to be." He shook his head again. "I was wrong about you on one other thing, as well. You're not a magnet for accidents—that's not a broad enough classification. You are a magnet for *trouble*. If there is anything dangerous within a ten-mile radius, it will invariably find you."

"And you put yourself into that category?" I guessed.

His face turned cold, expressionless. "Unequivocally."

I stretched my hand across the table again—ignoring him when he pulled back slightly once more—to touch the back of his hand shyly with my fingertips. His skin was cold and hard, like a stone.

"Thank you." My voice was fervent with gratitude. "That's twice now."

His face softened. "Let's not try for three, agreed?"

I scowled, but nodded. He moved his hand out from under mine, placing both of his under the table. But he leaned toward me.

"I followed you to Port Angeles," he admitted, speaking in a rush. "I've never tried to keep a specific person alive before, and it's much more troublesome than I would have believed. But that's probably just because it's you. Ordinary people seem to make it through the day without so many catastrophes." He paused. I wondered if it should bother me that he was following me; instead I felt a strange surge of pleasure. He stared, maybe wondering why my lips were curving into an involuntary smile.

"Did you ever think that maybe my number was up the first time, with the van, and that you've been interfering with fate?" I speculated, distracting myself.

"That wasn't the first time," he said, and his voice was hard to hear. I stared at him in amazement, but he was looking down. "Your number was up the first time I met you."

I felt a spasm of fear at his words, and the abrupt memory of his violent black glare that first day . . . but the overwhelming sense of safety I felt in his presence stifled it. By the time he looked up to read my eyes, there was no trace of fear in them.

"You remember?" he asked, his angel's face grave.

"Yes." I was calm.

"And yet here you sit." There was a trace of disbelief in his voice; he raised one eyebrow.

"Yes, here I sit . . . because of you." I paused. "Because somehow you knew how to find me today . . . ?" I prompted.

He pressed his lips together, staring at me through narrowed eyes, deciding again. His eyes flashed down to my full plate, and then back to me.

"You eat, I'll talk," he bargained.

I quickly scooped up another ravioli and popped it in my mouth.

"It's harder than it should be—keeping track of you. Usually I can find someone very easily, once I've heard their mind before." He looked at me anxiously, and I realized I had frozen. I made myself swallow, then stabbed another ravioli and tossed it in.

"I was keeping tabs on Jessica, not carefully—like I said, only you could find trouble in Port Angeles—and at first I didn't notice when you took off on your own. Then, when I realized that you weren't with her anymore, I went looking for you at the bookstore I saw in her head. I could tell that you hadn't gone in, and that you'd gone south . . . and I knew you would have to turn around soon. So I was just waiting for you, randomly searching through the thoughts of people on the street—to see if anyone had noticed you so I would know where you were. I had no reason to be worried . . . but I was strangely anxious. . . ." He was lost in thought, staring past me, seeing things I couldn't imagine.

"I started to drive in circles, still . . . listening. The sun was finally setting, and I was about to get out and follow you on foot. And then—" He stopped, clenching his teeth together in sudden fury. He made an effort to calm himself.

"Then what?" I whispered. He continued to stare over my head.

"I heard what they were thinking," he growled, his upper lip curling slightly back over his teeth. "I saw your face in his mind." He suddenly leaned forward, one elbow appearing on the table, his hand covering his eyes. The movement was so swift it startled me.

"It was very . . . hard—you can't imagine how hard—for me to simply take you away, and leave them . . . alive." His voice was muffled by his arm. "I could have let you go with Jessica and Angela, but I was afraid if you left me alone, I would go looking for them," he admitted in a whisper.

I sat quietly, dazed, my thoughts incoherent. My hands were folded in my lap, and I was leaning weakly against the back of the seat. He still had his face in his hand, and he was as still as if he'd been carved from the stone his skin resembled.

Finally he looked up, his eyes seeking mine, full of his own questions.

"Are you ready to go home?" he asked.

"I'm ready to leave," I qualified, overly grateful that we had the hour-long ride home together. I wasn't ready to say goodbye to him.

The waitress appeared as if she'd been called. Or watching.

"How are we doing?" she asked Edward.

"We're ready for the check, thank you." His voice was quiet, rougher, still reflecting the strain of our conversation. It seemed to muddle her. He looked up, waiting.

"S-sure," she stuttered. "Here you go." She pulled a small leather folder from the front pocket of her black apron and handed it to him.

There was a bill in his hand already. He slipped it into the folder and handed it right back to her.

"No change." He smiled. Then he stood up, and I scrambled awkwardly to my feet.

She smiled invitingly at him again. "You have a nice evening."

He didn't look away from me as he thanked her. I suppressed a smile.

He walked close beside me to the door, still careful not to touch me. I remembered what Jessica had said about her relationship with Mike, how they were almost to the first-kiss stage. I sighed. Edward seemed to hear me, and he looked down curiously. I looked at the sidewalk, grateful that he didn't seem to be able to know what I was thinking.

He opened the passenger door, holding it for me as I stepped in, shutting it softly behind me. I watched him walk around the front of the car, amazed, yet again, by how graceful he was. I probably should have been used to that by now—but I wasn't. I had a feeling Edward wasn't the kind of person anyone got used to.

Once inside the car, he started the engine and turned the heater on high. It had gotten very cold, and I guessed the good weather was at an end. I was warm in his jacket, though, breathing in the scent of it when I thought he couldn't see.

Edward pulled out through the traffic, apparently without a glance, flipping around to head toward the freeway.

"Now," he said significantly, "it's your turn."

9. THEORY

"Can I ask just one more?" I pleaded as Edward accelerated much too quickly down the quiet street. He didn't seem to be paying any attention to the road.

He sighed.

"One," he agreed. His lips pressed together into a cautious line.

"Well . . . you said you knew I hadn't gone into the bookstore, and that I had gone south. I was just wondering how you knew that."

He looked away, deliberating.

"I thought we were past all the evasiveness," I grumbled.

He almost smiled.

"Fine, then. I followed your scent." He looked at the road, giving me time to compose my face. I couldn't think of an acceptable response to that, but I filed it carefully away for future study. I tried to refocus. I wasn't ready to let him be finished, now that he was finally explaining things.

"And then you didn't answer one of my first questions . . ." I stalled.

He looked at me with disapproval. "Which one?"

"How does it work—the mind-reading thing? Can you read anybody's mind, anywhere? How do you do it? Can the rest of your family . . . ?" I felt silly, asking for clarification on make-believe.

"That's more than one," he pointed out. I simply intertwined my fingers and gazed at him, waiting.

"No, it's just me. And I can't hear anyone, anywhere. I have to be fairly close. The more familiar someone's ... 'voice' is, the farther away I can hear them. But still, no more than a few miles." He paused thoughtfully. "It's a little like being in a huge hall filled with people, everyone talking at once. It's just a hum—a buzzing of voices in the background. Until I focus on one voice, and then what they're thinking is clear.

"Most of the time I tune it all out—it can be very distracting. And then it's easier to seem *normal*"—he frowned as he said the word—"when I'm not accidentally answering someone's thoughts rather than their words."

"Why do you think you can't hear me?" I asked curiously.

He looked at me, his eyes enigmatic.

"I don't know," he murmured. "The only guess I have is that maybe your mind doesn't work the same way the rest of theirs do. Like your thoughts are on the AM frequency and I'm only getting FM." He grinned at me, suddenly amused.

"My mind doesn't work right? I'm a freak?" The words bothered me more than they should—probably because his speculation hit home. I'd always suspected as much, and it embarrassed me to have it confirmed.

"I hear voices in my mind and you're worried that *you're* the freak," he laughed. "Don't worry, it's just a theory...." His face tightened. "Which brings us back to you."

I sighed. How to begin?

"Aren't we past all the evasions now?" he reminded me softly.

I looked away from his face for the first time, trying to find words. I happened to notice the speedometer.

"Holy crow!" I shouted. "Slow down!"

"What's wrong?" He was startled. But the car didn't decelerate.

"You're going a hundred miles an hour!" I was still shouting. I shot a panicky glance out the window, but it was too dark to see much. The road was only visible in the long patch of bluish brightness from the headlights. The forest along both sides of the road was like a black wall—as hard as a wall of steel if we veered off the road at this speed.

"Relax, Bella." He rolled his eyes, still not slowing.

"Are you trying to kill us?" I demanded.

"We're not going to crash."

I tried to modulate my voice. "Why are you in such a hurry?"

"I always drive like this." He turned to smile crookedly at me.

"Keep your eyes on the road!"

"I've never been in an accident, Bella—I've never even gotten a ticket." He grinned and tapped his forehead. "Built-in radar detector."

"Very funny." I fumed. "Charlie's a cop, remember? I was raised to abide by traffic laws. Besides, if you turn us into a Volvo pretzel around a tree trunk, you can probably just walk away."

"Probably," he agreed with a short, hard laugh. "But you can't." He sighed, and I watched with relief as the needle gradually drifted toward eighty. "Happy?"

"Almost."

"I hate driving slow," he muttered.

"This is slow?"

"Enough commentary on my driving," he snapped. "I'm still waiting for your latest theory."

I bit my lip. He looked down at me, his honey eyes unexpectedly gentle.

"I won't laugh," he promised.

"I'm more afraid that you'll be angry with me."

"Is it that bad?"

"Pretty much, yeah."

He waited. I was looking down at my hands, so I couldn't see his expression.

"Go ahead." His voice was calm.

"I don't know how to start," I admitted.

"Why don't you start at the beginning...you said you didn't come up with this on your own."

"No."

"What got you started—a book? A movie?" he probed.

"No—it was Saturday, at the beach." I risked a glance up at his face. He looked puzzled.

"I ran into an old family friend—Jacob Black," I continued. "His dad and Charlie have been friends since I was a baby."

He still looked confused.

"His dad is one of the Quileute elders." I watched him carefully. His confused expression froze in place. "We went for a walk—" I edited all my scheming out of the story "—and he was telling me some old legends— trying to scare me, I think. He told me one..." I hesitated.

"Go on," he said.

"About vampires." I realized I was whispering. I couldn't look at his face now. But I saw his knuckles tighten convulsively on the wheel.

"And you immediately thought of me?" Still calm.

"No. He... mentioned your family."

He was silent, staring at the road.

I was worried suddenly, worried about protecting Jacob.

"He just thought it was a silly superstition," I said quickly. "He didn't expect me to think anything of it." It didn't seem like enough; I had to confess. "It was my fault, I forced him to tell me."

"Why?"

"Lauren said something about you—she was trying to provoke me. And an older boy from the tribe said your family didn't come to the reservation, only it sounded like he meant something different. So I got Jacob alone and I tricked it out of him," I admitted, hanging my head.

He startled me by laughing. I glared up at him. He was laughing, but his eyes were fierce, staring ahead.

"Tricked him how?" he asked.

"I tried to flirt—it worked better than I thought it would." Disbelief colored my tone as I remembered.

"I'd like to have seen that." He chuckled darkly. "And you accused me of dazzling people—poor Jacob Black."

I blushed and looked out my window into the night.

"What did you do then?" he asked after a minute.

"I did some research on the Internet."

"And did that convince you?" His voice sounded barely interested. But his hands were clamped hard onto the steering wheel.

"No. Nothing fit. Most of it was kind of silly. And then..." I stopped.

"What?"

"I decided it didn't matter," I whispered.

"It didn't *matter*?" His tone made me look up—I had finally broken through his carefully composed mask. His face was incredulous, with just a hint of the anger I'd feared.

"No," I said softly. "It doesn't matter to me what you are."

A hard, mocking edge entered his voice. "You don't care if I'm a monster? If I'm not *human*?"

"No."

He was silent, staring straight ahead again. His face was bleak and cold.

"You're angry," I sighed. "I shouldn't have said anything."

"No," he said, but his tone was as hard as his face. "I'd rather know what you're thinking—even if what you're thinking is insane."

"So I'm wrong again?" I challenged.

"That's not what I was referring to. 'It doesn't matter'!" he quoted, gritting his teeth together.

"I'm right?" I gasped.

"Does it *matter*?"

I took a deep breath.

"Not really." I paused. "But I *am* curious." My voice, at least, was composed.

He was suddenly resigned. "What are you curious about?"

"How old are you?"

"Seventeen," he answered promptly.

"And how long have you been seventeen?"

His lips twitched as he stared at the road. "A while," he admitted at last.

"Okay." I smiled, pleased that he was still being honest with me. He stared down at me with watchful eyes, much as he had before, when he was worried I would go into shock. I smiled wider in encouragement, and he frowned.

"Don't laugh—but how can you come out during the daytime?"

He laughed anyway. "Myth."

"Burned by the sun?"

"Myth."

"Sleeping in coffins?"

"Myth." He hesitated for a moment, and a peculiar tone entered his voice. "I can't sleep."

It took me a minute to absorb that. "At all?"

"Never," he said, his voice nearly inaudible. He turned to look at me with a wistful expression. The golden eyes held mine, and I lost my train of thought. I stared at him until he looked away.

"You haven't asked me the most important question yet." His voice was hard now, and when he looked at me again his eyes were cold.

I blinked, still dazed. "Which one is that?"

"You aren't concerned about my diet?" he asked sarcastically.

"Oh," I murmured, "that."

"Yes, that." His voice was bleak. "Don't you want to know if I drink blood?"

I flinched. "Well, Jacob said something about that."

"What did Jacob say?" he asked flatly.

"He said you didn't . . . hunt people. He said your family wasn't supposed to be dangerous because you only hunted animals."

"He said we weren't dangerous?" His voice was deeply skeptical.

"Not exactly. He said you weren't *supposed* to be dangerous. But the Quileutes still didn't want you on their land, just in case."

He looked forward, but I couldn't tell if he was watching the road or not.

"So was he right? About not hunting people?" I tried to keep my voice as even as possible.

"The Quileutes have a long memory," he whispered.

I took it as a confirmation.

"Don't let that make you complacent, though," he warned me. "They're right to keep their distance from us. We are still dangerous."

"I don't understand."

"We try," he explained slowly. "We're usually very good at what we do. Sometimes we make mistakes. Me, for example, allowing myself to be alone with you."

"This is a mistake?" I heard the sadness in my voice, but I didn't know if he could as well.

"A very dangerous one," he murmured.

We were both silent then. I watched the headlights twist with the curves of the road. They moved too fast; it didn't look real, it looked like a video game. I was aware of the time slipping away so quickly, like the black road beneath us, and I was hideously afraid that I would never have another chance to be with him like this again—openly, the walls between us gone for once. His words hinted at an end, and I recoiled from the idea. I couldn't waste one minute I had with him.

"Tell me more," I asked desperately, not caring what he said, just so I could hear his voice again.

He looked at me quickly, startled by the change in my tone. "What more do you want to know?"

"Tell me why you hunt animals instead of people," I suggested, my voice still tinged with desperation. I realized my eyes were wet, and I fought against the grief that was trying to overpower me.

"I don't *want* to be a monster." His voice was very low.

"But animals aren't enough?"

He paused. "I can't be sure, of course, but I'd compare it to living on tofu and soy milk; we call ourselves vegetarians, our little inside joke. It doesn't completely satiate the hunger—or rather thirst. But it keeps us strong enough to resist. Most of the time." His tone turned ominous. "Sometimes it's more difficult than others."

"Is it very difficult for you now?" I asked.

He sighed. "Yes."

"But you're not hungry now," I said confidently—stating, not asking.

"Why do you think that?"

"Your eyes. I told you I had a theory. I've noticed that people—men in particular—are crabbier when they're hungry."

He chuckled. "You are observant, aren't you?"

I didn't answer; I just listened to the sound of his laugh, committing it to memory.

"Were you hunting this weekend, with Emmett?" I asked when it was quiet again.

"Yes." He paused for a second, as if deciding whether or not to say something. "I didn't want to leave, but it was necessary. It's a bit easier to be around you when I'm not thirsty."

"Why didn't you want to leave?"

"It makes me...anxious...to be away from you." His eyes were gentle but intense, and they seemed to be making my bones turn soft. "I wasn't joking when I asked you to try not to fall in the ocean or get run over last Thursday. I was distracted all weekend, worrying about you. And after what happened tonight, I'm surprised that you did make it through a whole weekend unscathed." He shook his head, and then seemed to remember something. "Well, not totally unscathed."

"What?"

"Your hands," he reminded me. I looked down at my palms, at the almost-healed scrapes across the heels of my hands. His eyes missed nothing.

"I fell," I sighed.

"That's what I thought." His lips curved up at the corners. "I suppose, being you, it could have been much worse—and that possibility tormented me the entire time I was away. It was a very long three days. I really got on Emmett's nerves." He smiled ruefully at me.

"Three days? Didn't you just get back today?"

"No, we got back Sunday."

"Then why weren't any of you in school?" I was frustrated, almost angry as I thought of how much disappointment I had suffered because of his absence.

"Well, you asked if the sun hurt me, and it doesn't. But I can't go out in the sunlight—at least, not where anyone can see."

"Why?"

"I'll show you sometime," he promised.

I thought about it for a moment.

"You might have called me," I decided.

He was puzzled. "But I knew you were safe."

"But *I* didn't know where *you* were. I—" I hesitated, dropping my eyes.

"What?" His velvety voice was compelling.

"I didn't like it. Not seeing you. It makes me anxious, too." I blushed to be saying this out loud.

He was quiet. I glanced up, apprehensive, and saw that his expression was pained.

"Ah," he groaned quietly. "This is wrong."

I couldn't understand his response. "What did I say?"

"Don't you see, Bella? It's one thing for me to make myself miserable, but a wholly other thing for you to be so involved." He turned his anguished eyes to the road, his words flowing almost too fast for me to understand. "I don't want to hear that you feel that way." His voice was low but urgent. His words cut me. "It's wrong. It's not safe. I'm dangerous, Bella—please, grasp that."

"No." I tried very hard not to look like a sulky child.

"I'm serious," he growled.

"So am I. I told you, it doesn't matter what you are. It's too late."

His voice whipped out, low and harsh. "Never say that."

I bit my lip and was glad he couldn't know how much that hurt. I stared out at the road. We must be close now. He was driving much too fast.

"What are you thinking?" he asked, his voice still raw. I just shook my head, not sure if I could speak. I could feel his gaze on my face, but I kept my eyes forward.

"Are you crying?" He sounded appalled. I hadn't realized the moisture in my eyes had brimmed over. I quickly rubbed my hand across my cheek, and sure enough, traitor tears were there, betraying me.

"No," I said, but my voice cracked.

I saw him reach toward me hesitantly with his right hand, but then he stopped and placed it slowly back on the steering wheel.

"I'm sorry." His voice burned with regret. I knew he wasn't just apologizing for the words that had upset me.

The darkness slipped by us in silence.

"Tell me something," he asked after another minute, and I could hear him struggle to use a lighter tone.

"Yes?"

"What were you thinking tonight, just before I came around the corner? I couldn't understand your expression—you didn't look that scared, you looked like you were concentrating very hard on something."

"I was trying to remember how to incapacitate an attacker—you know, self-defense. I was going to smash his nose into his brain." I thought of the dark-haired man with a surge of hate.

"You were going to fight them?" This upset him. "Didn't you think about running?"

"I fall down a lot when I run," I admitted.

"What about screaming for help?"

"I was getting to that part."

He shook his head. "You were right—I'm definitely fighting fate trying to keep you alive."

I sighed. We were slowing, passing into the boundaries of Forks. It had taken less than twenty minutes.

"Will I see you tomorrow?" I demanded.

"Yes—I have a paper due, too." He smiled. "I'll save you a seat at lunch."

It was silly, after everything we'd been through tonight, how that little promise sent flutters through my stomach, and made me unable to speak.

We were in front of Charlie's house. The lights were on, my truck in its place, everything utterly normal. It was like waking from a dream. He stopped the car, but I didn't move.

"Do you *promise* to be there tomorrow?"

"I promise."

I considered that for a moment, then nodded. I pulled his jacket off, taking one last whiff.

"You can keep it—you don't have a jacket for tomorrow," he reminded me.

I handed it back to him. "I don't want to have to explain to Charlie."

"Oh, right." He grinned.

I hesitated, my hand on the door handle, trying to prolong the moment.

"Bella?" he asked in a different tone—serious, but hesitant.

"Yes?" I turned back to him too eagerly.

"Will you promise me something?"

"Yes," I said, and instantly regretted my unconditional agreement. What if he asked me to stay away from him? I couldn't keep that promise.

"Don't go into the woods alone."

I stared at him in blank confusion. "Why?"

He frowned, and his eyes were tight as he stared past me out the window.

"I'm not always the most dangerous thing out there. Let's leave it at that."

I shuddered slightly at the sudden bleakness in his voice, but I was relieved. This, at least, was an easy promise to honor. "Whatever you say."

"I'll see you tomorrow," he sighed, and I knew he wanted me to leave now.

"Tomorrow, then." I opened the door unwillingly.

"Bella?" I turned and he was leaning toward me, his pale, glorious face just inches from mine. My heart stopped beating.

"Sleep well," he said. His breath blew in my face, stunning me. It was the same exquisite scent that clung to his jacket, but in a more concentrated form. I blinked, thoroughly dazed. He leaned away.

I was unable to move until my brain had somewhat unscrambled itself. Then I stepped out of the car awkwardly, having to use the frame for support. I thought I heard him chuckle, but the sound was too quiet for me to be certain.

He waited till I had stumbled to the front door, and then I heard his engine quietly rev. I turned to watch the silver car disappear around the corner. I realized it was very cold.

I reached for the key mechanically, unlocked the door, and stepped inside.

Charlie called from the living room. "Bella?"

"Yeah, Dad, it's me." I walked in to see him. He was watching a baseball game.

"You're home early."

"Am I?" I was surprised.

"It's not even eight yet," he told me. "Did you girls have fun?"

"Yeah—it was lots of fun." My head was spinning as I tried to remember all the way back to the girls' night out I had planned. "They both found dresses."

"Are you all right?"

"I'm just tired. I did a lot of walking."

"Well, maybe you should go lie down." He sounded concerned. I wondered what my face looked like.

"I'm just going to call Jessica first."

"Weren't you just with her?" he asked, surprised.

"Yes—but I left my jacket in her car. I want to make sure she brings it tomorrow."

"Well, give her a chance to get home first."

"Right," I agreed.

I went to the kitchen and fell, exhausted, into a chair. I was really feeling dizzy now. I wondered if I was going to go into shock after all. Get a grip, I told myself.

The phone rang suddenly, startling me. I yanked it off the hook.

"Hello?" I asked breathlessly.

"Bella?"

"Hey, Jess, I was just going to call you."

"You made it home?" Her voice was relieved . . . and surprised.

"Yes. I left my jacket in your car—could you bring it to me tomorrow?"

"Sure. But tell me what happened!" she demanded.

"Um, tomorrow—in Trig, okay?"

She caught on quickly. "Oh, is your dad there?"

"Yes, that's right."

"Okay, I'll talk to you tomorrow, then. Bye!" I could hear the impatience in her voice.

"Bye, Jess."

I walked up the stairs slowly, a heavy stupor clouding my mind. I went through the motions of getting ready for bed without paying any attention to what I was doing. It wasn't until I was in the shower—the water too hot, burning my skin—that I realized I was freezing. I shuddered violently for several minutes before the steaming spray could finally relax my rigid muscles. Then I stood in the shower, too tired to move, until the hot water began to run out.

I stumbled out, wrapping myself securely in a towel, trying to hold the heat from the water in so the aching shivers wouldn't return. I dressed for bed swiftly and climbed under my quilt, curling into a ball, hugging myself to keep warm. A few small shudders trembled through me.

My mind still swirled dizzily, full of images I couldn't understand, and some I fought to repress. Nothing seemed clear at first, but as I fell gradually closer to unconsciousness, a few certainties became evident.

About three things I was absolutely positive. First, Edward was a vampire. Second, there was part of him—and I didn't know how potent that part might be—that thirsted for my blood. And third, I was unconditionally and irrevocably in love with him.

10. INTERROGATIONS

IT WAS VERY HARD, IN THE MORNING, TO ARGUE WITH THE PART OF ME that was sure last night was a dream. Logic wasn't on my side, or common sense. I clung to the parts I couldn't have imagined—like his smell. I was sure I could never have dreamed that up on my own.

It was foggy and dark outside my window, absolutely perfect. He had no reason not to be in school today. I dressed in my heavy clothes, remembering I didn't have a jacket. Further proof that my memory was real.

When I got downstairs, Charlie was gone again—I was running later than I'd realized. I swallowed a granola bar in three bites, chased it down with milk straight from the carton, and then hurried out the door. Hopefully the rain would hold off until I could find Jessica.

It was unusually foggy; the air was almost smoky with it. The mist was ice cold where it clung to the exposed skin on my face and neck. I couldn't wait to get the heat going in my truck. It was such a thick fog that I was a few feet down the driveway before I realized there was a car in it: a silver car. My heart thudded, stuttered, and then picked up again in double time.

I didn't see where he came from, but suddenly he was there, pulling the door open for me.

"Do you want to ride with me today?" he asked, amused by my expression as he caught me by surprise yet again. There was uncertainty in his voice.

He was really giving me a choice—I was free to refuse, and part of him hoped for that. It was a vain hope.

"Yes, thank you," I said, trying to keep my voice calm. As I stepped into the warm car, I noticed his tan jacket was slung over the headrest of the passenger seat. The door closed behind me, and, sooner than should be possible, he was sitting next to me, starting the car.

"I brought the jacket for you. I didn't want you to get sick or something." His voice was guarded. I noticed that he wore no jacket himself, just a light gray knit V-neck shirt with long sleeves. Again, the fabric clung to his perfectly muscled chest. It was a colossal tribute to his face that it kept my eyes away from his body.

"I'm not quite that delicate," I said, but I pulled the jacket onto my lap, pushing my arms through the too-long sleeves, curious to see if the scent could possibly be as good as I remembered. It was better.

"Aren't you?" he contradicted in a voice so low I wasn't sure if he meant for me to hear.

We drove through the fog-shrouded streets, always too fast, feeling awkward. I was, at least. Last night all the walls were down...almost all. I didn't know if we were still being as candid today. It left me tongue-tied. I waited for him to speak.

He turned to smirk at me. "What, no twenty questions today?"

"Do my questions bother you?" I asked, relieved.

"Not as much as your reactions do." He looked like he was joking, but I couldn't be sure.

I frowned. "Do I react badly?"

"No, that's the problem. You take everything so coolly—it's unnatural. It makes me wonder what you're really thinking."

"I always tell you what I'm really thinking."

"You edit," he accused.

"Not very much."

"Enough to drive me insane."

"You don't want to hear it," I mumbled, almost whispered. As soon as the words were out, I regretted them. The pain in my voice was very faint; I could only hope he hadn't noticed it.

He didn't respond, and I wondered if I had ruined the mood. His face was unreadable as we drove into the school parking lot. Something occurred to me belatedly.

"Where's the rest of your family?" I asked—more than glad to be alone with him, but remembering that his car was usually full.

"They took Rosalie's car." He shrugged as he parked next to a glossy red convertible with the top up. "Ostentatious, isn't it?"

"Um, wow," I breathed. "If she has *that,* why does she ride with you?"

"Like I said, it's ostentatious. We *try* to blend in."

"You don't succeed." I laughed and shook my head as we got out of the car. I wasn't late anymore; his lunatic driving had gotten me to school in plenty of time. "So why did Rosalie drive today if it's more conspicuous?"

"Hadn't you noticed? I'm breaking *all* the rules now." He met me at the front of the car, staying very close to my side as we walked onto campus. I wanted to close that little distance, to reach out and touch him, but I was afraid he wouldn't like me to.

"Why do you have cars like that at all?" I wondered aloud. "If you're looking for privacy?"

"An indulgence," he admitted with an impish smile. "We all like to drive fast."

"Figures," I muttered under my breath.

Under the shelter of the cafeteria roof's overhang, Jessica was waiting, her eyes about to bug out of their sockets. Over her arm, bless her, was my jacket.

"Hey, Jessica," I said when we were a few feet away. "Thanks for remembering." She handed me my jacket without speaking.

"Good morning, Jessica," Edward said politely. It wasn't really his fault that his voice was so irresistible. Or what his eyes were capable of.

"Er . . . hi." She shifted her wide eyes to me, trying to gather her jumbled thoughts. "I guess I'll see you in Trig." She gave me a meaningful look, and I suppressed a sigh. What on earth was I going to tell her?

"Yeah, I'll see you then."

She walked away, pausing twice to peek back over her shoulder at us.

"What are you going to tell her?" Edward murmured.

"Hey, I thought you couldn't read my mind!" I hissed.

"I can't," he said, startled. Then understanding brightened his eyes. "However, I can read hers—she'll be waiting to ambush you in class."

I groaned as I pulled off his jacket and handed it to him, replacing it with my own. He folded it over his arm.

"So what are you going to tell her?"

"A little help?" I pleaded. "What does she want to know?"

He shook his head, grinning wickedly. "That's not fair."

"No, you not sharing what you know—now *that's* not fair."

He deliberated for a moment as we walked. We stopped outside the door to my first class.

"She wants to know if we're secretly dating. And she wants to know how you feel about me," he finally said.

"Yikes. What should I say?" I tried to keep my expression very innocent. People were passing us on their way to class, probably staring, but I was barely aware of them.

"Hmmm." He paused to catch a stray lock of hair that was escaping the twist on my neck and wound it back into place. My heart spluttered hyperactively. "I suppose you could say yes to the first . . . if you don't mind—it's easier than any other explanation."

"I don't mind," I said in a faint voice.

"And as for her other question . . . well, I'll be listening to hear the answer to that one myself." One side of his mouth pulled up into my favorite uneven smile. I couldn't catch my breath soon enough to respond to that remark. He turned and walked away.

"I'll see you at lunch," he called over his shoulder. Three people walking in the door stopped to stare at me.

I hurried into class, flushed and irritated. He was such a cheater. Now I was even more worried about what I was going to say to Jessica. I sat in my usual seat, slamming my bag down in aggravation.

"Morning, Bella," Mike said from the seat next to me. I looked up to see an odd, almost resigned look on his face. "How was Port Angeles?"

"It was . . ." There was no honest way to sum it up. "Great," I finished lamely. "Jessica got a really cute dress."

"Did she say anything about Monday night?" he asked, his eyes brightening. I smiled at the turn the conversation had taken.

"She said she had a really good time," I assured him.

"She did?" he said eagerly.

"Most definitely."

Mr. Mason called the class to order then, asking us to turn in our papers. English and then Government passed in a blur, while I worried about how to explain things to Jessica and agonized over whether Edward would really be listening to what I said through the medium of Jess's thoughts. How very inconvenient his little talent could be—when it wasn't saving my life.

The fog had almost dissolved by the end of the second hour, but the day was still dark with low, oppressing clouds. I smiled up at the sky.

Edward was right, of course. When I walked into Trig Jessica was sitting in the back row, nearly bouncing off her seat in agitation. I reluctantly went to sit by her, trying to convince myself it would be better to get it over with as soon as possible.

"Tell me everything!" she commanded before I was in the seat.

"What do you want to know?" I hedged.

"What happened last night?"

"He bought me dinner, and then he drove me home."

She glared at me, her expression stiff with skepticism. "How did you get home so fast?"

"He drives like a maniac. It was terrifying." I hoped he heard that.

"Was it like a date—did you tell him to meet you there?"

I hadn't thought of that. "No—I was *very* surprised to see him there."

Her lips puckered in disappointment at the transparent honesty in my voice.

"But he picked you up for school today?" she probed.

"Yes—that was a surprise, too. He noticed I didn't have a jacket last night," I explained.

"So are you going out again?"

"He offered to drive me to Seattle Saturday because he thinks my truck isn't up to it—does that count?"

"Yes." She nodded.

"Well, then, yes."

"W-o-w." She exaggerated the word into three syllables. "Edward Cullen."

"I know," I agreed. "Wow" didn't even cover it.

"Wait!" Her hands flew up, palms toward me like she was stopping traffic. "Has he kissed you?"

"No," I mumbled. "It's not like that."

She looked disappointed. I'm sure I did, too.

"Do you think Saturday . . . ?" She raised her eyebrows.

"I really doubt it." The discontent in my voice was poorly disguised.

"What did you talk about?" She pushed for more information in a whisper. Class had started but Mr. Varner wasn't paying close attention and we weren't the only ones still talking.

"I don't know, Jess, lots of stuff," I whispered back. "We talked about the English essay a little." A very, very little. I think he mentioned it in passing.

"Please, Bella," she begged. "Give me some details."

"Well . . . okay, I've got one. You should have seen the waitress flirting with him—it was over the top. But he didn't pay any attention to her at all." Let him make what he could of that.

"That's a good sign," she nodded. "Was she pretty?"

"Very—and probably nineteen or twenty."

"Even better. He must like you."

"I *think* so, but it's hard to tell. He's always so cryptic," I threw in for his benefit, sighing.

"I don't know how you're brave enough to be alone with him," she breathed.

"Why?" I was shocked, but she didn't understand my reaction.

"He's so . . . intimidating. I wouldn't know what to say to him." She made a face, probably remembering this morning or last night, when he'd turned the overwhelming force of his eyes on her.

"I do have some trouble with incoherency when I'm around him," I admitted.

"Oh well. He *is* unbelievably gorgeous." Jessica shrugged as if this excused any flaws. Which, in her book, it probably did.

"There's a lot more to him than that."

"Really? Like what?"

I wished I had let it go. Almost as much as I was hoping he'd been kidding about listening in.

"I can't explain it right . . . but he's even more unbelievable *behind* the face." The vampire who wanted to be good—who ran around saving people's lives so he wouldn't be a monster . . . I stared toward the front of the room.

"Is that *possible*?" She giggled.

I ignored her, trying to look like I was paying attention to Mr. Varner.

"So you like him, then?" She wasn't about to give up.

"Yes," I said curtly.

"I mean, do you *really* like him?" she urged.

"Yes," I said again, blushing. I hoped that detail wouldn't register in her thoughts.

She'd had enough with the single syllable answers. "How *much* do you like him?"

"Too much," I whispered back. "More than he likes me. But I don't see how I can help that." I sighed, one blush blending into the next.

Then, thankfully, Mr. Varner called on Jessica for an answer.

She didn't get a chance to start on the subject again during class, and as soon as the bell rang, I took evasive action.

"In English, Mike asked me if you said anything about Monday night," I told her.

"You're kidding! What did you say?!" she gasped, completely sidetracked.

"I told him you said you had a lot of fun—he looked pleased."

"Tell me exactly what he said, and your exact answer!"

We spent the rest of the walk dissecting sentence structures and most of Spanish on a minute description of Mike's facial expressions. I wouldn't have helped draw it out for as long as I did if I wasn't worried about the subject returning to me.

And then the bell rang for lunch. As I jumped up out of my seat, shoving my books roughly in my bag, my uplifted expression must have tipped Jessica off.

"You're not sitting with us today, are you?" she guessed.

"I don't *think* so." I couldn't be sure that he wouldn't disappear inconveniently again.

But outside the door to our Spanish class, leaning against the wall—looking more like a Greek god than anyone had a right to—Edward was waiting for me. Jessica took one look, rolled her eyes, and departed.

"See you later, Bella." Her voice was thick with implications. I might have to turn off the ringer on the phone.

"Hello." His voice was amused and irritated at the same time. He had been listening, it was obvious.

"Hi."

I couldn't think of anything else to say, and he didn't speak—biding his time, I presumed—so it was a quiet walk to the cafeteria. Walking with Edward through the crowded lunchtime rush was a lot like my first day here; everyone stared.

He led the way into the line, still not speaking, though his eyes returned to my face every few seconds, their expression speculative. It seemed to me that irritation was winning out over amusement as the dominant emotion in his face. I fidgeted nervously with the zipper on my jacket.

He stepped up to the counter and filled a tray with food.

"What are you doing?" I objected. "You're not getting all that for me?"

He shook his head, stepping forward to buy the food.

"Half is for me, of course."

I raised one eyebrow.

He led the way to the same place we'd sat that one time before. From the other end of the long table, a group of seniors gazed at us in amazement as we sat across from each other. Edward seemed oblivious.

"Take whatever you want," he said, pushing the tray toward me.

"I'm curious," I said as I picked up an apple, turning it around in my hands, "what would you do if someone dared you to eat food?"

"You're always curious." He grimaced, shaking his head. He glared at me, holding my eyes as he lifted the slice of pizza off the tray, and deliberately bit off a mouthful, chewed quickly, and then swallowed. I watched, eyes wide.

"If someone dared you to eat dirt, you could, couldn't you?" he asked condescendingly.

I wrinkled my nose. "I did once...on a dare," I admitted. "It wasn't so bad."

He laughed. "I suppose I'm not surprised." Something over my shoulder seemed to catch his attention.

"Jessica's analyzing everything I do—she'll break it down for you later." He pushed the rest of the pizza toward me. The mention of Jessica brought a hint of his former irritation back to his features.

I put down the apple and took a bite of the pizza, looking away, knowing he was about to start.

"So the waitress was pretty, was she?" he asked casually.

"You really didn't notice?"

"No. I wasn't paying attention. I had a lot on my mind."

"Poor girl." I could afford to be generous now.

"Something you said to Jessica . . . well, it bothers me." He refused to be distracted. His voice was husky, and he glanced up from under his lashes with troubled eyes.

"I'm not surprised you heard something you didn't like. You know what they say about eavesdroppers," I reminded him.

"I warned you I would be listening."

"And I warned you that you didn't want to know everything I was thinking."

"You did," he agreed, but his voice was still rough. "You aren't precisely right, though. I do want to know what you're thinking—everything. I just wish . . . that you wouldn't be thinking some things."

I scowled. "That's quite a distinction."

"But that's not really the point at the moment."

"Then what is?" We were inclined toward each other across the table now. He had his large white hands folded under his chin; I leaned forward, my right hand cupped around my neck. I had to remind myself that we were in a crowded lunchroom, with probably many curious eyes on us. It was too easy to get wrapped up in our own private, tense little bubble.

"Do you truly believe that you care more for me than I do for you?" he murmured, leaning closer to me as he spoke, his dark golden eyes piercing.

I tried to remember how to exhale. I had to look away before it came back to me.

"You're doing it again," I muttered.

His eyes opened wide with surprise. "What?"

"Dazzling me," I admitted, trying to concentrate as I looked back at him.

"Oh." He frowned.

"It's not your fault," I sighed. "You can't help it."

"Are you going to answer the question?"

I looked down. "Yes."

"Yes, you are going to answer, or yes, you really think that?" He was irritated again.

"Yes, I really think that." I kept my eyes down on the table, my eyes tracing the pattern of the faux wood grains printed on the laminate. The silence dragged on. I stubbornly refused to be the first to break it this time, fighting hard against the temptation to peek at his expression.

Finally he spoke, voice velvet soft. "You're wrong."

I glanced up to see that his eyes were gentle.

"You can't know that," I disagreed in a whisper. I shook my head in doubt, though my heart throbbed at his words and I wanted so badly to believe them.

"What makes you think so?" His liquid topaz eyes were penetrating— trying futilely, I assumed, to lift the truth straight from my mind.

I stared back, struggling to think clearly in spite of his face, to find some way to explain. As I searched for the words, I could see him getting impatient; frustrated by my silence, he started to scowl. I lifted my hand from my neck, and held up one finger.

"Let me think," I insisted. His expression cleared, now that he was satisfied that I was planning to answer. I dropped my hand to the table, moving my left hand so that my palms were pressed together. I stared at my hands, twisting and untwisting my fingers, as I finally spoke.

"Well, aside from the obvious, sometimes..." I hesitated. "I can't be sure—*I* don't know how to read minds—but sometimes it seems like you're trying to say goodbye when you're saying something else." That was the best I could sum up the sensation of anguish that his words triggered in me at times.

"Perceptive," he whispered. And there was the anguish again, surfacing as he confirmed my fear. "That's exactly why you're wrong, though," he began to explain, but then his eyes narrowed. "What do you mean, 'the obvious'?"

"Well, look at me," I said, unnecessarily as he was already staring. "I'm absolutely ordinary—well, except for bad things like all the near-death experiences and being so clumsy that I'm almost disabled. And look at you." I waved my hand toward him and all his bewildering perfection.

His brow creased angrily for a moment, then smoothed as his eyes took on a knowing look. "You don't see yourself very clearly, you know. I'll admit you're dead-on about the bad things," he chuckled blackly, "but you didn't hear what every human male in this school was thinking on your first day."

I blinked, astonished. "I don't believe it...," I mumbled to myself.

"Trust me just this once—you are the opposite of ordinary."

My embarrassment was much stronger than my pleasure at the look that came into his eyes when he said this. I quickly reminded him of my original argument.

"But I'm not saying goodbye," I pointed out.

"Don't you see? That's what proves me right. I care the most, because if I can do it"—he shook his head, seeming to struggle with the thought—"if leaving is the right thing to do, then I'll hurt myself to keep from hurting you, to keep you safe."

I glared. "And you don't think I would do the same?"

"You'd never have to make the choice."

Abruptly, his unpredictable mood shifted again; a mischievous, devastating smile rearranged his features. "Of course, keeping you safe is beginning to feel like a full-time occupation that requires my constant presence."

"No one has tried to do away with me today," I reminded him, grateful for the lighter subject. I didn't want him to talk about goodbyes anymore. If I had to, I supposed I could purposefully put myself in danger to keep him close. . . . I banished that thought before his quick eyes read it on my face. That idea would definitely get me in trouble.

"Yet," he added.

"Yet," I agreed; I would have argued, but now I wanted him to be expecting disasters.

"I have another question for you." His face was still casual.

"Shoot."

"Do you really need to go to Seattle this Saturday, or was that just an excuse to get out of saying no to all your admirers?"

I made a face at the memory. "You know, I haven't forgiven you for the Tyler thing yet," I warned him. "It's your fault that he's deluded himself into thinking I'm going to prom with him."

"Oh, he would have found a chance to ask you without me—I just really wanted to watch your face," he chuckled. I would have been angrier if his laughter wasn't so fascinating. "If I'd asked you, would you have turned *me* down?" he asked, still laughing to himself.

"Probably not," I admitted. "But I would have canceled later—faked an illness or a sprained ankle."

He was puzzled. "Why would you do that?"

I shook my head sadly. "You've never seen me in Gym, I guess, but I would have thought you would understand."

"Are you referring to the fact that you can't walk across a flat, stable surface without finding something to trip over?"

"Obviously."

"That wouldn't be a problem." He was very confident. "It's all in the leading." He could see that I was about to protest, and he cut me off. "But you never told me—are you resolved on going to Seattle, or do you mind if we do something different?"

As long as the "we" part was in, I didn't care about anything else.

"I'm open to alternatives," I allowed. "But I do have a favor to ask."

He looked wary, as he always did when I asked an open-ended question. "What?"

"Can I drive?"

He frowned. "Why?"

"Well, mostly because when I told Charlie I was going to Seattle, he specifically asked if I was going alone and, at the time, I was. If he asked again, I probably wouldn't lie, but I don't think he *will* ask again, and leaving my truck at home would just bring up the subject unnecessarily. And also, because your driving frightens me."

He rolled his eyes. "Of all the things about me that could frighten you, you worry about my driving." He shook his head in disgust, but then his eyes were serious again. "Won't you want to tell your father that you're spending the day with me?" There was an undercurrent to his question that I didn't understand.

"With Charlie, less is always more." I was definite about that. "Where are we going, anyway?"

"The weather will be nice, so I'll be staying out of the public eye . . . and you can stay with me, if you'd like to." Again, he was leaving the choice up to me.

"And you'll show me what you meant, about the sun?" I asked, excited by the idea of unraveling another of the unknowns.

"Yes." He smiled, and then paused. "But if you don't want to be . . . alone with me, I'd still rather you didn't go to Seattle by yourself. I shudder to think of the trouble you could find in a city that size."

I was miffed. "Phoenix is three times bigger than Seattle—just in population. In physical size—"

"But apparently," he interrupted me, "your number wasn't up in Phoenix. So I'd rather you stayed near me." His eyes did that unfair smoldering thing again.

I couldn't argue, with the eyes or the motivation, and it was a moot point anyway. "As it happens, I don't mind being alone with you."

"I know," he sighed, brooding. "You should tell Charlie, though."

"Why in the world would I do that?"

His eyes were suddenly fierce. "To give me some small incentive to bring you back."

I gulped. But, after a moment of thought, I was sure. "I think I'll take my chances."

He exhaled angrily, and looked away.

"Let's talk about something else," I suggested.

"What do you want to talk about?" he asked. He was still annoyed.

I glanced around us, making sure we were well out of anyone's hearing. As I cast my eyes around the room, I caught the eyes of his sister, Alice, staring at me. The others were looking at Edward. I looked away swiftly, back to him, and I asked the first thing that came to mind.

"Why did you go to that Goat Rocks place last weekend...to hunt? Charlie said it wasn't a good place to hike, because of bears."

He stared at me as if I was missing something very obvious.

"Bears?" I gasped, and he smirked. "You know, bears are not in season," I added sternly, to hide my shock.

"If you read carefully, the laws only cover hunting with weapons," he informed me.

He watched my face with enjoyment as that slowly sank in.

"Bears?" I repeated with difficulty.

"Grizzly is Emmett's favorite." His voice was still off-hand, but his eyes were scrutinizing my reaction. I tried to pull myself together.

"Hmmm," I said, taking another bite of pizza as an excuse to look down. I chewed slowly, and then took a long drink of Coke without looking up.

"So," I said after a moment, finally meeting his now-anxious gaze. "What's your favorite?"

He raised an eyebrow and the corners of his mouth turned down in disapproval. "Mountain lion."

"Ah," I said in a politely disinterested tone, looking for my soda again.

"Of course," he said, and his tone mirrored mine, "we have to be careful not to impact the environment with injudicious hunting. We try to focus on areas with an overpopulation of predators—ranging as far away as we need. There's always plenty of deer and elk here, and they'll do, but where's the fun in that?" He smiled teasingly.

"Where indeed," I murmured around another bite of pizza.

"Early spring is Emmett's favorite bear season—they're just coming out of hibernation, so they're more irritable." He smiled at some remembered joke.

"Nothing more fun than an irritated grizzly bear," I agreed, nodding.

He snickered, shaking his head. "Tell me what you're really thinking, please."

"I'm trying to picture it—but I can't," I admitted. "How do you hunt a bear without weapons?"

"Oh, we have weapons." He flashed his bright teeth in a brief, threatening smile. I fought back a shiver before it could expose me. "Just not the kind they consider when writing hunting laws. If you've ever seen a bear attack on television, you should be able to visualize Emmett hunting."

I couldn't stop the next shiver that flashed down my spine. I peeked across the cafeteria toward Emmett, grateful that he wasn't looking my way. The thick bands of muscle that wrapped his arms and torso were somehow even more menacing now.

Edward followed my gaze and chuckled. I stared at him, unnerved.

"Are you like a bear, too?" I asked in a low voice.

"More like the lion, or so they tell me," he said lightly. "Perhaps our preferences are indicative."

I tried to smile. "Perhaps," I repeated. But my mind was filled with opposing images that I couldn't merge together. "Is that something I might get to see?"

"Absolutely not!" His face turned even whiter than usual, and his eyes were suddenly furious. I leaned back, stunned and—though I'd never admit it to him—frightened by his reaction. He leaned back as well, folding his arms across his chest.

"Too scary for me?" I asked when I could control my voice again.

"If that were it, I would take you out tonight," he said, his voice cutting. "You *need* a healthy dose of fear. Nothing could be more beneficial for you."

"Then why?" I pressed, trying to ignore his angry expression.

He glared at me for a long minute.

"Later," he finally said. He was on his feet in one lithe movement. "We're going to be late."

I glanced around, startled to see that he was right and the cafeteria was nearly vacant. When I was with him, the time and the place were such a muddled blur that I completely lost track of both. I jumped up, grabbing my bag from the back of my chair.

"Later, then," I agreed. I wouldn't forget.

11. COMPLICATIONS

EVERYONE WATCHED US AS WE WALKED TOGETHER TO OUR LAB TABLE. I noticed that he no longer angled the chair to sit as far from me as the desk would allow. Instead, he sat quite close beside me, our arms almost touching.

Mr. Banner backed into the room then—what superb timing the man had—pulling a tall metal frame on wheels that held a heavy-looking, outdated TV and VCR. A movie day—the lift in the class atmosphere was almost tangible.

Mr. Banner shoved the tape into the reluctant VCR and walked to the wall to turn off the lights.

And then, as the room went black, I was suddenly hyperaware that Edward was sitting less than an inch from me. I was stunned by the unexpected electricity that flowed through me, amazed that it was possible to be *more* aware of him than I already was. A crazy impulse to reach over and touch him, to stroke his perfect face just once in the darkness, nearly overwhelmed me. I crossed my arms tightly across my chest, my hands balling into fists. I was losing my mind.

The opening credits began, lighting the room by a token amount. My eyes, of their own accord, flickered to him. I smiled sheepishly as I realized his posture was identical to mine, fists clenched under his arms, right down to the eyes, peering sideways at me. He grinned back, his eyes somehow managing to smolder, even in the dark. I looked away before I could start hyperventilating. It was absolutely ridiculous that I should feel dizzy.

The hour seemed very long. I couldn't concentrate on the movie—I didn't even know what subject it was on. I tried unsuccessfully to relax, but the electric current that seemed to be originating from somewhere in his body never slackened. Occasionally I would permit myself a quick glance in his direction, but he never seemed to relax, either. The overpowering craving to touch him also refused to fade, and I crushed my fists safely against my ribs until my fingers were aching with the effort.

I breathed a sigh of relief when Mr. Banner flicked the lights back on at the end of class, and stretched my arms out in front of me, flexing my stiff fingers. Edward chuckled beside me.

"Well, that was interesting," he murmured. His voice was dark and his eyes were cautious.

"Umm," was all I was able to respond.

"Shall we?" he asked, rising fluidly.

I almost groaned. Time for Gym. I stood with care, worried my balance might have been affected by the strange new intensity between us.

He walked me to my next class in silence and paused at the door; I turned to say goodbye. His face startled me—his expression was torn, almost pained, and so fiercely beautiful that the ache to touch him flared as strong as before. My goodbye stuck in my throat.

He raised his hand, hesitant, conflict raging in his eyes, and then swiftly brushed the length of my cheekbone with his fingertips. His skin was as icy as ever, but the trail his fingers left on my skin was alarmingly warm—like I'd been burned, but didn't feel the pain of it yet.

He turned without a word and strode quickly away from me.

I walked into the gym, lightheaded and wobbly. I drifted to the locker room, changing in a trancelike state, only vaguely aware that there were other people surrounding me. Reality didn't fully set in until I was handed a racket. It wasn't heavy, yet it felt very unsafe in my hand. I could see a few of the other kids in class eyeing me furtively. Coach Clapp ordered us to pair up into teams.

Mercifully, some vestiges of Mike's chivalry still survived; he came to stand beside me.

"Do you want to be a team?"

"Thanks, Mike—you don't have to do this, you know." I grimaced apologetically.

"Don't worry, I'll keep out of your way." He grinned. Sometimes it was so easy to like Mike.

It didn't go smoothly. I somehow managed to hit myself in the head with my racket and clip Mike's shoulder on the same swing. I spent the rest of the hour in the back corner of the court, the racket held safely behind my back. Despite being handicapped by me, Mike was pretty good; he won three games out of four singlehandedly. He gave me an unearned high five when the coach finally blew the whistle ending class.

"So," he said as we walked off the court.

"So what?"

"You and Cullen, huh?" he asked, his tone rebellious. My previous feeling of affection disappeared.

"That's none of your business, Mike," I warned, internally cursing Jessica straight to the fiery pits of Hades.

"I don't like it," he muttered anyway.

"You don't have to," I snapped.

"He looks at you like . . . like you're something to eat," he continued, ignoring me.

I choked back the hysteria that threatened to explode, but a small giggle managed to get out despite my efforts. He glowered at me. I waved and fled to the locker room.

I dressed quickly, something stronger than butterflies battering recklessly against the walls of my stomach, my argument with Mike already a distant memory. I was wondering if Edward would be waiting, or if I should meet him at his car. What if his family was there? I felt a wave of real terror. Did they know that I knew? Was I supposed to know that they knew that I knew, or not?

By the time I walked out of the gym, I had just about decided to walk straight home without even looking toward the parking lot. But my worries were unnecessary. Edward was waiting, leaning casually against the side of the gym, his breathtaking face untroubled now. As I walked to his side, I felt a peculiar sense of release.

"Hi," I breathed, smiling hugely.

"Hello." His answering smile was brilliant. "How was Gym?"

My face fell a tiny bit. "Fine," I lied.

"Really?" He was unconvinced. His eyes shifted their focus slightly, looking over my shoulder and narrowing. I glanced behind me to see Mike's back as he walked away.

"What?" I demanded.

His eyes slid back to mine, still tight. "Newton's getting on my nerves."

"You weren't listening again?" I was horror-struck. All traces of my sudden good humor vanished.

"How's your head?" he asked innocently.

"You're unbelievable!" I turned, stomping away in the general direction of the parking lot, though I hadn't ruled out walking at this point.

He kept up with me easily.

"You were the one who mentioned how I'd never seen you in Gym—it made me curious." He didn't sound repentant, so I ignored him.

We walked in silence—a furious, embarrassed silence on my part—to his car. But I had to stop a few steps away—a crowd of people, all boys, were surrounding it. Then I realized they weren't surrounding the Volvo, they were actually circled around Rosalie's red convertible, unmistakable lust in their eyes. None of them even looked up as Edward slid between them to open his door. I climbed quickly in the passenger side, also unnoticed.

"Ostentatious," he muttered.

"What kind of car is that?" I asked.

"An M3."

"I don't speak *Car and Driver.*"

"It's a BMW." He rolled his eyes, not looking at me, trying to back out without running over the car enthusiasts.

I nodded—I'd heard of that one.

"Are you still angry?" he asked as he carefully maneuvered his way out.

"Definitely."

He sighed. "Will you forgive me if I apologize?"

"Maybe . . . if you mean it. *And* if you promise not to do it again," I insisted.

His eyes were suddenly shrewd. "How about if I mean it, *and* I agree to let you drive Saturday?" he countered my conditions.

I considered, and decided it was probably the best offer I would get. "Deal," I agreed.

"Then I'm very sorry I upset you." His eyes burned with sincerity for a protracted moment—playing havoc with the rhythm of my heart—and then turned playful. "And I'll be on your doorstep bright and early Saturday morning."

"Um, it doesn't help with the Charlie situation if an unexplained Volvo is left in the driveway."

His smile was condescending now. "I wasn't intending to bring a car."

"How—"

He cut me off. "Don't worry about it. I'll be there, no car."

I let it go. I had a more pressing question.

"Is it later yet?" I asked significantly.

He frowned. "I suppose it is later."

I kept my expression polite as I waited.

He stopped the car. I looked up, surprised—of course we were already at Charlie's house, parked behind the truck. It was easier to ride with him if I only looked when it was over. When I looked back at him, he was staring at me, measuring with his eyes.

"And you still want to know why you can't see me hunt?" He seemed solemn, but I thought I saw a trace of humor deep in his eyes.

"Well," I clarified, "I was mostly wondering about your reaction."

"Did I frighten you?" Yes, there was definitely humor there.

"No," I lied. He didn't buy it.

"I apologize for scaring you," he persisted with a slight smile, but then all evidence of teasing disappeared. "It was just the very thought of you being there . . . while we hunted." His jaw tightened.

"That would be bad?"

He spoke from between clenched teeth. "Extremely."

"Because . . . ?"

He took a deep breath and stared through the windshield at the thick, rolling clouds that seemed to press down, almost within reach.

"When we hunt," he spoke slowly, unwillingly, "we give ourselves over to our senses . . . govern less with our minds. Especially our sense of smell. If you were anywhere near me when I lost control that way . . ." He shook his head, still gazing morosely at the heavy clouds.

I kept my expression firmly under control, expecting the swift flash of his eyes to judge my reaction that soon followed. My face gave nothing away.

But our eyes held, and the silence deepened—and changed. Flickers of the electricity I'd felt this afternoon began to charge the atmosphere as he gazed unrelentingly into my eyes. It wasn't until my head started to swim that I realized I wasn't breathing. When I drew in a jagged breath, breaking the stillness, he closed his eyes.

"Bella, I think you should go inside now." His low voice was rough, his eyes on the clouds again.

I opened the door, and the arctic draft that burst into the car helped clear my head. Afraid I might stumble in my woozy state, I stepped carefully out of the car and shut the door behind me without looking back. The whir of the automatic window unrolling made me turn.

"Oh, Bella?" he called after me, his voice more even. He leaned toward the open window with a faint smile on his lips.

"Yes?"

"Tomorrow it's my turn."

"Your turn to what?"

He smiled wider, flashing his gleaming teeth. "Ask the questions."

And then he was gone, the car speeding down the street and disappearing around the corner before I could even collect my thoughts. I smiled as I walked to the house. It was clear he was planning to see me tomorrow, if nothing else.

That night Edward starred in my dreams, as usual. However, the climate of my unconsciousness had changed. It thrilled with the same electricity that had charged the afternoon, and I tossed and turned restlessly, waking often. It was only in the early hours of the morning that I finally sank into an exhausted, dreamless sleep.

When I woke I was still tired, but edgy as well. I pulled on my brown turtleneck and the inescapable jeans, sighing as I daydreamed of spaghetti straps and shorts. Breakfast was the usual, quiet event I expected. Charlie fried eggs for himself; I had my bowl of cereal. I wondered if he had forgotten about this Saturday. He answered my unspoken question as he stood up to take his plate to the sink.

"About this Saturday . . . ," he began, walking across the kitchen and turning on the faucet.

I cringed. "Yes, Dad?"

"Are you still set on going to Seattle?" he asked.

"That was the plan." I grimaced, wishing he hadn't brought it up so I wouldn't have to compose careful half-truths.

He squeezed some dish soap onto his plate and swirled it around with the brush. "And you're sure you can't make it back in time for the dance?"

"I'm not going to the dance, Dad." I glared.

"Didn't anyone ask you?" he asked, trying to hide his concern by focusing on rinsing the plate.

I sidestepped the minefield. "It's a girl's choice."

"Oh." He frowned as he dried his plate.

I sympathized with him. It must be a hard thing, to be a father; living in fear that your daughter would meet a boy she liked, but also having to worry if she didn't. How ghastly it would be, I thought, shuddering, if Charlie had even the slightest inkling of exactly what I *did* like.

Charlie left then, with a goodbye wave, and I went upstairs to brush my teeth and gather my books. When I heard the cruiser pull away, I could only wait a few seconds before I had to peek out of my window. The silver car was already there, waiting in Charlie's spot on the driveway. I bounded down the stairs and out the front door, wondering how long this bizarre routine would continue. I never wanted it to end.

He waited in the car, not appearing to watch as I shut the door behind me without bothering to lock the deadbolt. I walked to the car, pausing shyly before opening the door and stepping in. He was smiling, relaxed—and, as usual, perfect and beautiful to an excruciating degree.

"Good morning." His voice was silky. "How are you today?" His eyes roamed over my face, as if his question was something more than simple courtesy.

"Good, thank you." I was always good—much more than good—when I was near him.

His gaze lingered on the circles under my eyes. "You look tired."

"I couldn't sleep," I confessed, automatically swinging my hair around my shoulder to provide some measure of cover.

"Neither could I," he teased as he started the engine. I was becoming used to the quiet purr. I was sure the roar of my truck would scare me, whenever I got to drive it again.

I laughed. "I guess that's right. I suppose I slept just a little bit more than you did."

"I'd wager you did."

"So what did you do last night?" I asked.

He chuckled. "Not a chance. It's my day to ask questions."

"Oh, that's right. What do you want to know?" My forehead creased. I couldn't imagine anything about me that could be in any way interesting to him.

"What's your favorite color?" he asked, his face grave.

I rolled my eyes. "It changes from day to day."

"What's your favorite color today?" He was still solemn.

"Probably brown." I tended to dress according to my mood.

He snorted, dropping his serious expression. "Brown?" he asked skeptically.

"Sure. Brown is warm. I *miss* brown. Everything that's supposed to be brown—tree trunks, rocks, dirt—is all covered up with squashy green stuff here," I complained.

He seemed fascinated by my little rant. He considered for a moment, staring into my eyes.

"You're right," he decided, serious again. "Brown is warm." He reached over, swiftly, but somehow still hesitantly, to sweep my hair back behind my shoulder.

We were at the school by now. He turned back to me as he pulled into a parking space.

"What music is in your CD player right now?" he asked, his face as somber as if he'd asked for a murder confession.

I realized I'd never removed the CD Phil had given me. When I said the name of the band, he smiled crookedly, a peculiar expression in his eyes. He flipped open a compartment under his car's CD player, pulled out one of thirty or so CDs that were jammed into the small space, and handed it to me.

"Debussy to this?" He raised an eyebrow.

It was the same CD. I examined the familiar cover art, keeping my eyes down.

It continued like that for the rest of the day. While he walked me to English, when he met me after Spanish, all through the lunch hour, he questioned me relentlessly about every insignificant detail of my existence.

Movies I'd liked and hated, the few places I'd been and the many places I wanted to go, and books—endlessly books.

I couldn't remember the last time I'd talked so much. More often than not, I felt self-conscious, certain I must be boring him. But the absolute absorption of his face, and his never-ending stream of questions, compelled me to continue. Mostly his questions were easy, only a very few triggering my easy blushes. But when I did flush, it brought on a whole new round of questions.

Such as the time he asked my favorite gemstone, and I blurted out topaz before thinking. He'd been flinging questions at me with such speed that I felt like I was taking one of those psychiatric tests where you answer with the first word that comes to mind. I was sure he would have continued down whatever mental list he was following, except for the blush. My face reddened because, until very recently, my favorite gemstone was garnet. It was impossible, while staring back into his topaz eyes, not to remember the reason for the switch. And, naturally, he wouldn't rest until I'd admitted why I was embarrassed.

"Tell me," he finally commanded after persuasion failed—failed only because I kept my eyes safely away from his face.

"It's the color of your eyes today," I sighed, surrendering, staring down at my hands as I fiddled with a piece of my hair. "I suppose if you asked me in two weeks I'd say onyx." I'd given more information than necessary in my unwilling honesty, and I worried it would provoke the strange anger that flared whenever I slipped and revealed too clearly how obsessed I was.

But his pause was very short.

"What kinds of flowers do you prefer?" he fired off.

I sighed in relief, and continued with the psychoanalysis.

Biology was a complication again. Edward had continued with his quizzing up until Mr. Banner entered the room, dragging the audiovisual frame again. As the teacher approached the light switch, I noticed Edward slide his chair slightly farther away from mine. It didn't help. As soon as the room was dark, there was the same electric spark, the same restless craving to stretch my hand across the short space and touch his cold skin, as yesterday.

I leaned forward on the table, resting my chin on my folded arms, my hidden fingers gripping the table's edge as I fought to ignore the irrational longing that unsettled me. I didn't look at him, afraid that if he was looking at me, it would only make self-control that much harder. I sincerely tried to watch the movie, but at the end of the hour I had no idea what I'd just seen. I sighed in relief again when Mr. Banner turned the lights on, finally glancing at Edward; he was looking at me, his eyes ambivalent.

He rose in silence and then stood still, waiting for me. We walked toward the gym in silence, like yesterday. And, also like yesterday, he touched my face wordlessly—this time with the back of his cool hand, stroking once from my temple to my jaw—before he turned and walked away.

Gym passed quickly as I watched Mike's one-man badminton show. He didn't speak to me today, either in response to my vacant expression or because he was still angry about our squabble yesterday. Somewhere, in a corner of my mind, I felt bad about that. But I couldn't concentrate on him.

I hurried to change afterward, ill at ease, knowing the faster I moved, the sooner I would be with Edward. The pressure made me more clumsy than usual, but eventually I made it out the door, feeling the same release when I saw him standing there, a wide smile automatically spreading across my face. He smiled in reaction before launching into more cross-examination.

His questions were different now, though, not as easily answered. He wanted to know what I missed about home, insisting on descriptions of anything he wasn't familiar with. We sat in front of Charlie's house for hours, as the sky darkened and rain plummeted around us in a sudden deluge.

I tried to describe impossible things like the scent of creosote—bitter, slightly resinous, but still pleasant—the high, keening sound of the cicadas in July, the feathery barrenness of the trees, the very size of the sky, extending white-blue from horizon to horizon, barely interrupted by the low mountains covered with purple volcanic rock. The hardest thing to explain was why it was so beautiful to me—to justify a beauty that didn't depend on the sparse, spiny vegetation that often looked half dead, a beauty that had more to do with the exposed shape of the land, with the shallow bowls of valleys between the craggy hills, and the way they held on to the sun. I found myself using my hands as I tried to describe it to him.

His quiet, probing questions kept me talking freely, forgetting, in the dim light of the storm, to be embarrassed for monopolizing the conversation. Finally, when I had finished detailing my cluttered room at home, he paused instead of responding with another question.

"Are you finished?" I asked in relief.

"Not even close—but your father will be home soon."

"Charlie!" I suddenly recalled his existence, and sighed. I looked out at the rain-darkened sky, but it gave nothing away. "How late is it?" I wondered out loud as I glanced at the clock. I was surprised by the time—Charlie would be driving home now.

"It's twilight," Edward murmured, looking at the western horizon, obscured as it was with clouds. His voice was thoughtful, as if his mind were somewhere far away. I stared at him as he gazed unseeingly out the windshield.

I was still staring when his eyes suddenly shifted back to mine.

"It's the safest time of day for us," he said, answering the unspoken question in my eyes. "The easiest time. But also the saddest, in a way...the end of another day, the return of the night. Darkness is so predictable, don't you think?" He smiled wistfully.

"I like the night. Without the dark, we'd never see the stars." I frowned. "Not that you see them here much."

He laughed, and the mood abruptly lightened.

"Charlie will be here in a few minutes. So, unless you want to tell him that you'll be with me Saturday..." He raised one eyebrow.

"Thanks, but no thanks." I gathered my books, realizing I was stiff from sitting still so long. "So is it my turn tomorrow, then?"

"Certainly not!" His face was teasingly outraged. "I told you I wasn't done, didn't I?"

"What more is there?"

"You'll find out tomorrow." He reached across to open my door for me, and his sudden proximity sent my heart into frenzied palpitations.

But his hand froze on the handle.

"Not good," he muttered.

"What is it?" I was surprised to see that his jaw was clenched, his eyes disturbed.

He glanced at me for a brief second. "Another complication," he said glumly.

He flung the door open in one swift movement, and then moved, almost cringed, swiftly away from me.

The flash of headlights through the rain caught my attention as a dark car pulled up to the curb just a few feet away, facing us.

"Charlie's around the corner," he warned, staring through the downpour at the other vehicle.

I hopped out at once, despite my confusion and curiosity. The rain was louder as it glanced off my jacket.

I tried to make out the shapes in the front seat of the other car, but it was too dark. I could see Edward illuminated in the glare of the new car's headlights; he was still staring ahead, his gaze locked on something or someone I couldn't see. His expression was a strange mix of frustration and defiance.

Then he revved the engine, and the tires squealed against the wet pavement. The Volvo was out of sight in seconds.

"Hey, Bella," called a familiar, husky voice from the driver's side of the little black car.

"Jacob?" I asked, squinting through the rain. Just then, Charlie's cruiser swung around the corner, his lights shining on the occupants of the car in front of me.

Jacob was already climbing out, his wide grin visible even through the darkness. In the passenger seat was a much older man, a heavyset man with a memorable face—a face that overflowed, the cheeks resting against his shoulders, with creases running through the russet skin like an old leather jacket. And the surprisingly familiar eyes, black eyes that seemed at the same time both too young and too ancient for the broad face they were set in. Jacob's father, Billy Black. I knew him immediately, though in the more than five years since I'd seen him last I'd managed to forget his name when Charlie had spoken of him my first day here. He was staring at me, scrutinizing my face, so I smiled tentatively at him. His eyes were wide, as if in shock or fear, his nostrils flared. My smile faded.

Another complication, Edward had said.

Billy still stared at me with intense, anxious eyes. I groaned internally. Had Billy recognized Edward so easily? Could he really believe the impossible legends his son had scoffed at?

The answer was clear in Billy's eyes. Yes. Yes, he could.

12. BALANCING

"BILLY!" CHARLIE CALLED AS SOON AS HE GOT OUT OF THE CAR.

I turned toward the house, beckoning to Jacob as I ducked under the porch. I heard Charlie greeting them loudly behind me.

"I'm going to pretend I didn't see you behind the wheel, Jake," he said disapprovingly.

"We get permits early on the rez," Jacob said while I unlocked the door and flicked on the porch light.

"Sure you do," Charlie laughed.

"I have to get around somehow." I recognized Billy's resonant voice easily, despite the years. The sound of it made me feel suddenly younger, a child.

I went inside, leaving the door open behind me and turning on lights before I hung up my jacket. Then I stood in the door, watching anxiously as Charlie and Jacob helped Billy out of the car and into his wheelchair.

I backed out of the way as the three of them hurried in, shaking off the rain.

"This is a surprise," Charlie was saying.

"It's been too long," Billy answered. "I hope it's not a bad time." His dark eyes flashed up to me again, their expression unreadable.

"No, it's great. I hope you can stay for the game."

Jacob grinned. "I think that's the plan—our TV broke last week."

Billy made a face at his son. "And, of course, Jacob was anxious to see

Bella again," he added. Jacob scowled and ducked his head while I fought back a surge of remorse. Maybe I'd been too convincing on the beach.

"Are you hungry?" I asked, turning toward the kitchen. I was eager to escape Billy's searching gaze.

"Naw, we ate just before we came," Jacob answered.

"How about you, Charlie?" I called over my shoulder as I fled around the corner.

"Sure," he replied, his voice moving in the direction of the front room and the TV. I could hear Billy's chair follow.

The grilled cheese sandwiches were in the frying pan and I was slicing up a tomato when I sensed someone behind me.

"So, how are things?" Jacob asked.

"Pretty good." I smiled. His enthusiasm was hard to resist. "How about you? Did you finish your car?"

"No." He frowned. "I still need parts. We borrowed that one." He pointed with his thumb in the direction of the front yard.

"Sorry. I haven't seen any . . . what was it you were looking for?"

"Master cylinder." He grinned. "Is something wrong with the truck?" he added suddenly.

"No."

"Oh. I just wondered because you weren't driving it."

I stared down at the pan, pulling up the edge of a sandwich to check the bottom side. "I got a ride with a friend."

"Nice ride." Jacob's voice was admiring. "I didn't recognize the driver, though. I thought I knew most of the kids around here."

I nodded noncommittally, keeping my eyes down as I flipped sandwiches.

"My dad seemed to know him from somewhere."

"Jacob, could you hand me some plates? They're in the cupboard over the sink."

"Sure."

He got the plates in silence. I hoped he would let it drop now.

"So who was it?" he asked, setting two plates on the counter next to me.

I sighed in defeat. "Edward Cullen."

To my surprise, he laughed. I glanced up at him. He looked a little embarrassed.

"Guess that explains it, then," he said. "I wondered why my dad was acting so strange."

"That's right." I faked an innocent expression. "He doesn't like the Cullens."

"Superstitious old man," Jacob muttered under his breath.

"You don't think he'd say anything to Charlie?" I couldn't help asking, the words coming out in a low rush.

Jacob stared at me for a moment, and I couldn't read the expression in his dark eyes. "I doubt it," he finally answered. "I think Charlie chewed him out pretty good last time. They haven't spoken much since—tonight is sort of a reunion, I think. I don't think he'd bring it up again."

"Oh," I said, trying to sound indifferent.

I stayed in the front room after I carried the food out to Charlie, pretending to watch the game while Jacob chattered at me. I was really listening to the men's conversation, watching for any sign that Billy was about to rat me out, trying to think of ways to stop him if he began.

It was a long night. I had a lot of homework that was going undone, but I was afraid to leave Billy alone with Charlie. Finally, the game ended.

"Are you and your friends coming back to the beach soon?" Jacob asked as he pushed his father over the lip of the threshold.

"I'm not sure," I hedged.

"That was fun, Charlie," Billy said.

"Come up for the next game," Charlie encouraged.

"Sure, sure," Billy said. "We'll be here. Have a good night." His eyes shifted to mine, and his smile disappeared. "You take care, Bella," he added seriously.

"Thanks," I muttered, looking away.

I headed for the stairs while Charlie waved from the doorway.

"Wait, Bella," he said.

I cringed. Had Billy gotten something in before I'd joined them in the living room?

But Charlie was relaxed, still grinning from the unexpected visit.

"I didn't get a chance to talk to you tonight. How was your day?"

"Good." I hesitated with one foot on the first stair, searching for details I could safely share. "My badminton team won all four games."

"Wow, I didn't know you could play badminton."

"Well, actually I can't, but my partner is really good," I admitted.

"Who is it?" he asked with token interest.

"Um . . . Mike Newton," I told him reluctantly.

"Oh yeah—you said you were friends with the Newton kid." He perked up. "Nice family." He mused for a minute. "Why didn't you ask him to the dance this weekend?"

"Dad!" I groaned. "He's kind of dating my friend Jessica. Besides, you know I can't dance."

"Oh yeah," he muttered. Then he smiled at me apologetically. "So I guess it's good you'll be gone Saturday . . . I've made plans to go fishing with the guys from the station. The weather's supposed to be real warm. But if you wanted to put your trip off till someone could go with you, I'd stay home. I know I leave you here alone too much."

"Dad, you're doing a great job." I smiled, hoping my relief didn't show. "I've never minded being alone—I'm too much like you." I winked at him, and he smiled his crinkly-eyed smile.

I slept better that night, too tired to dream again. When I woke to the pearl gray morning, my mood was blissful. The tense evening with Billy and Jacob seemed harmless enough now; I decided to forget it completely. I caught myself whistling while I was pulling the front part of my hair back into a barrette, and later again as I skipped down the stairs. Charlie noticed.

"You're cheerful this morning," he commented over breakfast.

I shrugged. "It's Friday."

I hurried so I would be ready to go the second Charlie left. I had my bag ready, shoes on, teeth brushed, but even though I rushed to the door as soon as I was sure Charlie would be out of sight, Edward was faster. He was waiting in his shiny car, windows down, engine off.

I didn't hesitate this time, climbing in the passenger side quickly, the sooner to see his face. He grinned his crooked smile at me, stopping my breath and my heart. I couldn't imagine how an angel could be any more glorious. There was nothing about him that could be improved upon.

"How did you sleep?" he asked. I wondered if he had any idea how appealing his voice was.

"Fine. How was your night?"

"Pleasant." His smile was amused; I felt like I was missing an inside joke.

"Can I ask what you did?" I asked.

"No." He grinned. "Today is still *mine*."

He wanted to know about people today: more about Renée, her hobbies, what we'd done in our free time together. And then the one grandmother I'd known, my few school friends—embarrassing me when he asked about boys I'd dated. I was relieved that I'd never really dated anyone, so that particular conversation couldn't last long. He seemed as surprised as Jessica and Angela by my lack of romantic history.

"So you never met anyone you wanted?" he asked in a serious tone that made me wonder what he was thinking about.

I was grudgingly honest. "Not in Phoenix."

His lips pressed together into a hard line.

We were in the cafeteria at this point. The day had sped by in the blur that was rapidly becoming routine. I took advantage of his brief pause to take a bite of my bagel.

"I should have let you drive yourself today," he announced, apropos of nothing, while I chewed.

"Why?" I demanded.

"I'm leaving with Alice after lunch."

"Oh." I blinked, bewildered and disappointed. "That's okay, it's not that far of a walk."

He frowned at me impatiently. "I'm not going to make you walk home. We'll go get your truck and leave it here for you."

"I don't have my key with me," I sighed. "I really don't mind walking." What I minded was losing my time with him.

He shook his head. "Your truck will be here, and the key will be in the ignition—unless you're afraid someone might steal it." He laughed at the thought.

"All right," I agreed, pursing my lips. I was pretty sure my key was in the pocket of a pair of jeans I wore Wednesday, under a pile of clothes in the laundry room. Even if he broke into my house, or whatever he was planning, he'd never find it. He seemed to feel the challenge in my consent. He smirked, overconfident.

"So where are you going?" I asked as casually as I could manage.

"Hunting," he answered grimly. "If I'm going to be alone with you tomorrow, I'm going to take whatever precautions I can." His face grew morose . . . and pleading. "You can always cancel, you know."

I looked down, afraid of the persuasive power of his eyes. I refused to be convinced to fear him, no matter how real the danger might be. *It doesn't matter,* I repeated in my head.

"No," I whispered, glancing back at his face. "I can't."

"Perhaps you're right," he murmured bleakly. His eyes seemed to darken in color as I watched.

I changed the subject. "What time will I see you tomorrow?" I asked, already depressed by the thought of him leaving now.

"That depends . . . it's a Saturday, don't you want to sleep in?" he offered.

"No," I answered too fast. He restrained a smile.

"The same time as usual, then," he decided. "Will Charlie be there?"

"No, he's fishing tomorrow." I beamed at the memory of how conveniently things had worked out.

His voice turned sharp. "And if you don't come home, what will he think?"

"I have no idea," I answered coolly. "He knows I've been meaning to do the laundry. Maybe he'll think I fell in the washer."

He scowled at me and I scowled back. His anger was much more impressive than mine.

"What are you hunting tonight?" I asked when I was sure I had lost the glowering contest.

"Whatever we find in the park. We aren't going far." He seemed bemused by my casual reference to his secret realities.

"Why are you going with Alice?" I wondered.

"Alice is the most . . . supportive." He frowned as he spoke.

"And the others?" I asked timidly. "What are they?"

His brow puckered for a brief moment. "Incredulous, for the most part."

I peeked quickly behind me at his family. They sat staring off in different directions, exactly the same as the first time I'd seen them. Only now they were four; their beautiful, bronze-haired brother sat across from me, his golden eyes troubled.

"They don't like me," I guessed.

"That's not it," he disagreed, but his eyes were too innocent. "They don't understand why I can't leave you alone."

I grimaced. "Neither do I, for that matter."

Edward shook his head slowly, rolling his eyes toward the ceiling before he met my gaze again. "I told you—you don't see yourself clearly at all. You're not like anyone I've ever known. You fascinate me."

I glared at him, sure he was teasing now.

He smiled as he deciphered my expression. "Having the advantages I do," he murmured, touching his forehead discreetly, "I have a better than average grasp of human nature. People are predictable. But you . . . you never do what I expect. You always take me by surprise."

I looked away, my eyes wandering back to his family, embarrassed and dissatisfied. His words made me feel like a science experiment. I wanted to laugh at myself for expecting anything else.

"That part is easy enough to explain," he continued. I felt his eyes on my face but I couldn't look at him yet, afraid he might read the chagrin in my eyes. "But there's more . . . and it's not so easy to put into words—"

I was still staring at the Cullens while he spoke. Suddenly Rosalie, his blond and breathtaking sister, turned to look at me. No, not to look—to glare, with dark, cold eyes. I wanted to look away, but her gaze held me until Edward broke off mid-sentence and made an angry noise under his breath. It was almost a hiss.

Rosalie turned her head, and I was relieved to be free. I looked back at Edward—and I knew he could see the confusion and fear that widened my eyes.

His face was tight as he explained. "I'm sorry about that. She's just worried. You see . . . it's dangerous for more than just me if, after spending so much time with you so publicly . . ." He looked down.

"If?"

"If this ends . . . badly." He dropped his head into his hands, as he had that night in Port Angeles. His anguish was plain; I yearned to comfort him, but I was at a loss to know how. My hand reached toward him involuntarily; quickly, though, I dropped it to the table, fearing that my touch would only make things worse. I realized slowly that his words should frighten me. I waited for that fear to come, but all I could seem to feel was an ache for his pain.

And frustration—frustration that Rosalie had interrupted whatever he was about to say. I didn't know how to bring it up again. He still had his head in his hands.

I tried to speak in a normal voice. "And you have to leave now?"

"Yes." He raised his face; it was serious for a moment, and then his mood shifted and he smiled. "It's probably for the best. We still have fifteen minutes of that wretched movie left to endure in Biology—I don't think I could take any more."

I started. Alice—her short, inky hair in a halo of spiky disarray around her exquisite, elfin face—was suddenly standing behind his shoulder. Her slight frame was willowy, graceful even in absolute stillness.

He greeted her without looking away from me. "Alice."

"Edward," she answered, her high soprano voice almost as attractive as his.

"Alice, Bella—Bella, Alice," he introduced us, gesturing casually with his hand, a wry smile on his face.

"Hello, Bella." Her brilliant obsidian eyes were unreadable, but her smile was friendly. "It's nice to finally meet you."

Edward flashed a dark look at her.

"Hi, Alice," I murmured shyly.

"Are you ready?" she asked him.

His voice was aloof. "Nearly. I'll meet you at the car."

She left without another word; her walk was so fluid, so sinuous that I felt a sharp pang of jealousy.

"Should I say 'have fun,' or is that the wrong sentiment?" I asked, turning back to him.

"No, 'have fun' works as well as anything." He grinned.

"Have fun, then." I worked to sound wholehearted. Of course I didn't fool him.

"I'll try." He still grinned. "And you try to be safe, please."

"Safe in Forks—what a challenge."

"For you it *is* a challenge." His jaw hardened. "Promise."

"I promise to try to be safe," I recited. "I'll do the laundry tonight—that ought to be fraught with peril."

"Don't fall in," he mocked.

"I'll do my best."

He stood then, and I rose, too.

"I'll see you tomorrow," I sighed.

"It seems like a long time to you, doesn't it?" he mused.

I nodded glumly.

"I'll be there in the morning," he promised, smiling his crooked smile. He reached across the table to touch my face, lightly brushing along my cheekbone again. Then he turned and walked away. I stared after him until he was gone.

I was sorely tempted to ditch the rest of the day, at the very least Gym, but a warning instinct stopped me. I knew that if I disappeared now, Mike and others would assume I was with Edward. And Edward was worried about the time we'd spent together publicly . . . if things went wrong. I refused to dwell on the last thought, concentrating instead on making things safer for him.

I intuitively knew—and sensed he did, too—that tomorrow would be pivotal. Our relationship couldn't continue to balance, as it did, on the point of a knife. We would fall off one edge or the other, depending entirely upon his decision, or his instincts. My decision was made, made before I'd ever consciously chosen, and I was committed to seeing it through. Because there was nothing more terrifying to me, more excruciating, than the thought of turning away from him. It was an impossibility.

I went to class, feeling dutiful. I couldn't honestly say what happened in Biology; my mind was too preoccupied with thoughts of tomorrow. In Gym, Mike was speaking to me again; he wished me a good time in Seattle. I carefully explained that I'd canceled my trip, worried about my truck.

"Are you going to the dance with Cullen?" he asked, suddenly sulky.

"No, I'm not going to the dance at all."

"What are you doing, then?" he asked, too interested.

My natural urge was to tell him to butt out. Instead, I lied brightly.

"Laundry, and then I have to study for the Trig test or I'm going to fail."

"Is Cullen helping you study?"

"*Edward,*" I emphasized, "is not going to help me study. He's gone away somewhere for the weekend." The lies came more naturally than usual, I noted with surprise.

"Oh." He perked up. "You know, you could come to the dance with our group anyway—that would be cool. We'd all dance with you," he promised.

The mental image of Jessica's face made my tone sharper than necessary. "I'm *not* going to the dance, Mike, okay?"

"Fine." He sulked again. "I was just offering."

When the school day had finally ended, I walked to the parking lot without enthusiasm. I did not especially want to walk home, but I couldn't see how he would have retrieved my truck. Then again, I was starting to believe that nothing was impossible for him. The latter instinct proved correct— my truck sat in the same space he'd parked his Volvo in this morning. I shook my head, incredulous, as I opened the unlocked door and saw the key in the ignition.

There was a piece of white paper folded on my seat. I got in and closed the door before I unfolded it. Two words were written in his elegant script.

Be safe.

The sound of the truck roaring to life frightened me. I laughed at myself.

When I got home, the handle of the door was locked, the dead bolt unlocked, just as I'd left it this morning. Inside, I went straight to the laundry room. It looked just the same as I'd left it, too. I dug for my jeans and, after finding them, checked the pockets. Empty. Maybe I'd hung my key up after all, I thought, shaking my head.

Following the same instinct that had prompted me to lie to Mike, I called Jessica on the pretense of wishing her luck at the dance. When she offered the same wish for my day with Edward, I told her about the cancellation. She was more disappointed than really necessary for a third-party observer to be. I said goodbye quickly after that.

Charlie was absentminded at dinner, worried over something at work, I guessed, or maybe a basketball game, or maybe he was just really enjoying the lasagna—it was hard to tell with Charlie.

"You know, Dad...," I began, breaking into his reverie.

"What's that, Bell?"

"I think you're right about Seattle. I think I'll wait until Jessica or someone else can go with me."

"Oh," he said, surprised. "Oh, okay. So, do you want me to stay home?"

"No, Dad, don't change your plans. I've got a million things to do...

homework, laundry...I need to go to the library and the grocery store. I'll be in and out all day...you go and have fun."

"Are you sure?"

"Absolutely, Dad. Besides, the freezer is getting dangerously low on fish— we're down to a two, maybe three years' supply."

"You're sure easy to live with, Bella." He smiled.

"I could say the same thing about you," I said, laughing. The sound of my laughter was off, but he didn't seem to notice. I felt so guilty for deceiving him that I almost took Edward's advice and told him where I would be. Almost.

After dinner, I folded clothes and moved another load through the dryer. Unfortunately it was the kind of job that only keeps hands busy. My mind definitely had too much free time, and it was getting out of control. I fluctuated between anticipation so intense that it was very nearly pain, and an insidious fear that picked at my resolve. I had to keep reminding myself that I'd made my choice, and I wasn't going back on it. I pulled his note out of my pocket much more often than necessary to absorb the two small words he'd written. He wants me to be safe, I told myself again and again. I would just hold on to the faith that, in the end, that desire would win out over the others. And what was my other choice—to cut him out of my life? Intolerable. Besides, since I'd come to Forks, it really seemed like my life was *about* him.

But a tiny voice in the back of my mind worried, wondering if it would hurt *very* much...if it ended badly.

I was relieved when it was late enough to be acceptable for bedtime. I knew I was far too stressed to sleep, so I did something I'd never done before. I deliberately took unnecessary cold medicine—the kind that knocked me out for a good eight hours. I normally wouldn't condone that type of behavior in myself, but tomorrow would be complicated enough without me being loopy from sleep deprivation on top of everything else. While I waited for the drugs to kick in, I dried my clean hair till it was impeccably straight, and fussed over what I would wear tomorrow.

With everything ready for the morning, I finally lay in my bed. I felt hyper; I couldn't stop twitching. I got up and rifled through my shoebox of CDs until I found a collection of Chopin's nocturnes. I put that on very quietly and then lay down again, concentrating on relaxing individual parts of my body. Somewhere in the middle of that exercise, the cold pills took effect, and I gladly sank into unconsciousness.

I woke early, having slept soundly and dreamlessly thanks to my gratuitous drug use. Though I was well rested, I slipped right back into the same hectic frenzy from the night before. I dressed in a rush, smoothing my collar against my neck, fidgeting with the tan sweater till it hung right over my jeans. I sneaked a swift look out the window to see that Charlie was already gone. A thin, cottony layer of clouds veiled the sky. They didn't look very lasting.

I ate breakfast without tasting the food, hurrying to clean up when I was done. I peeked out the window again, but nothing had changed. I had just finished brushing my teeth and was heading back downstairs when a quiet knock sent my heart thudding against my rib cage.

I flew to the door; I had a little trouble with the simple deadbolt, but I yanked the door open at last, and there he was. All the agitation dissolved as soon as I looked at his face, calm taking its place. I breathed a sigh of relief—yesterday's fears seemed very foolish with him here.

He wasn't smiling at first—his face was somber. But then his expression lightened as he looked me over, and he laughed.

"Good morning," he chuckled.

"What's wrong?" I glanced down to make sure I hadn't forgotten anything important, like shoes, or pants.

"We match." He laughed again. I realized he had a long, light tan sweater on, with a white collar showing underneath, and blue jeans. I laughed with him, hiding a secret twinge of regret—why did he have to look like a runway model when I couldn't?

I locked the door behind me while he walked to the truck. He waited by the passenger door with a martyred expression that was easy to understand.

"We made a deal," I reminded him smugly, climbing into the driver's seat, and reaching over to unlock his door.

"Where to?" I asked.

"Put your seat belt on—I'm nervous already."

I gave him a dirty look as I complied.

"Where to?" I repeated with a sigh.

"Take the one-oh-one north," he ordered.

It was surprisingly difficult to concentrate on the road while feeling his gaze on my face. I compensated by driving more carefully than usual through the still-sleeping town.

"Were you planning to make it out of Forks before nightfall?"

"This truck is old enough to be your car's grandfather—have some respect," I retorted.

We were soon out of the town limits, despite his negativity. Thick underbrush and green-swathed trunks replaced the lawns and houses.

"Turn right on the one-ten," he instructed just as I was about to ask. I obeyed silently.

"Now we drive until the pavement ends."

I could hear a smile in his voice, but I was too afraid of driving off the road and proving him right to look over and be sure.

"And what's there, at the pavement's end?" I wondered.

"A trail."

"We're hiking?" Thank goodness I'd worn tennis shoes.

"Is that a problem?" He sounded as if he'd expected as much.

"No." I tried to make the lie sound confident. But if he thought my truck was slow . . .

"Don't worry, it's only five miles or so, and we're in no hurry."

Five miles. I didn't answer, so that he wouldn't hear my voice crack in panic. Five miles of treacherous roots and loose stones, trying to twist my ankles or otherwise incapacitate me. This was going to be humiliating.

We drove in silence for a while as I contemplated the coming horror.

"What are you thinking?" he asked impatiently after a few moments.

I lied again. "Just wondering where we're going."

"It's a place I like to go when the weather is nice." We both glanced out the windows at the thinning clouds after he spoke.

"Charlie said it would be warm today."

"And did you tell Charlie what you were up to?" he asked.

"Nope."

"But Jessica thinks we're going to Seattle together?" He seemed cheered by the idea.

"No, I told her you canceled on me—which is true."

"No one knows you're with me?" Angrily, now.

"That depends . . . I assume you told Alice?"

"That's very helpful, Bella," he snapped.

I pretended I didn't hear that.

"Are you so depressed by Forks that it's made you suicidal?" he demanded when I ignored him.

"You said it might cause trouble for you . . . us being together publicly," I reminded him.

"So you're worried about the trouble it might cause *me—if you* don't come *home?*" His voice was still angry, and bitingly sarcastic.

I nodded, keeping my eyes on the road.

He muttered something under his breath, speaking so quickly that I couldn't understand.

We were silent for the rest of the drive. I could feel the waves of infuriated disapproval rolling off of him, and I could think of nothing to say.

And then the road ended, constricting to a thin foot trail with a small wooden marker. I parked on the narrow shoulder and stepped out, afraid because he was angry with me and I didn't have driving as an excuse not to look at him. It was warm now, warmer than it had been in Forks since the day I'd arrived, almost muggy under the clouds. I pulled off my sweater and knotted it around my waist, glad that I'd worn the light, sleeveless shirt—especially if I had five miles of hiking ahead of me.

I heard his door slam, and looked over to see that he'd removed his sweater, too. He was facing away from me, into the unbroken forest beside my truck.

"This way," he said, glancing over his shoulder at me, eyes still annoyed. He started into the dark forest.

"The trail?" Panic was clear in my voice as I hurried around the truck to catch up to him.

"I said there was a trail at the end of the road, not that we were taking it."

"No trail?" I asked desperately.

"I won't let you get lost." He turned then, with a mocking smile, and I stifled a gasp. His white shirt was sleeveless, and he wore it unbuttoned, so that the smooth white skin of his throat flowed uninterrupted over the marble contours of his chest, his perfect musculature no longer merely hinted at behind concealing clothes. He was too perfect, I realized with a piercing stab of despair. There was no way this godlike creature could be meant for me.

He stared at me, bewildered by my tortured expression.

"Do you want to go home?" he said quietly, a different pain than mine saturating his voice.

"No." I walked forward till I was close beside him, anxious not to waste one second of whatever time I might have with him.

"What's wrong?" he asked, his voice gentle.

"I'm not a good hiker," I answered dully. "You'll have to be very patient."

"I can be patient—if I make a great effort." He smiled, holding my glance, trying to lift me out of my sudden, unexplained dejection.

I tried to smile back, but the smile was unconvincing. He scrutinized my face.

"I'll take you home," he promised. I couldn't tell if the promise was unconditional, or restricted to an immediate departure. I knew he thought it was fear that upset me, and I was grateful again that I was the one person whose mind he couldn't hear.

"If you want me to hack five miles through the jungle before sundown, you'd better start leading the way," I said acidly. He frowned at me, struggling to understand my tone and expression.

He gave up after a moment and led the way into the forest.

It wasn't as hard as I had feared. The way was mostly flat, and he held the damp ferns and webs of moss aside for me. When his straight path took us over fallen trees or boulders, he would help me, lifting me by the elbow, and then releasing me instantly when I was clear. His cold touch on my skin never failed to make my heart thud erratically. Twice, when that happened, I caught a look on his face that made me sure he could somehow hear it.

I tried to keep my eyes away from his perfection as much as possible, but I slipped often. Each time, his beauty pierced me through with sadness.

For the most part, we walked in silence. Occasionally he would ask a random question that he hadn't gotten to in the past two days of interrogation. He asked about my birthdays, my grade school teachers, my childhood pets—and I had to admit that after killing three fish in a row, I'd given up on the whole institution. He laughed at that, louder than I was used to—bell-like echoes bouncing back to us from the empty woods.

The hike took me most of the morning, but he never showed any sign of impatience. The forest spread out around us in a boundless labyrinth of ancient trees, and I began to be nervous that we would never find our way out again. He was perfectly at ease, comfortable in the green maze, never seeming to feel any doubt about our direction.

After several hours, the light that filtered through the canopy transformed, the murky olive tone shifting to a brighter jade. The day had turned sunny, just as he'd foretold. For the first time since we'd entered the woods, I felt a thrill of excitement—which quickly turned to impatience.

"Are we there yet?" I teased, pretending to scowl.

"Nearly." He smiled at the change in my mood. "Do you see the brightness ahead?"

I peered into the thick forest. "Um, should I?"

He smirked. "Maybe it's a bit soon for *your* eyes."

"Time to visit the optometrist," I muttered. His smirk grew more pronounced.

But then, after another hundred yards, I could definitely see a lightening in the trees ahead, a glow that was yellow instead of green. I picked up the pace, my eagerness growing with every step. He let me lead now, following noiselessly.

I reached the edge of the pool of light and stepped through the last fringe of ferns into the loveliest place I had ever seen. The meadow was small, perfectly round, and filled with wildflowers—violet, yellow, and soft white. Somewhere nearby, I could hear the bubbling music of a stream. The sun was directly overhead, filling the circle with a haze of buttery sunshine. I walked slowly, awestruck, through the soft grass, swaying flowers, and warm, gilded air. I halfway turned, wanting to share this with him, but he wasn't behind me where I thought he'd be. I spun around, searching for him with sudden alarm. Finally I spotted him, still under the dense shade of the canopy at the edge of the hollow, watching me with cautious eyes. Only then did I remember what the beauty of the meadow had driven from my mind—the enigma of Edward and the sun, which he'd promised to illustrate for me today.

I took a step back toward him, my eyes alight with curiosity. His eyes were wary, reluctant. I smiled encouragingly and beckoned to him with my hand, taking another step back to him. He held up a hand in warning, and I hesitated, rocking back onto my heels.

Edward seemed to take a deep breath, and then he stepped out into the bright glow of the midday sun.

13. CONFESSIONS

EDWARD IN THE SUNLIGHT WAS SHOCKING. I COULDN'T GET USED TO IT, though I'd been staring at him all afternoon. His skin, white despite the faint flush from yesterday's hunting trip, literally sparkled, like thousands of tiny diamonds were embedded in the surface. He lay perfectly still in the grass, his shirt open over his sculpted, incandescent chest, his scintillating arms bare. His glistening, pale lavender lids were shut, though of course he didn't sleep. A perfect statue, carved in some unknown stone, smooth like marble, glittering like crystal.

Now and then, his lips would move, so fast it looked like they were trembling. But, when I asked, he told me he was singing to himself; it was too low for me to hear.

I enjoyed the sun, too, though the air wasn't quite dry enough for my taste. I would have liked to lie back, as he did, and let the sun warm my face. But I stayed curled up, my chin resting on my knees, unwilling to take my eyes off him. The wind was gentle; it tangled my hair and ruffled the grass that swayed around his motionless form.

The meadow, so spectacular to me at first, paled next to his magnificence.

Hesitantly, always afraid, even now, that he would disappear like a mirage, too beautiful to be real...hesitantly, I reached out one finger and stroked the back of his shimmering hand, where it lay within my reach. I marveled again at the perfect texture, satin smooth, cool as stone. When I looked up again, his eyes were open, watching me. Butterscotch today, lighter, warmer after hunting. His quick smile turned up the corners of his flawless lips.

"I don't scare you?" he asked playfully, but I could hear the real curiosity in his soft voice.

"No more than usual."

He smiled wider; his teeth flashed in the sun.

I inched closer, stretched out my whole hand now to trace the contours of his forearm with my fingertips. I saw that my fingers trembled, and knew it wouldn't escape his notice.

"Do you mind?" I asked, for he had closed his eyes again.

"No," he said without opening his eyes. "You can't imagine how that feels." He sighed.

I lightly trailed my hand over the perfect muscles of his arm, followed the faint pattern of bluish veins inside the crease at his elbow. With my other hand, I reached to turn his hand over. Realizing what I wished, he flipped his palm up in one of those blindingly fast, disconcerting movements of his. It startled me; my fingers froze on his arm for a brief second.

"Sorry," he murmured. I looked up in time to see his golden eyes close again. "It's too easy to be myself with you."

I lifted his hand, turning it this way and that as I watched the sun glitter on his palm. I held it closer to my face, trying to see the hidden facets in his skin.

"Tell me what you're thinking," he whispered. I looked to see his eyes watching me, suddenly intent. "It's still so strange for me, not knowing."

"You know, the rest of us feel that way all the time."

"It's a hard life." Did I imagine the hint of regret in his tone? "But you didn't tell me."

"I *was* wishing I could know what you were thinking . . ." I hesitated.

"And?"

"I was wishing that I could believe that you were real. And I was wishing that I wasn't afraid."

"I don't want you to be afraid." His voice was just a soft murmur. I heard what he couldn't truthfully say, that I didn't need to be afraid, that there was nothing to fear.

"Well, that's not exactly the fear I meant, though that's certainly something to think about."

So quickly that I missed his movement, he was half sitting, propped up on his right arm, his left palm still in my hands. His angel's face was only a few inches from mine. I might have—should have—flinched away from his unexpected closeness, but I was unable to move. His golden eyes mesmerized me.

"What are you afraid of, then?" he whispered intently.

But I couldn't answer. As I had just that once before, I smelled his cool breath in my face. Sweet, delicious, the scent made my mouth water. It was unlike anything else. Instinctively, unthinkingly, I leaned closer, inhaling.

And he was gone, his hand ripped from mine. In the time it took my eyes to focus, he was twenty feet away, standing at the edge of the small meadow, in the deep shade of a huge fir tree. He stared at me, his eyes dark in the shadows, his expression unreadable.

I could feel the hurt and shock on my face. My empty hands stung.

"I'm . . . sorry . . . Edward," I whispered. I knew he could hear.

"Give me a moment," he called, just loud enough for my less sensitive ears. I sat very still.

After ten incredibly long seconds, he walked back, slowly for him. He stopped, still several feet away, and sank gracefully to the ground, crossing his legs. His eyes never left mine. He took two deep breaths, and then smiled in apology.

"I am so very sorry." He hesitated. "Would you understand what I meant if I said I was only human?"

I nodded once, not quite able to smile at his joke. Adrenaline pulsed through my veins as the realization of danger slowly sank in. He could smell that from where he sat. His smile turned mocking.

"I'm the world's best predator, aren't I? Everything about me invites you in—my voice, my face, even my *smell*. As if I need any of that!" Unexpectedly, he was on his feet, bounding away, instantly out of sight, only to appear beneath the same tree as before, having circled the meadow in half a second.

"As if you could outrun me," he laughed bitterly.

He reached up with one hand and, with a deafening crack, effortlessly ripped a two-foot-thick branch from the trunk of the spruce. He balanced it in that hand for a moment, and then threw it with blinding speed, shattering it against another huge tree, which shook and trembled at the blow.

And he was in front of me again, standing two feet away, still as a stone.

"As if you could fight me off," he said gently.

I sat without moving, more frightened of him than I had ever been. I'd never seen him so completely freed of that carefully cultivated façade. He'd never been less human . . . or more beautiful. Face ashen, eyes wide, I sat like a bird locked in the eyes of a snake.

His lovely eyes seemed to glow with rash excitement. Then, as the seconds passed, they dimmed. His expression slowly folded into a mask of ancient sadness.

"Don't be afraid," he murmured, his velvet voice unintentionally seductive. "I promise . . ." He hesitated. "I *swear* not to hurt you." He seemed more concerned with convincing himself than me.

"Don't be afraid," he whispered again as he stepped closer, with exaggerated slowness. He sat sinuously, with deliberately unhurried movements, till our faces were on the same level, just a foot apart.

"Please forgive me," he said formally. "I *can* control myself. You caught me off guard. But I'm on my best behavior now."

He waited, but I still couldn't speak.

"I'm not thirsty today, honestly." He winked.

At that I had to laugh, though the sound was shaky and breathless.

"Are you all right?" he asked tenderly, reaching out slowly, carefully, to place his marble hand back in mine.

I looked at his smooth, cold hand, and then at his eyes. They were soft, repentant. I looked back at his hand, and then deliberately returned to tracing the lines in his hand with my fingertip. I looked up and smiled timidly.

His answering smile was dazzling.

"So where were we, before I behaved so rudely?" he asked in the gentle cadences of an earlier century.

"I honestly can't remember."

He smiled, but his face was ashamed. "I think we were talking about why you were afraid, besides the obvious reason."

"Oh, right."

"Well?"

I looked down at his hand and doodled aimlessly across his smooth, iridescent palm. The seconds ticked by.

"How easily frustrated I am," he sighed. I looked into his eyes, abruptly grasping that this was every bit as new to him as it was to me. As many years of unfathomable experience as he had, this was hard for him, too. I took courage from that thought.

"I was afraid...because, for, well, obvious reasons, I can't *stay* with you. And I'm afraid that I'd like to stay with you, much more than I should." I looked down at his hands as I spoke. It was difficult for me to say this aloud.

"Yes," he agreed slowly. "That is something to be afraid of, indeed. Wanting to be with me. That's really not in your best interest."

I frowned.

"I should have left long ago," he sighed. "I should leave now. But I don't know if I can."

"I don't want you to leave," I mumbled pathetically, staring down again.

"Which is exactly why I should. But don't worry. I'm essentially a selfish creature. I crave your company too much to do what I should."

"I'm glad."

"Don't be!" He withdrew his hand, more gently this time; his voice was harsher than usual. Harsh for him, still more beautiful than any human voice. It was hard to keep up—his sudden mood changes left me always a step behind, dazed.

"It's not only your company I crave! Never forget *that*. Never forget I am more dangerous to you than I am to anyone else." He stopped, and I looked to see him gazing unseeingly into the forest.

I thought for a moment.

"I don't think I understand exactly what you mean—by that last part anyway," I said.

He looked back at me and smiled, his mood shifting yet again.

"How do I explain?" he mused. "And without frightening you again... hmmmm." Without seeming to think about it, he placed his hand back in mine; I held it tightly in both of mine. He looked at our hands.

"That's amazingly pleasant, the warmth." He sighed.

A moment passed as he assembled his thoughts.

"You know how everyone enjoys different flavors?" he began. "Some people love chocolate ice cream, others prefer strawberry?"

I nodded.

"Sorry about the food analogy—I couldn't think of another way to explain."

I smiled. He smiled ruefully back.

"You see, every person smells different, has a different essence. If you locked an alcoholic in a room full of stale beer, he'd gladly drink it. But he could resist, if he wished to, if he were a recovering alcoholic. Now let's say you placed in that room a glass of hundred-year-old brandy, the rarest, finest cognac—and filled the room with its warm aroma—how do you think he would fare then?"

We sat silently, looking into each other's eyes—trying to read each other's thoughts.

He broke the silence first.

"Maybe that's not the right comparison. Maybe it would be too easy to turn down the brandy. Perhaps I should have made our alcoholic a heroin addict instead."

"So what you're saying is, I'm your brand of heroin?" I teased, trying to lighten the mood.

He smiled swiftly, seeming to appreciate my effort. "Yes, you are *exactly* my brand of heroin."

"Does that happen often?" I asked.

He looked across the treetops, thinking through his response.

"I spoke to my brothers about it." He still stared into the distance. "To Jasper, every one of you is much the same. He's the most recent to join our family. It's a struggle for him to abstain at all. He hasn't had time to grow sensitive to the differences in smell, in flavor." He glanced swiftly at me, his expression apologetic.

"Sorry," he said.

"I don't mind. Please don't worry about offending me, or frightening me, or whichever. That's the way you think. I can understand, or I can try to at least. Just explain however you can."

He took a deep breath and gazed at the sky again.

"So Jasper wasn't sure if he'd ever come across someone who was as"—he hesitated, looking for the right word—"*appealing* as you are to me. Which makes me think not. Emmett has been on the wagon longer, so to speak, and he understood what I meant. He says twice, for him, once stronger than the other."

"And for you?"

"Never."

The word hung there for a moment in the warm breeze.

"What did Emmett do?" I asked to break the silence.

It was the wrong question to ask. His face grew dark, his hand clenched into a fist inside mine. He looked away. I waited, but he wasn't going to answer.

"I guess I know," I finally said.

He lifted his eyes; his expression was wistful, pleading.

"Even the strongest of us fall off the wagon, don't we?"

"What are you asking? My permission?" My voice was sharper than I'd intended. I tried to make my tone kinder—I could guess what his honesty must cost him. "I mean, is there no hope, then?" How calmly I could discuss my own death!

"No, no!" He was instantly contrite. "Of course there's hope! I mean, of course I won't..." He left the sentence hanging. His eyes burned into mine. "It's different for us. Emmett... these were strangers he happened across. It was a long time ago, and he wasn't as... practiced, as careful, as he is now."

He fell silent and watched me intently as I thought it through.

"So if we'd met... oh, in a dark alley or something..." I trailed off.

"It took everything I had not to jump up in the middle of that class full of children and—" He stopped abruptly, looking away. "When you walked past me, I could have ruined everything Carlisle has built for us, right then and there. If I hadn't been denying my thirst for the last, well, too many years, I wouldn't have been able to stop myself." He paused, scowling at the trees.

He glanced at me grimly, both of us remembering. "You must have thought I was possessed."

"I couldn't understand why. How you could hate me so quickly..."

"To me, it was like you were some kind of demon, summoned straight from my own personal hell to ruin me. The fragrance coming off your skin…I thought it would make me deranged that first day. In that one hour, I thought of a hundred different ways to lure you from the room with me, to get you alone. And I fought them each back, thinking of my family, what I could do to them. I had to run out, to get away before I could speak the words that would make you follow…."

He looked up then at my staggered expression as I tried to absorb his bitter memories. His golden eyes scorched from under his lashes, hypnotic and deadly.

"You would have come," he promised.

I tried to speak calmly. "Without a doubt."

He frowned down at my hands, releasing me from the force of his stare. "And then, as I tried to rearrange my schedule in a pointless attempt to avoid you, you were there—in that close, warm little room, the scent was maddening. I so very nearly took you then. There was only one other frail human there—so easily dealt with."

I shivered in the warm sun, seeing my memories anew through his eyes, only now grasping the danger. Poor Ms. Cope; I shivered again at how close I'd come to being inadvertently responsible for her death.

"But I resisted. I don't know how. I forced myself *not* to wait for you, *not* to follow you from the school. It was easier outside, when I couldn't smell you anymore, to think clearly, to make the right decision. I left the others near home—I was too ashamed to tell them how weak I was, they only knew something was very wrong—and then I went straight to Carlisle, at the hospital, to tell him I was leaving."

I stared in surprise.

"I traded cars with him—he had a full tank of gas and I didn't want to stop. I didn't dare to go home, to face Esme. She wouldn't have let me go without a scene. She would have tried to convince me that it wasn't necessary…

"By the next morning I was in Alaska." He sounded ashamed, as if admitting a great cowardice. "I spent two days there, with some old acquaintances…but I was homesick. I hated knowing I'd upset Esme, and the rest of them, my adopted family. In the pure air of the mountains it was hard to believe you were so irresistible. I convinced myself it was weak to run away. I'd dealt with temptation before, not of this magnitude, not even close, but I was strong. Who were you, an insignificant little girl"—he grinned suddenly—"to chase me from the place I wanted to be? So I came back...." He stared off into space.

I couldn't speak.

"I took precautions, hunting, feeding more than usual before seeing you again. I was sure that I was strong enough to treat you like any other human. I was arrogant about it.

"It was unquestionably a complication that I couldn't simply read your thoughts to know what your reaction was to me. I wasn't used to having to go to such circuitous measures, listening to your words in Jessica's mind . . . her mind isn't very original, and it was annoying to have to stoop to that. And then I couldn't know if you really meant what you said. It was all extremely irritating." He frowned at the memory.

"I wanted you to forget my behavior that first day, if possible, so I tried to talk with you like I would with any person. I was eager actually, hoping to decipher some of your thoughts. But you were too interesting, I found myself caught up in your expressions . . . and every now and then you would stir the air with your hand or your hair, and the scent would stun me again. . . .

"Of course, then you were nearly crushed to death in front of my eyes. Later I thought of a perfectly good excuse for why I acted at that moment—because if I hadn't saved you, if your blood had been spilled there in front of me, I don't think I could have stopped myself from exposing us for what we are. But I only thought of that excuse later. At the time, all I could think was, 'Not her.'"

He closed his eyes, lost in his agonized confession. I listened, more eager than rational. Common sense told me I should be terrified. Instead, I was relieved to finally understand. And I was filled with compassion for his suffering, even now, as he confessed his craving to take my life.

I finally was able to speak, though my voice was faint. "In the hospital?"

His eyes flashed up to mine. "I was appalled. I couldn't believe I had put us in danger after all, put myself in your power—you of all people. As if I needed another motive to kill you." We both flinched as that word slipped out. "But it had the opposite effect," he continued quickly. "I fought with Rosalie, Emmett, and Jasper when they suggested that now was the time . . . the worst fight we've ever had. Carlisle sided with me, and Alice."

He grimaced when he said her name. I couldn't imagine why. "Esme told me to do whatever I had to in order to stay." He shook his head indulgently.

"All that next day I eavesdropped on the minds of everyone you spoke to, shocked that you kept your word. I didn't understand you at all. But I knew that I couldn't become more involved with you. I did my very best to stay as far from you as possible. And every day the perfume of your skin, your breath, your hair... it hit me as hard as the very first day."

He met my eyes again, and they were surprisingly tender.

"And for all that," he continued, "I'd have fared better if I *had* exposed us all at that first moment, than if now, here—with no witnesses and nothing to stop me—I were to hurt you."

I was human enough to have to ask. "Why?"

"Isabella." He pronounced my full name carefully, then playfully ruffled my hair with his free hand. A shock ran through my body at his casual touch. "Bella, I couldn't live with myself if I ever hurt you. You don't know how it's tortured me." He looked down, ashamed again. "The thought of you, still, white, cold... to never see you blush scarlet again, to never see that flash of intuition in your eyes when you see through my pretenses... it would be unendurable." He lifted his glorious, agonized eyes to mine. "You are the most important thing to me now. The most important thing to me ever."

My head was spinning at the rapid change in direction our conversation had taken. From the cheerful topic of my impending demise, we were suddenly declaring ourselves. He waited, and even though I looked down to study our hands between us, I knew his golden eyes were on me.

"You already know how I feel, of course," I finally said. "I'm here... which, roughly translated, means I would rather die than stay away from you." I frowned. "I'm an idiot."

"You *are* an idiot," he agreed with a laugh. Our eyes met, and I laughed, too. We laughed together at the idiocy and sheer impossibility of such a moment.

"And so the lion fell in love with the lamb...," he murmured. I looked away, hiding my eyes as I thrilled to the word.

"What a stupid lamb," I sighed.

"What a sick, masochistic lion." He stared into the shadowy forest for a long moment, and I wondered where his thoughts had taken him.

"Why . . . ?" I began, and then paused, not sure how to continue.

He looked at me and smiled; sunlight glinted off his face, his teeth. "Yes?"

"Tell me why you ran from me before."

His smile faded. "You know why."

"No, I mean, *exactly* what did I do wrong? I'll have to be on my guard, you see, so I better start learning what I shouldn't do. This, for example"—I stroked the back of his hand—"seems to be all right."

He smiled again. "You didn't do anything wrong, Bella. It was my fault."

"But I want to help, if I can, to not make this harder for you."

"Well . . ." He contemplated for a moment. "It was just how close you were. Most humans instinctively shy away from us, are repelled by our alienness. . . . I wasn't expecting you to come so close. And the smell of your *throat*." He stopped short, looking to see if he'd upset me.

"Okay, then," I said flippantly, trying to alleviate the suddenly tense atmosphere. I tucked my chin. "No throat exposure."

It worked; he laughed. "No, really, it was more the surprise than anything else."

He raised his free hand and placed it gently on the side of my neck. I sat very still, the chill of his touch a natural warning—a warning telling me to be terrified. But there was no feeling of fear in me. There were, however, other feelings. . . .

"You see," he said. "Perfectly fine."

My blood was racing, and I wished I could slow it, sensing that this must make everything so much more difficult—the thudding of my pulse in my veins. Surely he could hear it.

"The blush on your cheeks is lovely," he murmured. He gently freed his other hand. My hands fell limply into my lap. Softly he brushed my cheek, then held my face between his marble hands.

"Be very still," he whispered, as if I wasn't already frozen.

Slowly, never moving his eyes from mine, he leaned toward me. Then abruptly, but very gently, he rested his cold cheek against the hollow at the base of my throat. I was quite unable to move, even if I'd wanted to. I listened to the sound of his even breathing, watching the sun and wind play in his bronze hair, more human than any other part of him.

With deliberate slowness, his hands slid down the sides of my neck. I shivered, and I heard him catch his breath. But his hands didn't pause as they softly moved to my shoulders, and then stopped.

His face drifted to the side, his nose skimming across my collarbone. He came to rest with the side of his face pressed tenderly against my chest.

Listening to my heart.

"Ah," he sighed.

I don't know how long we sat without moving. It could have been hours. Eventually the throb of my pulse quieted, but he didn't move or speak again as he held me. I knew at any moment it could be too much, and my life could end—so quickly that I might not even notice. And I couldn't make myself be afraid. I couldn't think of anything, except that he was touching me.

And then, too soon, he released me.

His eyes were peaceful.

"It won't be so hard again," he said with satisfaction.

"Was that very hard for you?"

"Not nearly as bad as I imagined it would be. And you?"

"No, it wasn't bad . . . for me."

He smiled at my inflection. "You know what I mean."

I smiled.

"Here." He took my hand and placed it against his cheek. "Do you feel how warm it is?"

And it was almost warm, his usually icy skin. But I barely noticed, for I was touching his face, something I'd dreamed of constantly since the first day I'd seen him.

"Don't move," I whispered.

No one could be still like Edward. He closed his eyes and became as immobile as stone, a carving under my hand.

I moved even more slowly than he had, careful not to make one unexpected move. I caressed his cheek, delicately stroked his eyelid, the purple shadow in the hollow under his eye. I traced the shape of his perfect nose, and then, so carefully, his flawless lips. His lips parted under my hand, and I could feel his cool breath on my fingertips. I wanted to lean in, to inhale the scent of him. So I dropped my hand and leaned away, not wanting to push him too far.

He opened his eyes, and they were hungry. Not in a way to make me fear, but rather to tighten the muscles in the pit of my stomach and send my pulse hammering through my veins again.

"I wish," he whispered, "I wish you could feel the...complexity...the confusion...I feel. That you could understand."

He raised his hand to my hair, then carefully brushed it across my face.

"Tell me," I breathed.

"I don't think I can. I've told you, on the one hand, the hunger—the thirst—that, deplorable creature that I am, I feel for you. And I think you can understand that, to an extent. Though"—he half-smiled—"as you are not addicted to any illegal substances, you probably can't empathize completely.

"But..." His fingers touched my lips lightly, making me shiver again. "There are other hungers. Hungers I don't even understand, that are foreign to me."

"I may understand *that* better than you think."

"I'm not used to feeling so human. Is it always like this?"

"For me?" I paused. "No, never. Never before this."

He held my hands between his. They felt so feeble in his iron strength.

"I don't know how to be close to you," he admitted. "I don't know if I can."

I leaned forward very slowly, cautioning him with my eyes. I placed my cheek against his stone chest. I could hear his breath, and nothing else.

"This is enough," I sighed, closing my eyes.

In a very human gesture, he put his arms around me and pressed his face against my hair.

"You're better at this than you give yourself credit for," I noted.

"I have human instincts—they may be buried deep, but they're there."

We sat like that for another immeasurable moment; I wondered if he could be as unwilling to move as I was. But I could see the light was fading, the shadows of the forest beginning to touch us, and I sighed.

"You have to go."

"I thought you couldn't read my mind."

"It's getting clearer." I could hear a smile in his voice.

He took my shoulders and I looked into his face.

"Can I show you something?" he asked, sudden excitement flaring in his eyes.

"Show me what?"

"I'll show you how *I* travel in the forest." He saw my expression. "Don't worry, you'll be very safe, and we'll get to your truck much faster." His mouth twitched up into that crooked smile so beautiful my heart nearly stopped.

"Will you turn into a bat?" I asked warily.

He laughed, louder than I'd ever heard. "Like I haven't heard *that* one before!"

"Right, I'm sure you get that all the time."

"Come on, little coward, climb on my back."

I waited to see if he was kidding, but, apparently, he meant it. He smiled as he read my hesitation, and reached for me. My heart reacted; even though he couldn't hear my thoughts, my pulse always gave me away. He then proceeded to sling me onto his back, with very little effort on my part, besides, when in place, clamping my legs and arms so tightly around him that it would choke a normal person. It was like clinging to a stone.

"I'm a bit heavier than your average backpack," I warned.

"Hah!" he snorted. I could almost hear his eyes rolling. I'd never seen him in such high spirits before.

He startled me, suddenly grabbing my hand, pressing my palm to his face, and inhaling deeply.

"Easier all the time," he muttered.

And then he was running.

If I'd ever feared death before in his presence, it was nothing compared to how I felt now.

He streaked through the dark, thick underbrush of the forest like a bullet, like a ghost. There was no sound, no evidence that his feet touched the earth. His breathing never changed, never indicated any effort. But the trees flew by at deadly speeds, always missing us by inches.

I was too terrified to close my eyes, though the cool forest air whipped against my face and burned them. I felt as if I were stupidly sticking my head out the window of an airplane in flight. And, for the first time in my life, I felt the dizzy faintness of motion sickness.

Then it was over. We'd hiked hours this morning to reach Edward's meadow, and now, in a matter of minutes, we were back to the truck.

"Exhilarating, isn't it?" His voice was high, excited.

He stood motionless, waiting for me to climb down. I tried, but my muscles wouldn't respond. My arms and legs stayed locked around him while my head spun uncomfortably.

"Bella?" he asked, anxious now.

"I think I need to lie down," I gasped.

"Oh, sorry." He waited for me, but I still couldn't move.

"I think I need help," I admitted.

He laughed quietly, and gently unloosened my stranglehold on his neck. There was no resisting the iron strength of his hands. Then he pulled me around to face him, cradling me in his arms like a small child. He held me for a moment, then carefully placed me on the springy ferns.

"How do you feel?" he asked.

I couldn't be sure how I felt when my head was spinning so crazily. "Dizzy, I think."

"Put your head between your knees."

I tried that, and it helped a little. I breathed in and out slowly, keeping my head very still. I felt him sitting beside me. The moments passed, and eventually I found that I could raise my head. There was a hollow ringing sound in my ears.

"I guess that wasn't the best idea," he mused.

I tried to be positive, but my voice was weak. "No, it was very interesting."

"Hah! You're as white as a ghost—no, you're as white as *me*!"

"I think I should have closed my eyes."

"Remember that next time."

"Next time!" I groaned.

He laughed, his mood still radiant.

"Show-off," I muttered.

"Open your eyes, Bella," he said quietly.

And he was right there, his face so close to mine. His beauty stunned my mind—it was too much, an excess I couldn't grow accustomed to.

"I was thinking, while I was running . . ." He paused.

"About not hitting the trees, I hope."

"Silly Bella," he chuckled. "Running is second nature to me, it's not something I have to think about."

"Show-off," I muttered again.

He smiled.

"No," he continued, "I was thinking there was something I wanted to try." And he took my face in his hands again.

I couldn't breathe.

He hesitated—not in the normal way, the human way.

Not the way a man might hesitate before he kissed a woman, to gauge her reaction, to see how he would be received. Perhaps he would hesitate to prolong the moment, that ideal moment of anticipation, sometimes better than the kiss itself.

Edward hesitated to test himself, to see if this was safe, to make sure he was still in control of his need.

And then his cold, marble lips pressed very softly against mine.

What neither of us was prepared for was my response.

Blood boiled under my skin, burned in my lips. My breath came in a wild gasp. My fingers knotted in his hair, clutching him to me. My lips parted as I breathed in his heady scent.

Immediately I felt him turn to unresponsive stone beneath my lips. His hands gently, but with irresistible force, pushed my face back. I opened my eyes and saw his guarded expression.

"Oops," I breathed.

"That's an understatement."

His eyes were wild, his jaw clenched in acute restraint, yet he didn't lapse from his perfect articulation. He held my face just inches from his. He dazzled my eyes.

"Should I . . . ?" I tried to disengage myself, to give him some room.

His hands refused to let me move so much as an inch.

"No, it's tolerable. Wait for a moment, please." His voice was polite, controlled.

I kept my eyes on his, watched as the excitement in them faded and gentled.

Then he smiled a surprisingly impish grin.

"There," he said, obviously pleased with himself.

"Tolerable?" I asked.

He laughed aloud. "I'm stronger than I thought. It's nice to know."

"I wish I could say the same. I'm sorry."

"You *are* only human, after all."

"Thanks so much," I said, my voice acerbic.

He was on his feet in one of his lithe, almost invisibly quick movements. He held out his hand to me, an unexpected gesture. I was so used to our standard of careful non-contact. I took his icy hand, needing the support more than I thought. My balance had not yet returned.

"Are you still faint from the run? Or was it my kissing expertise?" How lighthearted, how human he seemed as he laughed now, his seraphic face untroubled. He was a different Edward than the one I had known. And I felt all the more besotted by him. It would cause me physical pain to be separated from him now.

"I can't be sure, I'm still woozy," I managed to respond. "I think it's some of both, though."

"Maybe you should let me drive."

"Are you insane?" I protested.

"I can drive better than you on your best day," he teased. "You have much slower reflexes."

"I'm sure that's true, but I don't think my nerves, or my truck, could take it."

"Some trust, please, Bella."

My hand was in my pocket, curled tightly around the key. I pursed my lips, deliberated, then shook my head with a tight grin.

"Nope. Not a chance."

He raised his eyebrows in disbelief.

I started to step around him, heading for the driver's side. He might have let me pass if I hadn't wobbled slightly. Then again, he might not have. His arm created an inescapable snare around my waist.

"Bella, I've already expended a great deal of personal effort at this point to keep you alive. I'm not about to let you behind the wheel of a vehicle when you can't even walk straight. Besides, friends don't let friends drive drunk," he quoted with a chuckle. I could smell the unbearably sweet fragrance coming off his chest.

"Drunk?" I objected.

"You're intoxicated by my very presence." He was grinning that playful smirk again.

"I can't argue with that," I sighed. There was no way around it; I couldn't resist him in anything. I held the key high and dropped it, watching his hand flash like lightning to catch it soundlessly. "Take it easy—my truck is a senior citizen."

"Very sensible," he approved.

"And are you not affected at all?" I asked, irked. "By my presence?"

Again his mobile features transformed, his expression became soft, warm. He didn't answer at first; he simply bent his face to mine, and brushed his lips slowly along my jaw, from my ear to my chin, back and forth. I trembled.

"Regardless," he finally murmured, "I have better reflexes."

14. MIND OVER MATTER

HE COULD DRIVE WELL, WHEN HE KEPT THE SPEED REASONABLE, I HAD
to admit. Like so many things, it seemed to be effortless to him. He barely
looked at the road, yet the tires never deviated so much as a centimeter from
the center of the lane. He drove one-handed, holding my hand on the seat.
Sometimes he gazed into the setting sun, sometimes he glanced at me—my
face, my hair blowing out the open window, our hands twined together.

He had turned the radio to an oldies station, and he sang along with a
song I'd never heard. He knew every line.

"You like fifties music?" I asked.

"Music in the fifties was good. Much better than the sixties, or the seventies, ugh!" He shuddered. "The eighties were bearable."

"Are you ever going to tell me how old you are?" I asked, tentative, not
wanting to upset his buoyant humor.

"Does it matter much?" His smile, to my relief, remained unclouded.

"No, but I still wonder..." I grimaced. "There's nothing like an unsolved
mystery to keep you up at night."

"I wonder if it will upset you," he reflected to himself. He gazed into the
sun; the minutes passed.

"Try me," I finally said.

He sighed, and then looked into my eyes, seeming to forget the road completely for a time. Whatever he saw there must have encouraged him. He

looked into the sun—the light of the setting orb glittered off his skin in ruby-tinged sparkles—and spoke.

"I was born in Chicago in 1901." He paused and glanced at me from the corner of his eyes. My face was carefully unsurprised, patient for the rest. He smiled a tiny smile and continued. "Carlisle found me in a hospital in the summer of 1918. I was seventeen, and dying of the Spanish influenza."

He heard my intake of breath, though it was barely audible to my own ears. He looked down into my eyes again.

"I don't remember it well—it was a very long time ago, and human memories fade." He was lost in his thoughts for a short time before he went on. "I do remember how it felt, when Carlisle saved me. It's not an easy thing, not something you could forget."

"Your parents?"

"They had already died from the disease. I was alone. That was why he chose me. In all the chaos of the epidemic, no one would ever realize I was gone."

"How did he . . . save you?"

A few seconds passed before he answered. He seemed to choose his words carefully.

"It was difficult. Not many of us have the restraint necessary to accomplish it. But Carlisle has always been the most humane, the most compassionate of us. . . . I don't think you could find his equal throughout all of history." He paused. "For me, it was merely very, very painful."

I could tell from the set of his lips, he would say no more on this subject. I suppressed my curiosity, though it was far from idle. There were many things I needed to think through on this particular issue, things that were only beginning to occur to me. No doubt his quick mind had already comprehended every aspect that eluded me.

His soft voice interrupted my thoughts. "He acted from loneliness. That's usually the reason behind the choice. I was the first in Carlisle's family, though he found Esme soon after. She fell from a cliff. They brought her straight to the hospital morgue, though, somehow, her heart was still beating."

"So you must be dying, then, to become . . ." We never said the word, and I couldn't frame it now.

"No, that's just Carlisle. He would never do that to someone who had another choice." The respect in his voice was profound whenever he spoke of his father figure. "It is easier he says, though," he continued, "if the blood is weak." He looked at the now-dark road, and I could feel the subject closing again.

"And Emmett and Rosalie?"

"Carlisle brought Rosalie to our family next. I didn't realize till much later that he was hoping she would be to me what Esme was to him—he was careful with his thoughts around me." He rolled his eyes. "But she was never more than a sister. It was only two years later that she found Emmett. She was hunting—we were in Appalachia at the time—and found a bear about to finish him off. She carried him back to Carlisle, more than a hundred miles, afraid she wouldn't be able to do it herself. I'm only beginning to guess how difficult that journey was for her." He threw a pointed glance in my direction, and raised our hands, still folded together, to brush my cheek with the back of his hand.

"But she made it," I encouraged, looking away from the unbearable beauty of his eyes.

"Yes," he murmured. "She saw something in his face that made her strong enough. And they've been together ever since. Sometimes they live separately from us, as a married couple. But the younger we pretend to be, the longer we can stay in any given place. Forks seemed perfect, so we all enrolled in high school." He laughed. "I suppose we'll have to go to their wedding in a few years, *again*."

"Alice and Jasper?"

"Alice and Jasper are two very rare creatures. They both developed a conscience, as we refer to it, with no outside guidance. Jasper belonged to another . . . family, a *very* different kind of family. He became depressed, and he wandered on his own. Alice found him. Like me, she has certain gifts above and beyond the norm for our kind."

"Really?" I interrupted, fascinated. "But you said you were the only one who could hear people's thoughts."

"That's true. She knows other things. She *sees* things—things that might happen, things that are coming. But it's very subjective. The future isn't set in stone. Things change."

His jaw set when he said that, and his eyes darted to my face and away so quickly that I wasn't sure if I only imagined it.

"What kinds of things does she see?"

"She saw Jasper and knew that he was looking for her before he knew it himself. She saw Carlisle and our family, and they came together to find us. She's most sensitive to non-humans. She always sees, for example, when another group of our kind is coming near. And any threat they may pose."

"Are there a lot of . . . your kind?" I was surprised. How many of them could walk among us undetected?

"No, not many. But most won't settle in any one place. Only those like us, who've given up hunting you people"—a sly glance in my direction—"can live together with humans for any length of time. We've only found one other family like ours, in a small village in Alaska. We lived together for a time, but there were so many of us that we became too noticeable. Those of us who live . . . differently tend to band together."

"And the others?"

"Nomads, for the most part. We've all lived that way at times. It gets tedious, like anything else. But we run across the others now and then, because most of us prefer the North."

"Why is that?"

We were parked in front of my house now, and he'd turned off the truck. It was very quiet and dark; there was no moon. The porch light was off so I knew my father wasn't home yet.

"Did you have your eyes open this afternoon?" he teased. "Do you think I could walk down the street in the sunlight without causing traffic accidents? There's a reason why we chose the Olympic Peninsula, one of the most sun-less places in the world. It's nice to be able to go outside in the day. You wouldn't believe how tired you can get of nighttime in eighty-odd years."

"So that's where the legends came from?"

"Probably."

"And Alice came from another family, like Jasper?"

"No, and that *is* a mystery. Alice doesn't remember her human life at all. And she doesn't know who created her. She awoke alone. Whoever made her walked away, and none of us understand why, or how, he could. If she hadn't had that other sense, if she hadn't seen Jasper and Carlisle and known that she would someday become one of us, she probably would have turned into a total savage."

There was so much to think through, so much I still wanted to ask. But, to my great embarrassment, my stomach growled. I'd been so intrigued, I hadn't even noticed I was hungry. I realized now that I was ravenous.

"I'm sorry, I'm keeping you from dinner."

"I'm fine, really."

"I've never spent much time around anyone who eats food. I forget."

"I want to stay with you." It was easier to say in the darkness, knowing as I spoke how my voice would betray me, my hopeless addiction to him.

"Can't I come in?" he asked.

"Would you like to?" I couldn't picture it, this godlike creature sitting in my father's shabby kitchen chair.

"Yes, if it's all right." I heard the door close quietly, and almost simultaneously he was outside my door, opening it for me.

"Very human," I complimented him.

"It's definitely resurfacing."

He walked beside me in the night, so quietly I had to peek at him constantly to be sure he was still there. In the darkness he looked much more normal. Still pale, still dreamlike in his beauty, but no longer the fantastic sparkling creature of our sunlit afternoon.

He reached the door ahead of me and opened it for me. I paused halfway through the frame.

"The door was unlocked?"

"No, I used the key from under the eave."

I stepped inside, flicked on the porch light, and turned to look at him with my eyebrows raised. I was sure I'd never used that key in front of him.

"I was curious about you."

"You spied on me?" But somehow I couldn't infuse my voice with the proper outrage. I was flattered.

He was unrepentant. "What else is there to do at night?"

I let it go for the moment and went down the hall to the kitchen. He was there before me, needing no guide. He sat in the very chair I'd tried to picture him in. His beauty lit up the kitchen. It was a moment before I could look away.

I concentrated on getting my dinner, taking last night's lasagna from the fridge, placing a square on a plate, heating it in the microwave. It revolved, filling the kitchen with the smell of tomatoes and oregano. I didn't take my eyes from the plate of food as I spoke.

"How often?" I asked casually.

"Hmmm?" He sounded as if I had pulled him from some other train of thought.

I still didn't turn around. "How often did you come here?"

"I come here almost every night."

I whirled, stunned. "Why?"

"You're interesting when you sleep." He spoke matter-of-factly. "You talk."

"No!" I gasped, heat flooding my face all the way to my hairline. I gripped the kitchen counter for support. I knew I talked in my sleep, of course; my mother teased me about it. I hadn't thought it was something I needed to worry about here, though.

His expression shifted instantly to chagrin. "Are you very angry with me?"

"That depends!" I felt and sounded like I'd had the breath knocked out of me.

He waited.

"On?" he urged.

"What you heard!" I wailed.

Instantly, silently, he was at my side, taking my hands carefully in his.

"Don't be upset!" he pleaded. He dropped his face to the level of my eyes, holding my gaze. I was embarrassed. I tried to look away.

"You miss your mother," he whispered. "You worry about her. And when it rains, the sound makes you restless. You used to talk about home a lot, but it's less often now. Once you said, 'It's too *green*.'" He laughed softly, hoping, I could see, not to offend me further.

"Anything else?" I demanded.

He knew what I was getting at. "You did say my name," he admitted.

I sighed in defeat. "A lot?"

"How much do you mean by 'a lot,' exactly?"

"Oh no!" I hung my head.

He pulled me against his chest, softly, naturally.

"Don't be self-conscious," he whispered in my ear. "If I could dream at all, it would be about you. And I'm not ashamed of it."

Then we both heard the sound of tires on the brick driveway, saw the headlights flash through the front windows, down the hall to us. I stiffened in his arms.

"Should your father know I'm here?" he asked.

"I'm not sure . . ." I tried to think it through quickly.

"Another time then . . ."

And I was alone.

"Edward!" I hissed.

I heard a ghostly chuckle, then nothing else.

My father's key turned in the door.

"Bella?" he called. It had bothered me before; who else would it be? Suddenly he didn't seem so far off base.

"In here." I hoped he couldn't hear the hysterical edge to my voice. I grabbed my dinner from the microwave and sat at the table as he walked in. His footsteps sounded so noisy after my day with Edward.

"Can you get me some of that? I'm bushed." He stepped on the heels of his boots to take them off, holding the back of Edward's chair for support.

I took my food with me, scarfing it down as I got his dinner. It burned my tongue. I filled two glasses with milk while his lasagna was heating, and gulped mine to put out the fire. As I set the glass down, I noticed the milk trembling and realized my hand was shaking. Charlie sat in the chair, and the contrast between him and its former occupant was comical.

"Thanks," he said as I placed his food on the table.

"How was your day?" I asked. The words were rushed; I was dying to escape to my room.

"Good. The fish were biting . . . how about you? Did you get everything done that you wanted to?"

"Not really—it was too nice out to stay indoors." I took another big bite.

"It was a nice day," he agreed. What an understatement, I thought to myself.

Finished with the last bite of lasagna, I lifted my glass and chugged the remains of my milk.

Charlie surprised me by being observant. "In a hurry?"

"Yeah, I'm tired. I'm going to bed early."

"You look kinda keyed up," he noted. Why, oh why, did this have to be his night to pay attention?

"Do I?" was all I could manage in response. I quickly scrubbed my dishes clean in the sink, and placed them upside down on a dish towel to dry.

"It's Saturday," he mused.

I didn't respond.

"No plans tonight?" he asked suddenly.

"No, Dad, I just want to get some sleep."

"None of the boys in town your type, eh?" He was suspicious, but trying to play it cool.

"No, none of the boys have caught my eye yet." I was careful not to over-emphasize the word *boys* in my quest to be truthful with Charlie.

"I thought maybe that Mike Newton . . . you said he was friendly."

"He's *just* a friend, Dad."

"Well, you're too good for them all, anyway. Wait till you get to college to start looking." Every father's dream, that his daughter will be out of the house before the hormones kick in.

"Sounds like a good idea to me," I agreed as I headed up the stairs.

"'Night, honey," he called after me. No doubt he would be listening carefully all evening, waiting for me to try to sneak out.

"See you in the morning, Dad." See you creeping into my room tonight at midnight to check on me.

I worked to make my tread sound slow and tired as I walked up the stairs to my room. I shut the door loud enough for him to hear, and then sprinted on my tiptoes to the window. I threw it open and leaned out into the night. My eyes scanned the darkness, the impenetrable shadows of the trees.

"Edward?" I whispered, feeling completely idiotic.

The quiet, laughing response came from behind me. "Yes?"

I whirled, one hand flying to my throat in surprise.

He lay, smiling hugely, across my bed, his hands behind his head, his feet dangling off the end, the picture of ease.

"Oh!" I breathed, sinking unsteadily to the floor.

"I'm sorry." He pressed his lips together, trying to hide his amusement.

"Just give me a minute to restart my heart."

He sat up slowly, so as not to startle me again. Then he leaned forward and reached out with his long arms to pick me up, gripping the tops of my arms like I was a toddler. He sat me on the bed beside him.

"Why don't you sit with me," he suggested, putting a cold hand on mine. "How's the heart?"

"You tell me—I'm sure you hear it better than I do."

I felt his quiet laughter shake the bed.

We sat there for a moment in silence, both listening to my heartbeat slow. I thought about having Edward in my room, with my father in the house.

"Can I have a minute to be human?" I asked.

"Certainly." He gestured with one hand that I should proceed.

"Stay," I said, trying to look severe.

"Yes, ma'am." And he made a show of becoming a statue on the edge of my bed.

I hopped up, grabbing my pajamas from off the floor, my bag of toiletries off the desk. I left the light off and slipped out, closing the door.

I could hear the sound from the TV rising up the stairs. I banged the bathroom door loudly, so Charlie wouldn't come up to bother me.

I meant to hurry. I brushed my teeth fiercely, trying to be thorough *and* speedy, removing all traces of lasagna. But the hot water of the shower couldn't be rushed. It unknotted the muscles in my back, calmed my pulse. The familiar smell of my shampoo made me feel like I might be the same person I had been this morning. I tried not to think of Edward, sitting in my room, waiting, because then I had to start all over with the calming process. Finally, I couldn't delay anymore. I shut off the water, toweling hastily, rushing again. I pulled on my holey t-shirt and gray sweatpants. Too late to regret not packing the Victoria's Secret silk pajamas my mother got me two birthdays ago, which still had the tags on them in a drawer somewhere back home.

I rubbed the towel through my hair again, and then yanked the brush through it quickly. I threw the towel in the hamper, flung my brush and toothpaste into my bag. Then I dashed down the stairs so Charlie could see that I was in my pajamas, with wet hair.

"'Night, Dad."

"'Night, Bella." He did look startled by my appearance. Maybe that would keep him from checking on me tonight.

I took the stairs two at a time, trying to be quiet, and flew into my room, closing the door tightly behind me.

Edward hadn't moved a fraction of an inch, a carving of Adonis perched on my faded quilt. I smiled, and his lips twitched, the statue coming to life.

His eyes appraised me, taking in the damp hair, the tattered shirt. He raised one eyebrow. "Nice."

I grimaced.

"No, it looks good on you."

"Thanks," I whispered. I went back to his side, sitting cross-legged beside him. I looked at the lines in the wooden floor.

"What was all that for?"

"Charlie thinks I'm sneaking out."

"Oh." He contemplated that. "Why?" As if he couldn't know Charlie's mind much more clearly than I could guess.

"Apparently, I look a little overexcited."

He lifted my chin, examining my face.

"You look very warm, actually."

He bent his face slowly to mine, laying his cool cheek against my skin. I held perfectly still.

"Mmmmmm...," he breathed.

It was very difficult, while he was touching me, to frame a coherent question. It took me a minute of scattered concentration to begin.

"It seems to be...much easier for you, now, to be close to me."

"Does it seem that way to you?" he murmured, his nose gliding to the corner of my jaw. I felt his hand, lighter than a moth's wing, brushing my damp hair back, so that his lips could touch the hollow beneath my ear.

"Much, much easier," I said, trying to exhale.

"Hmm."

"So I was wondering...," I began again, but his fingers were slowly tracing my collarbone, and I lost my train of thought.

"Yes?" he breathed.

"Why is that," my voice shook, embarrassing me, "do you think?"

I felt the tremor of his breath on my neck as he laughed. "Mind over matter."

I pulled back; as I moved, he froze—and I could no longer hear the sound of his breathing.

We stared cautiously at each other for a moment, and then, as his clenched jaw gradually relaxed, his expression became puzzled.

"Did I do something wrong?"

"No—the opposite. You're driving me crazy," I explained.

He considered that briefly, and when he spoke, he sounded pleased. "Really?" A triumphant smile slowly lit his face.

"Would you like a round of applause?" I asked sarcastically.

He grinned.

"I'm just pleasantly surprised," he clarified. "In the last hundred years or so," his voice was teasing, "I never imagined anything like this. I didn't believe I would ever find someone I wanted to be with...in another way than my brothers and sisters. And then to find, even though it's all new to me, that I'm good at it...at being with you..."

"You're good at everything," I pointed out.

He shrugged, allowing that, and we both laughed in whispers.

"But how can it be so easy now?" I pressed. "This afternoon..."

"It's not *easy*," he sighed. "But this afternoon, I was still...undecided. I am sorry about that, it was unforgivable for me to behave so."

"Not unforgivable," I disagreed.

"Thank you." He smiled. "You see," he continued, looking down now, "I wasn't sure if I was strong enough...." He picked up one of my hands and pressed it lightly to his face. "And while there was still that possibility that I might be...overcome"—he breathed in the scent at my wrist—"I was... susceptible. Until I made up my mind that I *was* strong enough, that there was no possibility at all that I would...that I ever could..."

I'd never seen him struggle so hard for words. It was so...human.

"So there's no possibility now?"

"Mind over matter," he repeated, smiling, his teeth bright even in the darkness.

"Wow, that was easy," I said.

He threw back his head and laughed, quietly as a whisper, but still exuberantly.

"Easy for *you*!" he amended, touching my nose with his fingertip.

And then his face was abruptly serious.

"I'm trying," he whispered, his voice pained. "If it gets to be . . . too much, I'm fairly sure I'll be able to leave."

I scowled. I didn't like the talk of leaving.

"And it will be harder tomorrow," he continued. "I've had the scent of you in my head all day, and I've grown amazingly desensitized. If I'm away from you for any length of time, I'll have to start over again. Not quite from scratch, though, I think."

"Don't go away, then," I responded, unable to hide the longing in my voice.

"That suits me," he replied, his face relaxing into a gentle smile. "Bring on the shackles—I'm your prisoner." But his long hands formed manacles around *my* wrists as he spoke. He laughed his quiet, musical laugh. He'd laughed more tonight than I'd ever heard in all the time I'd spent with him.

"You seem more . . . optimistic than usual," I observed. "I haven't seen you like this before."

"Isn't it supposed to be like this?" He smiled. "The glory of first love, and all that. It's incredible, isn't it, the difference between reading about something, seeing it in the pictures, and experiencing it?"

"Very different," I agreed. "More forceful than I'd imagined."

"For example"—his words flowed swiftly now, I had to concentrate to catch it all—"the emotion of jealousy. I've read about it a hundred thousand times, seen actors portray it in a thousand different plays and movies. I believed I understood that one pretty clearly. But it shocked me. . . ." He grimaced. "Do you remember the day that Mike asked you to the dance?"

I nodded, though I remembered that day for a different reason. "The day you started talking to me again."

"I was surprised by the flare of resentment, almost fury, that I felt—I didn't recognize what it was at first. I was even more aggravated than usual that I couldn't know what you were thinking, why you refused him. Was it simply for your friend's sake? Was there someone else? I knew I had no right to care either way. I *tried* not to care."

"And then the line started forming," he chuckled. I scowled in the darkness.

"I waited, unreasonably anxious to hear what you would say to them, to watch your expressions. I couldn't deny the relief I felt, watching the annoyance on your face. But I couldn't be sure.

"That was the first night I came here. I wrestled all night, while watching you sleep, with the chasm between what I knew was *right,* moral, ethical, and what I *wanted.* I knew that if I continued to ignore you as I should, or if I left for a few years, till you were gone, that someday you would say yes to Mike, or someone like him. It made me angry.

"And then," he whispered, "as you were sleeping, you said my name. You spoke so clearly, at first I thought you'd woken. But you rolled over restlessly and mumbled my name once more, and sighed. The feeling that coursed through me then was unnerving, staggering. And I knew I couldn't ignore you any longer." He was silent for a moment, probably listening to the suddenly uneven pounding of my heart.

"But jealousy . . . it's a strange thing. So much more powerful than I would have thought. And irrational! Just now, when Charlie asked you about that vile Mike Newton . . ." He shook his head angrily.

"I should have known you'd be listening," I groaned.

"Of course."

"*That* made you feel jealous, though, really?"

"I'm new at this; you're resurrecting the human in me, and everything feels stronger because it's fresh."

"But honestly," I teased, "for that to bother you, after I have to hear that Rosalie—Rosalie, the incarnation of pure beauty, *Rosalie*—was meant for you. Emmett or no Emmett, how can I compete with that?"

"There's no competition." His teeth gleamed. He drew my trapped hands around his back, holding me to his chest. I kept as still as I could, even breathing with caution.

"I *know* there's no competition," I mumbled into his cold skin. "That's the problem."

"Of course Rosalie *is* beautiful in her way, but even if she wasn't like a sister to me, even if Emmett didn't belong with her, she could never have one tenth, no, one hundredth of the attraction you hold for me." He was serious now, thoughtful. "For almost ninety years I've walked among my kind, and yours . . . all the time thinking I was complete in myself, not realizing what I was seeking. And not finding anything, because you weren't alive yet."

"It hardly seems fair," I whispered, my face still resting on his chest, listening to his breath come and go. "I haven't had to wait at all. Why should I get off so easily?"

"You're right," he agreed with amusement. "I should make this harder for you, definitely." He freed one of his hands, released my wrist, only to gather it carefully into his other hand. He stroked my wet hair softly, from the top of my head to my waist. "You only have to risk your life every second you spend with me, that's surely not much. You only have to turn your back on nature, on humanity . . . what's that worth?"

"Very little—I don't feel deprived of anything."

"Not yet." And his voice was abruptly full of ancient grief.

I tried to pull back, to look in his face, but his hand locked my wrists in an unbreakable hold.

"What—" I started to ask, when his body became alert. I froze, but he suddenly released my hands, and disappeared. I narrowly avoided falling on my face.

"Lie down!" he hissed. I couldn't tell where he spoke from in the darkness.

I rolled under my quilt, balling up on my side, the way I usually slept. I heard the door crack open, as Charlie peeked in to make sure I was where I was supposed to be. I breathed evenly, exaggerating the movement.

A long minute passed. I listened, not sure if I'd heard the door close. Then Edward's cool arm was around me, under the covers, his lips at my ear.

"You are a terrible actress—I'd say that career path is out for you."

"Darn it," I muttered. My heart was crashing in my chest.

He hummed a melody I didn't recognize; it sounded like a lullaby.

He paused. "Should I sing you to sleep?"

"Right," I laughed. "Like I could sleep with you here!"

"You do it all the time," he reminded me.

"But I didn't *know* you were here," I replied icily.

"So if you don't want to sleep . . . ," he suggested, ignoring my tone. My breath caught.

"If I don't want to sleep . . . ?"

He chuckled. "What do you want to do then?"

I couldn't answer at first.

"I'm not sure," I finally said.

"Tell me when you decide."

I could feel his cool breath on my neck, feel his nose sliding along my jaw, inhaling.

"I thought you were desensitized."

"Just because I'm resisting the wine doesn't mean I can't appreciate the bouquet," he whispered. "You have a very floral smell, like lavender . . . or freesia," he noted. "It's mouthwatering."

"Yeah, it's an off day when I don't get *somebody* telling me how edible I smell."

He chuckled, and then sighed.

"I've decided what I want to do," I told him. "I want to hear more about you."

"Ask me anything."

I sifted through my questions for the most vital. "Why do you do it?" I said. "I still don't understand how you can work so hard to resist what you . . . *are*. Please don't misunderstand, of course I'm glad that you do. I just don't see why you would bother in the first place."

He hesitated before answering. "That's a good question, and you are not the first one to ask it. The others—the majority of our kind who are quite content with our lot—they, too, wonder at how we live. But you see, just because we've been . . . dealt a certain hand . . . it doesn't mean that we can't choose to rise above—to conquer the boundaries of a destiny that none of us wanted. To try to retain whatever essential humanity we can."

I lay unmoving, locked in awed silence.

"Did you fall asleep?" he whispered after a few minutes.

"No."

"Is that all you were curious about?"

I rolled my eyes. "Not quite."

"What else do you want to know?"

"Why can you read minds—why only you? And Alice, seeing the future . . . why does that happen?"

I felt him shrug in the darkness. "We don't really know. Carlisle has a theory . . . he believes that we all bring something of our strongest human traits with us into the next life, where they are intensified—like our minds, and our senses. He thinks that I must have already been very sensitive to the thoughts of those around me. And that Alice had some precognition, wherever she was."

"What did he bring into the next life, and the others?"

"Carlisle brought his compassion. Esme brought her ability to love passionately. Emmett brought his strength, Rosalie her...tenacity. Or you could call it pigheadedness," he chuckled. "Jasper is very interesting. He was quite charismatic in his first life, able to influence those around him to see things his way. Now he is able to manipulate the emotions of those around him—calm down a room of angry people, for example, or excite a lethargic crowd, conversely. It's a very subtle gift."

I considered the impossibilities he described, trying to take it in. He waited patiently while I thought.

"So where did it all start? I mean, Carlisle changed you, and then someone must have changed him, and so on...."

"Well, where did you come from? Evolution? Creation? Couldn't we have evolved in the same way as other species, predator and prey? Or, if you don't believe that all this world could have just happened on its own, which is hard for me to accept myself, is it so hard to believe that the same force that created the delicate angelfish with the shark, the baby seal and the killer whale, could create both our kinds together?"

"Let me get this straight—I'm the baby seal, right?"

"Right." He laughed, and something touched my hair—his lips?

I wanted to turn toward him, to see if it was really his lips against my hair. But I had to be good; I didn't want to make this any harder for him than it already was.

"Are you ready to sleep?" he asked, interrupting the short silence. "Or do you have any more questions?"

"Only a million or two."

"We have tomorrow, and the next day, and the next...," he reminded me. I smiled, euphoric at the thought.

"Are you sure you won't vanish in the morning?" I wanted this to be certain. "You are mythical, after all."

"I won't leave you." His voice had the seal of a promise in it.

"One more, then, tonight..." And I blushed. The darkness was no help— I'm sure he could feel the sudden warmth under my skin.

"What is it?"

"No, forget it. I changed my mind."

"Bella, you can ask me anything."

I didn't answer, and he groaned.

"I keep thinking it will get less frustrating, not hearing your thoughts. But it just gets worse and *worse*."

"I'm glad you can't read my thoughts. It's bad enough that you eavesdrop on my sleep-talking."

"Please?" His voice was so persuasive, so impossible to resist.

I shook my head.

"If you don't tell me, I'll just assume it's something much worse than it is," he threatened darkly. "Please?" Again, that pleading voice.

"Well," I began, glad that he couldn't see my face.

"Yes?"

"You said that Rosalie and Emmett will get married soon.... Is that... marriage... the same as it is for humans?"

He laughed in earnest now, understanding. "Is *that* what you're getting at?"

I fidgeted, unable to answer.

"Yes, I suppose it is much the same," he said. "I told you, most of those human desires are there, just hidden behind more powerful desires."

"Oh," was all I could say.

"Was there a purpose behind your curiosity?"

"Well, I did wonder... about you and me... someday..."

He was instantly serious, I could tell by the sudden stillness of his body. I froze, too, reacting automatically.

"I don't think that... that... would be possible for us."

"Because it would be too hard for you, if I were that... close?"

"That's certainly a problem. But that's not what I was thinking of. It's just that you are so soft, so fragile. I have to mind my actions every moment that we're together so that I don't hurt you. I could kill you quite easily, Bella, simply by accident." His voice had become just a soft murmur. He moved his icy palm to rest it against my cheek. "If I was too hasty... if for one second I wasn't paying enough attention, I could reach out, meaning to touch your face, and crush your skull by mistake. You don't realize how incredibly *breakable* you are. I can never, never afford to lose any kind of control when I'm with you."

He waited for me to respond, growing anxious when I didn't. "Are you scared?" he asked.

I waited for a minute to answer, so the words would be true. "No. I'm fine."

He seemed to deliberate for a moment. "I'm curious now, though," he said, his voice light again. "Have *you* ever...?" He trailed off suggestively.

"Of course not." I flushed. "I told you I've never felt like this about anyone before, not even close."

"I know. It's just that I know other people's thoughts. I know love and lust don't always keep the same company."

"They do for me. Now, anyway, that they exist for me at all," I sighed.

"That's nice. We have that one thing in common, at least." He sounded satisfied.

"Your human instincts...," I began. He waited. "Well, do you find me attractive, in *that* way, at all?"

He laughed and lightly rumpled my nearly dry hair.

"I may not be a human, but I am a man," he assured me.

I yawned involuntarily.

"I've answered your questions, now you should sleep," he insisted.

"I'm not sure if I can."

"Do you want me to leave?"

"No!" I said too loudly.

He laughed, and then began to hum that same, unfamiliar lullaby; the voice of an archangel, soft in my ear.

More tired than I realized, exhausted from the long day of mental and emotional stress like I'd never felt before, I drifted to sleep in his cold arms.

15. THE CULLENS

THE MUTED LIGHT OF YET ANOTHER CLOUDY DAY EVENTUALLY WOKE ME. I lay with my arm across my eyes, groggy and dazed. Something, a dream trying to be remembered, struggled to break into my consciousness. I moaned and rolled on my side, hoping more sleep would come. And then the previous day flooded back into my awareness.

"Oh!" I sat up so fast it made my head spin.

"Your hair looks like a haystack ... but I like it." His unruffled voice came from the rocking chair in the corner.

"Edward! You stayed!" I rejoiced, and thoughtlessly threw myself across the room and into his lap. In the instant that my thoughts caught up with my actions, I froze, shocked by my own uncontrolled enthusiasm. I stared up at him, afraid that I had crossed the wrong line.

But he laughed.

"Of course," he answered, startled, but seeming pleased by my reaction. His hands rubbed my back.

I laid my head cautiously against his shoulder, breathing in the smell of his skin.

"I was sure it was a dream."

"You're not that creative," he scoffed.

"Charlie!" I remembered, thoughtlessly jumping up again and heading to the door.

"He left an hour ago—after reattaching your battery cables, I might add. I have to admit I was disappointed. Is that really all it would take to stop you, if you were determined to go?"

I deliberated where I stood, wanting to return to him badly, but afraid I might have morning breath.

"You're not usually this confused in the morning," he noted. He held his arms open for me to return. A nearly irresistible invitation.

"I need another human minute," I admitted.

"I'll wait."

I skipped to the bathroom, my emotions unrecognizable. I didn't know myself, inside or out. The face in the mirror was practically a stranger—eyes too bright, hectic spots of red across my cheekbones. After I brushed my teeth, I worked to straighten out the tangled chaos that was my hair. I splashed my face with cold water, and tried to breathe normally, with no noticeable success. I half-ran back to my room.

It seemed like a miracle that he was there, his arms still waiting for me. He reached out to me, and my heart thumped unsteadily.

"Welcome back," he murmured, taking me into his arms.

He rocked me for a while in silence, until I noticed that his clothes were changed, his hair smooth.

"You left?" I accused, touching the collar of his fresh shirt.

"I could hardly leave in the clothes I came in—what would the neighbors think?"

I pouted.

"You were very deeply asleep; I didn't miss anything." His eyes gleamed. "The talking came earlier."

I groaned. "What did you hear?"

His gold eyes grew very soft. "You said you loved me."

"You knew that already," I reminded him, ducking my head.

"It was nice to hear, just the same."

I hid my face against his shoulder.

"I love you," I whispered.

"You are my life now," he answered simply.

There was nothing more to say for the moment. He rocked us back and forth as the room grew lighter.

"Breakfast time," he said eventually, casually—to prove, I'm sure, that he remembered all my human frailties.

So I clutched my throat with both hands and stared at him with wide eyes. Shock crossed his face.

"Kidding!" I snickered. "And you said I couldn't act!"

He frowned in disgust. "That wasn't funny."

"It was very funny, and you know it." But I examined his gold eyes carefully, to make sure that I was forgiven. Apparently, I was.

"Shall I rephrase?" he asked. "Breakfast time for the human."

"Oh, okay."

He threw me over his stone shoulder, gently, but with a swiftness that left me breathless. I protested as he carried me easily down the stairs, but he ignored me. He sat me right side up on a chair.

The kitchen was bright, happy, seeming to absorb my mood.

"What's for breakfast?" I asked pleasantly.

That threw him for a minute.

"Er, I'm not sure. What would you like?" His marble brow puckered.

I grinned, hopping up.

"That's all right, I fend for myself pretty well. Watch me hunt."

I found a bowl and a box of cereal. I could feel his eyes on me as I poured the milk and grabbed a spoon. I sat my food on the table, and then paused.

"Can I get you anything?" I asked, not wanting to be rude.

He rolled his eyes. "Just eat, Bella."

I sat at the table, watching him as I took a bite. He was gazing at me, studying my every movement. It made me self-conscious. I cleared my mouth to speak, to distract him.

"What's on the agenda for today?" I asked.

"Hmmm . . ." I watched him frame his answer carefully. "What would you say to meeting my family?"

I gulped.

"Are you afraid now?" He sounded hopeful.

"Yes," I admitted; how could I deny it—he could see my eyes.

"Don't worry." He smirked. "I'll protect you."

"I'm not afraid of *them*," I explained. "I'm afraid they won't . . . like me.

Won't they be, well, surprised that you would bring someone . . . like me . . . home to meet them? Do they know that I know about them?"

"Oh, they already know everything. They'd taken bets yesterday, you know"—he smiled, but his voice was harsh—"on whether I'd bring you back, though why anyone would bet against Alice, I can't imagine. At any rate, we don't have secrets in the family. It's not really feasible, what with my mind reading and Alice seeing the future and all that."

"And Jasper making you feel all warm and fuzzy about spilling your guts, don't forget that."

"You paid attention," he smiled approvingly.

"I've been known to do that every now and then." I grimaced. "So did Alice see me coming?"

His reaction was strange. "Something like that," he said uncomfortably, turning away so I couldn't see his eyes. I stared at him curiously.

"Is that any good?" he asked, turning back to me abruptly and eyeing my breakfast with a teasing look on his face. "Honestly, it doesn't look very appetizing."

"Well, it's no irritable grizzly . . . ," I murmured, ignoring him when he glowered. I was still wondering why he responded that way when I mentioned Alice. I hurried through my cereal, speculating.

He stood in the middle of the kitchen, the statue of Adonis again, staring abstractedly out the back windows.

Then his eyes were back on me, and he smiled his heartbreaking smile.

"And you should introduce me to your father, too, I think."

"He already knows you," I reminded him.

"As your boyfriend, I mean."

I stared at him with suspicion. "Why?"

"Isn't that customary?" he asked innocently.

"I don't know," I admitted. My dating history gave me few reference points to work with. Not that any normal rules of dating applied here. "That's not necessary, you know. I don't expect you to . . . I mean, you don't have to pretend for me."

His smile was patient. "I'm not pretending."

I pushed the remains of my cereal around the edges of the bowl, biting my lip.

"Are you going to tell Charlie I'm your boyfriend or not?" he demanded.

"Is that what you are?" I suppressed my internal cringing at the thought of Edward and Charlie and the word *boyfriend* all in the same room at the same time.

"It's a loose interpretation of the word 'boy,' I'll admit."

"I was under the impression that you were something more, actually," I confessed, looking at the table.

"Well, I don't know if we need to give him all the gory details." He reached across the table to lift my chin with a cold, gentle finger. "But he will need some explanation for why I'm around here so much. I don't want Chief Swan getting a restraining order put on me."

"Will you be?" I asked, suddenly anxious. "Will you really be here?"

"As long as you want me," he assured me.

"I'll always want you," I warned him. "Forever."

He walked slowly around the table, and, pausing a few feet away, he reached out to touch his fingertips to my cheek. His expression was unfathomable.

"Does that make you sad?" I asked.

He didn't answer. He stared into my eyes for an immeasurable period of time.

"Are you finished?" he finally asked.

I jumped up. "Yes."

"Get dressed—I'll wait here."

It was hard to decide what to wear. I doubted there were any etiquette books detailing how to dress when your vampire sweetheart takes you home to meet his vampire family. It was a relief to think the word to myself. I knew I shied away from it intentionally.

I ended up in my only skirt—long, khaki-colored, still casual. I put on the dark blue blouse he'd once complimented. A quick glance in the mirror told me my hair was entirely impossible, so I pulled it back into a ponytail.

"Okay." I bounced down the stairs. "I'm decent."

He was waiting at the foot of the stairs, closer than I'd thought, and I bounded right into him. He steadied me, holding me a careful distance away for a few seconds before suddenly pulling me closer.

"Wrong again," he murmured in my ear. "You are utterly indecent—no one should look so tempting, it's not fair."

"Tempting how?" I asked. "I can change..."

He sighed, shaking his head. "You are *so* absurd." He pressed his cool lips delicately to my forehead, and the room spun. The smell of his breath made it impossible to think.

"Shall I explain how you are tempting me?" he said. It was clearly a rhetorical question. His fingers traced slowly down my spine, his breath coming more quickly against my skin. My hands were limp on his chest, and I felt lightheaded again. He tilted his head slowly and touched his cool lips to mine for the second time, very carefully, parting them slightly.

And then I collapsed.

"Bella?" His voice was alarmed as he caught me and held me up.

"You...made...me...faint," I accused him dizzily.

"What am I going to do with you?" he groaned in exasperation. "Yesterday I kiss you, and you attack me! Today you pass out on me!"

I laughed weakly, letting his arms support me while my head spun.

"So much for being good at everything," he sighed.

"That's the problem." I was still dizzy. "You're *too* good. Far, far too good."

"Do you feel sick?" he asked; he'd seen me like this before.

"No—that wasn't the same kind of fainting at all. I don't know what happened." I shook my head apologetically. "I think I forgot to breathe."

"I can't take you anywhere like this."

"I'm fine," I insisted. "Your family is going to think I'm insane anyway, what's the difference?"

He measured my expression for a moment. "I'm very partial to that color with your skin," he offered unexpectedly. I flushed with pleasure, and looked away.

"Look, I'm trying really hard not to think about what I'm about to do, so can we go already?" I asked.

"And you're worried, not because you're headed to meet a houseful of vampires, but because you think those vampires won't approve of you, correct?"

"That's right," I answered immediately, hiding my surprise at his casual use of the word.

He shook his head. "You're incredible."

I realized, as he drove my truck out of the main part of town, that I had no idea where he lived. We passed over the bridge at the Calawah River, the road winding northward, the houses flashing past us growing farther apart, getting bigger. And then we were past the other houses altogether, driving through misty forest. I was trying to decide whether to ask or be patient, when he turned abruptly onto an unpaved road. It was unmarked, barely visible among the ferns. The forest encroached on both sides, leaving the road ahead only discernible for a few meters as it twisted, serpentlike, around the ancient trees.

And then, after a few miles, there was some thinning of the woods, and we were suddenly in a small meadow, or was it actually a lawn? The gloom of the forest didn't relent, though, for there were six primordial cedars that shaded an entire acre with their vast sweep of branches. The trees held their protecting shadow right up to the walls of the house that rose among them, making obsolete the deep porch that wrapped around the first story.

I don't know what I had expected, but it definitely wasn't this. The house was timeless, graceful, and probably a hundred years old. It was painted a soft, faded white, three stories tall, rectangular and well proportioned. The windows and doors were either part of the original structure or a perfect restoration. My truck was the only car in sight. I could hear the river close by, hidden in the obscurity of the forest.

"Wow."

"You like it?" He smiled.

"It . . . has a certain charm."

He pulled the end of my ponytail and chuckled.

"Ready?" he asked, opening my door.

"Not even a little bit—let's go." I tried to laugh, but it seemed to get stuck in my throat. I smoothed my hair nervously.

"You look lovely." He took my hand easily, without thinking about it.

We walked through the deep shade up to the porch. I knew he could feel my tension; his thumb rubbed soothing circles into the back of my hand.

He opened the door for me.

The inside was even more surprising, less predictable, than the exterior. It was very bright, very open, and very large. This must have originally been several rooms, but the walls had been removed from most of the first floor to create one wide space. The back, south-facing wall had been entirely replaced with glass, and, beyond the shade of the cedars, the lawn stretched bare to the wide river. A massive curving staircase dominated the west side of the room. The walls, the high-beamed ceiling, the wooden floors, and the thick carpets were all varying shades of white.

Waiting to greet us, standing just to the left of the door, on a raised portion of the floor by a spectacular grand piano, were Edward's parents.

I'd seen Dr. Cullen before, of course, yet I couldn't help but be struck again by his youth, his outrageous perfection. At his side was Esme, I assumed, the only one of the family I'd never seen before. She had the same pale, beautiful features as the rest of them. Something about her heart-shaped face, her billows of soft, caramel-colored hair, reminded me of the ingenues of the silent-movie era. She was small, slender, yet less angular, more rounded than the others. They were both dressed casually, in light colors that matched the inside of the house. They smiled in welcome, but made no move to approach us. Trying not to frighten me, I guessed.

"Carlisle, Esme," Edward's voice broke the short silence, "this is Bella."

"You're very welcome, Bella." Carlisle's step was measured, careful as he approached me. He raised his hand tentatively, and I stepped forward to shake hands with him.

"It's nice to see you again, Dr. Cullen."

"Please, call me Carlisle."

"Carlisle." I grinned at him, my sudden confidence surprising me. I could feel Edward's relief at my side.

Esme smiled and stepped forward as well, reaching for my hand. Her cold, stone grasp was just as I expected.

"It's very nice to know you," she said sincerely.

"Thank you. I'm glad to meet you, too." And I was. It was like meeting a fairy tale—Snow White, in the flesh.

"Where are Alice and Jasper?" Edward asked, but no one answered, as they had just appeared at the top of the wide staircase.

"Hey, Edward!" Alice called enthusiastically. She ran down the stairs, a streak of black hair and white skin, coming to a sudden and graceful stop in front of me. Carlisle and Esme shot warning glances at her, but I liked it. It was natural—for her, anyway.

"Hi, Bella!" Alice said, and she bounced forward to kiss my cheek. If Carlisle and Esme had looked cautious before, they now looked staggered.

There was shock in my eyes, too, but I was also very pleased that she seemed to approve of me so entirely. I was startled to feel Edward stiffen at my side. I glanced at his face, but his expression was unreadable.

"You do smell nice, I never noticed before," she commented, to my extreme embarrassment.

No one else seemed to know quite what to say, and then Jasper was there—tall and leonine. A feeling of ease spread through me, and I was suddenly comfortable despite where I was. Edward stared at Jasper, raising one eyebrow, and I remembered what Jasper could do.

"Hello, Bella," Jasper said. He kept his distance, not offering to shake my hand. But it was impossible to feel awkward near him.

"Hello, Jasper." I smiled at him shyly, and then at the others. "It's nice to meet you all—you have a very beautiful home," I added conventionally.

"Thank you," Esme said. "We're so glad that you came." She spoke with feeling, and I realized that she thought I was brave.

I also realized that Rosalie and Emmett were nowhere to be seen, and I remembered Edward's too-innocent denial when I'd asked him if the others didn't like me.

Carlisle's expression distracted me from this train of thought; he was gazing meaningfully at Edward with an intense expression. Out of the corner of my eye, I saw Edward nod once.

I looked away, trying to be polite. My eyes wandered again to the beautiful instrument on the platform by the door. I suddenly remembered my childhood fantasy that, should I ever win a lottery, I would buy a grand piano for my mother. She wasn't really good—she only played for herself on our secondhand upright—but I loved to watch her play. She was happy, absorbed—she seemed like a new, mysterious being to me then, someone outside the "mom" persona I took for granted. She'd put me through lessons, of course, but like most kids, I whined until she let me quit.

Esme noticed my preoccupation.

"Do you play?" she asked, inclining her head toward the piano.

I shook my head. "Not at all. But it's so beautiful. Is it yours?"

"No," she laughed. "Edward didn't tell you he was musical?"

"No." I glared at his suddenly innocent expression with narrowed eyes. "I should have known, I guess."

Esme raised her delicate eyebrows in confusion.

"Edward can do everything, right?" I explained.

Jasper snickered and Esme gave Edward a reproving look.

"I hope you haven't been showing off—it's rude," she scolded.

"Just a bit," he laughed freely. Her face softened at the sound, and they shared a brief look that I didn't understand, though Esme's face seemed almost smug.

"He's been too modest, actually," I corrected.

"Well, play for her," Esme encouraged.

"You just said showing off was rude," he objected.

"There are exceptions to every rule," she replied.

"I'd like to hear you play," I volunteered.

"It's settled then." Esme pushed him toward the piano. He pulled me along, sitting me on the bench beside him.

He gave me a long, exasperated look before he turned to the keys.

And then his fingers flowed swiftly across the ivory, and the room was filled with a composition so complex, so luxuriant, it was impossible to believe only one set of hands played. I felt my chin drop, my mouth open in astonishment, and heard low chuckles behind me at my reaction.

Edward looked at me casually, the music still surging around us without a break, and winked. "Do you like it?"

"You wrote this?" I gasped, understanding.

He nodded. "It's Esme's favorite."

I closed my eyes, shaking my head.

"What's wrong?"

"I'm feeling extremely insignificant."

The music slowed, transforming into something softer, and to my surprise I detected the melody of his lullaby weaving through the profusion of notes.

"You inspired this one," he said softly. The music grew unbearably sweet. I couldn't speak.

"They like you, you know," he said conversationally. "Esme especially."

I glanced behind me, but the huge room was empty now.

"Where did they go?"

"Very subtly giving us some privacy, I suppose."

I sighed. *"They* like me. But Rosalie and Emmett..." I trailed off, not sure how to express my doubts.

He frowned. "Don't worry about Rosalie," he said, his eyes wide and persuasive. "She'll come around."

I pursed my lips skeptically. "Emmett?"

"Well, he thinks *I'm* a lunatic, it's true, but he doesn't have a problem with you. He's trying to reason with Rosalie."

"What is it that upsets her?" I wasn't sure if I wanted to know the answer.

He sighed deeply. "Rosalie struggles the most with... with what we are. It's hard for her to have someone on the outside know the truth. And she's a little jealous."

"Rosalie is jealous of *me?"* I asked incredulously. I tried to imagine a universe in which someone as breathtaking as Rosalie would have any possible reason to feel jealous of someone like me.

"You're human." He shrugged. "She wishes that she were, too."

"Oh," I muttered, still stunned. "Even Jasper, though..."

"That's really my fault," he said. "I told you he was the most recent to try our way of life. I warned him to keep his distance."

I thought about the reason for that, and shuddered.

"Esme and Carlisle...?" I continued quickly, to keep him from noticing.

"Are happy to see me happy. Actually, Esme wouldn't care if you had a third eye and webbed feet. All this time she's been worried about me, afraid that there was something missing from my essential makeup, that I was too young when Carlisle changed me.... She's ecstatic. Every time I touch you, she just about chokes with satisfaction."

"Alice seems very... enthusiastic."

"Alice has her own way of looking at things," he said through tight lips.

"And you're not going to explain that, are you?"

A moment of wordless communication passed between us. He realized that I knew he was keeping something from me. I realized that he wasn't going to give anything away. Not now.

"So what was Carlisle telling you before?"

His eyebrows pulled together. "You noticed that, did you?"

I shrugged. "Of course."

He looked at me thoughtfully for a few seconds before answering. "He wanted to tell me some news—he didn't know if it was something I would share with you."

"Will you?"

"I have to, because I'm going to be a little . . . overbearingly protective over the next few days—or weeks—and I wouldn't want you to think I'm naturally a tyrant."

"What's wrong?"

"Nothing's wrong, exactly. Alice just sees some visitors coming soon. They know we're here, and they're curious."

"Visitors?"

"Yes . . . well, they aren't like us, of course—in their hunting habits, I mean. They probably won't come into town at all, but I'm certainly not going to let you out of my sight till they're gone."

I shivered.

"Finally, a rational response!" he murmured. "I was beginning to think you had no sense of self-preservation at all."

I let that one pass, looking away, my eyes wandering again around the spacious room.

He followed my gaze. "Not what you expected, is it?" he asked, his voice smug.

"No," I admitted.

"No coffins, no piled skulls in the corners; I don't even think we have cobwebs . . . what a disappointment this must be for you," he continued slyly.

I ignored his teasing. "It's so light . . . so open."

He was more serious when he answered. "It's the one place we never have to hide."

The song he was still playing, my song, drifted to an end, the final chords shifting to a more melancholy key. The last note hovered poignantly in the silence.

"Thank you," I murmured. I realized there were tears in my eyes. I dabbed at them, embarrassed.

He touched the corner of my eye, trapping one I missed. He lifted his finger, examining the drop of moisture broodingly. Then, so quickly I couldn't be positive that he really did, he put his finger to his mouth to taste it.

I looked at him questioningly, and he gazed back for a long moment before he finally smiled.

"Do you want to see the rest of the house?"

"No coffins?" I verified, the sarcasm in my voice not entirely masking the slight but genuine anxiety I felt.

He laughed, taking my hand, leading me away from the piano.

"No coffins," he promised.

We walked up the massive staircase, my hand trailing along the satin-smooth rail. The long hall at the top of the stairs was paneled with a honey-colored wood, the same as the floorboards.

"Rosalie and Emmett's room...Carlisle's office...Alice's room..." He gestured as he led me past the doors.

He would have continued, but I stopped dead at the end of the hall, staring incredulously at the ornament hanging on the wall above my head. Edward chuckled at my bewildered expression.

"You can laugh," he said. "It *is* sort of ironic."

I didn't laugh. My hand raised automatically, one finger extended as if to touch the large wooden cross, its dark patina contrasting with the lighter tone of the wall. I didn't touch it, though I was curious if the aged wood would feel as silky as it looked.

"It must be very old," I guessed.

He shrugged. "Early sixteen-thirties, more or less."

I looked away from the cross to stare at him.

"Why do you keep this here?" I wondered.

"Nostalgia. It belonged to Carlisle's father."

"He collected antiques?" I suggested doubtfully.

"No. He carved this himself. It hung on the wall above the pulpit in the vicarage where he preached."

I wasn't sure if my face betrayed my shock, but I returned to gazing at the simple, ancient cross, just in case. I quickly did the mental math; the cross was over three hundred and seventy years old. The silence stretched on as I struggled to wrap my mind around the concept of so many years.

"Are you all right?" He sounded worried.

"How old is Carlisle?" I asked quietly, ignoring his question, still staring up.

"He just celebrated his three hundred and sixty-second birthday," Edward said. I looked back at him, a million questions in my eyes.

He watched me carefully as he spoke.

"Carlisle was born in London, in the sixteen-forties, he believes. Time wasn't marked as accurately then, for the common people anyway. It was just before Cromwell's rule, though."

I kept my face composed, aware of his scrutiny as I listened. It was easier if I didn't try to believe.

"He was the only son of an Anglican pastor. His mother died giving birth to him. His father was an intolerant man. As the Protestants came into power, he was enthusiastic in his persecution of Roman Catholics and other religions. He also believed very strongly in the reality of evil. He led hunts for witches, werewolves...and vampires." I grew very still at the word. I'm sure he noticed, but he went on without pausing.

"They burned a lot of innocent people—of course the real creatures that he sought were not so easy to catch.

"When the pastor grew old, he placed his obedient son in charge of the raids. At first Carlisle was a disappointment; he was not quick to accuse, to see demons where they did not exist. But he was persistent, and more clever than his father. He actually discovered a coven of true vampires that lived hidden in the sewers of the city, only coming out by night to hunt. In those days, when monsters were not just myths and legends, that was the way many lived.

"The people gathered their pitchforks and torches, of course"—his brief laugh was darker now—"and waited where Carlisle had seen the monsters exit into the street. Eventually one emerged."

His voice was very quiet; I strained to catch the words.

"He must have been ancient, and weak with hunger. Carlisle heard him call out in Latin to the others when he caught the scent of the mob. He ran through the streets, and Carlisle—he was twenty-three and very fast—was in the lead of the pursuit. The creature could have easily outrun them, but Carlisle thinks he was too hungry, so he turned and attacked. He fell on Carlisle first, but the others were close behind, and he turned to defend himself. He killed two men, and made off with a third, leaving Carlisle bleeding in the street."

He paused. I could sense he was editing something, keeping something from me.

"Carlisle knew what his father would do. The bodies would be burned—anything infected by the monster must be destroyed. Carlisle acted instinctively to save his own life. He crawled away from the alley while the mob followed the fiend and his victim. He hid in a cellar, buried himself in rotting potatoes for three days. It's a miracle he was able to keep silent, to stay undiscovered.

"It was over then, and he realized what he had become."

I'm not sure what my face was revealing, but he suddenly broke off.

"How are you feeling?" he asked.

"I'm fine," I assured him. And, though I bit my lip in hesitation, he must have seen the curiosity burning in my eyes.

He smiled. "I expect you have a few more questions for me."

"A few."

His smile widened over his brilliant teeth. He started back down the hall, pulling me along by the hand. "Come on, then," he encouraged. "I'll show you."

16. CARLISLE

HE LED ME BACK TO THE ROOM THAT HE'D POINTED OUT AS CARLISLE'S office. He paused outside the door for an instant.

"Come in," Carlisle's voice invited.

Edward opened the door to a high-ceilinged room with tall, west-facing windows. The walls were paneled again, in a darker wood—where they were visible. Most of the wall space was taken up by towering bookshelves that reached high above my head and held more books than I'd ever seen outside a library.

Carlisle sat behind a huge mahogany desk in a leather chair. He was just placing a bookmark in the pages of the thick volume he held. The room was how I'd always imagined a college dean's would look—only Carlisle looked too young to fit the part.

"What can I do for you?" he asked us pleasantly, rising from his seat.

"I wanted to show Bella some of our history," Edward said. "Well, your history, actually."

"We didn't mean to disturb you," I apologized.

"Not at all. Where are you going to start?"

"The Waggoner," Edward replied, placing one hand lightly on my shoulder and spinning me around to look back toward the door we'd just come through. Every time he touched me, in even the most casual way, my heart had an audible reaction. It was more embarrassing with Carlisle there.

The wall we faced now was different from the others. Instead of bookshelves, this wall was crowded with framed pictures of all sizes, some in vibrant colors, others dull monochromes. I searched for some logic, some binding motif the collection had in common, but I found nothing in my hasty examination.

Edward pulled me toward the far left side, standing me in front of a small square oil painting in a plain wooden frame. This one did not stand out among the bigger and brighter pieces; painted in varying tones of sepia, it depicted a miniature city full of steeply slanted roofs, with thin spires atop a few scattered towers. A wide river filled the foreground, crossed by a bridge covered with structures that looked like tiny cathedrals.

"London in the sixteen-fifties," Edward said.

"The London of my youth," Carlisle added, from a few feet behind us. I flinched; I hadn't heard him approach. Edward squeezed my hand.

"Will *you* tell the story?" Edward asked. I twisted a little to see Carlisle's reaction.

He met my glance and smiled. "I would," he replied. "But I'm actually running a bit late. The hospital called this morning—Dr. Snow is taking a sick day. Besides, you know the stories as well as I do," he added, grinning at Edward now.

It was a strange combination to absorb—the everyday concerns of the town doctor stuck in the middle of a discussion of his early days in seventeenth-century London.

It was also unsettling to know that he spoke aloud only for my benefit.

After another warm smile for me, Carlisle left the room.

I stared at the little picture of Carlisle's hometown for a long moment.

"What happened then?" I finally asked, staring up at Edward, who was watching me. "When he realized what had happened to him?"

He glanced back to the paintings, and I looked to see which image caught his interest now. It was a larger landscape in dull fall colors—an empty, shadowed meadow in a forest, with a craggy peak in the distance.

"When he knew what he had become," Edward said quietly, "he rebelled against it. He tried to destroy himself. But that's not easily done."

"How?" I didn't mean to say it aloud, but the word broke through my shock.

"He jumped from great heights," Edward told me, his voice impassive. "He tried to drown himself in the ocean . . . but he was young to the new life, and very strong. It is amazing that he was able to resist . . . feeding . . . while he was still so new. The instinct is more powerful then, it takes over everything. But he was so repelled by himself that he had the strength to try to kill himself with starvation."

"Is that possible?" My voice was faint.

"No, there are very few ways we can be killed."

I opened my mouth to ask, but he spoke before I could.

"So he grew very hungry, and eventually weak. He strayed as far as he could from the human populace, recognizing that his willpower was weakening, too. For months he wandered by night, seeking the loneliest places, loathing himself.

"One night, a herd of deer passed his hiding place. He was so wild with thirst that he attacked without a thought. His strength returned and he realized there was an alternative to being the vile monster he feared. Had he not eaten venison in his former life? Over the next months his new philosophy was born. He could exist without being a demon. He found himself again.

"He began to make better use of his time. He'd always been intelligent, eager to learn. Now he had unlimited time before him. He studied by night, planned by day. He swam to France and—"

"He *swam* to France?"

"People swim the Channel all the time, Bella," he reminded me patiently.

"That's true, I guess. It just sounded funny in that context. Go on."

"Swimming is easy for us—"

"Everything is easy for *you*," I griped.

He waited, his expression amused.

"I won't interrupt again, I promise."

He chuckled darkly, and finished his sentence. "Because, technically, we don't need to breathe."

"You—"

"No, no, you promised." He laughed, putting his cold finger lightly to my lips. "Do you want to hear the story or not?"

"You can't spring something like that on me, and then expect me not to say anything," I mumbled against his finger.

He lifted his hand, moving it to rest against my neck. The speed of my heart reacted to that, but I persisted.

"You don't have to *breathe?*" I demanded.

"No, it's not necessary. Just a habit." He shrugged.

"How long can you go . . . without *breathing?*"

"Indefinitely, I suppose; I don't know. It gets a bit uncomfortable—being without a sense of smell."

"A bit uncomfortable," I echoed.

I wasn't paying attention to my own expression, but something in it made him grow somber. His hand dropped to his side and he stood very still, his eyes intent on my face. The silence lengthened. His features were immobile as stone.

"What is it?" I whispered, touching his frozen face.

His face softened under my hand, and he sighed. "I keep waiting for it to happen."

"For what to happen?"

"I know that at some point, something I tell you or something you see is going to be too much. And then you'll run away from me, screaming as you go." He smiled half a smile, but his eyes were serious. "I won't stop you. I want this to happen, because I want you to be safe. And yet, I want to be with you. The two desires are impossible to reconcile. . . ." He trailed off, staring at my face. Waiting.

"I'm not running anywhere," I promised.

"We'll see," he said, smiling again.

I frowned at him. "So, go on—Carlisle was swimming to France."

He paused, getting back into his story. Reflexively, his eyes flickered to another picture—the most colorful of them all, the most ornately framed, and the largest; it was twice as wide as the door it hung next to. The canvas overflowed with bright figures in swirling robes, writhing around long pillars and off marbled balconies. I couldn't tell if it represented Greek mythology, or if the characters floating in the clouds above were meant to be biblical.

"Carlisle swam to France, and continued on through Europe, to the universities there. By night he studied music, science, medicine—and found his calling, his penance, in that, in saving human lives." His expression became awed, almost reverent. "I can't adequately describe the struggle; it took Carlisle two centuries of torturous effort to perfect his self-control. Now he is all but immune to the scent of human blood, and he is able to do the work he loves without agony. He finds a great deal of peace there, at the hospital. . . ." Edward stared off into space for a long moment. Suddenly he seemed to recall his purpose. He tapped his finger against the huge painting in front of us.

"He was studying in Italy when he discovered the others there. They were much more civilized and educated than the wraiths of the London sewers."

He touched a comparatively sedate quartet of figures painted on the highest balcony, looking down calmly on the mayhem below them. I examined the grouping carefully and realized, with a startled laugh, that I recognized the golden-haired man.

"Solimena was greatly inspired by Carlisle's friends. He often painted them as gods," Edward chuckled. "Aro, Marcus, Caius," he said, indicating the other three, two black-haired, one snowy-white. "Nighttime patrons of the arts."

"What happened to them?" I wondered aloud, my fingertip hovering a centimeter from the figures on the canvas.

"They're still there." He shrugged. "As they have been for who knows how many millennia. Carlisle stayed with them only for a short time, just a few decades. He greatly admired their civility, their refinement, but they persisted in trying to cure his aversion to 'his natural food source,' as they called it. They tried to persuade him, and he tried to persuade them, to no avail. At that point, Carlisle decided to try the New World. He dreamed of finding others like himself. He was very lonely, you see.

"He didn't find anyone for a long time. But, as monsters became the stuff of fairy tales, he found he could interact with unsuspecting humans as if he were one of them. He began practicing medicine. But the companionship he craved evaded him; he couldn't risk familiarity.

"When the influenza epidemic hit, he was working nights in a hospital in Chicago. He'd been turning over an idea in his mind for several years, and he had almost decided to act—since he couldn't find a companion, he would create one. He wasn't absolutely sure how his own transformation had occurred, so he was hesitant. And he was loath to steal anyone's life the way his had been stolen. It was in that frame of mind that he found me. There was no hope for me; I was left in a ward with the dying. He had nursed my parents, and knew I was alone. He decided to try . . ."

His voice, nearly a whisper now, trailed off. He stared unseeingly through the west windows. I wondered which images filled his mind now, Carlisle's memories or his own. I waited quietly.

When he turned back to me, a gentle angel's smile lit his expression.

"And so we've come full circle," he concluded.

"Have you always stayed with Carlisle, then?" I wondered.

"Almost always." He put his hand lightly on my waist and pulled me with him as he walked through the door. I stared back at the wall of pictures, wondering if I would ever get to hear the other stories.

Edward didn't say any more as we walked down the hall, so I asked, "Almost?"

He sighed, seeming reluctant to answer. "Well, I had a typical bout of rebellious adolescence—about ten years after I was . . . born . . . created, whatever you want to call it. I wasn't sold on his life of abstinence, and I resented him for curbing my appetite. So I went off on my own for a time."

"Really?" I was intrigued, rather than frightened, as I perhaps should have been.

He could tell. I vaguely realized that we were headed up the next flight of stairs, but I wasn't paying much attention to my surroundings.

"That doesn't repulse you?"

"No."

"Why not?"

"I guess . . . it sounds reasonable."

He barked a laugh, more loudly than before. We were at the top of the stairs now, in another paneled hallway.

"From the time of my new birth," he murmured, "I had the advantage of knowing what everyone around me was thinking, both human and non-human alike. That's why it took me ten years to defy Carlisle—I could read his perfect sincerity, understand exactly why he lived the way he did.

"It took me only a few years to return to Carlisle and recommit to his vision. I thought I would be exempt from the . . . depression . . . that accompanies a conscience. Because I knew the thoughts of my prey, I could pass over the innocent and pursue only the evil. If I followed a murderer down a dark alley where he stalked a young girl—if I saved her, then surely I wasn't so terrible."

I shivered, imagining only too clearly what he described—the alley at night, the frightened girl, the dark man behind her. And Edward, Edward as he hunted, terrible and glorious as a young god, unstoppable. Would she have been grateful, that girl, or more frightened than before?

"But as time went on, I began to see the monster in my eyes. I couldn't escape the debt of so much human life taken, no matter how justified. And I went back to Carlisle and Esme. They welcomed me back like the prodigal. It was more than I deserved."

We'd come to a stop in front of the last door in the hall.

"My room," he informed me, opening it and pulling me through.

His room faced south, with a wall-sized window like the great room below. The whole back side of the house must be glass. His view looked down on the winding Sol Duc River, across the untouched forest to the Olympic Mountain range. The mountains were much closer than I would have believed.

The western wall was completely covered with shelf after shelf of CDs. His room was better stocked than a music store. In the corner was a sophisticated-looking sound system, the kind I was afraid to touch because I'd be sure to break something. There was no bed, only a wide and inviting black leather sofa. The floor was covered with a thick golden carpet, and the walls were hung with heavy fabric in a slightly darker shade.

"Good acoustics?" I guessed.

He chuckled and nodded.

He picked up a remote and turned the stereo on. It was quiet, but the soft jazz number sounded like the band was in the room with us. I went to look at his mind-boggling music collection.

"How do you have these organized?" I asked, unable to find any rhyme or reason to the titles.

He wasn't paying attention.

"Ummm, by year, and then by personal preference within that frame," he said absently.

I turned, and he was looking at me with a peculiar expression in his eyes. "What?"

"I was prepared to feel . . . relieved. Having you know about everything, not needing to keep secrets from you. But I didn't expect to feel more than that. I *like* it. It makes me . . . happy." He shrugged, smiling slightly.

"I'm glad," I said, smiling back. I'd worried that he might regret telling me these things. It was good to know that wasn't the case.

But then, as his eyes dissected my expression, his smile faded and his forehead creased.

"You're still waiting for the running and the screaming, aren't you?" I guessed.

A faint smile touched his lips, and he nodded.

"I hate to burst your bubble, but you're really not as scary as you think you are. I don't find you scary at all, actually," I lied casually.

He stopped, raising his eyebrows in blatant disbelief. Then he flashed a wide, wicked smile.

"You *really* shouldn't have said that," he chuckled.

He growled, a low sound in the back of his throat; his lips curled back over his perfect teeth. His body shifted suddenly, half-crouched, tensed like a lion about to pounce.

I backed away from him, glaring.

"You wouldn't."

I didn't see him leap at me—it was much too fast. I only found myself suddenly airborne, and then we crashed onto the sofa, knocking it into the wall. All the while, his arms formed an iron cage of protection around me— I was barely jostled. But I still was gasping as I tried to right myself.

He wasn't having that. He curled me into a ball against his chest, holding me more securely than iron chains. I glared at him in alarm, but he seemed well in control, his jaw relaxed as he grinned, his eyes bright only with humor.

"You were saying?" he growled playfully.

"That you are a very, very terrifying monster," I said, my sarcasm marred a bit by my breathless voice.

"Much better," he approved.

"Um." I struggled. "Can I get up now?"

He just laughed.

"Can we come in?" a soft voice sounded from the hall.

I struggled to free myself, but Edward merely readjusted me so that I was somewhat more conventionally seated on his lap. I could see it was Alice, then, and Jasper behind her in the doorway. My cheeks burned, but Edward seemed at ease.

"Go ahead." Edward was still chuckling quietly.

Alice seemed to find nothing unusual in our embrace; she walked—almost danced, her movements were so graceful—to the center of the room, where she folded herself sinuously onto the floor. Jasper, however, paused at the door, his expression a trifle shocked. He stared at Edward's face, and I wondered if he was tasting the atmosphere with his unusual sensitivity.

"It sounded like you were having Bella for lunch, and we came to see if you would share," Alice announced.

I stiffened for an instant, until I realized Edward was grinning—whether at her comment or my response, I couldn't tell.

"Sorry, I don't believe I have enough to spare," he replied, his arms holding me recklessly close.

"Actually," Jasper said, smiling despite himself as he walked into the room, "Alice says there's going to be a real storm tonight, and Emmett wants to play ball. Are you game?"

The words were all common enough, but the context confused me. I gathered that Alice was a bit more reliable than the weatherman, though.

Edward's eyes lit up, but he hesitated.

"Of course you should bring Bella," Alice chirped. I thought I saw Jasper throw a quick glance at her.

"Do you want to go?" Edward asked me, excited, his expression vivid.

"Sure." I couldn't disappoint such a face. "Um, where are we going?"

"We have to wait for thunder to play ball—you'll see why," he promised.

"Will I need an umbrella?"

They all three laughed aloud.

"Will she?" Jasper asked Alice.

"No." She was positive. "The storm will hit over town. It should be dry enough in the clearing."

"Good, then." The enthusiasm in Jasper's voice was catching, naturally. I found myself eager, rather than scared stiff.

"Let's go see if Carlisle will come." Alice bounded up and to the door in a fashion that would break any ballerina's heart.

"Like you don't know," Jasper teased, and they were swiftly on their way. Jasper managed to inconspicuously close the door behind them.

"What will we be playing?" I demanded.

"*You* will be watching," Edward clarified. "We will be playing baseball."

I rolled my eyes. "Vampires like baseball?"

"It's the American pastime," he said with mock solemnity.

17. THE GAME

IT WAS JUST BEGINNING TO DRIZZLE WHEN EDWARD TURNED ONTO MY street. Up until that moment, I'd had no doubt that he'd be staying with me while I spent a few interim hours in the real world.

And then I saw the black car, a weathered Ford, parked in Charlie's driveway—and heard Edward mutter something unintelligible in a low, harsh voice.

Leaning away from the rain under the shallow front porch, Jacob Black stood behind his father's wheelchair. Billy's face was impassive as stone as Edward parked my truck against the curb. Jacob stared down, his expression mortified.

Edward's low voice was furious. "This is crossing the line."

"He came to warn Charlie?" I guessed, more horrified than angry.

Edward just nodded, answering Billy's gaze through the rain with narrowed eyes.

I felt weak with relief that Charlie wasn't home yet.

"Let me deal with this," I suggested. Edward's black glare made me anxious.

To my surprise, he agreed. "That's probably best. Be careful, though. The child has no idea."

I bridled a little at the word *child*. "Jacob is not that much younger than I am," I reminded him.

He looked at me then, his anger abruptly fading. "Oh, I know," he assured me with a grin.

I sighed and put my hand on the door handle.

"Get them inside," he instructed, "so I can leave. I'll be back around dusk."

"Do you want my truck?" I offered, meanwhile wondering how I would explain its absence to Charlie.

He rolled his eyes. "I could *walk* home faster than this truck moves."

"You don't have to leave," I said wistfully.

He smiled at my glum expression. "Actually, I do. After you get rid of them"—he threw a dark glance in the Blacks' direction—"you still have to prepare Charlie to meet your new boyfriend." He grinned widely, showing all of his teeth.

I groaned. "Thanks a lot."

He smiled the crooked smile that I loved. "I'll be back soon," he promised. His eyes flickered back to the porch, and then he leaned in to swiftly kiss me just under the edge of my jaw. My heart lurched frantically, and I, too, glanced toward the porch. Billy's face was no longer impassive, and his hands clutched at the armrests of his chair.

"*Soon,*" I stressed as I opened the door and stepped out into the rain.

I could feel his eyes on my back as I half-ran through the light sprinkle toward the porch.

"Hey, Billy. Hi, Jacob." I greeted them as cheerfully as I could manage. "Charlie's gone for the day—I hope you haven't been waiting long."

"Not long," Billy said in a subdued tone. His black eyes were piercing. "I just wanted to bring this up." He indicated a brown paper sack resting in his lap.

"Thanks," I said, though I had no idea what it could be. "Why don't you come in for a minute and dry off?"

I pretended to be oblivious to his intense scrutiny as I unlocked the door, and waved them in ahead of me.

"Here, let me take that," I offered, turning to shut the door. I allowed myself one last glance at Edward. He was waiting, perfectly still, his eyes solemn.

"You'll want to put it in the fridge," Billy noted as he handed me the package. "It's some of Harry Clearwater's homemade fish fry—Charlie's favorite. The fridge keeps it drier." He shrugged.

"Thanks," I repeated, but with feeling this time. "I was running out of new ways to fix fish, and he's bound to bring home more tonight."

"Fishing again?" Billy asked with a subtle gleam in his eye. "Down at the usual spot? Maybe I'll run by and see him."

"No," I quickly lied, my face going hard. "He was headed someplace new . . . but I have no idea where."

He took in my changed expression, and it made him thoughtful.

"Jake," he said, still appraising me. "Why don't you go get that new picture of Rebecca out of the car? I'll leave that for Charlie, too."

"Where is it?" Jacob asked, his voice morose. I glanced at him, but he was staring at the floor, his eyebrows pulling together.

"I think I saw it in the trunk," Billy said. "You may have to dig for it."

Jacob slouched back out into the rain.

Billy and I faced each other in silence. After a few seconds, the quiet started to feel awkward, so I turned and headed to the kitchen. I could hear his wet wheels squeak against the linoleum as he followed.

I shoved the bag onto the crowded top shelf of the fridge, and spun around to confront him. His deeply lined face was unreadable.

"Charlie won't be back for a long time." My voice was almost rude.

He nodded in agreement, but said nothing.

"Thanks again for the fish fry," I hinted.

He continued nodding. I sighed and folded my arms across my chest.

He seemed to sense that I had given up on small talk. "Bella," he said, and then he hesitated.

I waited.

"Bella," he said again, "Charlie is one of my best friends."

"Yes."

He spoke each word carefully in his rumbling voice. "I noticed you've been spending time with one of the Cullens."

"Yes," I repeated curtly.

His eyes narrowed. "Maybe it's none of my business, but I don't think that is such a good idea."

"You're right," I agreed. "It *is* none of your business."

He raised his graying eyebrows at my tone. "You probably don't know this, but the Cullen family has an unpleasant reputation on the reservation."

"Actually, I did know that," I informed him in a hard voice. This surprised him. "But that reputation couldn't be deserved, could it? Because the Cullens never set foot on the reservation, do they?" I could see that my less than subtle reminder of the agreement that both bound and protected his tribe pulled him up short.

"That's true," he acceded, his eyes guarded. "You seem . . . well informed about the Cullens. More informed than I expected."

I stared him down. "Maybe even better informed than you are."

He pursed his thick lips as he considered that. "Maybe," he allowed, but his eyes were shrewd. "Is Charlie as well informed?"

He had found the weak chink in my armor.

"Charlie likes the Cullens a lot," I hedged. He clearly understood my evasion. His expression was unhappy, but unsurprised.

"It's not my business," he said. "But it may be Charlie's."

"Though it would be my business, again, whether or not I think that it's Charlie's business, right?"

I wondered if he even understood my confused question as I struggled not to say anything compromising. But he seemed to. He thought about it while the rain picked up against the roof, the only sound breaking the silence.

"Yes," he finally surrendered. "I guess that's your business, too."

I sighed with relief. "Thanks, Billy."

"Just think about what you're doing, Bella," he urged.

"Okay," I agreed quickly.

He frowned. "What I meant to say was, don't do what you're doing."

I looked into his eyes, filled with nothing but concern for me, and there was nothing I could say.

Just then the front door banged loudly, and I jumped at the sound.

"There's no picture anywhere in that car." Jacob's complaining voice reached us before he did. The shoulders of his shirt were stained with the rain, his hair dripping, when he rounded the corner.

"Hmm," Billy grunted, suddenly detached, spinning his chair around to face his son. "I guess I left it at home."

Jacob rolled his eyes dramatically. "Great."

"Well, Bella, tell Charlie"—Billy paused before continuing—"that we stopped by, I mean."

"I will," I muttered.

Jacob was surprised. "Are we leaving already?"

"Charlie's gonna be out late," Billy explained as he rolled himself past Jacob.

"Oh." Jacob looked disappointed. "Well, I guess I'll see you later, then, Bella."

"Sure," I agreed.

"Take care," Billy warned me. I didn't answer.

Jacob helped his father out the door. I waved briefly, glancing swiftly toward my now-empty truck, and then shut the door before they were gone.

I stood in the hallway for a minute, listening to the sound of their car as it backed out and drove away. I stayed where I was, waiting for the irritation and anxiety to subside. When the tension eventually faded a bit, I headed upstairs to change out of my dressy clothes.

I tried on a couple of different tops, not sure what to expect tonight. As I concentrated on what was coming, what had just passed became insignificant. Now that I was removed from Jasper's and Edward's influence, I began to make up for not being terrified before. I gave up quickly on choosing an outfit—throwing on an old flannel shirt and jeans—knowing I would be in my raincoat all night anyway.

The phone rang and I sprinted downstairs to get it. There was only one voice I wanted to hear; anything else would be a disappointment. But I knew that if *he* wanted to talk to me, he'd probably just materialize in my room.

"Hello?" I asked, breathless.

"Bella? It's me," Jessica said.

"Oh, hey, Jess." I scrambled for a moment to come back down to reality. It felt like months rather than days since I'd spoken to Jess. "How was the dance?"

"It was so much fun!" Jessica gushed. Needing no more invitation than that, she launched into a minute-by-minute account of the previous night. I *mmm*'d and *ahh*'d at the right places, but it wasn't easy to concentrate. Jessica, Mike, the dance, the school—they all seemed strangely irrelevant at the moment. My eyes kept flashing to the window, trying to judge the degree of light behind the heavy clouds.

"Did you hear what I said, Bella?" Jess asked, irritated.

"I'm sorry, what?"

"I said, Mike kissed me! Can you believe it?"

"That's wonderful, Jess," I said.

"So what did *you* do yesterday?" Jessica challenged, still sounding both-ered by my lack of attention. Or maybe she was upset because I hadn't asked for details.

"Nothing, really. I just hung around outside to enjoy the sun."

I heard Charlie's car in the garage.

"Did you ever hear anything more from Edward Cullen?"

The front door slammed and I could hear Charlie banging around under the stairs, putting his tackle away.

"Um." I hesitated, not sure what my story was anymore.

"Hi there, kiddo!" Charlie called as he walked into the kitchen. I waved at him.

Jess heard his voice. "Oh, your dad's there. Never mind—we'll talk tomor-row. See you in Trig."

"See ya, Jess." I hung up the phone.

"Hey, Dad," I said. He was scrubbing his hands in the sink. "Where's the fish?"

"I put it out in the freezer."

"I'll go grab a few pieces before they freeze—Billy dropped off some of Harry Clearwater's fish fry this afternoon." I worked to sound enthusiastic.

"He did?" Charlie's eyes lit up. "That's my favorite."

Charlie cleaned up while I got dinner ready. It didn't take long till we were sitting at the table, eating in silence. Charlie was enjoying his food. I was wondering desperately how to fulfill my assignment, struggling to think of a way to broach the subject.

"What did you do with yourself today?" he asked, snapping me out of my reverie.

"Well, this afternoon I just hung out around the house...." Only the very recent part of this afternoon, actually. I tried to keep my voice upbeat, but my stomach was hollow. "And this morning I was over at the Cullens'."

Charlie dropped his fork.

"Dr. Cullen's place?" he asked in astonishment.

I pretended not to notice his reaction. "Yeah."

"What were you doing there?" He hadn't picked his fork back up.

"Well, I sort of have a date with Edward Cullen tonight, and he wanted to introduce me to his parents...Dad?"

It appeared that Charlie was having an aneurysm.

"Dad, are you all right?"

"You are going out with Edward Cullen?" he thundered.

Uh-oh. "I thought you liked the Cullens."

"He's too old for you," he ranted.

"We're both juniors," I corrected, though he was more right than he dreamed.

"Wait..." He paused. "Which one is Edwin?"

"*Edward* is the youngest, the one with the reddish brown hair." The beautiful one, the godlike one...

"Oh, well, that's"—he struggled—"better, I guess. I don't like the look of that big one. I'm sure he's a nice boy and all, but he looks too...mature for you. Is this Edwin your boyfriend?"

"It's Edward, Dad."

"Is he?"

"Sort of, I guess."

"You said last night that you weren't interested in any of the boys in town." But he picked up his fork again, so I could see the worst was over.

"Well, Edward doesn't live in town, Dad."

He gave me a disparaging look as he chewed.

"And, anyways," I continued, "it's kind of at an early stage, you know. Don't embarrass me with all the boyfriend talk, okay?"

"When is he coming over?"

"He'll be here in a few minutes."

"Where is he taking you?"

I groaned loudly. "I hope you're getting the Spanish Inquisition out of your system now. We're going to play baseball with his family."

His face puckered, and then he finally chuckled. "*You're* playing baseball?"

"Well, I'll probably watch most of the time."

"You must really like this guy," he observed suspiciously.

I sighed and rolled my eyes for his benefit.

I heard the roar of an engine pull up in front of the house. I jumped up and started cleaning my dishes.

"Leave the dishes, I can do them tonight. You baby me too much."

The doorbell rang, and Charlie stalked off to answer it. I was half a step behind him.

I hadn't realized how hard it was pouring outside. Edward stood in the halo of the porch light, looking like a male model in an advertisement for raincoats.

"Come on in, Edward."

I breathed a sigh of relief when Charlie got his name right.

"Thanks, Chief Swan," Edward said in a respectful voice.

"Go ahead and call me Charlie. Here, I'll take your jacket."

"Thanks, sir."

"Have a seat there, Edward."

I grimaced.

Edward sat down fluidly in the only chair, forcing me to sit next to Chief Swan on the sofa. I quickly shot him a dirty look. He winked behind Charlie's back.

"So I hear you're getting my girl to watch baseball." Only in Washington would the fact that it was raining buckets have no bearing at all on the playing of outdoor sports.

"Yes, sir, that's the plan." He didn't look surprised that I'd told my father the truth. He might have been listening, though.

"Well, more power to you, I guess."

Charlie laughed, and Edward joined in.

"Okay." I stood up. "Enough humor at my expense. Let's go." I walked back to the hall and pulled on my jacket. They followed.

"Not too late, Bell."

"Don't worry, Charlie, I'll have her home early," Edward promised.

"You take care of my girl, all right?"

I groaned, but they ignored me.

"She'll be safe with me, I promise, sir."

Charlie couldn't doubt Edward's sincerity, it rang in every word.

I stalked out. They both laughed, and Edward followed me.

I stopped dead on the porch. There, behind my truck, was a monster Jeep. Its tires were higher than my waist. There were metal guards over the headlights and taillights, and four large spotlights attached to the crash bar. The hardtop was shiny red.

Charlie let out a low whistle.

"Wear your seat belts," he choked out.

Edward followed me around to my side and opened the door. I gauged the distance to the seat and prepared to jump for it. He sighed, and then lifted me in with one hand. I hoped Charlie didn't notice.

As he went around to the driver's side, at a normal, human pace, I tried to put on my seat belt. But there were too many buckles.

"What's all this?" I asked when he opened the door.

"It's an off-roading harness."

"Uh-oh."

I tried to find the right places for all the buckles to fit, but it wasn't going too quickly. He sighed again and reached over to help me. I was glad that the rain was too heavy to see Charlie clearly on the porch. That meant he couldn't see how Edward's hands lingered at my neck, brushed along my collarbones. I gave up trying to help him and focused on not hyperventilating.

Edward turned the key and the engine roared to life. We pulled away from the house.

"This is a . . . um . . . *big* Jeep you have."

"It's Emmett's. I didn't think you'd want to run the whole way."

"Where do you keep this thing?"

"We remodeled one of the outbuildings into a garage."

"Aren't you going to put on your seat belt?"

He threw me a disbelieving look.

Then something sunk in.

"Run the *whole* way? As in, we're still going to run part of the way?" My voice edged up a few octaves.

He grinned tightly. "You're not going to run."

"*I'm* going to be sick."

"Keep your eyes closed, you'll be fine."

I bit my lip, fighting the panic.

He leaned over to kiss the top of my head, and then groaned. I looked at him, puzzled.

"You smell so good in the rain," he explained.

"In a good way, or in a bad way?" I asked cautiously.

He sighed. "Both, always both."

I don't know how he found his way in the gloom and downpour, but he somehow found a side road that was less of a road and more of a mountain path. For a long while conversation was impossible, because I was bouncing up and down on the seat like a jackhammer. He seemed to enjoy the ride, though, smiling hugely the whole way.

And then we came to the end of the road; the trees formed green walls on three sides of the Jeep. The rain was a mere drizzle, slowing every second, the sky brighter through the clouds.

"Sorry, Bella, we have to go on foot from here."

"You know what? I'll just wait here."

"What happened to all your courage? You were extraordinary this morning."

"I haven't forgotten the last time yet." Could it have been only yesterday?

He was around to my side of the car in a blur. He started unbuckling me.

"I'll get those, you go on ahead," I protested.

"Hmmm . . . ," he mused as he quickly finished. "It seems I'm going to have to tamper with your memory."

Before I could react, he pulled me from the Jeep and set my feet on the ground. It was barely misting now; Alice was going to be right.

"Tamper with my memory?" I asked nervously.

"Something like that." He was watching me intently, carefully, but there was humor deep in his eyes. He placed his hands against the Jeep on either side of my head and leaned forward, forcing me to press back against the door. He leaned in even closer, his face inches from mine. I had no room to escape.

"Now," he breathed, and just his smell disturbed my thought processes, "what exactly are you worrying about?"

"Well, um, hitting a tree—" I gulped "—and dying. And then getting sick."

He fought back a smile. Then he bent his head down and touched his cold lips softly to the hollow at the base of my throat.

"Are you still worried now?" he murmured against my skin.

"Yes." I struggled to concentrate. "About hitting trees and getting sick."

His nose drew a line up the skin of my throat to the point of my chin. His cold breath tickled my skin.

"And now?" His lips whispered against my jaw.

"Trees," I gasped. "Motion sickness."

He lifted his face to kiss my eyelids. "Bella, you don't really think I would hit a tree, do you?"

"No, but *I* might." There was no confidence in my voice. He smelled an easy victory.

He kissed slowly down my cheek, stopping just at the corner of my mouth.

"Would I let a tree hurt you?" His lips barely brushed against my trembling lower lip.

"No," I breathed. I knew there was a second part to my brilliant defense, but I couldn't quite call it back.

"You see," he said, his lips moving against mine. "There's nothing to be afraid of, is there?"

"No," I sighed, giving up.

Then he took my face in his hands almost roughly, and kissed me in earnest, his unyielding lips moving against mine.

There really was no excuse for my behavior. Obviously I knew better by now. And yet I couldn't seem to stop from reacting exactly as I had the first time. Instead of keeping safely motionless, my arms reached up to twine tightly around his neck, and I was suddenly welded to his stone figure. I sighed, and my lips parted.

He staggered back, breaking my grip effortlessly.

"Damn it, Bella!" he broke off, gasping. "You'll be the death of me, I swear you will."

I leaned over, bracing my hands against my knees for support.

"You're indestructible," I mumbled, trying to catch my breath.

"I might have believed that before I met *you*. Now let's get out of here before I do something really stupid," he growled.

He threw me across his back as he had before, and I could see the extra effort it took for him to be as gentle as he was. I locked my legs around his waist and secured my arms in a choke hold around his neck.

"Don't forget to close your eyes," he warned severely.

I quickly tucked my face into his shoulder blade, under my own arm, and squeezed my eyes shut.

And I could hardly tell we were moving. I could feel him gliding along beneath me, but he could have been strolling down the sidewalk, the movement was so smooth. I was tempted to peek, just to see if he was really flying through the forest like before, but I resisted. It wasn't worth that awful dizziness. I contented myself with listening to his breath come and go evenly.

I wasn't quite sure we had stopped until he reached back and touched my hair.

"It's over, Bella."

I dared to open my eyes, and, sure enough, we were at a standstill. I stiffly unlocked my stranglehold on his body and slipped to the ground, landing on my backside.

"Oh!" I huffed as I hit the wet ground.

He stared at me incredulously, evidently not sure whether he was still too mad to find me funny. But my bewildered expression pushed him over the edge, and he broke into a roar of laughter.

I picked myself up, ignoring him as I brushed the mud and bracken off the back of my jacket. That only made him laugh harder. Annoyed, I began to stride off into the forest.

I felt his arm around my waist.

"Where are you going, Bella?"

"To watch a baseball game. You don't seem to be interested in playing anymore, but I'm sure the others will have fun without you."

"You're going the wrong way."

I turned around without looking at him, and stalked off in the opposite direction. He caught me again.

"Don't be mad, I couldn't help myself. You should have seen your face." He chuckled before he could stop himself.

"Oh, you're the only one who's allowed to get mad?" I asked, raising my eyebrows.

"I wasn't mad at you."

" 'Bella, you'll be the death of me'?" I quoted sourly.

"*That* was simply a statement of fact."

I tried to turn away from him again, but he held me fast.

"You were mad," I insisted.

"Yes."

"But you just said—"

"That I wasn't mad at *you*. Can't you see that, Bella?" He was suddenly intense, all trace of teasing gone. "Don't you understand?"

"See what?" I demanded, confused by his sudden mood swing as much as his words.

"I'm never angry with you—how could I be? Brave, trusting . . . warm as you are."

"Then why?" I whispered, remembering the black moods that pulled him away from me, that I'd always interpreted as well-justified frustration— frustration at my weakness, my slowness, my unruly human reactions. . . .

He put his hands carefully on both sides of my face. "I infuriate myself," he said gently. "The way I can't seem to keep from putting you in danger. My very existence puts you at risk. Sometimes I truly hate myself. I should be stronger, I should be able to—"

I placed my hand over his mouth. "Don't."

He took my hand, moving it from his lips, but holding it to his face.

"I love you," he said. "It's a poor excuse for what I'm doing, but it's still true."

It was the first time he'd said he loved me—in so many words. He might not realize it, but I certainly did.

"Now, please try to behave yourself," he continued, and he bent to softly brush his lips against mine.

I held properly still. Then I sighed.

"You promised Chief Swan that you would have me home early, remember? We'd better get going."

"Yes, ma'am."

He smiled wistfully and released all of me but one hand. He led me a few feet through the tall, wet ferns and draping moss, around a massive hemlock tree, and we were there, on the edge of an enormous open field in the lap of the Olympic peaks. It was twice the size of any baseball stadium.

I could see the others all there; Esme, Emmett, and Rosalie, sitting on a bare outcropping of rock, were the closest to us, maybe a hundred yards away. Much farther out I could see Jasper and Alice, at least a quarter of a mile apart, appearing to throw something back and forth, but I never saw any ball. It looked like Carlisle was marking bases, but could they really be that far apart?

When we came into view, the three on the rocks rose. Esme started toward us. Emmett followed after a long look at Rosalie's back; Rosalie had risen gracefully and strode off toward the field without a glance in our direction. My stomach quivered uneasily in response.

"Was that you we heard, Edward?" Esme asked as she approached.

"It sounded like a bear choking," Emmett clarified.

I smiled hesitantly at Esme. "That was him."

"Bella was being unintentionally funny," Edward explained, quickly settling the score.

Alice had left her position and was running, or dancing, toward us. She hurtled to a fluid stop at our feet. "It's time," she announced.

As soon as she spoke, a deep rumble of thunder shook the forest beyond us, and then crashed westward toward town.

"Eerie, isn't it?" Emmett said with easy familiarity, winking at me.

"Let's go." Alice reached for Emmett's hand and they darted toward the oversized field; she ran like a gazelle. He was nearly as graceful and just as fast—yet Emmett could never be compared to a gazelle.

"Are you ready for some ball?" Edward asked, his eyes eager, bright.

I tried to sound appropriately enthusiastic. "Go team!"

He snickered and, after mussing my hair, bounded off after the other two. His run was more aggressive, a cheetah rather than a gazelle, and he quickly overtook them. The grace and power took my breath away.

"Shall we go down?" Esme asked in her soft, melodic voice, and I realized I was staring openmouthed after him. I quickly reassembled my expression and nodded. Esme kept a few feet between us, and I wondered if she was still being careful not to frighten me. She matched her stride to mine without seeming impatient at the pace.

"You don't play with them?" I asked shyly.

"No, I prefer to referee—I like keeping them honest," she explained.

"Do they like to cheat, then?"

"Oh yes—you should hear the arguments they get into! Actually, I hope you don't, you would think they were raised by a pack of wolves."

"You sound like my mom," I laughed, surprised.

She laughed, too. "Well, I do think of them as my children in most ways. I never could get over my mothering instincts—did Edward tell you I had lost a child?"

"No," I murmured, stunned, scrambling to understand what lifetime she was remembering.

"Yes, my first and only baby. He died just a few days after he was born, the poor tiny thing," she sighed. "It broke my heart—that's why I jumped off the cliff, you know," she added matter-of-factly.

"Edward just said you f-fell," I stammered.

"Always the gentleman." She smiled. "Edward was the first of my new sons. I've always thought of him that way, even though he's older than I, in one way at least." She smiled at me warmly. "That's why I'm so happy that he's found you, dear." The endearment sounded very natural on her lips. "He's been the odd man out for far too long; it's hurt me to see him alone."

"You don't mind, then?" I asked, hesitant again. "That I'm . . . all wrong for him?"

"No." She was thoughtful. "You're what he wants. It will work out, somehow," she said, though her forehead creased with worry. Another peal of thunder began.

Esme stopped then; apparently, we'd reached the edge of the field. It looked as if they had formed teams. Edward was far out in left field, Carlisle stood between the first and second bases, and Alice held the ball, positioned on the spot that must be the pitcher's mound.

Emmett was swinging an aluminum bat; it whistled almost untraceably through the air. I waited for him to approach home plate, but then I realized, as he took his stance, that he was already there—farther from the pitcher's mound than I would have thought possible. Jasper stood several feet behind him, catching for the other team. Of course, none of them had gloves.

"All right," Esme called in a clear voice, which I knew even Edward would hear, as far out as he was. "Batter up."

Alice stood straight, deceptively motionless. Her style seemed to be stealth rather than an intimidating windup. She held the ball in both hands at her waist, and then, like the strike of a cobra, her right hand flicked out and the ball smacked into Jasper's hand.

"Was that a strike?" I whispered to Esme.

"If they don't hit it, it's a strike," she told me.

Jasper hurled the ball back to Alice's waiting hand. She permitted herself a brief grin. And then her hand spun out again.

This time the bat somehow made it around in time to smash into the invisible ball. The crack of impact was shattering, thunderous; it echoed off the mountains—I immediately understood the necessity of the thunderstorm.

The ball shot like a meteor above the field, flying deep into the surrounding forest.

"Home run," I murmured.

"Wait," Esme cautioned, listening intently, one hand raised. Emmett was a blur around the bases, Carlisle shadowing him. I realized Edward was missing.

"Out!" Esme cried in a clear voice. I stared in disbelief as Edward sprang from the fringe of the trees, ball in his upraised hand, his wide grin visible even to me.

"Emmett hits the hardest," Esme explained, "but Edward runs the fastest."

The inning continued before my incredulous eyes. It was impossible to keep up with the speed at which the ball flew, the rate at which their bodies raced around the field.

I learned the other reason they waited for a thunderstorm to play when Jasper, trying to avoid Edward's infallible fielding, hit a ground ball toward Carlisle. Carlisle ran into the ball, and then raced Jasper to first base. When they collided, the sound was like the crash of two massive falling boulders. I jumped up in concern, but they were somehow unscathed.

"Safe," Esme called in a calm voice.

Emmett's team was up by one—Rosalie managed to flit around the bases after tagging up on one of Emmett's long flies—when Edward caught the third out. He sprinted to my side, sparkling with excitement.

"What do you think?" he asked.

"One thing's for sure, I'll never be able to sit through dull old Major League Baseball again."

"And it sounds like you did so much of that before," he laughed.

"I am a little disappointed," I teased.

"Why?" he asked, puzzled.

"Well, it would be nice if I could find just one thing you didn't do better than everyone else on the planet."

He flashed his special crooked smile, leaving me breathless.

"I'm up," he said, heading for the plate.

He played intelligently, keeping the ball low, out of the reach of Rosalie's always-ready hand in the outfield, gaining two bases like lightning before Emmett could get the ball back in play. Carlisle knocked one so far out of the field—with a boom that hurt my ears—that he and Edward both made it in. Alice slapped them dainty high fives.

The score constantly changed as the game continued, and they razzed each other like any street ballplayers as they took turns with the lead. Occasionally Esme would call them to order. The thunder rumbled on, but we stayed dry, as Alice had predicted.

Carlisle was up to bat, Edward catching, when Alice suddenly gasped. My eyes were on Edward, as usual, and I saw his head snap up to look at her. Their eyes met and something flowed between them in an instant. He was at my side before the others could ask Alice what was wrong.

"Alice?" Esme's voice was tense.

"I didn't see—I couldn't tell," she whispered.

All the others were gathered by this time.

"What is it, Alice?" Carlisle asked with the calm voice of authority.

"They were traveling much quicker than I thought. I can see I had the perspective wrong before," she murmured.

Jasper leaned over her, his posture protective. "What changed?" he asked.

"They heard us playing, and it changed their path," she said, contrite, as if she felt responsible for whatever had frightened her.

Seven pairs of quick eyes flashed to my face and away.

"How soon?" Carlisle said, turning toward Edward.

A look of intense concentration crossed his face.

"Less than five minutes. They're running—they want to play." He scowled.

"Can you make it?" Carlisle asked him, his eyes flicking toward me again.

"No, not carrying—" He cut short. "Besides, the last thing we need is for them to catch the scent and start hunting."

"How many?" Emmett asked Alice.

"Three," she answered tersely.

"Three!" he scoffed. "Let them come." The steel bands of muscle flexed along his massive arms.

For a split second that seemed much longer than it really was, Carlisle deliberated. Only Emmett seemed unperturbed; the rest stared at Carlisle's face with anxious eyes.

"Let's just continue the game," Carlisle finally decided. His voice was cool and level. "Alice said they were simply curious."

All this was said in a flurry of words that lasted only a few seconds. I had listened carefully and caught most of it, though I couldn't hear what Esme now asked Edward with a silent vibration of her lips. I only saw the slight shake of his head and the look of relief on her face.

"You catch, Esme," he said. "I'll call it now." And he planted himself in front of me.

The others returned to the field, warily sweeping the dark forest with their sharp eyes. Alice and Esme seemed to orient themselves around where I stood.

"Take your hair down," Edward said in a low, even voice.

I obediently slid the rubber band out of my hair and shook it out around me.

I stated the obvious. "The others are coming now."

"Yes, stay very still, keep quiet, and don't move from my side, please." He hid the stress in his voice well, but I could hear it. He pulled my long hair forward, around my face.

"That won't help," Alice said softly. "I could smell her across the field."

"I know." A hint of frustration colored his tone.

Carlisle stood at the plate, and the others joined the game halfheartedly.

"What did Esme ask you?" I whispered.

He hesitated for a second before he answered. "Whether they were thirsty," he muttered unwillingly.

The seconds ticked by; the game progressed with apathy now. No one dared to hit harder than a bunt, and Emmett, Rosalie, and Jasper hovered in the infield. Now and again, despite the fear that numbed my brain, I was aware of Rosalie's eyes on me. They were expressionless, but something about the way she held her mouth made me think she was angry.

Edward paid no attention to the game at all, eyes and mind ranging the forest.

"I'm sorry, Bella," he muttered fiercely. "It was stupid, irresponsible, to expose you like this. I'm so sorry."

I heard his breath stop, and his eyes zeroed in on right field. He took a half step, angling himself between me and what was coming.

Carlisle, Emmett, and the others turned in the same direction, hearing sounds of passage much too faint for my ears.

18. THE HUNT

THEY EMERGED ONE BY ONE FROM THE FOREST EDGE, RANGING A DOZEN meters apart. The first male into the clearing fell back immediately, allowing the other male to take the front, orienting himself around the tall, dark-haired man in a manner that clearly displayed who led the pack. The third was a woman; from this distance, all I could see of her was that her hair was a startling shade of red.

They closed ranks before they continued cautiously toward Edward's family, exhibiting the natural respect of a troop of predators as it encounters a larger, unfamiliar group of its own kind.

As they approached, I could see how different they were from the Cullens. Their walk was catlike, a gait that seemed constantly on the edge of shifting into a crouch. They dressed in the ordinary gear of backpackers: jeans and casual button-down shirts in heavy, weatherproof fabrics. The clothes were frayed, though, with wear, and they were barefoot. Both men had cropped hair, but the woman's brilliant orange hair was filled with leaves and debris from the woods.

Their sharp eyes carefully took in the more polished, urbane stance of Carlisle, who, flanked by Emmett and Jasper, stepped guardedly forward to meet them. Without any seeming communication between them, they each straightened into a more casual, erect bearing.

The man in front was easily the most beautiful, his skin olive-toned beneath the typical pallor, his hair a glossy black. He was of a medium build, hard-muscled, of course, but nothing next to Emmett's brawn. He smiled an easy smile, exposing a flash of gleaming white teeth.

The woman was wilder, her eyes shifting restlessly between the men facing her, and the loose grouping around me, her chaotic hair quivering in the slight breeze. Her posture was distinctly feline. The second male hovered unobtrusively behind them, slighter than the leader, his light brown hair and regular features both nondescript. His eyes, though completely still, somehow seemed the most vigilant.

Their eyes were different, too. Not the gold or black I had come to expect, but a deep burgundy color that was disturbing and sinister.

The dark-haired man, still smiling, stepped toward Carlisle.

"We thought we heard a game," he said in a relaxed voice with the slightest of French accents. "I'm Laurent, these are Victoria and James." He gestured to the vampires beside him.

"I'm Carlisle. This is my family, Emmett and Jasper, Rosalie, Esme and Alice, Edward and Bella." He pointed us out in groups, deliberately not calling attention to individuals. I felt a shock when he said my name.

"Do you have room for a few more players?" Laurent asked sociably.

Carlisle matched Laurent's friendly tone. "Actually, we were just finishing up. But we'd certainly be interested another time. Are you planning to stay in the area for long?"

"We're headed north, in fact, but we were curious to see who was in the neighborhood. We haven't run into any company in a long time."

"No, this region is usually empty except for us and the occasional visitor, like yourselves."

The tense atmosphere had slowly subsided into a casual conversation; I guessed that Jasper was using his peculiar gift to control the situation.

"What's your hunting range?" Laurent casually inquired.

Carlisle ignored the assumption behind the inquiry. "The Olympic Range here, up and down the Coast Ranges on occasion. We keep a permanent residence nearby. There's another permanent settlement like ours up near Denali."

Laurent rocked back on his heels slightly.

"Permanent? How do you manage that?" There was honest curiosity in his voice.

"Why don't you come back to our home with us and we can talk comfortably?" Carlisle invited. "It's a rather long story."

James and Victoria exchanged a surprised look at the mention of the word "home," but Laurent controlled his expression better.

"That sounds very interesting, and welcome." His smile was genial. "We've been on the hunt all the way down from Ontario, and we haven't had the chance to clean up in a while." His eyes moved appreciatively over Carlisle's refined appearance.

"Please don't take offense, but we'd appreciate it if you'd refrain from hunting in this immediate area. We have to stay inconspicuous, you understand," Carlisle explained.

"Of course." Laurent nodded. "We certainly won't encroach on your territory. We just ate outside of Seattle, anyway," he laughed. A shiver ran up my spine.

"We'll show you the way if you'd like to run with us—Emmett and Alice, you can go with Edward and Bella to get the Jeep," he casually added.

Three things seemed to happen simultaneously while Carlisle was speaking. My hair ruffled with the light breeze, Edward stiffened, and the second male, James, suddenly whipped his head around, scrutinizing me, his nostrils flaring.

A swift rigidity fell on all of them as James lurched one step forward into a crouch. Edward bared his teeth, crouching in defense, a feral snarl ripping from his throat. It was nothing like the playful sounds I'd heard from him this morning; it was the single most menacing thing I had ever heard, and chills ran from the crown of my head to the back of my heels.

"What's this?" Laurent exclaimed in open surprise. Neither James nor Edward relaxed their aggressive poses. James feinted slightly to the side, and Edward shifted in response.

"She's with us." Carlisle's firm rebuff was directed toward James. Laurent seemed to catch my scent less powerfully than James, but awareness now dawned on his face.

"You brought a snack?" he asked, his expression incredulous as he took an involuntary step forward.

Edward snarled even more ferociously, harshly, his lip curling high above his glistening, bared teeth. Laurent stepped back again.

"I said she's with us," Carlisle corrected in a hard voice.

"But she's *human*," Laurent protested. The words were not at all aggressive, merely astounded.

"Yes." Emmett was very much in evidence at Carlisle's side, his eyes on James. James slowly straightened out of his crouch, but his eyes never left me, his nostrils still wide. Edward stayed tensed like a lion in front of me.

When Laurent spoke, his tone was soothing—trying to defuse the sudden hostility. "It appears we have a lot to learn about each other."

"Indeed." Carlisle's voice was still cool.

"But we'd like to accept your invitation." His eyes flicked toward me and back to Carlisle. "And, of course, we will not harm the human girl. We won't hunt in your range, as I said."

James glanced in disbelief and aggravation at Laurent and exchanged another brief look with Victoria, whose eyes still flickered edgily from face to face.

Carlisle measured Laurent's open expression for a moment before he spoke. "We'll show you the way. Jasper, Rosalie, Esme?" he called. They gathered together, blocking me from view as they converged. Alice was instantly at my side, and Emmett fell back slowly, his eyes locked on James as he backed toward us.

"Let's go, Bella." Edward's voice was low and bleak.

This whole time I'd been rooted in place, terrified into absolute immobility. Edward had to grip my elbow and pull sharply to break my trance. Alice and Emmett were close behind us, hiding me. I stumbled alongside Edward, still stunned with fear. I couldn't hear if the main group had left yet. Edward's impatience was almost tangible as we moved at human speed to the forest edge.

Once we were into the trees, Edward slung me over his back without breaking stride. I gripped as tightly as possible as he took off, the others close on his heels. I kept my head down, but my eyes, wide with fright, wouldn't close. They plunged through the now-black forest like wraiths. The sense of exhilaration that usually seemed to possess Edward as he ran was completely absent, replaced by a fury that consumed him and drove him still faster. Even with me on his back, the others trailed behind.

We reached the Jeep in an impossibly short time, and Edward barely slowed as he flung me in the backseat.

"Strap her in," he ordered Emmett, who slid in beside me.

Alice was already in the front seat, and Edward was starting the engine. It roared to life and we swerved backward, spinning around to face the winding road.

Edward was growling something too fast for me to understand, but it sounded a lot like a string of profanities.

The jolting trip was much worse this time, and the darkness only made it more frightening. Emmett and Alice both glared out the side windows.

We hit the main road, and though our speed increased, I could see much better where we were going. And we were headed south, away from Forks.

"Where are we going?" I asked.

No one answered. No one even looked at me.

"Dammit, Edward! Where are you taking me?"

"We have to get you away from here—far away—now." He didn't look back, his eyes on the road. The speedometer read a hundred and five miles an hour.

"Turn around! You have to take me home!" I shouted. I struggled with the stupid harness, tearing at the straps.

"Emmett," Edward said grimly.

And Emmett secured my hands in his steely grasp.

"No! Edward! No, you can't do this."

"I have to, Bella, now please be quiet."

"I won't! You have to take me back—Charlie will call the FBI! They'll be all over your family—Carlisle and Esme! They'll have to leave, to hide forever!"

"Calm down, Bella." His voice was cold. "We've been there before."

"Not over me, you don't! You're not ruining everything over me!" I struggled violently, with total futility.

Alice spoke for the first time. "Edward, pull over."

He flashed her a hard look, and then sped up.

"Edward, let's just talk this through."

"You don't understand," he roared in frustration. I'd never heard his voice so loud; it was deafening in the confines of the Jeep. The speedometer neared one hundred and fifteen. "He's a tracker, Alice, did you *see* that? He's a tracker!"

I felt Emmett stiffen next to me, and I wondered at his reaction to the word. It meant something more to the three of them than it did to me; I wanted to understand, but there was no opening for me to ask.

"Pull over, Edward." Alice's tone was reasonable, but there was a ring of authority in it I'd never heard before.

The speedometer inched past one-twenty.

"Do it, Edward."

"Listen to me, Alice. I saw his mind. Tracking is his passion, his obsession—and he wants her, Alice—*her,* specifically. He begins the hunt tonight."

"He doesn't know where—"

He interrupted her. "How long do you think it will take him to cross her scent in town? His plan was already set before the words were out of Laurent's mouth."

I gasped, knowing where my scent would lead. "Charlie! You can't leave him there! You can't leave him!" I thrashed against the harness.

"She's right," Alice said.

The car slowed slightly.

"Let's just look at our options for a minute," Alice coaxed.

The car slowed again, more noticeably, and then suddenly we screeched to a stop on the shoulder of the highway. I flew against the harness, and then slammed back into the seat.

"There are no options," Edward hissed.

"I'm not leaving Charlie!" I yelled.

He ignored me completely.

"We have to take her back," Emmett finally spoke.

"No." Edward was absolute.

"He's no match for us, Edward. He won't be able to touch her."

"He'll wait."

Emmett smiled. "I can wait, too."

"You didn't see—you don't understand. Once he commits to a hunt, he's unshakable. We'd have to kill him."

Emmett didn't seem upset by the idea. "That's an option."

"And the female. She's with him. If it turns into a fight, the leader will go with them, too."

"There are enough of us."

"There's another option," Alice said quietly.

Edward turned on her in fury, his voice a blistering snarl. "There—is—no—other—option!"

Emmett and I both stared at him in shock, but Alice seemed unsurprised. The silence lasted for a long minute as Edward and Alice stared each other down.

I broke it. "Does anyone want to hear my plan?"

"No," Edward growled. Alice glared at him, finally provoked.

"Listen," I pleaded. "You take me back."

"No," he interrupted.

I glared at him and continued. "You take me back. I tell my dad I want to go home to Phoenix. I pack my bags. We wait till this tracker is watching, and then we run. He'll follow us and leave Charlie alone. Charlie won't call the FBI on your family. Then you can take me any damned place you want."

They stared at me, stunned.

"It's not a bad idea, really." Emmett's surprise was definitely an insult.

"It might work—and we simply can't leave her father unprotected. You know that," Alice said.

Everyone looked at Edward.

"It's too dangerous—I don't want him within a hundred miles of her."

Emmett was supremely confident. "Edward, he's not getting through us."

Alice thought for a minute. "I don't see him attacking. He'll try to wait for us to leave her alone."

"It won't take long for him to realize that's not going to happen."

"I *demand* that you take me home." I tried to sound firm.

Edward pressed his fingers to his temples and squeezed his eyes shut.

"Please," I said in a much smaller voice.

He didn't look up. When he spoke, his voice sounded worn.

"You're leaving tonight, whether the tracker sees or not. You tell Charlie that you can't stand another minute in Forks. Tell him whatever story works. Pack the first things your hands touch, and then get in your truck. I don't care what he says to you. You have fifteen minutes. Do you hear me? Fifteen minutes from the time you cross the doorstep."

The Jeep rumbled to life, and he spun us around, the tires squealing. The needle on the speedometer started to race up the dial.

"Emmett?" I asked, looking pointedly at my hands.

"Oh, sorry." He let me loose.

A few minutes passed in silence, other than the roar of the engine. Then Edward spoke again.

"This is how it's going to happen. When we get to the house, if the tracker is not there, I will walk her to the door. Then she has fifteen minutes." He glared at me in the rearview mirror. "Emmett, you take the outside of the house. Alice, you get the truck. I'll be inside as long as she is. After she's out, you two can take the Jeep home and tell Carlisle."

"No way," Emmett broke in. "I'm with you."

"Think it through, Emmett. I don't know how long I'll be gone."

"Until we know how far this is going to go, I'm with you."

Edward sighed. "If the tracker *is* there," he continued grimly, "we keep driving."

"We're going to make it there before him," Alice said confidently.

Edward seemed to accept that. Whatever his problem with Alice was, he didn't doubt her now.

"What are we going to do with the Jeep?" she asked.

His voice had a hard edge. "You're driving it home."

"No, I'm not," she said calmly.

The unintelligible stream of profanities started again.

"We can't all fit in my truck," I whispered.

Edward didn't appear to hear me.

"I think you should let me go alone," I said even more quietly.

He heard that.

"Bella, please just do this my way, just this once," he said between clenched teeth.

"Listen, Charlie's not an imbecile," I protested. "If you're not in town tomorrow, he's going to get suspicious."

"That's irrelevant. We'll make sure he's safe, and that's all that matters."

"Then what about this tracker? He saw the way you acted tonight. He's going to think you're with me, wherever you are."

Emmett looked at me, insultingly surprised again. "Edward, listen to her," he urged. "I think she's right."

"Yes, she is," Alice agreed.

"I can't do that." Edward's voice was icy.

"Emmett should stay, too," I continued. "He definitely got an eyeful of Emmett."

"What?" Emmett turned on me.

"You'll get a better crack at him if you stay," Alice agreed.

Edward stared at her incredulously. "You think I should let her go alone?"

"Of course not," Alice said. "Jasper and I will take her."

"I can't do that," Edward repeated, but this time there was a trace of defeat in his voice. The logic was working on him.

I tried to be persuasive. "Hang out here for a week—" I saw his expression in the mirror and amended "—a few days. Let Charlie see you haven't kidnapped me, and lead this James on a wild-goose chase. Make sure he's completely off my trail. Then come and meet me. Take a roundabout route, of course, and then Jasper and Alice can go home."

I could see him beginning to consider it.

"Meet you where?"

"Phoenix." Of course.

"No. He'll hear that's where you're going," he said impatiently.

"And you'll make it look like that's a ruse, obviously. He'll know that we'll know that he's listening. He'll never believe I'm actually going where I say I am going."

"She's diabolical," Emmett chuckled.

"And if that doesn't work?"

"There are several million people in Phoenix," I informed him.

"It's not that hard to find a phone book."

"I won't go home."

"Oh?" he inquired, a dangerous note in his voice.

"I'm quite old enough to get my own place."

"Edward, we'll be with her," Alice reminded him.

"What are *you* going to do in *Phoenix?*" he asked her scathingly.

"Stay indoors."

"I kind of like it." Emmett was thinking about cornering James, no doubt.

"Shut up, Emmett."

"Look, if we try to take him down while she's still around, there's a much better chance that someone will get hurt—she'll get hurt, or you will, trying to protect her. Now, if we get him alone . . ." He trailed off with a slow smile. I was right.

The Jeep was crawling slowly along now as we drove into town. Despite my brave talk, I could feel the hairs on my arms standing up. I thought about Charlie, alone in the house, and tried to be courageous.

"Bella." Edward's voice was very soft. Alice and Emmett looked out their windows. "If you let anything happen to yourself—anything at all—I'm holding you personally responsible. Do you understand that?"

"Yes," I gulped.

He turned to Alice.

"Can Jasper handle this?"

"Give him some credit, Edward. He's been doing very, very well, all things considered."

"Can *you* handle this?" he asked.

And graceful little Alice pulled back her lips in a horrific grimace and let loose with a guttural snarl that had me cowering against the seat in terror.

Edward smiled at her. "But keep your opinions to yourself," he muttered suddenly.

19. GOODBYES

CHARLIE WAS WAITING UP FOR ME. ALL THE HOUSE LIGHTS WERE ON. MY mind was blank as I tried to think of a way to make him let me go. This wasn't going to be pleasant.

Edward pulled up slowly, staying well back from my truck. All three of them were acutely alert, ramrod straight in their seats, listening to every sound of the wood, looking through every shadow, catching every scent, searching for something out of place. The engine cut off, and I sat, motionless, as they continued to listen.

"He's not here," Edward said tensely. "Let's go."

Emmett reached over to help me get out of the harness. "Don't worry, Bella," he said in a low but cheerful voice, "we'll take care of things here quickly."

I felt moisture filling up my eyes as I looked at Emmett. I barely knew him, and yet, somehow, not knowing when I would see him again after tonight was anguishing. I knew this was just a faint taste of the goodbyes I would have to survive in the next hour, and the thought made the tears begin to spill.

"Alice, Emmett." Edward's voice was a command. They slithered soundlessly into the darkness, instantly disappearing. Edward opened my door and took my hand, then drew me into the protecting enclosure of his arm. He walked me swiftly toward the house, eyes always roving through the night.

"Fifteen minutes," he warned under his breath.

"I can do this." I sniffled. My tears had given me an inspiration.

I stopped on the porch and took hold of his face in my hands. I looked fiercely into his eyes.

"I love you," I said in a low, intense voice. "I will always love you, no matter what happens now."

"Nothing is going to happen to you, Bella," he said just as fiercely.

"Just follow the plan, okay? Keep Charlie safe for me. He's not going to like me very much after this, and I want to have the chance to apologize later."

"Get inside, Bella. We have to hurry." His voice was urgent.

"One more thing," I whispered passionately. "Don't listen to another word I say tonight!" He was leaning in, and so all I had to do was stretch up on my toes to kiss his surprised, frozen lips with as much force as I was capable of. Then I turned and kicked the door open.

"Go away, Edward!" I yelled at him, running inside and slamming the door shut in his still-shocked face.

"Bella?" Charlie had been hovering in the living room, and he was already on his feet.

"Leave me alone!" I screamed at him through my tears, which were flowing relentlessly now. I ran up the stairs to my room, throwing the door shut and locking it. I ran to my bed, flinging myself on the floor to retrieve my duffel bag. I reached swiftly between the mattress and box spring to grab the knotted old sock that contained my secret cash hoard.

Charlie was pounding on my door.

"Bella, are you okay? What's going on?" His voice was frightened.

"I'm going *home*," I shouted, my voice breaking in the perfect spot.

"Did he hurt you?" His tone edged toward anger.

"No!" I shrieked a few octaves higher. I turned to my dresser, and Edward was already there, silently yanking out armfuls of random clothes, which he proceeded to throw to me.

"Did he break up with you?" Charlie was perplexed.

"No!" I yelled, slightly more breathless as I shoved everything into the bag. Edward threw another drawer's contents at me. The bag was pretty much full now.

"What happened, Bella?" Charlie shouted through the door, pounding again.

"*I* broke up with *him*!" I shouted back, jerking on the zipper of my bag. Edward's capable hands pushed mine away and zipped it smoothly. He put the strap carefully over my arm.

"I'll be in the truck—go!" he whispered, and pushed me toward the door. He vanished out the window.

I unlocked the door and pushed past Charlie roughly, struggling with my heavy bag as I ran down the stairs.

"What happened?" he yelled. He was right behind me. "I thought you liked him."

He caught my elbow in the kitchen. Though he was still bewildered, his grip was firm.

He spun me around to look at him, and I could see in his face that he had no intention of letting me leave. I could think of only one way to escape, and it involved hurting him so much that I hated myself for even considering it. But I had no time, and I had to keep him safe.

I glared up at my father, fresh tears in my eyes for what I was about to do.

"I *do* like him—that's the problem. I can't do this anymore! I can't put down any more roots here! I don't want to end up trapped in this stupid, boring town like Mom! I'm not going to make the same dumb mistake she did. I hate it—I can't stay here another minute!"

His hand dropped from my arm like I'd electrocuted him. I turned away from his shocked, wounded face and headed for the door.

"Bells, you can't leave now. It's nighttime," he whispered behind me.

I didn't turn around. "I'll sleep in the truck if I get tired."

"Just wait another week," he pled, still shell-shocked. "Renée will be back by then."

This completely derailed me. "What?"

Charlie continued eagerly, almost babbling with relief as I hesitated. "She called while you were out. Things aren't going so well in Florida, and if Phil doesn't get signed by the end of the week, they're going back to Arizona. The assistant coach of the Sidewinders said they might have a spot for another shortstop."

I shook my head, trying to reassemble my now-confused thoughts. Every passing second put Charlie in more danger.

"I have a key," I muttered, turning the knob. He was too close, one hand extended toward me, his face dazed. I couldn't lose any more time arguing with him. I was going to have to hurt him further.

"Just let me go, Charlie." I repeated my mother's last words as she'd walked out this same door so many years ago. I said them as angrily as I could manage, and I threw the door open. "It didn't work out, okay? I really, really *hate* Forks!"

My cruel words did their job—Charlie stayed frozen on the doorstep, stunned, while I ran into the night. I was hideously frightened of the empty yard. I ran wildly for the truck, visualizing a dark shadow behind me. I threw my bag in the bed and wrenched the door open. The key was waiting in the ignition.

"I'll call you tomorrow!" I yelled, wishing more than anything that I could explain everything to him right then, knowing I would never be able to. I gunned the engine and peeled out.

Edward reached for my hand.

"Pull over," he said as the house, and Charlie, disappeared behind us.

"I can drive," I said through the tears pouring down my cheeks.

His long hands unexpectedly gripped my waist, and his foot pushed mine off the gas pedal. He pulled me across his lap, wrenching my hands free of the wheel, and suddenly he was in the driver's seat. The truck didn't swerve an inch.

"You wouldn't be able to find the house," he explained.

Lights flared suddenly behind us. I stared out the back window, eyes wide with horror.

"It's just Alice," he reassured me. He took my hand again.

My mind was filled with the image of Charlie in the doorway. "The tracker?"

"He heard the end of your performance," Edward said grimly.

"Charlie?" I asked in dread.

"The tracker followed us. He's running behind us now."

My body went cold.

"Can we outrun him?"

"No." But he sped up as he spoke. The truck's engine whined in protest.

My plan suddenly didn't feel so brilliant anymore.

I was staring back at Alice's headlights when the truck shuddered and a dark shadow sprung up outside the window.

My bloodcurdling scream lasted a fraction of a second before Edward's hand clamped down on my mouth.

"It's Emmett!"

He released my mouth, and wound his arm around my waist.

"It's okay, Bella," he promised. "You're going to be safe."

We raced through the quiet town toward the north highway.

"I didn't realize you were still so bored with small-town life," he said conversationally, and I knew he was trying to distract me. "It seemed like you were adjusting fairly well—especially recently. Maybe I was just flattering myself that I was making life more interesting for you."

"I wasn't being nice," I confessed, ignoring his attempt at diversion, looking down at my knees. "That was the same thing my mom said when she left him. You could say I was hitting below the belt."

"Don't worry. He'll forgive you." He smiled a little, though it didn't touch his eyes.

I stared at him desperately, and he saw the naked panic in my eyes.

"Bella, it's going to be all right."

"But it won't be all right when I'm not with you," I whispered.

"We'll be together again in a few days," he said, tightening his arm around me. "Don't forget that this was your idea."

"It was the best idea—of course it was mine."

His answering smile was bleak and disappeared immediately.

"Why did this happen?" I asked, my voice catching. "Why me?"

He stared blackly at the road ahead. "It's my fault—I was a fool to expose you like that." The rage in his voice was directed internally.

"That's not what I meant," I insisted. "I was there, big deal. It didn't bother the other two. Why did this James decide to kill *me*? There're people all over the place, why me?"

He hesitated, thinking before he answered.

"I got a good look at his mind tonight," he began in a low voice. "I'm not sure if there's anything I could have done to avoid this, once he saw you. It *is* partially your fault." His voice was wry. "If you didn't smell so appallingly luscious, he might not have bothered. But when I defended you . . .

well, that made it a lot worse. He's not used to being thwarted, no matter how insignificant the object. He thinks of himself as a hunter and nothing else. His existence is consumed with tracking, and a challenge is all he asks of life. Suddenly we've presented him with a beautiful challenge—a large clan of strong fighters all bent on protecting the one vulnerable element. You wouldn't believe how euphoric he is now. It's his favorite game, and we've just made it his most exciting game ever." His tone was full of disgust.

He paused a moment.

"But if I had stood by, he would have killed you right then," he said with hopeless frustration.

"I thought . . . I didn't smell the same to the others . . . as I do to you," I said hesitantly.

"You don't. But that doesn't mean that you aren't still a temptation to every one of them. If you *had* appealed to the tracker—or any of them—the same way you appeal to me, it would have meant a fight right there."

I shuddered.

"I don't think I have any choice but to kill him now," he muttered. "Carlisle won't like it."

I could hear the tires cross the bridge, though I couldn't see the river in the dark. I knew we were getting close. I had to ask him now.

"How can you kill a vampire?"

He glanced at me with unreadable eyes and his voice was suddenly harsh. "The only way to be sure is to tear him to shreds, and then burn the pieces."

"And the other two will fight with him?"

"The woman will. I'm not sure about Laurent. They don't have a very strong bond—he's only with them for convenience. He was embarrassed by James in the meadow. . . ."

"But James and the woman—they'll try to kill you?" I asked, my voice raw.

"Bella, don't you *dare* waste time worrying about me. Your only concern is keeping yourself safe and—please, please—*trying* not to be reckless."

"Is he still following?"

"Yes. He won't attack the house, though. Not tonight."

He turned off onto the invisible drive, with Alice following behind.

We drove right up to the house. The lights inside were bright, but they did little to alleviate the blackness of the encroaching forest. Emmett had my door open before the truck was stopped; he pulled me out of the seat, tucked me like a football into his vast chest, and ran me through the door.

We burst into the large white room, Edward and Alice at our sides. All of them were there; they were already on their feet at the sound of our approach. Laurent stood in their midst. I could hear low growls rumble deep in Emmett's throat as he set me down next to Edward.

"He's tracking us," Edward announced, glaring balefully at Laurent.

Laurent's face was unhappy. "I was afraid of that."

Alice danced to Jasper's side and whispered in his ear; her lips quivered with the speed of her silent speech. They flew up the stairs together. Rosalie watched them, and then moved quickly to Emmett's side. Her beautiful eyes were intense and—when they flickered unwillingly to my face—furious.

"What will he do?" Carlisle asked Laurent in chilling tones.

"I'm sorry," he answered. "I was afraid, when your boy there defended her, that it would set him off."

"Can you stop him?"

Laurent shook his head. "Nothing stops James when he gets started."

"We'll stop him," Emmett promised. There was no doubt what he meant.

"You can't bring him down. I've never seen anything like him in my three hundred years. He's absolutely lethal. That's why I joined his coven."

His coven, I thought, of course. The show of leadership in the clearing was merely that, a show.

Laurent was shaking his head. He glanced at me, perplexed, and back to Carlisle. "Are you sure it's worth it?"

Edward's enraged roar filled the room; Laurent cringed back.

Carlisle looked gravely at Laurent. "I'm afraid you're going to have to make a choice."

Laurent understood. He deliberated for a moment. His eyes took in every face, and finally swept the bright room.

"I'm intrigued by the life you've created here. But I won't get in the middle of this. I bear none of you any enmity, but I won't go up against James. I think I will head north—to that clan in Denali." He hesitated. "Don't underestimate James. He's got a brilliant mind and unparalleled senses. He's every bit as comfortable in the human world as you seem to be, and he won't come at you head on. . . . I'm sorry for what's been unleashed here. Truly sorry." He bowed his head, but I saw him flicker another puzzled look at me.

"Go in peace," was Carlisle's formal answer.

Laurent took another long look around himself, and then he hurried out the door.

The silence lasted less than a second.

"How close?" Carlisle looked to Edward.

Esme was already moving; her hand touched an inconspicuous keypad on the wall, and with a groan, huge metal shutters began sealing up the glass wall. I gaped.

"About three miles out past the river; he's circling around to meet up with the female."

"What's the plan?"

"We'll lead him off, and then Jasper and Alice will run her south."

"And then?"

Edward's tone was deadly. "As soon as Bella is clear, we hunt him."

"I guess there's no other choice," Carlisle agreed, his face grim.

Edward turned to Rosalie.

"Get her upstairs and trade clothes," Edward commanded. She stared back at him with livid disbelief.

"Why should I?" she hissed. "What is she to me? Except a menace—a danger you've chosen to inflict on all of us."

I flinched back from the venom in her voice.

"Rose . . . ," Emmett murmured, putting one hand on her shoulder. She shook it off.

But I was watching Edward carefully, knowing his temper, worried about his reaction.

He surprised me. He looked away from Rosalie as if she hadn't spoken, as if she didn't exist.

"Esme?" he asked calmly.

"Of course," Esme murmured.

Esme was at my side in half a heartbeat, swinging me up easily into her arms, and dashing up the stairs before I could gasp in shock.

"What are we doing?" I asked breathlessly as she set me down in a dark room somewhere off the second-story hall.

"Trying to confuse the smell. It won't work for long, but it might help get you out." I could hear her clothes falling to the floor.

"I don't think I'll fit..." I hesitated, but her hands were abruptly pulling my shirt over my head. I quickly stripped my jeans off myself. She handed me something, it felt like a shirt. I struggled to get my arms through the right holes. As soon as I was done she handed me her slacks. I yanked them on, but I couldn't get my feet out; they were too long. She deftly rolled the hems a few times so I could stand. Somehow she was already in my clothes. She pulled me back to the stairs, where Alice stood, a small leather bag in one hand. They each grabbed one of my elbows and half-carried me as they flew down the stairs.

It appeared that everything had been settled downstairs in our absence. Edward and Emmett were ready to leave, Emmett carrying a heavy-looking backpack over his shoulder. Carlisle was handing something small to Esme. He turned and handed Alice the same thing—it was a tiny silver cell phone.

"Esme and Rosalie will be taking your truck, Bella," he told me as he passed. I nodded, glancing warily at Rosalie. She was glowering at Carlisle with a resentful expression.

"Alice, Jasper—take the Mercedes. You'll need the dark tint in the south." They nodded as well.

"We're taking the Jeep."

I was surprised to see that Carlisle intended to go with Edward. I realized suddenly, with a stab of fear, that they made up the hunting party.

"Alice," Carlisle asked, "will they take the bait?"

Everyone watched Alice as she closed her eyes and became incredibly still.

Finally her eyes opened. "He'll track you. The woman will follow the truck. We should be able to leave after that." Her voice was certain.

"Let's go." Carlisle began to walk toward the kitchen.

But Edward was at my side at once. He caught me up in his iron grip, crushing me to him. He seemed unaware of his watching family as he pulled my face to his, lifting my feet off the floor. For the shortest second, his lips were icy and hard against mine. Then it was over. He set me down, still holding my face, his glorious eyes burning into mine.

His eyes went blank, curiously dead, as he turned away.

And they were gone.

We stood there, the others looking away from me as the tears streaked noiselessly down my face.

The silent moment dragged on, and then Esme's phone vibrated in her hand. It flashed to her ear.

"Now," she said. Rosalie stalked out the front door without another glance in my direction, but Esme touched my cheek as she passed.

"Be safe." Her whisper lingered behind them as they slipped out the door. I heard my truck start thunderously, and then fade away.

Jasper and Alice waited. Alice's phone seemed to be at her ear before it buzzed.

"Edward says the woman is on Esme's trail. I'll get the car." She vanished into the shadows the way Edward had gone.

Jasper and I looked at each other. He stood across the length of the entry-way from me . . . being careful.

"You're wrong, you know," he said quietly.

"What?" I gasped.

"I can feel what you're feeling now—and you *are* worth it."

"I'm not," I mumbled. "If anything happens to them, it will be for nothing."

"You're wrong," he repeated, smiling kindly at me.

I heard nothing, but then Alice stepped through the front door and came toward me with her arms held out.

"May I?" she asked.

"You're the first one to ask permission." I smiled wryly.

She lifted me in her slender arms as easily as Emmett had, shielding me protectively, and then we flew out the door, leaving the lights bright behind us.

20. IMPATIENCE

WHEN I WOKE UP I WAS CONFUSED. MY THOUGHTS WERE HAZY, STILL twisted up in dreams and nightmares; it took me longer than it should have to realize where I was.

This room was too bland to belong anywhere but in a hotel. The bedside lamps, bolted to the tables, were a dead giveaway, as were the long drapes made from the same fabric as the bedspread, and the generic watercolor prints on the walls.

I tried to remember how I got here, but nothing came at first.

I did remember the sleek black car, the glass in the windows darker than that on a limousine. The engine was almost silent, though we'd raced across the black freeways at more than twice the legal speed.

And I remembered Alice sitting with me on the dark leather backseat. Somehow, during the long night, my head had ended up against her granite neck. My closeness didn't seem to bother her at all, and her cool, hard skin was oddly comforting to me. The front of her thin cotton shirt was cold, damp with the tears that streamed from my eyes until, red and sore, they ran dry.

Sleep had evaded me; my aching eyes strained open even though the night finally ended and dawn broke over a low peak somewhere in California. The gray light, streaking across the cloudless sky, stung my eyes. But I couldn't close them; when I did, the images that flashed all too vividly, like still slides behind my lids, were unbearable. Charlie's broken expression—Edward's brutal snarl, teeth bared—Rosalie's resentful glare—the keen-eyed scrutiny of the tracker—the dead look in Edward's eyes after he kissed me the last time...I couldn't stand to see them. So I fought against my weariness and the sun rose higher.

I was still awake when we came through a shallow mountain pass and the sun, behind us now, reflected off the tiled rooftops of the Valley of the Sun. I didn't have enough emotion left to be surprised that we'd made a three-day journey in one. I stared blankly at the wide, flat expanse laid out in front of me. Phoenix—the palm trees, the scrubby creosote, the haphazard lines of the intersecting freeways, the green swaths of golf courses and turquoise splotches of swimming pools, all submerged in a thin smog and embraced by the short, rocky ridges that weren't really big enough to be called mountains.

The shadows of the palm trees slanted across the freeway—defined, sharper than I remembered, paler than they should be. Nothing could hide in these shadows. The bright, open freeway seemed benign enough. But I felt no relief, no sense of homecoming.

"Which way to the airport, Bella?" Jasper had asked, and I flinched, though his voice was quite soft and unalarming. It was the first sound, besides the purr of the car, to break the long night's silence.

"Stay on the I-ten," I'd answered automatically. "We'll pass right by it."

My brain had worked slowly through the fog of sleep deprivation.

"Are we flying somewhere?" I'd asked Alice.

"No, but it's better to be close, just in case."

I remembered beginning the loop around Sky Harbor International... but not ending it. I suppose that must have been when I'd fallen asleep.

Though, now that I'd chased the memories down, I did have a vague impression of leaving the car—the sun was just falling behind the horizon—my arm draped over Alice's shoulder and her arm firm around my waist, dragging me along as I stumbled through the warm, dry shadows.

I had no memory of this room.

I looked at the digital clock on the nightstand. The red numbers claimed it was three o'clock, but they gave no indication if it was night or day. No edge of light escaped the thick curtains, but the room was bright with the light from the lamps.

I rose stiffly and staggered to the window, pulling back the drapes.

It was dark outside. Three in the morning, then. My room looked out on a deserted section of the freeway and the new long-term parking garage for the airport. It was slightly comforting to be able to pinpoint time and place.

I looked down at myself. I was still wearing Esme's clothes, and they didn't fit very well at all. I looked around the room, glad when I discovered my duffel bag on top of the low dresser.

I was on my way to find new clothes when a light tap on the door made me jump.

"Can I come in?" Alice asked.

I took a deep breath. "Sure."

She walked in, and looked me over cautiously. "You look like you could sleep longer," she said.

I just shook my head.

She drifted silently to the curtains and closed them securely before turning back to me.

"We'll need to stay inside," she told me.

"Okay." My voice was hoarse; it cracked.

"Thirsty?" she asked.

I shrugged. "I'm okay. How about you?"

"Nothing unmanageable." She smiled. "I ordered some food for you, it's in the front room. Edward reminded me that you have to eat a lot more frequently than we do."

I was instantly more alert. "He called?"

"No," she said, and watched as my face fell. "It was before we left."

She took my hand carefully and led me through the door into the living room of the hotel suite. I could hear a low buzz of voices coming from the TV. Jasper sat motionlessly at the desk in the corner, his eyes watching the news with no glimmer of interest.

I sat on the floor next to the coffee table, where a tray of food waited, and began picking at it without noticing what I was eating.

Alice perched on the arm of the sofa and stared blankly at the TV like Jasper.

I ate slowly, watching her, turning now and then to glance quickly at Jasper. It began to dawn on me that they were too still. They never looked away from the screen, though commercials were playing now. I pushed the tray away, my stomach abruptly uneasy. Alice looked down at me.

"What's wrong, Alice?" I asked.

"Nothing's wrong." Her eyes were wide, honest . . . and I didn't trust them.

"What do we do now?"

"We wait for Carlisle to call."

"And should he have called by now?" I could see that I was near the mark. Alice's eyes flitted from mine to the phone on top of her leather bag and back.

"What does that mean?" My voice quavered, and I fought to control it. "That he hasn't called yet?"

"It just means that they don't have anything to tell us." But her voice was too even, and the air was harder to breathe.

Jasper was suddenly beside Alice, closer to me than usual.

"Bella," he said in a suspiciously soothing voice. "You have nothing to worry about. You are completely safe here."

"I know that."

"Then why are you frightened?" he asked, confused. He might feel the tenor of my emotions, but he couldn't read the reasons behind them.

"You heard what Laurent said." My voice was just a whisper, but I was sure they could hear me. "He said James was lethal. What if something goes wrong, and they get separated? If something happens to any of them, Carlisle, Emmett . . . Edward . . ." I gulped. "If that wild female hurts Esme . . ." My voice had grown higher, a note of hysteria beginning to rise in it. "How could I live with myself when it's my fault? None of you should be risking yourselves for me—"

"Bella, Bella, stop," he interrupted me, his words pouring out so quickly they were hard to understand. "You're worrying about all the wrong things, Bella. Trust me on this—none of us are in jeopardy. You are under too much strain as it is; don't add to it with wholly unnecessary worries. Listen to me!" he ordered, for I had looked away. "Our family is strong. Our only fear is losing you."

"But why should you—"

Alice interrupted this time, touching my cheek with her cold fingers. "It's been almost a century that Edward's been alone. Now he's found you. You can't see the changes that we see, we who have been with him for so long. Do you think any of us want to look into his eyes for the next hundred years if he loses you?"

My guilt slowly subsided as I looked into her dark eyes. But, even as the calm spread over me, I knew I couldn't trust my feelings with Jasper there.

It was a very long day.

We stayed in the room. Alice called down to the front desk and asked them to ignore our maid service for now. The windows stayed shut, the TV on, though no one watched it. At regular intervals, food was delivered for me. The silver phone resting on Alice's bag seemed to grow bigger as the hours passed.

My babysitters handled the suspense better than I did. As I fidgeted and paced, they simply grew more still, two statues whose eyes followed me imperceptibly as I moved. I occupied myself with memorizing the room; the striped pattern of the couches, tan, peach, cream, dull gold, and tan again. Sometimes I stared at the abstract prints, randomly finding pictures in the shapes, like I'd found pictures in the clouds as a child. I traced a blue hand, a woman combing her hair, a cat stretching. But when the pale red circle became a staring eye, I looked away.

As the afternoon wore on, I went back to bed, simply for something to do. I hoped that by myself in the dark, I could give in to the terrible fears that hovered on the edge of my consciousness, unable to break through under Jasper's careful supervision.

But Alice followed me casually, as if by some coincidence she had grown tired of the front room at the same time. I was beginning to wonder exactly what sort of instructions Edward had given her. I lay across the bed, and she sat, legs folded, next to me. I ignored her at first, suddenly tired enough to sleep. But after a few minutes, the panic that had held off in Jasper's presence began to make itself known. I gave up on the idea of sleep quickly then, curling up into a small ball, wrapping my arms around my legs.

"Alice?" I asked.

"Yes?"

I kept my voice very calm. "What do you think they're doing?"

"Carlisle wanted to lead the tracker as far north as possible, wait for him to get close, and then turn and ambush him. Esme and Rosalie were supposed to head west as long as they could keep the female behind them. If she turned around, they were to head back to Forks and keep an eye on your dad. So I imagine things are going well if they can't call. It means the tracker is close enough that they don't want him to overhear."

"And Esme?"

"I think she must be back in Forks. She won't call if there's any chance the female will overhear. I expect they're all just being very careful."

"Do you think they're safe, really?"

"Bella, how many times do we have to tell you that there's no danger to us?"

"Would you tell me the truth, though?"

"Yes. I will always tell you the truth." Her voice was earnest.

I deliberated for a moment, and decided she meant it.

"Tell me then . . . how do you become a vampire?"

My question caught her off guard. She was quiet. I rolled over to look at her, and her expression seemed ambivalent.

"Edward doesn't want me to tell you that," she said firmly, but I sensed she didn't agree.

"That's not fair. I think I have a right to know."

"I know."

I looked at her, waiting.

She sighed. "He'll be *extremely* angry."

"It's none of his business. This is between you and me. Alice, as a friend, I'm begging you." And we were friends now, somehow—as she must have known we would be all along.

She looked at me with her splendid, wise eyes . . . choosing.

"I'll tell you the mechanics of it," she said finally, "but I don't remember it myself, and I've never done it or seen it done, so keep in mind that I can only tell you the theory."

I waited.

"As predators, we have a glut of weapons in our physical arsenal—much, much more than really necessary. The strength, the speed, the acute senses, not to mention those of us like Edward, Jasper, and I, who have extra senses as well. And then, like a carnivorous flower, we are physically attractive to our prey."

I was very still, remembering how pointedly Edward had demonstrated the same concept for me in the meadow.

She smiled a wide, ominous smile. "We have another fairly superfluous weapon. We're also venomous," she said, her teeth glistening. "The venom doesn't kill—it's merely incapacitating. It works slowly, spreading through the bloodstream, so that, once bitten, our prey is in too much physical pain to escape us. Mostly superfluous, as I said. If we're that close, the prey doesn't escape. Of course, there are always exceptions. Carlisle, for example."

"So...if the venom is left to spread...," I murmured.

"It takes a few days for the transformation to be complete, depending on how much venom is in the bloodstream, how close the venom enters to the heart. As long as the heart keeps beating, the poison spreads, healing, changing the body as it moves through it. Eventually the heart stops, and the conversion is finished. But all that time, every minute of it, a victim would be wishing for death."

I shivered.

"It's not pleasant, you see."

"Edward said that it was very hard to do...I don't quite understand," I said.

"We're also like sharks in a way. Once we taste the blood, or even smell it for that matter, it becomes very hard to keep from feeding. Sometimes impossible. So you see, to actually bite someone, to taste the blood, it would begin the frenzy. It's difficult on both sides—the bloodlust on the one hand, the awful pain on the other."

"Why do you think you don't remember?"

"I don't know. For everyone else, the pain of transformation is the sharpest memory they have of their human life. I remember nothing of being human." Her voice was wistful.

We lay silently, wrapped in our individual meditations.

The seconds ticked by, and I had almost forgotten her presence, I was so enveloped in my thoughts.

Then, without any warning, Alice leaped from the bed, landing lightly on her feet. My head jerked up as I stared at her, startled.

"Something's changed." Her voice was urgent, and she wasn't talking to me anymore.

She reached the door at the same time Jasper did. He had obviously heard our conversation and her sudden exclamation. He put his hands on her shoulders and guided her back to the bed, sitting her on the edge.

"What do you see?" he asked intently, staring into her eyes. Her eyes were focused on something very far away. I sat close to her, leaning in to catch her low, quick voice.

"I see a room. It's long, and there are mirrors everywhere. The floor is wooden. He's in the room, and he's waiting. There's gold...a gold stripe across the mirrors."

"Where is the room?"

"I don't know. Something is missing—another decision hasn't been made yet."

"How much time?"

"It's soon. He'll be in the mirror room today, or maybe tomorrow. It all depends. He's waiting for something. And he's in the dark now."

Jasper's voice was calm, methodical, as he questioned her in a practiced way. "What is he doing?"

"He's watching TV...no, he's running a VCR, in the dark, in another place."

"Can you see where he is?"

"No, it's too dark."

"And the mirror room, what else is there?"

"Just the mirrors, and the gold. It's a band, around the room. And there's a black table with a big stereo, and a TV. He's touching the VCR there, but he doesn't watch the way he does in the dark room. This is the room where he waits." Her eyes drifted, then focused on Jasper's face.

"There's nothing else?"

She shook her head. They looked at each other, motionless.

"What does it mean?" I asked.

Neither of them answered for a moment, then Jasper looked at me.

"It means the tracker's plans have changed. He's made a decision that will lead him to the mirror room, and the dark room."

"But we don't know where those rooms are?"

"No."

"But we do know that he won't be in the mountains north of Washington, being hunted. He'll elude them." Alice's voice was bleak.

"Should we call?" I asked. They traded a serious look, undecided.

And the phone rang.

Alice was across the room before I could lift my head to look at it.

She pushed a button and held the phone to her ear, but she didn't speak first.

"Carlisle," she breathed. She didn't seem surprised or relieved, the way I felt.

"Yes," she said, glancing at me. She listened for a long moment.

"I just saw him." She described again the vision she'd seen. "Whatever made him get on that plane...it was leading him to those rooms." She paused. "Yes," Alice said into the phone, and then she spoke to me. "Bella?"

She held the phone out toward me. I ran to it.

"Hello?" I breathed.

"Bella," Edward said.

"Oh, Edward! I was so worried."

"Bella," he sighed in frustration, "I told you not to worry about anything but yourself." It was so unbelievably good to hear his voice. I felt the hovering cloud of despair lighten and drift back as he spoke.

"Where are you?"

"We're outside of Vancouver. Bella, I'm sorry—we lost him. He seems suspicious of us—he's careful to stay just far enough away that I can't hear what he's thinking. But he's gone now—it looks like he got on a plane. We think he's heading back to Forks to start over." I could hear Alice filling in Jasper behind me, her quick words blurring together into a humming noise.

"I know. Alice saw that he got away."

"You don't have to worry, though. He won't find anything to lead him to you. You just have to stay there and wait till we find him again."

"I'll be fine. Is Esme with Charlie?"

"Yes—the female has been in town. She went to the house, but while Charlie was at work. She hasn't gone near him, so don't be afraid. He's safe with Esme and Rosalie watching."

"What is she doing?"

"Probably trying to pick up the trail. She's been all through the town during the night. Rosalie traced her through the airport, all the roads around town, the school . . . she's digging, Bella, but there's nothing to find."

"And you're sure Charlie's safe?"

"Yes, Esme won't let him out of her sight. And we'll be there soon. If the tracker gets anywhere near Forks, we'll have him."

"I miss you," I whispered.

"I know, Bella. Believe me, I know. It's like you've taken half my self away with you."

"Come and get it, then," I challenged.

"Soon, as soon as I possibly can. I *will* make you safe first." His voice was hard.

"I love you," I reminded him.

"Could you believe that, despite everything I've put you through, I love you, too?"

"Yes, I can, actually."

"I'll come for you soon."

"I'll be waiting."

As soon as the phone went dead, the cloud of depression began to creep over me again.

I turned to give the phone back to Alice and found her and Jasper bent over the table, where Alice was sketching on a piece of hotel stationery. I leaned on the back of the couch, looking over her shoulder.

She drew a room: long, rectangular, with a thinner, square section at the back. The wooden planks that made up the floor stretched lengthwise across the room. Down the walls were lines denoting the breaks in the mirrors. And then, wrapping around the walls, waist high, a long band. The band Alice said was gold.

"It's a ballet studio," I said, suddenly recognizing the familiar shapes.

They looked at me, surprised.

"Do you know this room?" Jasper's voice sounded calm, but there was an undercurrent of something I couldn't identify. Alice bent her head to her work, her hand flying across the page now, the shape of an emergency exit taking shape against the back wall, the stereo and TV on a low table by the front right corner.

"It looks like a place I used to go for dance lessons—when I was eight or nine. It was shaped just the same." I touched the page where the square section jutted out, narrowing the back part of the room. "That's where the bathrooms were—the doors were through the other dance floor. But the stereo was here"—I pointed to the left corner—"it was older, and there wasn't a TV. There was a window in the waiting room—you would see the room from this perspective if you looked through it."

Alice and Jasper were staring at me.

"Are you sure it's the same room?" Jasper asked, still calm.

"No, not at all—I suppose most dance studios would look the same—the mirrors, the bar." I traced my finger along the ballet bar set against the mirrors. "It's just the shape that looked familiar." I touched the door, set in exactly the same place as the one I remembered.

"Would you have any reason to go there now?" Alice asked, breaking my reverie.

"No, I haven't been there in almost ten years. I was a terrible dancer—they always put me in the back for recitals," I admitted.

"So there's no way it could be connected with you?" Alice asked intently.

"No, I don't even think the same person owns it. I'm sure it's just another dance studio, somewhere."

"Where was the studio you went to?" Jasper asked in a casual voice.

"It was just around the corner from my mom's house. I used to walk there after school...," I said, my voice trailing off. I didn't miss the look they exchanged.

"Here in Phoenix, then?" His voice was still casual.

"Yes," I whispered. "Fifty-eighth Street and Cactus."

We all sat in silence, staring at the drawing.

"Alice, is that phone safe?"

"Yes," she reassured me. "The number would just trace back to Washington."

"Then I can use it to call my mom."

"I thought she was in Florida."

"She is—but she's coming home soon, and she can't come back to that house while..." My voice trembled. I was thinking about something Edward had said, about the red-haired female at Charlie's house, at the school, where my records would be.

"How will you reach her?"

"They don't have a permanent number except at the house—she's supposed to check her messages regularly."

"Jasper?" Alice asked.

He thought about it. "I don't think there's any way it could hurt—be sure you don't say where you are, of course."

I reached eagerly for the phone and dialed the familiar number. It rang four times, and then I heard my mom's breezy voice telling me to leave a message.

"Mom," I said after the beep, "it's me. Listen, I need you to do something. It's important. As soon as you get this message, call me at this number." Alice was already at my side, writing the number for me on the bottom of her picture. I read it carefully, twice. "Please don't go anywhere until you talk to me. Don't worry, I'm okay, but I have to talk to you right away, no matter how late you get this call, all right? I love you, Mom. Bye." I closed my eyes and prayed with all my might that no unforeseen change of plans would bring her home before she got my message.

I settled into the sofa, nibbling on a plate of leftover fruit, anticipating a long evening. I thought about calling Charlie, but I wasn't sure if I should be home by now or not. I concentrated on the news, watching out for stories about Florida, or about spring training—strikes or hurricanes or terrorist attacks—anything that might send them home early.

Immortality must grant endless patience. Neither Jasper nor Alice seemed to feel the need to do anything at all. For a while, Alice sketched the vague outline of the dark room from her vision, as much as she could see in the light from the TV. But when she was done, she simply sat, looking at the blank walls with her timeless eyes. Jasper, too, seemed to have no urge to pace, or peek through the curtains, or run screaming out the door, the way I did.

I must have fallen asleep on the couch, waiting for the phone to ring again. The touch of Alice's cold hands woke me briefly as she carried me to the bed, but I was unconscious again before my head hit the pillow.

21. PHONE CALL

I COULD FEEL IT WAS TOO EARLY AGAIN WHEN I WOKE, AND I KNEW I WAS getting the schedule of my days and nights slowly reversed. I lay in my bed and listened to the quiet voices of Alice and Jasper in the other room. That they were loud enough for me to hear at all was strange. I rolled till my feet touched the floor and then staggered to the living room.

The clock on the TV said it was just after two in the morning. Alice and Jasper were sitting together on the sofa, Alice sketching again while Jasper looked over her shoulder. They didn't look up when I entered, too engrossed in Alice's work.

I crept to Jasper's side to peek.

"Did she see something more?" I asked him quietly.

"Yes. Something's brought him back to the room with the VCR, but it's light now."

I watched as Alice drew a square room with dark beams across its low ceiling. The walls were paneled in wood, a little too dark, out of date. The floor had a dark carpet with a pattern in it. There was a large window against the south wall, and an opening through the west wall led to the living room. One side of that entrance was stone—a large tan stone fireplace that was open to both rooms. The focus of the room from this perspective, the TV and VCR, balanced on a too-small wooden stand, were in the southwest corner of the room. An aged sectional sofa curved around in front of the TV, a round coffee table in front of it.

"The phone goes there," I whispered, pointing.

Two pairs of eternal eyes stared at me.

"That's my mother's house."

Alice was already off the couch, phone in hand, dialing. I stared at the precise rendering of my mother's family room. Uncharacteristically, Jasper slid closer to me. He lightly touched his hand to my shoulder, and the physical contact seemed to make his calming influence stronger. The panic stayed dull, unfocused.

Alice's lips were trembling with the speed of her words, the low buzzing impossible to decipher. I couldn't concentrate.

"Bella," Alice said. I looked at her numbly.

"Bella, Edward is coming to get you. He and Emmett and Carlisle are going to take you somewhere, to hide you for a while."

"Edward is coming?" The words were like a life vest, holding my head above the flood.

"Yes, he's catching the first flight out of Seattle. We'll meet him at the airport, and you'll leave with him."

"But, my mother . . . he came here for my mother, Alice!" Despite Jasper, the hysteria bubbled up in my voice.

"Jasper and I will stay till she's safe."

"I can't win, Alice. You can't guard everyone I know forever. Don't you see what he's doing? He's not tracking me at all. He'll find someone, he'll hurt someone I love. . . . Alice, I can't—"

"We'll catch him, Bella," she assured me.

"And what if you get hurt, Alice? Do you think that's okay with me? Do you think it's only my human family he can hurt me with?"

Alice looked meaningfully at Jasper. A deep, heavy fog of lethargy washed over me, and my eyes closed without my permission. My mind struggled against the fog, realizing what was happening. I forced my eyes open and stood up, stepping away from Jasper's hand.

"I don't want to go back to sleep," I snapped.

I walked to my room and shut the door, slammed it really, so I could be free to go to pieces privately. This time Alice didn't follow me. For three and a half hours I stared at the wall, curled in a ball, rocking. My mind went around in circles, trying to come up with some way out of this nightmare. There was no escape, no reprieve. I could see only one possible end looming darkly in my future. The only question was how many other people would be hurt before I reached it.

The only solace, the only hope I had left, was knowing that I would see Edward soon. Maybe, if I could just see his face again, I would also be able to see the solution that eluded me now.

When the phone rang, I returned to the front room, a little ashamed of my behavior. I hoped I hadn't offended either of them, that they would know how grateful I was for the sacrifices they were making on my account.

Alice was talking as rapidly as ever, but what caught my attention was that, for the first time, Jasper was not in the room. I looked at the clock—it was five-thirty in the morning.

"They're just boarding their plane," Alice told me. "They'll land at nine-forty-five." Just a few more hours to keep breathing till he was here.

"Where's Jasper?"

"He went to check out."

"You aren't staying here?"

"No, we're relocating closer to your mother's house."

My stomach twisted uneasily at her words.

But the phone rang again, distracting me. She looked surprised, but I was already walking forward, reaching hopefully for the phone.

"Hello?" Alice asked. "No, she's right here." She held the phone out to me. Your mother, she mouthed.

"Hello?"

"Bella? Bella?" It was my mother's voice, in a familiar tone I had heard a thousand times in my childhood, anytime I'd gotten too close to the edge of the sidewalk or strayed out of her sight in a crowded place. It was the sound of panic.

I sighed. I'd been expecting this, though I'd tried to make my message as unalarming as possible without lessening the urgency of it.

"Calm down, Mom," I said in my most soothing voice, walking slowly away from Alice. I wasn't sure if I could lie as convincingly with her eyes on me. "Everything is fine, okay? Just give me a minute and I'll explain everything, I promise."

I paused, surprised that she hadn't interrupted me yet.

"Mom?"

"Be very careful not to say anything until I tell you to." The voice I heard now was as unfamiliar as it was unexpected. It was a man's tenor voice, a very pleasant, generic voice—the kind of voice that you heard in the background of luxury car commercials. He spoke very quickly.

"Now, I don't need to hurt your mother, so please do exactly as I say, and she'll be fine." He paused for a minute while I listened in mute horror. "That's very good," he congratulated. "Now repeat after me, and do try to sound natural. Please say, 'No, Mom, stay where you are.'"

"No, Mom, stay where you are." My voice was barely more than a whisper.

"I can see this is going to be difficult." The voice was amused, still light and friendly. "Why don't you walk into another room now so your face doesn't ruin everything? There's no reason for your mother to suffer. As you're walking, please say, 'Mom, please listen to me.' Say it now."

"Mom, please listen to me," my voice pleaded. I walked very slowly to the bedroom, feeling Alice's worried stare on my back. I shut the door behind me, trying to think clearly through the terror that gripped my brain.

"There now, are you alone? Just answer yes or no."

"Yes."

"But they can still hear you, I'm sure."

"Yes."

"All right, then," the agreeable voice continued, "say, 'Mom, trust me.'"

"Mom, trust me."

"This worked out rather better than I expected. I was prepared to wait, but your mother arrived ahead of schedule. It's easier this way, isn't it? Less suspense, less anxiety for you."

I waited.

"Now I want you to listen very carefully. I'm going to need you to get away from your friends; do you think you can do that? Answer yes or no."

"No."

"I'm sorry to hear that. I was hoping you would be a little more creative than that. Do you think you could get away from them if your mother's life depended on it? Answer yes or no."

Somehow, there had to be a way. I remembered that we were going to the airport. Sky Harbor International Airport: crowded, confusingly laid out . . .

"Yes."

"That's better. I'm sure it won't be easy, but if I get the slightest hint that you have any company, well, that would be very bad for your mother," the friendly voice promised. "You must know enough about us by now to realize how quickly I would know if you tried to bring anyone along with you. And how little time I would need to deal with your mother if that was the case. Do you understand? Answer yes or no."

"Yes." My voice broke.

"Very good, Bella. Now this is what you have to do. I want you to go to your mother's house. Next to the phone there will be a number. Call it, and I'll tell you where to go from there." I already knew where I would go, and where this would end. But I would follow his instructions exactly. "Can you do that? Answer yes or no."

"Yes."

"Before noon, please, Bella. I haven't got all day," he said politely.

"Where's Phil?" I asked tersely.

"Ah, be careful now, Bella. Wait until I ask you to speak, please."

I waited.

"It's important, now, that you don't make your friends suspicious when you go back to them. Tell them that your mother called, and that you talked her out of coming home for the time being. Now repeat after me, 'Thank you, Mom.' Say it now."

"Thank you, Mom." The tears were coming. I tried to fight them back.

"Say, 'I love you, Mom, I'll see you soon.' Say it now."

"I love you, Mom." My voice was thick. "I'll see you soon," I promised.

"Goodbye, Bella. I look forward to seeing you again." He hung up.

I held the phone to my ear. My joints were frozen with terror—I couldn't unbend my fingers to drop it.

I knew I had to think, but my head was filled with the sound of my mother's panic. Seconds ticked by while I fought for control.

Slowly, slowly, my thoughts started to break past that brick wall of pain. To plan. For I had no choices now but one: to go to the mirrored room and die. I had no guarantees, nothing to give to keep my mother alive. I could only hope that James would be satisfied with winning the game, that beating Edward would be enough. Despair gripped me; there was no way to bargain, nothing I could offer or withhold that could influence him. But I still had no choice. I had to try.

I pushed the terror back as well as I could. My decision was made. It did no good to waste time agonizing over the outcome. I had to think clearly, because Alice and Jasper were waiting for me, and evading them was absolutely essential, and absolutely impossible.

I was suddenly grateful that Jasper was gone. If he had been here to feel my anguish in the last five minutes, how could I have kept them from being suspicious? I choked back the dread, the anxiety, tried to stifle it. I couldn't afford it now. I didn't know when he would return.

I concentrated on my escape. I had to hope that my familiarity with the airport would turn the odds in my favor. Somehow, I had to keep Alice away. . . .

I knew Alice was in the other room waiting for me, curious. But I had to deal with one more thing in private, before Jasper was back.

I had to accept that I wouldn't see Edward again, not even one last glimpse of his face to carry with me to the mirror room. I was going to hurt him, and I couldn't say goodbye. I let the waves of torture wash over me, have their way for a time. Then I pushed them back, too, and went to face Alice.

The only expression I could manage was a dull, dead look. I saw her alarm and I didn't wait for her to ask. I had just one script and I'd never manage improvisation now.

"My mom was worried, she wanted to come home. But it's okay, I convinced her to stay away." My voice was lifeless.

"We'll make sure she's fine, Bella, don't worry."

I turned away; I couldn't let her see my face.

My eye fell on a blank page of the hotel stationery on the desk. I went to it slowly, a plan forming. There was an envelope there, too. That was good.

"Alice," I asked slowly, without turning, keeping my voice level. "If I write a letter for my mother, would you give it to her? Leave it at the house, I mean."

"Sure, Bella." Her voice was careful. She could see me coming apart at the seams. I *had* to keep my emotions under better control.

I went into the bedroom again, and knelt next to the little bedside table to write.

"Edward," I wrote. My hand was shaking, the letters were hardly legible.

I love you. I am so sorry. He has my mom, and I have to try. I know it may not work. I am so very, very sorry.

Don't be angry with Alice and Jasper. If I get away from them it will be a miracle. Tell them thank you for me. Alice especially, please.

And please, please don't come after him. That's what he wants, I think. I can't bear it if anyone has to be hurt because of me, especially you. Please, this is the only thing I can ask you now. For me.

I love you. Forgive me.

Bella.

I folded the letter carefully, and sealed it in the envelope. Eventually he would find it. I only hoped he would understand, and listen to me just this once.

And then I carefully sealed away my heart.

22. HIDE-AND-SEEK

IT HAD TAKEN MUCH LESS TIME THAN I'D THOUGHT—ALL THE TERROR, the despair, the shattering of my heart. The minutes were ticking by more slowly than usual. Jasper still hadn't come back when I returned to Alice. I was afraid to be in the same room with her, afraid that she would guess... and afraid to hide from her for the same reason.

I would have thought I was far beyond the ability to be surprised, my thoughts tortured and unstable, but I *was* surprised when I saw Alice bent over the desk, gripping the edge with two hands.

"Alice?"

She didn't react when I called her name, but her head was slowly rocking side to side, and I saw her face. Her eyes were blank, dazed. . . . My thoughts flew to my mother. Was I already too late?

I hurried to her side, reaching out automatically to touch her hand.

"Alice!" Jasper's voice whipped, and then he was right behind her, his hands curling over hers, loosening them from their grip on the table. Across the room, the door swung shut with a low click.

"What is it?" he demanded.

She turned her face away from me, into his chest. "Bella," she said.

"I'm right here," I replied.

Her head twisted around, her eyes locking on mine, their expression still strangely blank. I realized at once that she hadn't been speaking to me, she'd been answering Jasper's question.

"What did you see?" I said—and there was no question in my flat, uncaring voice.

Jasper looked at me sharply. I kept my expression vacant and waited. His eyes were confused as they flickered swiftly between Alice's face and mine, feeling the chaos...for I could guess what Alice had seen now.

I felt a tranquil atmosphere settle around me. I welcomed it, using it to keep my emotions disciplined, under control.

Alice, too, recovered herself.

"Nothing, really," she answered finally, her voice remarkably calm and convincing. "Just the same room as before."

She finally looked at me, her expression smooth and withdrawn. "Did you want breakfast?"

"No, I'll eat at the airport." I was very calm, too. I went to the bathroom to shower. Almost as if I were borrowing Jasper's strange extra sense, I could feel Alice's wild—though well-concealed—desperation to have me out of the room, to be alone with Jasper. So she could tell him that they were doing something wrong, that they were going to fail....

I got ready methodically, concentrating on each little task. I left my hair down, swirling around me, covering my face. The peaceful mood Jasper created worked its way through me and helped me think clearly. Helped me plan. I dug through my bag until I found my sock full of money. I emptied it into my pocket.

I was anxious to get to the airport, and glad when we left by seven. I sat alone this time in the back of the dark car. Alice leaned against the door, her face toward Jasper but, behind her sunglasses, shooting glances in my direction every few seconds.

"Alice?" I asked indifferently.

She was wary. "Yes?"

"How does it work? The things that you see?" I stared out the side window, and my voice sounded bored. "Edward said it wasn't definite...that things change?" It was harder than I would have thought to say his name. That must have been what alerted Jasper, why a fresh wave of serenity filled the car.

"Yes, things change...," she murmured—hopefully, I thought. "Some things are more certain than others...like the weather. People are harder. I only see the course they're on while they're on it. Once they change their minds—make a new decision, no matter how small—the whole future shifts."

I nodded thoughtfully. "So you couldn't see James in Phoenix until he decided to come here."

"Yes," she agreed, wary again.

And she hadn't seen me in the mirror room with James until I'd made the decision to meet him there. I tried not to think about what else she might have seen. I didn't want my panic to make Jasper more suspicious. They would be watching me twice as carefully now, anyway, after Alice's vision. This was going to be impossible.

We got to the airport. Luck was with me, or maybe it was just good odds. Edward's plane was landing in terminal four, the largest terminal, where most flights landed—so it wasn't surprising that his was. But it was the terminal I needed: the biggest, the most confusing. And there was a door on level three that might be the only chance.

We parked on the fourth floor of the huge garage. I led the way, for once more knowledgeable about my surroundings than they were. We took the elevator down to level three, where the passengers unloaded. Alice and Jasper spent a long time looking at the departing flights board. I could hear them discussing the pros and cons of New York, Atlanta, Chicago. Places I'd never seen. And would never see.

I waited for my opportunity, impatient, unable to stop my toe from tapping. We sat in the long rows of chairs by the metal detectors, Jasper and Alice pretending to people-watch but really watching me. Every inch I shifted in my seat was followed by a quick glance out of the corner of their eyes. It was hopeless. Should I run? Would they dare to stop me physically in this public place? Or would they simply follow?

I pulled the unmarked envelope out of my pocket and set it on top of Alice's black leather bag. She looked at me.

"My letter," I said. She nodded, tucking it under the top flap. He would find it soon enough.

The minutes passed and Edward's arrival grew closer. It was amazing how every cell in my body seemed to know he was coming, to long for his coming. That made it very hard. I found myself trying to think of excuses to stay, to see him first and then make my escape. But I knew that was impossible if I was going to have any chance to get away.

Several times Alice offered to go get breakfast with me. Later, I told her, not yet.

I stared at the arrival board, watching as flight after flight arrived on time. The flight from Seattle crept closer to the top of the board.

And then, when I had only thirty minutes to make my escape, the numbers changed. His plane was ten minutes early. I had no more time.

"I think I'll eat now," I said quickly.

Alice stood. "I'll come with you."

"Do you mind if Jasper comes instead?" I asked. "I'm feeling a little..." I didn't finish the sentence. My eyes were wild enough to convey what I didn't say.

Jasper stood up. Alice's eyes were confused, but—I saw to my relief—not suspicious. She must be attributing the change in her vision to some maneuver of the tracker's rather than a betrayal by me.

Jasper walked silently beside me, his hand on the small of my back, as if he were guiding me. I pretended a lack of interest in the first few airport cafés, my head scanning for what I really wanted. And there it was, around the corner, out of Alice's sharp sight: the level-three ladies' room.

"Do you mind?" I asked Jasper as we passed. "I'll just be a moment."

"I'll be right here," he said.

As soon as the door shut behind me, I was running. I remembered the time I had gotten lost from this bathroom, because it had two exits.

Outside the far door it was only a short sprint to the elevators, and if Jasper stayed where he said he would, I'd never be in his line of sight. I didn't look behind me as I ran. This was my only chance, and even if he saw me, I had to keep going. People stared, but I ignored them. Around the corner the elevators were waiting, and I dashed forward, throwing my hand between the closing doors of a full elevator headed down. I squeezed in beside the irritated passengers, and checked to make sure that the button for level one had been pushed. It was already lit, and the doors closed.

As soon as the door opened I was off again, to the sound of annoyed murmurs behind me. I slowed myself as I passed the security guards by the luggage carousels, only to break into a run again as the exit doors came into view. I had no way of knowing if Jasper was looking for me yet. I would have only seconds if he was following my scent. I jumped out the automatic doors, nearly smacking into the glass when they opened too slowly.

Along the crowded curb there wasn't a cab in sight.

I had no time. Alice and Jasper were either about to realize I was gone, or they already had. They would find me in a heartbeat.

A shuttle to the Hyatt was just closing its doors a few feet behind me.

"Wait!" I called, running, waving at the driver.

"This is the shuttle to the Hyatt," the driver said in confusion as he opened the doors.

"Yes," I huffed, "that's where I'm going." I hurried up the steps.

He looked askance at my luggage-less state, but then shrugged, not caring enough to ask.

Most of the seats were empty. I sat as far from the other travelers as possible, and watched out the window as first the sidewalk, and then the airport, drifted away. I couldn't help imagining Edward, where he would stand at the edge of the road when he found the end of my trail. I couldn't cry yet, I told myself. I still had a long way to go.

My luck held. In front of the Hyatt, a tired-looking couple was getting their last suitcase out of the trunk of a cab. I jumped out of the shuttle and ran to the cab, sliding into the seat behind the driver. The tired couple and the shuttle driver stared at me.

I told the surprised cabbie my mother's address. "I need to get there as soon as possible."

"That's in Scottsdale," he complained.

I threw four twenties over the seat.

"Will that be enough?"

"Sure, kid, no problem."

I sat back against the seat, folding my arms across my lap. The familiar city began to rush around me, but I didn't look out the windows. I exerted myself to maintain control. I was determined not to lose myself at this point, now that my plan was successfully completed. There was no point in indulging in more terror, more anxiety. My path was set. I just had to follow it now.

So, instead of panicking, I closed my eyes and spent the twenty minutes' drive with Edward.

I imagined that I had stayed at the airport to meet Edward. I visualized how I would stand on my toes, the sooner to see his face. How quickly, how gracefully he would move through the crowds of people separating us. And then I would run to close those last few feet between us—reckless as always—and I would be in his marble arms, finally safe.

I wondered where we would have gone. North somewhere, so he could be outside in the day. Or maybe somewhere very remote, so we could lay in the sun together again. I imagined him by the shore, his skin sparkling like the sea. It wouldn't matter how long we had to hide. To be trapped in a hotel room with him would be a kind of heaven. So many questions I still had for him. I could talk to him forever, never sleeping, never leaving his side.

I could see his face so clearly now . . . almost hear his voice. And, despite all the horror and hopelessness, I was fleetingly happy. So involved was I in my escapist daydreams, I lost all track of the seconds racing by.

"Hey, what was the number?"

The cabbie's question punctured my fantasy, letting all the colors run out of my lovely delusions. Fear, bleak and hard, was waiting to fill the empty space they left behind.

"Fifty-eight twenty-one." My voice sounded strangled. The cabbie looked at me, nervous that I was having an episode or something.

"Here we are, then." He was anxious to get me out of his car, probably hoping I wouldn't ask for my change.

"Thank you," I whispered. There was no need to be afraid, I reminded myself. The house was empty. I had to hurry; my mom was waiting for me, frightened, depending on me.

I ran to the door, reaching up automatically to grab the key under the eave. I unlocked the door. It was dark inside, empty, normal. I ran to the phone, turning on the kitchen light on my way. There, on the whiteboard, was a ten-digit number written in a small, neat hand. My fingers stumbled over the keypad, making mistakes. I had to hang up and start again.

I concentrated only on the buttons this time, carefully pressing each one in turn. I was successful. I held the phone to my ear with a shaking hand. It rang only once.

"Hello, Bella," that easy voice answered. "That was very quick. I'm impressed."

"Is my mom all right?"

"She's perfectly fine. Don't worry, Bella, I have no quarrel with her. Unless you didn't come alone, of course." Light, amused.

"I'm alone." I'd never been more alone in my entire life.

"Very good. Now, do you know the ballet studio just around the corner from your home?"

"Yes. I know how to get there."

"Well, then, I'll see you very soon."

I hung up.

I ran from the room, through the door, out into the baking heat.

There was no time to look back at my house, and I didn't want to see it as it was now—empty, a symbol of fear instead of sanctuary. The last person to walk through those familiar rooms was my enemy.

From the corner of my eye, I could almost see my mother standing in the shade of the big eucalyptus tree where I'd played as a child. Or kneeling by the little plot of dirt around the mailbox, the cemetery of all the flowers she'd tried to grow. The memories were better than any reality I would see today. But I raced away from them, toward the corner, leaving everything behind me.

I felt so slow, like I was running through wet sand—I couldn't seem to get enough purchase from the concrete. I tripped several times, once falling, catching myself with my hands, scraping them on the sidewalk, and then lurching up to plunge forward again. But at last I made it to the corner. Just another street now; I ran, sweat pouring down my face, gasping. The sun was hot on my skin, too bright as it bounced off the white concrete and blinded me. I felt dangerously exposed. More fiercely than I would have dreamed I was capable of, I wished for the green, protective forests of Forks . . . of home.

When I rounded the last corner, onto Cactus, I could see the studio, looking just as I remembered it. The parking lot in front was empty, the vertical blinds in all the windows drawn. I couldn't run anymore—I couldn't breathe; exertion and fear had gotten the best of me. I thought of my mother to keep my feet moving, one in front of the other.

As I got closer, I could see the sign inside the door. It was handwritten on hot pink paper; it said the dance studio was closed for spring break. I touched the handle, tugged on it cautiously. It was unlocked. I fought to catch my breath, and opened the door.

The lobby was dark and empty, cool, the air conditioner thrumming. The plastic molded chairs were stacked along the walls, and the carpet smelled like shampoo. The west dance floor was dark, I could see through the open viewing window. The east dance floor, the bigger room, was lit. But the blinds were closed on the window.

Terror seized me so strongly that I was literally trapped by it. I couldn't make my feet move forward.

And then my mother's voice called.

"Bella? Bella?" That same tone of hysterical panic. I sprinted to the door, to the sound of her voice.

"Bella, you scared me! Don't you ever do that to me again!" Her voice continued as I ran into the long, high-ceilinged room.

I stared around me, trying to find where her voice was coming from. I heard her laugh, and I whirled to the sound.

There she was, on the TV screen, tousling my hair in relief. It was Thanksgiving, and I was twelve. We'd gone to see my grandmother in California, the last year before she died. We went to the beach one day, and I'd leaned too far over the edge of the pier. She'd seen my feet flailing, trying to reclaim my balance. "Bella? Bella?" she'd called to me in fear.

And then the TV screen was blue.

I turned slowly. He was standing very still by the back exit, so still I hadn't noticed him at first. In his hand was a remote control. We stared at each other for a long moment, and then he smiled.

He walked toward me, quite close, and then passed me to put the remote down next to the VCR. I turned carefully to watch him.

"Sorry about that, Bella, but isn't it better that your mother didn't really have to be involved in all this?" His voice was courteous, kind.

And suddenly it hit me. My mother was safe. She was still in Florida. She'd never gotten my message. She'd never been terrified by the dark red eyes in the abnormally pale face before me. She was safe.

"Yes," I answered, my voice saturated with relief.

"You don't sound angry that I tricked you."

"I'm not." My sudden high made me brave. What did it matter now? It would soon be over. Charlie and Mom would never be harmed, would never have to fear. I felt almost giddy. Some analytical part of my mind warned me that I was dangerously close to snapping from the stress.

"How odd. You really mean it." His dark eyes assessed me with interest. The irises were nearly black, just a hint of ruby around the edges. Thirsty. "I will give your strange coven this much, you humans can be quite interesting. I guess I can see the draw of observing you. It's amazing—some of you seem to have no sense of your own self-interest at all."

He was standing a few feet away from me, arms folded, looking at me curiously. There was no menace in his face or stance. He was so very average-looking, nothing remarkable about his face or body at all. Just the white skin, the circled eyes I'd grown so used to. He wore a pale blue, long-sleeved shirt and faded blue jeans.

"I suppose you're going to tell me that your boyfriend will avenge you?" he asked, hopefully it seemed to me.

"No, I don't think so. At least, I asked him not to."

"And what was his reply to that?"

"I don't know." It was strangely easy to converse with this genteel hunter. "I left him a letter."

"How romantic, a last letter. And do you think he will honor it?" His voice was just a little harder now, a hint of sarcasm marring his polite tone.

"I hope so."

"Hmmm. Well, our hopes differ then. You see, this was all just a little too easy, too quick. To be quite honest, I'm disappointed. I expected a much greater challenge. And, after all, I only needed a little luck."

I waited in silence.

"When Victoria couldn't get to your father, I had her find out more about you. There was no sense in running all over the planet chasing you down when I could comfortably wait for you in a place of my choosing. So, after I talked to Victoria, I decided to come to Phoenix to pay your mother a visit. I'd heard you say you were going home. At first, I never dreamed you meant it. But then I wondered. Humans can be very predictable; they like to be somewhere familiar, somewhere safe. And wouldn't it be the perfect ploy, to go to the last place you should be when you're hiding—the place that you said you'd be.

"But of course I wasn't sure, it was just a hunch. I usually get a feeling about the prey that I'm hunting, a sixth sense, if you will. I listened to your message when I got to your mother's house, but of course I couldn't be sure where you'd called from. It was very useful to have your number, but you could have been in Antarctica for all I knew, and the game wouldn't work unless you were close by.

"Then your boyfriend got on a plane to Phoenix. Victoria was monitoring them for me, naturally; in a game with this many players, I couldn't be working alone. And so they told me what I'd hoped, that you were here after all. I was prepared; I'd already been through your charming home movies. And then it was simply a matter of the bluff.

"Very easy, you know, not really up to my standards. So, you see, I'm hoping you're wrong about your boyfriend. Edward, isn't it?"

I didn't answer. The bravado was wearing off. I sensed that he was coming to the end of his gloat. It wasn't meant for me anyway. There was no glory in beating me, a weak human.

"Would you mind, very much, if I left a little letter of my own for your Edward?"

He took a step back and touched a palm-sized digital video camera balanced carefully on top of the stereo. A small red light indicated that it was already running. He adjusted it a few times, widened the frame. I stared at him in horror.

"I'm sorry, but I just don't think he'll be able to resist hunting me after he watches this. And I wouldn't want him to miss anything. It was all for him, of course. You're simply a human, who unfortunately was in the wrong place, at the wrong time, and indisputably running with the wrong crowd, I might add."

He stepped toward me, smiling. "Before we begin..."

I felt a curl of nausea in the pit of my stomach as he spoke. This was something I had not anticipated.

"I would just like to rub it in, just a little bit. The answer was there all along, and I was so afraid Edward would see that and ruin my fun. It happened once, oh, ages ago. The one and only time my prey escaped me.

"You see, the vampire who was so stupidly fond of this little victim made the choice that your Edward was too weak to make. When the old one knew I was after his little friend, he stole her from the asylum where he worked—I *never* will understand the obsession some vampires seem to form with you humans—and as soon as he freed her he made her safe. She didn't even seem to notice the pain, poor little creature. She'd been stuck in that black hole of a cell for so long. A hundred years earlier and she would have been burned at the stake for her visions. In the nineteen-twenties it was the asylum and the shock treatments. When she opened her eyes, strong with her fresh youth, it was like she'd never seen the sun before. The old vampire made her a strong new vampire, and there was no reason for me to touch her then." He sighed. "I destroyed the old one in vengeance."

"Alice," I breathed, astonished.

"Yes, your little friend. I *was* surprised to see her in the clearing. So I guess her coven ought to be able to derive some comfort from this experience. I get you, but they get her. The one victim who escaped me, quite an honor, actually.

"And she did smell so delicious. I still regret that I never got to taste... She smelled even better than you do. Sorry—I don't mean to be offensive. You have a very nice smell. Floral, somehow..."

He took another step toward me, till he was just inches away. He lifted a lock of my hair and sniffed at it delicately. Then he gently patted the strand back into place, and I felt his cool fingertips against my throat. He reached up to stroke my cheek once quickly with his thumb, his face curious. I wanted so badly to run, but I was frozen. I couldn't even flinch away.

"No," he murmured to himself as he dropped his hand, "I don't understand." He sighed. "Well, I suppose we should get on with it. And then I can call your friends and tell them where to find you, and my little message."

I was definitely sick now. There was pain coming, I could see it in his eyes. It wouldn't be enough for him to win, to feed and go. There would be no quick end like I'd been counting on. My knees began to shake, and I was afraid I was going to fall.

He stepped back, and began to circle, casually, as if he were trying to get a better view of a statue in a museum. His face was still open and friendly as he decided where to start.

Then he slumped forward, into a crouch I recognized, and his pleasant smile slowly widened, grew, till it wasn't a smile at all but a contortion of teeth, exposed and glistening.

I couldn't help myself—I tried to run. As useless as I knew it would be, as weak as my knees already were, panic took over and I bolted for the emergency door.

He was in front of me in a flash. I didn't see if he used his hand or his foot, it was too fast. A crushing blow struck my chest—I felt myself flying backward, and then heard the crunch as my head bashed into the mirrors. The glass buckled, some of the pieces shattering and splintering on the floor beside me.

I was too stunned to feel the pain. I couldn't breathe yet.

He walked toward me slowly.

"That's a very nice effect," he said, examining the mess of glass, his voice friendly again. "I thought this room would be visually dramatic for my little film. That's why I picked this place to meet you. It's perfect, isn't it?"

I ignored him, scrambling on my hands and knees, crawling toward the other door.

He was over me at once, his foot stepping down hard on my leg. I heard the sickening snap before I felt it. But then I *did* feel it, and I couldn't hold back my scream of agony. I twisted up to reach for my leg, and he was standing over me, smiling.

"Would you like to rethink your last request?" he asked pleasantly. His toe nudged my broken leg and I heard a piercing scream. With a shock, I realized it was mine.

"Wouldn't you rather have Edward try to find me?" he prompted.

"No!" I croaked. "No, Edward, don't—" And then something smashed into my face, throwing me back into the broken mirrors.

Over the pain of my leg, I felt the sharp rip across my scalp where the glass cut into it. And then the warm wetness began to spread through my hair with alarming speed. I could feel it soaking the shoulder of my shirt, hear it dripping on the wood below. The smell of it twisted my stomach.

Through the nausea and dizziness I saw something that gave me a sudden, final shred of hope. His eyes, merely intent before, now burned with an uncontrollable need. The blood—spreading crimson across my white shirt, pooling rapidly on the floor—was driving him mad with thirst. No matter his original intentions, he couldn't draw this out much longer.

Let it be quick now, was all I could hope as the flow of blood from my head sucked my consciousness away with it. My eyes were closing.

I heard, as if from underwater, the final growl of the hunter. I could see, through the long tunnels my eyes had become, his dark shape coming toward me. With my last effort, my hand instinctively raised to protect my face. My eyes closed, and I drifted.

23. THE ANGEL

As I drifted, I dreamed.

Where I floated, under the dark water, I heard the happiest sound my mind could conjure up—as beautiful, as uplifting, as it was ghastly. It was another snarl; a deeper, wilder roar that rang with fury.

I was brought back, almost to the surface, by a sharp pain slashing my upraised hand, but I couldn't find my way back far enough to open my eyes.

And then I knew I was dead.

Because, through the heavy water, I heard the sound of an angel calling my name, calling me to the only heaven I wanted.

"Oh no, Bella, no!" the angel's voice cried in horror.

Behind that longed-for sound was another noise—an awful tumult that my mind shied away from. A vicious bass growling, a shocking snapping sound, and a high keening, suddenly breaking off . . .

I tried to concentrate on the angel's voice instead.

"Bella, please! Bella, listen to me, please, please, Bella, please!" he begged.

Yes, I wanted to say. Anything. But I couldn't find my lips.

"Carlisle!" the angel called, agony in his perfect voice. "Bella, Bella, no, oh please, no, no!" And the angel was sobbing tearless, broken sobs.

The angel shouldn't weep, it was wrong. I tried to find him, to tell him everything was fine, but the water was so deep, it was pressing on me, and I couldn't breathe.

There was a point of pressure against my head. It hurt. Then, as that pain broke through the darkness to me, other pains came, stronger pains. I cried out, gasping, breaking through the dark pool.

"Bella!" the angel cried.

"She's lost some blood, but the head wound isn't deep," a calm voice informed me. "Watch out for her leg, it's broken."

A howl of rage strangled on the angel's lips.

I felt a sharp stab in my side. This couldn't be heaven, could it? There was too much pain for that.

"Some ribs, too, I think," the methodical voice continued.

But the sharp pains were fading. There was a new pain, a scalding pain in my hand that was overshadowing everything else.

Someone was burning me.

"Edward." I tried to tell him, but my voice was so heavy and slow. I couldn't understand myself.

"Bella, you're going to be fine. Can you hear me, Bella? I love you."

"Edward," I tried again. My voice was a little clearer.

"Yes, I'm here."

"It hurts," I whimpered.

"I know, Bella, I know"—and then, away from me, anguished—"can't you do anything?"

"My bag, please.... Hold your breath, Alice, it will help," Carlisle promised.

"Alice?" I groaned.

"She's here, she knew where to find you."

"My hand hurts," I tried to tell him.

"I know, Bella. Carlisle will give you something, it will stop."

"My hand is burning!" I screamed, finally breaking through the last of the darkness, my eyes fluttering open. I couldn't see his face, something dark and warm was clouding my eyes. Why couldn't they see the fire and put it out?

His voice was frightened. "Bella?"

"The fire! Someone stop the fire!" I screamed as it burned me.

"Carlisle! Her hand!"

"He bit her." Carlisle's voice was no longer calm, it was appalled.

I heard Edward catch his breath in horror.

"Edward, you have to do it." It was Alice's voice, close by my head. Cool fingers brushed at the wetness in my eyes.

"No!" he bellowed.

"Alice," I moaned.

"There may be a chance," Carlisle said.

"What?" Edward begged.

"See if you can suck the venom back out. The wound is fairly clean." As Carlisle spoke, I could feel more pressure on my head, something poking and pulling at my scalp. The pain of it was lost in the pain of the fire.

"Will that work?" Alice's voice was strained.

"I don't know," Carlisle said. "But we have to hurry."

"Carlisle, I . . ." Edward hesitated. "I don't know if I can do that." There was agony in his beautiful voice again.

"It's your decision, Edward, either way. I can't help you. I have to get this bleeding stopped here if you're going to be taking blood from her hand."

I writhed in the grip of the fiery torture, the movement making the pain in my leg flare sickeningly.

"Edward!" I screamed. I realized my eyes were closed again. I opened them, desperate to find his face. And I found him. Finally, I could see his perfect face, staring at me, twisted into a mask of indecision and pain.

"Alice, get me something to brace her leg!" Carlisle was bent over me, working on my head. "Edward, you must do it now, or it will be too late."

Edward's face was drawn. I watched his eyes as the doubt was suddenly replaced with a blazing determination. His jaw tightened. I felt his cool, strong fingers on my burning hand, locking it in place. Then his head bent over it, and his cold lips pressed against my skin.

At first the pain was worse. I screamed and thrashed against the cool hands that held me back. I heard Alice's voice, trying to calm me. Something heavy held my leg to the floor, and Carlisle had my head locked in the vise of his stone arms.

Then, slowly, my writhing calmed as my hand grew more and more numb. The fire was dulling, focusing into an ever-smaller point.

I felt my consciousness slipping as the pain subsided. I was afraid to fall into the black waters again, afraid I would lose him in the darkness.

"Edward," I tried to say, but I couldn't hear my voice. They could hear me.

"He's right here, Bella."

"Stay, Edward, stay with me. . . ."

"I will." His voice was strained, but somehow triumphant.

I sighed contentedly. The fire was gone, the other pains dulled by a sleepiness seeping through my body.

"Is it all out?" Carlisle asked from somewhere far away.

"Her blood tastes clean," Edward said quietly. "I can taste the morphine."

"Bella?" Carlisle called to me.

I tried to answer. "Mmmmm?"

"Is the fire gone?"

"Yes," I sighed. "Thank you, Edward."

"I love you," he answered.

"I know," I breathed, so tired.

I heard my favorite sound in the world: Edward's quiet laugh, weak with relief.

"Bella?" Carlisle asked again.

I frowned; I wanted to sleep. "What?"

"Where is your mother?"

"In Florida," I sighed. "He tricked me, Edward. He watched our videos." The outrage in my voice was pitifully frail.

But that reminded me.

"Alice." I tried to open my eyes. "Alice, the video—he knew you, Alice, he knew where you came from." I meant to speak urgently, but my voice was feeble. "I smell gasoline," I added, surprised through the haze in my brain.

"It's time to move her," Carlisle said.

"No, I want to sleep," I complained.

"You can sleep, sweetheart, I'll carry you," Edward soothed me.

And I was in his arms, cradled against his chest—floating, all the pain gone.

"Sleep now, Bella" were the last words I heard.

24. AN IMPASSE

My eyes opened to a bright, white light. I was in an unfamiliar room, a white room. The wall beside me was covered in long vertical blinds; over my head, the glaring lights blinded me. I was propped up on a hard, uneven bed—a bed with rails. The pillows were flat and lumpy. There was an annoying beeping sound somewhere close by. I hoped that meant I was still alive. Death shouldn't be this uncomfortable.

My hands were all twisted up with clear tubes, and something was taped across my face, under my nose. I lifted my hand to rip it off.

"No, you don't." And cool fingers caught my hand.

"Edward?" I turned my head slightly, and his exquisite face was just inches from mine, his chin resting on the edge of my pillow. I realized again that I was alive, this time with gratitude and elation. "Oh, Edward, I'm so sorry!"

"Shhhh," he shushed me. "Everything's all right now."

"What happened?" I couldn't remember clearly, and my mind rebelled against me as I tried to recall.

"I was almost too late. I could have been too late," he whispered, his voice tormented.

"I was so stupid, Edward. I thought he had my mom."

"He tricked us all."

"I need to call Charlie and my mom," I realized through the haze.

"Alice called them. Renée is here—well, here in the hospital. She's getting something to eat right now."

"She's here?" I tried to sit up, but the spinning in my head accelerated, and his hand pushed me gently down onto the pillows.

"She'll be back soon," he promised. "And you need to stay still."

"But what did you tell her?" I panicked. I had no interest in being soothed. My mom was here and *I* was recovering from a vampire attack. "Why did you tell her I'm here?"

"You fell down two flights of stairs and through a window." He paused. "You have to admit, it could happen."

I sighed, and it hurt. I stared down at my body under the sheet, the huge lump that was my leg.

"How bad am I?" I asked.

"You have a broken leg, four broken ribs, some cracks in your skull, bruises covering every inch of your skin, and you've lost a lot of blood. They gave you a few transfusions. I didn't like it—it made you smell all wrong for a while."

"That must have been a nice change for you."

"No, I like how *you* smell."

"How did you do it?" I asked quietly. He knew what I meant at once.

"I'm not sure." He looked away from my wondering eyes, lifting my gauze-wrapped hand from the bed and holding it gently in his, careful not to disrupt the wire connecting me to one of the monitors.

I waited patiently for the rest.

He sighed without returning my gaze. "It was impossible . . . to stop," he whispered. "Impossible. But I did." He looked up finally, with half a smile. "I *must* love you."

"Don't I taste as good as I smell?" I smiled in response. That hurt my face.

"Even better—better than I'd imagined."

"I'm sorry," I apologized.

He raised his eyes to the ceiling. "Of all the things to apologize for."

"What *should* I apologize for?"

"For very nearly taking yourself away from me forever."

"I'm sorry," I apologized again.

"I know why you did it." His voice was comforting. "It was still irrational, of course. You should have waited for me, you should have told me."

"You wouldn't have let me go."

"No," he agreed in a grim tone, "I wouldn't."

Some very unpleasant memories were beginning to come back to me. I shuddered, and then winced.

He was instantly anxious. "Bella, what's wrong?"

"What happened to James?"

"After I pulled him off you, Emmett and Jasper took care of him." There was a fierce note of regret in his voice.

This confused me. "I didn't see Emmett and Jasper there."

"They had to leave the room . . . there was a lot of blood."

"But you stayed."

"Yes, I stayed."

"And Alice, and Carlisle . . . ," I said in wonder.

"They love you, too, you know."

A flash of painful images from the last time I'd seen Alice reminded me of something. "Did Alice see the tape?" I asked anxiously.

"Yes." A new sound darkened his voice, a tone of sheer hatred.

"She was always in the dark, that's why she didn't remember."

"I know. She understands now." His voice was even, but his face was black with fury.

I tried to reach his face with my free hand, but something stopped me. I glanced down to see the IV pulling at my hand.

"Ugh." I winced.

"What is it?" he asked anxiously—distracted, but not enough. The bleakness did not entirely leave his eyes.

"Needles," I explained, looking away from the one in my hand. I concentrated on a warped ceiling tile and tried to breathe deeply despite the ache in my ribs.

"Afraid of a needle," he muttered to himself under his breath, shaking his head. "Oh, a sadistic vampire, intent on torturing her to death, sure, no problem, she runs off to meet him. An *IV*, on the other hand . . ."

I rolled my eyes. I was pleased to discover that this reaction, at least, was pain-free. I decided to change the subject.

"Why are *you* here?" I asked.

He stared at me, first confusion and then hurt touching his eyes. His brows pulled together as he frowned. "Do you want me to leave?"

"No!" I protested, horrified by the thought. "No, I meant, why does my mother think you're here? I need to have my story straight before she gets back."

"Oh," he said, and his forehead smoothed back into marble. "I came to Phoenix to talk some sense into you, to convince you to come back to Forks." His wide eyes were so earnest and sincere, I almost believed him myself. "You agreed to see me, and you drove out to the hotel where I was staying with Carlisle and Alice—of course I was here with parental supervision," he inserted virtuously, "but you tripped on the stairs on the way to my room and . . . well, you know the rest. You don't need to remember any details, though; you have a good excuse to be a little muddled about the finer points."

I thought about it for a moment. "There are a few flaws with that story. Like no broken windows."

"Not really," he said. "Alice had a little bit too much fun fabricating evidence. It's all been taken care of very convincingly—you could probably sue the hotel if you wanted to. You have nothing to worry about," he promised, stroking my cheek with the lightest of touches. "Your only job now is to heal."

I wasn't so lost to the soreness or the fog of medication that I didn't respond to his touch. The beeping of the monitor jumped around erratically—now he wasn't the only one who could hear my heart misbehave.

"That's going to be embarrassing," I muttered to myself.

He chuckled, and a speculative look came into his eye. "Hmm, I wonder . . ."

He leaned in slowly; the beeping noise accelerated wildly before his lips even touched me. But when they did, though with the most gentle of pressure, the beeping stopped altogether.

He pulled back abruptly, his anxious expression turning to relief as the monitor reported the restarting of my heart.

"It seems that I'm going to have to be even more careful with you than usual." He frowned.

"I was not finished kissing you," I complained. "Don't make me come over there."

He grinned, and bent to press his lips lightly to mine. The monitor went wild.

But then his lips were taut. He pulled away.

"I think I hear your mother," he said, grinning again.

"Don't leave me," I cried, an irrational surge of panic flooding through me. I couldn't let him go—he might disappear from me again.

He read the terror in my eyes for a short second. "I won't," he promised solemnly, and then he smiled. "I'll take a nap."

He moved from the hard plastic chair by my side to the turquoise faux-leather recliner at the foot of my bed, leaning it all the way back, and closing his eyes. He was perfectly still.

"Don't forget to breathe," I whispered sarcastically. He took a deep breath, his eyes still closed.

I could hear my mother now. She was talking to someone, maybe a nurse, and she sounded tired and upset. I wanted to jump out of the bed and run to her, to calm her, promise that everything was fine. But I wasn't in any sort of shape for jumping, so I waited impatiently.

The door opened a crack, and she peeked through.

"Mom!" I whispered, my voice full of love and relief.

She took in Edward's still form on the recliner, and tiptoed to my bedside.

"He never leaves, does he?" she mumbled to herself.

"Mom, I'm so glad to see you!"

She bent down to hug me gently, and I felt warm tears falling on my cheeks.

"Bella, I was so upset!"

"I'm sorry, Mom. But everything's fine now, it's okay," I comforted her.

"I'm just glad to finally see your eyes open." She sat on the edge of my bed.

I suddenly realized I didn't have any idea *when* it was. "How long have they been closed?"

"It's Friday, hon, you've been out for a while."

"Friday?" I was shocked. I tried to remember what day it had been when . . . but I didn't want to think about that.

"They had to keep you sedated for a while, honey—you've got a lot of injuries."

"I know." I could feel them.

"You're lucky Dr. Cullen was there. He's such a nice man . . . very young, though. And he looks more like a model than a doctor. . . ."

"You met Carlisle?"

"And Edward's sister Alice. She's a lovely girl."

"She is," I agreed wholeheartedly.

She glanced over her shoulder at Edward, lying with his eyes closed in the chair. "You didn't tell me you had such good friends in Forks."

I cringed, and then moaned.

"What hurts?" she demanded anxiously, turning back to me. Edward's eyes flashed to my face.

"It's fine," I assured them. "I just have to remember not to move." He lapsed back into his phony slumber.

I took advantage of my mother's momentary distraction to keep the subject from returning to my less-than-candid behavior. "Where's Phil?" I asked quickly.

"Florida—oh, Bella! You'll never guess! Just when we were about to leave, the best news!"

"Phil got signed?" I guessed.

"Yes! How did you guess! The Suns, can you believe it?"

"That's great, Mom," I said as enthusiastically as I could manage, though I had little idea what that meant.

"And you'll like Jacksonville so much," she gushed while I stared at her vacantly. "I was a little bit worried when Phil started talking about Akron, what with the snow and everything, because you know how I hate the cold, but now Jacksonville! It's always sunny, and the humidity really isn't *that* bad. We found the cutest house, yellow, with white trim, and a porch just like in an old movie, and this huge oak tree, and it's just a few minutes from the ocean, and you'll have your own bathroom—"

"Wait, Mom!" I interrupted. Edward still had his eyes closed, but he looked too tense to pass as asleep. "What are you talking about? I'm not going to Florida. I live in Forks."

"But you don't have to anymore, silly," she laughed. "Phil will be able to be around so much more now . . . we've talked about it a lot, and what I'm going to do is trade off on the away games, half the time with you, half the time with him."

"Mom." I hesitated, wondering how best to be diplomatic about this. "I *want* to live in Forks. I'm already settled in at school, and I have a couple of girlfriends"—she glanced toward Edward again when I reminded her of friends, so I tried another direction—"and Charlie needs me. He's just all alone up there, and he can't cook *at all*."

"You want to stay in Forks?" she asked, bewildered. The idea was inconceivable to her. And then her eyes flickered back toward Edward. "Why?"

"I told you—school, Charlie—ouch!" I'd shrugged. Not a good idea.

Her hands fluttered helplessly over me, trying to find a safe place to pat. She made do with my forehead; it was unbandaged.

"Bella, honey, you hate Forks," she reminded me.

"It's not so bad."

She frowned and looked back and forth between Edward and me, this time very deliberately.

"Is it this boy?" she whispered.

I opened my mouth to lie, but her eyes were scrutinizing my face, and I knew she would see through that.

"He's part of it," I admitted. No need to confess how big a part. "So, have you had a chance to talk with Edward?" I asked.

"Yes." She hesitated, looking at his perfectly still form. "And I want to talk to you about that."

Uh-oh. "What about?" I asked.

"I think that boy is in love with you," she accused, keeping her voice low.

"I think so, too," I confided.

"And how do you feel about him?" She only poorly concealed the raging curiosity in her voice.

I sighed, looking away. As much as I loved my mom, this was not a conversation I wanted to have with her. "I'm pretty crazy about him." There— that sounded like something a teenager with her first boyfriend might say.

"Well, he *seems* very nice, and, my goodness, he's incredibly good-looking, but you're so young, Bella..." Her voice was unsure; as far as I could remember, this was the first time since I was eight that she'd come close to trying to sound like a parental authority. I recognized the reasonable-but-firm tone of voice from talks I'd had with her about men.

"I know that, Mom. Don't worry about it. It's just a crush," I soothed her.

"That's right," she agreed, easily pleased.

Then she sighed and glanced guiltily over her shoulder at the big, round clock on the wall.

"Do you need to go?"

She bit her lip. "Phil's supposed to call in a little while...I didn't know you were going to wake up...."

"No problem, Mom." I tried to tone down the relief so she wouldn't get her feelings hurt. "I won't be alone."

"I'll be back soon. I've been sleeping here, you know," she announced, proud of herself.

"Oh, Mom, you don't have to do that! You can sleep at home—I'll never notice." The swirl of painkillers in my brain was making it hard to concentrate even now, though, apparently, I'd been sleeping for days.

"I was too nervous," she admitted sheepishly. "There's been some crime in the neighborhood, and I don't like being there alone."

"Crime?" I asked in alarm.

"Someone broke into that dance studio around the corner from the house and burned it to the ground—there's nothing left at all! And they left a stolen car right out front. Do you remember when you used to dance there, honey?"

"I remember." I shivered, and winced.

"I can stay, baby, if you need me."

"No, Mom, I'll be fine. Edward will be with me."

She looked like that might be why she wanted to stay. "I'll be back tonight." It sounded as much like a warning as it sounded like a promise, and she glanced at Edward again as she said it.

"I love you, Mom."

"I love you, too, Bella. Try to be more careful when you walk, honey, I don't want to lose you."

Edward's eyes stayed closed, but a wide grin flashed across his face.

A nurse came bustling in then to check all my tubes and wires. My mother kissed my forehead, patted my gauze-wrapped hand, and left.

The nurse was checking the paper readout on my heart monitor.

"Are you feeling anxious, honey? Your heart rate got a little high there."

"I'm fine," I assured her.

"I'll tell your RN that you're awake. She'll be in to see you in a minute."

As soon as she closed the door, Edward was at my side.

"You stole a car?" I raised my eyebrows.

He smiled, unrepentant. "It was a good car, very fast."

"How was your nap?" I asked.

"Interesting." His eyes narrowed.

"What?"

He looked down while he answered. "I'm surprised. I thought Florida . . . and your mother . . . well, I thought that's what you would want."

I stared at him uncomprehendingly. "But you'd be stuck inside all day in Florida. You'd only be able to come out at night, just like a real vampire."

He almost smiled, but not quite. And then his face was grave. "I would stay in Forks, Bella. Or somewhere like it," he explained. "Someplace where I couldn't hurt you anymore."

It didn't sink in at first. I continued to stare at him blankly as the words one by one clicked into place in my head like a ghastly puzzle. I was barely conscious of the sound of my heart accelerating, though, as my breathing became hyperventilation, I *was* aware of the sharp aching in my protesting ribs.

He didn't say anything; he watched my face warily as the pain that had nothing to do with broken bones, pain that was infinitely worse, threatened to crush me.

And then another nurse walked purposefully into the room. Edward sat still as stone as she took in my expression with a practiced eye before turning to the monitors.

"Time for more pain meds, sweetheart?" she asked kindly, tapping the IV feed.

"No, no," I mumbled, trying to keep the agony out of my voice. "I don't need anything." I couldn't afford to close my eyes now.

"No need to be brave, honey. It's better if you don't get too stressed out; you need to rest." She waited, but I just shook my head.

"Okay," she sighed. "Hit the call button when you're ready."

She gave Edward a stern look, and threw one more anxious glance at the machinery, before leaving.

His cool hands were on my face; I stared at him with wild eyes.

"Shhh, Bella, calm down."

"Don't leave me," I begged in a broken voice.

"I won't," he promised. "Now relax before I call the nurse back to sedate you."

But my heart couldn't slow.

"Bella." He stroked my face anxiously. "I'm not going anywhere. I'll be right here as long as you need me."

"Do you swear you won't leave me?" I whispered. I tried to control the gasping, at least. My ribs were throbbing.

He put his hands on either side of my face and brought his face close to mine. His eyes were wide and serious. "I swear."

The smell of his breath was soothing. It seemed to ease the ache of my breathing. He continued to hold my gaze while my body slowly relaxed and the beeping returned to a normal pace. His eyes were dark, closer to black than gold today.

"Better?" he asked.

"Yes," I said cautiously.

He shook his head and muttered something unintelligible. I thought I picked out the word "overreaction."

"Why did you say that?" I whispered, trying to keep my voice from shaking. "Are you tired of having to save me all the time? Do you *want* me to go away?"

"No, I don't want to be without you, Bella, of course not. Be rational. And I have no problem with saving you, either—if it weren't for the fact that I was the one putting you in danger . . . that I'm the reason that you're here."

"Yes, you are the reason." I frowned. "The reason I'm here—*alive.*"

"Barely." His voice was just a whisper. "Covered in gauze and plaster and hardly able to move."

"I wasn't referring to my most recent near-death experience," I said, growing irritated. "I was thinking of the others—you can take your pick. If it weren't for you, I would be rotting away in the Forks cemetery."

He winced at my words, but the haunted look didn't leave his eyes.

"That's not the worst part, though," he continued to whisper. He acted as if I hadn't spoken. "Not seeing you there on the floor . . . crumpled and broken." His voice was choked. "Not thinking I was too late. Not even hearing you scream in pain—all those unbearable memories that I'll carry with me for the rest of eternity. No, the very worst was feeling...knowing that I couldn't stop. Believing that I was going to kill you myself."

"But you didn't."

"I could have. So easily."

I knew I needed to stay calm...but he was trying to talk himself into leaving me, and the panic fluttered in my lungs, trying to get out.

"Promise me," I whispered.

"What?"

"You know what." I was starting to get angry now. He was so stubbornly determined to dwell on the negative.

He heard the change in my tone. His eyes tightened. "I don't seem to be strong enough to stay away from you, so I suppose that you'll get your way...whether it kills you or not," he added roughly.

"Good." He hadn't promised, though—a fact that I had not missed. The panic was only barely contained; I had no strength left to control the anger. "You told me how you stopped...now I want to know why," I demanded.

"Why?" he repeated warily.

"*Why* you did it. Why didn't you just let the venom spread? By now I would be just like you."

Edward's eyes seemed to turn flat black, and I remembered that this was something he'd never intended me to know. Alice must have been preoccupied by the things she'd learned about herself...or she'd been very careful with her thoughts around him—clearly, he'd had no idea that she'd filled me in on the mechanics of vampire conversions. He was surprised, and infuriated. His nostrils flared, his mouth looked as if it was chiseled from stone.

He wasn't going to answer, that much was clear.

"I'll be the first to admit that I have no experience with relationships," I said. "But it just seems logical...a man and woman have to be somewhat equal...as in, one of them can't always be swooping in and saving the other one. They have to save each other *equally*."

He folded his arms on the side of my bed and rested his chin on his arms. His expression was smooth, the anger reined in. Evidently he'd decided he wasn't angry with *me*. I hoped I'd get a chance to warn Alice before he caught up with her.

"You *have* saved me," he said quietly.

"I can't always be Lois Lane," I insisted. "I want to be Superman, too."

"You don't know what you're asking." His voice was soft; he stared intently at the edge of the pillowcase.

"I think I do."

"Bella, you *don't* know. I've had almost ninety years to think about this, and I'm still not sure."

"Do you wish that Carlisle hadn't saved you?"

"No, I don't wish that." He paused before continuing. "But my life was over. I wasn't giving anything up."

"You *are* my life. You're the only thing it would hurt me to lose." I was getting better at this. It was easy to admit how much I needed him.

He was very calm, though. Decided.

"I can't do it, Bella. I won't do that to you."

"Why not?" My throat rasped and the words weren't as loud as I'd meant them to be. "Don't tell me it's too hard! After today, or I guess it was a few days ago . . . anyway, after *that,* it should be nothing."

He glared at me.

"And the pain?" he asked.

I blanched. I couldn't help it. But I tried to keep my expression from showing how clearly I remembered the feeling . . . the fire in my veins.

"That's my problem," I said. "I can handle it."

"It's possible to take bravery to the point where it becomes insanity."

"It's not an issue. Three days. Big deal."

Edward grimaced again as my words reminded him that I was more informed than he had ever intended me to be. I watched him repress the anger, watched as his eyes grew speculative.

"Charlie?" he asked curtly. "Renée?"

Minutes passed in silence as I struggled to answer his question. I opened my mouth, but no sound came out. I closed it again. He waited, and his expression became triumphant because he knew I had no true answer.

"Look, that's not an issue either," I finally muttered; my voice was as unconvincing as it always was when I lied. "Renée has always made the choices that work for her—she'd want me to do the same. And Charlie's resilient, he's used to being on his own. I can't take care of them forever. I have my own life to live."

"Exactly," he snapped. "And I won't end it for you."

"If you're waiting for me to be on my deathbed, I've got news for you! I was just there!"

"You're going to recover," he reminded me.

I took a deep breath to calm myself, ignoring the spasm of pain it triggered. I stared at him, and he stared back. There was no compromise in his face.

"No," I said slowly. "I'm not."

His forehead creased. "Of course you are. You may have a scar or two...."

"You're wrong," I insisted. "I'm going to die."

"Really, Bella." He was anxious now. "You'll be out of here in a few days. Two weeks at most."

I glared at him. "I may not die now... but I'm going to die sometime. Every minute of the day, I get closer. And I'm going to get *old*."

He frowned as what I was saying sunk in, pressing his long fingers to his temples and closing his eyes. "That's how it's supposed to happen. How it should happen. How it would have happened if I didn't exist—and *I shouldn't exist*."

I snorted. He opened his eyes in surprise. "That's stupid. That's like going to someone who's just won the lottery, taking their money, and saying, 'Look, let's just go back to how things should be. It's better that way.' And I'm not buying it."

"I'm hardly a lottery prize," he growled.

"That's right. You're much better."

He rolled his eyes and set his lips. "Bella, we're not having this discussion anymore. I refuse to damn you to an eternity of night and that's the end of it."

"If you think that's the end, then you don't know me very well," I warned him. "You're not the only vampire I know."

His eyes went black again. "Alice wouldn't dare."

And for a moment he looked so frightening that I couldn't help but believe it—I couldn't imagine someone brave enough to cross him.

"Alice already saw it, didn't she?" I guessed. "That's why the things she says upset you. She knows I'm going to be like you . . . someday."

"She's wrong. She also saw you dead, but that didn't happen, either."

"You'll never catch *me* betting against Alice."

We stared at each other for a very long time. It was quiet except for the whirring of the machines, the beeping, the dripping, the ticking of the big clock on the wall. Finally, his expression softened.

"So where does that leave us?" I wondered.

He chuckled humorlessly. "I believe it's called an *impasse*."

I sighed. "Ouch," I muttered.

"How are you feeling?" he asked, eyeing the button for the nurse.

"I'm fine," I lied.

"I don't believe you," he said gently.

"I'm not going back to sleep."

"You need rest. All this arguing isn't good for you."

"So give in," I hinted.

"Nice try." He reached for the button.

"No!"

He ignored me.

"Yes?" the speaker on the wall squawked.

"I think we're ready for more pain medication," he said calmly, ignoring my furious expression.

"I'll send in the nurse." The voice sounded very bored.

"I won't take it," I promised.

He looked toward the sack of fluids hanging beside my bed. "I don't think they're going to ask you to swallow anything."

My heart rate started to climb. He read the fear in my eyes, and sighed in frustration.

"Bella, you're in pain. You need to relax so you can heal. Why are you being so difficult? They're not going to put any more needles in you now."

"I'm not afraid of the needles," I mumbled. "I'm afraid to close my eyes."

Then he smiled his crooked smile, and took my face between his hands. "I told you I'm not going anywhere. Don't be afraid. As long as it makes you happy, I'll be here."

I smiled back, ignoring the ache in my cheeks. "You're talking about for-ever, you know."

"Oh, you'll get over it—it's just a crush."

I shook my head in disbelief—it made me dizzy. "I was shocked when Renée swallowed that one. I know *you* know better."

"That's the beautiful thing about being human," he told me. "Things change."

My eyes narrowed. "Don't hold your breath."

He was laughing when the nurse came in, brandishing a syringe.

"Excuse me," she said brusquely to Edward.

He got up and crossed to the end of the small room, leaning against the wall. He folded his arms and waited. I kept my eyes on him, still apprehen-sive. He met my gaze calmly.

"Here you go, honey." The nurse smiled as she injected the medicine into my tube. "You'll feel better now."

"Thanks," I mumbled, unenthusiastic. It didn't take long. I could feel the drowsiness trickling through my bloodstream almost immediately.

"That ought to do it," she muttered as my eyelids drooped.

She must have left the room, because something cold and smooth touched my face.

"Stay." The word was slurred.

"I will," he promised. His voice was beautiful, like a lullaby. "Like I said, as long as it makes you happy . . . as long as it's what's best for you."

I tried to shake my head, but it was too heavy. "'S not the same thing," I mumbled.

He laughed. "Don't worry about that now, Bella. You can argue with me when you wake up."

I think I smiled. "'Kay."

I could feel his lips at my ear.

"I love you," he whispered.

"Me, too."

"I know," he laughed quietly.

I turned my head slightly . . . searching. He knew what I was after. His lips touched mine gently.

"Thanks," I sighed.

"Anytime."

I wasn't really there at all anymore. But I fought against the stupor weakly. There was just one more thing I wanted to tell him.

"Edward?" I struggled to pronounce his name clearly.

"Yes?"

"I'm betting on Alice," I mumbled.

And then the night closed over me.

EPILOGUE: AN OCCASION

EDWARD HELPED ME INTO HIS CAR, BEING VERY CAREFUL OF THE WISPS of silk and chiffon, the flowers he'd just pinned into my elaborately styled curls, and my bulky walking cast. He ignored the angry set of my mouth.

When he had me settled, he got in the driver's seat and headed back out the long, narrow drive.

"At what point exactly are you going to tell me what's going on?" I asked grumpily. I really hated surprises. And he knew that.

"I'm shocked that you haven't figured it out yet." He threw a mocking smile in my direction, and my breath caught in my throat. Would I ever get used to his perfection?

"I did mention that you looked very nice, didn't I?" I verified.

"Yes." He grinned again. I'd never seen him dress in black before, and, with the contrast against his pale skin, his beauty was absolutely surreal. That much I couldn't deny, even if the fact that he was wearing a tuxedo made me very nervous.

Not quite as nervous as the dress. Or the shoe. Only one shoe, as my other foot was still securely encased in plaster. But the stiletto heel, held on only by satin ribbons, certainly wasn't going to help me as I tried to hobble around.

"I'm not coming over anymore if Alice is going to treat me like Guinea Pig Barbie when I do," I griped. I'd spent the better part of the day in Alice's staggeringly vast bathroom, a helpless victim as she played hairdresser and cosmetician. Whenever I fidgeted or complained, she reminded me that she didn't have any memories of being human, and asked me not to ruin her vicarious fun. Then she'd dressed me in the most ridiculous dress—deep blue, frilly and off the shoulders, with French tags I couldn't read—a dress more suitable for a runway than Forks. Nothing good could come of our formal attire, of that I was sure. Unless...but I was afraid to put my suspicions into words, even in my own head.

I was distracted then by the sound of a phone ringing. Edward pulled his cell phone from a pocket inside his jacket, looking briefly at the caller ID before answering.

"Hello, Charlie," he said warily.

"Charlie?" I frowned.

Charlie had been...difficult since my return to Forks. He had compartmentalized my bad experience into two defined reactions. Toward Carlisle he was almost worshipfully grateful. On the other hand, he was stubbornly convinced that Edward was at fault—because, if not for him, I wouldn't have left home in the first place. And Edward was far from disagreeing with him. These days I had rules that hadn't existed before: curfews...visiting hours.

Something Charlie was saying made Edward's eyes widen in disbelief, and then a grin spread across his face.

"You're kidding!" He laughed.

"What is it?" I demanded.

He ignored me. "Why don't you let me talk to him?" Edward suggested with evident pleasure. He waited for a few seconds.

"Hello, Tyler, this is Edward Cullen." His voice was very friendly, on the surface. I knew it well enough to catch the soft edge of menace. What was Tyler doing at my house? The awful truth began to dawn on me. I looked again at the inappropriate dress Alice had forced me into.

"I'm sorry if there's been some kind of miscommunication, but Bella is unavailable tonight." Edward's tone changed, and the threat in his voice was suddenly much more evident as he continued. "To be perfectly honest, she'll be unavailable every night, as far as anyone besides myself is concerned. No offense. And I'm sorry about your evening." He didn't sound sorry at all. And then he snapped the phone shut, a huge smirk on his face.

My face and neck flushed crimson with anger. I could feel the rage-induced tears starting to fill my eyes.

He looked at me in surprise. "Was that last part a bit too much? I didn't mean to offend you."

I ignored that.

"You're taking me to *the prom*!" I yelled.

It was embarrassingly obvious now. If I'd been paying any attention at all, I'm sure I would have noticed the date on the posters that decorated the school buildings. But I'd never dreamed he was thinking of subjecting me to this. Didn't he know me at all?

He wasn't expecting the force of my reaction, that was clear. He pressed his lips together and his eyes narrowed. "Don't be difficult, Bella."

My eyes flashed to the window; we were halfway to the school already.

"Why are you doing this to me?" I demanded in horror.

He gestured to his tuxedo. "Honestly, Bella, what did you think we were doing?"

I was mortified. First, because I'd missed the obvious. And also because the vague suspicions—expectations, really—that I'd been forming all day, as Alice tried to transform me into a beauty queen, were so far wide of the mark. My half-fearful hopes seemed very silly now.

I'd guessed there was some kind of occasion brewing. But *prom*! That was the furthest thing from my mind.

The angry tears rolled over my cheeks. I remembered with dismay that I was very uncharacteristically wearing mascara. I wiped quickly under my eyes to prevent any smudges. My hand was unblackened when I pulled it away; maybe Alice had known I would need waterproof makeup.

"This is completely ridiculous. Why are you crying?" he demanded in frustration.

"Because I'm *mad*!"

"Bella." He turned the full force of his scorching golden eyes on me.

"What?" I muttered, distracted.

"Humor me," he insisted.

His eyes were melting all my fury. It was impossible to fight with him when he cheated like that. I gave in with poor grace.

"Fine," I pouted, unable to glare as effectively as I would have liked. "I'll go quietly. But you'll see. I'm way overdue for more bad luck. I'll probably break my other leg. Look at this shoe! It's a death trap!" I held out my good leg as evidence.

"Hmmm." He stared at my leg longer than was necessary. "Remind me to thank Alice for that tonight."

"Alice is going to be there?" That comforted me slightly.

"With Jasper, and Emmett . . . and Rosalie," he admitted.

The feeling of comfort disappeared. There had been no progress with Rosalie, though I was on quite good terms with her sometimes-husband. Emmett enjoyed having me around—he thought my bizarre human reactions were hilarious . . . or maybe it was just the fact that I fell down a lot that he found so funny. Rosalie acted as if I didn't exist. While I shook my head to dispel the direction my thoughts had taken, I thought of something else.

"Is Charlie in on this?" I asked, suddenly suspicious.

"Of course." He grinned, and then chuckled. "Apparently Tyler wasn't, though."

I gritted my teeth. How Tyler could be so delusional, I couldn't imagine. At school, where Charlie couldn't interfere, Edward and I were inseparable—except for those rare sunny days.

We were at the school now; Rosalie's red convertible was conspicuous in the parking lot. The clouds were thin today, a few streaks of sunlight escaping through far away in the west.

He got out and walked around the car to open my door. He held out his hand.

I sat stubbornly in my seat, arms folded, feeling a secret twinge of smugness. The lot was crowded with people in formal dress: witnesses. He couldn't remove me forcibly from the car as he might have if we'd been alone.

He sighed. "When someone wants to kill you, you're brave as a lion—and then when someone mentions dancing . . ." He shook his head.

I gulped. Dancing.

"Bella, I won't let anything hurt you—not even yourself. I won't let go of you once, I promise."

I thought about that and suddenly felt much better. He could see that in my face.

"There, now," he said gently, "it won't be so bad." He leaned down and wrapped one arm around my waist. I took his other hand and let him lift me from the car.

He kept his arm tightly around me, supporting me as I limped toward the school.

In Phoenix, they held proms in hotel ballrooms. This dance was in the gym, of course. It was probably the only room in town big enough for a dance. When we got inside, I giggled. There were actual balloon arches and twisted garlands of pastel crepe paper festooning the walls.

"This looks like a horror movie waiting to happen," I snickered.

"Well," he muttered as we slowly approached the ticket table—he was carrying most of my weight, but I still had to shuffle and wobble my feet forward—"there are *more* than enough vampires present."

I looked at the dance floor; a wide gap had formed in the center of the floor, where two couples whirled gracefully. The other dancers pressed to the sides of the room to give them space—no one wanted to stand in contrast with such radiance. Emmett and Jasper were intimidating and flawless in classic tuxedos. Alice was striking in a black satin dress with geometric cut-outs that bared large triangles of her snowy white skin. And Rosalie was... well, Rosalie. She was beyond belief. Her vivid scarlet dress was backless, tight to her calves where it flared into a wide ruffled train, with a neckline that plunged to her waist. I pitied every girl in the room, myself included.

"Do you want me to bolt the doors so you can massacre the unsuspecting townsfolk?" I whispered conspiratorially.

"And where do you fit into that scheme?" He glared.

"Oh, I'm with the vampires, of course."

He smiled reluctantly. "Anything to get out of dancing."

"Anything."

He bought our tickets, then turned me toward the dance floor. I cringed against his arm and dragged my feet.

"I've got all night," he warned.

Eventually he towed me out to where his family was twirling elegantly— if in a style totally unsuitable to the present time and music. I watched in horror.

"Edward." My throat was so dry I could only manage a whisper. "I *honestly* can't dance!" I could feel the panic bubbling up inside my chest.

"Don't worry, silly," he whispered back. "I *can*." He put my arms around his neck and lifted me to slide his feet under mine.

And then we were whirling, too.

"I feel like I'm five years old," I laughed after a few minutes of effortless waltzing.

"You don't look five," he murmured, pulling me closer for a second, so that my feet were briefly a foot from the ground.

Alice caught my eye on a turn and smiled in encouragement—I smiled back. I was surprised to realize that I was actually enjoying myself . . . a little.

"Okay, this isn't half bad," I admitted.

But Edward was staring toward the doors, and his face was angry.

"What is it?" I wondered aloud. I followed his gaze, disoriented by the spinning, but finally I could see what was bothering him. Jacob Black, not in a tux, but in a long-sleeved white shirt and tie, his hair smoothed back into his usual ponytail, was crossing the floor toward us.

After the first shock of recognition, I couldn't help but feel bad for Jacob. He was clearly uncomfortable—excruciatingly so. His face was apologetic as his eyes met mine.

Edward snarled very quietly.

"Be*have*!" I hissed.

Edward's voice was scathing. "He wants to chat with you."

Jacob reached us then, the embarrassment and apology even more evident on his face.

"Hey, Bella, I was hoping you would be here." Jacob sounded like he'd been hoping the exact opposite. But his smile was just as warm as ever.

"Hi, Jacob." I smiled back. "What's up?"

"Can I cut in?" he asked tentatively, glancing at Edward for the first time. I was shocked to notice that Jacob didn't have to look up. He must have grown half a foot since the first time I'd seen him.

Edward's face was composed, his expression blank. His only answer was to set me carefully on my feet, and take a step back.

"Thanks," Jacob said amiably.

Edward just nodded, looking at me intently before he turned to walk away.

Jacob put his hands on my waist, and I reached up to put my hands on his shoulders.

"Wow, Jake, how tall are you now?"

He was smug. "Six-two."

We weren't really dancing—my leg made that impossible. Instead we swayed awkwardly from side to side without moving our feet. It was just as well; the recent growth spurt had left him looking gangly and uncoordinated, he was probably no better a dancer than I was.

"So, how did you end up here tonight?" I asked without true curiosity. Considering Edward's reaction, I could guess.

"Can you believe my dad paid me twenty bucks to come to your prom?" he admitted, slightly ashamed.

"Yes, I can," I muttered. "Well, I hope you're enjoying yourself, at least. Seen anything you like?" I teased, nodding toward a group of girls lined up against the wall like pastel confections.

"Yeah," he sighed. "But she's taken."

He glanced down to meet my curious gaze for just a second—then we both looked away, embarrassed.

"You look really pretty, by the way," he added shyly.

"Um, thanks. So why did Billy pay you to come here?" I asked quickly, though I knew the answer.

Jacob didn't seem grateful for the subject change; he looked away, uncomfortable again. "He said it was a 'safe' place to talk to you. I swear the old man is losing his mind."

I joined in his laughter weakly.

"Anyway, he said that if I told you something, he would get me that master cylinder I need," he confessed with a sheepish grin.

"Tell me, then. I want you to get your car finished." I grinned back. At least Jacob didn't believe any of this. It made the situation a bit easier. Against the wall, Edward was watching my face, his own face expressionless. I saw a sophomore in a pink dress eyeing him with timid speculation, but he didn't seem to be aware of her.

Jacob looked away again, ashamed. "Don't get mad, okay?"

"There's no way I'll be mad at you, Jacob," I assured him. "I won't even be mad at Billy. Just say what you have to."

"Well—this is so stupid, I'm sorry, Bella—he wants you to break up with your boyfriend. He asked me to tell you 'please.'" He shook his head in disgust.

"He's still superstitious, eh?"

"Yeah. He was . . . kind of over the top when you got hurt down in Phoenix. He didn't believe . . ." Jacob trailed off self-consciously.

My eyes narrowed. "I fell."

"I know that," Jacob said quickly.

"He thinks Edward had something to do with me getting hurt." It wasn't a question, and despite my promise, I was angry.

Jacob wouldn't meet my eyes. We weren't even bothering to sway to the music, though his hands were still on my waist, and mine around his neck.

"Look, Jacob, I know Billy probably won't believe this, but just so you know"—he looked at me now, responding to the new earnestness in my voice—"Edward really did save my life. If it weren't for Edward and his father, I'd be dead."

"I know," he claimed, but he sounded like my sincere words had affected him some. Maybe he'd be able to convince Billy of this much, at least.

"Hey, I'm sorry you had to come do this, Jacob," I apologized. "At any rate, you get your parts, right?"

"Yeah," he muttered. He was still looking awkward . . . upset.

"There's more?" I asked in disbelief.

"Forget it," he mumbled, "I'll get a job and save the money myself."

I glared at him until he met my gaze. "Just spit it out, Jacob."

"It's so bad."

"I don't care. Tell me," I insisted.

"Okay . . . but, geez, this sounds bad." He shook his head. "He said to tell you, no, to *warn* you, that—and this is his plural, not mine"—he lifted one hand from my waist and made little quotations marks in the air—"'We'll be watching.'" He watched warily for my reaction.

It sounded like something from a mafia movie. I laughed out loud.

"Sorry you had to do this, Jake," I snickered.

"I don't mind *that* much." He grinned in relief. His eyes were appraising as they raked quickly over my dress. "So, should I tell him you said to butt the hell out?" he asked hopefully.

"No," I sighed. "Tell him I said thanks. I know he means well."

The song ended, and I dropped my arms.

His hands hesitated at my waist, and he glanced at my bum leg. "Do you want to dance again? Or can I help you get somewhere?"

Edward answered for me. "That's all right, Jacob. I'll take it from here."

Jacob flinched, and stared wide-eyed at Edward, who stood just beside us.

"Hey, I didn't see you there," he mumbled. "I guess I'll see you around, Bella." He stepped back, waving halfheartedly.

I smiled. "Yeah, I'll see you later."

"Sorry," he said again before he turned for the door.

Edward's arms wound around me as the next song started. It was a little up-tempo for slow dancing, but that didn't seem to concern him. I leaned my head against his chest, content.

"Feeling better?" I teased.

"Not really," he said tersely.

"Don't be mad at Billy," I sighed. "He just worries about me for Charlie's sake. It's nothing personal."

"I'm not mad at Billy," he corrected in a clipped voice. "But his son is irritating me."

I pulled back to look at him. His face was very serious.

"Why?"

"First of all, he made me break my promise."

I stared at him in confusion.

He half-smiled. "I promised I wouldn't let go of you tonight," he explained.

"Oh. Well, I forgive you."

"Thanks. But there's something else." Edward frowned.

I waited patiently.

"He called you *pretty*," he finally continued, his frown deepening. "That's practically an insult, the way you look right now. You're much more than beautiful."

I laughed. "You might be a little biased."

"I don't think that's it. Besides, I have excellent eyesight."

We were twirling again, my feet on his as he held me close.

"So are you going to explain the reason for all of this?" I wondered.

He looked down at me, confused, and I glared meaningfully at the crepe paper.

He considered for a moment, and then changed direction, spinning me through the crowd to the back door of the gym. I caught a glimpse of Jessica and Mike dancing, staring at me curiously. Jessica waved, and I smiled back quickly. Angela was there, too, looking blissfully happy in the arms of little Ben Cheney; she didn't look up from his eyes, a head lower than hers. Lee and Samantha, Lauren, glaring toward us, with Conner; I could name every face that spiraled past me. And then we were outdoors, in the cool, dim light of a fading sunset.

As soon as we were alone, he swung me up into his arms, and carried me across the dark grounds till he reached the bench beneath the shadow of the madrone trees. He sat there, keeping me cradled against his chest. The moon was already up, visible through the gauzy clouds, and his face glowed pale in the white light. His mouth was hard, his eyes troubled.

"The point?" I prompted softly.

He ignored me, staring up at the moon.

"Twilight, again," he murmured. "Another ending. No matter how perfect the day is, it always has to end."

"Some things don't have to end," I muttered through my teeth, instantly tense.

He sighed.

"I brought you to the prom," he said slowly, finally answering my question, "because I don't want you to miss anything. I don't want my presence to take anything away from you, if I can help it. I want you to be *human*. I want your life to continue as it would have if I'd died in nineteen-eighteen like I should have."

I shuddered at his words, and then shook my head angrily. "In what strange parallel dimension would I *ever* have gone to prom of my own free will? If you weren't a thousand times stronger than me, I would never have let you get away with this."

He smiled briefly, but it didn't touch his eyes. "It wasn't so bad, you said so yourself."

"That's because I was with you."

We were quiet for a minute; he stared at the moon and I stared at him. I wished there was some way to explain how very uninterested I was in a normal human life.

"Will you tell me something?" he asked, glancing down at me with a slight smile.

"Don't I always?"

"Just promise you'll tell me," he insisted, grinning.

I knew I was going to regret this almost instantly. "Fine."

"You seemed honestly surprised when you figured out that I was taking you here," he began.

"I *was*," I interjected.

"Exactly," he agreed. "But you must have had some other theory... I'm curious—what did you *think* I was dressing you up for?"

Yes, instant regret. I pursed my lips, hesitating. "I don't want to tell you."

"You promised," he objected.

"I know."

"What's the problem?"

I knew he thought it was mere embarrassment holding me back. "I think it will make you mad—or sad."

His brows pulled together over his eyes as he thought that through. "I still want to know. Please?"

I sighed. He waited.

"Well... I assumed it was some kind of... occasion. But I didn't think it would be some trite human thing... prom!" I scoffed.

"Human?" he asked flatly. He'd picked up on the key word.

I looked down at my dress, fidgeting with a stray piece of chiffon. He waited in silence.

"Okay," I confessed in a rush. "So I was hoping that you might have changed your mind... that you were going to change *me*, after all."

A dozen emotions played across his face. Some I recognized: anger... pain... and then he seemed to collect himself and his expression became amused.

"You thought that would be a black tie occasion, did you?" he teased, touching the lapel of his tuxedo jacket.

I scowled to hide my embarrassment. "I don't know how these things work. To me, at least, it seems more rational than prom does." He was still grinning. "It's not funny," I said.

"No, you're right, it's not," he agreed, his smile fading. "I'd rather treat it like a joke, though, than believe you're serious."

"But I am serious."

He sighed deeply. "I know. And you're really that willing?"

The pain was back in his eyes. I bit my lip and nodded.

"So ready for this to be the end," he murmured, almost to himself, "for this to be the twilight of your life, though your life has barely started. You're ready to give up everything."

"It's not the end, it's the beginning," I disagreed under my breath.

"I'm not worth it," he said sadly.

"Do you remember when you told me that I didn't see myself very clearly?" I asked, raising my eyebrows. "You obviously have the same blindness."

"I know what I am."

I sighed.

But his mercurial mood shifted on me. He pursed his lips, and his eyes were probing. He examined my face for a long moment.

"You're ready now, then?" he asked.

"Um." I gulped. "Yes?"

He smiled, and inclined his head slowly until his cold lips brushed against the skin just under the corner of my jaw.

"Right now?" he whispered, his breath blowing cool on my neck. I shivered involuntarily.

"Yes," I whispered, so my voice wouldn't have a chance to break. If he thought I was bluffing, he was going to be disappointed. I'd already made this decision, and I was sure. It didn't matter that my body was rigid as a plank, my hands balled into fists, my breathing erratic...

He chuckled darkly, and leaned away. His face did look disappointed.

"You can't really believe that I would give in so easily," he said with a sour edge to his mocking tone.

"A girl can dream."

His eyebrows rose. "Is that what you dream about? Being a monster?"

"Not exactly," I said, frowning at his word choice. Monster, indeed. "Mostly I dream about being with you forever."

His expression changed, softened and saddened by the subtle ache in my voice.

"Bella." His fingers lightly traced the shape of my lips. "I *will* stay with you—isn't that enough?"

I smiled under his fingertips. "Enough for now."

He frowned at my tenacity. No one was going to surrender tonight. He exhaled, and the sound was practically a growl.

I touched his face. "Look," I said. "I love you more than everything else in the world combined. Isn't that enough?"

"Yes, it is enough," he answered, smiling. "Enough for forever."

And he leaned down to press his cold lips once more to my throat.

Please turn the book over to read . . .

To my boys, Gabe, Seth, and Eli, for letting me be a part of the teenage boy experience. I couldn't have written this without you.

⤙ ⤚

FOREWORD

⤙ ⤛

Hello, lovely reader!

Again, happy anniversary and welcome to the new tenth-anniversary bonus material!

First things first:

I'M SO SORRY.

I know there is going to be a lot of wailing and teeth gnashing because this new bonus material is (A) not entirely new, but mostly (B) not *Midnight Sun*. (If you are worried that I don't understand your pain quite enough, let me assure you that my mother has made it abundantly clear.) I will explain how this came about, and hopefully that will make things, if not better, at least understandable.

A very short time ago, my agent approached me and asked if there was anything I could do for the tenth-anniversary rerelease of *Twilight*. The publisher was looking for a foreword of some kind, a "happy anniversary" letter thing. It seemed . . . well, to be honest, really boring. What could I say that would be fun and exciting? Nothing. So I thought about other things I could do, and if it makes you feel better, *Midnight Sun* did come up. The problem was time—as in, there wasn't any. Certainly not enough to write a novel, or even half of one.

As I was musing on *Twilight* after being away from it for so long, and discussing the anniversary problem with friends, I started thinking about something I'd said before at signings and in interviews. You know, Bella has always gotten a lot of censure for getting rescued on multiple occasions, and people have complained about her being a typical *damsel in distress*. My answer to that has always been that Bella is a *human in distress*, a normal human being surrounded on all sides

by people who are basically superheroes and supervillains. She's also been criticized for being too consumed with her love interest, as if that's somehow just a girl thing. But I've always maintained that it would have made no difference if the human were male and the vampire female—it's still the same story. Gender and species aside, *Twilight* has always been a story about the magic and obsession and frenzy of first love.

So I thought to myself, *Well, what if I put that theory to the test?* That *might be fun.* As per my usual, I started out believing that I would do one or two chapters. (It's funny/sad how I still don't seem to know myself very well.) Remember how I said there was no time? Fortunately, this project was not only fun, but also really fast and easy. It turns out that there isn't much difference at all between a female human in love with a male vampire and a male human in love with a female vampire. And that's how Beau and Edythe were born.

A couple of notes on the conversion:

1. I've done a pretty straight-across-the-board gender swap with all the *Twilight* characters, but there are two exceptions.

- The biggest exception is Charlie and Renée, who have stayed Charlie and Renée. Here's the reason for that: Beau was born in 1987. It was a rare thing for a father to get primary custody of a child in those days—even more so when the child was just a baby. Most likely, the mother would have had to be proven unfit in some way. I have a really hard time believing that any judge at that time (or even now) would give a child to a transient, unemployed father over a mother with a steady job and strong ties to her community. Of course, these days if Charlie had fought for Bella, he probably could have taken her from Renée. Thus, the more unlikely scenario is the one that plays out in *Twilight*. Only the fact that a few decades ago a mother's rights were considered more important than a father's rights, as well as the fact that Charlie's not the vindictive type, made it possible for Renée to raise Bella—and, in this case, now Beau.

- The second exception is very small—just a few background characters mentioned only twice. The reason for this exception is my misplaced sense of justice for fictional people. There were two characters in the wider *Twilight* universe who really got the shaft in an ongoing sense. So instead of doing a swap with these characters, I gave them a *coup*. It adds nothing to the story. It was just me being weird and indulging my neurosis.

2. There are many more changes in the writing than were necessitated by Beau's status as a male person, so I thought I would break them down for you. These are, of course, rough estimates. I did not count all the words I changed, or do any actual math.

- 5% of the changes I made were because Beau is a boy.

- 5% of the changes were because Beau's personality developed just slightly differently than Bella's. The biggest variations are that he's more OCD, he's not nearly so flowery with his words and thoughts, and he's not as angry—he's totally missing the chip Bella carries around on her shoulder all the time.

- 70% of the changes I made were because I was allowed to do a new editing run ten years later. I got to fix almost every word that has bothered me since the book was printed, *and it was glorious*.

- 10% were things that I wished I had done the first time around but that hadn't occurred to me at the time. That might sound like the same thing as the preceding category, but it's slightly different. This isn't a case of a word that sounds clunky or awkward. This is an idea that I wish had been explored earlier, or conversations that *should* have happened but didn't.

- 5% were mythology issues—mistakes, actually—mostly related to visions. As I continued into the sequels to *Twilight*—and even *Midnight Sun*, where I got to look inside Alice's head with

Edward—the way Alice's visions worked was refined. It's more mystical in *Twilight*, and looking at it now, there are ways she should have been involved and wasn't. Whoops!

• Which leaves a 5% catchall, for the many miscellaneous changes that I made, each for a different, and no doubt selfish, reason.

I hope you have fun with Beau and Edythe's story, even though it's not something you were waiting for. I truly had the *best time ever* creating this new version. I love Beau and Edythe with a passion I did not see coming, and their story has made the fictional world of Forks fresh and happy for me again. I hope it does the same for you. If you get one tenth of the pleasure out of this that I did, it will be worth it.

Thank you for reading. Thank you for being a part of this world, and thank you for being such an amazing and unexpected source of joy in my life for the last decade.

Much love,
Stephenie

If his destiny be strange, it is also sublime.

Jules Verne, *Twenty Thousand Leagues Under the Sea*

PREFACE

I'D NEVER GIVEN MUCH THOUGHT TO DYING—THOUGH I'D HAD REASON enough in the last few months—but even if I had, I wouldn't have imagined it like this.

I stared across the long room, into the dark eyes of the hunter, and she looked pleasantly back at me.

At least it was a good way to die, in the place of someone else, someone I loved. Noble, even. That ought to count for something.

I knew that if I'd never gone to Forks, I wouldn't be about to die now. But, terrified as I was, I couldn't bring myself to regret the decision. When life offers you a dream so far beyond any of your expectations, it's not reasonable to grieve when it comes to an end.

The hunter smiled in a friendly way as she sauntered forward to kill me.

1. FIRST SIGHT

January 17, 2005

My mom drove me to the airport with the windows rolled down. Though it was January everywhere else, it was seventy-five degrees in Phoenix, and the sky was bright blue. I had on my favorite t-shirt—the Monty Python one with the swallows and the coconut that Mom got me two Christmases ago. It didn't quite fit anymore, but that didn't matter. I wouldn't be needing t-shirts again soon.

In the Olympic Peninsula of northwest Washington State, a small town named Forks exists under a near-constant cover of clouds. It rains on this insignificant town more than any other place in the United States of America. It was from this town and its depressing gloom that my mom escaped with me when I was only a few months old. It was in this town that I'd been forced to spend a month every summer until I was fourteen. That was the year I finally started making ultimatums; these past three summers, my dad, Charlie, vacationed with me in California for two weeks instead.

Yet somehow, I now found myself exiled to Forks for the rest of my high school education. A year and a half. Eighteen months. It felt like a prison sentence. Eighteen months, hard time. When I slammed the car door behind me, it made a sound like the *clang* of iron bars locking into place.

Okay, just a tad melodramatic there. I have an overactive imagination, as

my mom was fond of telling me. And, of course, this was my choice. Self-imposed exile.

Didn't make it any easier.

I loved Phoenix. I loved the sun and the dry heat and the big, sprawling city. And I loved living with my mom, where I was needed.

"You don't have to do this," my mom said to me—the last of a hundred times—just before I got to the TSA post.

My mom says we look so much alike that I could use her for a shaving mirror. It's not entirely true, though I don't look much like my dad at all. Her chin is pointy and her lips full, which is not like me, but we do have exactly the same eyes. On her they're childlike—so wide and pale blue—which makes her look like my sister rather than my mom. We get that all the time and though she pretends not to, she loves it. On me the pale blue is less youthful and more . . . unresolved.

Staring at those wide, worried eyes so much like my own, I felt panicked. I'd been taking care of my mom for my whole life. I mean, I'm sure there must have been a time, probably when I was still in diapers, that I wasn't in charge of the bills and paperwork and cooking and general level-headedness, but I couldn't remember it.

Was leaving my mom to fend for herself really the right thing to do? It had seemed like it was, during the months I'd struggled toward this decision. But it felt all kinds of wrong now.

Of course she had Phil these days, so the bills would probably get paid on time, there would be food in the fridge, gas in the car, and someone to call when she got lost. . . . She didn't need me as much anymore.

"I *want* to go," I lied. I'd never been a good liar, but I'd been saying this lie so much lately that it almost sounded convincing now.

"Tell Charlie I said hi."

"I will."

"I'll see you soon," she promised. "You can come home whenever you want—I'll come right back as soon as you need me."

But I knew what it would cost her to do that.

"Don't worry about me," I insisted. "It'll be great. I love you, Mom."

She hugged me tightly for a minute, and then I walked through the metal detectors, and she was gone.

It's a three-hour flight from Phoenix to Seattle, another hour in a small plane up to Port Angeles, and then an hour drive back down to Forks. Flying's never bothered me; the hour in the car with Charlie, though, I was a little worried about.

Charlie had really been pretty decent about the whole thing. He seemed genuinely pleased that I was coming to live with him sort of permanently for the first time. He'd already gotten me registered for high school, and was going to help me get a car.

But it would be awkward. Neither of us was what you'd call extroverted— probably a necessary thing for living with my mother. But aside from that, what was there to say? It wasn't like I'd kept the way I felt about Forks a secret.

When I landed in Port Angeles, it was raining. It wasn't an omen, just inevitable. I'd said my goodbyes to the sun.

Charlie was waiting for me with the cruiser. This I was expecting, too. Charlie is Police Chief Swan to the good people of Forks. My primary motivation behind buying a car, despite my serious lack of funds, was that I hated driving around town in a car with red and blue lights on top. Nothing slows down traffic like a cop.

I stumbled off the plane into Charlie's awkward, one-armed hug.

"It's good to see you, Beau," he said, smiling as he automatically steadied me. We patted each other's shoulders, embarrassed, and then stepped back. "You haven't changed much. How's Renée?"

"Mom's great. It's good to see you, too, Dad." I wasn't supposed to call him Charlie to his face.

"You really feel okay about leaving her?"

We both understood that this question wasn't about my own personal happiness. It was about whether I was shirking my responsibility to look after her. This was the reason Charlie'd never fought Mom about custody; he knew she needed me.

"Yeah. I wouldn't be here if I wasn't sure."

"Fair enough."

I only had two big duffel bags. Most of my Arizona clothes were too permeable for the Washington climate. My mom and I had pooled our resources to supplement my winter wardrobe, but it still wasn't much. I could handle both of them, but Charlie insisted on taking one.

It threw my balance off a little—not that I was ever really balanced, especially since the growth spurt. My foot caught on the lip of the exit door and the bag swung out and hit the guy trying to get in.

"Oh, sorry."

The guy wasn't much older than me, and he was a lot shorter, but he stepped up to my chest with his chin raised high. I could see tattoos on both sides of his neck. A small woman with hair dyed solid black stared menacingly at me from his other side.

"*Sorry?*" she repeated, like my apology had been offensive somehow.

"Er, yeah?"

And then the woman noticed Charlie, who was in uniform. Charlie didn't even have to say anything. He just looked at the guy, who backed up a half-step and suddenly seemed a lot younger, and then the girl, whose sticky red lips settled into a pout. Without another word, they ducked around me and headed into the tiny terminal.

Charlie and I both shrugged at the same time. It was funny how we had some of the same mannerisms when we didn't spend much time together. Maybe it was genetic.

"I found a good car for you, really cheap," Charlie announced when we were strapped into the cruiser and on our way.

"What kind of car?" I asked, suspicious of the way he said "good car for *you*" as opposed to just "good car."

"Well, it's a truck actually, a Chevy."

"Where did you find it?"

"Do you remember Bonnie Black down at La Push?" La Push is the small Indian reservation on the nearby coastline.

"No."

"She and her husband used to go fishing with us during the summer," Charlie prompted.

That would explain why I didn't remember her. I do a good job of blocking painful things from my memory.

"She's in a wheelchair now," Charlie continued when I didn't respond, "so she can't drive anymore, and she offered to sell me her truck cheap."

"What year is it?" I could see from the change in his expression that this was the question he was hoping I wouldn't ask.

"Well, Bonnie's had a lot of work done on the engine—it's only a few years old, really."

Did he think I would give up that easily?

"When did she buy it?"

"She bought it in 1984, I think."

"Did she buy it new?"

"Well, no. I think it was new in the early sixties—or late fifties at the earliest," he admitted sheepishly.

"Ch—Dad, I don't really know anything about cars. I wouldn't be able to fix anything that broke, and I couldn't afford a mechanic. . . ."

"Really, Beau, the thing runs great. They don't build them like that anymore."

The thing, I thought to myself . . . it had possibilities—as a nickname, at the very least.

"How cheap is cheap?" After all, that part was the deal killer.

"Well, son, I kind of already bought it for you. As a homecoming gift." Charlie glanced sideways at me with a hopeful expression.

Wow. Free.

"You didn't need to do that, Dad. I was going to buy myself a car."

"I don't mind. I want you to be happy here." He was looking ahead at the road when he said this. Charlie had never been comfortable with expressing his emotions out loud. Another thing we had in common. So I was looking straight ahead as I responded.

"That's amazing, Dad. Thanks. I really appreciate it." No need to add that he was talking about impossibilities. Wouldn't help anything for him to suffer along with me. And I never looked a free truck in the mouth—or rather engine.

"Well, now, you're welcome," he mumbled, embarrassed by my thanks.

We exchanged a few more comments on the weather, which was wet, and that was pretty much it for conversation. We stared out the windows.

It was probably beautiful or something. Everything was green: the trees were covered in moss, both the trunks and the branches, the ground blanketed with ferns. Even the air had turned green by the time it filtered down through the leaves.

It was too green—an alien planet.

Eventually we made it to Charlie's. He still lived in the small, two-bedroom house that he'd bought with my mother in the early days of their marriage. Those were the only kind of days their marriage had—the early ones. There, parked on the street in front of the house that never changed, was my new—well, new to me—truck. It was a faded red color, with big, curvy fenders and a rounded cab.

And I loved it. I wasn't really a car guy, so I was kind of surprised by my own reaction. I mean, I didn't even know if it would run, but I could see myself in it. Plus, it was one of those solid iron monsters that never gets damaged—the kind you see at the scene of an accident, paint unscratched, surrounded by the pieces of the foreign car it had just destroyed.

"Wow, Dad, it's awesome! Thanks!" Serious enthusiasm this time. Not only was the truck strangely cool, but now I wouldn't have to walk two miles in the rain to school in the morning. Or accept a ride in the cruiser, which was obviously worst-case scenario.

"I'm glad you like it," Charlie said gruffly, embarrassed again.

It took only one trip to get all my stuff upstairs. I got the west bedroom that faced out over the front yard. The room was familiar; it had belonged to me since I was born. The wooden floor, the light blue walls, the peaked ceiling, the faded blue-and-white checked curtains around the window— these were all a part of my childhood. The only changes Charlie had ever made were switching the crib for a bed and adding a desk as I grew. The desk now held a secondhand computer, with the phone line for the modem stapled along the floor to the nearest phone jack. This was one of my mother's requirements, so that we could stay in touch. The rocking chair from my baby days was still in the corner.

There was only one small bathroom at the top of the stairs, which I would have to share with Charlie, but I'd had to share with my mom before, and that was definitely worse. She had a lot more stuff, and she doggedly resisted all my attempts to organize any of it.

One of the best things about Charlie is he doesn't hover. He left me alone to unpack and get settled, which would have been totally impossible for my mom. It was nice to be alone, not to have to smile and look comfortable; a relief to stare out the window at the sheeting rain and let my thoughts get dark.

Forks High School had just three hundred and fifty-seven—now

fifty-eight—students; there were more than seven hundred people in my junior class alone back home. All of the kids here had grown up together—their grandparents had been toddlers together. I would be the new kid from the big city, something to stare at and whisper about.

Maybe if I had been one of the cool kids, I could make this work for me. Come in all popular, homecoming king–styles. But there was no hiding the fact that I was not *that guy*—not the football star, not the class president, not the bad boy on the motorcycle. I was the kid who looked like he should be good at basketball, until I started walking. The kid who got shoved into lockers until I'd suddenly shot up eight inches sophomore year. The kid who was too quiet and too pale, who didn't know anything about gaming or cars or baseball statistics or anything else I was supposed to be into.

Unlike the other guys, I didn't have a ton of free time for hobbies. I had a checkbook to balance, a clogged drain to snake, and a week's groceries to shop for.

Or I used to.

So I didn't relate well to people my age. Maybe the truth was that I didn't relate well to people, period. Even my mother, who I was closest to of anyone on the planet, never really understood me. Sometimes I wondered if I was seeing the same things through my eyes that the rest of the world was seeing through theirs. Like, maybe what I saw as green was what everyone else saw as red. Maybe I smelled vinegar when they smelled coconut. Maybe there was a glitch in my brain.

But the cause didn't matter. All that mattered was the effect. And tomorrow would be just the beginning.

I didn't sleep well that night, even after I finally got my head to shut up. The constant *whoosh*ing of the rain and wind across the roof wouldn't fade into the background. I pulled the old quilt over my head, and later added the pillow, too. But I couldn't fall asleep until after midnight, when the rain finally settled into a quiet drizzle.

Thick fog was all I could see out my window in the morning, and I could feel the claustrophobia creeping up on me. You could never see the sky here; it was like that prison cage I'd imagined.

Breakfast with Charlie was quiet. He wished me good luck at school. I

thanked him, knowing his hope was a waste of time. Good luck tended to avoid me. Charlie left first, off to the police station that was his wife and family. After he left, I sat at the old square oak table in one of the three unmatching chairs and stared at the familiar kitchen, with its dark paneled walls, bright yellow cabinets, and white linoleum floor. Nothing had changed. My mom had painted the cabinets eighteen years ago, trying to bring some sunshine into the house. Over the small fireplace in the adjoining, microscopic family room was a row of pictures. First a wedding picture of Charlie and my mom in Las Vegas, then one of the three of us in the hospital after I was born, taken by a helpful nurse, followed by the procession of my school pictures up to this year's. Those were embarrassing to look at—the bad haircuts, the braces years, the acne that had finally cleared up. I would have to see what I could do to get Charlie to put them somewhere else, at least while I was living here.

It was impossible, being in this house, not to realize that Charlie had never gotten over my mom. It made me uncomfortable.

I didn't want to be too early to school, but I couldn't stay in the house anymore. I put on my jacket—thick, non-breathing plastic, like a biohazard suit—and headed out into the rain.

It was just drizzling still, not enough to soak me through immediately as I reached for the house key that was always hidden under the eave by the door, and locked up. The sloshing of my new waterproof boots sounded weird. I missed the normal crunch of gravel as I walked.

Inside the truck, it was nice and dry. Either Bonnie or Charlie had obviously cleaned it up, but the tan upholstered seats still smelled faintly of tobacco, gasoline, and peppermint. The engine started quickly, which was a relief, but loudly, roaring to life and then idling at top volume. Well, a truck this old was bound to have a flaw. The antique radio worked, a bonus I hadn't expected.

Finding the school wasn't difficult; like most other things, it was just off the highway. It wasn't obvious at first that it was a school; only the sign, which declared it to be the Forks High School, clued me in. It looked like a collection of matching houses, built with maroon-colored bricks. There were so many trees and shrubs I couldn't see its size at first. Where was the feel

of the institution? I thought. Where were the chain-link fences, the metal detectors?

I parked by the first building, which had a small sign over the door reading FRONT OFFICE. No one else was parked there, so I was sure it was off limits, but I decided I would get directions inside instead of circling around in the rain like an idiot.

Inside, it was brightly lit, and warmer than I'd hoped. The office was small; there was a little waiting area with padded folding chairs, orange-flecked commercial carpet, notices and awards cluttering the walls, and a big clock ticking loudly. Plants grew everywhere in large plastic pots, as if there weren't enough greenery outside. The room was cut in half by a long counter, cluttered with wire baskets full of papers and brightly colored flyers taped to the front. There were three desks behind the counter; a round, balding man in glasses sat at one. He was wearing a t-shirt, which immediately made me feel overdressed for the weather.

The balding man looked up. "Can I help you?"

"I'm Beau Swan," I informed him, and saw the quick recognition in his eyes. I was expected, already the subject of gossip. The Chief's son, the one with the unstable mom, come home at last.

"Of course," he said. He dug through a leaning stack of papers on his desk till he found the ones he was looking for. "I have your schedule right here, Beaufort, and a map of the school." He brought several sheets to the counter to show me.

"Um, it's Beau, please."

"Oh, sure, Beau."

He went through my classes for me, highlighting the best route to each on the map, and gave me a slip to have each teacher sign, which I was to bring back at the end of the day. He smiled at me and hoped, like Charlie, that I would like it here in Forks. I smiled back as convincingly as I could.

When I went back out to my truck, other students were starting to arrive. I drove around the school, following the line of traffic. Most of the cars were older like mine, nothing flashy. At home, I'd lived in one of the few lower-income neighborhoods that were included in the Paradise Valley District. It was a common thing to see a new Mercedes or Porsche in the student lot. The nicest car here was a brand-new silver Volvo, and it stood

out. Still, I cut the engine as soon as I was in a spot, so that the earsplitting volume wouldn't draw attention to me.

I looked at the map in the truck, trying to memorize it now; hopefully I wouldn't have to walk around with it stuck in front of my nose all day. I stuffed everything in my backpack, slung the strap over my shoulder, and sucked in a huge breath. *It won't be that bad*, I lied to myself. Seriously, though, this wasn't a life and death situation—it was just high school. It's not like anyone was going to bite me. I finally exhaled, and stepped out of the truck.

I pulled my hood down over my face as I walked to the sidewalk, crowded with teenagers. My plain black jacket didn't stand out, I was glad to see, though there wasn't much I could do about my height. I hunched my shoulders and kept my head down.

Once I got around the cafeteria, building three was easy to spot. A large black "3" was painted on a white square on the east corner. I followed two unisex raincoats through the door.

The classroom was small. The people in front of me stopped just inside the door to hang up their coats on a long row of hooks. I copied them. They were two girls, one a porcelain-colored blonde, the other also pale, with light brown hair. At least my skin wouldn't be a standout here.

I took the slip up to the teacher, a narrow woman with thinning hair whose desk had a nameplate identifying her as Ms. Mason. She gawked at me when she saw my name—discouraging—and I could feel the blood rush into my face, no doubt forming unattractive splotches across my cheeks and neck. At least she sent me to an empty desk at the back without introducing me to the class. I tried to fold myself into the little desk as inconspicuously as possible.

It was harder for my new classmates to stare at me in the back, but somehow, they managed. I kept my eyes down on the reading list the teacher had given me. It was pretty basic: Brontë, Shakespeare, Chaucer, Faulkner. I'd already read everything. That was comforting . . . and boring. I wondered if my mom would send me my folder of old essays, or if she would think that was cheating. I went through different arguments with her in my head while the teacher droned on.

When the bell rang, a pale, skinny girl with skin problems and hair black as an oil slick leaned across the aisle to talk to me.

"You're Beaufort Swan, aren't you?" She gave off the vibe of an overly help-ful, chess club type.

"Beau," I corrected. Everyone within a three-seat radius turned to look at me.

"Where's your next class?" she asked.

I had to check in my bag. "Um, Government, with Jefferson, in building six."

There was nowhere to look without meeting curious eyes.

"I'm headed toward building four, I could show you the way. . . ." Defi-nitely over-helpful. "I'm Erica," she added.

I forced a smile. "Thanks."

We got our jackets and headed out into the rain, which had picked up. Several people seemed to be walking too close behind us—like they were trying to eavesdrop or something. I hoped I wasn't getting paranoid.

"So, this is a lot different than Phoenix, huh?" she asked.

"Very."

"It doesn't rain much there, does it?"

"Three or four times a year."

"Wow, what must that be like?" she wondered.

"Sunny," I told her.

"You don't look very tan."

"My mother is part albino."

She studied my face uneasily, and I stifled a groan. It looked like clouds and a sense of humor didn't mix. A few months of this and I'd forget how to use sarcasm.

We walked back around the cafeteria, to the south buildings by the gym. Erica followed me right to the door, though it was clearly marked.

"Well, good luck," she said as I touched the handle. "Maybe we'll have some other classes together." She sounded hopeful.

I smiled at her—in what I hoped was not an encouraging way—and went inside.

The rest of the morning passed in about the same way. My Trigonometry teacher, Ms. Varner, who I would have disliked anyway just because of the subject she taught, was the only one who made me stand in front of the class and introduce myself. I stammered, went splotchy red, and tripped over my own boots on the way to my seat.

After two classes, I started to recognize some of the faces in each room. There was always someone braver than the others who would introduce themselves and ask me questions about how I was liking Forks. I tried to be diplomatic, but mostly I just lied a lot. At least I never needed the map.

In every class, the teacher started out calling me Beaufort, and though I corrected them immediately, it was depressing. It had taken me years to live down Beaufort—thank you *so* much, Grandpa, for dying just months before I was born and making my mom feel obligated to honor you. No one at home even remembered that Beau was just a nickname anymore. Now I had to start all over again.

One guy sat next to me in both Trig and Spanish, and he walked with me to the cafeteria for lunch. He was short, not even up to my shoulder, but his crazy curly hair made up some of the difference between our heights. I couldn't remember his name, so I smiled and nodded as he rattled on about teachers and classes. I didn't try to keep up.

We sat at the end of a full table with several of his friends, who he introduced to me—couldn't complain about the manners here. I forgot all their names as soon as he said them. They seemed to think it was cool that he'd invited me. The girl from English, Erica, waved at me from across the room, and they all laughed. Already the butt of the joke. It was probably a new record for me. But none of them seemed mean-spirited about it.

It was there, sitting in the lunchroom, trying to make conversation with seven curious strangers, that I first saw them.

They were seated in the corner of the cafeteria, as far away from where I sat as possible in the long room. There were five of them. They weren't talking, and they weren't eating, though they each had a tray of food in front of them. They weren't gawking at me, unlike most of the other students, so it was safe to stare at them. But it was none of these things that caught my attention.

They didn't look anything alike.

There were three girls; one I could tell was super tall, even sitting down, maybe as tall as I was—her legs went on *forever*. She looked like she might be the captain of the volleyball team, and I was pretty sure you wouldn't want to get in the way of one of her spikes. She had dark, curly hair, pulled back in a messy ponytail.

Another had hair the color of honey hanging to her shoulders; she was not quite so tall as the brunette but still probably taller than most of the other guys at my table. There was something intense about her, edgy. It was kind of weird, but for some reason she made me think of this actress I'd seen in an action movie a few weeks ago, who took down a dozen guys with a machete. I remembered thinking then that I didn't buy it—there was no way the actress could have taken on that many bad guys and won. But I thought now that I might have bought it all if the character had been played by *this* girl.

The last girl was smaller, with hair somewhere between red and brown, but different than either, kind of metallic somehow, a bronze-y color. She looked younger than the other two, who could have been in college, easy.

The two guys were opposites. The taller one—who was definitely taller than me, I'd guess six-five or even more—was clearly the school's star athlete. And the prom king. And the guy who always had dibs on whatever equipment he wanted in the weight room. His straight gold hair was wound into a bun on the back of his head, but there was nothing feminine about it—somehow it made him look even more like a man. He was clearly too cool for this school, or any other I could imagine.

The shorter guy was wiry, his dark hair buzzed so short it was just a shadow across his scalp.

Totally different, and yet, they were all exactly alike. Every one of them was chalky pale, the palest of all the students living in this sunless town. Paler than me, the albino. They all had very dark eyes—from here they looked black—despite the range in their hair colors. There were deep shadows under all their eyes—purple shadows, like bruises. Maybe the five of them had just pulled an all-nighter. Or maybe they were recovering from broken noses. Except that their noses, all their features, were straight, angular.

But that wasn't why I couldn't look away.

I stared because their faces, so different, so similar, were all insanely, inhumanly beautiful. The girls and the guys both—beautiful. They were faces you never saw in real life—just airbrushed in magazines and on billboards. Or in a museum, painted by an old master as the face of an angel. It was hard to believe they were real.

I decided the most beautiful of all was the smaller girl with the bronze-

colored hair, though I expected the female half of the student body would vote for the movie-star blond guy. They would be wrong, though. I mean, all of them were gorgeous, but the girl was something more than just beautiful. She was absolutely perfect. It was an upsetting, disturbing kind of perfection. It made my stomach uneasy.

They were all looking away; away from each other, away from the rest of the students, away from anything in particular as far as I could tell. It reminded me of models posed oh so artistically for an ad—aesthetic ennui. As I watched, the wiry skinhead guy rose with his tray—unopened soda, untouched apple—and walked away with a quick, graceful lope that belonged on a runway. I watched, wondering if they had a dance company here in town, till he dumped his tray and glided through the back door, faster than I would have thought possible. My eyes darted back to the others, who hadn't changed.

"Who are *they*?" I asked the guy from my Spanish class, whose name I'd forgotten.

As he looked up to see who I meant—though he could probably guess from my tone—suddenly she looked at us, the perfect one. She looked at my neighbor for just a fraction of a second, and then her dark eyes flickered to mine. Long eyes, angled up at the corners, thick lashes.

She looked away quickly, faster than I could, though I dropped my stare as soon as she'd glanced our way. I could feel the patches of red start to bloom in my face. In that brief flash of a glance, her face wasn't interested at all—it was like he had called her name, and she'd looked up in involuntary response, already having decided not to answer.

My neighbor laughed once, uncomfortable, looking down at the table like I did.

He muttered his answer under his breath. "Those are the Cullens and the Hales. Edith and Eleanor Cullen, Jessamine and Royal Hale. The one who left was Archie Cullen. They live with Dr. Cullen and her husband."

I glanced sideways at the perfect girl, who was looking at her tray now, picking a bagel to pieces with thin, pale fingers. Her mouth was moving very quickly, her full lips barely opening. The other three looked away, but I still thought she might be speaking quietly to them.

Weird names. Old-fashioned. The kinds of names grandparents had—like

my name. Maybe that was the thing here? Small-town names? And then I finally remembered that my neighbor was named Jeremy. A totally normal name. There were two kids named Jeremy in my history class back home.

"They're all very . . . good-looking." What an understatement.

"Yeah!" Jeremy agreed with another laugh. "They're all *together*, though— Royal and Eleanor, Archie and Jessamine. Like dating, you know? And they *live* together." He snickered and wagged his eyebrows suggestively.

I didn't know why, but his reaction made me want to defend them. Maybe just because he sounded so judgmental. But what could I say? I didn't know anything about them.

"Which ones are the Cullens?" I asked, wanting to change the tone but not the subject. "They don't look related . . . well, I mean, sort of . . ."

"Oh, they're not. Dr. Cullen is really young. Early thirties. The Cullen kids are all adopted. The Hales—the blondes—*are* brother and sister, twins, I think, and they're some kind of foster kids."

"They look old for foster kids."

"They are now. Royal and Jessamine are both eighteen, but they've been with Mr. Cullen since they were little. He's their uncle, I think."

"That's actually kind of amazing—for them to take care of all those kids, when they're so young and everything."

"I guess so," Jeremy said, though it sounded like he'd rather not say anything positive. As if he didn't like the doctor and her husband for some reason . . . and the way he was looking at their adopted kids, I could guess there might be some jealousy involved. "I think Dr. Cullen can't have any kids, though," he added, as if that somehow made what they were doing less admirable.

Through all this conversation, I couldn't keep my eyes away from the strange family for more than a few seconds at a time. They continued to look at the walls and not eat.

"Have they always lived in Forks?" I asked. How could I never have noticed them during my summers here?

"No. They just moved down two years ago from somewhere in Alaska."

I felt a strange wave of pity, and relief. Pity because, as beautiful as they were, they were still outsiders, not accepted. Relief that I wasn't the only newcomer here, and definitely not the most interesting by any standard.

As I examined them again, the perfect girl, one of the Cullens, looked up and met my gaze, this time with obvious curiosity. As I immediately looked away, I thought that her look held some kind of unanswered expectation.

"Which one is the girl with the reddish brown hair?" I asked. I tried to glance casually in that direction, like I was just checking out the cafeteria; she was still staring at me, but not gawking like the other kids had today—she had this frustrated expression I didn't understand. I looked down again.

"That's Edith. She's hot, sure, but don't waste your time. She doesn't go out with anyone. Apparently none of the guys here are good enough for her," Jeremy said sourly, then grunted. I wondered how many times she'd turned him down.

I pressed my lips together to hide a smile. Then I glanced at her again. Edith. Her face was turned away, but I thought from the shape of her cheek that she might be smiling, too.

After a few more minutes, the four of them left the table together. They all were seriously graceful—even the golden prom king. It was a strange thing to watch them in motion together. Edith didn't look at me again.

I sat at the table with Jeremy and his friends longer than I would have if I'd been sitting alone. I didn't want to be late for class on my first day. One of my new acquaintances, who politely reminded me that his name was Allen, had Biology II with me the next hour. We walked to class together in silence. He was probably shy like me.

When we entered the classroom, Allen went to sit at a black-topped lab table exactly like the ones I was used to at home. He already had a neighbor. In fact, all the tables were filled but one. Next to the center aisle, I recognized Edith Cullen by her unusual metallic hair, sitting next to that single open seat.

My heart started pounding a little faster than usual.

As I walked down the aisle to do my required intro for the teacher and get my slip signed, I was watching her, trying to make it covert. Just as I passed, she suddenly went rigid in her seat. Her face jerked up toward mine so fast it surprised me, staring with the strangest expression—it was more than angry, it was furious, hostile. I looked away, stunned, going red again. I stumbled over a book in the walkway and had to catch myself on the edge of a table. The girl sitting there giggled.

I'd been right about the eyes. They were black—coal black.

Mrs. Banner signed my slip and handed me a book with no nonsense about introductions and no mention of my full name. I could tell we were going to get along. Of course, she had no choice but to send me to the one open seat in the middle of the room. I kept my eyes down as I went to sit by *her*, confused and awkward, wondering what I could have done to earn the antagonistic glare she'd given me.

I didn't look up as I set my book on the table and took my seat, but I saw her posture change from the corner of my eye. She was leaning away from me, sitting on the extreme edge of her chair and averting her face like she smelled something bad. Inconspicuously, I sniffed. My shirt smelled like laundry detergent. How could that be offensive? I scooted my chair to the right, giving her as much space as I could, and tried to pay attention to the teacher.

The lecture was on cellular anatomy, something I'd already studied. I took notes carefully anyway, always looking down.

I couldn't stop myself from shooting the occasional glance at the strange girl next to me. Throughout the entire class, she never relaxed her stiff position on the edge of her chair, sitting as far from me as possible, with her hair hiding most of her face. Her hand was clenched into a fist on top of her left thigh, tendons standing out under her pale skin. This, too, she never relaxed. She had the sleeves of her white henley pushed up to her elbows, and her forearm flexed with surprisingly hard muscle beneath her pale skin. I couldn't help but notice how perfect that skin was. Not one freckle, not one scar.

The class seemed to drag on longer than the rest. Was it because the day was finally ending, or because I was waiting for her tight fist to loosen? It never did; she continued to sit so still it looked like she wasn't even breathing. What was wrong with her? Was this how she usually acted? I questioned my quick judgment on Jeremy's sour grapes at lunch today. Maybe he wasn't just resentful.

This couldn't have anything to do with me. She didn't know me from Adam.

Mrs. Banner passed some quizzes back when the class was almost done. She handed me one to give to the girl. I glanced at the top automatically—one hundred percent . . . and I'd been spelling her name wrong in my head.

It was Edythe, not Edith. I'd never seen it spelled that way, but it fit her better.

I glanced down at her as I slid the paper over, and then instantly regretted it. She was glaring up at me again, her long, black eyes full of revulsion. As I flinched away from the hate radiating from her, the phrase *if looks could kill* suddenly ran through my mind.

At that moment, the bell rang loudly, making me jump, and Edythe Cullen was out of her seat. She moved like a dancer, every perfect line of her slim body in harmony with all the others, her back to me, and she was out the door before anyone else was out of their seat.

I sat frozen in my seat, staring blankly after her. She was so harsh. I began gathering up my things slowly, trying to block out the confusion and guilt that filled me. Why should I feel guilty? I hadn't done anything wrong. How could I have? I hadn't actually even met her.

"Aren't you Beaufort Swan?" a female voice asked.

I looked up to see a cute, baby-faced girl, her hair carefully flat-ironed into a pale blond curtain, smiling at me in a friendly way. She obviously didn't think I smelled bad.

"Beau," I corrected her, smiling back.

"I'm McKayla."

"Hi, McKayla."

"Do you need any help finding your next class?"

"I'm headed to the gym, actually. I think I can find it."

"That's my next class, too." She seemed thrilled, though it wasn't such a big coincidence in a school this small.

We walked to class together; she was a chatterer—she supplied most of the conversation, which made it easy for me. She'd lived in California till she was ten, so she got how I felt about the sun. It turned out she'd been in my English class also. She was the nicest person I'd met today.

But as we were entering the gym she asked, "So, did you stab Edythe Cullen with a pencil or what? I've never seen her act like that."

I winced. I guess I wasn't the only one who had noticed. And, apparently, that *wasn't* Edythe Cullen's usual behavior. I decided to play dumb.

"Was that the girl I sat next to in Biology?"

"Yeah," she said. "She looked like she was in pain or something."

"I don't know," I responded. "I never spoke to her."

"She's weird." McKayla lingered by me instead of heading to the dressing room. "If I got to sit by you, I would have talked to you."

I smiled at her before walking through the boys' locker room door. She was kind and seemed to like me. But that wasn't enough to make me forget the last strange hour.

The Gym teacher, Coach Clapp, found me a uniform, but she didn't make me dress down for today's class. At home, only two years of P.E. were required. Here P.E. was mandatory all four years. My own special version of hell.

I watched four volleyball games running simultaneously. Remembering how many injuries I had sustained—and inflicted—playing volleyball, I felt a little nauseated.

The final bell rang at last. I walked slowly to the office to return my paperwork. The rain had faded away, but the wind was strong, and colder. I zipped my jacket up and shoved my free hand into a pocket.

When I walked into the warm office, I almost turned around and walked back out.

Edythe Cullen stood at the desk in front of me. Impossible not to recognize her tangled bronze hair. She didn't seem to notice the sound of my entrance. I stood pressed against the back wall, waiting for the balding receptionist to be free.

She was arguing with him in a low, velvety voice. I quickly picked up the gist of the argument. She was trying to trade from sixth-hour Biology to another time—any other time.

This could *not* be about me. It had to be something else, something that happened before I got to the Biology room. The look on her face must have been about some other problem. It was impossible that a stranger could take such a sudden, intense dislike to me. I wasn't interesting enough to be worth that strong of a reaction.

The door opened again, and the cold wind suddenly gusted through the room, rustling the papers on the desk, waving through my hair. The girl who came in merely stepped to the desk, placed a note in the wire basket, and walked out again. But Edythe Cullen's back stiffened, and she turned slowly to glare at me—her face was ridiculously perfect, not even one tiny

flaw to make her seem human—with piercing, hate-filled eyes. For an instant, I felt the oddest thrill of genuine *fear*, raising the hair on my arms. As if she were going to pull a gun out and shoot me. The look only lasted a second, but it was colder than the freezing wind. She turned back to the receptionist.

"Never mind, then," she said quickly in a voice like silk. "I can see that it's impossible. Thank you so much for your help." And she turned on her heel without another look at me, and disappeared out the door.

I went robotically to the desk, my face white for once instead of red, and handed him the signed slip.

"How did your first day go, son?" he asked.

"Fine," I lied, my voice cracking. I could see I hadn't convinced him.

When I got to the truck, it was almost the last car in the lot. It seemed like a haven, already the closest thing to home I had in this wet, green hell. I sat inside for a while, just staring out the windshield blankly. But soon I was cold enough to want the heater, so I turned the key and the engine roared to life. I headed back to Charlie's house, trying to think of nothing at all.

2. OPEN BOOK

THE NEXT DAY WAS BETTER . . . AND WORSE.

It was better because it wasn't raining yet, though the clouds were dense and black. It was easier because I knew better what to expect of the day. McKayla came to sit by me in English, and walked with me to my next class, with Chess Club Erica glaring at her all the way there; that was kind of flattering. People didn't stare at me quite as much as they had yesterday. I sat with a big group at lunch that included McKayla, Erica, Jeremy, Allen, and several other people whose names and faces I now remembered. I began to feel like I might be treading water, instead of drowning in it.

It was worse because I was tired; I still couldn't sleep with the rain beating on the house. It was worse because Ms. Varner called on me in Trig when my hand wasn't raised and I had the wrong answer. It was miserable because I had to play volleyball, and the one time I didn't dodge out of the way of the ball, I hit two of my teammates in the head with one bad volley. And it was worse because Edythe Cullen wasn't in school at all.

All morning I was trying not to think about lunch, not wanting to remember those hate-filled stares. Part of me wanted to confront her and demand to know what her problem was. While I was lying awake in bed, I even imagined out what I would say. But I knew myself too well to think I would really have the guts to do it. Maybe if she hadn't been so abnormally beautiful.

But when I walked into the cafeteria with Jeremy—trying to keep my

eyes from sweeping the place for her and totally failing—I saw that her four adopted siblings were sitting together at the same table as before, and she was not with them.

McKayla intercepted us and steered us to her table. Jeremy seemed thrilled by the attention, and his friends quickly joined us. I tried to tune into the conversations around me, but I was still uncomfortable, waiting for Edythe's arrival. I hoped that she would simply ignore me when she came, and prove that I was making a big deal out of nothing.

She didn't come, and I got more and more tense.

I walked to Biology with more confidence when, by the end of lunch, she still hadn't showed. McKayla, who was starting to seem weirdly, I don't know, *territorial* about me, walked by my side to class. I hesitated for a second at the door, but Edythe Cullen wasn't here, either. I exhaled and went to my seat. McKayla followed, talking about an upcoming trip to the beach. She lingered by my desk till the bell rang, then she smiled at me wistfully and went to sit by a boy with braces and something close to a bowl cut.

I didn't want to be arrogant, but I was pretty sure she was into me, which was a strange feeling. Girls hadn't noticed me much at home. I wondered if I *wanted* her to like me. She was sort of pretty and everything, but her attention made me feel a little uncomfortable. Why was that? Because she'd picked me instead of the other way around? That was a stupid reason. Ego running wild, like it had to be my decision first. Still, it was not as stupid as the other possibility I'd thought of—I really hoped it wasn't because of the time I'd spent staring at Edythe Cullen yesterday, but I was kind of afraid that was it. Which was about the stupidest thing possible, really. If I based my reaction to a girl's looks off a face like Edythe's, I was doomed. That was fantasy, not reality.

I was glad that I had the desk to myself, that Edythe wasn't here. I told myself that again and again. Still, I couldn't get rid of this annoying feeling that I was the reason she was gone. It was ridiculous, and egotistical again, to think that I could affect anyone that much. It was impossible. But I couldn't stop worrying about it.

When the school day was finally done, and the patches of red were fading out of my face from the latest volleyball incident, I changed quickly back

into my jeans and heavy sweater. I rushed from the locker room, glad to find that I had successfully evaded McKayla for the moment. I hurried out to the parking lot. It was crowded now with fleeing students. I got in my truck and dug through my backpack to make sure I still had what I needed.

It was no secret that Charlie couldn't cook much besides fried eggs and bacon. Last night, I'd requested that I be assigned kitchen detail for the duration of my stay. He was willing enough to let me take over. A quick search revealed that he had no food in the house. So I had my grocery list and the cash from the jar in the cupboard labeled FOOD MONEY, and I was headed to the Thriftway.

I gunned the thunderous engine to life, ignoring the heads that turned in my direction, and backed into a place in the line of cars that were waiting to exit the parking lot. As I waited, trying to pretend that the earsplitting rumble was coming from someone else's car, I saw the two Cullens and the Hale twins walking up to their car. It was the shiny new Volvo. Of course. I hadn't noticed their clothes before—I'd been too mesmerized by their faces. Now that I looked, it was obvious that they were all wearing stuff that probably cost more than my entire wardrobe. Attractive as they all were, they could have worn garbage sacks and started a trend. It seemed like too much for them to have both looks and money. Though, as far as I could tell, life worked that way most of the time. It didn't look like it bought them any popularity here.

But I couldn't really believe that. The isolation had to be something they chose; I couldn't imagine any door their beauty wouldn't open for them.

They looked at my noisy truck as I passed them, just like everyone else. Except they weren't anything like anyone else. I saw that the big blond guy—Royal, it must be. Figured. Anyway, *Royal* had his hand casually on the hip of the really tall girl with the dark curly hair, who looked like she was just as familiar with the weight room as he was. He had to be a good two inches taller than even I was, but he only had a half-inch on her. Though he was obviously pretty sure of himself, I was still kind of surprised he felt comfortable doing that. Not that she wasn't hot—she was super, mega hot—but not . . . approachable. Like, not even the Rock would dare to whistle at her, if you know what I mean. The blond girl caught me looking, and the way her eyes narrowed made me turn straight ahead and punch the gas. The truck didn't go any faster, the engine just grumbled even louder.

The Thriftway was not far from the school, a few streets south, off the highway. It was nice to be inside the supermarket; it felt normal. I did most of the shopping at home, and I fell easily into the pattern of the familiar job. The store was big enough inside that I couldn't hear the tapping of the rain on the roof to remind me where I was.

When I got home, I unloaded all the groceries, reorganizing the cupboards till everything was in a place that made sense. Charlie's system was kind of haphazard. I hoped Charlie wouldn't mind, that he wasn't OCD about his kitchen the way I was. Once I was satisfied with the organization, I worked on the prep for dinner.

I kind of have a sixth sense about my mom. I realized, as I was sticking the marinade-covered steak into the fridge, that I hadn't let her know I'd made it yesterday. She was probably freaking out.

I ran up the stairs two at a time and fired up the old computer in my room. It took a minute to wheeze to life and then I had to wait for a connection. Once I was online, three messages showed up in my in-box. The first was from yesterday, while I was still en route.

"Beau," my mom wrote.

Write me as soon as you get in. Tell me how your flight was. Is it raining? I miss you already. I'm almost finished packing for Florida, but I can't find my pink blouse. Do you know where I put it? Phil says hi. Mom.

I sighed, and went to the next. It was sent six hours after the first.

Beau,
Why haven't you e-mailed me yet? What are you waiting for? Mom.

The last was from this morning.

Beaufort Swan,
If I haven't heard from you by 5:30 p.m. today I'm calling Charlie.

I checked the clock. I still had an hour, but Mom was known for jumping the gun.

Mom,
Calm down. I'm writing right now. Don't do anything crazy.
  Beau.

I sent that, and then started the next, beginning with a lie.

Everything is great. Of course it's raining. I was
waiting for something to write about. School isn't bad,
just a little repetitive. I met some okay kids who sit
by me at lunch.

Your shirt is at the dry cleaners—you were supposed to
pick it up Friday.

Charlie bought me a truck, can you believe it? It's
awesome. It's old, but really sturdy, which is good,
you know, for me.

I miss you, too. I'll write again soon, but I'm not going
to check my e-mail every five minutes. Relax, breathe. I
love you.
  Beau.

I heard the front door bang open, and I hurried downstairs to take the potatoes out and put the steak in to broil.

"Beau?" my father called out when he heard me on the stairs.

Who else? I thought to myself.

"Hey, Dad, welcome home."

"Thanks." He hung up his gun belt and stepped out of his boots as I moved around the kitchen. As far as I was aware, he'd never shot the gun on the job. But he kept it ready. When I'd come here as a child, he would always remove the bullets as soon as he walked in the door. I guess he

considered me old enough now not to shoot myself by accident, and not depressed enough to shoot myself on purpose.

"What's for dinner?" he asked warily. Mom was an imaginative cook, when she bothered, and her experiments weren't always edible. I was surprised, and sad, that he seemed to remember that far back.

"Steak and potatoes," I answered. Charlie looked relieved.

He obviously felt awkward standing in the kitchen doing nothing; he lumbered into the living room to watch TV while I worked. I think we were both more comfortable that way. I made a salad while the steak cooked, and set the table.

I called him in when dinner was ready, and he sniffed appreciatively as he walked into the room.

"Smells good, Beau."

"Thanks."

We ate in silence for a few minutes. It wasn't awkward. Both of us like quiet. In some ways, we were good roommates.

"So, how did you like school? Make any friends?" he asked as he was taking seconds.

"Well, I have a few classes with this guy named Jeremy. I sit with his friends at lunch. And there's this girl, McKayla, who's friendly. Everybody seems pretty nice." With one outstanding exception.

"That must be McKayla Newton. Nice girl—nice family. Her dad owns the sporting goods store just outside of town. He makes a good living off all the backpackers who come through here."

We ate in silence for a minute.

"Do you know the Cullen family?" I asked, trying to sound casual.

"Dr. Cullen's family? Sure. She's a great woman."

"They—the kids—are a little . . . different. They don't seem to fit in very well at school."

I was surprised to see Charlie's face get red, the way it does when he's angry.

"People in this town," he muttered. "Dr. Cullen is a brilliant surgeon who could probably work in any hospital in the world, make ten times the salary she gets here," he continued, getting louder. "We're lucky to have her—lucky that her husband wanted to live in a small town. She's an asset to the community,

and all of those kids are well behaved and polite. I had my doubts, when they first moved in, with all those adopted teenagers. I thought we might have some problems with them. But they're all very mature—I haven't had one speck of trouble from any of them. That's more than I can say for the children of some folks who have lived in this town for generations. And they stick together the way a family should—camping trips every other weekend. . . . Just because they're newcomers, people have to talk."

It was the longest speech I'd ever heard Charlie make. He must feel strongly about whatever people were saying.

I backpedaled. "They seemed nice enough to me. I just noticed they kept to themselves. They're all very attractive," I added, trying to be more complimentary.

"You should see the doctor," Charlie said, laughing. "It's a good thing she's happily married. A lot of the hospital staff have a hard time concentrating on their work with her around."

We lapsed back into silence as we finished eating. He cleared the table while I started on the dishes. He went back to the TV, and after I finished washing the dishes by hand—no dishwasher—I went upstairs to work on my math homework. I could feel a tradition in the making.

That night it was finally quiet. I fell asleep fast, exhausted.

The rest of the week was uneventful. I got used to the routine of my classes. By Friday I was able to recognize, if not name, almost all the kids at school. In Gym, the people on my team learned not to send the ball my direction. I stayed out of their way.

Edythe Cullen didn't come back to school.

Every day, I watched, pretending I wasn't looking, until the rest of the Cullens entered the cafeteria without her. Then I could relax and join in the conversation. Mostly it centered around a trip to the La Push Ocean Park in two weeks that McKayla was putting together. I was invited, and I agreed to go, more out of politeness than a strong urge to hit the beach. I believed beaches should be hot, and—aside from the ocean—dry.

By Friday I was totally comfortable entering my Biology class, no longer worried that Edythe would show. For all I knew, she'd dropped out of school. I tried not to think about her, but I couldn't totally erase the worry that I was responsible for her continued absence, ridiculous as it seemed.

My first weekend in Forks continued without incident. Charlie worked most of the time. I wrote my mom more fake cheerful e-mails, got ahead on my homework, and cleaned up the house—obviously OCD wasn't a problem for Charlie. I drove to the library Saturday, but I didn't even bother to get a card—there wasn't anything interesting I hadn't read; I would have to visit Olympia or Seattle soon, and find a good bookstore. I wondered idly what kind of gas mileage the truck got . . . and winced at the thought.

The rain stayed soft over the weekend, quiet, so I was able to sleep.

People greeted me in the parking lot Monday morning. I didn't know all their names, but I smiled at everyone. It was colder this morning, but at least it wasn't raining. In English, McKayla took her now-normal seat by my side. We had a pop quiz on *Wuthering Heights*. It was straightforward, very easy.

All in all, I was feeling a lot more comfortable than I had thought I would feel by this point. More comfortable than I had ever expected to feel here.

When we walked out of class, the air was full of swirling bits of white. I could hear people shouting excitedly to each other. The wind was freezing against my cheeks, my nose.

"Wow," McKayla said. "It's snowing."

I looked at the little cotton fluffs that were building up along the sidewalk and swirling erratically past my face.

"Ugh." Snow. There went my good day.

She looked surprised. "Don't you like snow?"

"Snow means it's too cold for rain." Obviously. "Besides, I thought it was supposed to come down in flakes—you know, each one unique and all that. These just look like the ends of Q-tips."

"Haven't you ever seen snow fall before?" she asked incredulously.

"Sure I have." I paused. "On TV."

McKayla laughed. And then a big, wet ball of dripping snow smacked into the back of her head. We both turned to see where it came from. I suspected Erica, who was walking away, her back toward us—in the wrong direction for her next class. McKayla had the same idea. She bent over and began scraping together a pile of white mush.

"I'll see you at lunch, okay?" I kept walking as I spoke. The last thing I wanted was a wad of dirty ice melting down my neck the rest of the day.

She just nodded, her eyes on Erica's back.

I kept a sharp lookout on the way to the cafeteria with Jeremy after Spanish. Mush balls were flying everywhere. I had a binder in my hands, ready to use it as a shield. Jeremy thought I was hilarious, but something in my expression kept him from lobbing a snowball at me himself.

McKayla caught up to us as we walked in the doors, laughing, her usually sleek hair turning frizzy from the wet. She and Jeremy were talking animatedly about the snow fight as we got in line to buy food. I glanced toward that table in the corner out of habit. And then I froze where I stood. There were five people at the table.

Jeremy pulled on my arm.

"Hey? Beau? What do you want?"

I looked down; my ears were hot. I had no reason to feel self-conscious, I reminded myself. I hadn't done anything wrong.

"What's with Beau?" McKayla asked Jeremy.

"Nothing," I answered. I grabbed a soda bottle as I caught up to the end of the line.

"Aren't you hungry?" Jeremy asked.

"Actually, I feel a little sick," I said.

He shuffled a few steps away from me.

I waited for them to get their food, and then followed them to the table, my eyes anywhere but the back corner of the cafeteria.

I drank my soda slowly, stomach churning. Twice McKayla asked, with a concerned tone that seemed a little over the top, how I was feeling. I told her it was nothing, but I was wondering if I *should* play it up and escape to the nurse's office for the next hour.

Ridiculous. I shouldn't have to run away. Why was I being such a coward? Was it so bad to be glared at? It wasn't like she was actually going to stab a knife in me.

I decided to allow myself one glance at the Cullen family's table. Just to read the mood.

I kept my head turned away and glanced out of the side of my eye. None of them were looking this way. I turned my head a little.

They were laughing. Edythe, Jessamine, and Eleanor all had their hair entirely saturated with melting snow. Archie and Royal were leaning away as Eleanor flipped her dripping hair toward them, leaving a wide arc of

splatters across the front of their jackets. They were enjoying the snowy day, just like everyone else—only they looked more like a scene from a movie than the rest of us.

But, aside from the laughter and playfulness, there was something different, and I couldn't quite figure out what that difference was. I examined Edythe, comparing her to my memory of last week. Her skin was less pale, I decided—flushed from the snow fight maybe—the circles under her eyes much less noticeable. Her hair was darker, wet and slicked down against her head. But there was something else. I forgot to pretend I wasn't staring as I tried to put my finger on the change.

"What are you staring at, Beau?" Jeremy asked.

At that precise moment, Edythe's eyes flashed over to meet mine.

I turned my head completely toward Jeremy, shifting my shoulders in his direction, too. Jeremy leaned away, surprised by my sudden invasion of his personal space.

I was sure, though, in the instant our eyes had met, that she didn't look angry or disgusted as she had the last time I'd seen her. She just looked curious again, unsatisfied in some way.

"Edythe Cullen is staring at you," Jeremy said, looking over my shoulder.

"She doesn't look angry, does she?" I couldn't help asking.

"No." Jeremy looked confused, then he suddenly smiled. "What did you do, ask her out?"

"No! I've never even talked to her. I just . . . don't think she likes me very much," I admitted. I kept my body angled toward Jeremy, but the back of my neck had goose bumps, like I could feel her eyes on me.

"The Cullens don't like anybody . . . well, they don't notice anybody enough to like them. But she's still staring at you."

"Stop looking at her," I insisted.

He snickered, but finally looked away.

McKayla interrupted us then—she was planning an epic battle of the blizzard in the parking lot after school and wanted us to join. Jeremy agreed enthusiastically. The way he looked at McKayla left little doubt that he would be up for anything she suggested. I kept silent. I wondered how many years I would have to live in Forks before I was bored enough to find frozen water exciting. Probably much longer than I planned to be here.

For the rest of the lunch hour I very carefully kept my eyes at my own table. Edythe didn't look like she was planning to murder me anymore, so it was no big thing to go to Biology. My stomach twisted at the thought of sitting next to her again.

I didn't really want to walk to class with McKayla as usual—she seemed to be a popular target for snowballs—but when we got to the door, everyone besides me groaned in unison. It was raining, washing all traces of the snow away in clear, icy ribbons down the side of the walkway. I pulled my hood up, hiding my smile. I would be free to go straight home after Gym.

McKayla kept up a string of complaints on the way to building four.

Once inside the classroom, I was relieved that Edythe's chair was still empty. It gave me a minute to settle myself. Mrs. Banner was walking around the room, distributing one microscope and box of slides to each table. Class still had a few minutes before it started, and the room buzzed with conversation. I kept my eyes away from the door, doodling idly on the cover of my notebook.

I heard very clearly when the chair next to me moved, but I kept my eyes focused on the pattern I was drawing.

"Hello," said a quiet, musical voice.

I looked up, shocked that she was speaking to me. She was sitting as far away from me as the desk allowed, but her chair was angled toward me. Her hair was dripping wet, tangled—even so, she looked like she'd just finished shooting a commercial. Her perfect face was friendly, open, a slight smile on her full, pink lips. But her long eyes were careful.

"My name is Edythe Cullen," she continued. "I didn't have a chance to introduce myself last week. You must be Beau Swan."

My mind was whirling with confusion. Had I made up the whole thing? She was totally polite now. I had to say something; she was waiting. But I couldn't think of anything normal to say.

"H-how do you know my name?" I stammered.

She laughed softly. "Oh, I think everyone knows your name. The whole town's been waiting for you to arrive."

I frowned, though it wasn't as if I hadn't guessed as much.

"No," I persisted like an idiot. "I meant, why did you call me Beau?"

She seemed confused. "Do you prefer Beaufort?"

"*Absolutely* not," I said. "But I think Charlie—I mean, my dad—must call me that behind my back—that's what everyone here seemed to know me as." The more I tried to explain, the more moronic it sounded.

"Oh." She let it drop. I looked away awkwardly.

Luckily, Mrs. Banner started class at that moment. I tried to concentrate as she explained the lab we would be doing today. The slides in the box were out of order. Working as lab partners, we had to separate the slides of onion root tip cells into the phases of mitosis they represented and label them accordingly. We weren't supposed to use our books. In twenty minutes, she would be coming around to see who had it right.

"Get started," she commanded.

"Ladies first, partner?" Edythe asked. I looked up to see her smiling a dimpled smile so perfect that I could only stare at her like a fool.

She raised her eyebrows.

"Uh, sure, go ahead," I sputtered.

I saw her eyes flash to the splotches blooming across my cheeks. Why couldn't my blood just stay in my veins where it belonged?

She looked away sharply, yanking the microscope to her side of the table.

She studied the first slide for a quarter of a second—maybe less.

"Prophase."

She switched out the slide for the next, then paused and looked up at me.

"Or did you want to check?" she challenged.

"Uh, no, I'm good," I said.

She wrote the word *Prophase* neatly on the top line of our worksheet. Even her handwriting was perfect, like she'd taken classes in penmanship or something. Did anyone still do that?

She barely glanced through the microscope at the second slide, then wrote *Anaphase* on the next line, looping her *A* like it was calligraphy, like she was addressing a wedding invitation. I'd had to do the invitations for my mom's wedding. I'd printed the labels in a fancy script font that didn't look anything as elegant as Edythe's handwriting.

She moved the next slide into place, while I took advantage of her diverted attention to stare. So close up, you'd think I'd be able to see something—a hint of a pimple, a stray eyebrow hair, a pore, *something*—wrong with her. But there was nothing.

Suddenly her head flipped up, eyes to the front of the class, just before Mrs. Banner called out, "Miss Cullen?"

"Yes, Mrs. Banner?" Edythe slid the microscope toward me as she spoke.

"Perhaps you should let Mr. Swan have an opportunity to learn?"

"Of course, Mrs. Banner."

Edythe turned and gave me a *well, go ahead then* look.

I bent down to look through the eyepiece. I could sense she was watching—only fair, considering how I'd been ogling her—but it made me feel awkward, like just inclining my head was a clumsy move.

At least the slide wasn't difficult.

"Metaphase," I said.

"Do you mind if I look?" she asked as I started to remove the slide. Her hand caught mine, to stop me, as she was speaking. Her fingers were ice cold, like she'd been holding them in a snowdrift before class. But that wasn't why I jerked my hand away so quickly. When she touched me, it stung my hand like a low-voltage electric shock.

"I'm sorry," she murmured, quickly pulling her hand back, though she continued to reach for the microscope. I watched her, a little dazed, as she examined the slide for another tiny fraction of a second.

"Metaphase," she agreed, then slid the microscope back to me.

I tried to exchange slides, but they were too small or my fingers were too big, and I ended up dropping both. One fell on the table and the other over the edge, but Edythe caught it before it could hit the ground.

"Ugh," I exhaled, mortified. "Sorry."

"Well, the last is no mystery, regardless," she said. Her tone was right on the edge of laughter. Butt of the joke again.

Edythe calligraphied the words *Metaphase* and *Telophase* onto the last two lines of the worksheet.

We were finished before anyone else was close. I could see McKayla and her partner comparing two slides again and again, and another pair had their book open under the table.

Which left me with nothing to do but try not to look at her . . . unsuccessfully. I glanced down, and she was staring at me, that same strange look of frustration in her eyes. Suddenly I identified that elusive difference in her face.

"Did you get contacts?" I blurted out.

She seemed puzzled by my apropos-of-nothing question. "No."

"Oh," I mumbled. "I thought there was something different about your eyes."

She shrugged, and looked away.

In fact, I *knew* there was something different. I had not forgotten one detail of that first time she'd glared at me like she wanted me dead. I could still see the flat black color of her eyes—so jarring against the background of her pale skin. Today, her eyes were a completely different color: a strange gold, darker than butterscotch, but with the same warm tone. I didn't understand how that was possible, unless she was lying for some reason about the contacts. Or maybe Forks was making me crazy in the literal sense of the word.

I looked down. Her hands were clenched into fists again.

Mrs. Banner came to our table then, looking over our shoulders to glance at the completed lab, and then stared more intently to check the answers.

"So, Edythe . . . ," Mrs. Banner began.

"Beau identified half of the slides," Edythe said before Mrs. Banner could finish.

Mrs. Banner looked at me now; her expression was skeptical.

"Have you done this lab before?" she asked.

I shrugged. "Not with onion root."

"Whitefish blastula?"

"Yeah."

Mrs. Banner nodded. "Were you in an advanced placement program in Phoenix?"

"Yes."

"Well," she said after a moment, "I guess it's good you two are lab partners." She mumbled something else I couldn't hear as she walked away. After she left, I started doodling on my notebook again.

"It's too bad about the snow, isn't it?" Edythe asked. I had the odd feeling that she was forcing herself to make small talk with me. It was like she had heard my conversation with Jeremy at lunch and was trying to prove me wrong. Which was impossible. I was turning paranoid.

"Not really," I answered honestly, instead of pretending to be normal like everyone else. I was still trying to shake the stupid feeling of suspicion, and I couldn't concentrate on putting up a socially acceptable front.

"You don't like the cold." It wasn't a question.

"Or the wet."

"Forks must be a difficult place for you to live," she mused.

"You have no idea," I muttered darkly.

She looked riveted by my response, for some reason I couldn't imagine. Her face was such a distraction that I tried not to look at it any more than courtesy absolutely demanded.

"Why did you come here, then?"

No one had asked me that—not straight out like she did, demanding.

"It's . . . complicated."

"I think I can keep up," she pressed.

I paused for a long moment, and then made the mistake of meeting her gaze. Her long, dark gold eyes confused me, and I answered without thinking.

"My mother got remarried," I said.

"That doesn't sound so complex," she disagreed, but her tone was suddenly softer. "When did that happen?"

"Last September." I couldn't keep the sadness out of my voice.

"And you don't like him," Edythe guessed, her voice still kind.

"No, Phil is fine. A little young, maybe, but he's a good guy."

"Why didn't you stay with them?"

I couldn't understand her interest, but she continued to stare at me with penetrating eyes, as if my dull life's story was somehow vitally important.

"Phil travels most of the time. He plays ball for a living." I half-smiled.

"Have I heard of him?" she asked, smiling in response, just enough for a hint of the dimples to show.

"Probably not. He doesn't play *well*. Just minor league. He moves around a lot."

"And your mother sent you here so that she could travel with him." She said it as an assumption again, not a question.

My hunched shoulders straightened automatically. "No, she didn't. I sent myself."

Her eyebrows pushed together. "I don't understand," she admitted, and she seemed more frustrated by that fact than she should be.

I sighed. Why was I explaining this to her? She stared at me, waiting.

"She stayed with me at first, but she missed him. It made her unhappy . . . so I decided it was time to spend some quality time with Charlie." My voice was glum by the time I finished.

"But now you're unhappy," she pointed out.

"And?" I challenged.

"That doesn't seem fair." She shrugged, but her eyes were still intense.

I laughed once. "Haven't you heard? Life isn't fair."

"I believe I *have* heard that somewhere before," she agreed dryly.

"So that's it," I insisted, wondering why she was still staring at me that way.

Her head tilted to the side, and her gold eyes seemed to laser right through the surface of my skin. "You put on a good show," she said slowly. "But I'd be willing to bet that you're suffering more than you let anyone see."

I shrugged. "I repeat . . . And?"

"I don't entirely understand you, that's all."

I frowned. "Why would you want to?"

"That's a very good question," she murmured, so quietly that I wondered if she was talking to herself. However, after a few seconds of silence, I decided that was the only answer I was going to get.

It was awkward, just looking at each other, but she didn't look away. I wanted to keep staring at her face, but I was afraid she was wondering what was wrong with me for staring so much, so finally I turned toward the blackboard. She sighed.

I glanced back, and she was still looking at me, but her expression was different . . . a little frustrated, or irritated.

"I'm sorry," I said quickly. "Did I . . . Am I annoying you?"

She shook her head and smiled with half her mouth so that one dimple popped out. "No, if anything, I'm annoyed with myself."

"Why?"

She cocked her head to the side. "Reading people . . . it usually comes very easily to me. But I can't—I guess I don't know quite what to make of you. Is that funny?"

I flattened out my grin. "More . . . unexpected. My mom always calls me her open book. According to her, you can all but read my thoughts printing out across my forehead."

Her smile vanished and she half-glared into my eyes, not angry like before, just intense. As if she was trying hard to read that printout my mom had seen. Then, switching gears just as abruptly, she was smiling again.

"I suppose I've gotten overconfident."

I didn't know what to say to that. "Um, sorry?"

She laughed, and the sound was like music, though I couldn't think of the instrument to compare it to. Her teeth were perfect—no surprise there—and blinding white.

Mrs. Banner called the class to order then, and I was relieved to give her my attention. It was a little too intense, making small talk with Edythe. I felt dizzy in a strange way. Had I really just detailed my boring life to this bizarre, beautiful girl who might or might not hate me? She'd seemed almost too interested in what I had to say, but now I could see, from the corner of my eye, that she was leaning away from me again, her hands gripping the edge of the table with unmistakable tension.

I tried to focus as Mrs. Banner went through the lab with transparencies on the overhead projector, but my thoughts were far away from the lecture.

When the bell rang, Edythe rushed as swiftly and as gracefully from the room as she had last Monday. And, like last Monday, I stared after her with my jaw hanging open.

McKayla got to my table almost as quickly.

"That was awful," she said. "They all looked exactly the same. You're lucky you had Edythe for a partner."

"Yeah, she seemed to know her way around an onion root."

"She was friendly enough today," McKayla commented as we shrugged into our raincoats. She didn't sound happy about it.

I tried to make my voice casual. "I wonder what was with her last Monday."

I couldn't concentrate on McKayla's chatter as we walked to Gym, and P.E. didn't do much to hold my interest, either. McKayla was on my team today. She helpfully covered my position as well as her own, so I only had to pay attention when it was my turn to serve; my team knew to get out of the way when I was up.

The rain was just a mist as I walked to the parking lot, but I was still pretty damp when I got in the truck. I turned the heat up as high as it could go, for once not caring about the mind-numbing roar of the engine.

As I looked around me to make sure the way was clear, I noticed the still, white figure. Edythe Cullen was leaning against the front door of the Volvo, three cars down from me, and staring intently in my direction. The smile was gone, but at least so was the murder—for now, anyway. I looked away and threw the truck into reverse, almost hitting a rusty Toyota Corolla in my rush. Lucky for the Toyota, I stomped on the brake in time. It was just the sort of car that my truck would make scrap metal of. I took a deep breath, still looking out the other side of my car, and cautiously pulled out again. This time I made it. I stared straight ahead as I passed the Volvo, but I could see enough in my peripheral vision to know that she was laughing.

3. PHENOMENON

WHEN I OPENED MY EYES IN THE MORNING, SOMETHING WAS DIFFERENT.

It was the light. It was still the gloomy light of a cloudy day in the forest, but it was clearer somehow. I realized there was no fog obscuring my window.

I jumped up to look outside, and then groaned.

A fine layer of snow covered the yard, dusted the top of my truck, and whitened the road. But that wasn't the worst part. All the rain from yesterday had frozen solid—coating the needles on the trees in crazy patterns, and making the driveway a deadly ice slick. I had enough trouble not falling down when the ground was dry; it might be safer for me to go back to bed now.

Charlie had left for work before I got downstairs. In a lot of ways, living with Charlie was like having my own place, and I found myself enjoying the space rather than feeling lonely.

I threw down a quick bowl of cereal and some orange juice from the carton. I felt excited to go to school, and that worried me. I knew it wasn't the stimulating learning environment I was anticipating, or seeing my new set of friends. If I was being honest with myself, I knew I was eager to get to school because I would see Edythe Cullen. And that was very, very stupid.

Maybe a few of the other girls were intrigued by the novelty of the new kid, but Edythe wasn't a McKayla or an Erica. I was well aware that my league and her league were spheres that did not touch. I was already worried

that just looking at her face was giving me unrealistic expectations that would haunt me for the rest of my life. Spending more time looking at her—watching her lips move, marveling at her skin, listening to her voice—was certainly not going to help with that. I didn't exactly trust her anyway—why lie about her eyes? And of course, there was the whole thing where she might have at one point wanted me dead. So I should definitely not be excited to see her again.

It took every ounce of my concentration to make it down the icy brick driveway alive. I almost lost my balance when I finally got to the truck, but I managed to cling on to the side mirror and save myself. The sidewalks at school would be complex today . . . so much potential for humiliation.

My truck seemed to have no problem with the black ice that covered the roads. I drove very slowly, though, not wanting to carve a path of destruction through Main Street.

When I got out of my truck at school, I discovered why I'd had so little trouble. Something silver caught my eye, and I walked to the back of the truck—carefully holding the side for support—to examine my tires. There were thin chains crisscrossed in diamond shapes around them. Charlie had gotten up who knows how early to put snow chains on my truck.

I frowned, surprised that my throat suddenly felt tight. That wasn't the way it was supposed to work. I probably should have been the one to think about putting chains on his tires, if I could figure out how to do that. Or at least I should have helped him with the chore. It wasn't his job. . . .

Except that, actually, it kind of was. He was the parent. He was taking care of me, his son. That was how it worked in books and on TV shows, but it made me feel upside down in a strange way.

I was standing by the back corner of the truck, struggling to contain the sudden wave of emotion the snow chains had brought on, when I heard a strange sound.

It was a high-pitched screech, and almost as soon as I registered it, the sound was already painfully loud. I looked up, startled.

I saw several things simultaneously. Nothing was moving in slow motion, the way it does in the movies. Instead, the adrenaline rush seemed to make my brain work faster, and I was able to absorb in clear detail a few things all at once.

Edythe Cullen was standing four cars down from me, mouth open in horror. Her face stood out from a sea of faces, all frozen in the same mask of shock. Also, a dark blue van was skidding, tires locked and squealing against the brakes, spinning wildly across the ice of the parking lot. It was going to hit the back corner of my truck, and I was standing between them. I didn't even have time to close my eyes.

Just before I heard the shattering crunch of the van folding around the truck bed, something hit me, hard, but not from the direction I was expecting. My head cracked against the icy blacktop, and I felt something solid and cold pinning me to the ground. I realized I was lying on the pavement behind the tan car I'd parked next to. But I didn't have a chance to notice anything else, because the van was still coming. It had curled gratingly around the end of the truck and, still spinning and sliding, was about to collide with me *again*.

"Come *on*!" She said the words so quickly I almost missed them, but the voice was impossible not to recognize.

Two thin, white hands shot out in front of me, and the van shuddered to a stop a foot from my face, her pale hands fitting exactly into a deep dent in the side of the van's body.

Then her hands moved so fast they blurred. One was suddenly gripping under the body of the van, and something was dragging me, swinging my legs around like a rag doll's, till they hit the tire of the tan car. There was a groaning metallic thud so loud it hurt my ears, and the van settled, glass popping, onto the asphalt—exactly where, a second ago, my legs had been.

It was absolutely silent for one long second. Then the screaming started. In the abrupt chaos, I could hear more than one person shouting my name. But more clearly than all the yelling, I could hear Edythe Cullen's low, frantic voice in my ear.

"Beau? Are you all right?"

"I'm fine." My voice sounded strange. I tried to sit up, and realized she was holding me against the side of her body. I must have been more traumatized than I realized, because I couldn't budge her arm at all. Was I weak with shock?

"Be careful," she warned as I struggled. "I think you hit your head pretty hard."

I became aware of a throbbing ache centered above my left ear.

"Ow," I said, surprised.

"That's what I thought." Nothing seemed funny to me, but it sounded like she was trying not to laugh.

"How in the . . ." I trailed off, trying to clear my head, get my bearings. "How did you get over here so fast?"

"I was standing right next to you, Beau," she said, her voice suddenly serious again.

I turned to sit up, and this time she helped me, but then she slid as far from me as she could in the limited space. I looked at her concerned, innocent expression, and was disoriented again by her gold-colored eyes. What was I asking her?

And then they found us, a crowd of people with tears streaming down their faces, shouting at each other, shouting at us.

"Don't move," someone instructed.

"Get Taylor out of the van!" someone else shouted. There was a flurry of activity around us. I tried to get up, but Edythe's hand pushed my shoulder down.

"Just stay put for now."

"But it's cold," I complained. It surprised me when she chuckled under her breath. There was an edge to the sound.

"You were over there," I suddenly remembered, and her chuckle stopped short. "You were by your car."

Her expression hardened abruptly. "No, I wasn't."

"I saw you." Everything around us was confusion. I could hear the lower voices of adults arriving on the scene. But I stubbornly held on to the argument; I was right, and she was going to admit it.

"Beau, I was standing with you, and I pulled you out of the way."

She stared at me, and something strange happened. It was like the gold of her eyes turned up, like her eyes were drugging me, hypnotizing me. It was devastating in a weird, exciting way. But her expression was anxious. I thought she was trying to communicate something crucial.

"But that's not what happened," I said weakly.

The gold in her eyes blazed again. "Please, Beau."

"Why?" I asked.

"Trust me?" she pleaded.

I could hear the sirens now. "Will you explain everything to me later?"

"Fine," she snapped, suddenly exasperated.

"Okay," I mumbled, unable to process her mood swings with everything else I was trying to come to terms with. What was I supposed to think, when what I remembered was impossible?

It took six EMTs and two teachers—Ms. Varner and Coach Clapp—to shift the van far enough away from us to bring the stretchers in. Edythe insisted she hadn't been touched, and I tried to do the same, but she was quick to contradict me. She told them I'd hit my head, and then made it sound worse than it was, throwing around words like *concussion* and *hemorrhage*. I wanted to die when they put on the neck brace. It looked like the entire school was there, watching soberly as they loaded me in the back of the ambulance. Edythe got to ride in the front. It was a thousand times more humiliating than I'd imagined today would be, and I hadn't even made it to the sidewalk.

To make matters worse, Chief Swan arrived before they could get me safely away.

"Beau!" he yelled in panic when he recognized me on the stretcher.

"I'm completely fine, Char—Dad," I sighed. "There's nothing wrong with me."

He rounded on the closest EMT for a second opinion. While the EMT tried to talk him down, I tuned them out to consider the jumble of absurd images churning in my head—images that were not possible. When they'd lifted me away from the car, I had seen the deep dent in the tan car's bumper—a very distinct dent that fit the slim shape of Edythe's shoulders . . . as if she had braced herself against the car with enough force to damage the metal frame. . . .

And then there was her family, looking on from a distance, with expressions that ranged from disapproval (Eleanor) to fury (Royal), but held no hint of concern for their little sister's safety.

I remembered the sensation of almost flying through the air . . . that hard mass that had pinned me to the ground . . . Edythe's hand under the frame of the van, like it was holding the van off the ground . . .

I tried to think of a logical explanation that could make sense of what I had just seen. All I could come up with was that I was having a psychotic episode. I didn't *feel* crazy, but maybe crazy people always felt sane.

Naturally, the ambulance got a police escort to the county hospital. I felt ridiculous the whole time they were unloading me. What made it worse was that Edythe simply glided through the hospital doors on her own.

They put me in the emergency room, a long room with a line of beds separated by pastel-patterned curtains. A nurse put a pressure cuff on my arm and a thermometer under my tongue. Since no one bothered pulling the curtain around to give me some privacy, I decided I wasn't obligated to wear the embarrassing neck brace anymore. As soon as the nurse walked away, I quickly unfastened the Velcro and threw it under the bed.

There was another flurry of hospital personnel, another stretcher brought to the bed next to me. I recognized Taylor Crowley from my Government class beneath the bloodstained bandages wrapped tightly around her head. Taylor looked a hundred times worse than I felt. But she was staring anxiously at me.

"Beau, I'm so sorry!"

"I'm fine, Taylor—you look awful, are you all right?" As we spoke, nurses began unwinding her bloody bandages, exposing dozens of shallow slices all over her forehead and left cheek.

She ignored me. "I thought I was going to kill you! I was going too fast, and I hit the ice wrong. . . ." She winced as one nurse started dabbing at her face.

"Don't worry about it; you missed me."

"How did you get out of the way so fast? You were there, and then you were gone. . . ."

"Umm . . . Edythe shoved me out of the way."

She looked confused. "Who?"

"Edythe Cullen—she was standing next to me." As usual, I didn't sound believable at all.

"Edythe? I didn't see her . . . wow, it was all so fast, I guess. Is she okay?"

"I think so. She's here somewhere, but they didn't make her use a stretcher."

I knew I wasn't crazy. What had happened? There was no way to explain away what I'd seen.

They wheeled me away then, to X-ray my head. I told them there was nothing wrong, and I was right. Not even a concussion. I asked if I could leave, but the nurse said I had to talk to a doctor first. So I was trapped in

the ER, harassed by Taylor's constant apologies and promises to make it up to me. No matter how many times I tried to convince her I was fine, she continued to beg for forgiveness. Finally, I closed my eyes and tried to ignore her.

"Is he sleeping?" a musical voice asked. My eyes flew open.

Edythe was standing at the foot of my bed, her expression more a smirk than a smile. I stared at her, trying to put the pieces together in my head. She didn't *look* like someone who could stop attacking vehicles with her bare hands. But then, she also didn't look like anyone I'd ever seen before.

"Hey, um, Edythe, I'm really sorry—" Taylor began.

Edythe lifted a hand to stop her.

"No blood, no foul," she said, flashing her bright white teeth. She moved to sit on the edge of Taylor's bed, facing me. She smirked again.

"So, what's the verdict?" she asked me.

"There's nothing wrong with me, but they won't let me go," I said. "How come you aren't strapped to a gurney like the rest of us?"

"It's all about who you know," she answered. "But don't worry, I came to spring you."

Then a doctor walked around the corner, and my mouth fell open. She was young, she was blond . . . and she was more beautiful than any movie star I'd ever seen. Like someone sliced up Audrey Hepburn, Grace Kelly, and Marilyn Monroe, took the best parts, and glued them together to form one goddess. She was pale, though, and tired-looking, with circles under her dark eyes. From Charlie's description, this had to be Edythe's mom.

"So, Mr. Swan," Dr. Cullen asked in a gentle voice, "how are you feeling?"

"I'm fine," I said, for the last time, I hoped.

She walked to the lightboard on the wall over my head, and turned it on.

"Your X-rays look good," she said. "Does your head hurt? Edythe said you hit it pretty hard."

"It's fine," I repeated with a sigh, throwing a quick, questioning look Edythe's way. She avoided my eyes.

The doctor's cool fingers probed lightly along my skull. She noticed when I winced.

"Tender?" she asked.

"Not really." I'd had worse.

I heard a low laugh, and looked over to see Edythe smiling.

"Well, your father is in the waiting room—you can go home with him now. But come back if you feel dizzy or have trouble with your eyesight at all."

"Can't I go back to school?" I asked, imagining Charlie trying to play nurse.

"Maybe you should take it easy today."

I glanced at Edythe. "Does she get to go to school?"

"Someone has to spread the good news that we survived," Edythe said blithely.

"Actually," Dr. Cullen corrected, "most of the school seems to be in the waiting room."

"Ugh," I moaned.

Dr. Cullen raised her eyebrows. "Do you want to stay?"

"No, no!" I insisted, throwing my legs over the side of the bed and hopping down quickly. Too quickly—I staggered, and Dr. Cullen caught me. She was sturdier than she looked.

"I'm fine," I assured her again. No need to explain that my balance problems had nothing to do with hitting my head.

"Take some Tylenol for the pain," she suggested as she steadied me.

"It doesn't hurt that bad," I insisted.

"It sounds like you were extremely lucky," Dr. Cullen said, smiling as she signed my chart with a flourish.

"Lucky Edythe just happened to be standing next to me," I amended, shooting another glance at the subject of my statement.

"Oh, well, yes," Dr. Cullen agreed, suddenly occupied with the papers in front of her. Then she looked away, at Taylor, and walked to the next bed. It made me sure the doctor was in on it.

"I'm afraid that *you'll* have to stay with us just a little bit longer," she said to Taylor, and began checking her cuts.

As soon as the doctor's back was turned, I moved to Edythe's side.

"Can I talk to you for a minute?" I whispered under my breath. She took a step back from me, her jaw suddenly clenched.

"Your father is waiting for you," she said through her teeth.

I glanced at Dr. Cullen and Taylor.

"I need to speak with you alone," I pressed.

She glared—but it wasn't the same as that first day, not nearly as homicidal, so I just waited. After a second, she turned her back and stalked quickly down the long room. Long as my legs are, I nearly had to run to keep up. As soon as we turned the corner into a short hallway, she spun around to face me.

"What do you want?" she asked, sounding annoyed. Her eyes were cold.

Her unfriendliness intimidated me. My words came out with less certainty than I'd planned. "You owe me an explanation," I reminded her.

"I saved your life—I don't owe you anything."

I flinched back from the resentment in her voice. "Why are you acting like this?"

"Beau, you hit your head, you don't know what you're talking about." Her tone was cutting.

Her anger only made me more sure that I was right, though. "There's nothing wrong with my head."

She turned up the heat of her glare. "What do you want from me, Beau?"

"I want to know the truth," I said. "I want to know why I'm lying for you."

"What do you *think* happened?" she snapped.

It was harder to say the words out loud, where I could hear the crazy. It shook my conviction, but I tried to keep my voice even and calm.

"I know that you weren't standing next to me—Taylor didn't see you, either, so it's not concussion damage. That van was going to crush us both—but it didn't. It looked like your hands left dents in the side of it—and your shoulders left a dent in the other car, but you're not hurt at all. The van should have smashed my legs, but you were holding it up. . . ." It just kept sounding worse and worse. I couldn't continue.

She was staring at me, her eyes wide and incredulous. But she couldn't entirely hide the tension, the defensiveness.

"You think I lifted a van off you?" Her tone questioned my sanity, but there was something off. It was like a line delivered by a skilled actor—so hard to doubt, but at the same time, the frame of the movie screen reminded you nothing was actually real.

I just nodded once.

She smiled, hard and mocking. "Nobody will believe that, you know."

"I'm not going to tell anybody."

Surprise flitted across her face, and the smile faded. "Then why does it matter?"

"It matters to me," I said. "I don't like to lie—so there'd better be a good reason why I'm doing it."

"Can't you just thank me and get over it?"

"Thank you," I said, and then folded my arms. Waiting.

"You're not going to let it go, are you?"

"Nope."

"In that case . . . I hope you enjoy disappointment."

She scowled at me, and I stared back, thoughts scattered by how beautiful her anger was. I was the first to speak, trying to keep myself focused. I was in danger of being totally distracted. It was like trying to stare down a destroying angel.

"If you were going to be like this about it," I said, "why did you even bother?"

She paused, and for a brief moment her perfect face was unexpectedly vulnerable.

"I don't know," she whispered.

And then she turned her back on me and walked away.

It took me a few minutes until I was able to move. When I could walk, I made my way slowly to the exit at the end of the hallway.

The waiting room was unpleasant, like I'd expected. It seemed like every face I knew in Forks was there, staring at me. Charlie rushed to my side; I put up my hands.

"There's nothing wrong with me," I assured him, abruptly aggravated by the whole crazy situation.

"What did the doctor say?"

"Dr. Cullen saw me, and she said I was fine and I could go home." McKayla, Jeremy, and Erica were all there, beginning to converge on us. "Let's go," I urged.

Charlie put one arm out toward me, like he thought I needed support. I retreated quickly toward the exit doors, waving halfheartedly at my friends. Hopefully they would forget about this by tomorrow.

Unlikely.

It was a huge relief—the first time I'd ever felt that way—to get into the cruiser.

We drove in silence. I was so wrapped up in my thoughts that I barely knew Charlie was there. I was positive that Edythe's defensive behavior in the hall was a confirmation of the bizarre things I still could hardly believe I'd seen.

When we got to the house, Charlie finally spoke.

"Um . . . you'll need to call Renée." He hung his head, guilty.

I was appalled. "You told *Mom?*"

"Sorry."

I slammed the cruiser's door a little harder than necessary on my way out.

My mom was in hysterics, of course. I had to tell her I felt fine at least thirty times before she would calm down. She begged me to come home—forgetting the fact that home was empty at the moment—but her pleas were easier to resist than I would have thought. I was consumed by the mystery Edythe presented. And more than a little obsessed with Edythe herself. Stupid, stupid, stupid. I wasn't as eager to escape Forks as I should be, as any normal, sane person would be.

I decided I might as well go to bed early that night. Charlie continued to watch me anxiously, and it was getting on my nerves. I stopped on my way to grab three Tylenol from the bathroom. They did help, and, as the pain eased, I drifted to sleep.

That was the first night I dreamed about Edythe Cullen.

4. INVITATIONS

IN MY DREAM IT WAS VERY DARK, AND WHAT DIM LIGHT THERE WAS seemed to be radiating from Edythe's skin. I couldn't see her face, just her back as she walked away from me, leaving me in the blackness. No matter how fast I ran, I couldn't catch up to her; no matter how loud I called, she never turned. I got more and more frantic to get to her, until that anxiety woke me. It was the middle of the night, but I couldn't sleep again for what seemed like a very long time. After that, she was in my dreams nearly every night, but always on the edges, never within reach.

The month that followed the accident was uneasy, tense, and, at first, embarrassing.

I found myself the center of attention for the rest of the week, which really sucked. Taylor Crowley was super annoying, following me around, coming up with different hypothetical ways to make it up to me. I tried to convince her that what I wanted more than anything else was for her to forget about it—especially since nothing had actually happened to me—but she wouldn't give up. She found me between classes and sat at our now-crowded lunch table. McKayla and Erica didn't seem to like that; they flashed more side-eye at her than they did at each other, which made me worry that I'd gained another unwelcome fan. Like being into the new kid was the latest fad.

No one was worried about Edythe—no one followed her around or asked for her eyewitness account. I always included her in my version; she was the

hero—she had pulled me out of the way and nearly been crushed, too, but all anyone ever said was that they hadn't even realized she was there until the van was pulled away.

I wondered a lot about why no one else had noticed her standing so far away by her car, before she was suddenly and impossibly saving my life. There was only one solution I could think of, and I didn't like it. It had to be because no one else was so aware of Edythe. No one watched her the way I did. It was pathetic, and kind of stalkerish.

People avoided Edythe the same way they usually did. The Cullens and the Hales sat at the same table they always sat at, not eating, talking only to each other. None of them ever glanced my way anymore.

When Edythe sat beside me in class, as far away as possible, like usual, she seemed totally unaware that I was sitting there next to her. Like my seat was empty. Only now and then, when her fists would suddenly ball up— skin stretched even whiter over her knuckles—did I wonder if she wasn't as entirely oblivious as she seemed.

I wanted very much to continue our conversation from the hospital hall-way, and the day after the accident I tried. She'd been so furious when we talked before. And, even though I really wanted to know what had actually happened and I thought I deserved the truth, I also knew I had been pretty pushy, considering that she had just saved my life and all. I didn't think I'd thanked her properly.

She was already in her chair when I got to Biology. She didn't turn when I sat down, just kept staring straight ahead. She showed no sign that she knew I was there.

"Hey, Edythe," I said.

She turned her head half an inch toward me, but her eyes stayed focused on the blackboard. She gave me one little half-nod, then turned her face away from me.

And that was the last contact I'd had with her, though she was there, a foot away from me, every day. I watched her sometimes, unable to stop myself—always from a distance, though, in the cafeteria or park-ing lot. I watched as her golden eyes grew noticeably darker day by day (then abruptly, they were honey-colored again. And the slow pro-gression toward black would start over). But in class I gave no more

notice that she existed than she showed toward me. It was miserable. And the dreams continued.

She wished she hadn't pushed me out of the way of Taylor's van. I couldn't think of any other explanation. Since she obviously preferred me dead, she was pretending that I was.

Despite my outright lies, the tone of my e-mails got my mom worked up. She called a few times, demanding to know I was okay. I tried to convince her it was just the rain that had me down.

McKayla, at least, was pleased by the obvious coolness between my lab partner and me. I guessed she'd been worried that the shared trauma would have bonded us or something. She got more confident, sitting on the edge of my table to talk before Biology class started, ignoring Edythe as completely as Edythe ignored us.

The snow washed away for good after that one dangerously icy day. McKayla complained that she'd never gotten to stage her big snowball fight, but she was happy that the beach trip would soon be possible. The rain continued heavily, though, and the weeks passed.

I hadn't really been aware of how much time was passing. Most days looked the same—gray, green, and more gray. My stepdad had always complained that Phoenix didn't have seasons, but as far as I could tell, Forks was much worse. I had no idea spring was anywhere near appearing until I was walking to the cafeteria with Jeremy one rainy morning.

"Hey, Beau?" he asked.

I wanted to hurry out of the rain, but Jeremy was barely shuffling forward. I slowed my pace to match his.

"What's up, Jeremy?"

"I was just wondering if anyone's asked you to the spring dance yet. You know, it's girls' choice."

"Oh. Um, no."

"Huh. Do you want . . . I mean, do you think McKayla will ask you?"

"I hope not," I said, maybe a little too fast.

He looked up at me, surprised. "Why not?"

"I don't do dances."

"Oh."

We shuffled forward for a minute in silence. He was thoughtful. I was impatient to get out of the drizzle.

"Do you mind if I tell her that?" he asked.

"No. That's probably a good idea. I don't want to have to tell anyone no if I don't have to."

"Okay."

"When's the dance again?"

We were close to the cafeteria now. He pointed to a bright yellow poster advertising the dance. I'd never noticed it before, but it was curling around the edges and a little washed out, like it had been up for a while.

"A week from Saturday," he said.

I was pretty sure Jeremy had already said something when, the next morning, McKayla was not her usual bubbly self in English. At lunch she sat away from both Jeremy and me, and she didn't say much to anyone. She stayed quiet as she walked with me to Biology, but she came over like usual to sit on the edge of my lab table. As always, I was too aware of Edythe sitting close enough to touch, but still so far away she might as well have been a product of my imagination.

"So," McKayla said, looking at the floor instead of at me. "Jeremy said that you don't do dances."

"Yeah, that's true."

She looked at me then, her expression hurt and a little angry. I hadn't even told her no yet, and I already felt guilty.

"Oh," she said. "I thought maybe he was making it up."

"Uh, sorry, no. Why would he make up a story like that?"

She frowned. "I think he wants me to ask him."

I forced a smile. "You should. Jeremy's great."

She shrugged. "I guess." Then she took a deep breath and looked me straight in the eye with a quick, nervous smile. "Would this 'I don't dance' thing change if I was the one asking you to go?"

From the corner of my eye, I saw Edythe's head suddenly tilt in my direction. Like she was listening to my answer, too.

It took me a little too long to respond. I still felt guilty, but mostly distracted. *Was* Edythe listening?

"Um, sorry, again."

McKayla's face fell. "Would it change if someone else asked you?"

Did Edythe see how McKayla's eyes flickered in her direction?

"No. It's a moot point anyway. I'm going to be in Seattle that day." I needed to get out of town—two Saturdays from now was the perfect time to go.

"Does it have to be *that* weekend?" McKayla asked.

"Yeah. But don't worry about me. You should take Jeremy. He's much more fun than I am."

"Yeah, I guess," she mumbled, and she turned to walk back to her seat. I watched her shoulders slump forward, and I felt horrible. I closed my eyes and pushed my fingers against my temples, trying to force McKayla's dejected posture out of my head. Mrs. Banner started talking. I sighed and opened my eyes.

Edythe was staring straight at me, that familiar expression of frustration even more obvious now in her black eyes.

I stared back, surprised, expecting her to look away. She didn't. Her eyes kept boring into mine, like she was trying to find something really important inside them. I continued to stare also, totally unable to break the connection, even if I wanted to. My hands started to shake.

"Miss Cullen?" the teacher called, looking for the answer to some question I hadn't heard.

"The Krebs Cycle," Edythe answered, seeming reluctant as she turned to look at Mrs. Banner.

I put my head down, pretending to stare at my book, as soon as her eyes released me. It bothered me—the rush of emotion pulsing through me, just because she'd happened to look at me for the first time in six weeks. It wasn't normal. It was actually pretty pathetic, and probably more than that. Unhealthy.

I tried hard not to be aware of her for the rest of the class, or, since that was impossible, at least not to let her know that I was aware of her. When the bell finally rang, I turned away from her to stack up my books, expecting her to rush out as usual.

"Beau?"

Her voice shouldn't sound so familiar, like I'd been hearing it all my life instead of just an hour here and there a few weeks ago.

I turned slowly toward her, not wanting to feel what I knew I *would* feel when I looked at her too-perfect face. I'm sure my expression was guarded; hers was unreadable. She didn't say anything.

"Yes?" I asked.

She just looked at me.

"So . . . um, are you . . . or are you not talking to me again?"

"Not," she said, but her lips curled up into a smile, her dimples flashing.

"Okay . . ." I looked away—down at my hands, then over toward the chalkboard. It was hard to concentrate when I looked at her, and this conversation wasn't making much sense.

"I'm sorry," she said, and there was no joke in her voice now. "I'm being very rude, I know. But it's better this way, really."

I looked at her again; her expression was totally serious now.

"I don't know what you mean."

"It's better if we're not friends," she explained. "Trust me."

My eyes narrowed. I'd heard that one before.

She seemed surprised by my reaction. "What are you thinking?" she asked.

"I guess . . . that it's too bad you didn't figure this out earlier, saved yourself the regret."

"Regret?" My answer seemed to have caught her off guard. "Regret for what?"

"For not letting Taylor's van crush me when it had the chance."

She looked completely shocked. She stared at me for a minute, wide-eyed, and when she finally spoke she almost sounded mad.

"You think I regret saving your life?" The words were quiet, just under her breath, but still pretty intense.

I glanced quickly toward the front of the room, where a couple of kids were still lingering. I caught one of them looking at us. He looked away and I turned back to Edythe.

"Yeah," I said, just as quietly. "I mean, what else? Seems kind of obvious."

She made the strangest sound—she exhaled through her teeth and it was like a *hiss*. She still looked mad.

"You're an idiot," she told me.

Well, that was my limit.

It was bad enough that I was so fixated on this girl, bad enough that I thought about her all the time, dreamed about her every night. I didn't need to sit here like the moron she thought I was and just stare while she insulted

me. I grabbed my books and lurched out of my chair, knowing all the while that she was right—I *was* an idiot, because I wanted to stay, even if all I got to hear was more abuse from her. I needed to get out of the room as fast as possible, so of course, I tripped over the threshold and half-fell through the doorway, my books scattering across the sidewalk. I stood there for a second with my eyes closed, thinking about leaving them. Then I sighed and bent to pick them up.

Edythe was there; she'd already stacked them in a pile, which she offered to me.

I took them without really looking at her.

"Thanks," I mumbled.

"You're welcome," she answered. Still mad, sounded like.

I straightened up, and hurried to Gym without looking back.

Gym didn't make my day any better. We'd moved on to basketball. On the first day, even though all of them had *seen* me play volleyball, the other kids still seemed to think I should be good. It didn't take them long to figure out the truth. They never passed to me now, which was good, but with all the running I still managed to have a few accidents per game. Today was worse than yesterday, because I couldn't concentrate on my feet. All I could think of was Edythe.

It was a relief, as usual, when I was finally free to leave. I couldn't wait to be back inside my truck, alone. The truck was in pretty decent shape, all things considered. I'd had to replace the taillights after the accident, but that was it. If the paint job weren't already hopeless, maybe I would have had to do something about the new scrapes. Taylor's parents had to sell her van for parts.

I rounded the corner and nearly had a heart attack. Someone small and thin was leaning against the side of my truck. I skidded to a stop, then took a deep breath. It was just Erica. I started walking again.

"Hey, Erica," I called.

"Hi, Beau."

"What's up?" I asked as I went to unlock the door. I glanced down at her, and fumbled my keys. She looked really uncomfortable.

"Um, I was wondering if you would go to the spring dance with me?"

I carefully inserted the car key into the lock.

"Sorry, Erica, I'm not going to the dance."

I had to look at her then. Her face was down, her black hair hiding her eyes.

"Oh, okay."

"Because I'm going to be in Seattle," I said quickly, trying to make her feel better. "It's the only day I can go. So, you know, oh well. I hope it's fun and all."

She glanced up from under her hair. "Okay," she repeated, but her voice was slightly more cheerful now. "Maybe next time."

"Sure," I agreed, and then immediately regretted it. Hopefully she wouldn't take that too literally.

"See ya," she said over her shoulder. She was already escaping. I waved, but she didn't see it.

I heard a low laugh.

Edythe was walking past the front of my truck, looking straight forward, her mouth not betraying even the hint of a smile.

I froze for a second. I wasn't prepared to be so close to her. I was used to bracing myself before Biology, but this was unexpected. She kept walking. I jerked the door open and climbed in, slamming it a little too hard behind me. I revved the deafening engine twice and reversed out into the aisle. Edythe was in her car already, two spaces down, sliding out into the lane in front of me, cutting me off. She stopped there—to wait for her family, I assumed. I could see the four of them walking this way, but they were still all the way back by the cafeteria. I looked in my rearview mirror. A line was beginning to form. Right behind me, Taylor Crowley was in her newly acquired used Sentra, waving. I ducked my head and pretended I couldn't see her.

While I was sitting there, focusing all my efforts on *not* staring at the driver in front of me, I heard a knock on my passenger side window. It was Taylor. I glanced in my mirror again, confused. Her Sentra was still running, the door left open. I leaned across the cab to crank the window down. It was stiff. I got it halfway there, then gave up.

"Sorry, Taylor, I can't move. I'm pinned in." I gestured to the Volvo. Obviously there was nothing I could do.

"Oh, I know—I just wanted to ask you something while we're trapped here." She grinned.

What was with this school? Was this some kind of practical joke? Hazing the new guy?

"Will you go to the spring dance with me?" she continued.

"I'm not going to be in town, Taylor." I realized I sounded too sharp. I had to remember it wasn't Taylor's fault that McKayla and Erica had already used up my patience.

"Yeah, McKayla told me that," she admitted.

"Then why—"

She shrugged. "I was hoping you were just letting her down easy."

Okay, it was totally her fault.

"Sorry, Taylor," I said, not feeling nearly as bad as I had with McKayla and Erica. "I'm not going to the dance."

"That's cool," she said, unfazed. "We still have prom."

Before I could say anything, she was walking back to her car. I could feel the red patches staining my face. Straight ahead, Archie, Royal, Eleanor, and Jessamine were all sliding into the Volvo. In the rearview mirror, I could see Edythe's eyes—staring at me. They were crinkled around the edges, and her shoulders were shaking with laughter. It was like she'd heard everything Taylor had said, and found my splotchy reaction hilarious. I revved my engine, wondering how much damage it would do to the Volvo and the black car beside it if I just muscled my way through and made my escape. I was pretty sure my truck could win that fight.

But they were all in, and Edythe was speeding away with her nearly silent engine.

I tried to concentrate on something else—anything else—as I drove home. Would McKayla ask Jeremy to the dance? Would he blame me if she didn't? Was Taylor serious about the prom? What would be my excuse for that one? Maybe I could work out a visit to my mom, or maybe she could come here. What was I going to make for dinner? We hadn't had chicken in a while.

But each time I finished answering my own question, my mind went right back to Edythe.

By the time I got home, I'd run out of new questions, so I gave up trying to think about something else. I decided to make chicken enchiladas because it would keep me busy for a while and I didn't have that much homework. It also forced me to concentrate on all the dicing—chicken, chilies, onions. All the while, though, I kept running through Biology class

again, trying to analyze every word she'd spoken to me. What did she mean, it was better if we weren't friends?

My stomach dropped when I realized the only thing she could have meant. She must know how obsessed I was with her—it wasn't like I was hiding it very well. She didn't want to lead me on . . . so we couldn't even be friends . . . because she didn't want to hurt my feelings the way I'd hurt McKayla and Erica today. (Taylor seemed fine.) Edythe didn't want to have to feel that guilt. Because she wasn't interested in me at all.

Which made perfect sense, obviously, because I wasn't *interesting*.

My eyes were starting to sting and tear from the onions. I grabbed a dish towel, ran it under the faucet, and then rubbed it across my eyes. It didn't really help.

I was boring—I knew this about myself. And Edythe was the opposite of boring. This wasn't about her secret, whatever it was, if I even remembered any of that insane moment clearly. At this point, I almost believed the story I'd told everyone else. It made a lot more sense than what I thought I'd seen.

But she didn't need a secret to be out of my league. She was also brilliant and mysterious and beautiful and completely perfect. If she was, in fact, able to lift a full-sized van with one hand, it really didn't matter. Either way, she was fantasy and I was the very most mundane kind of reality.

And that was fine. I could leave her alone. I *would* leave her alone. I would get through my self-imposed sentence here in purgatory, and then hope-fully some school in the Southwest, or possibly Hawaii, would offer me a scholarship.

I tried to think about palm trees and sun while I finished dinner.

Charlie seemed worried when he came home and smelled the green pep-pers, but he came around after the first bite. It was kind of a strange feeling, but also a good feeling, watching as he started to trust me in the kitchen.

"Dad?" I asked when he was almost done.

"Yeah, Beau?"

"Um, I just wanted to let you know that I'm going to Seattle a week from Saturday. Just for the day." I didn't want to ask permission—it set a bad prece-dent—but the statement form sounded rude, so I added, "If that's okay?"

"Why?" He sounded surprised, like he couldn't imagine any reason that would make someone want to leave Forks's town limits.

"Well, I wanted to get a few books—the library here is pretty limited. And maybe some warmer clothes." I had a little extra money, since, thanks to Charlie, I hadn't had to buy a car—though the truck did need a bigger gasoline budget than I'd expected—and the cold-weather clothes I'd picked up in Phoenix seemed to have been designed by people who'd never actually lived in temperatures below seventy but had once had such a climate described to them.

"That truck probably doesn't get very good gas mileage," he said, echoing my thoughts.

"I know, I'll stop in Montessano and Olympia—and Tacoma if I have to."

"Are you going all by yourself?"

"Yeah."

"Seattle is a big city—you could get lost," he warned.

"Dad, Phoenix is five times the size of Seattle—and I can read a map, don't worry about it."

"Do you want me to come with you?"

I wondered if he was really that worried about me, or if he just thought all the Saturdays he left me alone were adding up to neglect. Probably worried. I was sure that, in his head, he still pictured me as a five-year-old most of the time.

"That's okay. It's not going to be very exciting."

"Will you be back in time for the dance?"

I just stared back at him until he got it.

It didn't take him long. "Oh, right."

"Yeah," I said. I didn't get my balance issues from my mom.

The next morning at school, I parked as far as possible from the shiny silver Volvo. I would keep my distance. I wouldn't notice her anymore. She'd have nothing to complain about from here on out.

As I slammed the truck door shut, I lost my hold on the key and it splashed down in a puddle at my feet. As I bent to retrieve it, a pale hand flashed out and grabbed it first. I jerked upright, almost smacking my head into her. Edythe Cullen was right there, leaning casually against my truck.

"How do you *do* that?" I gasped.

"Do what?" She held out my key while she spoke. As I reached for it, she dropped it in my palm.

"Appear out of thin air?"

"Beau, it's not my fault if you are exceptionally unobservant." Her voice was just a murmur, muted velvet, and her lips were holding back a smile. Like she thought I was hilarious.

How was I supposed to ignore her when she wouldn't ignore me? That was what she wanted, right? Me, out of her long, bronze-y hair? Wasn't that what she'd said to me yesterday? We couldn't be friends. Then why was she talking to me? Was she sadistic? Was this her idea of fun—torture the idiotic kid she could never possibly care about?

I stared at her, frustrated. Her eyes were light again today, a deep, golden honey color. My thoughts got confused, and I had to look down. Her feet were just a half-foot from mine, oriented toward me, unmoving. Like she was waiting for a response.

I looked past her, toward the school, and said the first dumb things that came into my mind. "Why the traffic jam last night? I thought you were supposed to be pretending I don't exist."

"Ah. That was for Taylor's sake. She was figuratively dying for her chance at you."

I blinked. "What?" Irritation from yesterday's memory bled into my voice. I hadn't thought Edythe and Taylor were friends. Did Taylor ask her . . . ? That didn't seem likely.

"And I'm not pretending you don't exist," she continued like I hadn't spoken.

I met her eyes again, trying hard to keep my mind focused, no matter how golden they seemed, or how long her lashes were against her pale violet lids.

"I don't know what you want from me," I told her.

It was annoying how my thoughts seemed to explode straight through my lips when I was near her, like I had no filter at all. I would never have spoken this way to another girl.

The amused half-smile disappeared, and her face was suddenly guarded.

"Nothing," she said too quickly, almost like she was lying.

"Then you probably should have let the van take me out. Easier that way."

She stared for a second, and when she answered, her voice was cold. "Beau, you are utterly absurd."

I must be right about the torture thing. I was just a way for her to pass time in this boring town. An easy mark.

I was past her in one long stride.

"Wait," she said, but I forced myself to keep moving, not to look back.

"I'm sorry, that was rude," she said, somehow right next to me, keeping pace though my legs were probably twice as long as hers. "I'm not saying it wasn't true, but it was rude to say it out loud."

"Why won't you leave me alone?"

"I wanted to ask you something, but you sidetracked me."

I sighed and slowed, though she didn't seem like she was having a hard time keeping up. "Fine." I was such a sucker. "What do you want?"

"I was wondering if, a week from Saturday—you know, the day of the spring dance—"

I stopped, wheeling to look down at her. "Is this *funny* to you?"

She stared up at me, seeming oblivious to the drizzling rain that was falling. She was apparently wearing no makeup at all—nothing smudged or ran. Of course, her face was just that perfect naturally. For a second, I was actually angry—angry that she had to be so beautiful. Angry that her beauty had made her cruel. Angry that I was the object of her cruelty, and even though I knew it, I still couldn't successfully walk away from her.

Her amused expression was back, the hint of dimples threatening on her cheeks.

"Will you please allow me to finish?" she asked.

Walk away, I told myself.

I didn't move.

"I heard that you were going to Seattle that day, and I wondered if you wanted a ride."

That was not what I was expecting.

"Huh?"

"Do you want a ride to Seattle?"

I wasn't sure where her joke was heading now. "With who?"

"Myself, obviously." She enunciated every syllable, like she thought maybe English wasn't my first language.

"Why?" Where was the punch line?

"Well, I was planning to go to Seattle in the next few weeks, and to be honest, I'm not sure if your truck can make it."

Finally, I was able to start walking again, goaded by the insult to my truck.

"Make fun of me all you want, but leave the truck out of it," I said.

Again, she kept up easily. "Why would you think that I'm making fun of you?" she asked. "The invitation is genuine."

"My truck is great, thanks."

"Can your truck make it to Seattle on one tank of gas?"

Before the truck, I'd never cared one way or another about any car, but I could feel a prejudice against Volvos forming.

"I don't see how that's your problem."

"The wasting of finite resources is everyone's problem," she said primly.

"Seriously, Edythe." I felt a charge go through me as I said her name aloud, and I didn't like it. "I can't keep up with you. I thought you didn't want to be my friend."

"I said it would be better if we weren't friends, not that I didn't want to be."

"Oh, wow, great, so that's *all* cleared up." Thick sarcasm. I realized I had stopped walking again. I looked down at her rain-washed face, clean and perfect, and my thoughts stuttered to a halt.

"It would be more . . . *prudent* for you not to be my friend," she explained. "But I'm tired of trying to stay away from you, Beau."

There was no humor in her face now. Her eyes were intense, narrowed, the long lines of her lashes stark black against her skin. Her voice had a strange heat to it. I couldn't remember how to breathe.

"Will you accept a ride with me to Seattle?" she demanded, voice still burning.

I couldn't speak, so I just nodded.

A quick smile reshaped her face, and then she was serious again.

"You really *should* stay away from me," she warned. "I'll see you in class."

She spun on her heel and then walked quickly back the way we'd come.

5. BLOOD TYPE

I WALKED TO ENGLISH IN A KIND OF DAZE. I DIDN'T REALIZE WHEN I first came through the door that class had already started.

Ms. Mason's irritated voice was my first clue. "Thank you for joining us, Mr. Swan."

Patches of red formed on my face as I hurried to my seat.

It wasn't until class was over that I noticed McKayla wasn't sitting next to me like she usually did, and I remembered that I had hurt her feelings. But she and Erica waited at the door for me, so I hoped that meant I would be forgiven eventually. As we walked, McKayla seemed to become herself again, getting more enthusiastic as she talked about the weather report for the weekend. The rain was supposed to take a short break, so her beach trip would be possible. I tried to match her enthusiasm to make up for disappointing her yesterday, but I could tell I wasn't fooling either of them. Rain or no rain, we would be lucky if the temperature even got close to fifty degrees. Not my idea of a beach day.

The rest of the morning passed in a blur. It was hard to believe I wasn't imagining things again—that Edythe really had said those words, and that her eyes had looked that way when she was saying them. Something about her confused my reality. First I'd thought I'd seen her stop a van bare-handed, and now this. The original delusion seemed more likely than the second—that I appealed to her on any level. But here I was, walking into

this one with eyes wide open, and I didn't even care that the punch line was coming. At the moment, it seemed like a decent trade—her laughter later for that look in her eyes now.

I was both eager and nervous when I finally got to the cafeteria at lunch-time. Would she ignore me like usual? Would there be any sign from her that the conversation this morning had, in fact, happened? With a small percentage of my brain I listened to Jeremy. McKayla had asked him to the dance, and they were going to go with a few others—Allen and Erica, Logan and Taylor. I think I grunted in the right places, because he didn't seem to notice how little of my attention I was giving him.

My eyes went straight to her table as soon as I was through the door, and then disappointment hit like a punch to the gut. There were only four peo-ple there, and Edythe wasn't one of them. Was she going to disappear every time something significant happened?

Of course, the conversation this morning was only significant to me, I was sure.

I lost my appetite. I grabbed a bottle of lemonade for something to carry and followed Jeremy robotically through the line, wishing I were the kind of person who could just go home early, the kind who didn't worry about unexcused absences and detention and disappointed paren-tal figures.

"Edythe Cullen is staring at you again," Jeremy said. I was one hundred percent paying attention as soon as he said her name. "I wonder why she's sitting alone today."

My head snapped up and I quickly followed his line of sight. Edythe was sitting at an empty table across the cafeteria from where she usually sat. Her dimples flashed as soon as she knew I'd seen her. She raised one hand and motioned with her index finger for me to join her. As I stared, not entirely believing my own eyes, she winked.

"Does she mean *you?*" Jeremy asked. There was an insult in his astonish-ment, but I was past caring.

"Um, maybe she needs help with her Biology homework," I muttered. "I guess I should go see what she wants."

I could feel Jeremy staring after me as I walked away. I could also feel those ugly splotches of red start up my neck, and tried to calm myself.

When I got to her table I just stood there behind the chair across from her, awkward.

"Why don't you sit with me today?" she suggested through a wide smile.

I sat down automatically, watching her expression. Was this how the joke ended? She hadn't stopped smiling. I found that I still didn't care. Whatever got me more time this close to her.

She stared back at me, still smiling. Did she want me to say something?

"This is, uh, different," I finally managed.

"Well," she said, and then paused. I could tell there was more, so I waited. The rest of it followed in a rush, the words blurring together so that it took me a minute to decipher the meaning. "I decided as long as I was going to hell, I might as well do it thoroughly."

I kept waiting, thinking she would explain, but she didn't. The silence got more uncomfortable as the seconds passed.

"You know I don't understand what you mean, right?" I asked.

"I'm counting on it," she said, and then her eyes focused behind me. "I think your friends are upset that I've stolen you."

Suddenly I could feel all their eyes boring into my back. For once, it didn't bother me at all.

"They'll survive."

She grinned. "I may not give you back, though."

I swallowed too loud and she laughed.

"You look worried," she said.

"No." I stopped to swallow again, hearing the edge of a break in my voice. "But surprised, yes. What's this all about?" I gestured toward her and the rest of the empty table.

"I told you—I'm tired of trying to stay away from you. So I'm giving up." The smile was fading, and her eyes were serious by the end.

"Giving up?" I repeated.

"Yes—giving up trying to be good. I'm just going to do what I want now, and let the chips fall where they may." The smile disappeared completely, and a hard edge crept into her silky voice.

"You lost me again."

It looked like she found that funny. "I always say too much when I'm talking to you—that's one of the problems."

"Don't worry—I don't understand anything you say."

"Like I said—I'm counting on that."

We stared at each other for a few seconds, but the quiet wasn't awkward this time. It was more . . . charged. My face started to get hot again.

"So," I said, looking away so that I could catch my breath. "In plain English, are we friends now?"

"Friends . . . ," she murmured. She sounded like it wasn't her favorite word.

"Or not," I offered.

"Well, we can try, I suppose. But I'm warning you again that I'm not a good friend for you to have." Her smile was brittle now, the warning real.

"You say that a lot." Funny how my stomach was rolling. Was it because I was hungry after all? Because she was smiling at me? Or because I suddenly almost believed her? I could tell that *she* believed what she was saying.

"I do, because you're not listening. I'm still waiting for you to hear me. If you're smart, you'll avoid me."

Then I had to smile, and I watched as her smile automatically got bigger in response. "I thought we'd already come to the conclusion that I'm an idiot. Or absurd, or whatever."

"I did apologize—for the second one, at least. Will you forgive me for the first? I spoke without thinking."

"Yeah, of course. You don't have to apologize to me."

She sighed. "Don't I?"

I didn't know how to answer—it sounded like a rhetorical question anyway. I stared down at my hands wrapped around the lemonade bottle, not sure what to do. It was so strange to sit with her here—like normal people. I was sure only one of us was normal.

"What are you thinking?" she asked.

I looked up. She was staring again, her gold eyes curious and—like the first time I'd seen her—frustrated. Once again, my thoughts refused to pass through the appropriate filter.

"I'm wondering what you are."

Her smile tightened, like her teeth were suddenly clamped together, but she held it carefully in place.

"Are you having much luck with that?" Her voice was casual, like she didn't really care about my answer.

My neck got hot and—I assumed—unattractively blotchy. During the last month I'd given it some thought, but the only solutions I could come up with were completely ridiculous. Like Clark Kent and Peter Parker–level nonsense.

She tilted her head to the side, staring into my eyes as if she was trying to see *through* them, right into my brain. She smiled—inviting this time, impossible to resist.

"Won't you tell me?"

But I had to try to resist. She already thought I was an idiot. I shook my head. "Too embarrassing."

"That's *really* frustrating," she complained.

"Really?" I raised my eyebrows. "Like . . . someone refusing to tell you what she's thinking, even if all the while she's making cryptic little comments designed to keep you up at night wondering what she could possibly mean . . . Frustrating like that?"

She frowned, her lips pouting out in a distracting way. I worked to hold on to my focus.

"Or is it frustrating like, say, she's done a bunch of other strange things—for example, saving your life under impossible circumstances one day, then treating you like a pariah the next—and she never explained any of that, either, even after she promised? Frustrating like that?"

Her frown twitched, then settled into a deeper scowl. "You're really not over that yet?"

"Not quite yet."

"Would another apology help?"

"An explanation would be better."

She pursed her lips, then glanced past my left arm and laughed once.

"What?"

"Your girlfriend thinks I'm being mean to you—she's debating whether or not to come break up our fight."

"I don't have a girlfriend, and you're trying to change the subject."

She ignored the second half of my statement. "You might not think of her that way, but it's how she thinks of you."

"There's no way that's true."

"It is. I told you, most people are very easy to read."

"Except me."

"Yes, except for you." Her eyes shifted to me and intensified, drilling into mine. "I wonder why that is."

I had to look away. I concentrated on unscrewing the lid of my lemonade. I took a swig, staring at the table without seeing it.

"Aren't you hungry?" she asked.

Her stare was less penetrating now, I saw with relief. "No." I didn't think it was necessary to mention that my stomach wasn't steady enough for food. "You?" I looked at the empty table in front of her.

"No, I'm not hungry." She smiled like I was missing some inside joke.

"Can you do me a favor?" I asked, the words escaping before I could make sure they were allowed.

She got serious quickly. "That depends on what you want."

"It's not much," I promised.

She waited, still guarded but clearly curious.

"Could you warn me beforehand? The next time you decide to ignore me? For my own good, or whatever. Just so I'm prepared." I looked at the lemonade again as I asked, tracing the lip of the opening with one finger.

"That sounds fair."

She looked like she was trying not to laugh when I glanced up.

"Thanks."

"Can I have a favor in return?" she asked.

"Sure." It was my turn to be curious. What would she want from me?

"Tell me one of your theories."

Whoops. "No way."

"You promised me a favor."

"And you've broken promises before," I reminded her.

"Just one theory—I won't laugh."

"Yes, you will." I had no doubt about that.

She looked down, then glanced up at me through her thick lashes, her long gold eyes scorching underneath.

"Please?" she breathed, leaning toward me. Without permission, my body leaned closer to her, like she was a magnet and I was a paper clip, till her face was less than a foot from mine. My mind went totally blank.

I shook my head, trying to clear it, and forced myself to sit back. "Um . . . what?"

"One little theory," she purred. "Please?"

"Well, er, bitten by a radioactive spider?" Was she a hypnotist, too? Or was I just a hopeless pushover?

She rolled her eyes. "That's not very creative."

"Sorry, that's all I've got."

"You're not even close."

"No spiders?"

"No spiders."

"No radioactivity?"

"None at all."

"Huh," I mumbled.

She chuckled. "Kryptonite doesn't bother me, either."

"You're not supposed to laugh, remember?"

She pressed her lips together, but her shoulders shook from holding the laughter back.

"I'll figure it out eventually," I muttered.

Her humor vanished like a switch flipped off. "I wish you wouldn't try."

"How can I not wonder? I mean . . . you're impossible." I didn't say it like a criticism, just a statement. *You are not possible. You are more than what is possible.*

She understood. "But what if I'm not a superhero? What if I'm the villain?" She smiled as she said this, playfully, but her eyes were heavy with some burden I couldn't imagine.

"Oh," I said, surprised. Her many hints started adding up until they finally made sense. "Oh, okay."

She waited, suddenly rigid with stress. In that second, all of her walls seemed to disappear.

"What exactly does *okay* mean?" she asked so quietly it was almost a whisper.

I tried to order my thoughts, but her anxiety pushed me to answer faster. I said the words without preparing them first.

"You're dangerous?" It came out like a question, and there was doubt in my voice. She was smaller than I was, no more than my age, and delicately built. Under normal circumstances, I would have laughed at applying the word *dangerous* to someone like her. But she was not normal, and there *was* no one like her. I remembered the first time she'd glared at me with hate

in her eyes, and I'd felt genuinely afraid, though I hadn't understood that reaction in the moment, and I'd thought it foolish just seconds later. Now I understood. Under the doubt, outside the incongruity of the word *dangerous* applied to her slim and perfect body, I could feel the truth of the foundation. The danger was real, though my logical mind couldn't make sense of it. And she'd been trying to warn me all along.

"Dangerous," I murmured again, trying to fit the word to the person in front of me. Her porcelain face was still vulnerable, without walls or secrets. Her eyes were wide now, anticipating my reaction. She seemed to be bracing herself for some kind of impact. "But not the villain," I whispered. "No, I don't believe that."

"You're wrong." Her voice was almost inaudible. She looked down, reaching out to steal the lid for my lemonade, which she then spun like a top between her fingers. I took advantage of her inattention to stare some more. She meant what she was saying—that was obvious. She wanted me to be afraid of her.

What I felt most was . . . fascinated. There were some nerves, of course, being so close to her. Fear of making a fool of myself. But all I wanted was to sit here forever, to listen to her voice and watch the expressions fly across her face, so much faster than I could analyze them. So of course that was when I noticed that the cafeteria was almost empty.

I shoved my chair away from the table, and she looked up. She seemed . . . sad. But resigned. Like this was the reaction she'd been waiting for.

"We're going to be late," I told her, scrambling to my feet.

She was surprised for just a second, and then the now-familiar amusement was back.

"I'm not going to class today." Her fingers twirled the lid so fast that it was just a blur.

"Why not?"

She smiled up at me, but her eyes were not entirely disguised. I could still see the stress behind her façade.

"It's healthy to ditch class now and then," she said.

"Oh. Well, I guess . . . I should go?" Was there another option? I wasn't much for ditching, but if she asked me to . . .

She turned her attention back to her makeshift top. "I'll see you later, then."

That sounded like a dismissal, and I wasn't totally against being dismissed. There was so much to think about, and I didn't do my best thinking with her near. The first bell rang and I hurried to the door. I glanced back once to see that she hadn't moved at all, and the lid was still spinning in a tight circle like it would never stop.

As I half-ran to class, my head was spinning just as fast. So few questions had been answered—none, really, when I thought through it—but so many more had been raised.

I was lucky; the teacher wasn't in the room when I ran in late, face hot. Both Allen and McKayla were staring at me—Allen with surprise, almost awe, and McKayla with resentment.

Mrs. Banner made her entrance then, calling the class to order while juggling a bunch of cardboard boxes in her hands. She let the boxes fall onto McKayla's table, and asked her to start passing them around the class.

"Okay, guys, I want you all to take one piece from each box," she said as she produced a pair of rubber gloves from the pocket of her lab coat and pulled them on. The crack as the gloves snapped into place was strangely ominous. "The first should be an indicator card," she went on, grabbing a white card about the size of an index card and displaying it to us; it had four squares marked on it instead of lines. "The second is a four-pronged applicator"—she held up something that looked like a nearly toothless hair pick—"and the third is a sterile micro-lancet." She displayed a small piece of blue plastic before splitting it open. The barb was invisible from this distance, but my stomach plunged.

"I'll be coming around with a dropper of water to prepare your cards, so please don't start until I get to you. . . ." She began at McKayla's table again, carefully putting one drop of water in each of the four squares of McKayla's card.

"Then I want you to carefully prick your finger with the lancet. . . ." She grabbed McKayla's hand and jabbed the spike into the tip of McKayla's middle finger.

"Ouch," McKayla complained.

Clammy moisture broke out across my forehead and my ears began a faint ringing.

"Put a small drop of blood on each of the prongs. . . ." Mrs. Banner

demonstrated as she instructed, squeezing McKayla's finger till the blood flowed. I swallowed convulsively, and my stomach heaved.

"And then apply it to the card," she finished, holding up the dripping red card for us to see. I closed my eyes, trying to hear through the humming in my ears.

"The Red Cross is having a blood drive in Port Angeles next weekend, so I thought you should all know your blood type." She sounded proud of herself. "Those of you who aren't eighteen yet will need a parent's permission—I have slips at my desk."

She continued through the room with her water dropper. I put my cheek against the cool, black tabletop and tried to hold on as everything seemed to get farther away, slithering down a dark tunnel. The squeals, complaints, and giggles as my classmates skewered their fingers all sounded far off in the distance. I breathed slowly in and out through my mouth.

"Beau, are you all right?" Mrs. Banner asked. Her voice was close to my head, but still far away, and it sounded alarmed.

"I already know my blood type, Mrs. Banner. I'm O negative."

I couldn't open my eyes.

"Are you feeling faint?"

"Yes, ma'am," I muttered, wishing I could kick myself for not ditching when I had the chance.

"Can someone walk Beau to the nurse, please?" she called.

"I will." Even though it was far away, I recognized McKayla's voice.

"Can you walk?" Mrs. Banner asked me.

"Yes," I whispered. *Just let me get out of here*, I thought. *I'll crawl.*

I felt McKayla grab my hand—I was sure it was all sweaty and gross but I couldn't care about that yet—and I worked to get my eyes open while she tugged me up. I just had to get out of this room before it went full dark. I stumbled toward the door while McKayla put her arm around my waist, trying to steady me. I put my arm over her shoulders, but she was too short to help my balance much. I tried to carry my own weight as much as possible.

McKayla and I lumbered slowly across campus. When we were around the edge of the cafeteria, out of sight of building four in case Mrs. Banner was watching, I stopped fighting.

"Just let me sit for a minute, please?" I asked.

McKayla breathed out a sigh of relief as I settled clumsily on the edge of the walk.

"And whatever you do, keep your hand in your pocket," I said. Everything seemed to be swirling dizzily, even when I closed my eyes. I slumped over to one side, putting my cheek against the freezing, damp cement of the sidewalk. That helped.

"Wow, you're green, Beau," McKayla said nervously.

"Just gimme . . . a minute . . ."

"Beau?" a different voice called from the distance.

Oh, please no. Not this, too. Let me just be imagining that horribly familiar voice.

"What's wrong? Is he hurt?" The voice was closer now, and it sounded strangely fierce. I squeezed my eyes shut, hoping to die. Or, at the very least, not to throw up.

McKayla sounded stressed. "I think he fainted. I don't know what happened, he didn't even stick his finger."

"Beau, can you hear me?" Edythe's voice was right by my head now, and she sounded relieved.

"No," I groaned.

She laughed.

"I was trying to help him to the nurse," McKayla explained, defensive. "But he wouldn't go any farther."

"I'll take him," Edythe said, the smile still in her voice. "You can go back to class."

"What? No, I'm supposed to . . ."

And then a thin, strong arm was under both of mine, and I was on my feet without realizing how I got there. The strong arm, cold like the sidewalk, held me tight against a slim body, almost like a crutch. My eyes flipped open in surprise, but all I could see was her tangled bronze hair against my chest. She started moving forward, and my feet fumbled trying to catch up. I expected to fall, but she somehow kept me upright. She didn't so much as stagger when my full weight tugged us both forward.

Then again, I didn't weigh as much as a van.

"I'm good, I swear," I mumbled. Please, please let me not vomit on her.

"Hey," McKayla called after us, already ten paces behind.

Edythe ignored her. "You look simply awful," she told me. I could hear the grin.

"Just put me back on the sidewalk," I groaned. "I'll be fine in a few minutes."

She propelled us quickly forward while I tried to make my feet move in the right pattern to match her speed. A few times I could swear that my feet were actually dragging across the ground, but then, I couldn't feel them very well, so I wasn't sure.

"So you faint at the sight of blood?" she asked. Apparently, this was hilarious.

I didn't answer. I closed my eyes again and fought the nausea, lips clamped together. The most important thing was that I not vomit on her. I could survive everything else.

"And not even your own blood!" She laughed. It was like the sound of a bell ringing.

"I have a weak vasovagal system," I muttered. "It's just a neurally mediated syncope."

She laughed again. Apparently, the big words I'd memorized to explain these situations did not impress her the way they were supposed to.

I wasn't sure how she got the door open while dragging me, but suddenly it was warm—everywhere except where her body pressed against me. I wished I felt normal so that I could appreciate that more—her body touching mine. I knew that under normal circumstances I would be enjoying this.

"Oh my," a male voice gasped.

"He's having a neurally mediated syncope," Edythe explained brightly.

I opened my eyes. I was in the office, and Edythe was dragging me past the front counter toward the door at the back of the room. Mr. Cope, the balding receptionist, ran ahead of her to hold it open. He faltered when he heard the dire-sounding diagnosis.

"Should I call nine-one-one?" he gasped.

"It's just a fainting spell," I mumbled.

A grandfatherly old man—the school medic—looked up from a novel, shocked, as Edythe hauled me into the room. Did he notice that when she leaned me against the cot, she half-lifted me into place? The crackly paper complained as she pushed me down with one hand against my chest, then turned and swung my feet up onto the vinyl mattress.

This reminded me of the time she'd swung my feet out of the way of the van, and the memory made me dizzy.

"They're blood typing in Biology," Edythe explained to the nurse.

I watched the old man nod sagely. "There's always one."

Edythe covered her mouth and pretended her laugh was a cough. She'd gone to stand across the room from me. Her eyes were bright, excited.

"Just lie down for a minute, son," the old nurse told me. "It'll pass."

"I know," I muttered. In fact, the dizziness was already beginning to fade. Soon the tunnel would shorten and things would sound normal again.

"Does this happen a lot?" he asked.

I sighed. "I have a weak vasovagal system."

The nurse looked confused.

"Sometimes," I told him.

Edythe laughed again, not bothering to disguise it.

"You can go back to class now," the nurse said to her.

"I'm supposed to stay with him," Edythe answered. She said it with such confidence that—even though he pursed his lips—the nurse didn't argue it further.

"I'll get you some ice for your head," he said to me, and then he shuffled out of the room.

I let my eyelids fall shut again. "You were right."

"I usually am—but about what in particular this time?"

"Ditching *is* healthy." I worked to breathe in and out evenly.

"You scared me for a minute there," she admitted after a pause. The way she said it made it sound like she was confessing a weakness, something to be ashamed of. "I thought that Newton girl had poisoned you."

"Hilarious." I still had my eyes shut, but I was feeling more normal every minute.

"Honestly," she said, "I've seen corpses with better color. I was concerned that I might have to avenge your death."

"I bet McKayla's annoyed."

"She absolutely loathes me," Edythe said cheerfully.

"You don't know that," I countered, but then I wondered. . . .

"You should have seen her face. It was obvious."

"How did you even see us? I thought you were ditching."

I was pretty much fine now, though the queasiness would probably have passed faster if I'd eaten something for lunch. On the other hand, maybe it was lucky my stomach was empty.

"I was in my car, listening to a CD." Such a normal response—it surprised me.

I heard the door and opened my eyes to see the nurse with a cold compress in his hand.

"Here you go, son." He laid it across my forehead. "You're looking better," he added.

"I think I'm okay," I said, sitting up. Just a little ringing in my ears, no spinning. The mint green walls stayed where they should.

I could tell he was about to make me lie back down, but the door opened just then, and Mr. Cope stuck his head in.

"We've got another one," he warned.

I lurched off the cot to make room for the next victim and handed the compress back to the nurse. "Here, I don't need this."

And then McKayla staggered through the door, now supporting Leann Stephens, another girl in our Biology class. She was currently sallow green. Edythe and I drew back against the wall to give them room.

"Oh no," Edythe murmured. "Go out to the office, Beau."

I looked down at her, confused.

"Trust me—go."

I spun and caught the door before it closed, floundering out of the infirmary. I could feel Edythe right behind me.

"You actually listened to me," she said, surprised.

"I smelled the blood." Leann wasn't sick from just watching other people. Much less embarrassing, I thought.

"People can't smell blood," Edythe contradicted.

"I can—that's what makes me sick. It smells like rust . . . and salt."

She was staring at me with a wary expression.

"What?" I asked.

"It's nothing."

McKayla came through the door then, glancing from Edythe to me and back again.

"Thanks so much for your help, Edythe," she said, her sickly sweet tone

a pretty good indication that Edythe was right about the loathing thing. "I don't know what Beau here would have done without you."

"Don't mention it," Edythe replied with an amused smile.

"You look better," McKayla said to me in the same tone. "I'm so glad."

"Just keep your hand in your pocket," I cautioned her again.

"It's not bleeding anymore," she told me, her voice going back to normal. "Are you coming to class?"

"No thanks. I'd just have to turn around and come back."

"Yeah, I guess. . . . So are you going this weekend? To the beach?" While she spoke, she flashed a dark look toward Edythe, who was standing against the cluttered counter, motionless as a sculpture, staring off into space.

I didn't want to upset her more. "Sure, I said I was in."

"We're meeting at my parents' store at ten." Her eyes flickered to Edythe again, and I could tell she was worried she was giving out too much information. Her body language made it clear this wasn't an open invitation.

"I'll be there," I promised.

"I'll see you in Gym, then," she said, moving uncertainly toward the door.

"Yeah, see you," I replied.

She looked at me again, her round face slightly pouting, and then as she walked through the door, her shoulders slumped. Guilt lanced through me, the same as yesterday. I didn't *want* to hurt her feelings, but it seemed like it just kept happening. I thought about looking at her disappointed face all through Gym.

"Ugh, Gym," I muttered.

"I can take care of that." I hadn't heard Edythe walk over, but now she spoke from right beside me, making me jump. "Go sit down and look pale," she instructed in a whisper.

That wasn't a challenge; I was usually pale, and the recent episode had left a light sheen of sweat on my face. I sat in one of the creaky folding chairs and rested my head against the wall with my eyes closed. Fainting was exhausting.

I heard Edythe speaking softly at the counter.

"Mr. Cope?"

I hadn't heard the man return to his desk, but he answered, "Yes?"

"Beau has Gym next hour, and I don't think he feels well enough. Actually, I was thinking I should drive him home. Do you mind excusing him

from class?" Her voice was like melting honey. I could guess how much more overwhelming her eyes would be.

"Do you need to be excused, too, Edythe?" Mr. Cope's voice broke.

Why couldn't I do that to people?

"No, I have Mr. Goff," Edythe said. "He won't mind."

"Okay, it's all taken care of. You feel better, Beau," Mr. Cope called to me. I nodded weakly, hamming it up just a bit.

"Can you walk, or do you want me to help you again?" With her back to the receptionist, her expression turned sarcastic.

"I'll walk."

I stood carefully, and I was still fine. She opened the door for me, her smile polite but her eyes mocking. I felt stupid as I walked through the door, out into the cold, fine mist that had just begun to fall. But it felt good—the first time I'd enjoyed the never-ending moisture falling out of the sky—as it washed the sweat off my face.

"Thanks for that," I said when she'd followed me out. "It's almost worth getting sick to miss Gym."

"Anytime," she promised. She stared past me into the rain.

"So are you going? This Saturday—the beach trip?" I was hoping she would, though it seemed unlikely. I couldn't picture her loading up to car-pool with the rest of the kids from school; she didn't belong in the same world. But just wishing that she might gave me the first thrill of enthusiasm I'd felt for the outing.

"Where are you all going?" She was still staring ahead, expressionless, but her question made me hope she was considering it.

"Down to La Push, to First Beach."

I watched her face, trying to read it. I thought I saw her eyes narrow just slightly.

She finally looked up at me and smiled. "I really don't think I was invited."

"I just invited you."

"Let's you and I not antagonize poor McKayla any more this week. We don't want her to snap." Her eyes danced, like she was enjoying the idea more than she should.

"Fine, whatever," I grumbled, preoccupied by the way she'd said *you and I*. I liked it more than *I* should.

We were at the parking lot now, so I angled toward my truck. Something caught my jacket and yanked me back half a step.

"Where are you going?" she asked, surprised. Her little hand had a fistful of my jacket. She didn't look like she'd even planted her feet. For a second I couldn't answer. She denied being a superhero, but my mind couldn't seem to frame it another way. It was like Supergirl had left her cape at home.

I wondered if it was supposed to bother me that she was so much stronger than I was, but I hadn't been insecure about things like that for a long time. Ever since I'd outgrown my bullies, I'd been fairly well satisfied. Sure, I'd like to be coordinated, but it didn't bother me that I wasn't good at sports. I didn't have time for them anyway, and they'd always seemed a little child-ish. Why get so worked up about a bunch of people chasing a ball around? I was strong enough that I could make people leave me alone, and that was all I wanted.

So, this small girl was stronger than I was. A lot. But I was willing to bet she was stronger than everyone else I knew, kids and adults alike. She could take Schwarzenegger in his prime. I couldn't compete with that, and I didn't need to. She was special.

"Beau?" she asked, and I realized I hadn't answered her question.

"Uh, what?"

"I asked where you were going."

"Home. Or am I not?" Her expression confused me.

She smiled. "Didn't you hear me promise to take you safely home? Do you think I'm going to let you drive in your condition?"

"What condition?"

"I hate to be the bearer of bad news, but you have a weak vasovagal system."

"I think I'll survive," I said. I tried to take another step toward my truck, but her hand didn't free my jacket.

I stopped and looked down at her again. "Okay, why don't you tell me what you want me to do?"

Her smile got wider. "Very sensible. You're going to get into my car, and I am going to drive you home."

"I have two issues with that. One, it's not necessary, and two, what about my truck?"

"One, *necessary* is a subjective word, and two, I'll have Archie drop it off after school."

I was distracted by the casual reminder that she had siblings—strange, pale, beautiful siblings. Special siblings? Special like her?

"Are you going to put up a fuss?" she asked when I didn't speak.

"Is there any point in resisting?"

I tried to decipher all the layers to her smile, but I didn't get very far. "It warms my cold heart to see you learning so quickly. This way."

She dropped her fistful of jacket and turned. I followed her willingly. The smooth roll of her hips was just as hypnotic as her eyes. And there wasn't a downside to getting more time with her.

The inside of the Volvo was just as pristine as the outside. Instead of the smell of gasoline and tobacco, there was just a faint perfume. It was almost familiar, but I couldn't put my finger on it. Whatever it was, it smelled amazing.

As the engine purred quietly to life, she played with a few dials, turning the heat on and the music down.

"Is that 'Clair de Lune'?" I asked.

She glanced at me, surprised. "You're a fan of Debussy?"

I shrugged. "My mom plays a lot of classical stuff around the house. I only know my favorites."

"It's one of my favorites, too."

"Well, imagine that," I said. "We have something in common."

I expected her to laugh, but she only stared out through the rain.

I relaxed against the light gray seat, responding automatically to the familiar melody. Because I was mostly watching her from the corner of my eye, the rain blurred everything outside the window into gray and green smudges. It took me a minute to realize we were driving very fast; the car moved so smoothly I didn't feel the speed. Only the town flashing by gave it away.

"What's your mother like?" she asked suddenly.

Her butterscotch eyes studied me curiously while I answered.

"She kind of looks like me—same eyes, same color hair—but she's short. She's an extrovert, and pretty brave. She's also slightly eccentric, a little irresponsible, and a very unpredictable cook. She was my best friend." I stopped. It made me depressed to talk about her in the past tense.

"How old are you, Beau?" Her voice sounded frustrated for some reason I couldn't imagine.

The car stopped, and I realized we were at Charlie's house already. The rain had really picked up, so heavy now that I could barely see the house. It was like the car was submerged in a vertical river.

"I'm seventeen," I said, a little confused by her tone.

"You don't seem seventeen," she said—it was like an accusation.

I laughed.

"What?" she demanded.

"My mom always says I was born thirty-five years old and that I get more middle-aged every year." I laughed again, and then sighed. "Well, someone has to be the adult." I paused for a second. "You don't seem much like a junior in high school, either."

She made a face and changed the subject.

"Why did your mother marry Phil?"

I was surprised that she remembered Phil's name; I was sure I'd only said it once, almost two months ago. It took me a second to answer.

"My mom . . . she's very young for her age. I think Phil makes her feel even younger. Anyway, she's crazy about him." Personally I didn't see it, but did anyone ever think anyone was good enough for his mom?

"Do you approve?" she asked.

I shrugged. "I want her to be happy, and he's who she wants."

"That's very generous. . . . I wonder . . ."

"What?"

"Would she extend the same courtesy to you, do you think? No matter who your choice was?" Her eyes were suddenly intent, searching mine.

"I—I think so," I stuttered. "But she's the adult—on paper at least. It's a little different."

Her face relaxed. "No one too scary, then," she teased.

I grinned back. "What do you mean by scary? Tattoos and facial piercings?"

"That's one definition, I suppose."

"What's your definition?"

She ignored me and asked another question. "Do you think I could be scary?" She raised one eyebrow.

I pretended to examine her face for a minute, just as an excuse to stare at her, my favorite thing to do.

Her features were so delicate, so symmetrical. Her face would stop anyone in his tracks, but it wouldn't make him run in the other direction. The opposite.

"It's kind of hard to imagine that," I admitted.

She frowned to herself.

"But, I mean, I'm sure you could be, if you wanted to."

She tilted her head and gave me an exasperated smile, but didn't say anything else.

"So are you going to tell me about your family?" I asked. "It's got to be a much more interesting story than mine."

She was instantly cautious. "What do you want to know?"

"The Cullens adopted you?"

"Yes."

I hesitated for a minute. "What happened to your parents?"

"They died many years ago." Her tone was matter-of-fact.

"I'm sorry."

"I don't really remember them clearly. Carine and Earnest have been my parents for a long time now."

"And you love them." It wasn't a question. It was obvious in the way she said their names.

"Yes." She smiled. "I can't imagine two better people."

"Then you're very lucky."

"I know it."

"And your brother and sister?"

She glanced at the clock on the dashboard.

"My brother and sister, and Jessamine and Royal for that matter, are going to be quite upset if they have to stand in the rain waiting for me."

"Oh, sorry, I guess you have to go."

It was stupid, but I didn't want to get out of the car.

"And you probably want your truck back before Chief Swan gets home and you have to explain about the syncopal episode."

She was good with the medical jargon, but then, her mother was a doctor.

"I'm sure he's already heard. There are no secrets in Forks," I grumbled.

Apparently I'd said something funny, but I couldn't guess what it was, or why there was an edge to her laughter.

"Have fun at the beach," she said when she was finished. "Good weather for sunbathing." She gestured to the sheeting rain.

"Won't I see you tomorrow?"

"No. Eleanor and I are starting the weekend early."

"What are you going to do?" A friend could ask that, right? I hoped she couldn't hear the disappointment in my voice.

"We'll be hiking the Goat Rocks Wilderness, just south of Rainier."

"Oh, sounds fun."

She smiled. "Will you do something for me this weekend?" She turned to look me straight in the eyes, her own burning in their hypnotic way.

I nodded, helpless. *Anything*, I could have said, and it would have been true.

"Don't be offended, but you seem to be one of those people who just attract accidents like a magnet. Try not to fall into the ocean or get run over by anything, all right?"

She flashed her dimples at me, which took away some of the sting of being called incompetent.

"I'll see what I can do," I promised.

I jumped out into the vertical river and ran for the porch. By the time I turned around, the Volvo had disappeared.

"Oh!" I clutched at my jacket pocket, remembering that I'd forgotten to give her my key.

The pocket was empty.

6. SCARY STORIES

WHILE I TRIED TO CONCENTRATE ON THE THIRD ACT OF *Macbeth*, I WAS listening for my truck. I would have thought I'd hear the engine's roar even over the pounding rain. But when I went to look out the window again, it was suddenly there.

I wasn't super excited to get up on Friday, and it more than lived up to my negative expectations. Of course there were all the fainting comments. Jeremy especially seemed to get a kick out of that story. He laughed till he choked when Logan pretended to swoon at the lunch table. Luckily, McKayla had kept her mouth shut, and no one seemed to know about Edythe's involvement. Jeremy did have a lot of questions about yesterday's lunch, though.

"What did Edythe Cullen want?" he'd asked in Trig.

"Not sure." It was the truth. "She never really got to the point."

"She looked kind of mad."

I'd shrugged. "Did she?"

"I've never seen her sit with anyone but her family before. That was weird."

"Yeah, weird," I'd agreed.

He'd seemed kind of irritated that I didn't have better answers.

The worst part about Friday was that, even though I knew she wasn't going to be there, I still hoped. When I walked into the cafeteria with Jeremy and McKayla, I couldn't keep from looking at her table, where Royal, Archie, and Jessamine sat, talking with their heads close together. I wondered if

Archie had been the one to drive my truck home last night, and what he thought about the chore.

At my normal table, everyone was full of our plans for the next day. McKayla was animated again, putting a lot more trust in the local weatherman than I thought he deserved. I'd have to see his promised sun before I believed it. At least it was warmer today—almost sixty, though it was still wet. Maybe the trip wouldn't be totally miserable.

I caught a few unfriendly glances from Logan during lunch, which I didn't really understand. Just like everyone else, I'd laughed along with his fainting stunt. But I got some clarification as we walked out of the room. I guess he didn't realize how close I was behind him.

He ran a hand over his slicked-back, silver-blond hair. "I don't know why *Beaufort*"—he said my name with a sneer—"doesn't just sit with the Cullens now," I heard him mutter to McKayla. I'd never noticed before what a nasal voice he had, and I was surprised now by the malice in it. I really didn't know him well, not well enough for him to dislike me—or so I would have thought.

"He's my friend; he sits with us," McKayla snapped back. Loyal, but also territorial. I paused to let Jeremy and Allen pass. I didn't want to hear any more.

Later, at dinner, Charlie seemed excited about my trip to La Push in the morning. I guessed he felt guilty for leaving me home alone on the weekends, but he'd spent too many years building his habits to break them now. And I never minded the alone time.

Of course he knew the names of all the kids going, and their parents, and their great-grandparents, too, probably. He obviously approved. I wondered if he would approve of my plan to ride to Seattle with Edythe. He seemed to like the Cullens a lot. But there was no reason to tell him about it.

"Dad, do you know a place called Goat Rocks or something like that? I think it's south of Mount Rainier."

"Yeah, why?"

I shrugged. "Some kids were talking about camping there."

"It's not a very good place for camping." He sounded surprised. "Too many bears. Most people go there during hunting season."

"Huh. Maybe I got it wrong."

I meant to sleep in, but the light woke me. Instead of the same gloomy

half-light I'd gotten up to for the past two months, there was a bright, clear yellow streaming through my window. I couldn't believe it, but there it was—finally—the sun. It was in the wrong place, too low and not as close as it should be, but it was definitely the sun. Clouds still ringed the horizon, but a wide blue patch took up most of the sky. I threw on my clothes quickly, afraid the blue would disappear as soon as I turned my back.

Newton's Olympic Outfitters was just north of town. I'd seen the store but never stopped there—not having much desire for the supplies needed to intentionally stay outdoors over an extended period of time. In the parking lot I saw McKayla's Suburban and Taylor's Sentra. As I pulled up next to their vehicles, I saw the kids standing around in front of the Suburban. Erica was there, and two other girls I knew from class; I was pretty sure their names were Becca and Colleen. Jeremy was there, flanked by Allen and Logan. Three other guys stood with them, including one I remembered falling over in Gym on Friday. That one gave me a dirty look as I climbed out of the truck, and then said something to Logan. They laughed loudly, and Logan pretended he was passing out. The other guy caught him at first, then let him fall. They both busted up again, Logan just lying there on the pavement with his hands behind his head.

So it was going to be like that.

At least McKayla was happy to see me.

"You came!" she called, sounding thrilled. "And I promised it would be sunny, didn't I?"

"I told you I was coming."

"We're just waiting for Leann and Sean . . . unless you invited someone," she added.

"Nope, it's just me," I lied lightly, hoping I wouldn't get caught. But then again, it would be worth getting caught out if it meant I could spend the day with Edythe.

McKayla smiled. "Do you want to ride with me? It's either that or Leann's mom's minivan."

"Sure."

Her smile was huge. It was so easy to make her happy.

"You can have shotgun," she promised, and I saw Jeremy look up at us and then scowl. Not so easy to make McKayla and Jeremy happy at the same time.

The numbers worked out, though. Leann brought two extra people, so every space was necessary. I made Jeremy climb in before me so that he was wedged between McKayla and me in the front seat of the Suburban. McKayla could have been more gracious about it, but as least Jeremy seemed appeased.

It was only fifteen miles to La Push from Forks, with thick green forests edging the road most of the way and the wide Quillayute River snaking beneath it twice. I was glad I had the window seat. We'd rolled the windows down—the Suburban was claustrophobic with nine people in it—and I tried to absorb as much sunlight as possible.

I'd been to the beaches around La Push lots of times during my Forks summers with Charlie, so the mile-long crescent of First Beach was familiar. Still breathtaking, though. The water was dark gray, even in the sunlight, white-capped and heaving onto the rocky shore. Islands rose out of the steel harbor waters with sheer cliff sides, each with a spiky crown of black firs. The beach had only a thin border of actual sand at the water's edge; after that it was a million smooth rocks that looked uniformly gray from a distance, but close up were every color a stone could be. The tide line was piled with huge driftwood trees, bleached white by the salty waves—some piled together against the forest's edge, and some lying alone just out of reach of the waves.

There was a strong breeze coming off the waves, cool and briny. Pelicans floated on the swells while seagulls and a lone eagle circled above them. The clouds still crowded the edges of the sky, but for now the sun shone warmly in its backdrop of blue.

We trudged through the thick sand down to the beach, McKayla leading the way to a circle of driftwood logs that had clearly been used for parties before. There was a fire ring already in place, filled with black ashes. Erica and the girl I thought was named Becca gathered broken branches of driftwood from the driest piles against the forest edge, and soon had a teepee-shaped construction built atop the old cinders.

"Have you ever seen a driftwood fire?" McKayla asked me. I was sitting on one of the bleached benches; Jeremy and Allen sat on either side of me, but most of the other guys sat across the circle from us. McKayla knelt by the fire, holding a cigarette lighter to one of the smaller pieces of kindling.

"No," I said as she placed the blazing twig carefully against the teepee.

"You'll like this, then—watch the colors." She lit another small branch

and laid it alongside the first. The flames started to lick quickly up the dry wood.

"It's blue," I said in surprise.

"The salt does it. Cool, isn't it?" She lit one more piece, placed it where the fire hadn't yet caught, and then came to sit by me. Luckily, Jeremy was on her other side. He turned to McKayla and started asking her questions about the plan for the day. I watched the strange blue and green flames crackle upward.

After a half hour of talk, some of the girls wanted to hike to the nearby tide pools, but most of the guys wanted to head up to the one shop in the village for food.

I wasn't sure which side to join. I wasn't hungry, and I loved the tide pools— I'd loved them since I was just a kid; they were one of the only things I ever looked forward to when I had to come to Forks. On the other hand, I'd also fallen into them a lot. Not a big deal when you're seven and with your dad. It reminded me suddenly of Edythe—not that she wasn't always somewhere in my thoughts—and how she'd told me not to fall into the ocean.

Logan was the one who made my decision for me. He was the loudest voice in the argument, and he wanted food. The group splintered into three pieces—food, hiking, and staying put—with most people following Logan. I waited until Taylor and Erica had committed to going with him before I got up quietly to join the pro-hiking group. McKayla smiled wide when she saw that I was coming.

The hike was short, but I hated to lose the sun in the trees. The green light of the forest was a strange setting for the teenage laughter, too murky and menacing to be in harmony with the joking around me. I had to concentrate on my feet and head, avoiding roots below and branches above, and I fell behind. When I broke through the dark edge of the forest and found the rocky shore again, I was the last one. It was low tide, and a tidal river flowed past us on its way to the sea. Along its rocky banks, shallow pools that never completely drained were filled with tiny sea creatures.

I was cautious not to lean too far over the little ocean ponds. The others were reckless, leaping over the rocks, perching precariously on the edges. I found a stable-looking rock on the fringe of one of the largest pools and sat there, totally entertained by the natural aquarium below me. The bouquets of anemones rippled in the invisible current, hermit crabs scurried around the edges in their

spiraled shells, starfish stuck motionless to the rocks and each other, and one small black eel with white racing stripes wove through the bright green weeds, waiting for the sea to return. Watching took most of my attention, except for the small part of my mind that was wondering what Edythe was doing now, and trying to imagine what she would be saying if she were here instead.

Suddenly everyone was hungry, and I got up stiffly to follow them back. I tried to keep up better this time through the woods, so naturally I tripped. I got some shallow scrapes on my palms, but they didn't bleed much.

When we got back to First Beach, the group we'd left behind had multiplied. As we got closer I could see the shining, straight black hair and copper skin of the new arrivals, teenagers from the reservation come to socialize. Food was already being passed around, and the hikers hurried to claim a share. Erica introduced us to the new kids as we each entered the driftwood circle. Allen and I were the last to arrive, and, as Erica said our names, I noticed a younger girl sitting on the ground near the fire look up at me with interest. I sat down next to Allen, and McKayla joined us with sandwiches and sodas. The girl who looked to be the oldest of the visitors rattled off the names of the seven others with her. All I caught was that one of the boys was also named Jeremy, and the girl who noticed me was named Julie.

It was relaxing to sit next to Allen; he was an easy person to be around—he didn't feel the need to fill every silence with talk, leaving me free to think while we ate. And what I thought about was how strangely time seemed to flow in Forks, passing in a blur at times, with single images standing out more clearly than others. And then, at other times, every second was significant, etched into my mind. I knew exactly what caused the difference, and it was troubling.

During lunch the clouds started to move in, darting in front of the sun momentarily, casting long shadows across the beach, and blackening the waves. As they finished eating, people started to drift away in twos and threes. Some walked down to the edge of the waves, trying to skip rocks across the choppy surface. Others were gathering a second expedition to the tide pools. McKayla—with Jeremy shadowing her—headed up to the little store. Some of the local kids went with them; others went along on the hike. By the time they all had scattered, I was sitting alone on my driftwood log, with Logan and Taylor talking by the CD player someone had brought, and

three teenagers from the reservation, including the girl named Julie and the oldest girl, who had acted as spokesperson.

A few minutes after Allen left with the hikers, Julie came over to take his place by my side. She looked fourteen, maybe fifteen, and had long, glossy black hair pulled back with a rubber band at the nape of her neck. Her skin was really beautiful, like coppery silk, her dark eyes were wide-set above her high cheekbones, and her lips were curved like a bow. It was a very pretty face. However, my positive opinion was damaged by the first words out of her mouth.

"You're Beaufort Swan, aren't you?"

It was like the first day of school all over again.

"Beau," I sighed.

"Right," she said, like she'd already known that. "I'm Julie Black." She held out her hand. "You bought my mom's truck."

"Oh," I said, relieved, shaking her warm hand. "Bonnie's your mom. I probably should remember you."

"No, I'm the youngest of the family—you would remember my older brothers."

And suddenly I did. "Adam and Aaron." Charlie and Bonnie and Bonnie's husband—George, I remembered now; he'd died a few years back, car accident or something, and Charlie had been really sad—had thrown us together a lot during my visits, to keep us busy while they fished. We'd never made much progress as friends. Of course, I'd objected often enough to end the fishing trips by the time I was eleven. "Adam and Aaron and . . . Jules, wasn't it?"

She smiled. "You do remember. No one's called me that since my brothers left."

"They aren't here?" I examined the boys at the ocean's edge, wondering if I would be able to recognize them now.

Jules shook her head. "No, Adam got a scholarship to Washington State, and Aaron married a Samoan surfer—he lives in Hawaii now."

"Married. Wow." I was stunned. The twins were only a little over a year older than I was.

"So how do you like the truck?" she asked.

"I love it. It runs great."

"Yeah, but it's really slow," she laughed. "I was *so* relieved when Charlie

bought it. My mom wouldn't let me work on building another car when we had a perfectly good vehicle right there."

"It's not that slow," I objected.

"Have you tried to go over sixty?"

"No," I admitted.

"Good. Don't." She grinned.

I couldn't help grinning back. "It does great in a collision," I offered in my truck's defense.

"I don't think a tank could take out that old monster," she agreed with another laugh.

"So you build cars?" I asked, impressed.

"When I have free time, and parts. You wouldn't happen to know where I could get my hands on a master cylinder for a 1986 Volkswagen Rabbit?" she added jokingly. She had an interesting voice, warm and kind of throaty.

"Sorry," I laughed, "I haven't seen any lately, but I'll keep my eyes open for you." As if I knew what that was. She was very easy to talk with.

She flashed a brilliant smile, looking at me in a way I was learning to recognize. I wasn't the only one who noticed.

"You know Beaufort, Julie?" Logan asked. I should have known someone like Logan would notice how much I disliked my full name.

"Beau and I have sort of known each other since I was born," Jules said, smiling at me again.

"How nice for you," Logan said. I hadn't noticed before how fishy his pale green eyes were.

Jules raised her eyebrows at his tone. "Yes, isn't it wonderful?"

Her sarcasm seemed to throw Logan off, but he wasn't done with me yet. "Beau, Taylor and I were just saying that it was too bad none of the Cullens could come out today. Didn't anyone think to ask them?"

He looked at me like he *knew* I'd asked Edythe to come, and thought it was hilarious that she'd turned me down. Only, it hadn't felt like a rejection in the moment—it'd felt like she'd wanted to come with me, but couldn't. Had I read her wrong?

My worries were interrupted by a strong, clear voice.

"You mean Dr. Carine Cullen's family?"

It was the older girl who had first introduced the local kids. She was even

older than I'd thought, now that I looked at her closer. Not really a girl at all, but a woman. Unlike Julie's, her hair was cut short as a boy's. She was standing now, and I saw that she was almost as tall as I was.

Logan glared at her, glared *up* because he was shorter than she was, irritated because she'd spoken before I could respond. "Yes, do you know them?" he asked in a patronizing tone, only half-turned toward her.

"The Cullens don't come here," she said, and in her clear, forceful voice, it sounded less like an observation and more like . . . a command. She had ignored his question, but clearly the conversation was over.

Taylor, trying to win back Logan's attention, asked his opinion of the CD she held. He was distracted.

I stared at the woman—she stood with a confident, straight posture, looking away toward the dark forest. She'd said that the Cullens didn't come here, but her tone had implied something more—that they weren't allowed to come, that they were prohibited from coming here. Her manner left a strange impression with me that I couldn't shake.

Jules interrupted my meditation. "So, is Forks driving you insane yet?"

I frowned. Possibly, I was literally insane at this point. "I'd say that's an understatement."

She grinned sympathetically.

I was still turning over the woman's brief comment on the Cullens, and piecing it together with what I'd read from Edythe's reactions the other day. I looked at Jules, speculating.

"What?" she asked.

"You want to take a walk down the beach with me?"

She looked at Logan, then back to me with a quick grin. "Yeah, let's get out of here."

As we walked north toward the driftwood seawall, the clouds finally won. The sun disappeared, the sea turned black, and the temperature started to drop. I shoved my hands deep in the pockets of my jacket.

While we walked, I thought about the way Edythe could always get me to talk, how she would look at me from under her thick eyelashes and the gold of her eyes would burn and I would forget everything—my own name, how to breathe, everything but her. I eyed the girl walking alongside me now. Jules just had on a long-sleeved t-shirt, but she swung her arms as

she walked, not bothered by the cold. The wind whipped her silky black hair into twists and knots on her back. There was something very natural and open about her face. Even if I knew how to do that burning thing that Edythe did, this girl would probably just laugh at me. But not meanly, I didn't think. With Jules, you would always be in on the joke.

"Nice friends," she commented when we were far enough from the fire that the clattering of the stones beneath our feet was more than enough to drown out our voices.

"Not mine."

She laughed. "I could tell."

"Were those other kids your friends? That one seemed kind of . . . older."

"That's Samantha—Sam. She's nineteen, I think. I don't hang out with her. One of my friends was there before—Quil. I think she went up to the store."

"I don't remember which one she was."

She shrugged. "I didn't catch many names, either. I only remember yours because you used to pull my hair."

"I did? I'm so sorry!"

She laughed. "Your face. No—that was just my brothers. But I totally could have convinced you that you were guilty."

It was easy to laugh with her. "Guess so. Hey, can I ask you something?"

"Shoot."

"What did that girl—Sam—what did she mean about the doctor's family?"

Jules made a face and then looked away, toward the ocean. She didn't say anything.

Which had to mean that I was right. There was something more to what Sam had said. And Jules knew what it was.

She was still looking at the ocean.

"Hey, um, I didn't mean to be rude or anything."

Jules turned back with another smile, kind of apologetic. "No worries. It's just . . . I'm not really supposed to talk about that."

"Is it a secret?"

She pursed her curved lips. "Sort of."

I held my hands up. "Forget I asked."

"Already blew it, though, didn't I?"

"I wouldn't say *you* did—that girl Sam was a little . . . intense."

She laughed. "Cool. Sam's fault, then."

I laughed, too. "Not really, though. I'm totally confused."

She looked up at me, smiling like we already shared a secret of our own. "Can I trust you?"

"Of course."

"You won't go running to spill to your blond friend?"

"Logan? Oh yeah, I can't keep anything from that guy. We're like brothers."

She liked that. When she laughed, it made me feel like I was funnier than I really was.

Her husky voice dropped a little lower. "Do you like scary stories, Beau?"

For one second, I could hear Edythe's voice clearly in my head. *Do you think I could be scary?*

"How scary are we talking here?"

"You'll never sleep again," she promised.

"Well, now I have to hear it."

She chuckled and looked down, a smile playing around the edges of her lips. I could tell she would try to make this good.

We were near one of the beached logs now, a huge white skeleton with the upended roots all tangled out like a hundred spider legs. Jules climbed up to sit on one of the thicker roots while I sat beneath her on the body of the tree. I tried to seem only interested as I looked at her, not like I was taking any of this seriously.

"I'm ready to be terrified."

"Do you know any of our old stories, about where we come from—the Quileutes, I mean?" she began.

"Not really," I admitted.

"There are lots of legends, some of them claiming to date back to the Great Flood—supposedly, the ancient Quileutes tied their canoes to the tops of the tallest trees on the mountain to survive like Noah and the ark." She smiled, to show me she wasn't taking this seriously, either. "Another legend claims that we descended from wolves—and that the wolves are our sisters still. It's against tribal law to kill them.

"Then there are the stories about the *cold ones*." Her voice dropped even lower.

"The cold ones?" I asked. Did I look too interested now? Could she guess that the word *cold* would mean something to me?

"Yes. There are stories of the cold ones as old as the wolf legends, and some much more recent. According to legend, my own great-grandmother knew some of them. She was the one who made the treaty that kept them off our land." She rolled her eyes.

"Your great-grandmother?" I encouraged.

"She was a tribal elder, like my mother. You see, the cold ones are the natural enemies of the wolf—well, not the wolf, really, but the wolves that turn into women, like our ancestors. You could call them werewolves, I guess."

"Werewolves have enemies?"

"Only one."

I stared at her, too eager, trying to disguise my impatience as entertainment.

"So you see," Jules continued, "the cold ones are traditionally our enemies. But this pack that came to our territory during my great-grandmother's time was different. They didn't hunt the way others of their kind did—they weren't supposed to be dangerous to the tribe. So my great-grandmother made a truce with them. If they would promise to stay off our lands, we wouldn't expose them to the pale-faces." She winked at me.

"If they weren't dangerous, then why . . . ?"

"There's always a risk for humans to be around the cold ones, even if they're civilized like this clan alleged they were. You never know when they might get too hungry to resist." She deliberately worked a thick edge of menace into her tone.

"What do you mean, 'civilized'?"

"They claimed that they didn't hunt humans. They supposedly were somehow able to prey on animals instead."

I tried to keep my voice casual, but I was pretty sure I failed. "So how does it fit in with the Cullens? Are they like the cold ones your great-grandmother met?"

"No. . . ." She paused dramatically. "They are the *same* ones."

She must have thought the expression on my face meant only that I was engrossed in her story. She smiled, pleased, and continued.

"There are more of them now, a new female and a new male, but the rest are the same. In my great-grandmother's time they already knew of

the leader, Carine. She'd been here and gone before *your* people had even arrived." She was fighting another smile, trying to keep the tone serious.

"And what are they?" I finally asked. "What *are* the cold ones?"

"Blood drinkers," she replied in a chilling voice. "Your people call them vampires."

I stared out at the rough surf after she answered, not sure what my face was giving away. *Do you think I could be scary?* Edythe's voice repeated in my head.

"You have goose bumps on your neck," Jules laughed delightedly.

"You're a good storyteller," I told her, still staring into the waves.

"Thanks, but you're just cold. It's crazy stuff, isn't it? No wonder my mom doesn't want us to talk about it to anyone."

I couldn't control my expression enough to look at her yet. "Don't worry, I won't give you away."

"I guess I just violated the treaty." She threw her head back and laughed.

"I'll take it to the grave," I promised, and then a shiver ran down my spine.

"Seriously, though, don't say anything to Charlie. He was pretty mad at my mom when he heard that some of us weren't going to the hospital since Dr. Cullen started working there."

"I won't say anything to Charlie, of course not."

"So, do you think we're a bunch of superstitious natives or what?" she asked in a playful tone, but with a hint of worry. I still hadn't looked away from the ocean.

So I turned and smiled at her as normally as I could.

"No. I think you're very good at telling scary stories, though. I still have goose bumps, see?" I yanked back the sleeve of my jacket to show her.

"Cool." She grinned.

And then we both heard the sound of the beach rocks clattering against each other. Our heads snapped up at the same time to see McKayla and Jeremy about fifty yards away, walking toward us.

"There you are, Beau," McKayla called in relief, waving her arm over her head.

"Is that your girlfriend?" Jules asked, picking up the edge in McKayla's voice. I was surprised it was so obvious.

"No, *why* does everyone think that?"

Jules snorted. "Maybe because she wants them to."

I sighed.

"You ever need a break from these friends of yours, let me know."

"That sounds cool," I said, and I meant it. I didn't know if it was because we'd known each other longer, if not well, or if it was because Jules was so easygoing, but I already felt more comfortable with her than I did with any of the kids I'd be riding home with.

McKayla had reached us now, with Jeremy a few paces back, struggling to keep up. McKayla looked Jules up and down once, then turned to me in a move that was strangely dismissive of Jules. Jules snorted quietly again.

"Where have you been?" McKayla asked, though the answer was right in front of her.

"Jules here was just giving me the guided tour of First Beach." I smiled at Jules and she grinned back. Again, it was like we had a shared secret. Of course, that was true now.

"Well," McKayla said, eyeing Jules again. "We're packing up. Looks like it's going to rain."

We all glanced up—the clouds were thick and black and very wet-looking.

"Okay," I said. "I'm coming."

"It was nice to see you *again*," Jules emphasized, and I guessed she was messing with McKayla.

"It really was. Next time Charlie comes down to see Bonnie, I'll come with."

Her grin stretched across her entire face, showing her straight white teeth. "That would be cool."

"And thanks," I added in a low voice, not quite casual enough.

She winked at me.

I pulled up my hood as we trudged across the rocks toward the parking lot. A few drops were beginning to fall, making black spots on the stones where they landed. When we got to the Suburban the others were already loading everything back in. I crawled into the backseat by Allen and Taylor, announcing that I'd already had my turn in the shotgun position. Allen just stared out the window at the building storm, and Logan twisted around in the middle seat to occupy Taylor's attention, so I was free to lay my head back over the seat, close my eyes, and try very hard not to think.

7. NIGHTMARE

I TOLD CHARLIE I HAD A LOT OF HOMEWORK TO DO, AND THAT I'D FILLED up at La Push and didn't want dinner. There was a basketball game on that he was excited about, though of course I couldn't tell what was special about it, so he wasn't aware of anything off about my face.

Once in my room, I locked the door. I dug through my desk until I found my old headphones, and I plugged them into my little CD player. I picked up a CD that Phil had given to me for Christmas. It was one of his favorite bands, but they were a little heavy for my taste. I stuck it into place and lay down on my bed. I put on the headphones, hit Play, and turned up the volume until it hurt my ears. I closed my eyes, and then added a pillow over the top half of my face.

I concentrated only on the music, trying to make out the lyrics, to unravel the complicated drum patterns. By the third time I'd listened through the CD, I knew all the words to the choruses, at least. I was surprised to find that I really did like the band after all, once I got past the blaring noise. I'd have to thank Phil again.

And it worked. The eardrum-shattering beats made it impossible for me to think—which was the whole idea. I listened to the CD again and again, until I was singing along with all the songs, until, finally, I fell asleep.

I opened my eyes to a familiar place. Though part of my mind seemed to know that I was dreaming, most of me was just present in the green light

of the forest. I could hear the waves crashing against the rocks somewhere nearby, and I knew that if I found the ocean, I'd be able to see the sun. So I was trying to follow the sound, but then Jules was there, tugging on my hand, pulling me back toward the blackest part of the forest.

"Jules? What's wrong?" I asked. Her face was frightened as she yanked on my hand, trying to tow me back into the dark.

"Run, Beau, you have to run!" she whispered, terrified.

"This way, Beau!" It was McKayla's voice I heard now, calling from the thick of the trees, but I couldn't see her.

"Why?" I asked, still pulling against Jules's grasp. Finding the sun was really important to the dream me. It was all I could focus on.

And then Jules dropped my hand—she let out a strange yelp and, suddenly shaking, she fell twitching to the ground. I watched in horror, unable to move.

"Jules!" I yelled, but she was gone. In her place was a big, red-brown wolf with black eyes. The wolf faced away from me, pointing toward the shore, the hair on the back of her shoulders bristling, low growls issuing from between her exposed fangs.

"Beau, run!" McKayla cried out again from behind me. But I didn't turn. I was watching a light, coming toward me from the beach.

And then Edythe stepped out from the trees.

She wore a black dress. It hung all the way to the ground but exposed her arms to the shoulders and had a deep-cut V for a neckline. Her skin was faintly glowing, and her eyes were flat black. She held up one hand and beckoned me to come to her. Her nails were filed into sharp points and painted a red so dark they were almost as black as her dress. Her lips were the same color.

The wolf between us growled.

I took a step forward, toward Edythe. She smiled then, and between her dark lips her teeth were sharp, pointed, like her fingernails.

"Trust me," she purred.

I took another step.

The wolf launched herself across the space between me and the vampire, fangs aiming for the jugular.

"No!" I shouted, wrenching upright out of my bed.

My sudden movement caused the headphones to pull the CD player off the bedside table, and it clattered to the wooden floor.

My light was still on, and I was sitting fully dressed on the bed, with my shoes on. I glanced, disoriented, at the clock on my dresser. It was five-thirty in the morning.

I groaned, fell back, and rolled over onto my face, kicking off my boots. I was too uncomfortable to get anywhere near sleep, though. I rolled back over and unbuttoned my jeans, yanking them off awkwardly as I tried to stay horizontal. I pulled the pillow back over my eyes.

It was all no use, though. My subconscious had decided to wallow in the word I'd been trying so hard to avoid. I was going to have to deal with it now.

First things first, I thought to myself, glad to put it off as long as possible. I grabbed my bathroom stuff.

Showering didn't take very long. I couldn't tell if Charlie was still asleep, or if he'd left already. I went to the window, and the cruiser was gone. Early-morning fishing again.

I dressed slowly in yesterday's jeans and an old sweatshirt, and then made my bed—which was just stalling.

I couldn't put it off any longer. I went to my desk and switched on my old computer.

I hated using the Internet here. My modem belonged in a museum, and my free service really proved that you got what you paid for. Just dialing up took so long that I decided to grab a bowl of cereal while I waited.

I ate slowly, so the last bites were too soggy to finish. I washed the bowl and spoon, then put them away. My feet dragged as I climbed the stairs. I went to pick up my CD player first, then wound up the headphones' cord, and put them away in the desk drawer. I turned the same CD on, but turned it down till it was just background noise.

With a sigh, I turned to my computer, already feeling stupid before I could even finish typing the word.

Vampire.

I felt even more stupid looking at it.

The results were difficult to sift through. Most of it was entertainment— movies, TV shows, role-playing games, metal bands. . . . There were goth clothes and makeup, Halloween costumes, and convention schedules.

Eventually I found a promising site—Vampires A–Z—and waited impatiently for it to load. The final page was simple and academic-looking, black text on a white background. Two quotes greeted me on the home page:

Throughout the vast shadowy world of ghosts and demons there is no figure so terrible, no figure so dreaded and abhorred, yet dight with such fearful fascination, as the vampire, who is himself neither ghost nor demon, but yet who partakes the dark natures and possesses the mysterious and terrible qualities of both.—Rev. Montague Summers

If there is in this world a well-attested account, it is that of the vampires. Nothing is lacking: official reports, affidavits of well-known people, of surgeons, of priests, of magistrates; the judicial proof is most complete. And with all that, who is there who believes in vampires?—Rousseau

The rest of the site was an alphabetized listing of all the different myths of vampires found throughout the world. The first I clicked on, the *Danag*, was a Filipino vampire supposedly responsible for planting taro on the islands long ago. The myth continued that the *Danag* worked with humans for many years, but the partnership ended one day when a woman cut her finger and a *Danag* sucked her wound, enjoying the taste so much that it drained her body completely of blood.

I read carefully through the descriptions, looking for anything that sounded familiar, let alone plausible. It seemed that most vampire myths focused on beautiful women as demons and children as victims; they also seemed like excuses created to explain away the high mortality rates for young children, and to give guys an excuse for infidelity. Many of the stories were about bodiless spirits and warnings against improper burials. There wasn't much that sounded like the movies I remembered, and just a couple, like the Hebrew *Estrie* and the Polish *Upier*, who were even that interested in drinking blood.

Only three entries really caught my attention: the Romanian *Varacolaci*, a powerful undead being who could appear as a beautiful, pale-skinned human, the Slovak *Nelapsi*, a creature so strong and fast it could massacre an entire village in the single hour after midnight, and one other, the *Stregoni benefici*.

About this last there was only one brief sentence.

Stregoni benefici: An Italian vampire, said to be on the side of goodness, and a mortal enemy of all evil vampires.

It was a strange relief, that one small entry, the one myth among hundreds that claimed the existence of good vampires.

Overall, though, there wasn't much that fit with Jules's story or my own observations. I'd created a catalogue in my mind, and as I'd read I'd compared it with each myth. Beauty, speed, strength, pale skin, eyes that shift color; and then Jules's criteria: blood drinkers, enemies of the werewolf, cold-skinned, and immortal. There were very few myths that matched even one factor.

And then another problem, one that I'd remembered from the horror movies that I'd seen and that was backed up by today's reading—vampires couldn't come out in the daytime, the sun would burn them to a cinder. They slept in coffins all day and came out only at night.

Annoyed, I snapped off the computer's main power switch, not waiting to shut things down right. Through my irritation, I felt overwhelming embarrassment. It was all so stupid. I was sitting in my room, researching vampires. What was wrong with me?

I had to get out of the house, but there was nowhere I wanted to go that didn't involve a three-day drive. I pulled on my boots anyway, unclear where I was headed, and went downstairs. I shrugged into my raincoat without checking the weather and stomped out the door.

Overcast, but not raining yet. I ignored my truck and started east on foot, angling across Charlie's yard toward the nearby forest. It didn't take long till I was deep enough that the house and the road were invisible, and the only sound was the squish of the damp earth under my feet.

There was a narrow trail that led through the woods here; it wound deeper and deeper into the forest, mostly east as far as I could tell. It snaked around the spruces and the hemlocks, the yews and the maples. I only vaguely knew the names of the trees around me, and all I knew was thanks to Charlie pointing them out to me from the cruiser window a long time ago. There were lots I didn't know, and others I couldn't be sure about, because they were so covered in green parasites.

I followed the trail as long as my anger pushed me forward. As that started to fade, I slowed. A few drops of moisture trickled down from the canopy above me, but I couldn't be sure if it was beginning to rain, or if it was simply pools left over from yesterday, stored high in the leaves above, slowly dripping their way to the ground. A recently fallen tree—I knew it was recent because it wasn't entirely carpeted in moss—rested against the trunk of another, creating a sheltered little bench just a few feet off the trail. I stepped over the ferns and sat down, leaning my hooded head back against the living tree.

This was the wrong place to go. I should have known, but where else was there? The forest was deep green and far too much like the scene in last night's dream to make me comfortable. Now that there was no longer the sound of my soggy footsteps, the silence was piercing. The birds were quiet, too, the drops increasing in frequency, so it must be raining above. The ferns stood almost as high as my head, now that I was seated, and I knew someone could walk by on the path, three feet away, and not even see me.

Here in the trees it was much easier to believe the stupid words that embarrassed me indoors. Nothing had changed in this forest for thousands of years, and all the old myths and legends seemed much more likely in this ancient green maze than they had in my mundane bedroom.

I forced myself to focus on the two most important questions I had to answer.

First, I had to decide if it was possible that what Jules had said about the Cullens could be true.

Immediately, my mind responded with a loud and clear *No*. It was stupid to even consider the idea. These were silly stories. Just morbid old legends.

But what, then? I asked myself. There was no rational explanation for how I had survived the van. I listed again in my head the things I'd observed myself: the inhuman beauty, the impossible speed and strength, the eye color shifting from black to gold and back again, the pale, cold skin. And more—small things that registered slowly—how they never seemed to eat, the disturbing grace with which they moved. And the way *she* sometimes spoke, with unfamiliar cadences and phrases that better fit the style of the historical romances my mom loved than that of a twenty-first-century class-room. She had skipped class the day we'd done blood typing. She hadn't said

no to the beach trip till I told her where we were going. She seemed to know what everyone around her was thinking . . . except me. She'd told me she was the villain, dangerous. . . .

Could the Cullens be vampires?

Well, they were *something*. Something outside the boundaries of normal and sane was happening in this nothing little town. Whether it was Jules's *cold ones* or my own superhero theory, Edythe Cullen was not . . . human. She was something more.

So then—maybe. That would have to be my answer for now.

And then the most important question of all. What was I going to do about it?

If Edythe was a vampire—I could barely make myself think the word—then what should I do? Involving someone else was definitely out. I couldn't even believe myself; anyone I tried to talk to about it would have me committed.

Only two options seemed practical. The first was to take her advice: to be smart, to avoid her as much as possible. To cancel our plans, and to go back to ignoring her as far as I was able. To pretend there was an impenetrable glass wall between us in the one class where we were forced together. To tell her she was right, and then never talk to her again.

And it hurt—just the idea—more than it should. More than I felt I could stand. I switched gears, skipping on to the next option.

I could do nothing different. After all, if she was something . . . sinister, she'd done nothing too bad so far. In fact, I would be a dent in Taylor's fender if she hadn't acted so fast. So fast, I argued with myself, that it might have been sheer reflexes. But if it was a reflex to save lives, how bad could she be? My head spun in circular questions, no answers.

There was one thing I was sure of, if I was sure of anything. The black-gowned Edythe with the sharp teeth and nails was just the embodiment of the word Jules had said, and not the real Edythe. Even so, when I'd shouted in horror as the werewolf lunged, it wasn't fear for the wolf that had me screaming *No*. It was terror that *she* would be hurt. Even while she was calling to me with sharp-edged fangs, I was afraid for *her*.

And I knew that in that I had my answer. I didn't know if there ever was a choice, really. I was already in too deep. Now that I knew—*if* I knew—what

could I do about it? Because when I thought of her, of her voice, her hypnotic eyes, the magnetic way her body pulled mine toward her, all I wanted was to be with her right now. Even if . . . but I didn't want to think the word again. Not here, in the silent forest. Not while the rain made it dark as dusk under the canopy and made noises like footsteps across the matted ground. I shivered and jumped up, worried that somehow the path would have disappeared with the rain.

But it was there, winding its way out of the dripping green gloom. I took longer strides now, and I was surprised, as I nearly ran through the trees, at how far I had come. I started to wonder if I was heading out at all, or following the path farther into the forest. Before I could get too panicky, though, I began to see some open spaces through the branches. And then I could hear a car passing on the street, and I was suddenly free, Charlie's lawn under my feet.

It was just noon when I got back inside. I went upstairs and got dressed for the day, clean jeans and a t-shirt, since I was staying indoors. It didn't take too much effort to concentrate on my task for the day, a paper on *Macbeth* that was due Wednesday. I settled into outlining a rough draft, more relaxed than I'd felt since . . . well, since Thursday afternoon, if I was being honest.

That had always been my way, though. Making decisions was the painful part for me, the part I agonized over. But once the decision was made, I just followed through—relieved that the choice was made. Sometimes the relief was mixed with despair, like my decision to come to Forks. But it was still better than wrestling with the alternatives.

This decision was almost too easy to live with. Dangerously easy.

The rest of the day was quiet, productive—I finished my paper before eight. Charlie came home with a large catch, and I made a mental note to pick up a book of recipes for fish while I was in Seattle next week. The spikes of adrenaline I felt whenever I thought of that trip were no different than the ones I'd felt before I'd taken my walk with Jules. They should be different, but I didn't know how to make myself feel the right kind of fear.

I slept dreamlessly that night, beat from getting up so early. For the second time since arriving in Forks, I woke to the bright yellow light of a sunny day. I staggered to the window, stunned to see that there was hardly a cloud in the sky. I opened the window—surprised when it opened silently, without sticking, though I hadn't opened it in who knows how many years—and

sucked in the relatively dry air. It was nearly warm, and hardly windy at all. My blood drummed in my veins.

Charlie was finishing breakfast when I came downstairs, and he picked up on my mood immediately.

"Nice day out," he commented.

"Yeah," I agreed with a grin.

He smiled back, his brown eyes crinkling around the edges. When he smiled big like that, it was easier to imagine him as the man who had impulsively married a beautiful girl he barely knew when he was only three years older than I was now. There wasn't much of that guy left. He'd faded over the years, like the curly brown hair had receded from his forehead.

I ate breakfast with a smile on my face, watching the dust motes stirring in the sunlight that streamed in the back window. Charlie called out a goodbye, and I heard the cruiser pull away from the house. I hesitated on my way out the door, hand on my rain jacket. It would be tempting fate to leave it home. I folded it over my arm and stepped out into the brightest light I'd seen in months.

After a short battle, I was able to get both windows in the truck almost completely rolled down. I was one of the first ones to school; I hadn't even checked the clock in my hurry to get outside. I parked and headed toward the picnic benches on the south side of the cafeteria. The benches were still damp, so I sat on my jacket, glad to have a use for it. My homework was done, but there were a few Trig problems I wasn't sure I had right. I took out my book, but halfway through rechecking the first problem my mind was wandering, watching the sunlight play on the red-barked trees. I sketched mindlessly along the margins of my homework. After a few minutes, I realized I'd drawn five pairs of dark eyes staring off the page at me. I scrubbed them out with the eraser.

"Beau!" I heard someone call, and it sounded like McKayla. I looked around to see that the school had filled with kids while I'd been sitting here. Everyone was in t-shirts, some even in shorts though the temperature couldn't be over sixty. McKayla was coming toward me in a skirt that only reached the middle of her thighs and a tank top.

"Hey, McKayla," I answered.

She came to sit with me, the sun shimmering off her freshly straightened

hair, a grin stretching across her face. She was so happy to see me, I couldn't help but feel responsive.

"Great day, isn't it?"

"My kind of day," I agreed.

"What did you do yesterday?" There was an annoying sense of ownership in her question, and it reminded me of what Jules had said on Saturday. People thought I was her boyfriend because that was what McKayla wanted them to think.

But I was in too good of a mood to let it get to me now. "I mostly worked on my essay."

"Oh yeah—that's due Thursday, right?"

"Um, Wednesday, I think."

"Wednesday?" Her smile disappeared. "That's not good. I guess I'll have to get to work on that tonight." She frowned. "I was going to ask if you wanted to go out."

"Oh." I was thrown. Why couldn't I ever have a conversation with McKayla anymore without it getting awkward?

"Well, we still could go to dinner or something . . . and I could work on it later." She smiled at me hopefully.

"McKayla . . ." *Here comes the guilt*, I thought. "I don't think that would be the best idea."

Her face fell. "Why?" she asked, her eyes guarded. My thoughts flashed to Edythe, and I wondered if McKayla was thinking the same thing.

"Look, I'm breaking all kinds of man codes telling you this, so don't rat me out, okay?"

"Man codes?" she repeated, mystified.

"Jeremy's my friend, and if I went out with you, well, it would upset him." She stared at me.

"I never said any of this, okay? It's your word against mine."

"Jeremy?" she asked, her voice blank with surprise.

"Seriously, are you blind?"

"Oh," she exhaled—looking dazed. Time to escape.

I stuffed the book in my bag. "I don't want to be late again. I'm already on Mason's list."

We walked in silence to building three, her expression distracted. I hoped

whatever thoughts she was immersed in were leading her in the right direction.

When I saw Jeremy in Trig, he was just as fired up by the sunny day as I was. He, Allen, and Logan were headed into Port Angeles to catch a movie and order corsages for the dance, and I was invited. I was indecisive. It would be nice to get out of town, but Logan would be there. And who knew what I might be doing tonight. . . . But that was definitely the wrong thing to think about. Of course I was happy to see the sun again. But that wasn't totally responsible for the mood I was in, not even close.

So I gave him a maybe, lying about homework I had to catch up on.

Finally we were on our way to lunch. I was so anxious to see not just Edythe, but all the Cullens, that it was almost painful. I had to compare them with the suspicions that were haunting me. Maybe, when we were all together in one room, I would be able to feel sure that I was wrong, that there was nothing sinister about them. As I walked through the doors into the cafeteria, I felt the first tremor of actual fear roll through my stomach. Would they be able to know what I was thinking? And then a different feeling hit my stomach—would Edythe be waiting for me again?

As was my routine, I glanced first toward the Cullens' table. I felt a small rush of panic when I saw that it was empty. With fading hope, I scoured the rest of the cafeteria, hoping to find her there alone. The place was nearly filled—Spanish had run over—but there was no sign of Edythe or any of her family. Just like that, my good mood was reversed.

We were late enough that everyone was already at our table. I vaguely noticed that McKayla had saved a seat for Jeremy, and that his face lit up in response.

Allen asked a few quiet questions about the *Macbeth* paper, which I answered as naturally as I could while my mood was spiraling lower and lower. He invited me to go with them tonight, too, and I agreed now, looking for any distraction.

What if, somehow, Edythe knew what I'd done this weekend? What if digging deeper into her secrets had triggered her disappearance? What if I'd done this to myself?

I realized I'd been holding on to a little bit of hope when I walked into Biology, saw her empty seat, and felt a new wave of disappointment.

The rest of the day dragged. I couldn't follow the discussion in Biology, and I didn't even try to keep up with Coach Clapp's lecture on the rules of badminton. I was glad to finally leave campus, so I could stop pretending I was fine until it was time to go to Port Angeles. But right after I walked through my front door, the phone rang. It was Jeremy, canceling our plans. I tried to sound glad that McKayla had asked him to dinner, but I think I sounded irritated. The movie got rescheduled to Tuesday.

Which left me with no distractions. I put some fish in a marinade and then finished up my new homework, but that only took a half hour. I checked my e-mail and realized I'd been ignoring my mom. She wasn't happy about it.

```
Mom,
Sorry. I've been out. I went to the beach with some
friends. And I had to write a paper.
```

My excuses were pretty pathetic, so I gave up on that.

```
It's sunny outside today—I know, I'm shocked, too—so I'm
going to go outside and soak up as much vitamin D as I
can. Love you, Beau.
```

I had a small collection of my favorite books that I'd brought to Forks, and now I grabbed *Twenty Thousand Leagues Under the Sea*, plus an old quilt from the linen cupboard at the top of the stairs.

Outside, I threw the quilt into the middle of the sunniest spot in Charlie's small square yard, then threw myself on top of it. I flipped through the paperback, waiting for a word or phrase to catch my interest—usually a giant squid or narwhal would be adequate—but today I went through the book twice without finding anything intriguing enough to start me reading. I snapped the book shut. Fine, whatever. I'd get a sunburn instead. I rolled onto my back and closed my eyes.

I tried to reason with myself. There was no need to freak out. Edythe had said she was going camping. Maybe the others had been planning to join her

all along. Maybe they'd all decided to stay an extra day because the weather was so nice. Missing a few days wasn't going to affect any of her perfect grades. I could relax. I would see her again tomorrow for sure.

Even if she, or one of the others, *could* know what I was thinking, it was hardly a reason for skipping town. I didn't believe any of it myself, and it wasn't like I was going to say anything to someone else. It was stupid. I knew the whole idea was completely ridiculous. Obviously, there was no reason for anyone—vampire or not—to overreact.

It was just as ridiculous to imagine that someone could read my mind. I needed to stop being so paranoid. Edythe would be back tomorrow. No one had ever found neuroticism attractive, and I doubted she would be the first.

Mellow. Relaxed. Normal. I could handle that. Just breathe in and out.

The next thing I was aware of was the sound of Charlie's car turning onto the bricks of the driveway. I sat up, surprised that the light was gone and I was deep in the shadow of the trees now. I must have fallen asleep. I looked around, still half out of it, with the sudden feeling that I wasn't alone.

"Charlie?" I asked. But I could hear his door slamming in front of the house.

I jumped up, feeling edgy and also stupid for feeling that way, and grabbed the quilt and my book. I hurried inside to get some oil heating on the stove; thanks to my nap, dinner would be late. Charlie was hanging up his gun belt and stepping out of his boots when I came in.

"Sorry, dinner's not ready yet—I fell asleep outside." I yawned hugely.

"Don't worry about it," he said. "I wanted to catch the score on the game anyway."

I watched TV with Charlie after dinner, for something to do. There wasn't anything on I wanted to watch, but he knew I didn't care about baseball, so he turned it to some mindless sitcom that neither of us enjoyed. He seemed happy, though, to be doing something together. And it felt good, despite my idiotic depression, to make him happy.

"FYI, Dad," I said during a commercial, "I'm going to a movie with some of the guys from school tomorrow night, so you'll be on your own."

"Anyone I know?" he asked.

Who didn't he know here? "Jeremy Stanley, Allen Weber, and Logan whatever-his-last-name-is."

"Mallory," he told me.

"If you say so."

"Fine, but it's a school night, so don't go crazy."

"We're leaving right after school, so we won't be too late. You want me to put something out for your dinner?"

"Beau, I fed myself for seventeen years before you got here," he reminded me.

"I don't know how you survived," I muttered.

Everything felt less gloomy in the morning—it was sunny again—but I tried not to get my hopes up. I dressed for the warmer weather in a thin sweater—something I'd worn in the dead of winter in Phoenix.

I had planned my arrival at school so that I barely had time to make it to class. My mood quickly deteriorated while I circled the full lot looking for a space . . . and also searching for the silver Volvo that was clearly not there.

It was the same as yesterday—I just couldn't keep little sprouts of hope from budding in my mind, only to have them squashed painfully as I searched the lunchroom in vain and sat at my empty Biology table. What if she never came back? What if I never saw her again?

The Port Angeles plan was back on again for tonight, and it was all the more welcome because Logan couldn't make it. I couldn't wait to get out of town so I could stop glancing over my shoulder, hoping to see her appearing out of the blue the way she always did. I committed to being in a good mood so that I wouldn't annoy Jeremy and Allen. Maybe I could find a decent bookstore while I was out. I didn't want to think that I might be looking alone in Seattle this weekend. She wouldn't really cancel without even telling me, would she? But then, who knew what social rules vampires felt compelled to follow?

After school, Jeremy followed me home in his old white Mercury so that I could ditch my truck, and then we headed to Allen's. He was waiting for us. My mood started to lift as we drove out of the town limits.

8. PORT ANGELES

JEREMY DROVE FASTER THAN THE CHIEF, SO WE MADE IT TO PORT ANGE-les by four. He took us to the florist first, where the glossy woman behind the counter quickly upsold Allen from roses to orchids. Allen made decisions fast, but it took Jeremy a lot longer to figure out what he wanted. The saleswoman made it sound like all the details would be really important to the girls, but I had a hard time believing anyone could care that much.

While Jeremy debated ribbon colors with the woman, Allen and I sat on a bench by the plate glass windows.

"Hey, Allen . . ."

He looked up, probably noticing the edge in my voice. "Yeah?"

I tried to sound more like I was just randomly curious, like I didn't care what the answer was.

"Do the, uh, Cullens miss school a lot—I mean, is that normal for them?"

Allen looked over his shoulder through the window while he answered, and I was sure he was being nice. No doubt he could see how awkward I felt asking, despite how hard I was trying to play it cool.

"Yeah, when the weather's good they go backpacking all the time—even the doctor. They're all really into nature or something."

He didn't ask one question, or make one snide comment about my obvious and pathetic crush. Allen was probably the nicest kid at Forks High School.

"Oh," I said, and let it drop.

After what felt like a long time, Jeremy finally settled on white flowers with a white bow, kind of anticlimactic. But when the orders were signed and paid for, we still had extra time before the movie was set to start.

Jeremy wanted to see if there was anything new at the video game store a few blocks to the east.

"Do you guys mind if I run an errand? I'll meet you at the theater."

"Sure." Jeremy was already towing Allen up the street.

It was a relief to be alone again. The field trip was backfiring. Sure, Allen's answer had been encouraging, but I just couldn't force myself into a good mood. Nothing helped me think about Edythe less. Maybe a *really* good book.

I headed in the opposite direction from the others, wanting to be by myself. I found a bookstore a couple of blocks south of the florist, but it wasn't what I was looking for. The windows were full of crystals, dream-catchers, and books on spiritual healing. I thought about going inside to ask directions to another bookstore, but one look at the fifty-year-old hippie smiling dreamily behind the counter convinced me that I didn't need to have that conversation. I would find a normal bookstore on my own.

I wandered up another street, and then found myself on an angled byway that confused me. I hoped I was heading toward downtown again, but I wasn't sure if the road was going to curve back in the direction I wanted or not. I knew I should be paying more attention, but I couldn't stop thinking about what Allen had said, and about Saturday, and what I was supposed to do if she didn't come back, and then I looked up and saw someone's silver Volvo parked along the street—not a sedan, this was an SUV, but still—and suddenly I was mad. Were all vampires this unreliable?

I trudged off in what I *thought* was a northeasterly direction, heading for some glass-fronted buildings that looked promising, but when I got to them, it was just a vacuum repair shop—closed—and a vacant space. I walked around the corner of the repair shop to see if there were any other stores.

It was a wrong turn—just leading around to a side alley where the dumpsters were. But it wasn't empty. Staring at the huddled circle of people, I tripped on the curb and staggered forward noisily.

Six faces turned in my direction. There were four men and two women. One of the women and two of the men quickly turned their backs to me,

shoving their hands in their pockets, and I had the impression that they were hiding the things they'd been holding. The other woman had dark black hair, and she looked strangely familiar as she glared in my direction. But I didn't stop to figure out how I knew her. When one of the men had spun around, I'd gotten a quick glimpse of what looked a lot like a gun stuffed into the back of his jeans.

I started walking forward, crossing the mouth of the alley and heading on to the next street, like I hadn't noticed them there. Just as I was out of view, I heard a voice whisper behind me.

"It's a cop."

I glanced behind me, hoping to see someone in uniform, but there was no one else on the empty street. I was farther off the main road than I'd realized. Picking up the pace, I watched the pavement so I wouldn't trip again.

I found myself on a sidewalk leading past the backs of several gray warehouses, each with large bay doors for unloading trucks, padlocked for the night. The south side of the street had no sidewalk, only a chain-link fence topped with barbed wire protecting some kind of engine parts storage yard. I'd wandered far past the part of Port Angeles that guests were supposed to see. It was getting dark now—the clouds were back and piling up on the western horizon, creating an early sunset. I'd left my jacket in Jeremy's car, and a sharp wind made me shove my hands in my pockets. A single van passed me, and then the road was empty.

"Hey, pig," a woman's voice called from behind me.

I looked back, and it was the woman I'd seen before, the familiar one. Behind her were two of the men from the alley—a tall bald guy and the shorter man who I thought might be the one who'd had the gun.

"What?" I asked, slowing automatically. She was looking straight at me. "I'm sorry, do you mean me?"

"Sorry?" she repeated. They were still walking toward me, and I backed away, toward the south side of the road. "Is that your favorite word or something?"

"I—I'm . . . sorry. I don't know what you're talking about."

She pursed her lips—they were painted a dark, sticky red—and suddenly I knew where I'd seen her before. She was with the guy I'd knocked with

my bag when I first arrived in Port Angeles. I looked at the shorter guy, and sure enough, I could see the tops of the tattoos on either side of his neck.

"Aren't you gonna call for backup, *Officer?*" he asked.

I had to glance behind myself again. It was just me. "I think you've got the wrong guy."

"Sure we do," the woman said. "And you didn't see anything back there, either, did you?"

"See anything? No. No, I didn't see anything."

My heel caught on something as I backed away, and I started to wobble. I threw my arms out, trying to balance, and the taller man, the one I'd never seen before, reacted.

He was pointing a handgun at me.

I'd thought it was the shorter guy who'd had the gun. Maybe they all had guns.

"Hey, hey," I said, holding my hands higher so he could see they were empty. "I'm not a cop. I'm still in high school." I kept edging away until my back ran into the chain-link fence.

"You think I'm stupid?" the woman asked. "You think your plainclothes getup fools me? I saw you with your cop partner, Vice."

"What? No, that was my dad," I said, and my voice broke.

She laughed. "You're just a baby pig?"

"Sure, okay. So that's cleared up. I'll get out of your way now. . . ." I started sliding along the fence.

"Stop."

It was the bald man, still pointing the gun. I froze.

"What are you doing?" the short guy said to him. His voice was low, but the street was very quiet, and I could hear him easily.

"I don't believe him," the tall one said.

The woman smiled. "How's that pirate song go? Dead men tell no tales."

"What?" I croaked. "No, look, that's—that's not necessary. I'm not telling any tales. There's nothing to tell."

"That's right," she agreed. She looked up at the tall man and nodded.

"My wallet's right here in my pocket," I offered. "There's not much in it, but you're welcome to it. . . ." I started to reach for my pocket, but that was the wrong move. The gun jumped up an inch. I put my hand in the air again.

"We need to keep this quiet," the short one cautioned, and he bent to grab a broken piece of pipe from the gutter. "Put the gun away."

As soon as the gun was down, I was going to bolt, and the bald guy seemed to know that. He hesitated while the tattooed one started toward me.

Zigzag, that was what my dad had told me once. It was hard to hit a moving target, especially one that wasn't moving in a straight line. It would help if I weren't doomed to trip over something. Just once, let me be sure on my feet. I could do that once, right? Just once, when my life depended on it?

How much would a nonfatal bullet wound hurt? Would I be able to keep running through the pain? I hoped so.

I tried to unlock my knees. The man with the pipe was only a few paces away from me now.

A shrill squeal froze him in place. We all stared up as the noise turned piercing.

Headlights flew around the corner and then barreled right at me. The car was just inches from hitting the tattooed guy before he jumped out of the way. The chain-link rattled when he rammed into it. I turned to run, but the car unexpectedly fishtailed around, skidding to a stop with the passenger door flying open just a few feet from me.

"Get in," a furious voice hissed.

I dove into the Volvo's dark interior, not even questioning how she'd come to be here, relief and a new panic swamping me at the same time. What if she got hurt? I yanked the door shut behind me while I shouted.

"Drive, Edythe, get out of here. He's got a gun."

But the car didn't move.

"Keep your head *down*," she ordered, and I heard the driver's side door open.

I reached out blindly toward the sound of her voice, and my hand caught her slim, cold arm. She froze when I touched her. There was no give, though my fingers wrapped tight around the leather of her jacket.

"What are you *doing*?" I demanded. "Drive!"

My eyes were adjusting, and I could just make out her eyes in the reflected glow of the headlights. First they looked at my hand gripping her arm, then they narrowed and glared out the windshield toward where the man and the woman must be watching, evaluating. They could shoot at any second.

"Give me just a minute here, Beau." I could tell her teeth were clenched together.

I knew she would have no problem breaking free of my grasp, but she seemed to be waiting for me to let her go. That wasn't going to happen.

"If you go out there, I'm going with you," I said quietly. "I'm not letting you get shot."

Her eyes glared forward for another half-second, and then her door slammed shut and we were reversing at what felt like about sixty.

"Fine," she huffed.

The car spun in a tight arc as we raced backward around a corner, and then suddenly we were speeding forward.

"Put on your seat belt," she told me.

I had to drop her arm to obey, but that was probably a good idea anyway. It wasn't exactly a normal thing, holding on to a girl like that. Still . . . I was sad to let go.

The snap as the belt connected was loud in the darkness.

She took a sharp left, then blew through several stop signs without a pause.

But I felt oddly at ease, and totally unconcerned about where we were going. I stared at her face—lit only by the dim dashboard lights—and felt a profound relief that went beyond my lucky escape.

She was here. She was real.

It took me a few minutes of staring at her perfect face to realize more than that. To realize that she looked super, super pissed.

"Are you okay?" I asked, surprised by how hoarse my voice was.

"No," she snapped.

I waited in silence, watching her face while her eyes glared straight ahead.

The car came to a sudden, screeching stop. I glanced around, but it was too dark to see anything besides the vague outline of dark trees crowding the roadside. We weren't in town anymore.

"Are you hurt at all, Beau?" she asked, her voice hard.

"No." My voice was still rough. I tried to clear my throat quietly. "Are you?"

She looked at me then, with a kind of irritated disbelief. "Of course I'm not hurt."

"Good," I said. "Um, can I ask why you're so mad? Did I do something?"

She exhaled in a sudden gust. "Don't be stupid, Beau."

"Sorry."

She gave me another disbelieving look and then shook her head. "Do you think you would be all right if I left you here in the car for just a few—"

Before she could finish, I reached out to grab her hand where it rested on the gearshift. She reacted by freezing again; she didn't pull her hand away.

It was the first time I'd really touched her skin, when it wasn't accidental and just for a fraction of a second. Though her hand was as cold as I expected, my hand seemed to burn from the contact. Her skin was so smooth.

"You're not going anywhere without me."

She glared at me, and like before, it was as if she were waiting for me to let go instead of just yanking free like she could easily have done.

After a moment, she closed her eyes.

"Fine," she said again. "Give me a moment."

I was okay with that. I kept my hand lightly on hers, taking advantage of her closed eyes to stare openly. Slowly, the tension in her face started to relax until it was smooth and blank as a statue. A beautiful statue, carved by an artistic genius. Aphrodite, maybe. Was that the one who was supposed to be the goddess of beauty?

There was that faint fragrance in the car again—something elusive that I couldn't quite put my finger on.

Then her eyes opened, and she looked slowly down at my hand.

"Do you . . . want me to let go?" I asked.

Her voice was careful. "I think that might be for the best."

"You're not going anywhere?" I checked.

"I suppose not, if you're that opposed."

Unwillingly, I pulled my hand from hers. It felt like I'd been holding a handful of ice cubes.

"Better?" I asked.

She took a deep breath. "Not really."

"What is it, Edythe? What's wrong?"

She almost smiled, but there was no humor in her eyes. "This may come as a surprise to you, Beau, but I have a little bit of a temper. Sometimes it's hard for me to forgive easily when someone . . . offends me."

"Did I—"

"Stop, Beau," she said before I could even get the second word fully out. "I'm not talking about you." She looked up at me with her eyes wide. "Do you realize that they were serious? That they were actually going to *kill* you?"

"Yeah, I kinda figured they were going to try."

"It's completely ridiculous!" It seemed like she was working herself up again. "Who gets murdered in *Port Angeles*? What *is* it with you, Beau? Why does everything deadly come looking for *you*?"

I blinked. "I . . . I have no answer for that."

She tilted her head to one side and pursed her lips, exhaling through her nose. "So I'm not allowed to go teach those thugs a lesson in manners?"

"Um, no. Please?"

She sighed a long, slow sigh, and her eyes closed again. "How disagreeable."

We sat in silence for a moment while I tried to think of something to say that would make up for . . . I guess, disappointing her? That was what it seemed like—that she was disappointed I was asking her not to go looking for multiple armed gangsters who had . . . *offended* her by threatening me. It didn't make much sense—and even less so when you factored in that she had asked me to stay in the car. She was planning to go on foot? We'd driven miles away.

For the first time since I'd seen her tonight, the word Jules had said popped into my mind.

Her eyes opened at the same moment, and I wondered if she'd somehow known what I was thinking. But she just looked at the clock and sighed again.

"Your friends must be worried about you," she said.

It was past six-thirty. I was sure she was right.

Without another word, she started the engine and spun the car around. Then we were speeding back toward town. We were under the streetlights in no time at all, still going too fast, weaving easily through the cars slowly cruising the boardwalk. She parallel parked against the curb in a space I would have thought much too small for the Volvo, but she slid in with one try. I looked out the window to see the theater's brightly lit marquee. Jeremy and Allen were just leaving, pacing away from us.

"How did you know where . . . ?" I started, but then I just shook my head.

"Stop them before I have to track them down, too. I won't be able to restrain myself if I run into your other friends again."

It was strange how her silky voice could sound so . . . menacing.

I jumped out of the car but kept my hand on the frame. Like before, holding her here.

"Jer! Allen!" I shouted.

They weren't very far away. They both turned, and I waved my free arm over my head. They rushed back, the relief on both their faces turning to surprise when they took in the car I was standing next to. Allen stared into the recesses of the car, and then his eyes popped wide in recognition.

"What happened to you?" Jeremy demanded. "We thought you took off."

"No, I just got lost. And then I ran into Edythe."

She leaned forward and smiled through the windshield. Now Jeremy's eyes bugged out.

"Oh, hi . . . Edythe," Allen said.

She waved at him with two fingers, and he swallowed loudly.

"Uh, hey," Jeremy said in her direction; then he stared at me—I must have looked odd, my one hand locked on the frame of the open door, but I wasn't letting go. "So . . . the movie's already started, I think."

"Sorry about that," I said.

He checked his watch. "It's probably still just running previews. Did you . . ." He eyed my hand on the car. ". . . still want to come?"

I hesitated, glancing at Edythe.

"Would you like to come . . . Edythe?" Allen asked politely, though he had a little trouble getting her name out.

Edythe opened her door and stepped out, shaking her long hair back from her face. She leaned on the frame and threw her dimples at them. Jeremy's mouth fell open.

"I've already seen this one, but thank you, Allen," she said.

Allen blinked and seemed to forget how to speak. It made me feel a little better for always being so stupid around her. Who could help it?

Edythe glanced over at me. "On a scale of one to ten, how much do you want to see this movie now?" she murmured.

Negative five thousand, I thought. "Er, not that much," I whispered back.

She smiled directly at Jeremy now. "Will it ruin your night if I make Beau take me to dinner?" she asked.

Jeremy just shook his head. He hadn't remembered how to close his mouth yet.

"Thanks," she told him, dimpling again. "I'll give Beau a ride home."

She slid back inside.

"Get in the car, Beau," she said.

Allen and Jeremy stared. I shrugged quickly and then ducked into the passenger seat.

"The *hell?*" I heard Jeremy breathe as I slammed my door.

I didn't get another look at their reactions. She was already racing away.

"Did you really want dinner?" I asked her.

She looked at me questioningly. Was she thinking what I was thinking—that I'd never actually seen her eat anything?

"I thought you might," she finally said.

"I'm good," I told her.

"If you'd rather go home . . ."

"No, no," I said too quickly. "I can do dinner. I just mean it doesn't have to be that. Whatever you'd like."

She smiled and stopped the car. We were parked right in front of an Italian place.

My palms started to sweat a little as I jumped out of the car, hurrying to hold the restaurant's door for her. I'd never really been on a date like this—a real *date* date. I'd gotten roped into some group things back in Phoenix, but I could honestly say that I hadn't cared one way or another if I ever saw any of those girls again. This was different. I nearly had a panic attack anytime I thought this girl might disappear.

She smiled at me as she walked past, and my heart did this weird double-beat thing.

The restaurant wasn't crowded—this was the off-season in Port Angeles. The host was a meticulously groomed guy a few years older than me, about my height but thicker through the shoulders. His eyes did that same thing that Allen's and Jeremy's had, bugging out for a second before he got control of his expression. Then it was his smarmiest smile and a goofy deep bow, all for her. I was pretty sure he didn't even know I was standing there next to her.

"What can I do for you?" he asked as he straightened up, still looking only at her.

"A table for two, please."

For the first time, he seemed to realize I was there. The look he gave me

was quick and dismissive. His eyes shifted back to her immediately, not that I could blame him for that.

"Of course, er, *mademoiselle*." He grabbed two leather folders and gestured for Edythe to follow. I rolled my eyes. *Signorina* was probably what he'd been looking for.

He led us to a four-top in the middle of the most crowded part of the dining room. I reached for a chair, but Edythe shook her head at me.

"Perhaps something more private?" she said quietly to the host. It looked like she brushed the top of his hand with her fingers, which I already knew was unlike her—she didn't touch people if she could help it—but then I saw him slide that hand to a pocket inside his suit coat, and I realized that she must have given him a tip. I'd never seen anyone refuse a table like that except in old movies.

"Of course," the host said, sounding as surprised as I was. He led us around a partition to a small ring of booths, all of them empty. "How is this?"

"Perfect," she said, and unleashed her smile on him.

Like a deer in headlights, the host froze for a long second, and then he slowly turned and staggered back toward the main floor, our menus still in the crook of his arm.

Edythe slid into one side of the closest booth, sitting close to the edge so that my only option was to sit facing her with the length of the table between us. After a second of hesitation, I sat, too.

Something thudded a couple of times on the other side of the partition, like the sound of someone tripping over his own feet and then recovering. It was a sound I was familiar with.

"That wasn't very nice."

She stared at me, surprised. "What do you mean?"

"Whatever that thing you do is—with the dimples and the hypnotizing or whatever. That guy could hurt himself trying to get back to the door."

She half-smiled. "I do a *thing*?"

"Like you don't know the effect you have on people."

"I suppose I can think of a few effects. . . ." Her expression went dark for a tiny second, but then it cleared and she smiled. "But no one's ever accused me of hypnotism by dimples before."

"Do you think other people get their way so easily?"

She tilted her head to the side, ignoring my question. "Does it work on you—this *thing* you think I do?"

I sighed. "Every time."

And then our server arrived with an expectant expression, which quickly shifted to awe. Whatever the host had told him, it had been an understatement.

"Hello," he said, surprise making his voice monotone as he mechanically recited his lines. "My name is Sal, and I'll be taking care of you tonight. What can I get you to drink?"

Like the host's, his eyes never strayed from her face.

"Beau?" she prompted.

"Um, a Coke?"

I might as well not have spoken at all. The waiter just kept staring at Edythe. She flashed a grin at me before turning to him.

"Two Cokes," she told him, and, almost like an experiment, she smiled a wide, dimpled smile right into his face.

He actually wobbled, like he was going to keel over.

She pressed her lips together, trying not to laugh. The waiter shook his head and blinked, trying to reorient. I watched sympathetically. I knew just how he felt.

"And a menu?" she added when he didn't move.

"Yes, of course, I'll be right back with that." He was still shaking his head as he walked out of sight.

"You've seriously never noticed that before?" I asked her.

"It's been a while since I cared what anyone thought about me," she said. "And I don't usually smile so much."

"Probably safer that way—for everyone."

"Everyone but you. Shall we talk about what happened tonight?"

"Huh?"

"Your near-death experience? Or did you already forget?"

"Oh." Actually, I had.

She frowned. "How do you feel?"

"What do you mean?" I hoped she didn't turn on the hypnotist eyes and make me tell the truth, because what I felt right now was . . . euphoria. She was right here, with me—on purpose—I'd gotten to touch her hand, and I

probably had a few hours ahead to spend with her, too, since she'd promised to drive me home. I'd never felt so happy and so off-balance at the same time.

"Are you cold, dizzy, sick . . . ?"

The way she listed the words reminded me of a doctor's exam. And I didn't feel cold or sick . . . or dizzy in a medical way. "Should I?"

She laughed. "I'm wondering if you're going to go into shock," she admitted. "I've seen it happen with less provocation."

"Oh. No, I think I'm fine, thanks." Honestly, almost being murdered was not the most interesting thing that had happened to me tonight, and I hadn't really thought much about it.

"Just the same, I'll feel better when you have some food in you."

On cue, the waiter appeared with our drinks and a basket of breadsticks. He stood with his back to me while he placed them on the table, then handed Edythe a menu. Done with her experiments, she didn't so much as look at him this time. She just pushed the menu across the table to me.

He cleared his throat nervously. "There are a few specials. Um, we have a mushroom ravioli and—"

"Sounds great," I interrupted; I didn't care what I got—food was the last thing on my mind. "I'll have that." I spoke a little louder than necessary, but I wasn't sure he really knew I was sitting here.

He finally threw a surprised glance my way, and then his attention was back to her.

"And for you . . . ?"

"That's all we need. Thank you."

Of course.

He waited for a second, hoping for another smile, I thought. A glutton for punishment. When Edythe kept her eyes on me, he gave up and walked away.

"Drink," Edythe said. It sounded like an order.

I took a sip obediently, then another bigger gulp, surprised to find that I was actually pretty thirsty. I'd sucked down the entire glass before I knew it, and she slid her glass toward me.

"No, I'm fine," I told her.

"*I'm* not going to drink it," she said, and her tone added the *duh*.

"Right," I said and, because I *was* still thirsty, I downed hers, too.

"Thanks," I muttered, while the word I didn't want to think swirled around my head again. The cold from the soda was radiating through my chest, and I had to shake off a shiver.

"You're cold?" she asked, serious now. Like a doctor again.

"It's just the Coke," I explained, fighting another shiver.

"Don't you have a jacket?"

"Yeah." Automatically, I patted the empty seat next to me. "Oh—I left it in Jeremy's car," I realized. I shrugged, and then shivered.

Edythe started unwinding a bone-colored scarf from around her neck. I realized that I'd never once really noticed what she was wearing—not just tonight, but ever. The only thing I could remember was the black gown from my nightmare. . . . But though I hadn't processed the particulars, I knew that in reality she always wore light colors. Like tonight—under the scarf she had on a pale gray leather jacket, cut short like motorcycle gear, and a thin white turtleneck sweater. I was pretty sure she usually kept her skin covered, which made me think of the deep V of the black dream gown again, and that was a mistake. A patch of warmth started to bloom on the side of my neck.

"Here," she said, tossing the scarf to me.

I pushed it back. "Really, I'm fine."

She cocked her head to the side. "The hairs on the back of your neck are standing up, Beau," she stated. "It's not a lady's scarf, if that's what's bothering you. I stole it from Archie."

"I don't need it," I insisted.

"Fine, Royal has a jacket in the trunk, I'll be right—"

She started to move, and I reached out, trying to catch her hand, to keep her there. She evaded my grasp, folding her hands under the table, but didn't get up.

"Don't go," I said softly. I knew my voice sounded too intense—she was just going out to her car, not disappearing forever—but I couldn't make it sound normal. "I'll wear the scarf. See?"

I grabbed the scarf from the table—it was very soft, and not at all warm, the way it should be after coming off someone's body—and started to wrap it around my neck. I'd never worn a scarf that I could remember, so I just

wound it in a circle until I ran out of fabric. At least it would cover the red on my neck. Maybe I *should* own a scarf.

This one smelled amazing, and familiar. I realized this was a hint of the fragrance from the car. It must be her.

"Did I do it right?" I asked her. The soft knit was already warming to my skin, and it did help.

"It suits you," she said, but then she laughed, so I guessed that meant the answer was no.

"Do you steal a lot of things from, um, Archie?"

She shrugged. "He has the best taste."

"You never told me about your family. We ran out of time the other day." Was it only last Thursday? It seemed like a lot longer.

She pushed the basket of breadsticks toward me.

"I'm not going into shock," I told her.

"Humor me?" she said, and then she did the thing with the smile and the eyes that always won.

"Ugh," I grumbled as I grabbed a breadstick.

"Good boy," she laughed.

I just gave her a dark look as I chewed.

"I don't know how you can be so blasé about this," she said. "You don't even look shaken. A normal person—" She shook her head. "But then you're not so normal, are you?"

I shook my head and swallowed. "I'm the most normal person I know."

"Everyone thinks that about themselves."

"Do you think that about *yourself*?" I challenged.

She pursed her lips.

"Right," I said. "Do you ever consider answering any of my questions, or is that not even on the table?"

"It depends on the question."

"So tell me one I'm allowed to ask."

She was still thinking about that when the waiter came around the partition with my food. I realized we'd been unconsciously leaning toward each other across the table, because we both straightened up as he approached. He set the dish in front of me—it looked pretty good—and turned quickly to Edythe.

"Did you change your mind?" he asked. "Isn't there anything I can get you?" I didn't think I was imagining the double meaning in his offer.

"Some more soda would be nice," she said, gesturing to the empty glasses without looking away from me.

The waiter stared at me now, and I could tell he was wondering why someone like Edythe would be looking at someone like me that way. Well, it was a mystery to me, too.

He grabbed the glasses and stalked off.

"I imagine you have a lot of questions for me," Edythe murmured.

"Just a couple thousand," I said.

"I'm sure. . . . Can I ask you one first? Is that unfair?"

Did that mean she was going to answer mine? I nodded eagerly. "What do you want to know?"

She stared down at the table now, her eyes hidden under her black lashes. Her hair fell forward, shielding more of her face.

The words weren't much more than a whisper. "We spoke before, about how you were . . . trying to figure out what I am. I was just wondering if you'd made any more progress with that."

I didn't answer, and finally she looked up. I was glad for the scarf again, though it couldn't hide the red I could feel creeping up into my face now.

What could I say? Had I made progress? Or just stumbled into another theory even more stupid than radioactive spiders? How could I say that word out loud, the one I'd been trying not to think all night?

I don't know what my face must have looked like, but her expression suddenly softened.

"It's that bad, then?" she asked.

"Can I—can we not talk about it here?" I glanced at the thin partition that separated us from the rest of the restaurant.

"Very bad," she murmured, half to herself. There was something very sad and . . . almost *old* about her eyes. Tired, defeated. It hurt me in a strange way to see her unhappy.

"Well," I said, trying to make my voice lighter. "Actually, if I answer your question first, I know you won't answer mine. You never do. So . . . you first."

Her face relaxed. "An exchange, then?"

"Yes."

The waiter returned with the Cokes. He set them on the table without a word this time and disappeared. I wondered if he could feel the tension as strongly as I could.

"I suppose we can try that," Edythe murmured. "But no promises."

"Okay. . . ." I started with the easy one. "So what brings you to Port Angeles tonight?"

She looked down, folding her hands carefully on the empty table in front of her. She glanced up at me from under the thick lashes, and there was a hint of a smile on her face.

"Next," she said.

"But that's the easiest one!"

She shrugged. "Next?"

I looked down, frustrated. I unrolled my silverware, picked up my fork, and carefully speared a ravioli. I put it in my mouth slowly, still looking down, chewing while I thought. The mushrooms were good. I swallowed and took a sip of Coke before I looked up.

"Fine, then." I glared at her, and continued slowly. "Let's say, hypothetically, that . . . someone . . . could know what people are thinking, read minds, you know—with just a few exceptions." It sounded so stupid. There was no way, if she wouldn't comment on the first one . . .

But then she looked at me calmly and said, "Just *one* exception. Hypothetically."

Well, damn.

It took me a minute to recover. She waited patiently.

"Okay." I worked to sound casual. "Just one exception, then. How would something like that work? What are the limitations? How would . . . that someone . . . find someone else at exactly the right time? How would she even know I was in trouble?" My convoluted questions weren't making any sense by the end.

"Hypothetically?" she asked.

"Right."

"Well, if . . . that someone—"

"Call her *Jane*," I suggested.

She smiled wryly. "If your Hypothetical Jane had been paying better attention, the timing wouldn't have needed to be quite so exact." She rolled

her eyes. "I'm still not over how this could happen at all. How does anyone get into so much trouble, so consistently, and in such unlikely places? You would have devastated Port Angeles's crime rate statistics for a decade, you know."

"I don't see how this is my fault."

She stared at me, that familiar frustration in her eyes. "I don't, either. But I don't know who to blame."

"How did you know?"

She locked eyes with me, torn, and I guessed she was wrestling against the desire to just tell me the truth.

"You can trust me, you know," I whispered. I reached forward slowly, to put my hand on top of hers, but she slid them back an inch, so I let my hand fall empty to the table.

"It's what I *want* to do," she admitted, her voice even quieter than mine. "But that doesn't mean it's right."

"Please?" I asked.

She hesitated one more second, and then it came out in a rush.

"I followed you to Port Angeles. I've never tried to keep a specific person alive before, and it's much more troublesome than I would have believed. But that's probably just because it's you. Ordinary people seem to make it through the day without so many catastrophes. I was wrong before, when I said you were a magnet for accidents. That's not a broad enough classification. You are a magnet for *trouble*. If there is anything dangerous within a ten-mile radius, it will invariably find you."

It didn't bother me at all that she was following me; instead I felt a strange surge of pleasure. She was here for *me*. She stared, waiting for me to react.

I thought about what she'd said—tonight, and before. . . . *Do you think I could be scary?*

"You put yourself into that category, don't you?" I guessed.

Her face turned hard, expressionless. "Unequivocally."

I stretched across the table again, ignoring her when she pulled back slightly once more, and laid my hand on top of hers. She kept them very still. It made them feel like stone—cold, hard, and now motionless. I thought of the statue again.

"That's twice now," I said. "Thank you."

She just stared at me, her mouth twitching into a frown.

I tried to ease the tension, make a joke. "I mean, did you ever think that maybe my number was up the first time, with the van, and you're messing with fate? Like those *Final Destination* movies?"

My joke fell flat. Her frown deepened.

"Edythe?"

She angled her face down again, her hair falling across her cheeks, and I could barely hear her answer.

"That wasn't the first time," she said. "Your number was up the first day I met you. It's not twice you've almost died, it's three times. The first time I saved you . . . it was from myself."

As clearly as if I were back in my first Biology class, I could see Edythe's murderous black glare. I heard again the phrase that had run through my head in that moment: *If looks could kill . . .*

"You remember?" she asked. She stared at me now, her perfect face very serious. "You understand?"

"Yes."

She waited for more, for another reaction. When I didn't say anything, her eyebrows pulled together.

"You can leave, you know," she told me. "Your friends are still at the movie."

"I don't want to leave."

She was suddenly irritated. "How can you say that?"

I patted her hands, totally calm. This was something I had already decided. It didn't matter to me if she was . . . something dangerous. But *she* mattered. Where she was, was where I wanted to be.

"You didn't finish answering my question," I reminded her, ignoring the anger. "How did you find me?"

She glared at me for a moment, like she was willing me to be angry, too. When that didn't work, she shook her head and huffed a sigh.

"I was keeping tabs on Jeremy's thoughts," she said, like it was the most normal thing. "Not carefully—like I said, it's not just anybody who could get themselves murdered in Port Angeles. At first I didn't notice when you set off on your own. Then, when I realized that you weren't with him any- more, I drove around looking for someone who had seen you. I found the bookstore you walked to, but I could tell that you hadn't gone inside. You'd

gone south, and I knew you'd have to turn around soon. So I was just wait-ing for you, randomly searching through the thoughts of everyone I could hear—to see if anyone had noticed you so I would know where you were. I had no reason to be worried . . . but I started to feel anxious. . . ." She was lost in thought now, staring past me. "I started to drive in circles, still . . . listening. The sun was finally setting, and I was about to get out and fol-low you on foot. And then—" She stopped suddenly, her teeth clenching together with an audible snap.

"Then what?"

She refocused on my face. "I heard what she was thinking. I saw your face in her head, and I knew what she was planning to do."

"But you got there in time."

She inclined her head slightly. "It was harder than you know for me to drive away, to just let them get away with that. It was the right thing, I know it was, but still . . . very difficult."

I tried not to picture what she would have done if I hadn't made her drive away. I didn't want to let my imagination run wild down that particular path.

"That's one reason I made you go to dinner with me," she admitted. "I could have let you go to the movie with Jeremy and Allen, but I was afraid that if I wasn't with you, I would go looking for those people."

My hand still rested on top of hers. My fingers were starting to feel numb, but I didn't care. If she didn't object, I'd never move again. She kept watch-ing me, waiting for a reaction that wasn't going to come.

I knew she was trying to warn me off with all this honesty, but she was wasting the effort.

She took a deep breath. "Are you going to eat anything else?" she asked.

I blinked at my food. "No, I'm good."

"Do you want to go home now?"

I paused. "I'm not in any hurry."

She frowned like my answer bothered her.

"Can I have my hands back now?" she asked.

I snatched my hand away. "Sure. Sorry."

She shot me a glance while she pulled something from her pocket. "Is it possible to go fifteen minutes without an unnecessary apology?"

If it was unnecessary for me to apologize for touching her, did that mean she liked it? Or just wasn't actually offended by it?

"Um, probably not," I admitted.

She laughed once, and then the waiter showed up.

"How are you do—" he started to ask.

She cut him off. "We're finished, thank you very much, that ought to cover it, no change, thanks."

She was already out of her seat.

I fumbled for my wallet. "Um, let me—you didn't even get anything—"

"My treat, Beau."

"But—"

"Try not to get caught up in antiquated gender roles."

She walked away, and I rushed to follow, leaving the stunned waiter behind me with what looked like a hundred-dollar bill on the table in front of him.

I passed her, hurrying again to get the door, ignoring what she'd said about antiquated roles. I knew she was faster than I could probably imagine, but the half-filled room of watching people forced her to act like she was one of them. She gave me a strange look when I held the door open—like she was kind of touched by the gesture, but also annoyed by it at the same time. I decided to overlook the annoyed part, and I scrambled past her to hold the car door, too. It opened easily—she'd never locked it. Her expression was more amused than anything at this point, so I took that as a good sign.

I almost ran to the passenger side of the car, trailing my hand across the hood as I moved. I had the nerve-wracking feeling that she was regretting telling me so much, and she might just drive off without me and disappear into the night. Once I was inside, she looked pointedly at my seat belt until I put it on again. I wondered for a second if she was some kind of safety-first absolutist—until I noticed that she hadn't bothered with hers, and we were racing off into the light traffic without a hint of caution on her part.

"Now," she said with a grim smile, "it's your turn."

9. THEORY

"Can—can I ask just one more?" I stuttered quickly as she accel-erated much too fast down the quiet street.

I was in no hurry to answer her question.

She shook her head. "We had a deal."

"It's not really a question," I argued. "Just a clarification of something you said before."

She rolled her eyes. "Make it quick."

"Well . . . you said you knew I hadn't gone into the bookstore, and that I had gone south. I was just wondering how you knew that."

She thought about it for a moment, deliberating again.

"I thought we were past all these evasions," I said.

She gave me a kind of *you asked for it* look. "Fine, then. I followed your scent."

I didn't have a response to that. I stared out the window, trying to process it.

"Your turn, Beau."

"But you didn't answer my other question."

"Oh, come *on*."

"I'm serious. You didn't tell me how it works—the mind-reading thing. Can you read anybody's mind, anywhere? How do you do it? Can the rest of your family do the same thing?"

It was easier to talk about this in the dark car. The streetlights were

behind us already, and in the low gleam from the dashboard, all the crazy stuff seemed just a little more possible.

It seemed like she felt the same sense of non-reality, like normality was on hold for as long as we were in this space together. Her voice was casual as she answered.

"No, it's just me. And I can't hear anyone, anywhere. I have to be fairly close. The more familiar someone's . . . 'voice' is, the farther away I can hear him. But still, no more than a few miles." She paused thoughtfully. "It's a little like being in a huge hall filled with people, everyone talking at once. It's just a hum—a buzzing of voices in the background. Until I focus on one voice, and then what he's thinking is clear.

"Most of the time I tune it all out—it can be very distracting. And then it's easier to seem *normal*"—she frowned as she said the word—"when I'm not accidentally answering someone's thoughts rather than their words."

"Why do you think you can't hear me?" I asked curiously.

She stared at me, eyes seeming to bore right through mine, with that frustrated look I knew well. I realized now that each time she'd looked at me this way, she must have been trying to hear my thoughts, and failing. Her expression relaxed as she gave up.

"I don't know," she murmured. "Maybe your mind doesn't work the same way the rest of theirs do. Like your thoughts are on the AM frequency and I'm only getting FM." She grinned at me, suddenly amused.

"My mind doesn't work right? I'm a freak?" Her speculation hit home. I'd always suspected as much, and it embarrassed me to have it confirmed.

"I hear voices in my mind and you're worried that *you're* the freak." She laughed. "Don't worry, it's just a theory. . . ." Her face tightened. "Which brings us back to you."

I frowned. How was I going to say this out loud?

"I thought we were past all these evasions," she reminded me softly.

I looked away from her face, trying to gather my thoughts into words, and my eyes wandered across the dashboard . . . stopped at the speedometer.

"Holy crow!" I shouted.

"What's wrong?" she asked, looking right and left, rather than straight ahead where she should be looking. The car didn't decelerate.

"You're doing one-ten!" I was still shouting.

I shot a panicked glance out the window, but it was too dark to see much. The road was only visible in the long patch of bluish brightness from the headlights. The forest along both sides of the road was like a black wall—as hard as a wall of steel if we veered off the road at this speed.

"Relax, Beau." She rolled her eyes, still not slowing.

"Are you trying to kill us?" I demanded.

"We're not going to crash."

I carefully modulated my voice. "Why are we in such a hurry, Edythe?"

"I always drive like this." She turned to flash a smile at me.

"Keep your eyes on the road!"

"I've never been in an accident, Beau—I've never even gotten a ticket." She grinned and tapped her forehead. "Built-in radar detector."

"Hands on the wheel, Edythe!"

She sighed, and I watched with relief as the needle gradually drifted toward eighty. "Happy?"

"Almost."

"I hate driving slow," she muttered.

"This is slow?"

"Enough commentary on my driving," she snapped. "I'm still waiting for you to answer my question."

I forced my eyes away from the road in front of us, but I didn't know where to look. It was hard to look at her face, knowing the word I was going to have to say now. My anxiety must have been pretty obvious.

"I promise I won't laugh this time," she said gently.

"I'm not worried about that."

"Then what?"

"That you'll be . . . upset. Unhappy."

She lifted her hand off the gearshift and held it out toward me—just a few centimeters. An offer. I glanced up quickly, to make sure I understood, and her eyes were soft.

"Don't worry about me," she said. "I can handle it."

I took her hand, and she curled her fingers very lightly around mine for one short second, then dropped her hand back to the gearshift. Carefully, I placed my hand over the top of hers again. I ran my thumb along the outside of her

hand, tracing from her wrist to the tip of her pinkie finger. Her skin was so *soft*—not that it had any give at all, no, but soft like satin. Smoother, even.

"The suspense is killing me, Beau," she whispered.

"I'm sorry. I don't know how to start."

Another long moment of silence, just the purr of the engine and the sound of my hitching breath. I couldn't hear hers at all. I traced back down the side of her perfect hand.

"Why don't you start at the beginning," she suggested, her voice more normal now. Practical. "Is this something you thought up on your own, or did something make you think of it—a comic book, maybe, or a movie?"

"Nothing like that," I said. "But I didn't think of it on my own."

She waited.

"It was Saturday—down at the beach."

I risked a glance up at her face. She looked confused.

"I ran into an old family friend—Jules, Julie Black. Her mom, Bonnie, and Charlie have been close since before I was born."

She still looked confused.

"Bonnie's one of the Quileute leaders. . . ."

Her confused expression froze in place. It was like all the planes of her face had suddenly hardened into ice. Oddly, she was even more beautiful like that, a goddess again in the light of the dashboard dials. She didn't look very human, though.

She stayed frozen, so I felt compelled to explain the rest.

"There was this Quileute woman on the beach—Sam something. Logan made a comment about you—trying to make fun of me. And this Sam said your family didn't come to the reservation, only it sounded like she meant something more than that. Jules seemed like she knew what the woman was talking about, so I got her alone and kept bugging her until she told me . . . told me the old Quileute legends."

I was surprised when she spoke—her face was so still, and her lips barely moved.

"And what were those legends? What did Jules Black tell you I was?"

I half-opened my mouth, then closed it again.

"What?"

"I don't want to say it," I admitted.

"It's not my favorite word, either." Her face had warmed up a little; she looked human again. "Not saying it doesn't make it go away, though. Sometimes . . . I think *not* saying it makes it more powerful."

I wondered if she was right.

"Vampire?" I whispered.

She flinched.

Nope. Saying it out loud didn't make it any less powerful.

Funny how it didn't sound stupid anymore, like it had in my room. It didn't feel like we were talking about impossible things, about old legends or silly horror movies or paperback books. It felt real.

And very powerful.

We drove in silence for another minute, and the word *vampire* seemed to get bigger and bigger inside the car. It didn't feel like it belonged to her, really, but more like it had the power to hurt her. I tried to think of something, anything to say to erase the sound of it.

Before I could come up with anything, she spoke.

"What did you do then?"

"Oh—um, I did some research on the Internet."

"And that convinced you?" She was very matter-of-fact now.

"No. Nothing fit. Lots of it was really stupid. But I just—"

I stopped abruptly. She waited, then stared at me when I didn't finish.

"You what?" she pushed.

"Well, I mean, it doesn't matter, right? So I just let it go."

Her eyes grew wider and wider, and then suddenly they were narrowed into little slits, glaring at me. I didn't want to point out to her again that she should probably be watching where she was going, but her speed had crept up to past ninety-five now, and she seemed totally unaware of the twisting road ahead of us.

"Um, Edythe—"

"It doesn't *matter*?" she half-shouted at me, her voice going shrill and almost . . . metallic. "*It doesn't matter?*"

"No. Not to me, anyway."

"You don't care if I'm a monster? If I'm not *human*?"

"No."

Finally she stared at the road again, her eyes still long slashes of anger across her face. I could feel the car accelerating under me.

"You're upset. See, I shouldn't have said anything," I mumbled.

She shook her head, then answered through her teeth. "No, I'd rather know what you're thinking, even if what you're thinking is insane."

"Sorry."

She blew out an exasperated sigh, and then it was quiet again for a few minutes. I stroked my thumb slowly up and down her hand.

"What are you thinking about now?" she asked. Her voice was calmer.

"Um . . . nothing, really."

"It drives me crazy, not knowing."

"I don't want to . . . I don't know, offend you."

"Spit it out, Beau."

"I have lots of questions. But you don't have to answer them. I'm just curious."

"About what?"

"How old you are."

"Seventeen."

I stared at her for a minute, till half her mouth twitched up into a smile.

"How long have you been seventeen?" I asked.

"A while," she admitted.

I smiled. "Okay."

She looked at me like I'd lost my mind.

This was better, though. Easier, with her just being herself, not worrying about keeping me in the dark. I liked being on the inside. Her world was where I wanted to be.

"Don't laugh—but how do you come outside in the daytime?"

She laughed anyway. "Myth."

The sound of her laughter was warm. It made me feel like I had swallowed a bunch of sunlight. My smile got bigger.

"Burned by the sun?"

"Myth."

"Sleeping in coffins?"

"Myth." She hesitated for a moment, and then added softly, "I can't sleep."

It took me a minute to absorb that. "At all?"

"Never," she murmured. She turned to look at me with a wistful expression. I held her gaze, my eyes getting trapped in her golden stare. After a few seconds, I'd completely lost my train of thought.

Suddenly she turned away, her eyes narrowing again. "You haven't asked me the most important question yet."

"The most important question?" I echoed. I couldn't think of what she meant.

"Aren't you *curious* about my diet?" she asked, her tone mocking.

"Oh. That one."

"Yes. That one," she said bleakly. "Don't you want to know if I drink blood?"

I winced. "Well, Jules said something about that."

"Did she now?"

"She said you didn't . . . hunt people. Your family wasn't supposed to be dangerous because you only hunted animals."

"She said we weren't dangerous?" Her voice was deeply skeptical.

"Not exactly. Jules said you weren't *supposed* to be dangerous. But the Quileutes still didn't want you on their land, just in case."

She looked forward, but I couldn't tell if she was watching the road or not.

"So, was she right? About not hunting people?" I tried to keep my voice as even as possible.

"The Quileutes have a long memory," she whispered.

I took that as a confirmation.

"Don't let that make you complacent, though," she warned me. "They're right to keep their distance from us. We are still dangerous."

"I don't understand."

"We . . . try," she explained. Her voice got heavier and slower. "We're usually very good at what we do. Sometimes we make . . . mistakes. Me, for example, allowing myself to be alone with you."

"This is a mistake?" I heard the hurt in my voice, but I didn't know if she could, too.

"A very dangerous one," she murmured.

We were both silent then. I watched the headlights twist with the curves of the road. They moved too fast; it didn't look real, it looked like a video game. I was aware of the time slipping away so quickly, like the black road underneath us, and I was suddenly terrified that I would never have another chance to be with her like this again—openly, the walls between us gone for once. What she was saying kind of sounded like . . . goodbye. My hand tightened over hers. I couldn't waste one minute I had with her.

"Tell me more." I didn't really care what she said, I just wanted to listen to her voice.

She looked at me quickly, seeming startled by the change in my tone. "What more do you want to know?"

"Tell me why you hunt animals instead of people," I said. It was the first question I could think of. My voice sounded thick. I double-blinked the extra moisture from my eyes.

Her answer was very low. "I don't *want* to be a monster."

"But animals aren't enough?"

She paused. "I can't be sure, but I'd compare it to living on tofu and soy milk; we call ourselves vegetarians, our little inside joke. It doesn't completely satiate the hunger—or rather thirst. But it keeps us strong enough to resist. Most of the time." Her tone darkened. "Sometimes it's more difficult than others."

"Is it very difficult for you now?" I asked.

She sighed. "Yes."

"But you're not hungry now," I said—stating, not asking.

"Why do you think that?"

"Your eyes. I have a theory about that. Seems like the color is linked to your mood—and people are generally crabbier when they're hungry, right?"

She laughed. "You're more observant than I gave you credit for."

I listened to the sound of her laugh, committing it to memory.

"So everything I thought I saw—that day with the van. That all happened for real. You *caught* the van."

She shrugged. "Yes."

"How strong are you?"

She glanced at me from the side of her eye. "Strong enough."

"Like, could you lift five thousand pounds?"

She looked a little thrown by my enthusiasm. "If I needed to. But I'm not much into feats of strength. They just make Eleanor competitive, and I'll never be *that* strong."

"How strong?"

"Honestly, if she wanted to, I think she could lift a mountain over her head. But I would never say that around her, because then she would have to try." She laughed, and it was a relaxed sound. Affectionate.

"Were you hunting this weekend, with, uh, Eleanor?" I asked when it was quiet again.

"Yes." She paused for a second, as if deciding whether or not to say something. "I didn't want to leave, but it was necessary. It's a bit easier to be around you when I'm not thirsty."

"Why didn't you want to leave?"

"It makes me . . . anxious . . . to be away from you." Her eyes were gentle, but intense, and they made it hard to breathe in and out like normal. "I wasn't joking when I asked you to try not to fall in the ocean or get run over last Thursday. I was distracted all weekend, worrying about you. And after what happened tonight, I'm surprised that you did make it through a whole weekend unscathed." She shook her head, and then seemed to remember something. "Well, not totally unscathed."

"What?"

"Your hands," she reminded me. I looked down at my palms, at the almost-healed scrapes across the heels of my hands. She didn't miss anything.

"I fell."

"That's what I thought." Her lips curved up at the corners. "I suppose, being you, it could have been much worse—and that was the possibility that tormented me the entire time I was away. It was a very long three days. I really got on Eleanor's nerves."

"Three days? Didn't you just get back today?"

"No, we got back Sunday."

"Then why weren't you at school?" I was frustrated, almost angry as I thought of how much her absence had affected me.

"Well, you asked if the sun hurt me, and it doesn't. But I can't go out in the sunlight—at least, not where anyone can see."

"Why?"

"I'll show you sometime," she promised.

I thought about it for a moment. "You could have told me."

She was puzzled. "But I knew you were fine."

"Yeah, but I didn't know where you were. I—" I hesitated, dropping my eyes.

"What?" Her silky voice was as hypnotic as her eyes.

"It's going to sound stupid . . . but, well, it kind of freaked me out. I

thought you might not come back. That somehow you knew that I knew and . . . I was afraid you would disappear. I didn't know what I was going to do. I *had* to see you again." My cheeks started heating up.

She was quiet. I glanced up—she looked pained, like something was hurting her.

"Edythe, are you okay?"

"Ah," she groaned quietly. "This is wrong."

I couldn't understand her response. "What did I say?"

"Don't you see, Beau? It's one thing for me to make myself miserable, but a wholly other thing for you to be so involved." She turned her anguished eyes to the road, her words flowing almost too fast for me to understand. "I don't want to hear that you feel that way. It's wrong. It's not safe. I'll hurt you, Beau. You'll be lucky to get out alive."

"I don't care."

"That's a really stupid thing to say."

"Maybe, but it's true. I told you, it doesn't matter to me what you are. It's too late."

Her voice whipped out, low and sharp. "Never say that. It's *not* too late. I can put things back the way they were. I *will*."

I stared straight ahead, glad again for the scarf. My neck was a mass of crimson splotches, I was sure.

"I don't want things back the way they were," I mumbled. I wondered if I was supposed to move my hand. I held it still. Maybe she would forget it was there.

"I'm sorry I've done this to you." Her voice burned with real regret.

The darkness slipped by us in silence. I realized the car was slowing, and even in the dark I recognized the landmarks. We were passing into the boundaries of Forks. It had taken less than twenty minutes.

"Will I see you tomorrow?"

"Do you want to?" she whispered.

"More than anything else I've ever wanted." It was pathetic how obviously true the words were. So much for playing hard to get.

She closed her eyes. The car didn't deviate so much as half an inch from the center of the lane.

"Then I'll be there," she finally said. "I do have a paper to turn in."

She looked at me then, and her face was calmer, but her eyes were troubled.

We were suddenly in front of Charlie's house. The lights were on, my truck in its place, everything totally normal. It was like waking up from a dream—the kind you didn't want to lose, the kind you kept your eyes closed tight for, rolled over and covered your head with a pillow for, trying to find a way back in. She shut off the engine, but I didn't move.

"Save me a seat at lunch?" I asked hesitantly.

I was rewarded with a wide smile. "That's easy enough."

"You promise?" I couldn't keep the tone light enough.

"I promise."

I stared into her eyes and it was like she was a magnet again, like she was pulling me toward her and I had no power to resist. I didn't want to try. The word *vampire* was still there between us, but it was easier to ignore than I would have thought possible. Her face was so unbearably perfect, it hurt in a strange way to look at it. At the same time, I never wanted to look away. I wanted to know if her lips were as silky smooth as the skin of her hand—

Suddenly her left hand was there, palm forward, an inch from my face, warning me back, and she was cringing against the car door, her eyes wide and frightened and her teeth clenched together.

I jerked away from her.

"Sorry!"

She stared at me for a long moment, and I would swear she wasn't breathing. After a long moment, she relaxed a little.

"You have to be more careful than that, Beau," she said finally in a dull voice.

Cautiously—like I was made of glass or something—her left hand lifted mine off her right and then let it go. I crossed my arms over my chest.

"Maybe—" she began.

"I can do better than that," I interrupted quickly. "Just tell me the rules, and I'll follow them. Whatever you want from me."

She sighed.

"Seriously. Tell me to do something, and I'll do it."

I regretted the words the second they were out of my mouth. What if she

asked me to forget about her? There were some things that weren't in my power to do.

But she smiled. "All right, I've got one."

"Yeah?" I asked, wary.

"Don't go in the woods alone again."

I could feel the surprise on my face. "How did you know that?"

She touched the tip of her nose.

"Really? You must have an *incredible* sense—"

"Are you going to agree to what I ask or not?" she interrupted.

"Sure, that one's easy. Can I ask why?"

She frowned, her eyes tight again as she stared out the window past me. "I'm not always the most dangerous thing out there. Let's leave it at that."

The sudden bleakness in her voice made me shiver, but I was relieved, too. She could have asked for something much harder. "Whatever you say."

She sighed. "I'll see you tomorrow, Beau."

I knew she wanted me to leave now. I opened the door unwillingly.

"Tomorrow," I emphasized. I started to climb out.

"Beau?"

I turned and ducked back awkwardly, and she was leaning toward me, her pale goddess face just inches from mine. My heart stopped beating.

"Sleep well," she said. Her breath blew into my face—it was the same compelling scent that haunted her car, but in a more concentrated form. I blinked, totally stunned. She leaned away.

It took me a few seconds till my brain unscrambled and I was able to move again. I backed out of the car, having to use the frame for balance. I thought she might have laughed, but the sound was too quiet for me to be sure.

She waited till I'd stumbled to the front door, and then her engine quietly revved. I turned to watch the silver car disappear around the corner. It was suddenly really cold.

I reached for the key automatically and unlocked the front door.

"Beau?" my dad called from the living room.

"Yeah, Dad, it's me." I locked the door and then went to find him. He was on his favorite couch, a baseball game on the TV.

"Movie over so early?"

"Is it early?" It seemed like I'd been with her for days . . . or maybe it was just a few seconds. Not long enough.

"It's not even eight yet," he told me. "Was the show any good?"

"Er, not very memorable, actually."

"What is that around your neck?"

I grabbed the scarf I'd forgotten and tried to yank it off, but it was wrapped too many times around my neck, and I just choked myself.

"Uh—I forgot a coat—and someone lent me a scarf."

"It looks goofy."

"Yeah, I figured. But it's warm."

"Are you okay? You look kind of pale."

"Aren't I always kind of pale?"

"Guess so."

Actually, my head was starting to spin a little, and I was still cold, though I knew the room was warm.

Wouldn't it be just like me if I did end up going into shock? *Get a grip.*

"I, uh, didn't sleep great last night," I said to Charlie. "Think I'm gonna hit the sack early."

"'Night, kid."

I walked up the stairs slowly, a sort of stupor starting to cloud my mind. I had no reason to be so exhausted—or so cold. I brushed my teeth and splashed some hot water on my face; it made me shiver. I didn't bother changing, just kicked off my shoes, then climbed into the bed fully dressed—the second time in a week. I wrapped my quilt tightly around me and fought through a couple of small shudders.

My mind swirled like I was dizzy. It was full of impressions and images, some I wished I could see more clearly, and some I didn't want to remember at all. The road whipping by too fast, the dim yellow light at the restaurant glinting in her metallic hair, the shape of her lips when she smiled . . . when she frowned . . . Jeremy's eyes bugging half out of his head, the headlights screaming toward me, the gun pointed at my face while cold sweat beaded on my forehead. My bed shook under me as I shivered again.

No, there were too many things I wanted to remember, wanted to cement into my head, to waste time with the unpleasant stuff. I pulled the scarf I was still wearing up over my nose and inhaled her scent. Almost immediately,

my body relaxed, the tremors stilling. I pictured her face in my head—every angle, every expression, every mood.

There were a few things I knew for sure. For one, Edythe was an actual vampire. For another, there was a part of her that saw me as food. But in the end, none of that mattered. All that mattered was that I loved her, more than I'd ever imagined it was possible to love anything. She was everything I wanted, the only thing I would ever want.

10. INTERROGATIONS

IT WAS DIFFERENT IN THE MORNING.

All the things that had seemed possible last night in the dark sounded like bad jokes when the sun was up, even inside my own head.

Did that really happen? Did I remember the words right? Had she really said those things to me? Had I really been brave enough to say the things I thought I'd said?

Her scarf—her brother's stolen scarf—was folded on top of my backpack, and I had to keep walking over to touch it. That part was real, at least.

It was foggy and dark outside my window, absolutely perfect. She had no reason to miss school today. I dressed in layers, remembering I didn't have my jacket and hoping I wouldn't get soaked all the way through before I could find it again.

When I got downstairs, Charlie was gone—I was running later than I'd realized. I swallowed a granola bar in three bites, chased it down with milk straight from the carton, and then hurried out the door. Hopefully the rain would hold off until I saw Jeremy. Hopefully my jacket was still in his car.

It was really foggy; the air looked like it was filled with smoke. The mist was ice cold where it touched my face, and I couldn't wait to get the heat going in my truck. It was such a thick fog that I was a few feet down the driveway before I realized there was another car in it: a familiar silver car. My heart did the weird double-thump thing, and I hoped I wasn't developing some kind of aortic issue.

The passenger window was down, and she was leaning toward me, trying not to laugh at my *I might be having a heart attack* face.

"Would you like a ride to school?" she asked.

Though she was smiling, there was uncertainty in her voice. She didn't mean this to be a no-brainer for me, she wanted me to really think about what I was doing. Maybe she even wanted me to say no. But that wasn't going to happen.

"Yeah, thanks," I said, trying to sound casual. As I ducked into the warm car, I noticed a light tan jacket slung over the headrest of the passenger seat.

"What's this?"

"Royal's jacket. I didn't want you to catch a cold or something."

I set the jacket carefully on the backseat. She didn't seem to mind borrowing her brothers' stuff, but who knew how *they* felt about it? One of the confused images I remembered from the car accident, however many weeks ago it was now, was the faces of her siblings, watching from a distance. The word that had best summed up Royal's face was *fury*.

I might have a hard time being afraid of Edythe, but I didn't think I'd have the same problem with Royal.

I pulled the scarf from my bag and laid it on top of the jacket.

"I'm good," I told her, and thumped my fist against my chest twice. "Immune system in top form."

She laughed, but I wasn't sure if it was because she thought I was funny, or ridiculous. Oh well. Just as long as I got to hear her laugh.

She drove through the foggy streets, always too fast, barely looking at the road. She wasn't wearing a jacket, either, just a pale lavender sweater with the sleeves pushed up. The sweater hugged her body, and I tried not to stare. Her hair was wound up into a twist on the back of her head—messy, with strands falling out everywhere—and the way it exposed the slender column of her neck was also distracting. I wanted to brush my fingertips down the length of her throat. . . .

But I had to be more careful, like she'd warned me last night. I wasn't entirely sure what she meant, but I would do my best, because it was something she obviously needed from me. I wouldn't do anything that would scare her away.

"What, no Twenty Questions today?" she asked me.

"Was that annoying last night?"

"Not annoying, just . . . confusing."

I was surprised she felt that way. It seemed like I was the one in the dark. "What does that mean?"

"Your reactions—I don't understand them."

"My reactions?"

She glanced at me, raising an eyebrow. "Yes, Beau. When someone tells you they drink blood, you're supposed to get upset. Make a cross with your fingers, throw holy water, run away screaming, that sort of thing."

"Oh. Um . . . I'll do better next time?"

"By all means, please work on your expressions of horror."

"Horror isn't exactly how I'd describe last night."

She exhaled through her nose, irritated. I didn't know what to say. Nothing could make me see her as something to run away from.

"So, um, where's the rest of your family?"

I didn't actually want to think about her family. I didn't want to deal with the idea of *more* vampires—vampires who weren't Edythe. Vampires who might inspire real horror.

But the fact was that usually her car was full, and today it wasn't. Of course, I was grateful. It was hard to imagine something that would keep me out of a car when Edythe invited me in, but a bunch of furious vampires in the backseat might complicate things.

She was just pulling into the school parking lot. Already.

"They took Royal's car." She gestured to a glossy red convertible with the top up as she swerved into the spot next to it. "Ostentatious, isn't it?"

"If he's got *that*, why does he ride with you?"

"Like I said, it's ostentatious. We *try* to blend in."

I laughed as I opened the car door. "No offense, but you're totally failing there."

She rolled her eyes.

I wasn't late anymore. Her lunatic driving had gotten us to school with time to spare. "Why did Royal drive today if it's more conspicuous?"

"My fault—as usual, Royal would say. Haven't you noticed, Beau? I'm breaking *all* the rules now."

She met me at the front of the car, staying very close to my side as we walked onto campus. I wanted to close that little distance, to reach out and

touch her hand again, to put my arm around her shoulders, but I was afraid that wouldn't be *careful* enough for her.

"Why do you even have cars like that?" I wondered aloud. "If you're looking for privacy, there are plenty of used Hondas available."

"It's an indulgence," she admitted with a little half-smile. "We all like to drive fast."

"Of course," I muttered.

Under the shelter of the cafeteria roof's overhang, Jeremy was waiting with his eyes popping out again. Over his arm was my jacket.

"Hey, Jer," I called when we were a few feet away. "Thanks for bringing that."

He handed me the jacket without speaking.

"Good morning, Jeremy," Edythe said politely. I could tell she wasn't *trying* to overwhelm him, but even her smallest smile was hard to take in stride.

"Er . . . hi." Jeremy shifted his wide eyes to me, trying to reorder his scrambled brains. "Guess I'll see you in Trig."

"Yeah, see you then."

He walked away, pausing to glance back at us twice.

"What are you going to tell him?" she murmured.

"Huh?" I looked at her, then at Jeremy's back. "Oh. What's he thinking?"

Her mouth pulled to one side. "I don't know if it's entirely ethical for me to tell you that. . . ."

"What's not *ethical* is for you to hoard your unfair advantages for yourself."

She grinned a mischievous smile. "He wants to know if we're secretly dating. And exactly which base you've gotten to with me."

The blood rushed to my face so fast I was sure it was beet red before a full second had passed.

She looked away, her face suddenly as uncomfortable as mine felt. She took a small step away from me and gritted her teeth.

It took me a minute to realize that the flush that embarrassed me so much was probably something else entirely to her.

That helped cool me down.

"Um, what should I say?"

She started walking, and I followed, not paying attention to where she was leading.

After a second, she looked up at me, her face relaxed and smiling again. "That's a good question. I can't *wait* to hear what you come up with."

"*Edythe . . .*"

She grinned, and then her little hand shot up and brushed a piece of hair off my forehead. Just as quickly her hand was back at her side. My heart spluttered like it was in actual distress.

"See you at lunch," she said, brandishing the dimples.

I stood there like I'd been Tasered while she pivoted and walked off in the other direction.

After a second, I recovered enough to see that I was standing right outside the English classroom. Three people had paused by the doorway, staring at me with varying shades of surprise and awe. I ducked my head and brushed past them into the room.

Was Jeremy really going to ask me that? Would Edythe really be eavesdropping on my reaction?

"Morning, Beau."

McKayla was already in her normal seat. Her greeting wasn't as enthusiastic as I was used to. She was smiling, but it felt like a polite thing, not like she was really happy to see me.

"Hey, McKayla. Uh, how're things?"

"Good. How was the movie last night?"

"Oh, right, yeah. I didn't actually see it. I got lost and . . ."

"Yeah, I heard," she said.

I blinked, startled. "How?"

"I saw Jeremy before school."

"Oh."

"He said you didn't miss much. The movie was lame."

"That's good, I guess."

She was suddenly really interested in her fingernails. She started chipping the purple paint off one. "Did you have, like, plans before you went? I mean, Jeremy thought you might have, and I wondered—why even go through the charade, you know?"

"No, no, I was totally planning on the movie. I didn't expect that . . . I would get lost and . . . stuff."

McKayla sniffed once like she didn't believe me, and then looked up at the

clock. Ms. Mason was working on something at her desk and didn't seem in a hurry to start class.

"That was really cool that you went out with Jeremy on Monday," I said, changing the subject. "He said it was great." Or I was sure he would have, if I'd asked about it.

She looked at her nails again, but her ears started to turn a little pink. "He did?" she asked in a completely different tone.

"Yeah." I dropped my voice to a whisper. "Remember, I didn't tell you anything. Like, I totally didn't tell you that he thinks you're the coolest girl he's ever known."

Her ears were even pinker now. "Man code. Right."

"I said nothing."

She finally smiled a real smile.

Ms. Mason got up then and asked us to open our books.

I thought maybe I was off the hook with McKayla, but when class was over, I saw her and Erica exchange a look, and then McKayla was picking at her nails again while we walked outside.

"So," she said.

"Yeah?"

"I was just curious if, you know, we were going to see you at the dance after all? Like, you could totally hang with our group, if you wanted to."

"The dance?" I looked at her blankly. "No. No, I'm still going to Seattle."

She seemed surprised, but then she relaxed. "Okay. Oh well. Maybe we can get a group thing together for prom. Share a limo."

I stopped walking.

"Uh, I wasn't really planning on prom. . . ."

"Really? Shocking!" McKayla laughed. "You might want to mention it to Taylor, though. She says you're taking her."

I felt my jaw fall open. McKayla cracked up.

"That's what I thought," she said.

"Are you serious?" I demanded when I had control of my face again. "I mean, she was probably joking."

"Logan and Jeremy were talking about getting started early and putting together a big thing for prom, and then Taylor said she was out because she already had plans—with you. That's why Logan's being so . . . you know . . . about you.

He has a thing for Taylor. I figure you deserved a heads-up. After all, you broke the man code for me."

"What am I supposed to do?"

"Tell her you're not taking her."

"I can't just . . . What would I even say?"

She smiled like she was enjoying this. "Man up, Beau. Or rent a tux. Your choice."

So I didn't get much out of Government after that. Was it really my responsibility to uninvite Taylor to the prom? I tried to remember what I'd said to her in the parking lot when she'd asked me to the girls' choice. I was almost positive I had not agreed to anything.

The sky was like lead as I walked to Trig, dark gray and kind of heavy-looking. Last week, I would have found it depressing. Today I smiled. There was something better than sunshine.

When I saw Jeremy sitting by an empty desk in the back row, watching the door, waiting for me, I remembered that Taylor wasn't the only problem I had right now. My neck started feeling warm, and I wished I'd kept the scarf.

There was another open chair two rows forward . . . but it was probably better to get this over with and be done with it.

Ms. Varner wasn't in the room yet. What was with all the tardy teachers today? It was like nobody even cared if we were educated.

I sat next to Jeremy. He didn't keep me waiting.

"*Dang*, son," he said. "Who knew you had that kind of game?"

I rolled my eyes. "I have no game."

"Please." He punched my arm. "*Edythe Cullen.* C'mon. How did you swing *that*?"

"I didn't do anything."

"How long has this been happening? Is it some kind of secret? Like, she doesn't want her family to know? Is that why you pretended you were going to the movie with us?"

"I wasn't pretending anything. I had no idea she was in Port Angeles last night. She was the *last* person I expected to see."

He seemed deflated by my obvious honesty.

"Have you ever been out with her before last night?"

"Never."

"Huh. Just a total coincidence?"

"I guess."

It was obvious when I was telling the truth—and obvious when I was evading it. The suspicious, knowing look came back to his face.

"Because, you know, it's not a secret that you've been, like, obsessed with her since you got here."

I winced. "It's not?"

"So, I have to wonder how you turned that around. Do you have a genie in a lamp? Did you find some blackmail on her? Or did you trade your soul to the devil or something?"

"Whatever, man."

"Exactly how much did you get in the bargain? Bet it was a pretty wild night, eh?"

I was starting to get pissed, but I knew he would twist whatever reaction I showed to make it seem like something else.

I answered calmly, "It was an early night. Home by eight."

"Are you serious?"

"It was just dinner and a ride home, Jeremy."

"What about this morning, though? You were still with her."

"*Still?* No! What—you thought she was with me all night?"

"She wasn't?"

"No."

"But you were in her car—"

"She picked me up for school this morning."

"Why?"

"I have no idea. She offered me a ride. I wasn't going to say no."

"And that's it?"

I shrugged.

"Really? Please tell me you at least made out with her—anything."

I scowled at him. "It's not like that."

He made a disgusted face. "That is, hands down, the most disappointing story I've ever heard in my entire life. I take back everything I said about your game. Obviously, it's just some pity thing."

"Yeah, probably."

"Maybe I should try to look more pathetic. If that's what Edythe is into."

"Go for it."

"It won't take her long to get bored with you, I bet."

My façade slipped for a second. He caught the change and grinned, a little smug.

"Yeah," I said. "I'm sure you're right."

Ms. Varner showed up then, and the general chatter started to die down while she began writing equations across the board.

"You know what, though?" Jeremy said under his breath. "I think I'd rather be with a normal girl."

I was already irritated. I didn't like the way he talked about Edythe in general, and the way he said *normal* really bugged me. No, Edythe wasn't normal, but that wasn't because, like his tone seemed to imply, she was something . . . off or wrong. She was beyond normal, above it. Surpassing it by so much that normal and Edythe weren't even on the same plane of existence.

"That's probably for the best," I muttered in a hard voice. "Keep your expectations low."

He shot me a startled look, but I turned to face the teacher. I could feel him staring at me suspiciously again, until Ms. Varner noticed and called on him for an answer. He started flipping spastically through his book, trying to figure out what she'd asked him.

Jeremy walked ahead of me on the way to Spanish, but I didn't care. I was still annoyed. He didn't talk to me again until the end of class when I started shoving my books—a little too enthusiastically—into my backpack.

"You're not sitting with us at lunch today, are you?"

His face was suspicious again, and more guarded now. Obviously, he'd thought I'd be eager to show off, to sell Edythe out to make myself look cooler. After all, Jeremy and I had been friends for a little while. Guys told each other this kind of stuff. It was probably part of the man code thing I'd invented. He'd assumed my loyalty would be with him . . . but now he knew he was wrong.

"Um, not sure," I said. No point in being overconfident. I remembered too clearly what it felt like whenever she disappeared. I didn't want to jinx myself.

He walked off without waiting for me, but then he did a little stutter step and paused on the threshold of the classroom.

"Seriously, *what the hell*," Jeremy said loud enough that I could hear him— as did everyone else within a ten-foot radius.

He glanced back at me, shook his head, then stalked away.

I was in a hurry to get out the door—to see what *that* was about—but so was everyone else. One by one, they all stopped to look back at me before exiting. By the time I got out, I didn't know what to expect. Irrationally, I was half-expecting to see Taylor in a sparkly prom dress and tiara.

But outside the door to my Spanish class, leaning against the wall—looking a thousand times more beautiful than anyone had a right to—Edythe was waiting for me. Her wide gold eyes looked amused, and the corners of her lips were right on the point of smiling. Her hair was still coiled up in that messy twist, and I had the oddest urge to reach down and pull the pins out of it.

"Hello, Beau."

"Hi."

Part of me was aware we had an audience, but I was past caring.

"Hungry?" she asked.

"Sure." Actually, I had no idea if I was. My whole body felt like it was being electrocuted in a strange and very pleasant way. My nerves couldn't process more than that.

She turned toward the cafeteria, swinging her bag into place.

"Hey, let me get that for you," I offered.

She looked up at me with doe eyes. "Does it look too heavy for me?"

"Well, I mean . . ."

"Sure," she said. She slid the bag down her arm and then held it out to me, very deliberately using just the tip of her pinkie finger.

"Er, thanks," I said, and she let the strap fall into my hand.

I guess I should have known it would be twice as heavy as my own. I caught it before it could hit the sidewalk, then hefted it over my free shoulder.

"Do you always bring your own cinder blocks to school?"

She laughed. "Archie asked me to grab a few things for him this morning."

"Is Archie your favorite brother?"

She looked at me. "It's not nice to have favorites."

"Only child," I said. "I'm everyone's favorite."

"It shows. Anyway, why do you think that?"

"Seems like you talk about him most easily."

She thought about that for a moment but didn't comment.

Once we were in the cafeteria, I followed her to the food line. I couldn't

help staring at the back corner of the cafeteria the way I did every day. Her family was all present and accounted for, paying attention only to each other. They either didn't notice Edythe with me, or they didn't care. I thought about the idea Jeremy had come up with—that Edythe and I were seeing each other in secret to keep it from her family's notice. It didn't look like she was hiding anything from them, but I couldn't help but wonder what they thought about me.

I wondered what I thought about them.

Just then Archie looked up and smiled across the room at me. Automatically, I smiled back, then glanced down to see if he'd actually meant the smile for Edythe. She was aware of him, but she wasn't responding in kind. She looked sort of angry. My eyes cut back and forth between the two of them as they had some kind of silent conversation. First, Archie smiled wider, showing off teeth so white they were bright even across the length of the room. Edythe raised her eyebrows in a sort of challenge, her upper lip curling back just a tiny bit. He rolled his eyes to the ceiling and held his hands up like he was saying *I surrender.* Edythe turned her back to him and moved forward in the line. She grabbed a tray and started loading it up.

"I'm pretty close with all my family, but Archie and I do have the most in common," she said, finally answering my question in a low voice. I had to duck my head down to hear her. "Some days he's really annoying, though."

I glanced back at him; he was laughing now. Though he wasn't looking at us, I thought he might be laughing at her.

I was paying so much attention to this little exchange that I didn't notice what she had on the tray till the lunch lady was ringing us up.

"That'll be twenty-four thirty-three," she said.

"What?" I looked down at the tray and then did a double take.

Edythe was already paying, and then gliding off toward the table where we'd sat together last week.

"Hey," I hissed, jogging a few steps to catch up with her. "I can't eat all that."

"Half is for me, of course."

She sat down and pushed the overflowing tray to the center of the table.

I raised my eyebrows. "Really."

"Take whatever you want."

I sank into the seat across from her, letting the dead weight of her bag

slide to the floor with mine. At the other end of the long table, a group of seniors watched her with wide eyes.

"I'm curious. What would you do if someone dared you to eat food?"

"You're always curious." She made a face, then daintily tore the tip off a piece of pizza, popped it in her mouth, and started chewing with a martyred expression. After a second, she swallowed, then gave me a superior look.

"If someone dared you to eat dirt, you could, couldn't you?" she asked.

I grinned at her. "I did once . . . on a dare. It wasn't so bad."

"Somehow, I'm not surprised. Here." She shoved the rest of the pizza to me.

I took a bite. I wondered if it really tasted like dirt to her. It wasn't the best pizza I'd ever had, but it was decent. While I was chewing, she glanced over my shoulder and laughed.

I swallowed quickly. "What?"

"You've got Jeremy *so* confused."

"Tough."

"He really let his mind run wild when he saw you get out of my car."

I shrugged and took another bite.

She tilted her head to the side. "Do you truly agree with him?"

I had to swallow fast again, and I almost choked. She half-rose, but I held my hand up and recovered. "I'm fine. Agree with him about what?"

"Why I'm here with you."

It took me a minute to think through the conversation. I remembered things I hoped she hadn't been paying attention to—like the fact that apparently everyone knew I'd been obsessed with her from day one.

"I'm not sure what you mean."

She frowned. "*Obviously, it's just some pity thing?*" she quoted.

I was surprised that she looked irritated. "It's as good an explanation as any."

"And I'll be getting bored soon, will I?"

That one stung a little—this was my biggest fear, and it seemed all too likely—but I tried to hide it with another shrug.

"Beau, you're being ridiculous again."

"Am I?"

She smiled a funny half-smile, half-frown. "There are several things I am currently worried about. Boredom is not one of them." She cocked her head to the side, her eyes drilling into mine. "Don't you believe me?"

"Um, sure, I guess. If you say so."

Her eyes narrowed. "Well, that was an overwhelming affirmative."

I took another bite of pizza, chewing slowly and deliberately this time. She waited, watching me with the intense little scowl that I knew meant she was trying to get inside my head. When I took a second bite without speaking, she blew an angry breath out her nose.

"I truly loathe it when you do that."

I took a second to swallow. "What? Not tell you every single stupid thought that passes through my head?"

I could tell she wanted to smile, but she didn't give in. "Precisely."

"I don't know what to say. Do I think you'll get bored with me? Yeah, I do. I honestly don't know why you're still here. But I was trying *not* to say that out loud, because I didn't want to point something out that you might not have thought of yet."

The smile escaped. "So very true. I never would have realized it myself, but now that you mention it, I really ought to be moving along. That Jeremy suddenly seems alluringly pathetic—" And then she cut off and the smile vanished. "Beau? You know that I'm joking."

I wondered what my face was doing. I nodded.

Her forehead creased. After a second, she hesitantly stretched her arm across the table toward me, leaving her hand in easy reach.

I covered it with mine.

She smiled, but then she winced.

"Sorry," I said, pulling away.

"No," she objected. "It's not you. Here."

As carefully as if my hand were blown from the thinnest glass, she rested her fingers on my palm. Copying her caution, I folded my hand gently around them.

"What was wrong just now?" I half-whispered.

"Many different reactions." Her forehead wrinkled again. "Royal has a particularly strident mental voice."

I couldn't help it; I automatically glanced across the room, and then was very sorry I had.

Royal was glaring daggers at Edythe's unprotected back, and Eleanor, across from him, was turned around to glower at Edythe, too. When I looked, Royal shifted his furious eyes to me.

My eyes darted to Edythe, the hair standing up on the back of my arms, but she was glaring back at Royal now, her upper lip pulled back off her teeth in a menacing scowl. To my surprise, Eleanor turned around at once and Royal dropped his threatening stare. He looked down at the table with a suddenly sulky expression.

Archie looked like he was enjoying it all hugely. Jessamine never turned.

"Did I just piss off—" I swallowed before I could finish. *A bunch of vampires?*

"No," she said fiercely, then sighed. "But I did."

I glanced at Royal again for a fraction of a second. He hadn't moved. "Look, are you in trouble because of me? What can I do?" The memory of his livid eyes trained on her small body had a wave of panic rolling through me.

She shook her head and smiled. "You don't need to worry about me," she reassured me, a little smug. "I'm not saying that Royal couldn't take me in a fair fight, but I *am* saying that I never *have* fought fair and I don't intend to start now. He knows better than to try anything with me."

"Edythe . . ."

She laughed. "A joke. It's really nothing, Beau. Normal sibling issues. An only child couldn't understand."

"If you say so."

"I do."

I looked at our hands, still folded so very carefully together. It was the first time I'd really held her hand, but wrapped up in the wonder of that was the memory of why she'd offered it to me in the first place.

"Back to what you were thinking," she said, as if she could read my thoughts.

I sighed.

"Would it help if you knew you weren't the only one who had been accused of obsession?"

I groaned. "You heard that, too. Great."

She laughed. "I was entranced from start to finish."

"Sorry," I said.

"Why are you apologizing? It makes me feel better to know I'm not the only one."

I stared at her, skeptical.

"Let me put it this way." She pursed her lips thoughtfully. "Though you are the one person I can't be *sure* about, I'd still be willing to place a very large wager that I spend more time thinking about you than you do about me."

"Ha," I laughed, startled. "You would totally lose that bet."

She raised an eyebrow and then spoke so low that I had to lean in to hear. "Ah, but you're only conscious for roughly sixteen hours in any given twenty-four-hour period. That gives me quite a lead, don't you think?"

"You're not factoring in dreams, though."

She sighed. "Do nightmares count as dreams?"

Red started creeping up my neck. "When I dream about you . . . it's definitely not a nightmare."

Her mouth opened just a tiny bit in surprise, and her face was suddenly vulnerable. "Really?" she asked.

It was obvious that she was pleased, so I said, "Every single night."

She closed her eyes for just a minute, but when she opened them, her smile was teasing again.

"REM cycles are the shortest of all the sleep stages. I'm still hours ahead."

I frowned. It was difficult to process. "You really think about *me*?"

"Why is that hard for you to believe?"

"Well, look at me," I said, unnecessarily, as she already was. "I'm absolutely ordinary—well, except for bad things like all the near-death experiences and being so uncoordinated that I can barely walk. And look at you." I waved my free hand toward her and all her unsettling perfection.

She smiled a slow smile. It started small but ended with the full array of dimples—like the grand finale at the end of a fireworks show on the Fourth of July.

"I can't argue with you about the bad things."

"Well, there you go."

"But you're the least ordinary person I've ever met."

Our eyes held for a long moment. Mine searched hers, as I tried to believe she could see something important enough to keep her here. It always felt like she was just about to slip away, to disappear like she was only a myth after all.

"But why . . ." I didn't know how to phrase it.

She tilted her head, waiting.

"Last night . . ." I stopped and shook my head.

She frowned. "Do you do that on purpose? The unfinished thought as a way to drive me mad?"

"I don't know if I can explain it right."

"Please try."

I took a deep breath. "Okay. You're claiming I don't bore you and you aren't thinking of moving on to Jeremy anytime soon."

She nodded, fighting a grin.

"But last night . . . it was like . . ." She was anxious now. The rest came out in a rush. "Like you were already looking for a way to say goodbye."

"Perceptive," she whispered. And there was the anguish again, surfacing as she confirmed my worst fear.

Her fingers ever so gently squeezed mine.

"Those two things are unrelated, however."

"Which two things?"

"The depth of my feelings for you, and the necessity of leaving. Well, they *are* related, but inversely."

The necessity of leaving. My stomach plunged. "I don't understand."

She stared into my eyes again, and hers burned, mesmerizing. Her voice was barely audible. "The more I care about you, the more crucial it is that I find a way to . . . keep you safe. From me. Leaving would be the right thing to do."

I shook my head. *"No."*

She took a deep breath, and her eyes seemed to darken in an odd way. "Well, I wasn't very good at leaving you alone when I tried. I don't know *how* to do it."

"Will you do me a favor? Stop trying to figure that one out."

She half-smiled. "I suppose, given the frequency of your near-death experiences, it's actually safer for me to stay close."

"True story. You never know when another rogue van might attack."

She frowned.

"You're still going to Seattle with me, right? Lots of vans in Seattle. Waiting in ambush around literally every corner."

"Actually, I have a question for you on that subject. Did you really need to go to Seattle this Saturday, or was that just an excuse to get out of saying a definitive no to your bevy of admirers?"

"Um."

"That's what I thought."

"You know, you actually put me in kind of a difficult position with the whole thing in the parking lot with Taylor."

"You mean because you're taking her to prom now?"

My mouth fell open, and then I ground my teeth together.

She was trying not to laugh now. "Oh, Beau."

I could tell there was more. "What?"

"She already has her dress."

I had no words for that.

She must have read the panic in my eyes. "It could be worse—she actually bought it before she claimed you for the date. It was secondhand, also, not a large investment. She couldn't pass up the deal."

I still couldn't talk. She squeezed my hand again. "You'll figure it out."

"I don't do dances," I said sadly.

"If *I'd* asked you to the spring dance, would you have told me no?"

I looked at her long gold eyes and tried to imagine refusing her anything she wanted. "Probably not, but I would have found a reason to cancel later. I would have broken my leg if I had to."

She looked mystified. "Why would you do that?"

I shook my head sadly. "You've never seen me in Gym, I guess, but I would have thought you would understand."

"Are you referring to the fact that you can't walk across a flat, stable surface without finding something to trip over?"

"Got it in one."

"I'm a very good teacher, Beau."

"I don't think coordination is a learnable skill."

She shook her head. "Back to the question. Must you go to Seattle, or would you mind if we did something different?"

As long as the *we* part was in, I didn't care about anything else.

"I'm open to alternatives," I allowed. "But I do have another favor to ask."

She looked wary, like she always did when I asked an open-ended question. "What?"

"Can I drive?"

She frowned. "Why?"

"Well, mostly because you're a terrifying driver. But also because I told Charlie I was going alone, and I don't want him to get curious."

She rolled her eyes. "Of all the things about me that could frighten you, you worry about my driving." She shook her head in disgust, but then her eyes were serious again. "Won't you want to tell your father that you're spending the day with me?" There was an undercurrent to her question that I didn't understand.

"With Charlie, less is always more." I was definite about that. "Where are we going, anyway?"

"Archie says the weather will be nice, so I'll be staying out of the public eye . . . and you can stay with me, if you'd like to." Again, she was leaving the choice up to me.

"And you'll show me what you meant, about the sun?" I asked, excited by the idea of solving another of the unknowns.

"Yes." She smiled, then hesitated. "But if you don't want to be . . . alone with me, I'd still rather you didn't go to Seattle by yourself. I shudder to think of all the *vans*."

"As it happens, I don't mind being alone with you."

"I know," she sighed. "You should tell Charlie, though."

I shook my head at the thought of explaining my personal life to Charlie. "Why on earth would I do that?"

Her eyes were suddenly fierce. "To give me some small incentive to bring you back."

I waited for her to relax. When she didn't, I said, "I'll take my chances."

She exhaled angrily, and looked away.

"So that's settled. New topic?"

My attempt to change the subject didn't help much.

"What do you want to talk about?" she asked through her teeth, still annoyed.

I glanced around us, making sure we were well out of anyone's hearing. In the back corner, Archie was leaning forward, talking to Jessamine. Eleanor sat beside her, but Royal was gone.

"Why did you go to that Goat Rocks place last weekend . . . to hunt? Charlie said it wasn't a good place to hike, because of bears."

She stared at me as if I was missing something very obvious.

"Bears?" I gasped.

She smirked.

"You know, bears are not in season," I added sternly, to cover my shock.

"If you read carefully, the laws only cover hunting with weapons," she informed me.

She watched my face with enjoyment as that slowly sank in.

"Bears?" I repeated with difficulty.

"Grizzly is Eleanor's favorite." Her voice was still offhand, but her eyes were scrutinizing my reaction. I tried to pull myself together.

"Hmmm," I said, taking another bite of pizza as an excuse to look down. I chewed slowly, then swallowed.

"So," I said after a moment. "What's your favorite?"

She raised an eyebrow and the corners of her mouth turned down like she didn't approve of my question. "Mountain lion."

"Sure, that makes sense." I nodded, like she'd just said something totally normal.

"Of course"—her tone mirrored mine, nothing out of the ordinary—"we have to be careful not to impact the environment with injudicious hunting. We try to focus on areas with an overpopulation of predators—ranging as far away as we need. There are always plenty of deer and elk here, and they'll do, but where's the fun in that?"

She smiled.

"So not fun," I murmured around another bite of pizza.

"Early spring is El's favorite bear season—they're just coming out of hibernation, so they're more irritable." She smiled at some remembered joke.

"Nothing better than an irritated grizzly bear," I agreed, nodding.

She laughed, then shook her head. "Tell me what you're really thinking, please."

"I'm trying to picture it—but I can't," I admitted. "How do you hunt a bear without weapons?"

"Oh, we have weapons." She flashed her bright teeth with a wide grin that wasn't really a *smile*. "Just not the kind they consider when writing hunting laws. If you've ever seen a bear attack on television, you should be able to visualize Eleanor hunting."

I glanced across the cafeteria toward Eleanor, grateful that she wasn't look-ing my way. The long, smooth lines of muscle that ran down her arms and legs were suddenly much more than intimidating. I pictured her gripping under the edge of a mountain, then lifting . . .

Edythe followed my gaze and chuckled. I stared back at her, unnerved.

"Is it dangerous?" I asked in a low voice. "Do you ever get hurt?"

Her laughter pealed like a bell. "Oh, Beau. About as dangerous as your slice."

I looked at the pizza crust and said, "Yikes. So . . . are you . . . like a bear attack?"

"More like the lion, or so they tell me," she said lightly. "Perhaps our pref-erences are indicative."

"Perhaps," I repeated. I tried to smile, but my mind was struggling to fit the paradoxical images together, and failing. "Is that something I might get to see?"

"Never!" she whispered. Her face turned even whiter than usual, and her eyes were suddenly horrified. She pulled her hand gently from mine and wrapped her arms tightly around her body.

My hand lay there empty on the table, numb from the cold.

"What did I say?" I asked.

She closed her eyes for a moment, regaining control. When she met my stare at last, she looked angry. "I almost wish it were possible. You don't seem to understand the realities present. It might be beneficial for you to see exactly how dangerous I actually am."

"Okay, then, why not?" I pressed, trying to ignore her hard expression.

She glared at me for a long minute.

"Later," she finally said. She was on her feet in one lithe movement. "We're going to be late."

I glanced around, startled to see that she was right and the cafeteria was nearly vacant. When I was with her, the time and the place were such minor details that I completely lost track of both. I jumped up, grabbing our bags from the floor.

"Later, then," I agreed. I wouldn't forget.

11. COMPLICATIONS

EVERYONE WATCHED US AS WE WALKED TOGETHER TO OUR LAB TABLE. This time she didn't angle the chair to sit as far from me as the desk would allow. Instead, she sat right next to me, our arms almost touching. Her hair brushed my skin.

Mrs. Banner backed into the room then, pulling an outdated TV and VCR on a wheeled frame. It seemed like everyone in the room relaxed at the same time. I was relieved, too. I knew I wouldn't have been able to pay attention to a lecture today. I had too much to sort through inside my head already.

Mrs. Banner shoved the old tape into the VCR, then walked across the room to turn off the lights. And then suddenly, as the room went black, things got weird.

It wasn't like I wasn't already hyperaware that Edythe was right there, just an inch away from me. I wouldn't have imagined that I could be *more* aware of her. But in the dark, somehow . . . It was like an electrical current was flowing through her body into mine, like those miniature lightning bolts that jump between live circuits were dancing up and down the small gap between our bodies. Where her hair touched my arm, it was almost painful.

A crazy strong impulse to reach over and touch her—to stroke her perfect face just once in the darkness—almost overwhelmed me. What was wrong with me? You couldn't just go around touching people because the lights were off. I crossed my arms tightly over my ribs and balled my hands into fists.

The opening credits started, and the room got a fraction brighter. I couldn't stop myself from peeking over at her.

She was sitting exactly like I was—arms crossed, hands clenched, just glancing over to me. When she saw me looking, too, she smiled, almost like she was embarrassed. Even in the dark, her eyes still burned. I had to look away before I did something stupid—something that would definitely not conform to her idea of *careful*.

It was a very long hour. I couldn't concentrate on the movie. I didn't have any idea what it was about. I tried to act normal, to make my muscles relax, but the electrical current never let up. Now and then, I let myself take a quick glance in her direction, but she never seemed to relax, either. The feeling that I just *had* to touch her face also refused to go away. I kept my fists crushed safely against my ribs until my fingers were aching with the effort.

I sighed with relief when Mrs. Banner flicked the lights back on at the end of class, and stretched my arms down at my sides, flexing my stiff fingers. Edythe laughed once.

"Well, that was . . . interesting," she murmured. Her voice was low and her eyes were cautious.

"Umm," was all I was able to respond.

"Shall we?" she asked, on her feet in one liquid movement. She scooped her bag up with one finger.

I stood carefully, worried I wouldn't be able to walk straight after all that.

She walked with me to Gym in silence, and then paused at the door. I looked down to say goodbye but choked on the word. Her face—it was torn, almost pained, and so unbearably beautiful that the ache to touch her hit me even more intensely than it had before. It was all I could do to just stare.

She raised one hand, hesitant, conflict clear in her eyes, and then quickly brushed her fingertips across the line of my jaw. Her fingers were icy like always, but the trail they left on my skin was almost like a burn that hadn't turned painful yet.

She spun without a word and walked swiftly away from me.

I stumbled into the gym, lightheaded and unstable, and dressed down in a trance, barely aware of the other people around me. Reality didn't fully set in until I was handed a racket.

It wasn't very heavy, but I knew that didn't matter. In my hands, it was

dangerous. I could see a few of the other kids eyeing me and the racket. Then Coach Clapp ordered us to choose our own partners, and I figured I was about to be the last guy up against the wall.

But I'd underestimated McKayla's loyalty. She came to stand next to me right away.

"You don't have to do this, you know," I told her.

She grinned. "Don't worry, I'll keep out of your way."

Sometimes it was really easy to like McKayla.

It didn't go smoothly. I'm not sure how I did it, but I managed to hit myself in the head with my racket and clip McKayla's shoulder on the same swing. I spent the rest of the hour in the back corner of the court, the racket held behind my back. Despite being handicapped by me, McKayla was pretty good; she won three games out of four single-handedly, then gave me an unearned high five when the coach finally blew the whistle ending class.

"So," she started as we walked off the court.

"So?"

"You and Edythe Cullen, huh?" Her tone was just slightly hostile.

"Yeah, me and Edythe Cullen," I replied. I'm sure she could hear the sound of wonder in my voice.

"I don't like it," she muttered.

"Well, you don't actually have to."

"So she just snaps her fingers and you heel?"

"Guess so."

She scowled at me. I turned my back on her and walked away. I knew I would be last against the wall tomorrow, but I didn't care. By the time I was dressed I'd forgotten all about McKayla. Would Edythe be outside, or should I go wait by her car? What if her family was there? She'd parked right next to Royal's car. Just thinking about Royal's face in the cafeteria had me wondering if I should walk home. Had she told them that I knew? Was I supposed to know that they knew that I knew? What was the etiquette on vampire acknowledgments? Did a nod work?

But when I walked out of the gym, Edythe was there. She stood in the shade of the gym building, though the clouds were still black, with her hands laced together in front of her. Her face was peaceful now, a small smile turning

up just the corners of her lips. The thin sweater didn't look like enough, and though I knew it was stupid, I wanted to take my jacket off and wrap it around her. As I walked to her side, I felt a strange sense of harmony—like everything was right in the world as long as I was close to her.

"Hi." I could feel the huge, goofy smile on my face.

"Hello." Her answering smile was brilliant. "How was Gym?"

I was suddenly suspicious. "Fine."

"Really?" Her eyebrows shot up. "How's your head?"

"You didn't."

She started walking slowly toward the parking lot. I automatically fell into step with her.

"You were the one who mentioned how I'd never seen you in Gym—it made me curious."

"Great," I said. "Fantastic. Well, sorry about that. I don't mind walking home if you don't want to be seen with me."

She laughed musically. "It was very entertaining. Though I wouldn't have minded if you'd hit that girl just a little harder."

"What?"

As she glanced behind us, her mouth flattened into a straight line. I turned to see what she was looking at—McKayla's blond hair bobbing as she walked away.

"It's been a while since someone besides family thought those kinds of words about me. I don't think I like it."

I felt a sudden pang of anxiety for McKayla.

Edythe read my expression and laughed again. "Don't worry, I wouldn't hurt your friend. If I did, who else would agree to be your badminton partner?"

It was hard to process. Edythe was just so . . . delicate. But when she said this, it was clear that she was more than confident in her abilities. If she wanted McKayla—or anyone—hurt, it would be very bad news for that person. She was dangerous, I knew this, but I kept running into a wall when I tried to believe it. I changed the subject.

"What kinds of words has your family been thinking about you?"

She shook her head. "It's not fair to judge people on their thoughts. Those are supposed to be private. It's actions that count."

"I don't know. . . . If you know someone can hear, isn't that the same thing as saying it out loud?"

"Easy for you to say." She grinned. "Controlling your thoughts is very difficult. When Royal and I butt heads, I think much worse things about him, and I *do* say those words out loud." She laughed her ringing laugh again.

I hadn't been watching where we were going, so I was surprised when we had to slow, blocked from Edythe's car by a crowd of kids. There was a circle around Royal's red convertible, two deep, mostly guys. Some of them looked about to drool. None of her family was around, and I wondered if she'd asked them to give her some space.

None of the car enthusiasts even looked up when I edged by them to get Edythe's door.

"Ostentatious," she muttered as she slid past me.

I hurried around to the passenger side and climbed in.

"What kind of car is that?"

"An M3," she said as she tried to back out of the space without hitting anybody.

"Um, I don't speak *Car and Driver*."

She carefully maneuvered her way free. "It's a BMW."

"Okay, I know that one."

We pulled away from the school and it was just the two of us. The privacy felt like freedom. There was no one watching or listening here.

"Is it later yet?" I asked her.

She didn't miss the significance in my tone.

She frowned. "I suppose it is."

I kept my expression neutral while I waited for her to explain. She watched the road, pretending like she actually needed to, and I watched her face. A few different expressions flickered across it, but they changed so fast I wasn't able to interpret them. I was starting to wonder if she was just going to ignore my question when she stopped the car. I looked up, surprised. We were already at Charlie's house, parked behind my truck. It was easier to ride with her, I decided, when I didn't look until it was over.

She was staring at me when I looked back, seeming to measure me with her eyes.

"And you want to know why you can't see me hunt?" she asked. Her voice

was serious, but her expression was a little amused. Not at all like it had been in the cafeteria earlier.

"Yes. And why you seemed so . . . mad when I asked."

She raised her eyebrows. "Did I frighten you?" The question sounded hopeful.

"Did you want to?"

She tilted her head to one side. "Maybe I did."

"Okay then, sure, I was terrified."

She smiled, shook her head, and then her face was serious again. "I apologize for reacting like that. It was just the thought of you being near . . . while we hunted." Her jaw tightened.

"That would be bad?"

She answered through her teeth. "Extremely."

"Because . . . ?"

She took a deep breath and stared through the windshield at the thick, rolling clouds that seemed to press down, almost within reach.

"When we hunt"—she spoke slowly, unwillingly—"we give ourselves over to our senses . . . govern less with our minds. Especially our sense of smell. If you were anywhere near me when I lost control that way . . ." She shook her head, still staring unhappily at the heavy clouds.

I kept my expression empty, expecting the swift flash of her eyes to judge my reaction that followed. But our eyes held, and the silence deepened—changed. Flickers of the electricity I'd felt this afternoon began to charge the atmosphere as she gazed without blinking into my eyes. It wasn't until my head started to swim that I realized I wasn't breathing. When I drew in a jagged breath, breaking the silence, she closed her eyes.

"Beau, I think you should go inside now." Her low voice wasn't so smooth—more like raw silk now—and her eyes were on the clouds again.

I opened the door, and the arctic draft that burst into the car helped clear my head. Afraid I was so lightheaded that I might stumble, I stepped carefully out of the car and shut the door behind me without looking back. The whir of the automatic window unrolling made me turn.

"Oh, Beau?" she called after me. She leaned toward the open window with a small smile on her lips.

"Yeah?"

"Tomorrow it's my turn."

"Your turn to what?"

She smiled wider, flashing her gleaming teeth. "Ask the questions."

And then she was gone, the car speeding down the street and disappearing around the corner before I could even put my thoughts in order. I smiled as I walked to the house. It was clear she was planning to see me tomorrow, if nothing else.

That night Edythe starred in my dreams, as usual. However, the climate of my unconsciousness had changed. It thrilled with the same electricity that had charged the afternoon, and I tossed and turned restlessly, waking often. It was only in the early hours of the morning that I finally sank into an exhausted, dreamless sleep.

When my alarm went off, I was still beat, but wired at the same time. After I showered, I stared at myself in the bathroom mirror while I combed through my wet hair. I looked the same as always, and yet there was something different. My hair was dark and too thick, my skin too pale, and my bones were all shaped the same underneath, no change there. My eyes were the same light blue staring back at me . . . but I realized they were the culprits. I'd always thought it was the color that made them—and by extension, the rest of my face—look so uncertain, but though the color hadn't changed, the lack of resolve had. The boy who looked back at me today was determined, sure of his course. I wondered when that had happened. I thought I could probably guess.

Breakfast was the usual, quiet event I expected. Charlie fried eggs for himself; I had my bowl of cereal. I wondered if he had forgotten about this Saturday.

"About this Saturday . . . ," he began, like he could read my mind. I was getting really paranoid about that specific concern.

"Yes, Dad?"

He walked across the kitchen and turned on the faucet. "Are you still set on going to Seattle?"

"That was the plan." I frowned, wishing he hadn't brought it up so I wouldn't have to compose careful half-truths.

He squeezed some dish soap onto his plate and swirled it around with the brush. "And you're sure you can't make it back in time for the dance?"

"I'm not going to the dance, Dad."

"Didn't anyone ask you?" he asked, his eyes focused on the plate.

"It's not my thing," I reminded him.

"Oh." He frowned as he dried his plate.

I wondered if he was worried about me being a social outcast. Maybe I should have told him I had lots of invitations. But that would obviously backfire. He wouldn't be very happy if he knew I'd turned them all down. Then I would have to tell him that there was a girl . . . who hadn't asked me . . . and obviously I didn't want to get into that.

Which got me thinking about prom and Taylor and the dress she already had and Logan's attitude toward me and that whole mess. I wasn't sure what I was supposed to do. In any universe, I wasn't going to prom. In a universe where Edythe Cullen existed, I wasn't going to be interested in any other girl. It wasn't fair to just go along with Taylor's plan when my heart wasn't in it. The problem was figuring out *how*. . . .

Charlie left then, with a goodbye wave, and I went upstairs to brush my teeth and gather my books. When I heard the cruiser pull away, I could only wait a few seconds before I had to look out of my window. The silver car was already there, waiting in Charlie's spot on the driveway. I took the stairs three at a time and was out the door in seconds. I wondered how long this strange routine would continue. I never wanted it to end.

She waited in the car, not appearing to watch as I shut the door behind me without bothering to lock the deadbolt. I walked to the car, then hesitated for just a second before I opened the door and climbed in. She was smiling, relaxed—and, as usual, so perfect it was painful.

"Good morning. How are you today?" Her eyes roamed over my face, like the question was something more than simple courtesy.

"Good, thank you." I was always good—much more than good—when I was close to her.

Her gaze lingered on the circles under my eyes. "You look tired."

"I couldn't sleep," I admitted.

She laughed. "Neither could I."

The engine purred quietly to life. I was getting used to the sound. The roar of my truck would probably scare me the next time I drove it.

"I guess that's right," I said. "I probably did get more sleep than you."

"I would wager you did."

"So what did you do last night?"

She laughed. "Not a chance. It's my day to ask questions."

"Oh, that's right." My forehead creased. I couldn't imagine anything about me that would be interesting to her. "What do you want to know?"

"What's your favorite color?" she asked, totally serious.

I shrugged. "It changes."

"What is it today?"

"Um, probably . . . gold, I guess."

"Is there anything material behind your choice, or is it random?"

I cleared my throat self-consciously. "It's the color of your eyes today. If you asked me in a week, I'd probably say black."

She gave me a look that I didn't entirely understand, but before I could ask, she was on to her next question.

"What music is in your CD player right now?"

I had to think about that one for a second, until I remembered that the last thing I'd listened to was the CD Phil had given me. When I said the name of the band, she smiled and opened a hatch under the car's CD player. She pulled out one of the dozens of CDs that were packed into the small space, and handed it to me. It was the same CD.

"Debussy to this?" she asked, raising an eyebrow.

It continued like that for the rest of the day. While we walked between classes and all through the lunch hour, she questioned me without a break. She wanted to know about every insignificant detail of my existence. Movies I'd liked and hated, the few places I'd been and the many places I wanted to go, and books—so many questions about books.

I couldn't remember the last time I'd talked so much. I felt self-conscious the whole time, knowing I had to be boring her. But she always seemed on the edge of her seat waiting for my answers, she always had a follow-up question, she always wanted more. So I went along with the psychoanalysis, since it seemed to matter to her.

When the first bell rang, I sighed deeply. It was time. "There's one question you haven't asked me yet."

"More than one, actually, but which specific one are you looking for?"

"The most embarrassing thing I've ever done."

She grinned. "Is it a spectacular story?"

"I'm not sure yet. I'll tell you in five minutes."

I shoved away from the table. Her eyes were bright with curiosity.

At my usual table, my friends were all just getting to their feet. I walked toward them.

Patches of red flared in my cheeks, but that was probably okay. I was supposed to look emotional. Anyway, the pretty guy in the melodramatic soap my mom used to watch religiously looked fired up when he did this scene. Thanks to him, at least I had a general outline for my script, embellished by something I'd once thought about Edythe; I wanted to keep this flattering.

Jeremy noticed me first, and his eyes were speculative. They flashed from my red face to where Edythe was and back to me.

"Taylor, can I have a minute?" I said as I walked up to her. I didn't say it quietly.

She was right in the very middle of the cluster. Logan turned to glower at me with his fishy green eyes.

"Sure, Beau," Taylor said, looking confused.

"Look," I said, "I can't do this anymore."

Everyone fell silent. Jeremy's eyes got all round. Allen looked embarrassed. McKayla shot me a critical glance, like she couldn't believe I was doing it this way. But she didn't know exactly what I was doing, or why I needed this audience.

Taylor was shocked. "What?"

I scowled. It was easy—I was pretty angry right now that I hadn't talked myself out of this, or come up with a better way. But it was too late for improv now.

"I'm tired of being a pawn in your game, Taylor. Do you even realize that I have feelings of my own? And all I can do is watch while you use me to make someone else jealous." My eyes darted quickly to Logan, whose mouth was hanging open, and back to Taylor. "You don't care if you break my heart in the process. Is it being beautiful that's made you so cruel?"

Taylor's eyes were wide, her mouth open in a little o.

"I'm not going to play anymore. This whole prom charade? I'm out. Go with the person you really want to be with." A longer glare this time at Logan.

And then I stalked away, slamming through the cafeteria doors in what I hoped was a dramatic way.

I was never going to live this down.

But at least I was free. Probably worth it.

Suddenly Edythe was right next to me, keeping pace like we'd been walking together all along.

"That truly was spectacular," she said.

I took a deep breath. "Maybe a little over the top. Did it work?"

"Like a charm. Taylor's feeling quite the femme fatale, and she's not even sure why. If Logan doesn't ask her to prom by Monday, I'll be surprised."

"Good," I grunted.

"And now back to you . . ."

Edythe kept up the quiz until we were in Biology and Mrs. Banner arrived, dragging the audiovisual frame again. When she was finished with her prep and turned toward the light switch, I saw Edythe slide her chair a half-inch farther away from mine. It didn't help. As soon as the room was dark, there was that same electric tension, the same restless craving to stretch my hand across the short space and touch her cold, smooth skin.

It was like an itch that just got more and more demanding. I couldn't pay attention to anything else. Hopefully whatever movie it was that we were watching wouldn't be on the final.

After a little while, maybe fifteen minutes—or maybe it was only two and it just felt so long because of the electricity—I shifted my chair over and slowly leaned to the side until my arm was just touching her shoulder. She didn't move away.

I thought that little contact would help, that it would take away the nagging *want*, but it kind of backfired. The little frisson of electricity got stronger, changed into bigger jolts. I was suddenly dying to put my arm around her, to pull her into my side and hold her against me. I wanted to run my fingers down the length of her hair, to bury my face in it. I wanted to trace the shape of her lips, the line of her cheekbone, the length of her throat. . . .

Not really appropriate for a classroom full of people.

I leaned forward, folding my arms on the table and gripping under the

edge with my fingers, trying to hold myself in place. I didn't look at her, afraid that if she was looking back at me, it would only make self-control that much harder. I tried to make myself watch the movie, but the patches of color just wouldn't resolve into coherent images.

I sighed in relief again when Mrs. Banner hit the lights, and then finally I looked at Edythe; she was staring back, her eyes ambivalent.

Like yesterday, we walked toward the gym in silence. And also like yesterday, she touched my face wordlessly—this time with the back of her cool hand, stroking once from my temple to my jaw—before she turned and walked away.

Gym passed quickly. To save time, Coach Clapp told us to keep the same partners, so McKayla was forced to be my teammate again. I watched her one-woman badminton show without participating—for both our safety. She didn't talk to me, but whether that was because of the scene in the cafeteria, or our falling-out yesterday, or because my expression was so vacant, I didn't know. Somewhere in the back of my mind, I felt bad about that. But I couldn't concentrate on her any more than I could make sense of the movie in Biology.

I felt the same sense of harmony when I walked out the gym door and saw Edythe in the shadow of the gym. Everything was right in my world. A wide smile spread automatically across my face. She smiled back, then launched into more cross-examination.

Her questions were different now, not as easily answered. She wanted to know what I missed about my home, insisting on descriptions of anything she wasn't familiar with. We sat in front of Charlie's house for hours, as the sky darkened and rain plummeted around us in a sudden cloudburst.

I tried to describe impossible things like the scent of creosote—bitter, kind of resinous, but still pleasant—the high, keening sound of the cicadas in July, the gaunt, feathery trees, the enormous sky, extending white-blue from horizon to horizon. The hardest thing to explain was why it was so beautiful to me—to justify a beauty that didn't depend on the spiny vegetation that mostly looked half dead, a beauty that had something to do with the exposed shape of the land, with the shallow bowls of valleys between the craggy hills, and the way they held on to the sun. I found myself using my hands as I tried to describe it to her.

Her quiet, probing questions kept me talking freely, forgetting to be

embarrassed for monopolizing the conversation. Finally, when I had finished detailing my old room at home, she paused instead of responding with another question.

"Are you finished?" I asked in relief.

"Not even close—but your father will be home soon."

"How late is it?" I wondered out loud as I glanced at the clock. I was surprised by the time.

"It's twilight," Edythe murmured, looking toward the western horizon, hidden behind the clouds. Her voice was thoughtful, as if her mind were far away. I stared at her as she stared out the windshield.

I was still staring when her eyes suddenly shifted back to mine.

"It's the safest time of day for us," she said, answering the unspoken question in my eyes. "The easiest time. But also the saddest, in a way . . . the end of another day, the return of the night. Darkness is so predictable, don't you think?" She smiled wistfully.

"I *like* the night. Without the dark, you'd never see the stars." I frowned. "Not that you see them here much."

She laughed, and the mood abruptly lightened.

"Charlie will be here in a few minutes. So, unless you want to tell him that you'll be with me Saturday . . ." She looked at me hopefully.

"Thanks, but no thanks." I gathered my books, stiff from sitting still so long. "So is it my turn tomorrow, then?"

"Certainly not!" She pretended to be outraged. "I told you I wasn't done, didn't I?"

"What more is there?"

She displayed the dimples. "You'll find out tomorrow."

I stared at her, a little dazed, as usual.

I'd always thought I didn't really have a type; my former crowd back home all had something—one liked blondes and one only cared about the legs and one had to have blue eyes. I'd thought I was less particular; a pretty girl was a pretty girl. But I realized now that I must have been the most difficult to please of them all. Apparently, my type was extremely specific—I'd just never known it. I hadn't known my favorite hair color was this metallic shade of bronze, because I'd never seen it before. I hadn't known I was looking for eyes the color of honey, because I'd never seen

those, either. I didn't know a girl's lips had to be curved just this way and her cheekbones high under the long slash of her black lashes. All along, there had only been one shape, one face that would move me.

Like an idiot, warnings forgotten, I reached for her face, leaning in.

She recoiled.

"Sorr—" I started to say as my hand dropped.

But her head whipped forward, and she was staring into the rain again.

"Oh no," she breathed.

"What's wrong?"

Her jaw was clenched, her brows pulled down into a hard line over her eyes. She glanced at me for one brief second.

"Another complication," she told me glumly.

She leaned across me and flung my door open in one quick movement—her proximity sent my heart racing in an uneven gallop—and then she almost cringed away from me.

Headlights flashed through the rain. I looked up, expecting Charlie and a bunch of explanations to follow, but it was a dark sedan I didn't recognize.

"Hurry," she urged.

She was glaring through the downpour at the other vehicle.

I jumped out immediately, though I didn't understand. The rain lashed against my face; I pulled my hood up.

I tried to make out the shapes in the front seat of the other car, but it was too dark. I could see Edythe illuminated in the blaze of the new car's headlights; she was still staring ahead, her gaze locked on something or someone I couldn't see. Her expression was a strange mix of frustration and defiance.

Then she revved the engine, and the tires squealed against the wet pavement. The Volvo was out of sight in seconds.

"Hey, Beau," called a familiar, husky voice from the driver's side of the little black car.

"Jules?" I asked, squinting through the rain. Just then, Charlie's cruiser swung around the corner, his lights shining on the occupants of the car in front of me.

Jules was already climbing out, her wide grin visible even through the darkness. In the passenger seat was a much older woman, an imposing woman with an unusual face—it was stern and stoic, with creases that ran

through the russet skin like an old leather jacket. And the surprisingly familiar eyes, set deep under the heavy brows, black eyes that seemed at the same time both too young and too ancient to match the face. Jules's mother, Bonnie Black. I knew her immediately, though in the more than five years since I'd seen her last I'd managed to forget her name when Charlie had spoken of her my first day here. She was staring at me, scrutinizing my face, so I smiled tentatively at her. Then I processed more—that her eyes were wide, as if in shock or fear, her nostrils flared—and my smile faded.

Another complication, Edythe had said.

Bonnie still stared at me with intense, anxious eyes. Had Bonnie recognized Edythe so easily? Could she really believe the impossible legends her daughter had scoffed at?

The answer was clear in Bonnie's eyes. Yes. Yes, she could.

12. BALANCING

"BONNIE!" CHARLIE CALLED AS SOON AS HE GOT OUT OF HIS CAR.

I turned toward the house, motioning to Jules for her to follow as I ducked under the porch. I heard Charlie greeting her loudly behind me.

"I'm going to pretend I didn't see you behind the wheel, young lady."

"We get permits early on the rez," Jules said while I unlocked the door and flicked on the porch light.

Charlie laughed. "Sure you do."

"I have to get around somehow." I recognized Bonnie's deep voice easily, despite the years. The sound of it made me feel suddenly younger, just a child.

I went inside, leaving the door open behind me and turning on lights before I hung up my jacket. Then I stood in the door, watching anxiously as Charlie and Jules helped Bonnie out of the car and into her wheelchair.

I backed out of the way as the three of them hurried in, shaking off the rain.

"This is a surprise," Charlie was saying.

"It's been too long," Bonnie answered. "I hope it's not a bad time." Her dark eyes flashed up to me again, their expression unreadable.

"No, it's great. I hope you can stay for the game."

Jules grinned. "I think that's the plan—our TV broke last week."

Bonnie made a face at her daughter. "And, of course, Jules was eager to see Beau again," she added. Jules returned the scowl.

"Are you hungry?" I asked, turning toward the kitchen. Bonnie's searching gaze made me uncomfortable.

"Naw, we ate just before we came," Jules answered.

"How about you, Charlie?" I called over my shoulder as I escaped around the corner.

"Sure," he replied, his voice moving in the direction of the front room and the TV. I could hear Bonnie's chair follow.

The grilled cheese sandwiches were in the frying pan and I was slicing up a tomato when I sensed someone behind me.

"So, how are things?" Jules asked.

"Pretty good." I smiled. Her enthusiasm was hard to resist. "How about you? Did you finish your car?"

"No." She frowned. "I still need parts. We borrowed that one." She pointed with her thumb in the direction of the front yard.

"Sorry. I haven't seen any . . . what was it you were looking for?"

"Master cylinder." She grinned. "Is something wrong with the truck?" she added suddenly.

"No."

"Oh. I just wondered because you weren't driving it."

I stared down at the pan, pulling up the edge of a sandwich to check on the bottom side. "I got a ride with a friend."

"Nice ride." Jules's voice was admiring. "I didn't recognize the driver, though. I thought I knew most of the kids around here."

I nodded noncommittally, keeping my eyes down as I flipped sandwiches.

"My mom seemed to know her from somewhere."

"Jules, could you hand me some plates? They're in the cupboard over the sink."

"Sure."

She got the plates in silence. I hoped she would let it drop now.

"So who was it?" she asked, setting two plates on the counter next to me.

I sighed in defeat. "Edythe Cullen."

To my surprise, she laughed. I glanced down at her. She looked a little embarrassed.

"Guess that explains it, then," she said. "I wondered why my mom was acting so strange."

I faked an innocent expression. "That's right. She doesn't like the Cullens."

"Superstitious old bat," Jules muttered under her breath.

"You don't think she'd say anything to Charlie?" I couldn't help asking, the words coming out in a low rush.

Jules stared at me for a minute, and I couldn't read the expression in her dark eyes. "I doubt it," she finally answered. "I think Charlie chewed her out pretty good last time. They haven't spoken much since—tonight is sort of a reunion, I think. I don't think she'd bring it up again."

"Oh," I said, trying to sound like it didn't matter much to me either way.

I stayed in the front room after I carried the food out to Charlie, pretending to watch the game while chatting absently with Jules. Mostly I was listening to the adults' conversation, watching for any sign that Bonnie was about to rat me out, trying to think of ways to stop her if she started.

It was a long night. I had a lot of homework that was going undone, but I was afraid to leave Bonnie alone with Charlie. Finally, the game ended.

"Are you and your friends coming back to the beach soon?" Jules asked as she pushed her mother over the lip of the threshold.

"Uh, I'm not sure," I hedged.

"That was fun, Charlie," Bonnie said.

"Come up for the next game," Charlie encouraged.

"Sure, sure," Bonnie said. "We'll be here. Have a good night." Her eyes shifted to mine, and her smile disappeared. "You take care, Beau," she added seriously.

"Thanks," I muttered, looking away.

I headed for the stairs while Charlie waved from the doorway.

"Wait, Beau," he said.

I cringed. Had Bonnie gotten something in before I'd joined them in the living room?

But Charlie was relaxed, still grinning from the unexpected visit.

"I didn't get a chance to talk to you tonight. How was your day?"

"Good." I hesitated with one foot on the first stair, trying to think of details I could safely share. "My badminton team won all four games."

"Wow, I didn't know you could play badminton."

"Well, actually I can't, but my partner is really good," I admitted.

"Who is it?" he asked with token interest.

"Um . . . McKayla Newton."

"Oh yeah—you said you were friends with the Newton girl." He perked up. "Nice family." He mused for a minute. "She didn't want to go with you to the dance this weekend?"

"Dad!" I groaned. "She's kind of dating my friend Jeremy. Besides, you know I can't dance."

"Oh yeah," he muttered. Then he smiled at me apologetically. "So I guess it's good you'll be gone Saturday. . . . I've made plans to go fishing with the guys from the station. The weather's supposed to be real warm. But if you wanted to put your trip off till someone could go with you, I'd stay home. I know I leave you here alone too much."

"Dad, you're doing a great job," I said, hoping my relief didn't show. "I've never minded being alone—I'm too much like you." I grinned at him, and he smiled his crinkly-eyed smile.

I slept better that night, too tired to dream again. When I woke to the pearl gray morning, I felt almost high, my mood was so optimistic. The tense evening with Bonnie and Jules seemed harmless enough now; I decided to forget it completely. I caught myself whistling while I was yanking a comb through my hair, and later again as I hurtled down the stairs. Charlie noticed.

"You're cheerful this morning," he commented over breakfast.

I shrugged. "It's Friday."

I hurried so I would be ready to go the second Charlie left. I had my bag packed, shoes on, teeth brushed, but even though I rushed to the door as soon as I was sure Charlie would be out of sight, Edythe was faster. She was waiting, windows down, engine off.

I didn't hesitate this time as I climbed into the passenger seat. She flourished her dimples, and my chest did its mini–heart attack thing. I couldn't imagine anything more beautiful—human, goddess, or angel. There was nothing about her that could be improved upon.

"How did you sleep?" she asked. I wondered if she knew just how irresistible her voice was, if she made it that way on purpose.

"Fine. How was your night?"

"Pleasant."

"Can I ask what you did?"

"No." She grinned. "Today is still *mine*."

She wanted to know about people today: more about my mom, her hobbies, what we'd done in our free time together. And then the one grandmother I'd known, my few school friends—and then I was going red in patches when she asked about girls I'd dated. I was relieved that I'd never really dated anyone, so that particular conversation couldn't last long. She seemed surprised at my lack of romantic history.

"So you never met anyone you wanted?" she asked in a serious tone that made me wonder what she was thinking about.

"Not in Phoenix."

Her lips pressed together into a thin line.

We were in the cafeteria at this point. The day had sped by in the pattern that was rapidly becoming routine. I took advantage of her brief pause to take a bite of my sandwich.

"I should have let you drive yourself today," she said suddenly.

I swallowed. "Why?"

"I'm leaving with Archie after lunch."

"Oh." I blinked, disappointed. "That's okay, it's not that far of a walk."

She frowned at me impatiently. "I'm not going to make you walk home. We'll go get your truck and leave it here for you."

"I don't have my key with me." I sighed. "I really don't mind walking." What I minded was losing my time with her.

She shook her head. "Your truck will be here, and the key will be in the ignition—unless you're afraid someone might steal it." She laughed at the thought.

"Okay," I agreed. I was pretty sure my key was in the pocket of a pair of jeans I wore Wednesday, under a pile of clothes in the laundry room. Even if she broke into my house, or whatever she was planning, she'd never find it. She seemed to feel the challenge in my consent. She smirked, overconfident.

"So where are you going?" I asked as casually as I could manage.

"Hunting," she answered grimly. "If we're going to be alone together tomorrow, I'm going to take whatever precautions I can." Her face was suddenly sad . . . and pleading. "You can always cancel, you know."

I looked down, afraid of the persuasive power of her eyes. I would not let

her talk me out of our day alone, no matter how real the danger might be. *It doesn't matter*, I repeated in my head.

"No," I whispered, glancing back at her face. "I can't."

"Perhaps you're right," she murmured. Her eyes almost seemed to darken in color as I watched.

I changed the subject. "What time tomorrow?" I asked, already depressed by the thought of her leaving now.

"That depends. . . . It's a Saturday. Don't you want to sleep in?" she offered.

"No," I answered too fast, and she grinned.

"Same time as usual, then?"

I nodded. "Where should I pick you up?"

"I'll come to your place, also as usual."

"Um, it doesn't help with the Charlie situation if an unexplained Volvo is left in the driveway."

Her smile was superior now. "I wasn't intending to bring a car."

"How—"

She cut me off. "Don't worry about it. I'll be there, no car. No chance that Charlie will see anything out of the ordinary." Her voice turned hard. "And then, if you don't come home, it will be a complete mystery, won't it?"

"Guess so," I said, shrugging. "Maybe I'll get on the news and everything."

She scowled at me and I ignored it, chewing another bite of my lunch.

When her face finally relaxed—though she still didn't look happy—I asked, "What are you hunting tonight?"

"Whatever we find in the park. We aren't going far." She stared at me, a little frustrated and a little amused by my casual reference to her unusual life.

"Why are you going with Archie? Didn't you say he was being annoying?"

She frowned. "He's still the most . . . supportive."

"And the rest of them?" I asked hesitantly, not sure I really wanted to know. "What are they?"

Her brow puckered. "Incredulous, for the most part."

I glanced toward them. They sat staring off in different directions, exactly the same as the first time I'd seen them. Only now there were just the four of them; their perfect, bronze-haired sister was mine, for this hour at least.

"They don't like me," I guessed.

"That's not it," she disagreed, but her eyes were too innocent. "They don't understand why I can't leave you alone."

I frowned. "Me, either."

She smiled. "You're not like anyone I've ever known, Beau. You fascinate me."

Part of me was sure she was making fun of me—the part that couldn't escape the fact that I was the most boring person I knew. "I can't understand that," I said.

"Having the advantages I do," she murmured, touching one finger to her forehead, "I have a better-than-average grasp of human nature. People are predictable. But you . . . you never do what I expect. You always take me by surprise."

I looked away, my eyes hitting their default position—the back corner of the cafeteria where her family sat. Her words made me feel like a science experiment. I wanted to laugh at myself for expecting anything else.

"That part is easy enough to explain." I felt her eyes on my face, but I couldn't look at her yet. I was sure she would see the self-contempt in my eyes. "But there's more," she went on, "and it's not so easy to put into words—"

I was still staring absently at the Cullens while she spoke. Suddenly Royal turned his head to look directly at me. Not to look—to glare, with dark, cold eyes. I wanted to look away, but I was frozen by his overt antagonism until Edythe broke off mid-sentence and made an angry noise under her breath—a kind of hiss.

Royal turned his head, and I was relieved to be free. I looked back at Edythe, my eyes wide.

"That was definitely dislike," I muttered.

Her expression was pained. "I'm sorry about that. He's just worried. You see . . . it's dangerous for more than just me if, after spending so much time with you so publicly . . ." She looked down.

"If?"

"If this ends . . . badly." She dropped her head into her hands, obviously in anguish. I wanted to comfort her somehow, to tell her that nothing bad would ever happen to her, but I didn't know the right words. Automatically, I reached out to place my hand lightly against her elbow. She was wearing

just a long-sleeved t-shirt, and the cold soaked through to my hand immediately. She didn't move, and as I sat there I slowly realized that what she'd said should frighten me. I waited for that fear to come, but all I could feel was an ache for her pain.

She still had her face in her hands.

I tried to speak in a normal voice. "And you have to leave now?"

"Yes." She let her hands drop. I kept my hand against her forearm. She looked at the place where we were connected, and she sighed. Suddenly her mood shifted and she grinned. "It's probably for the best. We still have fifteen minutes of that wretched movie left to endure in Biology—I don't think I could take any more."

I jumped, yanking my hand back. Archie—taller than I'd thought, his hair just a shadow of dark stubble against his scalp, his eyes dark as ink—was suddenly standing behind Edythe's shoulder.

Edythe greeted him without looking away from me. "Archie."

"Edythe," he answered, imitating her tone with a mocking twist. His voice was a soft tenor, velvety like hers.

"Archie, Beau—Beau, Archie," she introduced us, a wry smile on her face.

"Hello, Beau." His eyes glittered like black diamonds, but his smile was friendly. "It's nice to finally meet you." Just the lightest stress on the *finally*.

Edythe flashed a dark look at him.

It was not hard for me to believe that Archie was a vampire. Standing two feet away from me. With dark, hungry eyes. I felt a bead of sweat roll down the back of my neck.

"Um, hey, Archie."

"Are you ready?" he asked her.

Her voice was cold. "Nearly. I'll meet you at the car."

He left without another word; the way he moved was so fluid, so sinuous, it made me think of dancers again, though it wasn't really that human.

I swallowed. "Should I say 'have fun,' or is that the wrong sentiment?"

"'Have fun' works as well as anything." She grinned.

"Have fun, then." I tried to sound enthusiastic, but of course she wasn't fooled.

"I'll try. And you try to be safe, please."

I sighed. "Safe in Forks—what a challenge."

Her jaw tightened. "For you it *is* a challenge. Promise."

"I promise to try to be safe," I recited. "I was meaning to deal with the laundry . . . or is that too hazardous a task? I mean, I could fall in or something."

Her eyes narrowed.

"Okay, okay, I'll do my best."

She stood, and I rose, too.

"I'll see you tomorrow." I sighed.

She smiled a wistful smile. "It seems like a long time to you, doesn't it?"

I nodded glumly.

"I'll be there in the morning," she promised, and then she walked to my side, touched the back of my hand lightly, and turned to walk away. I stared after her until she was gone.

I really did not want to go to class, and I thought about a little healthy ditching, but I decided it would be irresponsible. I knew that if I disappeared now, McKayla and the others would assume I'd gone with Edythe. And Edythe was worried about the time we'd spent together publicly . . . if things went wrong. I wasn't going to think about what that would mean, or how painful it might be. I just worked out the ways I could make things safer for her. Which meant going to class.

I felt certain—and I thought she did, too—that tomorrow would change everything for us. She and I . . . if we were going to be together, we had to face this square on. We couldn't keep trying to balance on this precarious edge of almost-together. We would fall to one side or the other, and it all depended on her. I was all in, before I'd even consciously chosen, and I was committed to seeing this through. Because there was nothing more terrifying to me, more painful, than the idea of never seeing her again.

It didn't help my concentration so much that she wasn't next to me in Biology. The tension and electricity were gone, but my mind was too wrapped around the idea of tomorrow to pay attention.

In Gym, McKayla seemed to have forgiven me. She said she hoped I had a good time in Seattle. I carefully explained that I'd canceled the trip due to truck issues.

She was suddenly sulky again. "Are you taking Edythe to the dance?"

"No. I told you I wasn't going."

"What are you doing, then?"

I lied cheerfully. "Laundry, and then I have to study for the Trig test or I'm going to fail."

She frowned. "Is Edythe helping you 'study'?"

I could hear the quotation marks she put around the last word.

"Don't I wish," I said, smiling. "She's so much smarter than I am. But she's gone away somewhere with her brother for the weekend." It was funny how much easier than usual the lies were coming. Maybe because I was lying for someone else, and not for myself.

McKayla perked up. "Oh. You know, you could still come to the dance with us all. That would be cool. We'd all dance with you," she promised.

The mental image of Jeremy's face made my tone sharper than necessary. "I'm not going to the dance, McKayla, okay?"

"Fine," she snapped. "I was just offering."

When Gym was finally over, I walked to the parking lot without enthusiasm. I wasn't looking forward to walking home in the rain, but I couldn't think of how she would have been able to get my truck. Then again, was anything impossible for her?

And there it was—parked in the same spot where she'd parked the Volvo this morning. I shook my head, amazed, as I opened the door and found the key in the ignition as promised.

There was a piece of white paper folded on my seat. I got in and closed the door before I opened it. Two words were written in her fancy calligraphy handwriting.

Be safe.

The sound of the truck roaring to life startled me, and I laughed at myself.

When I got home, the handle of the door was locked, the deadbolt unlocked, just as I'd left it this morning. Inside, I went straight to the laundry room. It looked just the same as I'd left it, too. I dug for my jeans and, after finding them, checked the pockets. Empty. Maybe I'd hung my key up after all, I thought, shaking my head.

Charlie was absentminded at dinner, worried over something at work, I guessed, or maybe a basketball game, or maybe he was just really enjoying his lasagna—it was hard to tell with Charlie.

"You know, Dad . . . ," I began, breaking into his reverie.

"What's that, Beau?"

"I think you're right about Seattle. I think I'll wait until Jeremy or someone else can go with me."

"Oh," he said, surprised. "Oh, okay. So, do you want me to stay home?"

"No, Dad, don't change your plans. I've got a hundred things to do . . . homework, laundry. . . . I need to go to the library and the grocery store. I'll be in and out all day. . . . You go and have fun."

"Are you sure?"

"Absolutely, Dad. Besides, the freezer is getting dangerously low on fish—we're down to a two, maybe three years' supply."

He smiled. "You're sure easy to live with, Beau."

"I could say the same thing about you," I said, laughing. The sound of my laughter was off, but he didn't seem to notice. I felt so guilty for deceiving him that I almost took Edythe's advice and told him where I would be. Almost.

As I worked on the mindless chore of folding laundry, I wondered if, with this lie, I was choosing Edythe over my own father—after all, I was protecting her and leaving him to face . . . exactly what, I wasn't sure. Would I just vanish? Would the police find some . . . piece of me? I knew I wasn't able to process exactly how devastating that would be for him, that losing a child—even one he hadn't seen much for the last decade—was a bigger tragedy than I was able to understand.

But if I told him I would be with Edythe, if I implicated her in whatever followed, how did that help Charlie? Would it make the loss more bearable if he had someone to blame? Or would it just put him in more danger? I remembered how Royal had glared at me today. I remembered Archie's glittering black eyes, Eleanor's arms, like long lines of steel, and Jessamine, who—for some reason I couldn't define—was the most frightening of them all. Did I really want my father to know something that would make them feel threatened?

So really, the only thing that could help Charlie at all would be if I taped a note to the door tomorrow that read *I changed my mind*, and then got in my truck and drove to Seattle after all. I knew Edythe wouldn't be angry, that a part of her was hoping for exactly that.

But I also knew that I wasn't going to write that note. I couldn't even imagine doing it. When she came, I would be waiting.

So I guess I *was* choosing her over everything. And though I knew I should feel bad—wrong, guilty, sorry—I didn't. Maybe because it didn't feel like a choice at all.

But all of this was only if things went badly, and I was nearly ninety percent sure that they wouldn't. Part of it was that I still couldn't make myself be afraid of Edythe, even when I tried to picture her as the sharp-fanged Edythe from my nightmare. I had her note in my back pocket, and I pulled it out and read it again and again. She wanted me to be safe. She'd dedicated a lot of personal effort lately to ensuring my survival. Wasn't that who she was? When all the safeties were off, wouldn't that part of her win?

The laundry wasn't the best job for keeping my mind busy. As much as I tried to focus on the Edythe I knew, the one I loved, I couldn't help picturing what *ending badly* might look like. Might feel like. I'd seen enough horror flicks to have some preconceived notions, and it didn't look like the very *worst* way to go. Most of the victims just seemed sort of limp and out of it while they were . . . drained. But then I remembered what Edythe had said about bears, and I guessed that the realities of vampire attacks were not much like the Hollywood version.

But it was *Edythe.*

I was relieved when it was late enough to be acceptable for bedtime. I knew I would never get to sleep with all this crazy in my head, so I did something I'd never done before. I deliberately took unnecessary cold medicine—the kind that knocked me out for a good eight hours. I knew it was not the most responsible choice, but tomorrow would be complicated enough without me being loopy from sleep deprivation on top of everything else. While I waited for the drugs to kick in, I listened to Phil's CD again. The familiar screaming was oddly comforting, and somewhere in the middle of it, I drifted off.

I woke early, having slept soundly and dreamlessly thanks to the drug abuse. Though I was well rested, I was on edge and jittery—now and then, almost panicked. I showered and threw clothes on, dressing in layers out of habit, though Edythe had promised sun today. I checked out the window; Charlie was already gone and a thin layer of clouds, white and cottony, covered the

sky in a temporary-looking way. I ate without tasting the food, rushing to clean up when I was done. I'd just finished brushing my teeth when a quiet knock had me vaulting my way down the stairs.

My hands were suddenly too big for the simple deadbolt, and it took me a second, but finally I threw the door open, and there she was.

I took a deep breath. All the nerves faded to nothing, and I was totally calm.

She wasn't smiling at first—her face was serious, even wary. But then she looked me over and her expression lightened. She laughed.

"Good morning," she chuckled.

"What's wrong?" I glanced down to make sure I hadn't forgotten anything important, like shoes, or pants.

"We match." She laughed again.

She had on a light tan sweater with a scoop neck, a white t-shirt on underneath, and jeans. My sweater was the exact same shade, though that and my white tee both had crew necks. My jeans were the same color blue, too. Only, she looked like a runway model, and I knew that I did not.

I locked the door behind me while she walked to the truck. She waited by the passenger door with a martyred expression that was easy to understand.

"You agreed to this," I reminded her as I unlocked her door and opened it. She gave me a dark look as she climbed past me.

I got in my side and tried not to cringe as I revved the engine very loudly to life.

"Where to?" I asked.

"Put your seat belt on—I'm nervous already."

I rolled my eyes but did what she asked. "Where to?" I repeated.

"Take the one-oh-one north."

It was surprisingly difficult to concentrate on the road while feeling her eyes on my face. I compensated by driving more carefully than usual through the still-sleeping town.

"Were you planning to make it out of Forks before nightfall?"

"This truck is old enough to be the Volvo's grandfather—have a little respect."

We were soon out of the town limits, despite her pessimism. Thick underbrush and dense forest replaced the lawns and houses.

"Turn right on the one-ten," she instructed just as I was about to ask. I obeyed silently.

"Now we drive until the pavement ends."

I could hear a smile in her voice, but I was too afraid of driving off the road and proving her right to look over and be sure.

"And what's there, at the pavement's end?" I wondered.

"A trail."

"We're hiking?"

"Is that a problem?"

"No." I tried to make the lie sound confident. But if she thought my truck was slow . . .

"Don't worry, it's only five miles or so and we're in no hurry."

Five miles. I didn't answer, so that she wouldn't hear the panic in my voice. How far had I hiked last Saturday—a mile? And how many times had I managed to trip in that distance? This was going to be humiliating.

We drove in silence for a while. I was imagining what her expression would look like the twentieth time I face-planted.

"What are you thinking?" she asked impatiently after a few minutes.

I lied again. "Just wondering where we're going."

"It's a place I like to go when the weather is nice." We both glanced out the windows at the thinning clouds.

"Charlie said it would be warm today."

"And did you tell Charlie what you were up to?" she asked.

"Nope."

"But you probably said something to Jeremy about me driving you to Seattle," she said thoughtfully.

"No, I didn't."

"No one knows you're with me?" Angrily, now.

"That depends. . . . I assume you told Archie?"

"That's very helpful, Beau," she snapped.

I pretended I didn't hear that.

"Is it the weather? Seasonal affective disorder? Has Forks made you so depressed you're actually suicidal?"

"You said it might cause problems for you . . . us being together publicly," I explained.

"So you're worried about the trouble it might cause *me*—if *you* don't come *home*?" Her voice was a mix of ice and acid.

I nodded, keeping my eyes on the road.

She muttered something under her breath, the words flowing so quickly that I couldn't understand them.

It was silent for the rest of the drive. I could feel the waves of fury and disapproval rolling off her, and I couldn't think of the right way to apologize when I wasn't sorry.

The road ended at a small wooden marker. I could see the thin foot trail stretching away into the forest. I parked on the narrow shoulder and stepped out, not sure what to do because she was angry and I didn't have driving as an excuse not to look at her anymore.

It was warm now, warmer than it had been in Forks since the day I'd arrived, almost muggy under the thin clouds. I yanked off my sweater and tossed it into the cab, glad I'd worn the t-shirt—especially with five miles of hiking ahead of me.

I heard her door slam, and looked over to see that she'd removed her sweater, too, and twisted her hair into another messy bun. All she had on was a thin tank top. She was facing away from me, staring into the forest, and I could see the delicate shapes of her shoulder blades almost like furled wings under her pale skin. Her arms were so thin; it was hard to believe they contained the strength that I knew was in them.

"This way," she said, glancing over her shoulder at me, still annoyed. She started walking into the dark forest directly to the east of the truck.

"The trail?" I asked, trying to hide the panic in my voice as I hurried around the front of the truck to catch up to her.

"I said there was a trail at the end of the road, not that we were taking it."

"No trail? Really?"

"I won't let you get lost."

She turned then, with a mocking half-smile, and I couldn't breathe.

I'd never seen so much of her skin. Her pale arms, her slim shoulders, the fragile-looking twigs of her collarbones, the vulnerable hollows above them, the swanlike column of her neck, the gentle swell of her breasts—*don't stare, don't stare*—and the ribs I could nearly count under the thin cotton. She was

too perfect, I realized with a crushing wave of despair. There was no way this goddess could ever belong with me.

She stared at me, shocked by my tortured expression.

"Do you want to go home?" she asked quietly, a different pain than mine saturating her voice.

"No."

I walked forward till I was close beside her, anxious not to waste one second of the obviously numbered hours I had with her.

"What's wrong?" she asked, her voice still soft.

"I'm not a fast hiker," I answered dully. "You'll have to be very patient."

"I can be patient—if I make a great effort." She smiled, holding my gaze, trying to pull me out of my suddenly glum mood.

I tried to smile back, but I could feel that the smile was less than convincing. She searched my face.

"I'll take you home," she promised, but I couldn't tell if the promise was unconditional, or restricted to an immediate departure. Obviously, she thought it was fear of my impending demise that had upset me, and I was glad that I was the one person whose mind she couldn't hear.

"If you want me to hack five miles through the jungle before sundown, you'd better start leading the way," I said bitterly. Her eyebrows pulled down as she tried to understand my tone and expression.

She gave up after a moment and led the way into the forest.

It wasn't as hard as I'd been afraid it would be. The way was mostly flat, and she seemed content to go at my pace. Twice I tripped over roots, but each time her hand shot out and steadied my elbow before I could fall. When she touched me, my heart thudded and stuttered like usual. I saw her expression the second time that happened, and I was suddenly sure she could hear it.

I tried to keep from looking at her; every time I did, her beauty filled me with the same sadness. Mostly we walked in silence. Occasionally, she would ask a random question that she hadn't gotten to in the last two days of interrogation. She asked about birthdays, grade school teachers, childhood pets—and I had to admit that after killing three fish in a row, I'd given up on the practice. She laughed at that, louder than usual, the bell-like echoes bouncing back to me from the trees.

The hike took me most of the morning, but she never seemed impatient.

The forest spread out around us in a labyrinth of identical trees, and I started to get nervous that we wouldn't be able to find our way out again. She was perfectly at ease in the green maze, never showing any doubt about our direction.

After several hours, the green light that filtered down through the canopy brightened into yellow. The day had turned sunny, just as promised. For the first time since we'd started, I felt excitement again.

"Are we there yet?" I asked.

She smiled at the change in my mood. "Nearly. Do you see the clearer light ahead?"

I stared into the thick forest. "Um, should I?"

"Maybe it is a bit soon for *your* eyes."

"Time to visit the optometrist." I sighed and she grinned.

And then, after another hundred yards, I could definitely see a brighter spot in the trees ahead, a glow that was yellow-white instead of yellow-green. I picked up the pace, and she let me lead now, following noiselessly.

I reached the edge of the pool of light and stepped through the last fringe of ferns into the most beautiful place I had ever seen.

The meadow was small, perfectly round, and filled with wildflowers— violet, yellow, and white. Somewhere nearby, I could hear the liquid rush of a stream. The sun was directly overhead, filling the circle with a haze of buttery sunshine. I walked slowly forward through the soft grass, swaying flowers, and warm, gilded air. After that first minute of awe, I turned, wanting to share this with her, but she wasn't behind me where I thought she'd be. I spun around, searching for her, suddenly anxious. Finally I found her, still under the dense shade of the canopy at the edge of the hollow, watching me with cautious eyes, and I remembered why we were here. The mystery of Edythe and the sun—which she'd promised to solve for me today.

I took a step back, my hand stretched out toward her. Her eyes were wary, reluctant—oddly, it reminded me of stage fright. I smiled encouragingly and started walking back to her. She held up a warning hand and I stopped, rocking back onto my heels.

Edythe took a deep breath, closed her eyes, then stepped out into the bright glare of the midday sun.

13. CONFESSIONS

EYES CLOSED, EDYTHE STEPPED BLINDLY INTO THE LIGHT.

My heart jumped into my throat and I started sprinting toward her.

"Edythe!"

It was only when her eyes flashed open and I got close enough to begin to understand what I was seeing that I realized she hadn't caught on fire. She threw up her hand again, palm forward, and I stumbled to a stop, almost falling to my knees.

The light blazed off her skin, danced in prism-like rainbows across her face and neck, down her arms. She was so bright that I had to squint, like I was trying to stare at the sun.

I thought about falling to my knees on purpose. This was the kind of beauty you worshipped. The kind you built temples for and offered sacrifices to. I wished I had something in my empty hands to give her, but what would a goddess want from a mediocre mortal like me?

It took me a while to see past her incandescence to the expression on her face. She was watching me with wide eyes—it almost looked like she was afraid of something. I took a step toward her, and she cringed just slightly.

"Does that hurt you?" I whispered.

"No," she whispered back.

I took another step toward her—she was the magnet again, and I was just a helpless piece of dull metal. She let her warning hand drop to her side. As

she moved, the fire shimmered down her arm. Slowly, I circled around her, keeping my distance, just needing to absorb this, to see her from every angle. The sun played off her skin, refracting and magnifying every color light could hold. My eyes were adjusting, and they opened wide with wonder.

I knew that she'd chosen her clothes with care, that she'd been determined to show me this, but the way she held herself now, shoulders tight, legs braced, made me wonder if she wasn't second-guessing the decision now.

I finished my circle, then closed the last few feet between us. I couldn't stop staring, even to blink.

"Edythe," I breathed.

"Are you scared now?" she whispered.

"*No.*"

She stared searchingly into my eyes, trying to hear what I was thinking.

I reached toward her, deliberately unhurried, watching her face for permission. Her eyes opened even wider, and she froze. Carefully, slowly, I let my fingertips graze the glistening skin on the back of her arm. I was surprised to find it just as cold as ever. While my fingers were touching her, the reflections of the fire flickered against my skin, and suddenly my hand wasn't mediocre anymore. She was so astonishing that she could make even me less ordinary.

"What are you thinking?" she whispered.

I struggled to find words. "I am . . . I didn't know . . ." I took a deep breath, and the words finally came. "I've never seen anything more beautiful—never imagined anything so beautiful could exist."

Her eyes were still wary. Like she thought I was saying what I thought she wanted to hear. But it was only the truth, maybe the truest, most uncensored thing I'd ever said in my life. I was too overwhelmed to filter or pretend.

She started to lift her hand, then dropped it. The shimmer flared. "It's very strange, though," she murmured.

"Amazing," I breathed.

"Aren't you repulsed by my flagrant lack of humanity?"

I shook my head. "Not repulsed."

Her eyes narrowed. "You should be."

"I'm feeling like humanity is pretty overrated."

She pulled her arm from under my fingertips and folded it behind her

back. Rather than take her cue, I took a half-step closer to her. I could feel the reflected shine on my face.

And she was suddenly ten feet away from me, her warning hand up again and her jaw clenched.

"I'm sorry," I said.

"I need some time," she told me.

"I'll be more careful."

She nodded, then walked to the middle of the meadow, making a little arc when she passed me, keeping those ten feet always between us. She sat down with her back to me, the sunlight incandescent across her shoulder blades, reminding me of wings again. I walked slowly closer, and then sat down facing her when I was about five feet away.

"Is this all right?"

She nodded, but she didn't look sure. "Just let me . . . concentrate."

I sat, silent, and after a few seconds, she shut her eyes again. I was fine with that. Seeing her like this—it wasn't something you could get tired of. I watched her, trying to understand the phenomenon, and she ignored me.

It was about a half hour later that suddenly she lay back on the grass with one hand behind her head. The grass was long enough to partially obscure my view.

"Can I . . . ?" I asked.

She patted the ground beside her.

I moved a few feet closer, then another foot when she didn't object. Another few inches.

Her eyes were still closed, lids glistening pale lavender over the dark fan of lashes. Her chest rose and fell evenly, almost like she was asleep, except there was somehow a sense of effort and control to the motion. She seemed very *aware* of the process of breathing in and out.

I sat with my legs folded under me, my elbows on my knees and my chin on my hands. It was very warm—the sun felt strange on my skin now that I was so used to the rain—and the meadow was still lovely, but it was just background now. It didn't stand out. I had a new definition of beauty.

Her lips moved, and the light glittered off them while they . . . almost trembled. I thought she might have spoken, but the words were too quiet, and too fast.

"Did you . . . say something?" I whispered. Sitting next to her like this, watching her shine, made me feel the need for quiet. For reverence, even.

"Just singing to myself," she murmured. "It calms me."

We didn't move for a long time—except for her lips, every now and then singing too low for me to hear. An hour might have passed, maybe more. Very gradually, the tension that I hadn't totally processed at first drained quietly away, till everything was so peaceful that I was almost sleepy. Every time I shifted my weight, I would end up another half-inch nearer to her.

I leaned closer, studying her hand, trying to find the facets in her smooth skin. Without even thinking about it, I reached out with one finger to stroke the back of her hand, awed again by the satin-smooth texture, cool like stone. I felt her eyes on me and I looked up, my finger frozen.

Her eyes were peaceful, and she was smiling.

"I still don't scare you, do I?"

"Nope. Sorry."

She smiled wider. Her teeth flashed in the sun.

I inched closer again, stretched out my whole hand to trace the shape of her forearm with my fingertips. I saw that my fingers were trembling. Her eyes closed again.

"Do you mind?" I asked.

"No. You can't imagine how that feels."

I lightly trailed my hand over the delicate structure of her arm, followed the faint pattern of bluish veins inside the crease at her elbow. I reached to turn her hand over, and when she realized what I wanted, she flipped her palm up in a movement so fast it didn't exist. My fingers froze.

"Sorry," she murmured, and then smiled because that was my line. Her eyes slid closed again. "It's too easy to be myself with you."

I lifted her hand, turning it this way and that I as watched the sun shimmer across her palm. I held it closer to my face, trying again to find the facets.

"Tell me what you're thinking," she whispered. She was watching me again, her eyes as light as I'd ever seen them. Pale honey. "It's still so strange for me, not knowing."

"The rest of us feel that way all the time, you know."

"It's a hard life," she said, and there was a forlorn note in her tone. "But you didn't tell me."

"I was wishing I could know what *you* were thinking. . . ."

"And?"

"I was wishing that I could believe that you were real. I'm afraid. . . ."

"I don't want you to be afraid." Her voice was just a low murmur. We both heard what she hadn't said—that I didn't need to be afraid, that there was nothing to fear.

"That's not the kind of fear I meant."

So quickly that I missed the movement completely, she was half-sitting, propped up on her right arm, her left palm still in my hands. Her angel's face was only a few inches from mine. I should have leaned away. I was supposed to be careful.

Her honey eyes burned.

"Then what are you afraid of?" she whispered.

I couldn't answer. I smelled her sweet, cool breath in my face, like I had just the one time before. Unthinkingly, I leaned closer, inhaling.

And she was gone, her hand ripped from mine so fast that they stung. In the time it took my eyes to focus, she was twenty feet away, standing at the edge of the small meadow, deep in the shade of a huge fir tree. She stared at me, eyes dark in the shadows, her expression unreadable.

I could feel the shock on my face, and my hands burned.

"Edythe. I'm . . . sorry." My voice was just a whisper, but I knew she could hear me.

"Give me a moment," she called, just loud enough for my less sensitive ears.

I sat very still.

After ten very long seconds, she walked back, slowly for her. She stopped when she was still several feet away and sank gracefully to the ground, crossing her legs underneath her. Her eyes never left mine. She took two deep breaths, then smiled apologetically.

"I am so very sorry." She hesitated. "Would you understand what I meant if I said I was only human?"

I nodded, not quite able to smile at her joke. Adrenaline pushed through my system as I realized what had almost happened. She could smell that from where she sat. Her smile turned mocking.

"I'm the world's best predator, aren't I? Everything about me invites you in—my voice, my face, even my *smell*. As if I needed any of that!"

Suddenly she was just a blur. I blinked and she'd vanished; then she was standing beneath the same tree as before, having circled the entire meadow in a fraction of a second.

"As if you could outrun me," she said bitterly.

She leaped a dozen feet straight up, grabbing a two-foot-thick branch and wrenching it away from the trunk without any sign of effort. She was back on the ground in the same instant, balancing the huge, gnarled lance in one hand for just a second. Then with blinding speed she swung it—one-handed—like a bat at the tree she'd ripped it from.

With an explosive boom, both the branch and the tree shattered in half.

Before I even had time to shy away from the detonation, before the tree could even fall to the ground, she was right in front of me again, just two feet away, still as a sculpture.

"As if you could fight me off," she said gently. Behind her, the sound of the tree crashing to the earth echoed through the forest.

I'd never seen her so completely freed of her careful human façade. She'd never been less human . . . or more beautiful. I couldn't move, like a bird trapped by the eyes of a snake.

Her eyes seemed to glow with excitement. Then, as the seconds passed, they dimmed. Her expression slowly folded into a mask of sadness. She looked like she was about to cry, and I struggled up to my knees, one hand reaching toward her.

She held out her hand, cautioning me. "Wait."

I froze again.

She took one step toward me. "Don't be afraid," she murmured, and her velvet voice was unintentionally seductive. "I promise . . ." She hesitated. "I *swear* I will not hurt you." She seemed like she was trying to convince herself just as much as she was trying to convince me.

"You don't have to be afraid," she whispered again as she stepped closer with exaggerated slowness. She stopped just a foot away and gently touched her hand to the one I still had stretched toward her. I wrapped mine around hers tightly.

"Please forgive me," she said in a formal tone. "I can control myself. You caught me off guard. I'm on my best behavior now."

She waited for me to respond, but I just knelt there in front of her, staring, my brain totally scrambled.

"I'm not thirsty today, honestly." She winked.

That made me laugh, though my laugh sounded a little winded.

"Are you all right?" she asked, reaching out—slowly, carefully—to put her other hand on top of mine.

I looked at her smooth, marble hand, and then at her eyes. They were soft, repentant, but I could see some of the sadness still in them.

I smiled up at her so widely that my cheeks hurt. Her answering smile was dazzling.

With a deliberately unhurried, sinuous movement, she sank down, curling her legs beneath her. Awkwardly I copied her, till we were sitting facing each other, knees touching, our hands still wrapped together between us.

"So where were we, before I behaved so rudely?"

"I honestly have no idea."

She smiled, but her face was ashamed. "I think we were talking about why you were afraid, besides the obvious reason."

"Oh, right."

"Well?"

I looked down at our hands, turning mine so that the light would glisten across hers.

"How easily frustrated I am," she sighed.

I looked into her eyes, suddenly realizing that this was every bit as new to her as it was to me. However many years of experience she'd had before we'd met, this was hard for her, too. That made me braver.

"I was afraid . . . because for, well, obvious reasons, I probably can't *stay* with you, can I? And that's what I want, much more than I should."

"Yes," she agreed slowly. "Being with me has never been in your best interest."

I frowned.

"I should have left that first day and not come back. I should leave now." She shook her head. "I might have been able to do it then. I don't know how to do it now."

"Don't. Please."

Her face turned brittle. "Don't worry. I'm essentially a selfish creature. I crave your company too much to do what I should."

"Good!"

She glared, carefully extricating her hands from mine and then folding them across her chest. Her voice was harsher when she spoke again.

"You should never forget that it's not only your company I crave. Never forget that I am more dangerous to you than I am to anyone else." She stared unseeingly into the forest.

I thought for a moment.

"I don't think I understand exactly what you mean by that last part."

She looked back and smiled at me, her unpredictable mood shifting again.

"How do I explain? And without horrifying you?"

Without seeming to think about it, she placed her hand back in mine. I held it tightly. She looked at our hands.

"That's amazingly pleasant, the warmth."

A moment passed while she seemed to be arranging her thoughts.

"You know how everyone enjoys different flavors?" she began. "Some people love chocolate ice cream, others prefer strawberry?"

I nodded.

"I apologize for the food analogy—I couldn't think of another way to explain."

I grinned and she grinned back, but her smile was rueful.

"You see, every person has their own scent, their own essence. . . . If you locked an alcoholic in a room full of stale beer, she'd drink it. But she could resist, if she wished to, if she were a recovering alcoholic. Now let's say you placed in that room a glass of hundred-year-old brandy, the rarest, finest cognac—and filled the room with its warm aroma—how do you think our alcoholic would fare then?"

We sat in silence for a minute, staring into each other's eyes, trying to read each other's thoughts.

She broke the silence first.

"Maybe that's not the right comparison. Maybe it would be too easy to turn down the brandy. Perhaps I should have made our alcoholic a heroin addict instead."

"So what you're saying is, I'm your brand of heroin?" I teased, trying to lighten the mood.

She smiled swiftly, seeming to appreciate my effort. "Yes, you are *exactly* my brand of heroin."

"Does that happen often?" I asked.

She looked across the treetops, thinking through her response.

"I spoke to my sisters about it." She still stared into the distance. "To Jessamine, every one of you is much the same. She's the most recent to join our family. It's a struggle for her to abstain at all. She hasn't had time to grow sensitive to the differences in smell, in flavor." She glanced swiftly at me. "I'm sorry."

"It's fine. Look, don't worry about offending me, or horrifying me, or whatever. That's the way you think. I can understand, or I can try to at least. Just explain however it makes sense to you."

She took a deep breath and stared past me.

"So Jessamine wasn't sure if she'd ever come across someone who was as"—she hesitated, looking for the right word—"*appealing* as you are to me. Which makes me think not." Her eyes flickered to me. "She would remember *this*."

She looked away again. "El has been on the wagon longer, so to speak, and she understood what I meant. She says twice, for her, once stronger than the other."

"And for you?"

"Never before this."

We stared at each other again. This time I broke the silence.

"What did Eleanor do?"

It was the wrong question to ask. She cringed, and her face was suddenly tortured. I waited, but she didn't add anything.

"Okay, so I guess that was a dumb question."

She stared at me with eyes that pleaded for understanding. "Even the strongest of us fall off the wagon, don't we?"

"Are you . . . asking for my permission?" I whispered. A shiver rolled down my spine that had nothing to do with my freezing hands.

Her eyes flew wide in shock. "No!"

"But you're saying there's no hope, right?"

I knew it wasn't normal, facing death like this without any real sense of fear. It wasn't that I was super brave, I knew that. It was just that I wouldn't have chosen differently, even knowing it would end this way.

She looked angry again, but I didn't think she was angry with me. "Of

course there's hope. Of course I won't . . ." She left the sentence hanging. Her eyes felt like they were physically burning mine. "It's different for us. El . . . these were strangers she happened across. It was a long time ago. She wasn't as practiced, as careful as she is now. And she's never been as good at this as I am."

She fell silent, watching me intently as I thought it through.

"So if we'd met . . . oh, in a dark alley or something . . ."

"It took everything I had—every single year of practice and sacrifice and effort—not to jump up in the middle of that class full of children and—" She broke off, her eyes darting away from me. "When you walked past me, I could have ruined everything Carine has built for us, right then and there. If I hadn't been denying my thirst for the last . . . too many years, I wouldn't have been able to stop myself."

She stared at me grimly, both of us remembering.

"You must have thought I was possessed."

"I couldn't understand why. How you could hate me, just like that . . ."

"To me, it was like you were some kind of demon, summoned straight from my own personal hell to ruin me. The fragrance coming off your skin . . . I thought it would make me deranged that first day. In that one hour, I thought of a hundred different ways to lure you from the room with me, to get you alone. And I fought them each back, thinking of my family, what I could do to them. I had to run out, to get away before I could speak the words that would make you follow. . . ."

She looked up then, her golden eyes scorching from under her lashes, hypnotic and deadly.

"You would have come," she promised.

I tried to speak calmly. "No doubt about it."

She frowned at our hands. "And then, as I tried to rearrange my schedule in a pointless attempt to avoid you, there you were—in that close, warm little room, the scent was maddening. I so very nearly took you then. There was only one other frail human there—so easily dealt with."

It was so strange, seeing my memories again, but this time with subtitles. Understanding for the first time what it had all meant, understanding the danger. Poor Mr. Cope. I flinched at the thought of how close I'd come to being inadvertently responsible for his death.

"But I resisted. I don't know how. I forced myself *not* to wait for you, *not* to follow you from the school. It was easier outside, when I couldn't smell you anymore, to think clearly, to make the right decision. I left the others near home—I was too ashamed to tell them how weak I was, they only knew something was very wrong—and then I went straight to Carine, at the hospital, to tell her I was leaving."

I stared in surprise.

"I traded cars with her—she had a full tank of gas and I was afraid to stop. I didn't dare to go home, to face Earnest. He wouldn't have let me go without a fight. He would have tried to convince me that it wasn't necessary. . . .

"By the next morning I was in Alaska." She sounded ashamed, as if she was admitting some huge display of cowardice. "I spent two days there, with some old acquaintances . . . but I was homesick. I hated knowing I'd upset Earnest, and the rest of them, my adopted family. In the pure air of the mountains it was hard to believe you were so irresistible. I convinced myself it was weak to run away. I'd dealt with temptation before, not of this magnitude, not even close, but I was strong. Who were you, an insignificant human boy"— she grinned suddenly—"to chase me from the place I wanted to be? Ah, the deadly sin of pride." She shook her head. "So I came back. . . ."

I couldn't speak.

"I took precautions, hunting, feeding more than usual before seeing you again. I was sure that I was strong enough to treat you like any other human. I was arrogant about it.

"It was unquestionably a complication that I couldn't simply read your thoughts to know what your reaction was to me. I wasn't used to having to go to such circuitous measures, listening to your words in Jeremy's mind. . . . His mind isn't very original, and it was annoying to have to stoop to that. And then I couldn't know if you really meant what you were saying, or just saying what you thought your audience wanted to hear. It was all extremely irritating." She frowned at the memory.

"I wanted you to forget my behavior that first day, if possible, so I tried to talk with you like I would with any person. I was eager, actually, hoping to decipher some of your thoughts. But you were too interesting, I found myself caught up in your expressions . . . and every now and then you would move and the air would stir around you. . . . The scent would stun me again. . . .

"Of course, then you were nearly crushed to death in front of my eyes. Later I thought of a perfectly good excuse for why I acted at that moment—because if I hadn't saved you, if your blood had been spilled there in front of me, I don't think I could have stopped myself from exposing us for what we are. But I only thought of that excuse later. At the time, all I could think was, *Not him.*"

She shut her eyes, her expression agonized. For a long moment she was silent. I waited eagerly, which probably wasn't the brightest reaction. But it was such a relief to finally understand the other half of the story.

"In the hospital?" I asked.

Her eyes flashed up to mine. "I was appalled. I couldn't believe I had put us in danger after all, put myself in your power—*you* of all people. As if I needed another motive to kill you." We both flinched as that word slipped out, and she continued quickly. "But the disaster had the opposite effect. I fought with Royal, El, and Jessamine when they suggested that now was the time . . . the worst fight we've ever had. Carine sided with me, and Archie." She frowned sourly when she said his name. I couldn't imagine why. "Earnest told me to do whatever I had to in order to stay." She shook her head, a little indulgent smile on her lips.

"All that next day I eavesdropped on the minds of everyone you spoke to, shocked that you kept your word. I didn't understand you at all. But I knew that I couldn't become more involved with you. I did my very best to stay as far from you as possible. And every day the perfume of your skin, your breath . . . it hit me as hard as the very first day."

She met my eyes again, and hers were oddly tender.

"And for all that," she continued, "I'd have fared better if I *had* exposed us all at that first moment, than if now, here—with no witnesses and nothing to stop me—I were to hurt you."

"Why?"

"Oh, Beau." She touched my cheekbone lightly with her fingertips. A shock ran through me at this casual contact. "Beau, I couldn't survive hurting you. You don't know how it's tortured me"—she looked down, ashamed again—"the thought of you, still, white, cold . . . to never see your face turn red again, to never see that flash of intuition in your eyes when you see through my pretenses . . . I couldn't bear it." She lifted her glorious,

agonized eyes to mine. "You are the most important thing to me now. The most important thing to me ever."

My head was spinning at this rapid change in direction. Just minutes ago I'd thought we were talking about my imminent death. Now, suddenly, we were making declarations.

I gripped her hand tighter, staring into her golden eyes.

"You already know how I feel. I'm here because I would rather die with you than live without you." I realized how melodramatic that sounded. "Sorry, I'm an idiot."

"You are an idiot," she agreed with a laugh, and I laughed with her. This whole situation was idiocy—and impossibility and magic.

"And so the lion fell in love with the lamb," she murmured. The word was like another electric jolt to my system.

I tried to cover my reaction. "What a stupid lamb."

She sighed. "What a sick, masochistic lion."

She stared into the forest for a long time, and I wondered what she was thinking.

"Why . . . ?" I began, but then paused, not sure how to continue.

She looked at me and smiled; sunlight shimmered off her face, her teeth. "Yes?"

"Tell me why you ran away from me before."

Her smile faded. "You know why."

"No, I mean, *exactly* what did I do wrong? I need to learn how to make this easier for you, what I should and shouldn't do. This, for example"—I stroked my thumb across her wrist—"seems to be all right."

"You didn't do anything wrong, Beau. It was my fault."

"But I want to help."

"Well . . ." She thought for a moment. "It was just how close you were. Most humans instinctively shy away from us, are repelled by our alienness. . . . I wasn't expecting you to come so close. And the smell of your *throat*—" She broke off, looking to see if she'd upset me.

"Okay." I tucked my chin. "No throat exposure."

She grinned. "No, really, it was more the surprise than anything else."

She raised her free hand and placed it gently on the side of my neck. I held very still, recognizing that the chill of her touch was supposed to be a

natural warning, and wondering why I couldn't feel that. I felt something else entirely.

"You see?" she said. "Perfectly fine."

My blood was racing, and I wished I could slow it down. It must make everything so much more difficult for her—the thudding pulse in my veins.

"I love that," she murmured. She carefully freed her other hand. My hands fell limp into my lap. Softly she brushed her hand across the warm patch in my cheek, then held my face between her small, cold hands.

"Be very still," she whispered.

I was paralyzed as she suddenly leaned into me, resting her cheek against my chest—listening to my heart. I could feel the ice of her skin through my thin shirt. With deliberate slowness her hands moved to my shoulders and her arms wrapped around my neck, holding me tight against her. I listened to the sound of her careful, even breathing, which seemed to be keeping time with my heartbeats. One breath in for every three beats, one breath out for another three.

"Ah," she said.

I don't know how long we sat without moving. It could have been hours. Eventually, the throb of my pulse quieted. I knew at any moment it could be too much, and my life could end—so quickly that I might not even notice. And I still wasn't afraid. I couldn't think of anything, except that she was touching me.

And then, too soon, she unwrapped her arms from around my neck and leaned away. Her eyes were peaceful again.

"It won't be so hard again," she said with satisfaction.

"Was that very hard for you?"

"Not nearly as bad as I imagined it would be. And you?"

"No, that wasn't . . . bad for me."

We smiled at each other.

"Here." She picked up my hand—easily, like she didn't even have to think about it—and placed it against her cheek. "Do you feel how warm you've made me?"

And it was almost warm, her usually icy skin. But I barely noticed, because I was touching her face, something I'd been dreaming and fantasizing about constantly since the first day I'd seen her.

"Don't move," I whispered.

No one could be still like a vampire. She closed her eyes and turned into a statue.

I moved even more slowly than she had, careful not to make one unexpected move. I stroked her cheek, let my fingertips graze across her lavender eyelids, the shadows in the hollows under her eyes. I traced the shape of her straight nose, and then, so carefully, her perfect lips. Her lips parted and I could feel her cool breath on my fingertips. I wanted to lean in, to inhale her scent, but I knew that might be too much. If she could control herself, so could I—if only on a much smaller scale.

I tried to move in slow motion so that she could guess everything I would do before I did it. I let my palms slide down the sides of her slender neck, let them rest on her shoulders while my thumbs followed the impossibly fragile curve of her collarbones.

She was much stronger than I was, in so many ways. I seemed to lose control of my hands as they skimmed over the points of her shoulders and down across her sharp shoulder blades. I couldn't stop myself as my arms wrapped around her, pulling her against my chest again. My hands crossed behind her and wrapped around either side of her waist.

She leaned into me, but that was the only movement. She wasn't breathing.

So that gave me a time limit.

I bent down to press my face into her hair for one long second, inhaling a deep lungful of her scent. Then I forced myself to peel my hands off her and move away. One of my hands wouldn't obey completely; it trailed down her arm and settled on her wrist.

"Sorry," I muttered.

She opened her eyes, and they were hungry. Not in a way to make me afraid, but in a way that made the muscles in the pit of my stomach tighten into knots and sent my pulse hammering through my veins again.

"I wish . . . ," she whispered, "I wish that you could feel the . . . complexity . . . the confusion . . . I feel. That you could understand."

She raised her hand to my face, then ran her fingers quickly through my hair.

"Tell me," I breathed.

"I don't know if I can. You know, on the one hand, the hunger—the thirst—that, being what I am, I feel for you. And I think you can understand

that, to an extent. Though"—and she half-smiled—"as you are not addicted to any illegal substances, you probably can't empathize completely.

"But . . ." Her fingers touched my lips lightly, and my heart raced. "There are other things I want, other hungers. Hungers I don't even understand myself."

"I might understand that better than you think."

"I'm not used to feeling so human. Is it always like this?"

"For me?" I paused. "No, never. Never before this."

She put her hands on both sides of my face. "I don't know how to be close to you. I don't know if I can."

I put my hand over hers, then leaned forward slowly till my forehead was touching hers.

"This is enough," I sighed, closing my eyes.

We sat like that for a moment, and then her fingers moved into my hair. She angled her face up and pressed her lips to my forehead. The rhythm of my pulse exploded into a jagged sprint.

"You're a lot better at this than you give yourself credit for," I said when I could speak again.

She leaned away, taking my hands again. "I was born with human instincts—they may be buried deep, but they exist."

We stared at each other for another immeasurable moment; I wondered if she was as unwilling to move as I was. But the light was fading, the shadows of the trees almost touching us.

"You have to go."

"I thought you couldn't read my mind."

She smiled. "It's getting clearer."

A sudden excitement flared in her eyes. "Can I show you something?"

"Anything."

She grinned. "How about a faster way back to the truck?"

I looked at her warily.

"Don't you want to see how *I* travel in the forest?" she pressed. "I promise it's safe."

"Will you . . . turn into a bat?"

She burst into laughter. "Like I haven't heard *that* one before!"

"Right, I'm sure you get that all the time."

She was on her feet in another invisibly fast motion. She offered me her hand, and I jumped up next to her. She whirled around and looked back at me over her shoulder.

"Climb on my back."

I blinked. "Huh?"

"Don't be a coward, Beau, I promise this won't hurt."

She stood there waiting with her back toward me, totally serious.

"Edythe, I don't . . . I mean, *how?*"

She spun back to me, one eyebrow raised. "Surely you're familiar with the concept of a piggyback ride?"

I shrugged. "Sure, but . . ."

"What's the problem, then?"

"Well . . . you're so *small.*"

She blew out an exasperated breath, then vanished. This time I felt the wind from her passage. A second later, she was back with a boulder in one hand.

An actual boulder. One that she must have ripped out of the ground, because the bottom half was covered in clinging dirt and spidery roots. It would be as high as her waist if she set it down. She tilted her head to one side.

"That's not what I meant. I'm not saying you're not *strong* enough—"

She flipped the boulder lightly over her shoulder, and it sailed well past the edge of the forest and then crashed down to earth with the sound of shattering wood and stone.

"Obviously," I went on. "But I . . . How would I fit?" I looked at my too-long legs and then back to her delicate frame.

She turned her back to me again. "Trust me."

Feeling like the stupidest, most awkward person in all of history, I hesitantly put my arms around her neck.

"Come on," she said impatiently. She reached back with one hand and grabbed my leg, yanking my knee up past her hip.

"Whoa!"

But she already had my other leg, and instead of toppling backward, she easily supported my weight. She moved my legs into position around her waist. My face was burning, and I knew I must look like a gorilla on a greyhound.

"Am I hurting you?"

"*Please*, Beau."

Embarrassed as I was, I was also very aware that my arms and legs were wrapped tightly around her slender body.

Suddenly she grabbed my hand and pressed my palm to her face. She inhaled deeply.

"Easier all the time," she said.

And then she was running.

For the first time, I felt actual fear for my life. Terror.

She streaked through the forest like a bullet, like a ghost. There was no sound, no evidence that her feet ever touched the ground. Her breathing never changed, never indicated any effort. But the trees flew by at deadly speeds, always missing us by inches.

I was too shocked to close my eyes, though the cool air whipped against my face and burned them. It felt like I was sticking my head out the window of an airplane in flight.

Then it was over. We'd hiked hours this morning to reach Edythe's meadow, and now, in a matter of minutes—not even minutes, *seconds*—we were back to the truck.

"Exhilarating, isn't it?" Her voice was high, excited.

She stood motionless, waiting for me to unwind my legs and step away from her. I did try, but I couldn't get my muscles to unfreeze. My arms and legs stayed locked while my head spun uncomfortably.

"Beau?" she asked, anxious now.

"I might need to lie down," I gasped.

"Oh. I'm sorry."

It took me a few seconds to remember how to loosen my fingers. Then everything seemed to come undone at the same time, and I half-fell off her, stumbling backward until I lost my footing and finished the other half of the fall.

She held out her hand, trying not to laugh, but I refused her offer. Instead, I stayed down and put my head between my knees. My ears were ringing and my head whirled in queasy circles.

A cold hand rested lightly against the back of my neck. It helped.

"I guess that wasn't the best idea," she mused.

I tried to be positive, but my voice was hollow. "No, it was very interesting."

"Hah! You're as white as a ghost—no, worse, you're as white as *me*!"

"I think I should have closed my eyes."

"Remember that next time."

I looked up, startled. "Next time?"

She laughed, her mood still flying.

"Show-off," I muttered, and put my head down again.

After a half-minute, the swirling motion slowed.

"Look at me, Beau."

I lifted my head, and she was right there, her face just inches from mine. Her beauty was like a sucker punch that left me stunned. I couldn't get used to it.

"I was thinking, while I was running—"

"About not hitting trees, I hope," I interrupted breathlessly.

"Silly Beau. Running is second nature to me. It's not something I have to think about."

"Show-off," I muttered again.

She smiled. "No, I was thinking there was something I wanted to try." She put her hands on my face again.

I couldn't breathe.

She hesitated. It felt like a test, making sure this was safe, that she was still in control of herself.

And then her cold, perfect lips pressed very softly against mine.

Neither of us was ready for my reaction.

Blood boiled under my skin, burned in my lips. My breath came in a wild gasp. My fingers tangled in her hair, locking her face to mine. My lips opened as I breathed in her heady scent.

Immediately, she turned to unresponsive stone beneath my lips. Her hands gently, but forcibly, pushed my face back. I opened my eyes and saw her expression.

"Whoops," I said.

"That's an understatement."

Her eyes were wild, her jaw clenched in restraint. My face was still just inches from hers, my fingers twisted through her hair.

"Should I . . . ?" I tried to disengage myself, to give her some room.

Her hands didn't release me.

"No, it's tolerable. Wait for a moment, please." Her voice was polite, controlled.

I kept my eyes on hers, watching as the excitement in them faded and gentled.

She grinned, obviously pleased with herself. "There."

"Tolerable?" I asked.

She laughed. "I'm stronger than I thought. It's nice to know."

"And I'm not. Sorry."

"You *are* only human, after all."

I sighed. "Yeah."

She freed her hair from my fingers, and then she was on her feet in one of her lithe, nearly invisible movements. She held her hand out again, and this time I took it and pulled myself up. I needed the support; my balance hadn't returned yet. I wobbled slightly as I took a step away from her.

"Are you still reeling from the run, or was it my kissing expertise?" She seemed very human as she laughed now, careless and lighthearted. She was a new Edythe, different than the one I'd known, and I was even more besotted by her. It would cause me physical pain to be separated from her now.

"Both."

"Maybe you should let me drive."

"Uh, I think I've had enough of your need for speed for today. . . ."

"I can drive better than you on your best day," she said. "You have much slower reflexes."

"I believe you, but I don't think my truck could handle your driving."

"Some trust, please, Beau."

My hand curled around the key in my pocket. I pursed my lips, like I was deliberating, then shook my head with a tight grin.

"Nope. Not a chance."

She raised her eyebrows, grabbed a fistful of my t-shirt, and yanked. I nearly stumbled into her, catching myself with one hand against her shoulder.

"Beau, I've already expended a great deal of personal effort at this point to keep you alive. I'm not about to let you get behind the wheel of a vehicle when you can't even walk straight. Friends don't let friends drive drunk."

"Drunk?" I objected.

She leaned up on her tiptoes so that her face was closer to mine. I could smell the unbearably sweet fragrance of her breath. "You're intoxicated by my very presence."

"I can't argue with that." I sighed. There was no way around it—I couldn't resist her in anything. I held the key high and dropped it, watching her hand flash like lightning to catch it without a sound. "Take it easy. My truck is a senior citizen."

"Very sensible."

She dropped my shirt and ducked out from under my hand.

"So you're not affected at all? By my presence?"

She turned back and reached for my hand, holding it to her face again. She leaned into my palm, her eyes sliding closed. She took a slow, deep breath.

"Regardless . . . ," she murmured. Her eyes flashed open and she grinned. "I have better reflexes."

14. MIND OVER MATTER

HER DRIVING WAS JUST FINE, I HAD TO ADMIT—WHEN SHE KEPT THE speed reasonable. Like so many things, it seemed to be effortless for her. She barely looked at the road, yet the truck was always perfectly centered in her lane. She drove one-handed, because I was holding her other hand between us. Sometimes she gazed into the setting sun, which glittered off her skin in ruby-tinged shimmers. Sometimes she glanced at me—stared into my eyes or looked down at our hands twined together.

She had tuned the radio to an oldies station, and she sang along with a song I'd never heard. Her voice was as perfect as everything else about her, soaring an octave above the melody. She knew every line.

"You like fifties music?" I asked.

"Music in the fifties was good. Much better than the sixties, or the seventies, ugh!" She shuddered delicately. "The eighties were bearable."

"Are you ever going to tell me how old you are?"

I wondered if my question would upset her buoyant mood, but she just smiled.

"Does it matter very much?"

"No, but I want to know everything about you."

"I wonder if it will upset you," she said to herself. She stared straight into the sun; a minute passed.

"Try me," I finally said.

She looked into my eyes, seeming to forget the road completely for a

while. Whatever she saw must have encouraged her. She turned to face the last bloodred rays of the dying sun and sighed.

"I was born in Chicago in 1901." She paused and glanced at me from the corner of her eye. My face was carefully arranged, unsurprised, patient for the rest. She smiled a tiny smile and continued. "Carine found me in a hospital in the summer of 1918. I was seventeen, and I was dying of the Spanish influenza."

She heard my gasp and looked up into my eyes again.

"I don't remember it very well. It was a long time ago, and human memories fade." She seemed lost in thought for a minute, but before I could prompt her, she went on. "I do remember how it felt when Carine saved me. It's not an easy thing, not something you could forget."

"Your parents?"

"They had already died from the disease. I was alone. That's why she chose me. In all the chaos of the epidemic, no one would ever realize I was gone."

"How did she . . . save you?"

A few seconds passed, and when she spoke again she seemed to be choosing her words very carefully.

"It was difficult. Not many of us have the restraint necessary to accomplish it. But Carine has always been the most humane, the most compassionate of all of us. . . . I don't think you could find her equal anywhere in history." She paused. "For me, it was merely very, very painful."

She set her jaw, and I could tell she wasn't going to say anything more about it. I filed it away for later. My curiosity on the subject was hardly idle. There were lots of angles I needed to think through on this particular issue, angles that were only beginning to occur to me.

Her soft voice interrupted my thoughts. "She acted from loneliness. That's usually the reason behind the choice. I was the first in Carine's family, though she found Earnest soon after. He fell from a cliff. They took him straight to the hospital morgue, though, somehow, his heart was still beating."

"So you have to be dying, then. . . ."

"No, that's just Carine. She would never do that to someone who had another choice, any other choice." The respect in her voice was profound whenever she spoke of her adoptive mother. "It is easier, she says, though, if the heart is weak." She stared at the now-dark road, and I could feel the subject closing again.

"And Eleanor and Royal?"

"Carine brought Royal into our family next. I didn't realize till much later that she was hoping he would be to me what Earnest was to her—she was careful with her thoughts around me." She rolled her eyes. "But he was never more than a brother. It was only two years later that he found Eleanor. He was hunting—we were in Appalachia at the time—and found a bear about to finish her off. He carried her back to Carine, more than a hundred miles, afraid he wouldn't be able to do it himself. I'm only beginning to guess how difficult that journey was for him." She threw a pointed glance in my direction and raised our hands, still folded together, to brush her cheek against my hand.

"But he made it."

"Yes. He saw something in her face that made him strong enough. And they've been together ever since. Sometimes they live separately from us, as a married couple. But the younger we pretend to be, the longer we can stay in any given place. Forks is perfect in many ways, so we all enrolled in high school." She laughed. "I suppose we'll have to go to the wedding in a few years. Again."

"Archie and Jessamine?"

"Archie and Jessamine are two very rare creatures. They both developed a *conscience*, as we refer to it, with no outside guidance. Jessamine belonged to another . . . family, a very different kind of family. She became depressed, and she wandered on her own. Archie found her. Like me, he has certain gifts."

"Really?" I interrupted, fascinated. "But you said you were the only one who could hear people's thoughts."

"That's true. He knows other things. He *sees* things—things that might happen, things that are coming. But it's very subjective. The future isn't set in stone. Things change."

Her jaw set when she said that, and her eyes darted to my face and away so quickly that I wasn't sure if I'd only imagined it.

"What kinds of things does he see?"

"He saw Jessamine and knew that she was looking for him before she knew it herself. He saw Carine, and our family, and they came together to find us. He's most sensitive to non-humans. He always knows, for example, when another group of our kind is coming near. And any threat they may pose."

"Are there a lot of . . . your kind?" I was surprised. How many of them could walk around with us all totally oblivious?

My mind got caught on one word she'd said. *Threat*. It was the first time

she'd ever said anything to hint that her world wasn't just dangerous for humans. It made me anxious, and I was about to ask a new question, but she was already answering my first.

"No, not many. But most won't settle in any one place. Only those like us, who've given up hunting you people"—a sly glance in my direction—"can live together with humans for any length of time. We've only found one other family like ours, in a small village in Alaska. We lived together for a time, but there were so many of us that we became too noticeable. Those of us who live . . . differently, tend to band together."

"And the others?"

"Nomads, for the most part. We've all lived that way at times. It gets tedious, like anything else. But we run across the others now and then, because most of us prefer the North."

"Why is that?"

We were parked in front of my house now, and she turned off the truck. The silence that followed its roar felt intense. It was very dark; there was no moon. The porch light was off, so I knew my dad wasn't home yet.

"Did you have your eyes open this afternoon?" she teased. "Do you think I could walk down the street in the sunlight without causing traffic accidents?"

I thought to myself that she could stop traffic even without all the pyrotechnics.

"There's a reason why we chose the Olympic Peninsula, one of the most sunless places in the world. It's nice to be able to go outside in the day. You wouldn't believe how tired you can get of nighttime in eighty-odd years."

"So that's where the legends came from?"

"Probably."

"And Archie came from another family, like Jessamine?"

"No, and that *is* a mystery. Archie doesn't remember his human life at all. And he doesn't know who created him. He awoke alone. Whoever made him walked away, and none of us understand why, or how, he could. If Archie hadn't had that other sense, if he hadn't seen Jessamine and Carine and known that he would someday become one of us, he probably would have turned into a total savage."

There was so much to think through, so much I still wanted to ask. But just then my stomach growled. I'd been so interested, I hadn't even noticed I was hungry. I realized now that I was starving.

"I'm sorry, I'm keeping you from dinner."

"I'm fine, really."

"I don't spend a lot of time around people who eat food. I forget."

"I want to stay with you." It was easier to say in the darkness, knowing how my voice would betray me, my hopeless addiction to her.

"Can't I come in?" she asked.

"Would you like to?" I couldn't picture it, a goddess sitting in my dad's shabby kitchen chair.

"Yes, if you don't mind."

I smiled. "I do not."

I climbed out of the truck and she was already there; then she flitted ahead and disappeared. The lights turned on inside.

She met me at the door. It was so surreal to see her inside my house, framed by the boring physical details of my humdrum life. I remembered a game my mother used to play with me when I was maybe four or five. *One of these things is not like the others.*

"Did I leave that unlocked?" I wondered.

"No, I used the key from under the eave."

I hadn't thought I'd used that key in front of her. I remembered how she'd found my truck key, and shrugged.

"You're hungry, right?" And she led the way to the kitchen, as if she'd been here a million times before. She turned on the kitchen light and then sat in the same chair I'd just tried to picture her in. The kitchen didn't look so dingy anymore. But maybe that was because I couldn't really look at anything but her. I stood there for a moment, trying to wrap my mind around her presence here in the middle of mundania.

"Eat something, Beau."

I nodded and turned to scavenge. There was lasagna left over from last night. I put a square on a plate, changed my mind, and added the rest that was in the pan, then set the plate in the microwave. I washed the pan while the microwave revolved, filling the kitchen with the smell of tomatoes and oregano. My stomach growled again.

"Hmm," she said.

"What's that?"

"I'm going to have to do a better job in the future."

I laughed. "What could you possibly do better than you already do?"

"Remember that you're human. I should have, I don't know, packed a picnic or something today."

The microwave dinged and I pulled the plate out, then set it down quickly when it burned my hand.

"Don't worry about it."

I found a fork and started eating. I was *really* hungry. The first bite scalded my mouth, but I kept chewing.

"Does that taste good?" she asked.

I swallowed. "I'm not sure. I think I just burned my taste buds off. It tasted good yesterday."

She didn't look convinced.

"Do you ever miss food? Ice cream? Peanut butter?"

She shook her head. "I hardly remember food. I couldn't even tell you what my favorites were. It doesn't smell . . . edible now."

"That's kind of sad."

"It's not such a huge sacrifice." She said it sadly, like there were other things on her mind, sacrifices that *were* huge.

I used the dish towel as a hot pad and carried the plate to the table so I could sit by her.

"Do you miss other parts about being human?"

She thought about that for a second. "I don't actually *miss* anything, because I'd have to remember it to be able to miss it, and like I said, my human life is hard to remember. But there are things I think I'd like. I suppose you could say things I was jealous of."

"Like what?"

"Sleep is one. Never-ending consciousness gets tedious. I think I'd enjoy temporary oblivion. It looks interesting."

I ate a few bites, thinking about that. "Sounds hard. What do you do all night?"

She hesitated, then pursed her lips. "Do you mean in general?"

I wondered why she sounded like she didn't want to answer. Was it too broad a question?

"No, you don't have to be general. Like, what are you going to do tonight after you leave?"

It was the wrong question. I could feel my high start to slip. She was going to have to leave. It didn't matter how short the separation was—I dreaded it.

She didn't seem to like the question, either, at first I thought for the same reason. But then her eyes flashed to my face and away, like she was uncomfortable.

"What?"

She made a face. "Do you want a pleasant lie or a possibly disturbing truth?"

"The truth," I said quickly, though I wasn't entirely sure.

She sighed. "I'll come back here after you and your father are asleep. It's sort of my routine lately."

I blinked. Then I blinked again.

"You come *here?*"

"Almost every night."

"Why?"

"You're interesting when you sleep," she said casually. "You talk."

My mouth popped open. Heat flashed up my neck and into my face. I knew I talked in my sleep, of course; my mother teased me about it. I hadn't thought it was something I needed to worry about here.

She watched my reaction, staring up at me apprehensively from under her lashes.

"Are you very angry with me?"

Was I? I didn't know. The potential for humiliation was strong. And I didn't understand—she'd been listening to me babble in my sleep from where? The window? I couldn't understand.

"How do you . . . Where do you . . . What did I . . . ?" I couldn't finish any of my thoughts.

She put her hand on my cheek. The blood under her fingers felt burning hot next to her cold hand. "Don't be upset. I didn't mean any harm. I promise, I was very much in control of myself. If I'd thought there was any danger, I would have left immediately. I just . . . wanted to be where you were."

"I . . . That's not what I'm worried about."

"What are you worried about?"

"What did I *say?*"

She smiled. "You miss your mother. When it rains, the sound makes you restless. You used to talk about home a lot, but it's less often now. Once you said, 'It's too *green.*'" She laughed softly, hoping not to offend me again.

"Anything else?" I demanded.

She knew what I was getting at. "You did say my name," she admitted.

I sighed in defeat. "A lot?"

"Define 'a lot.'"

"Oh no," I groaned.

Like it was easy, natural, she put her arms around my shoulders and leaned her head against my chest. Automatically, my arms came up to wrap around her. To hold her there.

"Don't be self-conscious," she whispered. "You already told me that you dream about me, remember?"

"That's different. I knew what I was saying."

"If I could dream at all, it would be about you. And I'm not ashamed of it."

I stroked her hair. I guessed I really didn't mind, when it came down to it. It wasn't like I expected her to follow normal human rules anyway. The rules she'd made for herself seemed like enough.

"I'm not ashamed," I whispered.

She hummed, almost like a purr, her cheek pressed over my heart.

Then we both heard the sound of tires on the brick driveway, saw the headlights flash through the front windows, down the hall to us. I jumped, and dropped my arms as she pulled away.

"Do you want your father to know that I'm here?" she asked.

I tried to think it through quickly. "Um . . ."

"Another time, then . . ."

And I was alone.

"*Edythe?*" I whispered.

I heard a quiet laugh, and then nothing else.

My father's key turned in the door.

"Beau?" he called. I remembered finding that funny before; who else would it be? Suddenly he didn't seem so far off base.

"In here."

Was my voice too agitated? I took another bite of my lasagna so I could be chewing when he came in. His footsteps sounded extra noisy after I'd spent the day with Edythe.

"Did you take all the lasagna?" he asked, looking at my plate.

"Oh, sorry. Here, have some."

"No worries, Beau. I'll make myself a sandwich."

"Sorry," I mumbled again.

Charlie banged around the kitchen getting what he needed. I worked on eating my giant plate of food as fast as was humanly possible while not choking to death. I was thinking about what Edythe had just said—*Do you want your father to know that I'm here?* Which was not the same as *Do you want your father to know that I was here?* in the past tense. So did that mean she hadn't actually left? I hoped so.

Sandwich in hand, Charlie sat in the chair across from me. It was hard to imagine Edythe sitting in the same place just minutes ago. Charlie fit. The memory of her was like a dream that couldn't possibly have been real.

"How was your day? Did you get everything done that you wanted to?"

"Um, not really. It was . . . too nice out to stay indoors. Were the fish biting?"

"Yep. They like the good weather, too."

I scraped the last of the lasagna into one huge mouthful and started chewing.

"Got plans for tonight?" he asked suddenly.

I shook my head, maybe a little too emphatically.

"You look kinda keyed up," he noted.

Of course he would have to pay attention tonight.

I swallowed. "Really?"

"It's Saturday," he mused.

I didn't respond.

"I guess you're missing that dance tonight. . . ."

"As intended," I said.

He nodded. "Sure, dancing, I get it. But maybe next week—you could take that Newton girl out for dinner or something. Get out of the house. Socialize."

"I told you, she's dating my friend."

He frowned. "Well, there're lots of other fish in the sea."

"Not at the rate you're going."

He laughed. "I do my best. . . . So you're not going out tonight?" he asked again.

"Nowhere to go," I told him. "Besides, I'm tired. I'm just going to go to bed early again."

I got up and took my plate to the sink.

"Uh-huh," he said, chewing thoughtfully. "None of the girls in town are your type, eh?"

I shrugged as I scrubbed the plate.

I could feel him staring at me, and I tried really hard to keep the blood out of my neck. I wasn't sure I was succeeding.

"Don't be too hard on a small town," he said. "I know we don't have the variety of a big city—"

"There's plenty of variety, Dad. Don't worry about me."

"Okay, okay. None of my business anyway." He sounded kind of dejected.

I sighed. "Well, I'm done. I'll see you in the morning."

"'Night, Beau."

I tried to make my footsteps drag as I walked up the stairs, like I was super tired. I wondered if he bought my bad acting. I hadn't actually lied to him or anything. I definitely wasn't planning on going out tonight.

I shut my bedroom door loud enough for him to hear downstairs, then sprinted as quietly as I could to the window. I shoved it open and leaned out into the dark. I couldn't see anything, just the shadow of the treetops.

"Edythe?" I whispered, feeling completely idiotic.

The quiet, laughing response came from behind me. "Yes?"

I spun around so fast I knocked a book off my desk. It fell with a thud to the floor.

She was lying across my bed, hands behind her head, ankles crossed, a huge dimpled smile on her face. She looked the color of frost in the darkness.

"Oh!" I breathed, reaching out to grab the desk for support.

"I'm sorry," she said.

"Just give me a second to restart my heart."

She sat up—moving slowly like she did when she was either trying to act human or trying not to startle me—and dangled her legs over the edge of the bed. She patted the space next to her.

I walked unsteadily to the bed and sat down beside her. She put her hand on mine.

"How's your heart?"

"You tell me—I'm sure you hear it better than I do."

She laughed quietly.

We sat there for a moment in silence, both listening to my heartbeat slow. I thought about Edythe in my room . . . and my father's suspicious questions . . . and my lasagna breath.

"Can I have a minute to be human?"

"Certainly."

I stood, and then looked at her, sitting there all perfect on the edge of my bed, and I thought that maybe I was just hallucinating everything.

"You'll be here when I get back, right?"

"I won't move a muscle," she promised.

And then she became totally motionless, a statue again, perched on the edge of my bed.

I grabbed my pajamas out of their drawer and hurried to the bathroom, banging the door so Charlie would know it was occupied.

I brushed my teeth twice. Then I washed my face and traded clothes. I always just wore a pair of holey sweatpants and an old t-shirt to bed—it was from a barbecue place that my mom liked, and it had a pig smiling between two buns. I wished I had something less . . . me. But I really hadn't been expecting guests, and then it was probably dumb to worry anyway. If she hung out here at night, she already knew what I wore to sleep.

I brushed my teeth one more time.

When I opened the door, I had another small heart attack. Charlie was at the top of the stairs; I almost walked into him.

"Huh!" I coughed out.

"Oh, sorry, Beau. Didn't mean to scare you."

I took a deep breath. "I'm good."

He looked at my pajamas, and then made a little *harrumph* sound in the back of his throat like he was surprised.

"You heading to bed, too?" I asked.

"Yeah, I guess. I've got an early one again tomorrow."

"Okay. 'Night."

"Yeah."

I walked into my room, glad that the bed wasn't visible from where Charlie was standing, then shut the door firmly behind me.

Edythe hadn't moved even a fraction of an inch. I smiled and her lips twitched; she relaxed, and she was suddenly human again. Or close enough. I went back to sit next to her. She twisted to face me, pulling her legs up and crossing them.

"I'm not sure how I feel about that shirt," she said. Her voice was so quiet that I didn't have any worries that Charlie would hear us.

"I can change."

She rolled her eyes. "Not you wearing it—its entire existence." She reached out and brushed her fingers across the smiling pig. My pulse spiked, but she politely ignored that. "Should he be so happy to be food?"

I had to grin. "Well, we don't know his side of the story, do we? He might have a reason to smile."

She looked at me like she was doubting my sanity.

I reached out to hold her hand. It felt really natural, but at the same time, I couldn't believe I was so lucky. What had I ever done to deserve this?

"Your dad thinks you might be sneaking out," she told me.

"I know. Apparently I look *keyed up*."

"Are you?"

"A little more than that, I think. Thank you. For staying."

"It's what I wanted, too."

My heart started beating . . . not faster exactly, but *stronger* somehow. For some reason I would never understand, she wanted to be with me.

Moving at human speed, she unfolded her legs and draped them across mine. Then she curled up against my chest again the way she seemed to prefer, with her ear against my heart, which was reacting probably more than was necessary. I folded my arms around her and pressed my lips to her hair.

"Mmm," she hummed.

"This . . . ," I murmured into her hair, ". . . is much easier than I thought it would be."

"Does it seem easy to you?" It sounded like she was smiling. She angled her face up, and I felt her nose trace a cold line up the side of my neck.

"Well," I said breathlessly. Her lips were brushing the edge of my jaw. "It seems to be easier than it was this morning, at least."

"Hmm," she said. Her arms slid over my shoulders and then wrapped around my neck. She pulled herself up until her lips were brushing my ear.

"Why is that"—my voice shook embarrassingly—"do you think?"

"Mind over matter," she breathed right into my ear.

A tremor ran down my body. She froze, then leaned carefully back. One hand brushed across the skin just under the sleeve of my t-shirt.

"You're cold," she said. I could feel the goose bumps rise under her fingertips.

"I'm fine."

She frowned and climbed back to her original position. My arms weren't willing to let her go. As she slid out of them, my hands stayed on her hips.

"Your whole body is shivering."

"I don't think that's from being cold," I told her.

We looked at each other for a second in the dark.

"I'm not sure what I'm allowed to do," I admitted. "How careful do I need to be?"

She hesitated. "It's not easier," she said finally, answering my earlier question. Her hand brushed across my forearm, and I felt goose bumps again. "But this afternoon . . . I was still undecided. I'm sorry, it was unforgivable for me to behave as I did."

"I forgive you," I murmured.

"Thank you." She smiled and then was serious as she looked down at the bumps on my arm. "You see . . . I wasn't sure if I was strong enough. . . ." She lifted my hand and pressed it to her cheek, still looking down. "And while there was still that possibility that I might be . . . overcome"—she breathed in the scent at my wrist—"I was . . . susceptible. Until I made up my mind that I *was* strong enough, that there was no possibility at all that I would . . . that I ever could . . ."

I'd never seen her struggle so hard for words. It was so *human*.

"So there's no possibility now?"

She looked up at me finally and smiled. "Mind over matter."

"Sounds easy," I said, grinning so that she knew I was teasing.

"Rather than *easy* I would say . . . *herculean, but possible.* And so . . . in answer to your other question . . ."

"Sorry," I said.

She laughed quietly. "Why do you apologize?" It was a rhetorical question, and she went on quickly, putting a finger to my lips just in case I felt like I needed to explain. "It is *not* easy, and so, if it is acceptable to you, I would prefer if you would . . . follow my lead?" She let her finger drop. "Is that fair?"

"Of course," I said quickly. "Whatever you want." As usual, I meant that literally.

"If it gets to be . . . too much, I'm sure I will be able to make myself leave."

I frowned. "I will make sure it's not too much."

"It will be harder tomorrow," she said. "I've had the scent of you in my head all day, and I've grown amazingly desensitized. If I'm away from you for any length of time, I'll have to start over again. Not quite from scratch, though, I think."

"Never go away," I suggested.

Her face relaxed into a smile. "That suits me. Bring on the shackles—I am your prisoner." While she spoke, she laced her cold fingers around my wrist like a manacle. "And now, if you don't mind, may I borrow a blanket?"

It took me a second. "Oh, um, sure. Here."

I reached behind her with my free hand and snagged the old quilt that was folded over the foot of my bed, then offered it to her. She dropped my wrist, took the blanket and shook it out, then handed it back to me.

"I'd be happier if I knew you were comfortable."

"I'm *very* comfortable."

"Please?"

Quickly, I threw the quilt over my shoulders like a cape.

She chuckled quietly. "Not exactly what I was thinking." She was already on her feet, rearranging the blanket over my legs and pulling it all the way up to my shoulders. Before I could understand what she was doing, she had climbed onto my lap again and nestled against my chest. The quilt made a barrier between any place that our skin might touch.

"Better?" she asked.

"I'm not sure about that."

"Good enough?"

"Better than that."

She laughed. I stroked her hair. That seemed careful.

"It's so strange," she said. "You read about something . . . you hear about it in other people's minds, you watch it happen to them . . . and it doesn't prepare you even in the slightest for experiencing it yourself. The glory of first love. It's more than I was expecting."

"Much more," I agreed fervently.

"And other emotions, too—jealousy, for example. I thought I understood that one clearly. I've read about it a hundred thousand times, seen actors portray it in a thousand plays and movies, listened to it in the minds around me daily—even felt it myself in a shallow way, wishing I had what I didn't. . . .

But I was *shocked*." She scowled. "Do you remember the day that McKayla asked you to the dance?"

I nodded, though that day was most memorable to me for a different reason. "The day you started talking to me again."

"I was stunned by the flare of resentment, almost fury, that I felt—I didn't recognize what it was at first. I didn't know jealousy could be so powerful . . . so painful. And then you refused her, and I didn't know why. It was more aggravating than usual that I couldn't just hear what you were thinking. Was there someone else? Was it simply for Jeremy's sake? I knew I had no right to care either way. I *tried* not to care.

"And then the line started forming."

I groaned, and she laughed.

"I waited," she went on, "more anxious than I should be to hear what you would say to them, to try to decipher your expressions. I couldn't deny the relief I felt, watching the annoyance on your face. But I couldn't be sure. I didn't know what your answer would have been, if I'd asked. . . ."

She looked up at me. "That was the first night I came here. I wrestled all night, watching you sleep, with the chasm between what I knew was *right*, moral, ethical, honorable, and what I *wanted*. I knew that if I continued to ignore you as I should, or if I left for a few years, till you were gone, that someday you would find someone you wanted, someone human like McKayla. It made me sad.

"And then"—her voice dropped to an even quieter whisper—"as you were sleeping, you said my name. You spoke so clearly, at first I thought you'd woken. But you rolled over restlessly and mumbled my name once more, and sighed. The emotion that coursed through me then was unnerving . . . staggering. And I knew I couldn't ignore you any longer."

She was quiet for a moment, probably listening to the uneven pounding of my heart.

"But jealousy . . . it's so irrational. Just now, when Charlie asked you about that annoying girl . . ."

"*That* made you jealous. Really?"

"I'm new at this. You're resurrecting the human in me, and everything feels stronger because it's fresh."

"Honestly, though, for that to bother you, after I have to hear that

Royal—male model of the year, Royal, Mr. Perfect, Royal—was meant for you. Eleanor or no Eleanor, how can I compete with that?"

Her teeth gleamed and her arms wove around my neck again. "There's no competition."

"That's what I'm afraid of." Tentatively, I folded my arms around her. "Is this okay?" I checked.

"Very." She sighed happily. "Of course Royal *is* beautiful in his way, but even if he wasn't like a brother to me, even if he didn't belong with Eleanor, he could never have one tenth, no, one hundredth of the attraction you hold for me." She was serious now, thoughtful. "For almost ninety years I've walked among my kind, and yours . . . all the time thinking I was complete in myself, not realizing what I was seeking. And not finding anything, because you weren't alive yet."

"It doesn't seem fair," I whispered into her hair. "I haven't had to wait at all. Why do I get off so easily?"

"You're right," she agreed. "I should make this harder for you, definitely." Her hand stroked my cheek. "You only have to risk your life every second you spend with me, surely that's not much. You only have to turn your back on nature, on humanity . . . what is that worth?"

"I'm not feeling deprived."

She turned her face into my chest and whispered, "Not yet."

"What—" I started, but then her body was suddenly motionless. I froze, but she was gone, my arms wrapped around the empty air.

"Lie down," she hissed, but I couldn't tell where she was in the darkness.

I threw myself back on the bed, shaking the quilt out and then rolling on my side, the way I usually slept. I heard the door crack open. Charlie was checking up on me. I breathed evenly, exaggerating the movement.

A long minute passed. I listened for the door to close. Suddenly Edythe was next to me. She lifted my arm and placed it over her shoulders as she burrowed herself closer to me.

"You're a terrible actor—I'd say that career path is out for you."

"There goes my ten-year plan," I muttered. My heart was being obnoxious. She could probably *feel* it as well as hear it, careening around inside my ribs like it might bust one of them.

She hummed a melody I didn't recognize. It reminded me of a lullaby. Then she paused. "Should I sing you to sleep?"

"Right," I laughed. "Like I could sleep with you here."

"You do it all the time," she reminded me.

"Not with you *here*," I disagreed, tightening my arm around her.

"You have a point. So if you don't want to sleep, what do you want to do, then?"

"Honestly? A lot of things. None of them careful."

She didn't say anything; it didn't sound like she was breathing. I went on quickly.

"But since I promised to be careful, what I'd like is . . . to know more about you."

"Ask me anything." I could hear that she was smiling now.

I sifted through my questions for the most important. "Why do you do it?" I asked. "I still don't understand why you work so hard to resist what you . . . *are*. Don't misunderstand, of course I'm glad that you do—I've never been happier to be alive. I just don't see why you would bother in the first place."

She answered slowly. "That's a good question, and you are not the first one to ask it. The others—the vast majority of our kind who are quite content with our lot—they, too, wonder at how we live. But you see, just because we've been . . . dealt a certain hand . . . it doesn't mean that we can't choose to rise above—to conquer the boundaries of a destiny that none of us wanted. To try to retain whatever essential humanity we can."

I lay still, feeling kind of awed. She was a better person than I would ever be.

"Did you fall asleep?" she murmured almost silently after a few minutes.

"No."

"Is that all you were curious about?"

I rolled my eyes. "Not quite."

"What else do you want to know?"

"Why can you read minds—why only you? And Archie, seeing the future and everything . . . why does that happen?"

I felt her shrug under my arm. "We don't really know. Carine has a theory . . . she believes that we all bring something of our strongest human traits with us into the next life, where they are intensified—like our minds, and our senses. She thinks that I must have already been very sensitive to the thoughts of those around me. And that Archie had some precognition, wherever he was."

"What did she bring into the next life, and the others?"

"Carine brought her compassion. Earnest brought his ability to love passionately. Eleanor brought her strength, Royal his . . . tenacity. Or you could call it pigheadedness," she chuckled. "Jessamine is very interesting. She was quite charismatic in her first life, able to influence those around her to see things her way. Now she is able to manipulate the emotions of those near her—calm down a room of angry people, for example, or excite a lethargic crowd, conversely. It's a very subtle gift."

I considered the impossibilities she described, trying to take it in. She waited patiently while I thought.

"So where did it all start? I mean, Carine changed you, and then someone must have changed her, and so on. . . ."

"Well, where did you come from? Evolution? Creation? Couldn't we have evolved in the same way as other species, predator and prey? Or, if you don't believe that all this world could have just happened on its own, which is hard for me to accept myself, is it so hard to believe that the same force that created the delicate angelfish with the shark, the baby seal and the killer whale, could create both our kinds together?"

"Let me get this straight—I'm the baby seal, right?"

"Correct." She laughed, and her fingers brushed across my lips. "Aren't you tired? It's been a rather long day."

"I just have a few million more questions."

"We have tomorrow, and the next day, and the next. . . ."

A feeling of euphoria, of pure bliss, filled up my chest until I thought I might explode. I couldn't imagine there was a drug addict in the world who wouldn't trade his favorite fix for this feeling.

It was a minute before I could talk again. "Are you sure you won't vanish in the morning? You are mythical, after all."

"I won't leave you," she promised solemnly, and that same feeling, even stronger than before, washed through me.

When I could speak, I said, "One more, then, tonight. . . ." And then the blood rushed up my neck. The darkness was no help. I was sure she could feel the heat.

"What is it?"

"Um, nope, forget it. I changed my mind."

"Beau, you can ask me anything."

I didn't speak, and she groaned.

"I keep thinking it will get less frustrating, not hearing your thoughts. But it just gets worse and *worse*."

"It's bad enough that you eavesdrop on my sleep-talking," I muttered.

"Please tell me?" she murmured, her velvet voice taking on that mesmerizing intensity that I never could resist.

I tried. I shook my head.

"If you don't tell me, I'll just assume it's something much worse than it is," she threatened.

"I shouldn't have brought it up," I said, then locked my teeth.

"Please?" Again in that hypnotic voice.

I sighed. "You won't get . . . offended?"

"Of course not."

I took a deep breath. "Well . . . so, obviously, I don't know a lot that's true about vampires"—the word slipped out accidentally, I was just thinking so hard about how to ask my question, and then I realized what I'd said and I froze.

"Yes?"

She sounded normal, like the word didn't mean anything.

I exhaled in relief.

"Okay, I mean, I just know the things you've told me, and it seems like we're pretty . . . different. Physically. You *look* human—only better—but you don't eat or sleep, you know. You don't need the same things."

"Debatable on some levels, but there are definitely truths in what you're saying. What's your question?"

I took a deep breath. "I'm sorry."

"Ask me."

I blurted it all out in a rush. "So I'm just an ordinary human guy, and you're the most beautiful girl I've ever seen, and I am just . . . overwhelmed by you, and a part of that, naturally, is that I'm *insanely* attracted to you, which I'm sure you can't have helped but notice, what with your being, like, super aware of my circulatory system, but what I don't know is, if it's like that for you. Or is it like sleeping and eating, which you don't need and I do—though I don't *want* them nearly as much as I want you? You said that Eleanor and Royal go off and live like a married couple, but does that even mean the same thing for

vampires? And this question is totally offside, completely not first date appropriate, and I'm sorry and you don't have to answer."

I sucked in a huge breath.

"Hmm . . . I would have said this was our second date."

"You're right."

She laughed. "Are you asking me about sex, Beau?"

My face got hot again. "Yes. I shouldn't have."

She laughed again. "I *did* climb into your bed, Beau. I believe that makes this line of inquiry quite understandable."

"You still don't have to answer."

"I told you that you could ask me anything." She paused, and then her voice was different. Kind of formal, like a teacher lecturing. "So . . . in the general sense—Sex and Vampires One-Oh-One. We all started out human, Beau, and most of those human desires are still there—just obscured behind more powerful desires. But we're not thirsty all the time, and we tend to form . . . very strong bonds. Physical as well as emotional. Royal and Eleanor are just like any human couple who are attracted to each other, by which I mean, very, very annoying for those of us who have to live with them, and even more so for the one who can hear their minds."

I laughed quietly, and she joined in.

"Awkward," I murmured.

"You have no idea," she said darkly, then sighed. "And now in the specific sense . . . Sex and Vampires One-Oh-Two, Beau and Edythe." She sighed again, more slowly this time. "I don't think . . . that would be possible for us."

"Because I would have to get too . . . close?" I guessed.

"That would be a problem, but that's not the *main* problem. Beau, you don't know how . . . well, *fragile* you are. I don't mean that as an insult to your manliness, anyone human is fragile to me. I have to mind my actions every moment that we're together so that I don't hurt you. I could kill you quite easily, simply by accident."

I thought about the first few times that she'd touched me, how cautiously she'd moved, how much it had seemed to frighten her. How she would ask me to move my hand, rather than just pulling hers out from under it . . .

Now she put her palm against my cheek.

"If I were too hasty . . . if I were at all distracted, I could reach out, meaning to touch your face, and crush your skull by mistake. You don't realize how incredibly *breakable* you are. I can never, never afford to lose any kind of control when I'm with you."

If her life were in my hands that way, would I have already killed her? I cringed at the thought.

"I think I could be *very* distracted by you," she murmured.

"I am never *not* distracted by you."

"Can I ask you something now—something potentially offensive?"

"It's your turn."

"Do you have any experience with sex and humans?"

I was a little surprised that my face didn't go hot again. It felt natural to tell her everything. "Not even a little bit. This is all firsts for me. I told you, I've never felt like this about anyone before, not even close."

"I know. It's just that I hear what other people think. I know that love and lust don't always keep the same company."

"They do for me."

"That's nice. We have that one thing in common, at least."

"Oh." When she'd been talking before, about how *we tend to form very strong bonds, physical as well as emotional,* I couldn't help but wonder if she was speaking from experience. I found that I was surprisingly relieved to know that wasn't the case.

"So, you *do* find me distracting?"

"Indeed." She was smiling again. "Would you like me to tell you the things that distract me?"

"You don't have to."

"It was your eyes first. You have lovely eyes, Beau, like a sky without clouds. I've spent all my life in rainy climates and so I often miss the sky, but not when I'm with you."

"Er, thanks?"

She giggled. "I'm not alone. Six of your ten admirers started with your eyes, too."

"*Ten?*"

"They're not all so forward as Taylor and McKayla. Do you want a list? You have options."

"I think you're making fun of me. And either way, there is no other option." And never would be again.

"Next it was your arms—I'm *very* fond of your arms, Beau—this includes your shoulders and hands." She ran her hand down my arm, then back up to my shoulder, and back down to my hand again. "Or maybe it was your chin that was second . . ." Her fingers touched my face, like she thought I might not know what she meant. "I'm not entirely sure. It all took me quite by surprise when I realized that not only did I find you delicious, but also beautiful."

My face and neck were burning. I knew it couldn't be true, but in the moment, she was pretty convincing.

"Oh, and I didn't even mention your *hair*." Her fingernails combed against my scalp.

"Okay, now I *know* you're making fun."

"I'm truly not. Did you know your hair is just precisely the same shade as a teak inlaid ceiling in a monastery I once stayed at in . . . I think it would be Cambodia now?"

"Um, no, I did not." I yawned involuntarily.

She laughed. "Did I answer your question to your satisfaction?"

"Er, yes."

"Then you should sleep."

"I'm not sure if I can."

"Do you want me to leave?"

"No!" I said a little too loudly.

She laughed, then began to hum that same unfamiliar lullaby—her voice was like an angel's, soft in my ear.

More tired than I realized, exhausted from a day of mental and emotional stress like I'd never felt before, I drifted to sleep with her cold body in my arms.

15. THE CULLENS

THE MUTED LIGHT OF ANOTHER CLOUDY DAY EVENTUALLY WOKE ME. I lay with my arm across my eyes, groggy and dazed. Something, a dream trying to be remembered, struggled to break into my consciousness. I moaned and rolled on my side, hoping more sleep would come. And then yesterday came flooding back into my memory.

"Oh!" I sat up so fast it made my head spin.

"Your hair also has the ability to defy gravity." Her amused voice came from the rocking chair in the corner. "It's like your own superpower."

Automatically, I reached up to pat my hair down.

She sat crossed-legged in the chair, a perfect smile on her perfect face.

"You stayed." It was like I hadn't woken up after all.

"Of course. That's what you wanted, correct?"

I nodded.

She smiled wider. "It's what I wanted, too."

I staggered out of the bed, not sure where I was going, only that I needed to be closer to her. She waited for me, and there was no surprise in her face when I sank to my knees in front of her. I reached up slowly and laid my palm against the side of her face. She leaned into my hand, her eyes slipping closed.

"Charlie?" I asked. We'd both been speaking at normal volume.

"He left an hour ago, with an amazing amount of gear."

He'd be gone all day. So it was just me and Edythe, in an empty house,

with no need to go anywhere. So much time. I felt like some crazy old miser, gloating over his piles of gold coins, only instead of coins, it was seconds that I hoarded.

It was only then that I realized she'd changed her clothes. Instead of the thin-strapped tank top, she wore a peach-colored sweater.

"You left?" I asked.

She opened her eyes and smiled, putting one of her hands up to keep mine against her face. "I could hardly leave in the clothes I came in—what would the neighbors think? In any case, I was only gone for a few minutes and you were very deeply asleep at that point, so I know I didn't miss anything."

I groaned. "What did I say?"

Her eyes got a little wider, her face more vulnerable. "You said you loved me," she whispered.

"You already knew that."

"It was different, hearing the words."

I stared into her eyes. "I love you," I said.

She leaned down and rested her forehead carefully against mine. "You are my life now."

We sat like that for a long time, until finally my stomach grumbled. She sat up, laughing.

"Humanity is *so* overrated," I complained.

"Should we begin with breakfast?"

I threw my free hand over my jugular, my eyes wild.

She flinched; then her eyes narrowed and she scowled at me.

I laughed. "Come on, you know that was funny."

She was still frowning. "I disagree. Shall I rephrase? Breakfast time for the human?"

"Okay. I need another human minute first, if you don't mind."

"Of course."

"Stay."

She smiled.

I brushed my teeth twice again, then rushed through my shower. I ripped through my wet hair with a comb, trying to make it lie flat. It ignored me pretty thoroughly. And then I hit a wall. I'd forgotten to bring clothes with me.

I hesitated for a minute, but I was too impatient to panic long. There was

no help for it. I tucked the towel securely around my waist and then marched into the hall with my face blazing red. Even better—the patch of red on my chest was exposed, too. I stuck my head around the edge of the doorframe.

"Um . . ."

She was still in the rocking chair. She laughed at my expression.

"Shall we meet in the kitchen, then?"

"Yes, please."

She was past me in a rush of cool air, down the stairs before a second had passed. I was barely able to follow the motion—she was just a streak of pale color, then nothing.

"Thanks," I called after her, then hurried to my dresser.

I knew I should probably put some thought into what I wore, but I was in a hurry to get downstairs. I did think to grab a pullover, so she wouldn't worry about me getting cold.

I raked my fingers through my hair to calm it again, then ran down the stairs.

She was leaning against the counter, looking very at home.

"What's for breakfast?" I asked.

That threw her for a minute. Her brows pulled together. "I'm not sure. . . . What would you like?"

I laughed. "That's all right, I fend for myself pretty well. You're allowed to watch *me* hunt."

I got a bowl and a box of cereal. She returned to the chair she'd sat in last night, watching as I poured the milk and grabbed a spoon. I set my food on the table, then paused. The empty space in front of her on the table made me feel rude.

"Um, can I . . . get you anything?"

She rolled her eyes. "Just eat, Beau."

I sat at the table, watching her as I took a bite. She was gazing at me, studying my every movement. It made me self-conscious. I swallowed so I could speak, wanting to distract her.

"Anything on the agenda today?"

"Maybe," she said. "That depends on whether or not you like my idea."

"I'll like it," I promised as I took a second bite.

She pursed her lips. "Are you open to meeting my family?"

I choked on my cereal.

She jumped up, one hand stretched toward me helplessly, probably thinking about how she could crush my lungs if she tried to give me the Heimlich. I shook my head and motioned for her to sit while I coughed the milk out of my windpipe.

"I'm good, I'm good," I said when I could speak.

"Please don't do that to me again, Beau."

"Sorry."

"Maybe we should have this conversation after you're done eating."

"Okay." I needed a minute anyway.

She was apparently serious. And I guess I'd already met Archie and it hadn't been that bad. And Dr. Cullen, too. But that had been back before I'd known Dr. Cullen was a vampire, which changed things. And while I *had* known with Archie, I didn't know if he knew that I knew, and that felt like kind of an important distinction to me. Also, Archie was the most *supportive*, according to Edythe.

There were others who were obviously not as generous.

"I've finally done it," she murmured when I swallowed the last bite and pushed the bowl away.

"What did you do?"

"Scared you."

I thought about that for a moment, then held up my hand, fingers spread, and waved it from side to side in the international symbol for *Kinda, yeah.*

"I wouldn't let anyone hurt you," she assured me.

But that just made me worry more that someone—Royal—would want to, and she would get in between to rescue me. I didn't care what she said about holding her own and not fighting fair, that idea really freaked me out.

"No one would try, Beau, that was a joke."

"I don't want to cause you any problems. Do they even know that I know?"

She rolled her eyes. "Oh, they're quite up to date. It's not really possible to keep secrets in my house, what with our various parlor tricks. Archie had already seen that your dropping by was a possibility."

I could feel a variety of expressions rippling across my face before I could control it. What all did Archie *see*? Yesterday . . . last night . . . My face got hot.

I saw her eyes narrow the way they did when she was trying to read my mind.

"Just thinking about what Archie might have seen," I explained before she could ask.

She nodded. "It can feel invasive. But he doesn't do it on purpose. And he sees so many different possibilities . . . he doesn't know which will happen. For example, he saw over a hundred different ways that yesterday *could* have gone, and you only survived about seventy-five percent of the scenarios." Her voice got very hard at the last part, her posture brittle. "They'd taken bets, you know, as to whether I would kill you."

"Oh."

Her expression was still rigid. "Do you want to know who sided for and against?"

"Um, maybe not. Tell me after I meet them. I don't want to go into this prejudiced."

Surprise erased the anger from her face. "Oh. You'll go, then?"

"It seems like . . . the respectful thing to do. I don't want them to think I'm shady."

She laughed, a long, bell-like peal. I couldn't help but smile.

"Does that mean I get to meet Charlie, too, then?" she asked eagerly. "He's already suspicious, and I'd rather not be *shady*, either."

"I mean, sure, but what should we tell him? I mean, how do I explain . . . ?"

She shrugged. "I doubt he'll struggle *too* hard with the idea of your having a girlfriend. Though it's a loose interpretation of the word *girl*, I'll admit."

"*Girlfriend*," I mumbled. "It sounds . . . not enough." Mostly, it sounded transitory. Something that didn't last.

She stroked one finger down the side of my face. "Well, I don't know if we need to give him all the gory details, but he will need some explanation for why I'm around here so much. I don't want Chief Swan putting a restraining order on me."

"Will you really be here?" I asked, suddenly anxious. It seemed too good to be true, something only a fool would count on.

"As long as you want me."

"I'll always want you," I warned her. "I'm talking about forever here."

She put her fingers against my lips, and her eyes closed. It was almost like she wished I hadn't said that.

"Does that make you . . . sad?" I asked, trying to put a name to the expression on her face. *Sad* seemed closest.

Her eyes opened slowly. She didn't answer, she just stared into my eyes for a long time. Finally she sighed.

"Shall we?"

I glanced at the clock on the microwave automatically. "Isn't it a little ear—wait, forget I asked that."

"Forgotten."

"Is this okay?" I wondered, gesturing to my clothes. Should I dress up more?

"You look . . ." She suddenly dimpled up. "Delicious."

"So you're saying I should change?"

She laughed and shook her head. "Never change, Beau."

Then she stood and took a step toward me, so that her knees were pressed against mine. She put her hands on either side of my face and leaned down till her face was just an inch from mine.

"Carefully," she reminded me.

She tilted her head to the side and closed the distance between us. With the lightest pressure, her lips touched mine.

Carefully! I shouted in my head. *Just don't move.* My hands balled into fists. I knew she would feel the blood pulsing into my face.

Slowly, her lips moved against mine. As she got more sure of herself, her lips were firmer. I felt them part slightly, and her breath washed cool across my mouth. I didn't inhale. I knew how her scent made me do stupid things.

Her fingers stroked from my temples to my chin, and then hooked under my jaw and pulled my lips tighter to hers.

Careful! I shouted at myself.

And then, out of nowhere, the dizzy, hollow ringing sound started up in my ears. At first I couldn't concentrate on anything but her lips, but then I started to fall down the tunnel and her lips were getting farther and farther away.

"Beau? Beau?"

"Hey," I tried to say.

"What happened? Are you all right?" The sound of her anxiety helped

bring me around. I wasn't totally gone, so it was fairly easy. I took two deep breaths and opened my eyes.

"I'm fine," I told her. She was leaning away, but her arms were stretched out to me; one hand was cold on my forehead, the other on the back of my neck. Her face looked paler than usual. "Just . . . kind of forgot to breathe for a minute there. Sorry." I took another deep breath.

She eyed me doubtfully. "You forgot to breathe?"

"I was trying to be careful."

Suddenly she was angry. "What am I supposed to *do* with you, Beau? Yesterday, I kiss you, and you attack me! Today, you pass out!"

"Sorry."

She sighed deeply, then darted in suddenly to kiss my forehead. "It's a good thing that it's physically impossible for me to have a heart attack," she grumbled.

"That *is* good," I agreed.

"I can't take you anywhere like this."

"No, I'm fine, really. Totally back to normal. Besides, your family is going to think I'm insane anyway, so what's the difference if I'm a little unsteady?"

She frowned. "You mean more unsteady than usual?"

"Sure. Look, I'm trying not to think about what we're going to do now, so it would help if we could get going."

She shook her head but took my hand and pulled me out of the chair.

This time she didn't even ask, she just headed straight for the driver's side of my truck. I figured there was no point in arguing after my latest embarrassing episode, and anyway, I had no idea where she lived.

She drove respectfully, without any complaints about what my truck could handle. She took us north out of town, over the bridge at the Calawah River, and continued till we were past all the houses and on to close-packed trees. I was starting to wonder how far we were going when she abruptly steered right onto an unpaved road. The turnoff was unmarked, and almost totally hidden by thick ferns. The trees leaned close on both sides, so you could only see a few yards ahead before the road twisted out of sight.

We drove down this road for a least a few miles, mostly east. I was trying to fit this lane into the vague map I had in my head, not very successfully,

when there was suddenly some thinning of the forest. She drove into a meadow . . . or was it a lawn? It didn't get much brighter, though. There were six enormous cedars—maybe the biggest trees I'd ever seen—whose branches shaded an entire acre. They pushed right up against the house in the middle of the lawn—hiding it.

I don't know what I expected, but it definitely wasn't this. The house was probably a hundred years old, three stories high and kind of . . . *graceful*, if that word could be applied to a house. It was painted a soft, faded white and all the windows and doors looked original, but they were probably in too good shape for that to be true. My truck was the only car in sight. When Edythe shut off the engine, I could hear the sound of a river somewhere close by.

"Wow."

"You like it?"

"It's . . . really something."

Suddenly she was outside my door. I opened it slowly, starting to feel the nerves I'd been trying to suppress.

"Are you ready?"

"Nope. Let's do this."

She laughed, and I tried to laugh with her, but the sound seemed to get stuck in my throat. I mashed my hair flat.

"You look great," she said, then took my hand casually, like she didn't even have to think about it anymore. It wasn't a big thing, but it distracted me—made me feel just a little bit less panicky.

We walked through the deep shade up to the porch. I knew she could feel my tension. She reached across her body to put her free hand on my forearm for a second. Then she opened the front door and walked inside, towing me behind her.

The inside was even less like what I was expecting than the outside. It was very bright, very open, and very big. It must have started out as several rooms, but most of the walls had been removed from the first floor to create one wide space. The back, south-facing wall had been entirely replaced with glass. Past the cedars the lawn was open, and it stretched down to a wide river. A massive staircase dominated the west side of the room. The walls, the high ceiling, the wooden floors, and the thick carpets were all different shades of white.

Edythe's parents were waiting for us. They stood just to the left of the door on a little platform in front of a huge grand piano. It was also white.

I'd seen Dr. Cullen before, of course, but it hit me again how young she was, and how outrageously beautiful. She was holding hands with Earnest, I assumed—he was the only one of the family I'd never seen before. He seemed about the same age as Dr. Cullen, maybe a few years older, and had the same pale, perfect features as the rest of them. He had wavy hair, the color of caramel, a few inches longer than mine. There was something really . . . *kind* about his face, but I couldn't put my finger on what it was that made me think that. They were both dressed casually in light colors that matched the inside of the house.

They smiled, but made no move to approach. I thought they were probably trying not to scare me.

"Carine, Earnest, this is Beau," Edythe said.

"You're very welcome, Beau." Carine stepped forward, slow and careful. She raised her hand hesitantly. I stepped forward to shake, and I was kind of surprised by how okay it felt to do that. Maybe it was because she reminded me of Edythe in a lot of ways.

"It's nice to see you again, Dr. Cullen."

"Please, call me Carine."

I grinned at her, surprised that I felt pretty confident. "Carine," I repeated. Edythe squeezed my hand lightly.

Earnest stepped forward as well, offering his hand. His cold, stone grasp was just what I expected.

"It's very nice to know you," he said sincerely.

"Thank you, I'm glad to meet you, too." And I was. This felt right. This was Edythe's home, her family. It was good to be a part of it.

"Where are Archie and Jess?" Edythe asked.

No one answered, because they'd just appeared at the top of the stairs.

"Hey, Edy's home!" Archie called, and then he streaked down the stairs, just a blur of pale skin, coming to a sudden stop right in front of us. I saw Carine and Earnest shoot warning glances at him, but I kind of liked it. It was natural for him—how they moved when they didn't have to worry about strangers watching.

"Beau!" he greeted me, enthusiastic like we were old friends. He held out

his hand, and when I went to shake it, he pulled me into one of those one-armed bro-hugs, thumping me lightly on the back.

"Hey, Archie," I said; my voice sounded winded. I was shocked, but also a little pleased that he really did seem supportive—more than that, like he already *liked* me.

When he stepped back, I saw that I wasn't the only one who was shocked. Carine and Earnest were watching my face with wide eyes, like they were waiting for me to make a run for it. Edythe's jaw was locked, but I couldn't tell if she was worried or mad.

"You do smell good, I never noticed before," Archie commented. My face got hot, and then hotter when I thought what that must look like to *them*, and nobody seemed to know what to say.

Then Jessamine was there. Edythe had compared herself to a hunting lion, which was hard for me to picture, but I could easily picture Jessamine that way. There was something like a lion about her now, when she was just standing there. But despite that, I was suddenly totally comfortable. It felt like I was in my own place surrounded by people I knew well. Easy—kind of like when Jules was around. It was strange to feel that here, and then I remembered what Edythe had told me about what Jessamine could do. That was weird to think about. It didn't *feel* like someone was using magic or whatever on me.

"Hello, Beau," Jessamine said. She didn't approach or offer to shake my hand, but it didn't feel awkward.

"Hello, Jessamine." I smiled at her, and then the others. "It's nice to meet you all—you have a very beautiful home," I added conventionally.

"Thank you," Earnest said. "We're so glad that you came." He spoke with feeling, and I realized that he thought I was brave.

I also realized that Royal and Eleanor were nowhere to be seen, and while I was relieved, I was also kind of disappointed. It would have been nice to get that out of the way with Jessamine here, making me feel calm.

I noticed Carine gazing meaningfully at Edythe with a pretty intense expression. Out of the corner of my eye, I saw Edythe nod just slightly.

I felt like I was eavesdropping, so I looked away. My eyes wandered over to the beautiful piano on the platform. I suddenly remembered a childhood fantasy that, when I was older and somehow a millionaire, I was going to

buy a grand piano for my mother. She wasn't really good—she only played for herself on our secondhand upright—but I loved to watch her play. She was happy, absorbed—she seemed like a new, mysterious person to me then. She'd put me in lessons, of course, but like most kids, I whined until she let me quit.

Earnest noticed my stare.

"Do you play?" he asked.

I shook my head. "Not at all. But it's really beautiful. Is it yours?"

"No," he laughed. "Didn't Edythe tell you she was musical?"

"Uh, she hasn't mentioned it. But I guess I should have known, right?"

Earnest raised his eyebrows, confused.

"Is there anything she's not good at?" I asked rhetorically.

Jessamine barked out a laugh, Archie rolled his eyes, and Earnest gave Edythe a very fatherly look, which was impressive considering how young he seemed.

"I hope you haven't been showing off," he said. "It's rude."

"Oh, just a little bit." Edythe laughed—the sound was infectious, and everyone smiled, including me. Earnest smiled the widest, though, and he and Edythe shared a brief look.

"Edythe, you should play for him," Earnest said.

"You just said showing off was rude."

"Make an exception." He smiled at me. "I'm being selfish. She doesn't play enough, and I love to hear her."

"I'd like to hear you play," I told her.

She gave Earnest a long, exasperated look, then turned the same look on me. When that was done, she dropped my hand and walked up to sit on the bench. She patted the spot next to her and then looked back at me.

"Oh," I mumbled, and went to join her.

As soon as I sat down, her fingers started flowing across the keys, filling the room with a piece so complex and full it was impossible to believe only one person was playing. My mouth fell open in shock, and I heard chuckling behind me.

Edythe looked at me casually while the music surged around us without a break. "Do you like it?"

I got it immediately. Of course. "You wrote this."

She nodded. "It's Earnest's favorite."

I sighed.

"What's wrong?"

"I'm just . . . feeling a little insignificant."

She thought about that for a minute, and then the music changed slowly into something softer . . . something familiar. It was the lullaby she'd hummed to me, only a thousand times more intricate.

"I thought of this one," she said quietly, "while I watched you sleeping. It's *your* song."

The song turned even softer and sweeter. I couldn't speak.

Then her voice was normal again. "They like you quite a bit, you know. Earnest especially."

I glanced behind me, and the big room was empty.

"Where did they go?"

"Giving us some privacy. Subtle, aren't they?"

I laughed, then frowned. "It's nice that they like me. I like *them*. But Royal and Eleanor . . ."

Her expression tightened. "Don't worry about Royal. He's always the last to come around."

"Eleanor?"

She laughed sharply. "El thinks *I'm* a lunatic, it's true, but she doesn't have a problem with you. She's off trying to reason with Royal now."

"What did I do?" I had to ask. "I mean, I've never even spoken to—"

"You didn't do anything, Beau, honestly. Royal struggles the most with what we are. It's hard for him to have someone on the outside know the truth. And he's a little jealous."

"*Hah!*"

She shrugged. "You're human. He wishes he were, too."

That brought me up short. "Oh."

I listened to the music, my music. It kept changing and evolving, but the heart of it stayed the same. I wasn't sure how she did it. She didn't seem to be paying much attention to her hands.

"That thing Jessamine does feels really . . . *not* strange, I guess. It was kind of incredible."

She laughed. "Words don't fully do it justice, do they?"

"Not really. But . . . does she like me? She seemed . . ."

"That was my fault. I told you she was the most recent to try our way of life. I warned her to keep her distance."

"Oh."

"Indeed."

I worked hard not to shudder.

"Carine and Earnest think you're wonderful," she told me.

"Huh. I really didn't do anything very exciting. Shook a few hands."

"They're happy to see me happy. Earnest probably wouldn't care if you had a third eye and webbed feet. All this time he's been worrying about me, afraid I was too young when Carine changed me, that there was something missing from my essential makeup. He's so relieved. Every time I touch you, he practically bursts into applause."

"Archie's enthusiastic."

She made a face. "Archie has his own special perspective on life."

I looked at her for a moment, weighing her expression.

"What?" she asked.

"You're not going to explain what you mean by that, are you?"

Her eyes narrowed as she stared back at me, and a moment of wordless communication passed between us—almost like what I'd seen between her and Carine before, except without the benefit of mind reading. I knew she wasn't telling me something about Archie, something her attitude toward him had been hinting at for a long time. And she knew that I knew, but she wasn't going to give anything away. Not now.

"Okay," I said, like we'd spoken all that out loud.

"Hmm," she said.

And because I'd just thought of it . . . "So what was Carine telling you before?"

She was looking at the keys now. "You noticed that, did you?"

I shrugged. "Of course."

She stared at me thoughtfully for a moment before she answered. "She wanted to tell me some news. She didn't know if it was something I would share with you."

"Will you?"

"It's probably a good idea. My behavior might be a little . . . odd for the next few days—or weeks. A little maniacal. So it's best if I explain myself beforehand."

"What's wrong?"

"Nothing's wrong, exactly. Archie just sees some visitors coming soon. They know we're here, and they're curious."

"Visitors?"

"Yes . . . like us, but not. Their hunting habits are not like ours, I mean. They probably won't come into town at all, but I won't be letting you out of my sight till they're gone."

"Wow. Shouldn't we . . . I mean, is there a way to warn people?"

Her face was serious and sad. "Carine will ask them not to hunt nearby, as a courtesy, and most likely they won't have a problem with that. But we can't do more, for a variety of reasons." She sighed. "They won't be hunting here, but they'll be hunting somewhere. That's just how things are when you live in a world with monsters."

I shivered.

"Finally, a rational response," she murmured. "I was beginning to think you had no sense of self-preservation at all."

I let that one pass, looking away, my eyes wandering again around the big white room.

"It's not what you expected, is it?" she asked, and her voice was amused again.

"No," I admitted.

"No coffins, no piled skulls in the corners; I don't even think we have cobwebs . . . what a disappointment this must be for you."

I ignored her teasing. "I didn't expect it to be so light and so . . . open."

She was more serious when she answered. "It's the one place we never have to hide."

My song drifted to an end, the final chords shifting to a more melancholy key. The last note lingered for a long moment, and something about the sound of that single note was so sad that a lump formed in my throat.

I cleared it out, then said, "Thank you."

It seemed like the music had affected her, too. She stared searchingly at me for a long moment, and then she shook her head and sighed.

"Would you like to see the rest of the house?" she asked.

"Will there be piled skulls in any corners?"

"Sorry to disappoint."

"Well, okay, but my expectations are pretty low now."

We walked up the wide staircase hand in hand. My free hand trailed along the satin-smooth rail. The hall at the top of the stairs was paneled in wood the same pale color as the floorboards.

She gestured as we passed the doors. "Royal and Eleanor's room . . . Carine's office . . . Archie's room . . ."

She would have continued, but I stopped dead at the end of the hall, staring with raised eyebrows at the ornament hanging on the wall above my head. Edythe laughed at my expression.

"Ironic, I know," she said.

"It must be very old," I guessed. I kind of wanted to touch it, to see if the dark patina was as silky as it looked, but I could tell it was pretty valuable.

She shrugged. "Early sixteen-thirties, more or less."

I looked away from the cross to stare at her.

"Why do you have this here?"

"Nostalgia. It belonged to Carine's father."

"He collected antiques?"

"No. He carved this himself. It hung on the wall above the pulpit in the vicarage where he preached."

I turned back to stare at the cross while I did the mental math. The cross was over three hundred and seventy years old. The silence stretched on as I struggled to wrap my mind around the concept of so many years.

"Are you all right?" she asked.

"How old is Carine?" I asked quietly, still staring up.

"She just celebrated her three hundred and sixty-second birthday," Edythe said. She watched my expression carefully as she continued, and I tried to pull it together. "Carine was born in London in the sixteen-forties, she believes. Time wasn't marked as accurately then, for the common people anyway. It was just before Cromwell's rule, though."

The name pulled up a few disjointed facts in my head, from a World History class I'd had last year. I should have paid more attention.

"She was the only daughter of an Anglican pastor. Her mother died in

childbirth. Her father was . . . a hard man. Driven. He believed very strongly in the reality of evil. He led hunts for witches, werewolves . . . and vampires."

It was strange how the word shifted things, made the story sound less like a history lesson.

"They burned a lot of innocent people—of course, the real creatures that he sought were not so easy to catch.

"Carine did what she could to protect those innocents. She was always a believer in the scientific method, and she tried to convince her father to look past superstition to true evidence. He discouraged her involvement. He did love her, and those who defended monsters were often lumped in with them.

"Her father was persistent . . . and obsessive. Against the odds, he tracked some evidence of real monsters. Carine begged him to be careful, and he listened, to an extent. Rather than charge in blindly, he waited and watched for a long time. He spied on a coven of true vampires who lived in the city sewers, only coming out by night to hunt. In those days, when monsters were not just myths and legends, that was the way many lived.

"His people gathered their pitchforks and torches, of course"—she laughed darkly—"and waited where the pastor had seen the monsters exit into the street. There were two access points. The pastor and a few of his men poured a vat of burning pitch into one, while the others waited beside the second for the monsters to emerge."

I realized I was holding my breath again, and made myself exhale.

"Nothing happened. They waited a long time, and then left disappointed. The pastor was angry—there must have been other exits, and the vampires had obviously fled in fear. Of course, the men with their crude spears and axes weren't any kind of danger to a vampire, but he didn't know that. Now that they were warned, how would he ever find his monsters again?"

Her voice got lower. "It wasn't hard. He must have annoyed them. Vampires can't afford notoriety, or these probably would have simply massacred the entire mob. Instead, one of them followed him home.

"Carine remembers the night clearly—for a human memory. It was the kind of thing that would stick in your mind. Her father came home very late, or rather very early. Carine had waited up, worried. He was furious, ranting and raving about his loss. Carine tried to calm him, but he ignored her. And then there was a man in the middle of their small room.

"Carine says he was ragged, dressed like a beggar, but his face was beautiful and he spoke in Latin. Because of her father's vocation and her own curiosity, Carine was unusually educated for a woman in those days—she understood what the man said. He told her father that he was a fool and he would pay for the damage he had caused. The preacher threw himself in front of his daughter to protect her. . . .

"I often wonder about that moment. If he hadn't revealed what he loved most, would all our stories have changed?"

She was thoughtful for a few seconds, and then she continued. "The vampire smiled. He told the preacher, 'Go to your hell knowing this—that what you love will become all that you hate.'

"He tossed the preacher to the side and grabbed Carine—"

She'd seemed lost in the story, but now she stopped short. Her eyes came back to the present, and she looked at me like she'd said something wrong. Or maybe she thought she'd upset me.

"What happened?" I whispered.

When she spoke, it was like she was choosing each word carefully. "He made sure that the preacher knew what would happen to Carine, and then he killed the preacher very slowly while Carine watched, writhing in pain and horror."

I recoiled. She nodded in sympathy.

"The vampire left. Carine knew her fate if someone found her in this condition. Anything infected by the monster would have to be destroyed. She acted instinctively to save her own life. Despite the pain she was in, she crawled into the cellar and buried herself in a pile of rotting potatoes for three days. It's a miracle she was able to keep silent, to stay undiscovered.

"It was over then, and she realized what she had become."

I wasn't sure what my face was doing, but she suddenly broke off again.

"How are you feeling?" she asked.

"I'm good—what happened next?"

She half-smiled at my intensity, then turned back down the hall, pulling me with her.

"Come on, then," she said. "I'll show you."

16. CARINE

She led me back to the room that she'd pointed out as Carine's office. She paused outside the door for a second.

"Come in," Carine called from inside.

Edythe opened the door to a tall room with long windows that stretched the entire height of the walls. The room was lined by bookshelves reaching to the ceiling and holding more books than I'd ever seen outside a library.

Carine sat behind a huge desk; she was just placing a bookmark in the pages of the book she held. The room was how I'd always imagined a college dean's would look—only Carine looked too young to fit the part.

Knowing what she'd been through—having just watched it all in my imagination while knowing that my imagination wasn't up to the job and it was probably much worse than I'd pictured it—made me look at her differently.

"What can I do for you?" she asked with a smile, rising from her seat.

"I wanted to show Beau some of our history," Edythe said. "Well, your history, actually."

"We didn't mean to disturb you," I apologized.

"Not at all," she said to me, and then to Edythe, "Where are you going to start?"

"The Waggoner," Edythe said. She pulled me around in a circle, so that we were facing the door we'd just walked through.

This wall was different from the others. Instead of bookshelves, it was covered by dozens and dozens of framed paintings. They were all different sizes and styles, some dull, some blazing with color. I scanned quickly, looking for some kind of logic, something they all had in common, but I couldn't find any link.

Edythe pulled me to the far left side, then put both her hands on my arms and positioned me directly in front of one of the paintings. My heart reacted the way it always did when she touched me—even in the most casual way. It was more embarrassing knowing Carine would hear it, too.

The painting she wanted me to look at was a small square canvas in a plain wooden frame; it did not stand out among the bigger and brighter pieces. Painted in different shades of brown, it showed a miniature city full of steeply slanted roofs. A river filled the foreground, crossed by a bridge covered with structures that looked like tiny cathedrals.

"London in the sixteen-fifties," Edythe said.

"The London of my youth," Carine added from a few feet behind us. I jumped a little—I hadn't heard her approach. Edythe took my hand and squeezed it lightly.

"Will you tell the story?" Edythe asked. I turned to see Carine's reaction.

She met my glance and smiled. "I would, but I'm actually running a bit late. The hospital called this morning—Dr. Snow is taking a sick day. But Beau won't miss anything." She smiled at Edythe now. "You know the stories as well as I do."

It was a strange combination to absorb—the everyday life of a small-town doctor mixed up with a discussion of her early days in seventeenth-century London.

It was also kind of unsettling to realize that she probably was only speaking out loud for my benefit.

With another warm smile, Carine left the room.

I stared at the picture of her hometown for a long minute.

"What came next?" I asked again. "When she knew what had happened to her?"

She nudged me over a half-step, her eyes on a bigger landscape. It was done in dull fall colors and showed an empty meadow in a gloomy forest, a black mountain peak in the distance.

"When she knew what she had become," Edythe said quietly, "she despaired . . . and then rebelled. She tried to destroy herself. But that's not easily done."

"How?" I didn't mean to say that out loud, but I was so shocked, it slipped out.

Edythe shrugged. "She jumped from great heights. She tried to drown herself in the ocean. But she was young to the new life, and very strong. It is amazing that she was able to resist . . . feeding . . . while she was still so new. The instinct is more powerful then, it takes over everything. But she was so repelled by herself that she had the strength to try to kill herself with starvation."

"Is that possible?" I asked quietly.

"No, there are very few ways we can be killed."

I opened my mouth to ask, but she spoke before I could.

"So she grew very hungry, and eventually weak. She strayed as far as she could from the human populace, recognizing that her willpower was weakening, too. For months she wandered by night, seeking the loneliest places, loathing herself.

"One night, a herd of deer passed beneath her hiding place. She was so wild with thirst that she attacked without a thought. Her strength returned and she realized there was an alternative to being the vile monster she feared. Had she not eaten venison in her former life? Over the next months, her new philosophy was born. She could exist without being a demon. She found herself again.

"She began to make better use of her time. She'd always been intelligent, eager to learn. Now she had unlimited time before her. She studied by night, planned by day. She swam to France and—"

"She *swam* to France?"

"People swim the Channel all the time, Beau," she reminded me patiently.

"That's true, I guess. It just sounded funny in that context. Go on."

"Swimming is easy for us—"

"Everything is easy for *you*," I muttered.

She waited with her eyebrows raised.

"Sorry. I won't interrupt again, I promise."

She smiled darkly and finished her sentence. "Because, technically, we don't need to breathe."

"You—"

"No, no, you promised," she laughed, placing her cold finger against my lips. "Do you want to hear the story or not?"

"You can't spring something like that on me, and then expect me not to say anything," I mumbled against her finger.

She lifted her hand, moving it to rest against my chest. The speed of my heart reacted to that, but I ignored it.

"You don't have to *breathe?*" I demanded.

"No, it's not necessary. Just a habit." She shrugged.

"How long can you go . . . without *breathing?*"

"Indefinitely, I suppose; I don't know. It gets a bit uncomfortable—being without a sense of smell."

"A bit uncomfortable," I echoed.

I wasn't paying attention to my own expression, but something in it made her suddenly serious. Her hand fell to her side and she stood very still, watching my face. The silence stretched out. Her features turned to stone.

"What is it?" I whispered, carefully touching her frozen face.

Her face came back to life, and she smiled a tiny, wan smile. "I know that at some point, something I tell you or something you see is going to be too much. And then you'll run away from me, screaming as you go." Her smile faded. "I won't stop you when that happens. I *want* it to happen, because I want you to be safe. And yet, I want to be with you. The two desires are impossible to reconcile. . . ." She trailed off, staring at my face.

"I'm not running anywhere," I promised.

"We'll see," she said, smiling again.

I frowned at her. "Back to the story—Carine was swimming to France."

She paused, settling into the story again. Reflexively, her eyes flickered to another picture—the most colorful of them all, the most ornately framed, and the largest; it was twice as wide as the door it hung next to. The canvas overflowed with bright figures in swirling robes, writhing around long pillars and off marbled balconies. I couldn't tell if it represented Greek mythology, or if the characters floating in the clouds above were meant to be biblical.

"Carine swam to France, and continued on through Europe, to the universities there. By night she studied music, science, medicine—and found her

calling, her penance, in that, in saving human lives." Her expression became reverent. "I can't adequately describe the struggle; it took Carine two centuries of torturous effort to perfect her self-control. Now she is all but immune to the scent of human blood, and she is able to do the work she loves without agony. She finds a great deal of peace there, at the hospital. . . ." Edythe stared off into space for a long moment. Suddenly she seemed to remember the story. She tapped her finger against the huge painting in front of us.

"She was studying in Italy when she discovered the others there. They were much more civilized and educated than the wraiths of the London sewers."

She pointed up to a comparatively dignified group of figures painted on the highest balcony, looking down calmly on the mayhem below them. I looked carefully at the little assembly and realized, with a startled laugh, that I recognized the golden-haired woman standing off to one side.

"Solimena was greatly inspired by Carine's friends. He often painted them as gods." Edythe laughed. "Sulpicia, Marcus, and Athenodora," she said, indicating the other three. "Nighttime patrons of the arts."

The first woman and man were black-haired, the second woman was pale blond. All wore richly colored gowns, while Carine was painted in white.

"What about that one?" I asked, pointing to a small, nondescript girl with light brown hair and clothes. She was on her knees clinging to the other woman's skirts—the woman with the elaborate black curls.

"Mele," she said. "A . . . servant, I suppose you could call her. Sulpicia's little thief."

"What happened to them?" I wondered aloud, my fingertip hovering a centimeter from the figures on the canvas.

"They're still there." She shrugged. "As they have been for millennia. Carine stayed with them only for a short time, just a few decades. She admired their civility, their refinement, but they persisted in trying to cure her aversion to *her natural food source*, as they called it. They tried to persuade her, and she tried to persuade them, to no avail. Eventually, Carine decided to try the New World. She dreamed of finding others like herself. She was very lonely, you see.

"She didn't find anyone for a long time. But as monsters became the stuff of fairy tales, she found she could interact with unsuspecting humans as if she were one of them. She began working as a nurse—though her learning

and skill exceeded that of the surgeons of the day, as a woman, she couldn't be accepted in another role. She did what she could to save patients from less able doctors when no one was looking. But though she worked closely with humans, the companionship she craved evaded her; she couldn't risk familiarity.

"When the influenza epidemic hit, she was working nights in a hospital in Chicago. She'd been turning over an idea in her mind for several years, and she had almost decided to act—since she couldn't find a companion, she would create one. She wasn't sure which parts of her own transformation were actually necessary, and which were simply for the enjoyment of her sadistic creator, so she was hesitant. And she was loath to steal anyone's life the way hers had been stolen. It was in that frame of mind that she found me. There was no hope for me; I was left in a ward with the dying. She had nursed my parents, and knew I was alone. She decided to try. . . ."

Her voice, nearly a whisper now, trailed off. She stared unseeingly through the long windows. I wondered which images filled her mind now, Carine's memories or her own. I waited.

She turned back to me, smiling softly. "And now we've come full circle."

"So you've always been with Carine?"

"Almost always."

She took my hand again and pulled me back out into the hallway. I looked back toward the pictures I couldn't see anymore, wondering if I'd ever get to hear the other stories.

She didn't add anything as we walked down the hall, so I asked, "Almost?"

Edythe sighed, pursed her lips, and then looked up at me from the corner of her eye.

"You don't want to answer that, do you?" I said.

"It wasn't my finest hour."

We started up another flight of stairs.

"You can tell me anything."

She paused when we got to the top of the stairs and stared into my eyes for a few seconds.

"I suppose I owe you that. You should know who I am."

I got the feeling that what she was saying now was directly connected to what she'd said before, about me running away screaming. I carefully set my face and braced myself.

She took a deep breath. "I had a typical bout of rebellious adolescence—about ten years after I was . . . born . . . created, whatever you want to call it. I wasn't sold on Carine's life of abstinence, and I resented her for curbing my appetite. So . . . I went off on my own for a time."

"Really?" This didn't shock me the way she thought it would. It only made me more curious.

"That doesn't repulse you?"

"No."

"Why not?"

"I guess . . . it sounds reasonable."

She laughed one sharp laugh and then started pulling me forward again, through a hall similar to the one downstairs, walking slowly. "From the time of my new birth, I had the advantage of knowing what everyone around me was thinking, both human and non-human alike. That's why it took me ten years to defy Carine—I could read her perfect sincerity, understand exactly why she lived the way she did.

"It took me only a few years to return to Carine and recommit to her vision. I thought I would be exempt from the . . . depression . . . that accompanies a conscience. Because I knew the thoughts of my prey, I could pass over the innocent and pursue only the evil. If I followed a murderer down a dark alley where he stalked a young girl—if I saved her, then surely I wasn't so terrible."

I tried to imagine what she was describing. What would she have looked like, coming silent and pale out of the shadows? What would the murderer have thought when he saw her—perfect, beautiful, more than human? Would he even have known to be afraid?

"But as time went on, I began to see the monster in my eyes. I couldn't escape the debt of so much human life taken, no matter how justified. And I went back to Carine and Earnest. They welcomed me back like the prodigal. It was more than I deserved."

We'd come to a stop in front of the last door in the hall.

"My room," she said, opening it and pulling me through.

Her room faced south, with a wall-sized window like the great room below. The whole back side of the house must be glass. Her view looked down on the wide, winding river, which I figured had to be the Sol Duc, and

across the forest to the white peaks of the Olympic Mountain range. The mountains were much closer than I would have thought.

Her western wall was covered with shelf after shelf of CDs; the room was better stocked than a music store. In the corner was a sophisticated-looking sound system, the kind I was afraid to touch because I'd be sure to break something. There was no bed, only a deep black leather sofa. The floor was covered with a thick, gold-colored carpet, and the walls were upholstered with heavy fabric in a slightly darker shade.

"Good acoustics?" I guessed.

She laughed and nodded.

She picked up a remote and turned the stereo on. It was quiet, but the soft jazz number sounded like the band was in the room with us. I went to look at her mind-boggling music collection.

"How do you have these organized?" I asked, unable to find any rhyme or reason to the titles.

"Ummm, by year, and then by personal preference within that frame," she said absently.

I turned, and she was looking at me with an expression in her eyes that I couldn't read.

"What?"

"I was prepared to feel . . . relieved. Having you know about everything, not needing to keep secrets from you. But I didn't expect to feel more than that. I *like* it. It makes me . . . happy." She shrugged and smiled.

"I'm glad," I said, smiling back. I'd worried that she might regret telling me these things. It was good to know that wasn't the case.

But then, as her eyes dissected my expression, her smile faded and her eyebrows pulled together.

"You're still waiting for the running and the screaming, aren't you?" I asked.

She nodded, fighting a smile.

"I really hate to burst your bubble, but you're just not as scary as you think you are. I honestly can't imagine being afraid of you," I said casually.

She raised her eyebrows, and then a slow smile started spreading across her face.

"You probably shouldn't have said that," she told me.

And then she *growled*—a low sound that ripped up the back of her throat and didn't sound human at all. Her smile got wider until it changed from a smile into a display of teeth. Her body shifted, and she was half-crouched, her back stretched long and curved in, like a cat tensed to pounce.

"Um . . . Edythe?"

I didn't see her attack—it was much too fast. I couldn't even understand what was happening. For half a second I was airborne and the room rolled around me, upside down and then right side up again. I didn't feel the landing, but suddenly I was on my back on the black couch and Edythe was on top of me, her knees tight against my hips, her hands planted on either side of my head so that I couldn't move, and her bared teeth just inches from my face. She made another soft noise that was halfway between a growl and a purr.

"Wow," I breathed.

"You were saying?" she asked.

"Um, that you are a very, very terrifying monster?"

She grinned. "Much better."

"And that I am *so* completely in love with you."

Her face went soft, her eyes wide, all the walls down again.

"Beau," she whispered.

"Can we come in?" a low voice asked from the door.

I flinched and probably would have smacked my forehead against Edythe's if she hadn't been so much faster than I was. In another fraction of a second, she'd pulled me up so that I was sitting on the sofa and she was next to me, her legs draped over mine.

Archie stood in the doorway, Jessamine behind him in the hall. Red started creeping up my neck, but Edythe was totally relaxed.

"Please," she said to Archie.

Archie didn't seem to have noticed that we were doing anything unusual. He walked to the center of the room and folded himself onto the floor in a motion so graceful it was kind of surreal. Jessamine stayed by the door, and, unlike Archie, she looked a little shocked. She stared at Edythe's face, and I wondered what the room felt like to her.

"It sounded like you were having Beau for lunch," Archie said, "and we came to see if you would share."

I stiffened until I saw Edythe grin—whether because of Archie's comment or my reaction, I couldn't tell.

"Sorry," she replied, throwing a possessive arm around my neck. "I'm not in a mood to share."

Archie shrugged. "Fair enough."

"Actually," Jessamine said, taking a hesitant step into the room, "Archie says there's going to be a real storm tonight, and Eleanor wants to play ball. Are you game?"

The words were all normal, but I didn't quite understand the context. It sounded like Archie might be a little more reliable than the weatherman, though.

Edythe's eyes lit up, but she hesitated.

"Of course you should bring Beau," Archie said. I thought I saw Jessamine throw a quick glance at him.

"Do you want to go?" Edythe asked. Her expression was so eager that I would have agreed to anything.

"Sure. Um, where are we going?"

"We have to wait for thunder to play ball—you'll see why," she promised.

"Should I bring an umbrella?"

All three of them laughed out loud.

"Should he?" Jessamine asked Archie.

"No." Archie seemed positive. "The storm will hit over town. It'll be dry enough in the clearing."

"Good," Jessamine said, and the enthusiasm in her voice was—unsurprisingly—catching. I found myself getting excited about the idea, though I wasn't even sure what it was.

"Let's call Carine and see if she's in," Archie said, and he was on his feet in another liquid movement that made me stare.

"Like you don't already know," Jessamine teased, and then they were gone.

"So . . . what are we playing?" I asked.

"*You* will be watching," Edythe clarified. "*We* will be playing baseball."

I looked at her skeptically. "Vampires like baseball?"

She smiled up at me. "It's the American pastime."

17. THE GAME

IT WAS JUST BEGINNING TO RAIN WHEN EDYTHE TURNED ONTO MY street. Up until that moment, I'd had no doubt that she'd be staying with me while I spent a few hours in the real world.

And then I saw the black, weathered sedan parked in Charlie's driveway—and heard Edythe mutter something angry under her breath.

Leaning away from the rain under the shallow front porch, Jules Black stood behind her mother's wheelchair. Bonnie's face was impassive as rock while Edythe parked my truck against the curb. Jules stared down, looking mortified.

Edythe's low voice was furious. "This is crossing the line."

"She came to warn Charlie?" I guessed, more horrified than angry.

Edythe just nodded, answering Bonnie's stare with narrowed eyes.

At least Charlie wasn't home yet. Maybe the disaster could be averted.

"Let me deal with this," I suggested. Edythe's glare looked a little too . . . serious.

I was surprised that she agreed. "That's probably best. Be careful, though. The child has no idea."

"*Child?* You know, Jules is not that much younger than I am."

She looked at me then, her anger gone. She grinned. "Oh, I know."

I sighed.

"Get them inside so I can leave," she told me. "I'll be back around dusk."

"You can take the truck," I offered.

She rolled her eyes. "I could *walk* home faster than this truck moves."

I didn't want to leave her. "You don't have to go."

She touched my frown and smiled. "Actually, I do. After you get rid of them"—she glared in the Blacks' direction—"you still have to prepare Charlie to meet your new girlfriend."

She laughed at my face—I guess she could see exactly how excited I was for that.

It wasn't that I didn't want Charlie to know about Edythe. I knew he liked the Cullens, and how could he not like Edythe? He'd probably be insultingly impressed. But it just seemed like pushing my luck. Trying to drag this too-beautiful fantasy down into the sludge of boring, ordinary life didn't feel safe. How could the two coexist for long?

"I'll be back soon," she promised. Her eyes flickered over to the porch, and then she darted in swiftly to press her lips to the side of my neck. My heart bounced around inside my ribs while I, too, glanced at the porch. Bonnie's face was no longer impassive, and her hands clutched at the armrests of her chair.

"*Soon,*" I said as I opened my door and stepped out into the rain. I could feel her eyes on my back as I jogged to the porch.

"Hey, Jules. Hi, Bonnie," I greeted them, as cheerfully as I could manage. "Charlie's gone for the day—I hope you haven't been waiting long."

"Not long," Bonnie said in a subdued tone. Her dark eyes were piercing. "I just wanted to bring this up." She gestured to a brown paper sack resting on her lap.

"Thanks," I said automatically, though I had no idea what it could be. "Why don't you come in for a minute and dry off?"

I pretended I didn't notice her intense scrutiny as I unlocked the door and waved them inside ahead of me. Jules gave me a half-smile as she walked by.

"Let me take that," I offered as I turned to shut the door. I exchanged one last look with Edythe—she was perfectly still as she waited, her eyes serious.

"You'll want to put that in the fridge," Bonnie instructed as she handed me the package. "It's a batch of Holly Clearwater's homemade fish fry. Charlie's favorite. The fridge keeps it drier."

"Thanks," I repeated with more emotion. "I was running out of ways to cook fish, and he's bound to bring more home tonight."

"Fishing again?" Bonnie asked. She was suddenly intent. "Down at the usual spot? Maybe I'll run by and see him."

"No," I lied quickly. "He was headed someplace new . . . but I have no idea where."

She stared at my face, her eyes narrowing. It was always so obvious when I tried to lie.

"Julie," she said, still eyeing me. "Why don't you go get that new picture of Aaron out of the car? I'll leave that for Charlie, too."

"Where is it?" Jules asked. Her voice sounded kind of down. I glanced at her, but she was staring at the floor, her black brows pulling together.

"I think I saw it in the trunk," Bonnie said. "You may have to dig for it."

Jules stalked back out into the rain.

Bonnie and I faced each other in silence. After a few seconds, the quiet started to feel awkward, so I turned and headed to the kitchen. I could hear her wet wheels squeak against the linoleum as she followed.

I fit the paper bag into a space on the top shelf of the fridge, and then turned slowly to meet the eyes I could feel boring into me.

"Charlie won't be back for a long time." My voice was almost rude.

She nodded in agreement, but said nothing.

"Thanks again for the fish fry," I hinted.

She continued nodding. I sighed and leaned back against the counter.

"Beau," she said, and then she hesitated.

I waited.

"Beau," she said again, "Charlie is one of my best friends."

"Yes."

She spoke each word carefully in her deep voice. "I noticed you've been spending time with one of the Cullens."

"Yes," I repeated.

Her eyes narrowed again. "Maybe it's none of my business, but I don't think that is such a good idea."

"You're right," I agreed. "It *is* none of your business."

She raised her thick eyebrows at my tone. "You probably don't know this, but the Cullen family has an unpleasant reputation on the reservation."

"Actually, I did know that," I said in a hard voice. She looked surprised. "But that reputation couldn't be deserved, could it? Because the Cullens

never set foot on the reservation, do they?" I could see that my less-than-subtle reminder of the agreement that both bound and protected her tribe pulled her up short.

"That's true," she agreed, her eyes guarded. "You seem . . . well informed about the Cullens. More informed than I expected."

I stared her down. "Maybe even better informed than you are."

She pursed her thick lips as she considered that. "Maybe," she allowed, but her eyes were shrewd. "Is Charlie as well informed?"

She had found the weak spot in my armor.

"Charlie likes the Cullens a lot," I said. She obviously understood my evasion. Her expression was unhappy, but not surprised.

"It's not my business," she said. "But it may be Charlie's."

"Though it would be my business, again, whether or not I think that it's Charlie's business, right?"

I wondered if she even understood my confused question as I struggled not to say anything compromising. But she seemed to. She thought about it while the rain picked up against the roof, the only sound breaking the silence.

"Yes." She finally surrendered. "I guess that's your business, too."

I sighed with relief. "Thanks, Bonnie."

"Just think about what you're doing, Beau," she urged.

"Okay," I agreed quickly.

She frowned. "What I meant to say was, don't do what you're doing."

I looked into her eyes, filled only with concern for me, and there was nothing I could say.

The front door banged loudly.

"There's no picture anywhere in that car." Jules's complaining voice reached us before she did. She rounded the corner. The shoulders of her t-shirt were stained with the rain, her long hair dripping.

"Hmm," Bonnie grunted, suddenly detached, spinning her chair around to face her daughter. "I guess I left it at home."

Jules rolled her eyes dramatically. "Great."

"Well, Beau, tell Charlie"—Bonnie paused before continuing—"that we stopped by, I mean."

"I will," I muttered.

Jules was surprised. "Are we leaving already?"

"Charlie's gonna be out late," Bonnie explained as she rolled herself past Jules.

"Oh." Jules looked disappointed. "Well, I guess I'll see you later, then, Beau."

"Sure," I agreed.

"Take care," Bonnie warned me. I didn't answer.

Jules helped her mother out the door. I waved briefly, glancing swiftly toward my now-empty truck, and then shut the door before they were gone.

And then I had nothing to do but wait. After a few seconds staring at the empty kitchen, I sighed and started cleaning. At least it kept my hands busy. Not so much my thoughts. Now that I was away from Jessamine's mood fix, I was able to really stress out about what I'd agreed to. But how hard could it be? Edythe said I wouldn't have to play. I tried to convince myself it would be fine while scrubbing just a little too hard.

I was just finishing the bathroom when I finally heard Charlie's car in the drive. I stacked the cleaning supplies in alphabetical order under the sink while listening to him come in the front door. He started banging around under the stairs, stowing his tackle.

"Beau?" he called.

"Hey, Dad," I yelled back.

When I got downstairs, he was scrubbing his hands in the kitchen sink.

"Where's the fish?" I asked.

"Out in the deep freeze."

"I'll go grab a couple while they're fresh—Bonnie dropped off some of Holly Clearwater's fish fry this afternoon." I tried to sound enthusiastic.

"She did?" Charlie's eyes lit up. "That's my favorite!"

Charlie cleaned up while I got dinner ready. It wasn't long before we were both at the table, eating in silence. Charlie was obviously enjoying the food. I was wondering how on earth I was supposed to broach the subject of my new . . . girlfriend.

"What did you do with yourself today?" he asked, snapping me out of my thoughts.

"Well, this afternoon I just hung out around the house. . . ." Only the very

recent part of this afternoon, actually. I tried to keep my voice upbeat, but my stomach was hollow. "And this morning I was over at the Cullens'."

Charlie dropped his fork.

"Dr. Cullen's place?" he asked in astonishment.

I pretended not to notice his reaction. "Yeah."

"What were you doing there?" He hadn't picked his fork back up.

"Well, I sort of have a date with Edythe Cullen tonight, and she wanted to introduce me to her parents."

He stared at me like I'd just announced that I'd spent the day knocking over liquor stores.

"What, Dad? Didn't you just tell me that you wanted me to socialize?"

He blinked a few times, then picked up his fork. "Yeah, I guess I did." He took another bite, chewed slowly, and swallowed. "And didn't you just tell me that none of the girls in town are your type?"

"*I* didn't say that, *you* did."

"Don't get touchy with me, kid, you know what I mean. Why didn't you say something? Was I being too nosey?"

"No, Dad, it's just . . . this is all kind of new, okay? I didn't want to jinx it."

"Huh." He reflected for a minute while he ate another bite. "So you went to meet her folks, eh?"

"Er, yeah. I mean, I already knew Dr. Cullen. But I got to meet her father."

"Earnest Cullen is great—quiet, but very . . . kind, I guess is the best word for it. There's something about him."

"Yeah, I noticed that."

"Meeting the parents, though. Isn't that kind of serious? Does that mean she's your girlfriend?"

"Yeah." This wasn't as hard as I'd thought it would be. I felt a strange sense of pride, being able to claim her this way. Kind of Neanderthal of me, but there it was. "Yeah, she's my girlfriend."

"Wow."

"You're telling me."

"Do I get a visit, too?"

I raised one eyebrow. "Will you be on your best behavior?"

He lifted both hands. "What, me? Have I ever embarrassed you before?"

"Have I ever brought a girl over before?"

He huffed, then changed the subject. "When are you picking her up?"

"Um, she's meeting me here. See—you do get a visit. She'll probably be here soon, actually."

"Where are you taking her?"

"Well, I guess the plan is that we're going to go . . . play baseball with her family."

Charlie stared at me for one second, and then he busted up. I rolled my eyes and waited for him to finish. Eventually, he pretended to wipe tears out of his eyes.

"I hope you're getting that out of your system now."

"Baseball, huh? You must really like this girl."

I thought about just shrugging that off, but I figured he'd see through me anyway. "Yeah," I said. "I really do."

I heard an unfamiliar engine roar up to the house, and I looked up in surprise.

"That her?"

"Maybe . . ."

After a few seconds, the doorbell rang, and Charlie jumped up. I ran around him and beat him to the door.

"Pushy much?" he muttered under his breath.

I hadn't realized how hard it was pouring outside. Edythe stood in the halo of the porch light, looking like a model in an ad for raincoats.

I heard Charlie's breath catch in surprise. I wondered if he'd ever seen her up close before. It was kind of unnerving.

Even when you were used to it. I just stared at her, gobsmacked.

She laughed. "Can I come in?"

"Yeah! Of course." I jumped back out of her way, knocking into Charlie in the process.

After a few seconds of bumbling around, I had her jacket hung up and had both her and Charlie sitting down in the living room. She was in the armchair, so I went to sit next to Charlie on the sofa.

"So, Edythe, how are your parents?"

"Excellent, thank you, Chief Swan."

"You can call me Charlie. I'm off the clock."

"Thanks, Charlie." She unleashed the dimples, and his face went blank.

It took him a second to recover. "So, um, you're playing baseball tonight?"

It didn't seem to occur to either of them that the buckets of water falling out of the sky right now should impact these plans. Only in Washington.

"Yes. Hopefully Beau doesn't mind hanging out with my family too much."

Charlie jumped in before I could respond. "I'd say it was the baseball he'd mind more."

They both laughed. I shot my dad a look. Where was the best behavior I'd been promised?

"Should we be on our way?" I suggested.

"We're not in any hurry," Edythe said with a grin.

I hit Charlie with my elbow. Edythe's smile got wider.

"Oh, uh, yeah," Charlie said. "You kids go ahead, I've got a . . . a bunch of stuff to get to. . . ."

Edythe was on her feet in a fluid move. "It was lovely to see you, Charlie."

"Yes. You come visit anytime, Edythe."

"Thank you, you're very kind."

Charlie ran a hand through his hair self-consciously. I didn't think I'd ever seen him so flustered.

"Will you kids be out super late?"

I looked at her.

"No, we'll be reasonable."

"Don't wait up, though," I added.

I handed her coat to her and then held the door. As she passed, Charlie gave me a wide-eyed look. I shrugged my shoulders and raised my eyebrows. I didn't know how I'd gotten so lucky, either.

I followed her out onto the porch, then stopped dead.

There, behind my truck, was a monster Jeep. Its tires were as high as my waist. There were metal guards over the headlights and taillights, and four large spotlights attached to the crash bar. The hardtop was shiny red.

Charlie let out a low whistle. "Wear your seat belts."

I went to the driver's side to get the door for Edythe. She was inside in one efficient little leap, though I was glad we were on the far side of the Jeep from Charlie, because it didn't look entirely natural. I went to my side and

climbed gracelessly into my seat. She had the engine running now, and I recognized the roar that had surprised me earlier. It wasn't as loud as my truck, but it sounded a lot more brawny.

Out of habit—she wasn't going to start driving until I was buckled in—I reached for my seat belt.

"What—er—what is all this? How do I . . . ?"

"Off-roading harness," she explained.

"Um."

I tried to find all the right connectors, but it wasn't going too fast. And then her hands were there, flashing around at a barely visible speed, and gone again. I was glad the rain was too thick to see Charlie clearly on the porch, because that meant he couldn't see me clearly, either.

"Er, thanks."

"You're welcome."

I knew better than to ask if she was going to put her own harness on.

She pulled away from the house.

"This is a . . . um . . . large Jeep you have."

"It's Eleanor's. She let me borrow it so we wouldn't have to run the whole way."

"Where do you keep this thing?"

"We remodeled one of the outbuildings into a garage."

Suddenly her first answer sank in.

"Wait. Run the *whole* way? As in, we're still going to run part of the way?" I demanded.

She pursed her lips like she was trying not to smile. "You're not going to run."

I groaned. "I'm going to puke in front of your family."

"Keep your eyes closed, you'll be fine."

I shook my head, sighed, then reached over and took her hand. "Hi. I missed you."

She laughed—it was a trilling sound, not quite human. "I missed you, too. Isn't that strange?"

"Why strange?"

"You'd think I'd have learned more patience over the last hundred years. And here I am, finding it difficult to pass an afternoon without you."

"I'm glad it's not just me."

She leaned over to swiftly kiss my cheek, then pulled back quickly and sighed. "You smell even better in the rain."

"In a good way or a bad way?"

She frowned. "Always both."

I don't know how she even knew where we were going with the downpour—it was like a liquid gray curtain around the Jeep—but she somehow found a side road that was more or less a mountain path. For a long while conversation was impossible, because I was bouncing up and down on the seat like a jackhammer. She seemed to enjoy the ride, though, smiling hugely the whole way.

And then we came to the end of the road; the trees formed green walls on three sides of the Jeep. The rain was a mere drizzle, slowing every second, the sky brighter through the clouds.

"Sorry, Beau, we have to go on foot from here."

"You know what? I'll just wait here."

"What happened to all your courage? You were extraordinary this morning."

"I haven't forgotten the last time yet." Was it really only yesterday?

She was around to my side of the car in a blur, and she started on the harness.

"I'll get those, you go on ahead," I protested. She was finished before I got the first few words out.

I sat in the car, looking at her.

"You don't trust me?" she asked, hurt—or pretending to be hurt, I thought.

"That really isn't the issue. Trust and motion sickness have zero relationship to each other."

She looked at me for a minute, and I felt pretty stupid sitting there in the Jeep, but all I could think about was the most sickening roller-coaster ride I'd ever been on.

"Do you remember what I was saying about mind over matter?" she asked.

"Yes . . ."

"Maybe if you concentrated on something else."

"Like what?"

Suddenly she was in the Jeep with me, one knee on the seat next to my

leg, her hands on my shoulders. Her face was only inches away. I had a light heart attack.

"Keep breathing," she told me.

"How?"

She smiled, and then her face was serious again. "When we're running—and yes, that part is nonnegotiable—I want you to concentrate on this."

Slowly, she moved in closer, turning her face to the side so that we were cheek to cheek, her lips at my ear. One of her hands slid down my chest to my waist.

"Just remember us . . . like this. . . ."

Her lips pulled softly on my earlobe, then moved slowly across my jaw and down my neck.

"Breathe, Beau," she murmured.

I sucked in a loud lungful.

She kissed under the edge of my jaw, and then along my cheekbone. "Still worried?"

"Huh?"

She chuckled. Her hands were holding my face now, and she lightly kissed one eyelid and then the next.

"Edythe," I breathed.

Then her lips were on mine, and they weren't quite as gentle and cautious as they always had been before. They moved urgently, cold and unyielding, and though I knew better, I couldn't think coherently enough to make good decisions. I didn't consciously tell my hands to move, but my arms were wrapped around her waist, trying to pull her closer. My mouth moved with hers and I was gasping for air, gasping in her scent with every breath.

"Dammit, Beau!"

And then she was gone—slithering easily out of my grasp—already standing ten feet away outside the car by the time I'd blinked my way back to reality.

"Sorry," I gasped.

She stared warily at me with her eyes so wide the white showed all the way around the gold. I half-fell awkwardly from the car, then took a step toward her.

"I truly do think you'll be the death of me, Beau," she said quietly.

I froze. "What?"

She took a deep breath, and then she was right next to me. "Let's get out of here before I do something *really* stupid," she muttered.

She turned her back to me, staring back over her shoulder with a *get on with it* look.

And how was I supposed to reject her now? Feeling like a gorilla again, only even more ridiculous than before, I climbed onto her back.

"Keep your eyes shut," she warned, and then she was off.

I forced my eyes closed, trying not to think about the speed of the wind that was pushing the skin flat against my skull. Other than that tell, it was hard to believe we were really flying through the forest like we had before. The motion of her body was so smooth, I would have thought she was just strolling down the sidewalk—with a gorilla on her back. Her breath came and went evenly.

I wasn't entirely sure we had stopped when she reached back and touched my face.

"It's over, Beau."

I opened my eyes, and sure enough, we were at a standstill. In my hurry to get off her, I lost my balance. She turned just in time to watch as I—arms windmilling wildly—fell hard on my butt.

For a second she stared like she wasn't sure if she was still too mad to find me funny, but then she must have decided that she was *not* too mad.

She burst into long peals of laughter, throwing her head back and holding her arms across her stomach.

I got up slowly and brushed the mud and weeds off the back of my jeans the best I could while she kept laughing.

"You know, it would probably be more humane for you to just dump me now," I said glumly. "It's not going to get any easier for me over time."

She took a few deep breaths, trying to get control of herself.

I sighed and started walking in the most path-like direction I could see.

Something caught the back of my sweater, and I smiled. I looked over my shoulder. She had a fistful of sweater, the same way she'd grabbed me outside the nurse's office.

"Where are you going, Beau?"

"Wasn't there a baseball game happening?"

"It's the other way."

I pivoted. "Okay."

She took my hand and we started walking slowly toward a dark patch of forest.

"I'm sorry I laughed."

"I would have laughed at me, too."

"No, I was just a little . . . agitated. I needed the catharsis."

We walked silently for a few seconds.

"At least tell me it worked—the mind-over-matter experiment."

"Well . . . I didn't get sick."

"Good, but . . . ?"

"I wasn't thinking about . . . in the car. I was thinking about after."

She didn't say anything.

"I know I already apologized, but . . . sorry. Again. I will learn how to do better, I know—"

"Beau, stop. Please, you make me feel even more guilty when you apologize."

I looked down at her. We'd both stopped walking. "Why should *you* feel guilty?"

She laughed again, but this time there was an almost hysterical edge to her laugh. "Oh, indeed! Why should *I* feel guilty?"

The darkness in her eyes made me anxious. There was pain there, and I didn't know how to make it better. I put my hand against her cheek. "Edythe, I don't understand what you're saying."

She closed her eyes. "I just can't seem to stop putting you in danger. I *think* I'm in control of myself, and then it gets so close—I don't know how to not be *this* anymore." Eyes still closed, she gestured to herself. "My very existence puts you at risk. Sometimes I truly hate myself. I should be stronger, I should be able to—"

I moved my hand to cover her mouth. "Stop."

Her eyes opened. She peeled my hand off her mouth and placed it over her cheek again.

"I love you," she said. "It's a poor excuse for what I'm doing, but it's still true."

It was the first time she'd ever said she loved me—in so many words. Like she'd said this morning, it was different, hearing the words out loud.

"I love *you*," I told her when I'd caught my breath. "I don't want you to be anything other than what you are."

She sighed. "Now, be a good boy," she said, and stretched up on her tiptoes. I held very still while she brushed her lips softly against mine.

We stared at each other for a minute.

"Baseball?" she asked.

"Baseball," I agreed much more confidently than I felt.

She took my hand and led me a few feet through the tall ferns and around a massive hemlock tree, and we were suddenly there, on the edge of an enormous clearing on the side of a mountain. It was twice the size of any baseball stadium.

All of the others were there. Earnest, Eleanor, and Royal were sitting on an outcropping of rock, maybe a hundred yards away. Much farther out I could see Jessamine and Archie standing at least a quarter of a mile apart. It was almost like they were pantomiming playing catch; I never saw any ball. It looked like Carine was marking bases, but that couldn't be right. The points were much too far apart.

When we walked into view, the three on the rocks stood. Earnest started toward us. Royal walked away, toward where Carine was setting up. Eleanor followed Earnest after a long look at Royal's back.

I was staring at Royal's back, too. It made me nervous.

"Was that you we heard before, Edythe?" Earnest asked.

"Sounded like a hyena choking to death," Eleanor added.

I smiled tentatively at Earnest. "That was her."

"Beau was being funny," Edythe explained.

Archie had left off his game of catch and was running toward us—it was like his feet never touched the ground. In half a heartbeat he was there, hurtling to a stop right in front of us.

"It's time," he announced.

The second he spoke, a deep rumble of thunder shook the forest behind us and then crashed westward toward town.

"Eerie, isn't it?" Eleanor said to me. When I turned to look at her, surprised that she was so casual with me, she winked.

"Let's go!" Archie took Eleanor's hand and they darted toward the oversized diamond. Archie almost . . . bounded—like a stag, but closer to the ground. Eleanor was just as fast and nearly as graceful, but she was something altogether different. Something that *charged*, not bounded.

"Are you ready for some ball?" Edythe asked, her eyes bright.

It was impossible not to be enthusiastic about something that clearly made her happy. "Go team!"

She laughed, quickly ran her fingers through my hair, then raced off after the other two. Her run was more aggressive than either of the others', like a cheetah to a gazelle—but still supple and heartbreakingly beautiful. She quickly caught up to and then passed the others.

"Shall we go watch?" Earnest asked in his soft tenor voice. I realized that I was staring openmouthed after them. I quickly reassembled my expression and nodded. Earnest kept a few feet farther away than was exactly normal for two people walking together, and I figured he was still being careful not to frighten me. He matched his stride to mine without seeming impatient at the pace.

"You don't play with them?" I asked.

"No, I prefer to referee. I like keeping them honest."

"Do they cheat?"

"Oh yes—and you should hear the arguments they get into! Actually, I hope you don't, you would think they were raised by a pack of wolves."

"You sound like my dad," I laughed.

He laughed, too. "Well, I do think of them as my children in most ways. I never could get over—" He broke off, and then took a deep breath. "Did Edythe tell you I lost my daughter?"

"Er, no," I murmured, stunned, scrambling to understand what lifetime he was remembering.

"My only child—my Grace. She died when she was barely two. It broke my heart—that's why I jumped off the cliff, you know," he added calmly.

"Oh, um, Edythe just said you fell. . . ."

"Always so polite." Earnest smiled. "Edythe was the first of my new children. My second daughter. I've always thought of her that way—though she's older than I, in one way at least—and wondered if my Grace would have grown into such an amazing person." He looked at me and smiled warmly. "I'm so happy she's found you, Beau. She's been the odd man out for far too long. It's hurt me to see her alone."

"You don't mind, then?" I asked, hesitant again. "That I'm . . . all wrong for her?"

"No," he said thoughtfully. "You're what she wants. It will all work out, somehow." But his forehead creased with worry.

Another peal of thunder began.

Earnest stopped then; apparently, we'd reached the edge of the field. It looked as if they had formed teams. Edythe was far out in left field, Carine stood between the first and second bases, and Archie held the ball, positioned on the spot that must be the pitcher's mound.

Eleanor was swinging an aluminum bat; it whistled almost untraceably through the air. I waited for her to approach home plate, but then I realized, as she leaned into her stance, that she was already there—farther from the pitcher's mound than I would have thought possible. Jessamine stood several feet behind her, catching for the other team. Of course, none of them had gloves.

"All right," Earnest called in a clear voice, which I guessed even Edythe would hear, as far out as she was. "Batter up."

Archie stood straight, still as a statue. His style seemed to be stealth rather than an intimidating windup. He held the ball in both hands at his waist, and then, like the strike of a cobra, his right hand flicked out and the ball smacked into Jessamine's hand with a sound like a gunshot.

"Was that a strike?" I whispered to Earnest.

"If they don't hit it, it's a strike," he told me.

Jessamine hurled the ball back to Archie's waiting hand. He permitted himself a brief grin. And then his hand spun out again.

This time the bat somehow made it around in time to smash into the invisible ball. The crack of impact was shattering, thunderous; it echoed off the mountainside—I immediately understood the need for the storm.

I was barely able to follow the ball, shooting like a meteor above the field, flying deep into the surrounding forest.

"Home run," I muttered.

"Wait," Earnest said. He was listening intently, one hand raised. Eleanor was a blur around the bases, Carine shadowing her. I realized Edythe was missing.

"Out!" Earnest cried. I stared in disbelief as Edythe sprang from the fringe of the trees, ball in her upraised hand, her wide grin visible even to me.

"Eleanor hits the hardest," Earnest explained, "but Edythe runs the fastest."

It was like watching superheroes play. It was impossible to keep up with the speed at which the ball flew, the rate at which their bodies raced around the field.

I learned the other reason they waited for a thunderstorm to play when Jessamine, trying to avoid Edythe's infallible fielding, hit a ground ball toward Carine. Carine ran into the ball, and then raced Jessamine to first base. When they collided, the sound was like the crash of two massive falling boulders. I jumped up, afraid someone would be hurt, but they were both totally fine.

"Safe," Earnest called in a calm voice.

Eleanor's team was up by one—Royal managed to tear around the bases after tagging up on one of Eleanor's long flies—when Edythe caught the third out. She sprinted to my side, beaming with excitement.

"What do you think?" she asked.

"One thing's for sure, I'll never be able to sit through dull old Major League Baseball again."

"And it sounds like you did so much of that before," she laughed.

"I am a little disappointed," I teased.

"Why?"

"Well, it would be nice if I could find just one thing you didn't do better than everyone else on the planet."

She flashed her dimples, leaving me breathless.

"I'm up," she said, heading for the plate.

She played intelligently, keeping the ball low, out of the reach of Royal's always-ready hand in the outfield, gaining two bases like lightning before Eleanor could get the ball back in play. Carine knocked one so far out of the field—with a boom that hurt my ears—that she and Edythe both made it in. Archie slapped them high fives.

The score constantly changed as the game continued, and they razzed each other like street ballplayers as they took turns with the lead. Occasionally Earnest would call them to order. The thunder rumbled on, but we stayed dry, as Archie had predicted.

Carine was up to bat, Edythe catching, when Archie suddenly gasped. My

eyes were on Edythe, as usual, and I saw her head snap up to look at him. Their eyes met and something flowed between them in half a second. She was at my side before the others could ask Archie what was wrong.

"Archie?" Earnest asked, tense.

"I didn't see," Archie whispered. "I couldn't tell."

They were all gathered in now.

Carine was calm, authoritative. "What is it, Archie?"

"They were traveling much quicker than I thought. I can see I had the perspective wrong before," he murmured.

Jessamine put her arm around him, her posture protective. "What changed?" she asked.

"They heard us playing, and it changed their path," Archie said, contrite, as if he felt responsible for whatever had happened.

Seven pairs of quick eyes flashed to my face and away.

"How soon?" Carine asked.

A look of intense concentration crossed his face.

"Less than five minutes. They're running—they want to play." He scowled.

"Can you make it?" Carine asked Edythe, her eyes flicking toward me again.

"No, not carrying—" She cut short. "Besides, the last thing we need is for them to catch the scent and start hunting."

"How many?" Eleanor asked Archie.

"Three."

"Three!" she scoffed. "Let them come." The long bands of muscle flexed down her arms.

For a split second that seemed much longer than it really was, Carine deliberated. Only Eleanor seemed relaxed; the rest stared at Carine's face, obviously anxious.

"Let's just continue the game," Carine finally decided. Her voice was cool and level. "Archie said they were simply curious."

The entire conference lasted only a few seconds, but I had listened carefully and thought I'd caught most of it. I couldn't hear what Earnest asked Edythe now with just an intense look. I only saw the slight shake of her head and the look of relief on his face.

"You catch, Earnest," she said. "I'll call it now."

She stood right next to me as the others returned to the field, all of their eyes sweeping the forest. Archie and Earnest seemed to orient themselves around where I stood.

I stated the obvious. "The others are coming now."

"Yes, stay very still, keep quiet, and don't move from my side, please." I could hear the stress in her voice, though she tried to hide it.

"That won't help," Archie murmured. "I could smell him across the field."

"I know," Edythe snapped.

Carine stood at the plate, and the others joined the game halfheartedly.

"What did Earnest ask you?" I whispered.

She hesitated a second before she answered. "Whether they were thirsty,"

The seconds dragged by while the game progressed apathetically. No one dared to hit harder than a bunt, and Eleanor, Royal, and Jessamine hovered in the infield. Now and again, I was aware of Royal's eyes on me. They were expressionless, but something about the way he held his mouth made me sure he was angry.

Edythe paid no attention to the game at all, eyes and mind scanning the forest.

"I'm sorry, Beau," she muttered fiercely. "It was stupid, irresponsible, to expose you like this. I'm so sorry."

I heard her breath stop, and her eyes zeroed in on right field. She took a half-step, angling herself between me and what was coming. It made me start to panic, like I had before, imagining her between me and Royal—Edythe in danger. I was pretty sure whatever was coming now was worse than Royal.

18. THE HUNT

THEY EMERGED ONE BY ONE FROM THE EDGE OF THE FOREST, A DOZEN meters apart. The first woman in the clearing fell back immediately, allowing another woman to take the lead, aligning herself behind the tall, dark-haired woman in a manner that made it clear who led the pack. The third was a man; from this distance, all I could see was that his hair was blazing red.

They closed ranks before they continued cautiously toward Edythe's family. It was like a wildlife show—a troop of predators exhibiting natural respect as it encounters a larger, unfamiliar group of its own kind.

As they approached, I could see how different they were from the Cullens. Their walk was catlike, a gait that seemed constantly on the edge of shifting into a crouch. They were dressed in ordinary backpacking gear: jeans and casual button-down shirts in heavy, weatherproof fabrics. The clothes were frayed with wear, though, and they were barefoot. Their hair was filled with leaves and debris from the woods.

The woman in the lead analyzed Carine as she stepped forward, flanked by Eleanor and Jessamine, to meet them, and she straightened out of her half-crouch. The other two copied her.

The woman in front was easily the most beautiful. Her skin was pale but had an olive tone to it, and her hair was glossy black. She wasn't tall, but she looked strong—though not strong like Eleanor. She smiled easily, exposing a flash of gleaming white teeth.

The man was wilder. His eyes darted restlessly between the Cullens, and his posture was oddly feline. The second woman stayed unobtrusive in the back, smaller than the leader, with bland brown hair and a forgettable face. Her eyes were the calmest, the most still. But I had a strange feeling that she was seeing more than the others.

It was their eyes that made them the most different. They weren't gold or black like I was used to, but a deep, vivid red.

The dark-haired woman, still smiling, stepped toward Carine.

"We thought we heard a game," she said. There was the hint of a French accent in her voice. "I'm Lauren, these are Victor and Joss."

"I'm Carine. This is my family, Eleanor and Jessamine, Royal, Earnest and Archie, Edythe and Beau." She pointed us out in groups, deliberately not calling attention to individuals. I felt a shock when she said my name.

"Do you have room for a few more players?" Lauren asked.

Carine matched Lauren's friendly tone. "Actually, we were just finishing up. But we'd certainly be interested another time. Are you planning to stay in the area for long?"

"We're headed north, in fact, but we were curious to see who was in the neighborhood. We haven't run into any company in a long time."

"No, this region is usually empty except for us and the occasional visitor, like yourselves."

The tense atmosphere had slowly subsided into a casual conversation; I figured Jessamine was using her strange gift to control the situation.

"What's your hunting range?" Lauren casually inquired.

Carine ignored the assumption. "The Olympic Range here, up and down the Coast Ranges on occasion. We keep a permanent residence nearby. There's another permanent settlement like ours up near Denali."

Lauren rocked back on her heels slightly.

"Permanent? How do you manage that?" There was honest curiosity in her voice.

"Why don't you come back to our home with us and we can talk comfortably?" Carine invited. "It's a rather long story."

Victor and Joss exchanged a surprised look at the mention of the word *home*, but Lauren controlled her expression better.

"That sounds very interesting, and welcome." She smiled. "We've been on

the hunt all the way down from Ontario, and we haven't had the chance to clean up in a while." Her eyes moved appreciatively over Carine's clothes.

"Please don't take offense, but we'd appreciate it if you'd refrain from hunting in this immediate area. We have to stay inconspicuous, you understand," Carine explained.

"Of course." Lauren nodded. "We certainly won't encroach on your territory. We just ate outside of Seattle, anyway." She laughed. A shiver ran up my spine.

"We'll show you the way if you'd like to run with us—Eleanor and Archie, you can go with Edythe and Beau to get the Jeep," Carine casually added.

Three things seemed to happen at the same time when Carine finished. A light breeze ruffled my hair, Edythe stiffened, and the second woman, Joss, suddenly whipped her head around, scrutinizing me, her nostrils flaring.

Everyone went rigid as Joss lurched one step forward into a crouch. Edythe bared her teeth, coiling in front of me, a feral snarl ripping from her throat. It was nothing at all like the playful growls I'd heard her make before; it was the most menacing sound I'd ever heard. Chills ran from the crown of my head to the back of my heels.

"What's this?" Lauren asked, shocked. Neither Edythe nor Joss relaxed their aggressive stance. Joss feinted slightly to the side, but Edythe had already shifted to answer her move.

"He's with us," Carine said directly to Joss, her voice cold.

Lauren seemed to catch my scent then, though less powerfully than Joss, and understanding lit her face. "You brought a snack?" She took a step forward.

Edythe snarled even more harshly, her lip curled back high above her bared teeth. Lauren stepped back again.

"I said he's with us," Carine snapped.

"But he's *human*," Lauren protested. She didn't say it with any aggression, she just sounded surprised.

Eleanor leaned forward, suddenly very *there* at Carine's side. "Yes." Her eyes were locked on Joss.

Joss slowly straightened out of her crouch, but her eyes never left me, her nostrils still wide. Edythe stayed tensed in front of me. I wanted to pull her back—this Joss vampire wasn't messing around—but I could guess exactly

how well that would go over. She'd told me to stay still, so I would . . . unless someone tried to hurt her.

When Lauren spoke, her tone was soothing—trying to defuse the sudden hostility. "It appears we have a lot to learn about each other."

"Indeed." Carine's voice was still cool.

"But we'd like to accept your invitation." Her eyes flicked toward me and back to Carine. "And, of course, we will not harm the human boy. We won't hunt in your range, as I said."

Joss glanced at Lauren in disbelief and exchanged a brief look with Victor, whose eyes still flickered edgily from face to face.

Carine measured Lauren's sincere expression for a second before she spoke. "We'll show you the way. Jess, Royal, Earnest?" she called. They gathered together, blocking me from view as they converged. Archie was instantly at my side, while Eleanor moved more slowly, her eyes locked on Joss as she backed toward us.

"Let's move, Beau," Edythe said, low and bleak. She gripped my elbow and pulled me forward. Archie and Eleanor stayed close behind us, hiding me from whoever might still be watching. I stumbled alongside Edythe, trying to keep up with the pace she set. I couldn't hear if the main group had left yet. Edythe's impatience was almost tangible as we moved at human speed to the edge of the forest.

"I'm faster," she snapped, answering someone's thought.

Then we were in the trees and Edythe pulled my arm around her neck while we were still half-jogging forward. I realized what she wanted and, too shocked still to feel self-conscious, climbed into place. We were running before I was set.

I couldn't make my eyes close, but the forest was pretty much black now anyway. I couldn't see or hear Eleanor and Archie running alongside us. Like Edythe, they moved through the forest as if they were ghosts.

We were at the Jeep in seconds. Edythe barely slowed, she just spun and whipped me into the backseat.

"Strap him in," she hissed at Eleanor, who climbed in next to me.

Archie was already in the front seat, and Edythe revved the engine. She swerved backward, spinning around to face the winding road.

Edythe was growling something so fast I couldn't tell what she was saying,

but it kind of sounded like a string of profanities. The jolting ride was much worse this time, in the dark. Eleanor and Archie glared out the side windows.

We hit the main road. The Jeep raced faster. It was dark, but I recognized the direction we were headed. South, away from Forks.

"Where are we going?" I asked.

No one answered. No one even looked at me.

"Is anyone going to tell me what's happening?"

Edythe kept her eyes on the road as she spoke. The speedometer read one-oh-five. "We have to get you away from here—far away—now."

"What? But I have to go home."

"You can't go home, Beau." The way she said it sounded kind of permanent.

"I don't understand. Edythe? What do you mean?"

Archie spoke for the first time. "Pull over, Edythe."

She flashed him a hard look and gunned the engine.

"Edythe," Archie said. "Look at all the different ways this can go. We need to think this through." There was a warning in his voice, and I wondered what he was seeing in his head, what he was showing Edythe.

"You don't understand," Edythe nearly howled in frustration. The speed-ometer was at one hundred and fifteen. "She's a tracker, Archie! Did you *see* that? She's a tracker!"

I felt Eleanor stiffen next to me, and I wondered what the word meant to her. Obviously it meant a lot more to the three of them than it did to me. I wanted to understand, but there was no opening for me to ask.

"Pull over, Edythe." Archie's voice was harder now, steely.

The speedometer inched past one-twenty.

"Do it," he barked.

"Archie—listen! I saw her mind. Tracking is her passion, her obsession—and she wants him, Archie—*him*, specifically. She's already begun."

"She doesn't know where—"

"How long do you think it will take her to cross Beau's scent in town? Her plan was already set before the words were out of Lauren's mouth."

It was like a punch to the gut. I couldn't breathe for a second as what she was say-ing finally made concrete sense. Up till now, it had all felt like something abstract, like a word problem in Math. It didn't seem to connect to me in any real way.

I knew where my scent would lead.

"Charlie," I gasped. And then I yelled. "Charlie! We have to go back. We have to get Charlie!"

I started ripping at the buckles that held me in place, until Eleanor grabbed my wrists. Trying to yank them back was like trying to pull out of handcuffs that were bolted into concrete.

"Edythe! Turn around!" I shouted.

"He's right," Archie said.

The car slowed a tiny bit.

"Let's just look at our options for a minute," Archie coaxed.

The car slowed again, more noticeably, and then suddenly we screeched to a stop on the shoulder of the highway. I flew against the harness and then slammed back into the seat.

"There are no options," Edythe snarled.

"We're not leaving Charlie!" I yelled.

She ignored me completely.

Eleanor finally spoke. "We have to take him back."

"No."

"She's no match for us, Edy. She won't be able to touch him."

"She'll wait."

Eleanor smiled a cold, strangely eager smile. "I can wait, too."

Edythe huffed out a breath, exasperated. "You didn't see! You don't understand! Once she commits to a hunt, she's unshakable. We can't reason with her. We can't scare her off. We'd have to kill her."

This didn't bother Eleanor. "Yes."

"And the male. He's with her. If it turns into a fight, Lauren will side with them, too."

"There are enough of us."

"There's another option," Archie said quietly.

Edythe turned on him, furious, her voice a blistering snarl. "There—is—no—other—option!"

Eleanor and I both stared at her in shock, but Archie didn't seem surprised. The silence lasted for a long minute as Edythe and Archie stared each other down.

"Does anyone want to hear my idea?" I asked.

"No," Edythe snapped. Archie glared at her.

"Listen," I said. "You take me back."

"No!"

"Yes! You take me back. I tell my dad I want to go home to Phoenix. I pack my bags. We wait till this tracker is watching, and *then* we run. She'll follow us and leave Charlie alone. Then you can take me any damned place you want."

They stared at me with wide eyes.

"It's not a bad idea, really." Eleanor sounded so surprised, it was an insult.

"It might work—and we can't just leave his father unprotected," Archie said. "You know that, Edythe."

Everyone looked at Edythe.

"It's too dangerous—I don't want her within a hundred miles of Beau."

"She's not getting through us." Eleanor was very confident.

Archie closed his eyes for a second. "I don't see her attacking. She's the kind that goes around, not through. She'll wait for us to leave him unprotected."

"It won't take long for her to realize that's not going to happen," Edythe said.

"I *have* to go home, Edythe."

She pressed her fingers to her temples and squeezed her eyes shut for a second. Then she was glaring at me.

"Your plan takes too long. We've got no time for the packing charade."

"If I don't give him some kind of excuse, he'll make trouble for your family. Maybe call the FBI or something if he thinks you've . . . I don't know, kidnapped me."

"That doesn't matter."

"Yes. It does. There's a way to keep everyone safe, and that's what we're going to do."

The Jeep rumbled to life, and she spun us around, the tires squealing. The needle on the speedometer started to race up the dial.

"You're leaving tonight," Edythe said, and her voice sounded worn. "Whether the tracker sees or not. Tell Charlie whatever you want—as long as it's quick. Pack the first things your hands touch, then get in your truck. I don't care what Charlie says. You have fifteen minutes. Fifteen minutes from the time you cross the doorstep or I carry you out."

A few minutes passed in silence, other than the roar of the engine.

"Eleanor?" I asked, looking at my hands.

"Oh, sorry." She let me loose.

"This is how it's going to happen," Edythe said. "When we get to the house, if the tracker is not there, I will walk Beau to the door. Then he has fifteen minutes." She glared at me in the rearview mirror. "Eleanor, you take the outside of the house. Archie, you get the truck. I'll be inside as long as he is. After he's out, you two can take the Jeep home and tell Carine."

"No way," Eleanor broke in. "I'm with you."

"Think it through, El. I don't know how long I'll be gone."

"Until we know how far this is going to go, I'm with you."

Edythe sighed. "If the tracker *is* there," she continued grimly, "we keep driving."

"We're going to make it there before him," Archie said confidently.

Edythe seemed to accept that. Whatever her problem with Archie was, she didn't doubt him now.

"What are we going to do with the Jeep?" he asked.

Edythe's voice had a hard edge. "You're driving it home."

"No, I'm not," he said calmly.

The unintelligible stream of profanities started again.

"We can't all fit in my truck," I mumbled.

Edythe didn't seem to hear me.

"I think you should let me go alone," I said even more quietly.

She heard that.

"Beau, don't be stupid," she said between clenched teeth.

"Listen, Charlie's not an imbecile," I argued. "If you're not in town tomorrow, he's going to get suspicious."

"That's irrelevant. We'll make sure he's safe, and that's all that matters."

"Then what about this tracker? She saw how you acted tonight. She's going to think you're with me, wherever you are."

Eleanor looked at me, insultingly surprised again. "Edythe, listen to him," she urged. "I think he's right."

"He is," Archie agreed.

"I can't do that." Edythe's voice was icy.

"Eleanor should stay, too," I continued. "She definitely got an eyeful of Eleanor."

"What?" Eleanor turned on me, looking betrayed.

"You'll get a better crack at her if you stay," Archie agreed.

Edythe stared at him incredulously. "You think I should let him go alone?"

"Of course not," Archie said. "Jess and I will take him."

"I can't do that," Edythe repeated, but this time she sounded defeated. The logic was working on her.

I tried to be persuasive. "Hang out here for a week"—I saw her expression in the mirror and amended—"a few days. Let Charlie see you, and lead this hunter on a wild-goose chase. Make sure she's completely off the trail. Then come and meet me. Take a roundabout route, of course, and then Jessamine and Archie can go home."

She was beginning to consider it.

"Meet you where?"

"Phoenix."

"No," she said impatiently. "She'll hear that's where you're going."

"And you'll make it look like that's a trick, obviously. She'll know that *you'll* know that she's listening. She'll never believe I'm actually going where I say I am going."

"He's diabolical," Eleanor laughed.

"And if that doesn't work?"

"There are several million people in Phoenix," I informed her.

"It's not that hard to find a phone book."

"It's called a hotel, Edythe."

"Edythe, we'll be with him," Archie reminded her.

"What are *you* going to do in *Phoenix*?" she asked Archie scathingly.

"Stay indoors."

"I kind of like it." Eleanor was thinking about cornering Joss, no doubt.

"Shut up, El."

"Look, if we try to take her down while Beau's still around, there's a much better chance that someone will get hurt—he'll get hurt, or you will, trying to protect him. Now, if we get her alone . . ." She trailed off with a slow smile. I was right.

The Jeep was crawling slowly along now as we drove into town. I could feel the hairs on my arms standing up. I thought about Charlie, alone in the house, and my knee was bouncing with impatience.

"Beau," Edythe said in a very soft voice. Archie and Eleanor looked out

their windows. "If you let anything happen to yourself—anything at all—I'm holding you personally responsible. Do you understand that?"

I stared at her eyes in the mirror. "Ditto, Edythe."

She turned to Archie.

"Can Jessamine handle this?"

"Give her some credit, Edythe. She's been doing very, very well, all things considered."

"Can *you* handle this?"

Archie pulled his lips back in a horrific grimace and let loose a guttural snarl that had me wincing into the seat.

Edythe smiled at him. "But keep your opinions to yourself," she muttered suddenly.

19. GOODBYES

It looked like Charlie was waiting up for me. All the house lights were on. My mind went blank as I tried to think of a way to pull this off.

Edythe stopped a car length back from my truck. All three of them were ramrod straight in their seats, listening to every sound of the forest, looking through every shadow around the house, searching for something out of place. The engine died and I sat quietly as they continued to listen.

"She's not here," Edythe hissed. "Let's go."

Eleanor reached over to undo the harness. "Don't worry, Beau," she said in a low but cheerful voice. "We'll take care of things here quickly."

I felt the strangest sense of sadness as I looked at Eleanor's gorgeous and terrifying face. I barely knew her, but somehow, not knowing when I would see her again was awful. I knew this was the easiest goodbye I would have to survive in the next hour, and the thought made my stomach churn.

"Archie, El." Edythe's voice was a command. They slipped soundlessly into the darkness and were gone.

I crawled out after Eleanor, and Edythe was already there.

"Fifteen minutes," she said through her teeth.

I nodded, then stopped.

"Hurry, Beau."

"One thing." I bent down and kissed her once hard. "I love you. Whatever happens now, that doesn't change."

"Nothing is going to happen to you, Beau."

"Keep Charlie safe for me."

"Done. Hurry."

I nodded again, and then, with one backward glance at her, I jumped onto the porch and threw the front door open with a loud bang. I lurched inside and kicked the door shut behind me.

I suddenly knew what I was going to do, and I was already horrified at myself.

Charlie's face appeared in the hallway. "Beau?"

"Leave me alone," I snapped.

My eyes were starting to feel red and wet, and I knew I was going to have to get it together if I was going to do this right—protect Charlie, protect the Cullens, and make this plan work. It would be easier if I wasn't looking at him.

I wheeled and ran up the stairs, then slammed my bedroom door closed and locked it. I threw myself on the floor and yanked a duffel bag out from under the bed. Then I shoved my hand between the mattress and box spring, searching till I found the knotted tube sock with my cash hoard.

Charlie pounded on my door. "Beau, are you okay? What's going on?"

"I'm going home!" I yelled.

I turned to the dresser, and Edythe was already there, silently yanking out armfuls of clothes that she then threw at me. I caught what I could and stuffed it into the bag.

"So I guess your date didn't go so well." Charlie's voice was confused but calmer.

"Ugh, stay *out* of it, Charlie," I growled.

"Did she break up with you?"

"I broke up with her."

Edythe didn't react to what I was saying. She was totally focused. She swept my stuff off the top of the dresser and into the bag with one arm.

"Why?" Charlie asked, surprised. "I thought you really liked this girl."

"I do—too much."

"Um . . . that's not how that works, son."

Edythe zipped the bag up—apparently my packing time was over. She hung the strap on my shoulder.

"I'll be in the truck—go!" she whispered, and she pushed me toward the door. She vanished out the window.

I unlocked the door and shoved past Charlie. My bag knocked a picture off the wall as I hurtled down the stairs.

Charlie ran after me and grabbed the strap of my bag, hauling me back a step.

"Are you doing drugs, Beau?" he demanded.

"No!"

"Slow down. I don't understand. Tell me what happened."

He had a tight grip on the strap. I could leave it, but that would put a hole in my story. I was going to have to do this the hard way.

I turned to look at him, hoping the red in my eyes looked like anger.

"I'll tell you what happened," I said in the hardest voice I could manage. "I had a great night with the prettiest girl I've ever seen—and we talked about the future. The way she sees it—it's just like *you*. She's going to stay here the rest of her life. She's going to get married and have kids and never leave. And for a second, that all actually made *sense* to me. I'm losing myself here—I'm getting sucked in. If I don't run now, I'll never get out!"

"Beau, you can't leave now," he whispered. "It's nighttime."

"I'll sleep in the truck if I get tired."

"Just wait another week," he pleaded, looking shell-shocked. "Renée will be back by then."

This completely derailed me. "What?"

Relief flashed across Charlie's face when I hesitated. "She called while you were out. Things aren't going so well in Florida, and if Phil doesn't get signed by the end of the week, they're going back to Arizona. The assistant coach of the Sidewinders said they might have a spot for another shortstop."

I shook my head, trying to get back on track. Every passing second put Charlie in more danger.

"I have a key," I muttered, turning the knob. He was too close, one hand still locked on my bag, his face dazed. I couldn't lose any more time arguing with him. I was going to have to hurt him further.

"Just let me go, Charlie," I said through my teeth. I threw the door open. "It didn't work out, okay? I really, really *hate* Forks!"

The cruel words did their job—Charlie's hand dropped from my bag. His mouth fell open with surprise while a deep pain surfaced in his eyes. I turned my back on him and stalked out the door. I couldn't let him see my face now.

I tried to keep my walk angry, but I wanted to sprint. The dark yard seemed full of extra shadows that I was *pretty* sure were just my imagination. But not totally positive. I hurled my bag into the bed of the truck and wrenched the door open. The key was waiting in the ignition.

"I'll call you tomorrow!" I yelled.

I would never be able to explain this to him, never be able to make it right again. I gunned the engine and peeled out.

Edythe reached for my hand.

"Pull over," she said as Charlie and the house disappeared behind us.

I kept my eyes on the road, trying to control my face. "I can drive."

Suddenly she was sliding over my lap, her hands on the wheel and her foot pushing mine off the gas. She moved into the space between my leg and the door, then shoved me over with her hip. The truck didn't swerve an inch and she was in the driver's seat.

"You wouldn't be able to find the house," she explained.

Lights flared behind us. I jumped, and stared out the back window.

"It's just Archie," she said. She took my hand again.

When I closed my eyes, all I could see was Charlie standing in the doorway.

"The tracker?"

"She caught the end of your performance. She's running behind us now—about a mile back."

My body felt cold. "Can we outrun her?"

"No." But she sped up as she spoke. The truck's engine whined.

My plan wasn't feeling so brilliant anymore.

I was staring back at Archie's headlights when the truck shuddered and a dark shadow sprang up outside the window.

"E—!"

Her hand clamped over my mouth before I could finish shouting the warning.

"It's Eleanor!"

She dropped her hand to my knee.

"It's okay, Beau," she promised.

We raced out of town, headed north.

"I didn't realize you were still so bored with small-town life," she said conversationally, and I knew she was trying to distract me. "It seemed like you were adjusting fairly well—especially recently. Maybe I was just flattering myself that I was making life more interesting for you."

"That was below the belt," I confessed, staring at my knees. "Those were the last words my mother said to him when she left. It would have done less damage if I'd punched him."

"He'll forgive you," she promised.

I closed my eyes.

"Beau, it's going to be all right."

I looked down at her. "It won't be all right when we're not together."

"It's only a few days. Don't forget this was your idea."

"That makes it worse. Why did this happen? I don't understand."

She stared at the road ahead, her eyebrows pulling low over her eyes. "It's my fault. I shouldn't have exposed you like that."

I grabbed her hand. "No, that's not what I'm talking about. Okay, I was there. Big deal. It didn't bother the other two. Why did Joss decide to kill *me*? There are people all over the place—people who are a lot easier to get to." I glanced over my shoulder at Eleanor's shadow. "Why am I worth all this trouble?"

Edythe hesitated, thinking before she answered. "I got a good look at her mind tonight," she said in a low voice. "I'm not sure if there's anything I could have done to avoid this, once she caught your scent. It *is* partially your fault." She looked at me from the side of her eye for a second. "If you didn't smell so ridiculously delicious, she might not have bothered. But when I defended you . . . well, that made it a lot worse. She's not used to being thwarted, no matter how insignificant the object. She thinks of herself as a hunter—as *the* hunter. Her life is consumed with tracking, and a challenge is what she loves best in life. Suddenly we've presented her with an amazing challenge—a large clan of strong fighters, all determined to protect the one vulnerable element. You don't know how euphoric she is right now. It's her

favorite game, and we've just created the most exciting round ever." Her tone was full of disgust. She took a deep breath. "But if I had stood by, she would have killed you right then!" she hissed with frustration.

"I thought . . . I didn't smell the same to the others . . . as I do to you."

"You don't. But that doesn't mean that you aren't still a temptation to every one of them. If you *had* appealed to the tracker—or any of them—the same way you appeal to me, it would have meant a fight right there."

I shuddered.

"I don't think I have any choice but to kill her now," she muttered. "Carine won't like it."

"I don't like it," I whispered.

She looked at me, surprised. "You want me to spare her?"

I blinked. "No—I mean, yes. I don't care if she . . . dies. I mean, that would be a relief, right? I just don't want you . . . What if you get hurt?"

Her face went hard. "You don't have to worry about me. I don't fight fair."

I could hear the tires cross the bridge, though I couldn't see the river in the dark. I knew we were getting close.

"How do you kill a vampire?" I asked in a low voice.

She glanced at me—her eyes were hard to read. When she spoke her voice was harsh. "The only way to be sure is to tear her to shreds, and then burn the pieces."

"And the other two will fight with her?"

"The male will. I'm not sure about Lauren. They don't have a very strong bond—she's only with them for convenience. She was embarrassed by Joss's behavior in the meadow. . . ."

"But Joss and Victor—they'll be trying to kill you?" My voice was raw, like I'd sandblasted the back of my throat.

"Stop. You focus on staying safe. You do whatever Archie tells you."

"How am I supposed to not worry about you? What does that even mean—that you don't fight fair?"

She half-smiled. It didn't touch her eyes. "Have you ever tried to act without thinking of that act first? Aside from involuntary muscle actions like breathing and blinking, it's terribly difficult to do. Especially in a fight. I'll see every single thing she plans, every hole in her defense. The only one who can hold his own against me is Archie—since he can see what I decide to

do, but then I can hear how he'll react. It's usually a draw. Eleanor says it's cheating."

She seemed relaxed—like the idea of fighting the hunter and her partner was the easiest part of this whole mess. It made my stomach twist and plunge.

"Should Archie stay with you, then?" I asked. "If he's a better fighter than the others?"

"Eleanor can hear all this, you know. She's offended, and also not thrilled with that idea. It's been a while since she was allowed to really brawl, no holds barred. She plans to keep me and my cheating ways out of this as much as possible."

That made me feel a little bit better, which wasn't fair to Eleanor. I looked over my shoulder again, but I couldn't see her expression.

"Is she still following?" I asked.

Edythe knew I wasn't talking about Eleanor. "Yes. She won't attack the house, though. Not tonight."

She turned off onto the invisible drive. Archie's headlights followed. We drove right up to the house. The lights inside were bright, but they didn't do much to light up the surrounding trees. The yard was still black. Eleanor had my door open before the truck was stopped. She pulled me out of the seat, ducked under my arm, threw her arm around my waist, than ran me through the front door with my feet a foot off the ground, like I was a giant rag doll.

She burst into the big white room with Edythe and Archie on either side. All of them were there, already on their feet. Lauren stood in the middle of their circle. A low snarl rumbled in Eleanor's chest as she set me next to Edythe.

"She's tracking us," Edythe hissed, glaring at Lauren.

Lauren's expression was unhappy. "I was afraid of that."

Archie darted to Jessamine's side and whispered in her ear. They flew up the stairs together. Royal watched them, then moved quickly to Eleanor's side. His eyes were intense and—when they flickered unwillingly to my face—hostile.

"What will she do?" Carine asked Lauren.

"I'm sorry," she answered. "I was afraid, when your girl there defended him, that it would set Joss off."

"Can you stop her?"

Lauren shook her head. "Nothing stops Joss when she gets started."

"We'll stop her," Eleanor promised. There was no doubt what she meant.

"You can't bring her down," Lauren answered. "I've never seen anything like her in my three hundred years. She's absolutely lethal. That's why I joined her coven."

Her coven, I thought, of course. That whole show of leadership in the clearing was just that—a show.

Lauren was shaking her head. She glanced at me, obviously confused. "Are you sure this is all worth it?"

Edythe's furious growl tore through the room. Lauren cringed away from her.

Carine looked at Lauren. "I'm afraid you're going to have to make a choice."

Lauren understood. She hesitated for a minute. She looked at every face, then at the bright room.

"I'm intrigued by the life you've created here. But I won't get in the middle of this. I bear none of you any enmity, but I won't go up against Joss. I think I will head north—to that clan in Denali." She paused. "Don't underestimate Joss. She's got a brilliant mind and unparalleled senses. She looks wild, but she's every bit as comfortable in the human world as you seem to be. She won't come at you head on. . . . I'm sorry for what's been unleashed here. Truly sorry." She bowed her head, but I saw her flicker another puzzled look at me.

"Go in peace," Carine said.

Lauren took one more long look around the room, and then she disappeared through the door.

The silence lasted less than a second.

Carine looked at Edythe. "How close?"

Earnest was already moving. His hand touched a keypad on the wall, and with a groan, huge metal shutters began sealing up the glass wall. My mouth fell open.

"About three miles out past the river. She's circling around to meet up with the male."

"What's the plan?"

"We lead her off, then Archie and Jessamine will run him south."

"And then?"

Edythe's voice turned icy. "As soon as Beau is clear, we hunt her."

"I guess she's left us no other choice," Carine agreed, her expression grim.

Edythe looked at Royal. "Get him upstairs and trade clothes."

Royal stared back at her, incredulous.

"And why would I do that?" he asked. "What is he to me?"

"Roy . . . ," Eleanor murmured, putting one hand on his shoulder. He shook it off.

My eyes were on Edythe, worried that this would set off her temper, but she surprised me. She looked away from Royal like he hadn't spoken, like he didn't exist.

"Earnest?" she asked calmly.

"Of course."

As he was speaking, he was already at my side and ducking to grab me in a fireman's hold. We were up the stairs before I could register what was happening.

"What are we doing?" I asked as he set me down in a dark room somewhere off the second-story hall.

"Trying to confuse the scent trail. It won't work for long, but it might give you a head start." His voice was muffled as he pulled his shirt over his head.

I yanked my sweater off and held it out to him. He switched mine for his. I struggled to get my arms through the right holes, then yanked my jeans off. We traded. His pants were a little too short, but otherwise fit fine. He pulled me back to the hall. Earnest looked smaller in my clothes; he'd rolled the bottoms of my jeans. Archie was suddenly there; a leather satchel hung over his arm. They each grabbed one of my elbows and flew down the stairs.

It looked like everything had been settled. Edythe and Eleanor were ready to leave, Eleanor carrying a big backpack over her shoulder. Carine handed something small to Earnest. She turned to Archie and handed him the same thing—a tiny silver cell phone.

"Earnest and Royal will be taking your truck, Beau," she told me as she passed. I nodded, glancing warily at Royal. He was glaring at Carine, resentful.

"Archie, Jess, take the Mercedes. You'll need the dark tint in the South."

They nodded.

"We'll take the Jeep."

Carine stopped next to Edythe. I realized that this was the hunting party, and I felt like I was going to throw up. How did it get to this point? Why had they listened to my idea? It was obviously wrong.

"Archie, will they take the bait?"

Everyone watched Archie as he closed his eyes and became incredibly still. A few seconds later his eyes opened again.

"She'll track you. The man will follow the truck. We'll be able to leave after that." He was positive.

"Let's go," Carine said, heading for the kitchen.

But Edythe came back for me. She stared up at me, her gold eyes huge and deep and full of a million words she didn't have time to say, and reached up to put her hands on my face. I leaned down, my hands already in her hair. For the shortest second, her lips were icy and hard against mine.

Then it was over. She pushed my shoulders back. Her eyes went blank, dead, just before she turned away from me.

They were gone.

We stood there, no one looking at me while I stared after them. It felt like someone had ripped all the skin off my face. My eyes burned.

The silent moment dragged. Archie's eyes were closed again. Then Earnest's phone vibrated in his hand, and Archie nodded once. The phone flashed to Earnest's ear.

"Now," Earnest said. Royal stalked out the front door without another glance in my direction, but Earnest touched my shoulder as he passed.

"Be safe." His whisper lingered behind them as they slipped out the door. I heard the truck start thunderously, and then the sound faded away.

Jessamine and Archie waited. Then Archie lifted his phone to his ear just before it buzzed.

"Edythe says the man is on Earnest's trail. I'll get the car." He vanished into the shadows the way Edythe had gone.

Jessamine and I looked at each other. She stood across the length of the entryway from me.

"You're wrong, you know," she said.

"Huh?"

"I can feel what you're feeling now—and you *are* worth it."

The feeling of being slowly skinned didn't let up. "If anything happens to them, it will be for nothing," I whispered.

She smiled kindly. "You're wrong," she repeated.

Archie stepped through the front door and walked straight toward me, one arm out.

"May I?" he asked.

"You're the first one to ask permission," I mumbled.

Archie slung me up into a fireman's carry like Earnest had and, with Jessamine shielding us protectively, flew out the door, leaving the lights on behind us.

20. IMPATIENCE

WHEN I WOKE UP, I WAS CONFUSED. IT TOOK ME LONGER THAN IT SHOULD have to remember where I was.

The room was too bland to belong anywhere but a hotel. The bedside lamps were bolted to the tables, and the drapes were made from the same fabric as the bedspread.

I tried to remember how I'd gotten to this room, but nothing came at first.

I remembered the black car, the glass in the windows darker than that on a limousine. The engine was almost silent, though we'd raced across the black freeways at more than twice the legal limit.

And I remembered Archie on the seat next to me, rather than up front with Jessamine. I remembered realizing suddenly that he was there as my bodyguard, that the front seat was apparently not close enough. It should have made the danger seem more real, but it all felt a million miles away. The danger I was in personally wasn't the danger I was worried about.

I made Archie keep up a strange stream-of-consciousness future watch all night long. There weren't any details so small they didn't interest me. He'd told me turn by turn how Edythe, Carine, and Eleanor would be moving through the forest, and though I didn't know any of the landmarks he referenced, I'd been riveted by every word. And then he would go back and describe the same sequence differently, as some decision remapped the future. This happened over

and over again, and it was impossible to follow, but I didn't care. As long as the future never put Edythe and Joss in the same place, I'd been able to keep breathing.

Sometimes he would switch to Earnest for me. Earnest and Royal were in my truck, heading east. Which meant the red-haired man was still on their trail.

Archie'd had a more difficult time seeing Charlie. "Humans are harder than vampires," he told me. And I'd remembered that Edythe had said something to me about that once. It had seemed like years ago, when it had been only days. I remembered being disoriented by the way I couldn't make sense of the time.

I remembered the sun coming up over a low peak somewhere in California. The light had stung my eyes, but I'd tried not to close them. When I did, the images that flashed behind my lids like still slides were too much. I'd rather my eyes burn than see them again. Charlie's broken expression . . . Edythe's bared teeth . . . Royal's furious glare . . . the red eyes of the tracker staring at me . . . the dead look in Edythe's eyes when she'd turned away from me . . .

I kept my eyes open, and the sun moved across the sky.

I remembered my head feeling heavy and light at the same time as we raced through a shallow mountain pass and the sun, behind us now, reflected off the tiled rooftops of my hometown. I hadn't had enough emotion left to be surprised that we'd made a three-day journey in one. I'd stared blankly at the city laid out in front of us, realizing slowly that it was supposed to mean something to me. The scrubby creosote, the palm trees, the green golf course amoebas, the turquoise splotches of swimming pools—these were supposed to be familiar. I was supposed to feel like I was home.

The shadows of the streetlights had slanted across the freeway with lines that were sharper than I remembered. So little darkness. There was no place to hide in these shadows.

"Which way to the airport?" Jessamine had asked—the first time she'd spoken since we'd gotten in the car.

"Stay on the I-ten," I'd answered automatically. "We'll pass right by it."

It had taken me a few seconds more to process the implications of her question. My brain was foggy with exhaustion.

"Are we flying somewhere?" I'd asked Archie. I couldn't think of the plan. This didn't sound right, though.

"No, but it's better to be close, just in case."

I remembered starting the loop around Sky Harbor International . . . but not ending it. That must have been when my brain had finally crashed.

Though, now that I'd chased the memories down, I did have a vague impression of leaving the car—the sun behind the horizon, my arm draped over Archie's shoulder, his arm dragging me along as I stumbled through the warm, dry shadows.

I had no memory of this room.

I looked at the digital clock on the nightstand. The red numbers claimed it was three o'clock, but there was no way to tell if that meant a.m. or p.m. No light showed around the edges of the thick curtains, but the room was bright with the light from the lamps.

I rose stiffly and staggered to the window, pulling back the drapes.

It was dark outside. Three in the morning, then. The room looked out on a deserted section of the freeway and the new long-term parking garage for the airport. It made me feel better—by a very small amount—to be able to pinpoint time and place.

I looked down. I was still wearing Earnest's shirt and too-short pants. I looked around the room and was glad when I saw my duffel bag on top of the low dresser.

A light tap on the door made me jump.

"Can I come in?" Archie asked.

I took a deep breath. "Sure."

He walked in and looked me over. "You look like you could sleep longer."

I shook my head.

He darted silently to the window and pulled the curtains shut.

"We'll need to stay inside," he told me.

"Okay." My voice was hoarse; it cracked.

"Thirsty?" he asked.

I shrugged. "I'm okay. How about you?"

He smiled. "Nothing unmanageable. I ordered some food for you—it's in the front room. Edythe reminded me that you have to eat a lot more frequently than we do."

I was instantly more alert. "She called?"

"No." He watched my face fall. "It was before we left. She gave me lots of instructions. Come eat something."

He was out of the room before I could protest that I wasn't hungry. I followed slowly behind him.

There was a living room attached to the bedroom. A low buzz of voices was coming from the TV. Jessamine sat at the desk in the corner, her eyes on the TV, but no interest in her expression. Archie went to stand by her. He ran his hand over her honey-colored hair.

"What's the latest?" I asked.

"Earnest and Royal are back in Forks. The redhead gave up chasing them."

I opened my mouth, but Archie was faster.

"They're watching your father. The redhead won't get past them."

"What is he doing?"

"Working his way through town, looking for you as far as I can tell—he spent some time at the school."

My eyes bulged. "Did he hurt anyone?"

Archie shook his head. "They seem pretty committed to the hunt they already started."

"Edythe?"

"Frustrated, it looks like. They turned on the tracker, but she was already running. She's kept going north. They're chasing her."

I stood there, not sure what to do.

Edythe was chasing Joss. Sure, she had Carine and Eleanor with her, but Edythe was the fastest. . . .

"Eat something, Beau. Edythe gets really difficult when she thinks her instructions aren't being followed to the letter."

There was a tray on the coffee table with a couple of stainless steel covers over the plates on it. I couldn't think of anything to do besides follow Archie's order. I sat on the floor next to the table and pulled off the first plate cover. I didn't look at the food, I just grabbed something and started eating. I was probably hungry. We hadn't stopped for food during our drive.

They were quiet and motionless while I ate. I stared at the TV, but I couldn't make sense of what was happening. Was it a news show? Was it an

infomercial? I wasn't sure. I ate until the plates were empty. I didn't taste any of it.

When there was nothing left to eat, I stared at the wall.

All I could see was Edythe in the forest, faster than a cheetah—faster than a bullet. It was obvious she would catch up with the tracker first.

Lauren's words echoed in my head. *You can't bring her down. She's absolutely lethal.*

Suddenly Jessamine was standing over me, closer than usual.

"Beau," she said in a soothing voice. "You have nothing to worry about. You are completely safe here."

"I know."

"Then why are you frightened?" She sounded confused. She might feel my emotions, but she couldn't see the reasons behind them.

"You heard what Lauren said. Joss is lethal. What if something goes wrong, and they get separated? If anything happens, if Carine or Eleanor—or Edythe—" My voice broke. "If that crazy redhead hurts Earnest—how do I live with myself when it's my fault? None of you should be risking your lives for—"

"Stop, Beau, stop," she interrupted, her words pouring out so quickly they were hard to understand. "You're worrying about all the wrong things, Beau. Trust me on this—none of *us* are in jeopardy. You are under enough strain as it is; don't add to it with imaginary worries. Listen to me!" she ordered—I'd looked away. "Our family is strong. Our only fear is losing you."

"But why should you—"

Archie was there then, his arm around Jessamine's waist. "It's been almost a century that Edythe's been alone. Now she's found you. You can't see the changes that we see, we who have been with her for so long. Do you think any of us want to look into her eyes for the next hundred years if she loses you?"

My guilt started to ease. But even though the calm that spread over me felt totally natural, like it came from inside, I knew better.

"You know I'd do this anyway," Archie added. "Even if Edythe hadn't ask me to."

"Why?"

He grinned. "It's hard to explain without sounding slightly schizo-

phrenic. . . . Time doesn't mean the same thing to me that it does to you—or Jess, or anyone else." Jessamine grinned and tweaked his ear. "So this won't make sense to you. But for me, it's like we've already been friends for a long time, Beau. The first second you became a part of Edythe's life, for me it was like we'd already spent hundreds of hours together. We've laughed at Edythe's overreactions together, we've annoyed Royal right out of the house together, we've stayed up all night talking with Carine together. . . ."

I stared and he shrugged. "It's how I experience the world."

"We're friends?" I asked, my voice full of wonder.

"Best friends," he told me. "Someday. It was nice of my favorite sister, don't you think, to fall in love with my best friend? I guess I owe her one."

"Huh," was all I could think to say.

Archie laughed.

Jessamine rolled her eyes. "Thanks so much, Archie. I just got him calm."

"No, I'm good," I promised. Archie could be lying to make me feel better, but either way it worked. It wasn't so bad if Archie wanted to help me, too. If he wasn't just doing it for Edythe.

"So what do we do now?" I asked.

"We wait for something to change."

It was a very long day.

We stayed in the room. Archie called down to the front desk and asked them to suspend our housekeeping service. The curtains stayed shut, the TV on, though no one watched it. At regular intervals, food was delivered for me.

It was funny how I was suddenly comfortable with Archie. It was like his vision of our friendship, spoken out loud, had made it real. He sat in the chair next to the sofa where I sprawled, and answered all the questions I'd been too nervous to ask before. Sometimes he'd answer them before I asked them. It was a little weird, but I figured that was how everyone else felt around Edythe all the time.

"Yes," he said, when I thought about asking him that. "It's exactly the same. She tries hard not to be obnoxious about it."

He told me about waking up.

"I only remembered one thing, but I'm not even sure it *was* a memory. I thought I remembered someone saying my name—calling me Archie. But

maybe I was remembering something that hadn't happened yet—seeing that someday someone *would* call me Archie." He smiled at my expression. "I know, it's a circular dilemma, isn't it?"

"The hair?" He ran a hand over his scalp, unselfconscious. The stubble was just long enough to see that his hair would have been dark brown, nearly black, like his eyebrows. "It was a rather extreme look for 1920. A little too early for me to have been a skinhead, thank heavens. My best guess is disease or bad behavior."

"Bad behavior?" I asked.

He shrugged. "I might have been in prison."

"You couldn't have been much older than me," I protested.

He steepled his fingers thoughtfully. "I like to believe that if I *was* a criminal, I was both a mastermind and a prodigy."

Jessamine—back at the desk and mostly silent—laughed with me.

"It wasn't confusing the way it probably *should* have been," Archie said when I asked him what his first visions were like. "It seemed normal—I knew what I was seeing hadn't happened. I think maybe I'd seen things before I was changed. Or maybe I just adapt quickly." He smiled, already knowing the question I had waiting. "It was Jess. She was the first thing I saw." And then, "No, I didn't actually meet her in person until much later."

Something about his tone made me wonder. "How long?"

"Twenty-eight years."

"Twenty-eight . . . ? You had to wait twenty-eight *years*? But couldn't you . . . ?"

He nodded. "I could have found her earlier. I knew where she was. But she wasn't ready for me yet. If I'd come too early, she would have killed me."

I gasped and stared at her. She raised an eyebrow at me, and I looked back at Archie. He laughed.

"But Edythe said you were the only one who could hold your own against her—?"

Jessamine hissed—not like she was mad, like she was annoyed. I glanced at her again and she was rolling her eyes.

"We'll never know," Archie said. "If Jess was really trying to kill Edythe, rather than just playing . . . ? Well, Jess has a lot of experience. Seeing the future isn't the only reason why I can keep up with Edythe—it's also

because it was Jess who taught me how to fight. Lauren's coven all had their eyes on Eleanor—she's pretty spectacular, I grant you. But if it had come to a fight, Eleanor wouldn't have been their problem. If they'd taken a closer look at my darling"—he blew her a kiss—"they would have forgotten all about the strong girl."

I remembered the first time I'd seen Jessamine, in the cafeteria with her family. Beautiful, like the others, but with that edge. Even before I'd put it into words inside my own head, I'd sensed there was something about her that matched up with what Archie was telling me now.

I looked at Archie.

"You can ask her," he said. "But it's not going to happen."

"He wants to know my story?" Jessamine guessed. She laughed once—it was a dark sound. "You're not ready for that, Beau. Believe me."

And though I was still curious, I did believe her.

"You said humans were harder . . . but you seem to see me pretty well," I noted.

"I'm paying attention, and you're right here," Archie said. "Also, the two-second head starts are simpler than the weather. It's the long term that won't hold still. Even an hour complicates things."

Archie kept me updated on what was happening with the others—which was mostly nothing. Joss was good at running away. There were tricks, Archie told me. Scents couldn't be tracked through water, for example. Joss seemed to know the tricks. A half dozen times the trail took them back toward Forks, only to race off in the other direction again. Twice Archie called Carine to give her instructions. Once it was something about the direction in which Joss had jumped off a cliff, the other time it was where they would find her scent on the other side of a river. From the way he described it, he wasn't seeing the hunter, he was seeing Edythe and Carine. I guessed he would see his family the most clearly. I wanted to ask for the phone, but I knew there wasn't time for me to hear Edythe's voice. They were hunting.

I also knew I was supposed to be rooting for Edythe and the others to succeed, but I could only feel relieved as the distance between her and Joss got larger, despite Archie's help. If it meant I would be stuck here in this hotel room forever, I wouldn't complain. Whatever kept her safe.

There was one question that I wanted to ask more than the others, but I hesitated. I think if Jessamine hadn't been there, I might have done it sooner.

I didn't feel the same ease in her presence that I did now with Archie. Which was probably only because she wasn't *trying* to make me feel that way.

When I was eating—dinner? Maybe, I couldn't remember which meal I was on—I was thinking about different ways to ask. And then I caught a look on Archie's face and I knew that he already knew what I was trying to ask, and unlike my dozens of other questions, he was choosing not to answer this one.

My eyes narrowed.

"Was this on Edythe's lists of instructions?" I asked sourly.

I thought I heard a very faint sigh from Jessamine's corner. It was probably annoying listening to half a conversation. But she should be used to that. I'd bet Edythe and Archie never had to speak out loud at all when they talked to each other.

"It was implied," Archie answered.

I thought about their fight in the Jeep. Was this what it was about?

"I don't suppose our future friendship is enough to shift your loyalties?"

He frowned. "Edythe is my sister."

"Even if you disagree with her on this?"

We stared at each other for a minute.

"That's what you saw," I realized. I felt my eyes get bigger. "And then she got so upset. You already saw it, didn't you?"

"It was only one future among many. I also saw you die," he reminded me.

"But you saw it. It's a possibility."

He shrugged.

"Don't you think I deserve to know, then? Even if there's only the slightest chance?"

He stared at me, deliberating.

"You do," he finally said. "You have the right to know."

I waited.

"You don't know fury like Edythe when she's thwarted," he warned me.

"It's none of her business. This is between you and me. As your friend, I'm begging you."

He paused, then made his choice. "I can tell you the mechanics of it, but I don't remember it myself, and I've never done it or seen it done, so keep in mind that I can only tell you the theory."

"How does someone become a vampire?"

"Oh, is *that* all?" Jessamine muttered behind me. I'd forgotten she was listening.

I waited.

"As predators," Archie began, "we have a glut of weapons in our physical arsenal—much, much more than we need for hunting easy prey like humans. Strength, speed, acute senses, not to mention those of us like Edythe, Jessamine, and me who have extra senses as well. And then, like a carnivorous flower, we are physically attractive to our prey."

I was seeing it all in my head again—how Edythe had illustrated the same concept for me in the meadow.

He smiled wide—his teeth glistened. "We have one more, fairly superfluous weapon. We're also venomous. The venom doesn't kill—it's merely incapacitating. It works slowly, spreading through the bloodstream, so that, once bitten, our prey is in too much physical pain to escape us. Mostly superfluous, as I said. If we're that close, our prey doesn't escape. Of course, unless we want it to."

"Carine," I said quietly. The holes in the story Edythe had told me were filling themselves in. "So . . . if the venom is left to spread . . . ?"

"It takes a few days for the transformation to be complete, depending on how much venom is in the bloodstream, how close the venom enters to the heart—Carine's creator bit her on the hand on purpose to make it worse. As long as the heart keeps beating, the poison spreads, healing, changing the body as it moves through it. Eventually the heart stops, and the conversion is finished. But all that time, every minute of it, a victim would be wishing for death—screaming for it."

I shuddered.

"It's not pleasant, no."

"Edythe said it was very hard to do . . . but that sounds simple enough."

"We're also like sharks in a way. Once we taste blood, or even smell it for that matter, it becomes very hard to keep from feeding. Impossible, even. So you see, to actually bite someone, to taste the blood, it would begin the frenzy. It's difficult on both sides—the bloodlust on the one hand, the awful pain on the other."

"It sounds like something you would remember," I said.

"For everyone else, the pain of transformation is the sharpest memory they have of their human life. I don't know why I'm different."

Archie stared past me, motionless. I wondered what it would be like, not to know who you were. To look in the mirror and not recognize the person looking back.

It was hard for me to believe that Archie could have been a criminal, though; there was something intrinsically *good* about his face. Royal was the showy one, the one the girls at school stared at, but there was something better than perfection about Archie's face. It was totally pure.

"There are positives to being different," Archie said suddenly. "I don't remember anyone I left behind. I got to skip that pain, too." He looked at me, and his eyes narrowed a little bit. "Carine, Edythe, and Earnest all lost everyone who mattered to them before they left being human behind. So there was grief, but not regret. It was different for the others. The physical pain is a quick thing, comparatively, Beau. There are slower ways to suffer. . . ."

"Royal had parents who loved him and depended on him—two little sisters he adored. He could never see them again after he was changed. And then he outlived them all. That kind of pain is very, very slow."

I wondered if he was trying to make me feel bad for Royal—to cut the guy some slack even if he hated me. Well . . . it was working.

He shook his head, like he knew I wasn't getting it.

"That's part of the process, Beau. I haven't experienced it. I can't tell you what it feels like. But it's a part of the process."

And then I understood what he was telling me.

He was perfectly still again. I put my arm behind my head and stared up at the ceiling.

If . . . if ever, someday, Edythe wanted me that way . . . what would that mean for Mom? What would that mean for Charlie?

There were so many things to think about. Things I didn't even know I didn't know to think about.

But some things seemed obvious. For whatever reason, Edythe didn't want me thinking about any of this. Why? It hurt my stomach when I tried to come up with an answer to that question.

Then Archie sprang to his feet.

I looked up at him, startled by the sudden movement, then alarmed again when I saw his face.

It was totally blank—empty, his mouth half open.

Then Jessamine was there, gently pushing him back into the chair.

"What do you see?" she asked in a low, soothing voice.

"Something's changed," Archie said, even more quietly.

I leaned closer.

"What is it?"

"A room. It's long—there are mirrors everywhere. The floor is wood. The tracker is in the room, and she's waiting. There's a gold stripe across the mirrors."

"Where is the room?"

"I don't know. Something is missing—another decision hasn't been made yet."

"How much time?"

"It's soon. She'll be in the mirror room today, or maybe tomorrow. It all depends. She's waiting for something." His face went blank again. "And she's in the dark now."

Jessamine's voice was calm, methodical. "What is she doing?"

"She's watching TV . . . no, she's running a VCR, in the dark, in another place."

"Can you see where she is?"

"No, the space is too dark."

"And the mirror room, what else is there?"

"Just the mirrors, and the gold. It's a band, around the room. And there's a black table with a big stereo, and a TV. She's touching the VCR there, but she doesn't watch the way she does in the dark room. This is the room where she waits." His eyes drifted, then focused on Jessamine's face.

"There's nothing else?"

He shook his head. They looked at each other, motionless.

"What does it mean?" I asked.

Neither of them answered for a moment, then Jessamine looked at me.

"It means the tracker's plans have changed. She's made a decision that will lead her to the mirror room, and the dark room."

"But we don't know where those rooms are?"

"No."

"But we do know that she won't be in the mountains north of Washington, being hunted. She'll elude them." Archie's voice was bleak.

He picked up the phone just as it vibrated.

"Carine," he said. And then he glanced at me. "Yes." He listened for another long moment, then said, "I just saw her." He described the vision like he had for Jessamine. "Whatever made her take that plane . . . it was leading her to those rooms." He paused. "Yes."

He held out the phone to me. "Beau?"

I yanked it out of his hand. "Hello?"

"Beau," Edythe breathed.

"Oh, Edythe," I said. "Where are you?"

"Outside of Vancouver. I'm sorry, Beau—we lost her. She seems suspicious of us—she stays just far enough away that I can't hear her. She's gone now—looks like she stole a small plane. We think she's heading back to Forks to start over."

I could hear Archie filling Jessamine in behind me.

"I know. Archie saw that she got away."

"You don't have to worry, though. You've left no trail for her to follow. You just have to stay with Archie and wait till we find her again. Archie will get a bead on her soon enough."

"I'll be fine. Is Earnest with Charlie?"

"Yes—the male's been in town. He went to the house, but while Charlie was at work. He hasn't gone near your father. Don't worry—Charlie's safe with Earnest and Royal watching."

Somehow, Royal's presence didn't comfort me much.

"What do you think Victor is doing?"

"Trying to pick up the trail. He's been all through the area during the night. Royal traced him up to the airport in Port Angeles, all the roads around town, the school . . . he's digging, Beau, but there's nothing to find."

"And you're sure Charlie's safe?"

"Yes. Earnest won't let him out of his sight. I'll be there soon. If the tracker gets anywhere near Forks, I'll have her."

I swallowed. "Be careful. Stay with Carine and Eleanor."

"I know what I'm doing."

"I miss you," I said.

"I know, believe me, I know. It's like you've taken half of my self away with you."

"Come and get it, then."

"As soon as I possibly can. I *will* make this right first." Her voice got hard.

"I love you."

"Could you believe that, despite everything I've put you through, I love you, too?"

"Yes, I can."

"I'll come for you soon."

"I'll wait for you."

The phone went dead, and a sudden wave of depression crashed over me. Jessamine looked up sharply, and the feeling dissipated.

Jessamine went back to watching Archie. He was on the couch, leaning over the table with the free hotel pen in his hand. I walked over to see what he was doing.

He was sketching on a piece of hotel stationery. I leaned on the back of the couch, looking over his shoulder.

He drew a room: long, rectangular, with a thinner, square section at the back. He drew lines to show how the wooden planks that made up the floor stretched lengthwise across the room. Down the walls were more lines denoting the breaks in the mirrors. I hadn't been picturing them like that—covering the whole wall that way. And then, wrapping around the walls, waist high, a long band. The band Archie said was gold.

"It's a ballet studio," I said, suddenly recognizing the familiar shapes.

They both looked up at me, surprised.

"Do you know this room?" Jessamine's voice sounded calm, but there was an undercurrent to it. Archie leaned closer to the paper, his hand flying across the page now. An emergency exit took shape against the back wall just where I knew it would be; the stereo and TV filled in the right corner foreground.

"It looks like a place where my mom used to teach dance lessons—she didn't stick with it for very long. It was shaped just the same." I touched the page where the square section jutted out, narrowing the back part of the room. "That's where the bathrooms were—the doors were through the other dance floor. But the stereo was here"—I pointed to the left corner—"it was

older, and there wasn't a TV. There was a window in the waiting room—you could see the room from this perspective if you looked through it."

Archie and Jessamine were staring at me.

"Are you sure it's the same room?" Jessamine asked with the same unnatural calm.

"No, not at all. I mean, most dance studios would look the same—the mirrors, the bar." I leaned over the couch and traced my finger along the ballet bar set against the mirrors. "It's just the shape that looked familiar."

"Would you have any reason to go there now?" Archie asked.

"No. I haven't been back since my mom quit—it's probably been ten years."

"So there's no way it could be connected with you?" Archie asked intently.

I shook my head. "I don't even think the same person owns it. I'm sure it's just another dance studio, somewhere else."

"Where was the studio your mother went to?" Jessamine asked, her voice much more casual than Archie's.

"Just around the corner from our house. It's why she took the job—so I could meet her there when I walked home from school. . . ." My voice trailed off as I watched the look they exchanged.

"Here in Phoenix, then?" she asked, still casual.

"Yes," I whispered. "Fifty-eighth and Cactus."

We all stared in silence at the drawing.

"Archie, is that phone safe?" I asked.

"The number just traces back to Washington," he told me.

"Then I can use it to call my mom."

"She's in Florida, right? She should be safe there."

"She is—but she's coming home soon, and she can't come back to that house while . . ." A tremor ran through my voice. I was thinking about Victor searching Charlie's house, the school in Forks where my records were.

"What's her number?" Archie asked. He had the phone in his hand.

"They don't have a permanent number except at the house. She's supposed to check her messages regularly."

"Jess?" Archie asked.

She thought about it. "I don't think it could hurt—don't say where you are, obviously."

I nodded, reaching for the phone. I dialed the familiar number, then waited through four rings until my mother's breezy voice came on, telling me to leave a message.

"Mom," I said after the beep, "it's me. Listen, I need you to do something. It's important. As soon as you get this message, call me at this number." Archie pointed to the number already written on the bottom of his picture. I read it carefully, twice. "Please don't go anywhere until you talk to me. Don't worry, I'm okay, but I have to talk to you right away, no matter how late you get this call, all right? I love you, Mom. Bye." I closed my eyes and prayed that no unforeseen change of plans would bring her home before she got my message.

Then we were back to waiting.

I thought about calling Charlie, but I wasn't sure what I could say. I watched the news, concentrating now, watching for stories about Florida, or about spring training—strikes or hurricanes or terrorist attacks—anything that might send them home early.

It seemed like immortality granted endless patience, too. Neither Jessamine nor Archie seemed to feel the need to do anything at all. For a while, Archie sketched the vague outline of the dark room from his vision, as much as he could see in the light from the TV. But when he was done, he simply sat, looking at the blank walls. Jessamine, too, seemed to have no urge to pace, or to peek through the curtains, or to punch holes in the wall, the way I did.

I fell asleep on the couch, waiting for the phone to ring.

21. PHONE CALL

WHEN I WOKE UP, I KNEW IT WAS TOO EARLY. I WAS GETTING MY DAYS and nights reversed. The TV was on—the only light in the room—but the sound was muted. The clock on the TV said it was just after two in the morning. I could hear the sound of quiet voices speaking too quickly, and I figured that was what had woken me. I lay still on the couch for a minute, waiting for my eyes and ears to adjust.

I realized that it was strange that they were talking loud enough to wake me, and I sat up.

Archie was leaning over the desk, Jessamine next to him with her hand on his back. He was sketching again.

I got up and walked over to them. Neither one of them looked up, too engrossed in Archie's work.

I went around to Archie's other side to see.

"He saw something else," I said quietly to Jessamine.

"Something's brought the tracker back to the room with the VCR, but it's light now," she answered.

I watched as Archie drew a square room with dark beams across its low ceiling. The walls were paneled in wood, a little too dark, out of date. The floor had a dark carpet with a pattern in it. There was a large window against the south wall, and an opening through the west wall led to the living room. One side of that entrance was stone—a large tan stone fireplace that was open to both

rooms. The focus of the room from this perspective, the TV and VCR, balanced on a too-small wooden stand, were in the southwest corner of the room. An old sectional sofa curved around in front of the TV, a round coffee table in front of it.

"The phone goes there," I whispered, pointing.

They both stared at me.

"That's my mom's house."

Archie was across the room, phone in hand, dialing. I stared at the faithful rendering of my family room. Uncharacteristically, Jessamine slid closer to me. She lightly touched her hand to my shoulder, and the physical contact seemed to make her calming influence stronger. The panic stayed dull, unfocused.

Archie's lips blurred, he was talking so fast—his voice was just a low buzzing impossible to understand.

"Beau," he said. I looked at him numbly.

"Beau, Edythe is coming. She and Eleanor and Carine are going to take you somewhere, hide you for a while."

"Edythe is coming?"

"Yes, she's catching the first flight out of Seattle. We'll meet her at the airport, and you'll leave with her."

"But—my mom! She came here for my mom, Archie!" Even with Jessamine touching me, I could feel the panic seizing up my chest.

"Jess and I will stay till she's safe again."

"We can't win, Archie! You can't guard everyone I know forever. Don't you see what she's doing? She's not even tracking me. She'll find someone—she'll hurt someone I love! Archie, I can't—"

"We'll catch her, Beau."

"And what if you get hurt, Archie? Do you think that's okay with me? Do you think it's only my human family she can hurt me with?"

Archie raised his eyebrows at Jessamine. A heavy fog of exhaustion washed over me, and my eyes closed without my permission. I struggled against the fog, knowing what was happening. I forced my eyes open and stepped away from Jessamine's hand.

"I don't need sleep," I snapped.

I went back to the bedroom, slamming the door behind me. Archie didn't follow me, the way I half-expected him to. Maybe he could see what his reception would be.

For almost four hours I sat on the floor and stared at the wall, my hands clenched into fists. My mind went around in circles, trying to come up with some way out of this nightmare. I couldn't see any escape—just one possible end. The only question was how many other people would get hurt before I reached it.

The only hope I had left was knowing that I would see Edythe soon. Maybe, if I could see her face again, I would be able to see a solution, too. Things were always clearer when we were together.

When the phone rang, I went back to the front room, a little ashamed of my behavior. I hoped I hadn't offended anyone. I hoped they realized that I was nothing but grateful for the sacrifices they were making for me.

Archie was talking at high speed into the phone again. I looked around, but Jessamine was gone. The clock said it was five-thirty in the morning.

"They're just boarding their plane," Archie told me. "They'll land at nine-forty-five."

Just a few more hours to keep myself together till she was here.

"Where's Jessamine?"

"She went to check out."

"You aren't staying here?"

"No, we're relocating closer to your mother's house."

I felt like I wanted to throw up, but then the phone rang again. Archie looked at the number, then held it out to me. I yanked it from his hand.

"Mom?"

"Beau? Beau?" It was my mom's voice—that familiar tone I'd heard a thousand times in my childhood, anytime I'd gotten too close to the edge of the sidewalk or strayed out of her sight in a crowded place. It was the sound of panic.

"Calm down, Mom," I said in my most soothing voice, walking slowly away from Archie, back to the bedroom. I wasn't sure if I could lie convincingly with him watching. "Everything is fine, okay? Just give me a minute and I'll explain everything, I promise."

I paused, surprised that she hadn't interrupted me yet.

"Mom?"

"Be very careful not to say anything until I tell you to." The voice I heard now was as unfamiliar as it was unexpected. It was a woman's voice, but not my

mom's. It was a soft alto voice, a very pleasant, generic voice—the kind of voice that you heard in the background of luxury car commercials. She spoke quickly.

"Now, I don't *need* to hurt your mother, so please do exactly as I say, and she'll be fine." She paused for a minute while I listened in mute horror. "That's very good," she congratulated. "Now repeat after me, and do try to sound natural. Please say, 'No, Mom, stay where you are.'"

"No, Mom, stay where you are." My voice was barely more than a whisper.

"I can see this is going to be difficult." The voice was amused, still light and friendly. "Why don't you walk into another room now so your face doesn't ruin everything? There's no reason for your mother to suffer. As you're walking, say, 'Mom, please listen to me.' Say it now."

"Mom, please listen to me," I pleaded. I walked slowly through the bedroom door, feeling Archie's worried stare on my back. I shut the door behind me, trying to think clearly through the terror that immobilized my brain.

"There now, are you alone? Just answer yes or no."

"Yes."

"But they can still hear you, I'm sure."

"Yes."

"All right, then," the agreeable voice continued, "say, 'Mom, trust me.'"

"Mom, trust me."

"This worked out rather better than I expected. I was prepared to wait, but your mother arrived ahead of schedule. It's easier this way, isn't it? Less suspense, less anxiety for you."

I waited.

"Now I want you to listen very carefully. I'm going to need you to get away from your friends; do you think you can do that? Answer yes or no."

"No."

"I'm sorry to hear that. I was hoping you would be a little more creative. Do you think you could get away from them if your mother's life depended on it? Answer yes or no."

Somehow, there had to be a way.

"Yes," I said through my teeth.

"Very good, Beau. Now this is what you have to do. I want you to go to your mother's house. Next to the phone there will be a number. Call it, and I'll tell you where to go from there." I already knew where I would go, and

where this would end. But I would follow her instructions exactly. "Can you do that? Answer yes or no."

"Yes."

"Before noon, please, Beau. I haven't got all day," she said.

"Where's Phil?" I hissed.

"Ah, be careful now, Beau. Wait until I ask you to speak, please."

I waited.

"It's important that you don't make your friends suspicious when you go back to them. Tell them that your mother called, and that you talked her out of coming home for the time being. Now repeat after me, 'Thank you, Mom.' Say it now."

"Thank you, Mom." It was hard to understand the words. My throat was closing up.

"Say, 'I love you, Mom, I'll see you soon.' Say it now."

"I love you, Mom," I choked out. "I'll see you soon," I promised.

"Goodbye, Beau. I look forward to seeing you again." She hung up.

I held the phone to my ear. My joints were frozen with horror—I couldn't unbend my fingers to drop it.

I knew I had to think, but my head was filled with the sound of my mother's panic. Seconds ticked by while I fought for control.

Slowly, slowly, my thoughts started to break past that brick wall of pain. To plan. Because I had no choices now but one: to go to the mirrored room and die. I had no guarantees that doing what she wanted would keep my mother alive. I could only hope that Joss would be satisfied with winning the game, that beating Edythe would be enough. Despair was like a noose pulling tight around my neck; there was no way to bargain, nothing I could offer or withhold that would influence her. But I still had no choice. I had to try.

I pushed the terror back as well as I could. My decision was made. It did no good to waste time agonizing over it. I had to think clearly, because Archie and Jessamine were waiting for me, and deceiving them was absolutely essential, and absolutely impossible.

I was suddenly grateful that Jessamine was gone. If she had been here to feel my anguish in the last five minutes, how could I have kept them in the dark? I fought back the fear, the horror, tried to force a lid on it all. I couldn't afford to feel now. I didn't know when she would be back.

I tried to concentrate on my escape, then immediately realized that I couldn't plan anything. I had to be undecided. No doubt Archie would see the change soon, if he hadn't already. I couldn't let him see how it happened. *If* it happened. How could I get away? Especially when I couldn't even think about it.

I wanted to go see what Archie had made of all this—if he'd seen any changes yet—but I knew I had to deal with one more thing alone before Jessamine got back.

I had to accept that I would never see Edythe again. Not even one last look at her face to take with me to the mirror room. I was going to hurt her, and I couldn't say goodbye. It was like being tortured. I burned in it for a minute, let it break me. And then I had to pull my shell together to go face Archie.

The only expression I could manage was a blank, dead look, but I felt like that was understandable. I walked into the living room, my script ready to go.

Archie was bent over the desk, gripping the edge with two hands. His face—

At first the panic broke through my mask, and I jumped around the couch to get to him. While I was still in motion, I realized what he must be seeing. It brought me up short a few feet away from him.

"Archie," I said dully.

He didn't react when I called his name. His head rocked slowly from side to side. His expression brought the panic back again—maybe this wasn't about me, maybe he was watching my mother.

I took another step forward, reaching out to touch his arm.

"Archie!" Jessamine's voice whipped from the door, and then she was right behind Archie, her hands curling over his, loosening them from their grip on the table. Across the room, the door swung shut with a low click.

"What is it?" she demanded. "What did you see?"

He turned his empty face away from me, looking blindly into Jessamine's eyes.

"Beau," he said.

"I'm right here."

His head twisted, his eyes locked on mine, their expression still blank. I realized that he hadn't been speaking to me—he'd been answering Jessamine's question.

22. HIDE-AND-SEEK

"WHAT WAS IT?" I'D LOST CONTROL OF MY VOICE—IT WAS FLAT, UNCARING.

Jessamine stared at me. I kept my expression vacant and waited. Her eyes flickered between Archie's face and mine, feeling the chaos. I knew what Archie had seen.

A peaceful atmosphere settled around me. I didn't fight it. I used it to keep my emotions under control.

Archie recovered, too. His face snapped back to its normal expression.

"Nothing," he said, his voice amazingly calm and convincing. "Just the same room as before." He looked at me, focusing for the first time. "Did you want breakfast?"

"I'll eat at the airport." I was calm, too. Almost like I was borrowing Jessamine's extra sense, I could feel Archie's well-concealed desperation to get me out of the room, so that he could be alone with her. So he could tell her that they were doing something wrong, that they were going to fail.

Archie was still focused on me.

"Is your mother all right?"

I had to swallow back a throatful of bile. I could only follow the script I'd planned earlier.

"My mom was worried," I said in a monotone voice. "She wanted to come home. It's okay. I convinced her to stay in Florida for now."

"That's good."

"Yes," I agreed robotically.

I turned and walked slowly to the bedroom, feeling their eyes following the whole way. I shut the door behind me, and then I did what I could. I showered and got dressed in clothes that fit me. I dug through the duffel bag until I found my sock full of money—I emptied it into my pocket.

I stood there for a minute, staring at nothing, trying to think of things I was allowed to think about. I came up with one idea.

I knelt by the little bedside table and opened the top drawer. Underneath the complimentary copy of the Bible, there was a stash of stationery and a pen. I took a sheet of paper and an envelope out of the drawer.

"Edythe," I wrote. My hand was shaking. The letters were barely legible.

I love you.

Sorry—again. So sorry.

She has my mom, and I have to try. I know it may not work. I am so very, very sorry.

Don't be mad at Archie and Jessamine. If I get away from them it will be a miracle. Tell them thank you for me. Archie especially.

And please, please don't come after her. That's what she wants. I can't stand it if anyone else has to be hurt because of me, especially you. Please, this is the only thing I can ask you now. For me.

I'm not sorry that I met you. I'll never be sorry that I love you.

Forgive me.

Beau.

I folded the paper into thirds, and then sealed it into the envelope. Eventually she would find it. I hoped she would understand. I hoped she would forgive. And most of all, I hoped she would listen.

When I walked back out to the living room, they were ready.

I sat alone this time in the back of the car. Jessamine kept shooting glances

at me in the mirror when she thought I wouldn't notice. She kept me calm, which I appreciated.

Archie leaned against the passenger door, his face pointed at Jessamine, but I knew he was watching me in his peripheral vision. How much had he seen? Was he expecting me to try something? Or was he focused on the tracker's moves?

"Archie?" I asked.

He was wary. "Yes?"

"I wrote a note for my mom," I said slowly. "Would you give it to her? Leave it at the house, I mean?"

"Of course, Beau." His voice was careful—the way you spoke to someone standing on a ledge. They could both see me coming apart. I had to control myself better.

We got to the airport quickly. Jessamine parked in the center of the garage's fourth floor; the sun couldn't reach this deep into the concrete block. We never had to leave the shadows as we made our way to the terminal. It was terminal four, the biggest one, the most confusing. Maybe that would help.

I led the way, for once more knowledgeable about our surroundings than they were. We took the elevator down to level three, where the passengers unloaded. Archie and Jessamine spent a while looking at the departing flights board. I could hear them discussing the pros and cons of New York, Atlanta, Chicago. Places I'd never been. Places where I would never go, now.

I tried not to think about my escape. We sat in the long row of chairs by the metal detectors, and my knee kept bouncing. Jessamine and Archie pretended to people-watch, but they were really just watching me. Every inch I shifted in my seat was followed by a quick glance out of the corner of their eyes. This was hopeless. Should I run? Would they dare to stop me physically with all these people around? Or would they just follow?

Whatever I did, I was going to have to time it right. If I waited till Edythe and Carine were close, Archie would have to wait for them, right? But I couldn't let it get too close. I was pretty sure Edythe wouldn't care about the human witnesses when she started tracking me.

Part of me was able to make these calculated judgments. The other part was so aware that Edythe was almost here. Like every cell in my body was pulling toward her. That made it harder. I found myself trying to think

of excuses to stay, to see her first and then make my escape. But that was impossible if I was going to have any chance at all to run.

Several times Archie offered to go get breakfast with me. Later, I told him. Not yet.

I stared at the arrival board, watching as flight after flight arrived on time. The flight from Seattle crept closer to the top of the board.

And then, when I had only thirty-five minutes to make my escape, the numbers changed. Her plane was ten minutes early. I had no more time.

I pulled the unmarked envelope out of my pocket and handed it to Archie. "You'll get this to her?"

He nodded, taking the letter and slipping it into his backpack.

"I think I'll eat now," I said.

Archie stood. "I'll come with you."

"Do you mind if Jessamine comes instead?" I asked. "I'm feeling a little . . ." I didn't finish the sentence. My eyes were wild enough to convey the point.

Jessamine stood up. Archie looked confused, but—I saw with huge relief—not suspicious. He must be attributing the change in his vision to some maneuver of the tracker's rather than a betrayal by me. He wasn't watching me, he was watching Joss.

Jessamine walked silently beside me, her hand on the small of my back, as if she were guiding me. I pretended a lack of interest in the first few airport cafés, my head scanning for something, anything. There had to be a window, an opportunity I could use.

I saw a sign, and had an idea. Inspiration in desperation.

There was one place Jessamine wouldn't follow me.

I had to move quickly, before Archie saw something.

"Do you mind?" I asked Jessamine, nodding to the door. "I'll be right back."

"I'll be here," she promised.

As soon as I was around the corner of the doorless entry, out of sight, I was running.

It was an even better solution than I'd first thought. I remembered this room. My stride lengthened.

The one place Jessamine wouldn't follow me—the men's room. They

mostly had two entrances, but usually they were close to each other. My first plan, to slide out behind someone else, would never have worked.

But this room—I'd been here before. Gotten lost here once, because the other exit was straight through, coming out in a totally different hallway. I couldn't have planned it better.

I was already in the hall now, sprinting to the elevators. If Jessamine stayed where she said she would, I'd never be in her line of sight. I didn't look behind me as I ran. This was my only chance, and even if she was after me, I had to keep going. People stared, but they didn't look too shocked. There were lots of reasons to run in an airport.

I dashed up to the elevators, throwing my hand between the closing doors of a full car headed down. I squeezed in beside the irritated passengers, and checked to make sure that the button for level one had been pushed. It was already lit, and the doors closed.

As soon as the doors opened I was off again, to the sound of annoyed murmurs behind me. I slowed myself as I passed the security guards by the luggage carousels, only to break into a stumbling run again as the exit doors came into view. I had no way of knowing if Jessamine was looking for me yet. I would have only seconds if she was following my scent. I threw myself at the automatic doors, nearly smacking into the glass when they opened too slowly.

Along the crowded curb there wasn't a cab in sight.

I had no time. Archie and Jessamine were either about to realize I was gone, or they already had. They would find me in a heartbeat.

A boxy white shuttle was just closing its doors a few feet behind me.

"Wait!" I yelled, running, waving at the driver.

"This is the shuttle to the Hyatt," the driver said in confusion as he opened the doors.

"Yeah," I huffed, "that's where I'm going." I jumped up the steps.

He raised an eyebrow at my lack of luggage, but then shrugged, not caring enough to ask.

Most of the seats were empty. I sat as far from the other travelers as possible, and watched out the window as first the sidewalk, and then the airport, got smaller and smaller behind me. I couldn't stop imagining Edythe, where she would stand at the edge of the road when she found the end of my trail.

Don't lose it yet, I told myself. *You still have a long way to go.*

My luck held. In front of the Hyatt, a tired-looking couple was getting their last suitcase out of the trunk of a cab. I jumped out of the shuttle and ran to the cab, sliding into the seat behind the driver. The tired couple and the shuttle driver stared at me.

I told the surprised cabbie my address. "I need to get there as soon as possible."

"That's in Scottsdale," she complained.

I threw four twenties over the seat.

"Will that be enough?"

"Sure, kid, no problem."

I sat back against the seat, folding my arms across my chest. My city began to rush around me, but I didn't look out the windows. I had to fight to maintain control. There was no point in breaking down now, it wouldn't help anything. Against the odds, I'd escaped. I was able now to do everything I could for my mom. My path was set. I just had to follow it.

So, instead of panicking, I closed my eyes and spent the twenty-minute drive with Edythe.

I imagined that I had stayed at the airport to meet her. I visualized how I would have stood right at the do-not-cross line, the first person she would see as she came down the long hallway from the gates. She would move too fast through the other passengers—and they would stare because she was so graceful. She would dart across those last few feet—not quite human—and then she'd throw her arms around my waist. And I wouldn't bother with *careful*.

I wondered where we would have gone. North somewhere, so she could be outside in the day. Or maybe somewhere very remote, so we could lie in the sun together again. I imagined her by the shore, her skin sparkling like the sea. It wouldn't matter how long we had to hide. To be trapped in a hotel room with *her* would be like heaven. So many things I still wanted to know about her. I could listen to her talk forever, never sleeping, never leaving her side.

I could see her face so clearly now . . . almost hear her voice. And, despite everything, for a second I was actually happy. I was so involved in my escapist daydream, I lost all track of the racing seconds.

"Hey, what was the number?"

The cabbie's question punctured my fantasy. The fear I'd controlled for a few minutes took control again.

"Fifty-eight twenty-one." My voice sounded strangled. The cabbie looked at me like she was nervous that I was having an episode or something.

"Here we are, then." She was anxious to get me out of her car, probably hoping I wouldn't ask for my change.

"Thank you," I whispered. There was no need to be afraid, I reminded myself. I knew the house was empty. I had to hurry; my mom was waiting for me, terrified, maybe hurt already, in pain, depending on me.

I ran to the door, reaching up automatically to grab the key under the eave. It was dark inside, empty, normal. The smell was so familiar, it almost incapacitated me. It felt like my mother must be close, just in the other room, but I knew that wasn't true.

I ran to the phone, turning on the kitchen light on my way. There, on the whiteboard, was a ten-digit number written in a small, neat hand. My fingers stumbled over the keypad, making mistakes. I had to hang up and start again. I concentrated on just the buttons this time, carefully pressing each one in turn. I was successful. I held the phone to my ear with a shaking hand. It rang only once.

"Hello, Beau," that easy voice answered. "That was very quick. I'm impressed."

"Is my mom okay?"

"She's perfectly fine. Don't worry, Beau, I have no quarrel with her. Unless you didn't come alone, of course." Light, amused.

"I'm alone." I'd never been more alone in my entire life.

"Very good. Now, do you know the ballet studio just around the corner from your home?"

"Yeah. I know how to get there."

"Well, then, I'll see you very soon."

I hung up.

I ran from the room, through the door, out into the morning heat.

From the corner of my eye, I could almost see my mother standing in the shade of the big eucalyptus tree where I'd played as a kid. Or kneeling by the little plot of dirt around the mailbox, the cemetery of all the flowers

she'd tried to grow. The memories were better than any reality I would see today. But I raced away from them.

I felt so slow, like I was running through wet sand—I couldn't seem to get enough purchase from the concrete. I tripped over my feet several times, once falling, catching myself with my hands, scraping them on the sidewalk, and then lurching up to plunge forward again. At last I made it to the corner. Just another street now; I ran, sweat pouring down my face, gasping. The sun was hot on my skin, too bright as it bounced off the white concrete and blinded me.

When I rounded the last corner, onto Cactus, I could see the studio, looking just as I remembered it. The parking lot in front was empty, the vertical blinds in all the windows drawn. I couldn't run anymore—I couldn't breathe; fear had gotten the best of me. I thought of my mother to keep my feet moving, one in front of the other.

As I got closer, I could see the sign taped inside the door. It was handwritten on bright pink paper; it said the dance studio was closed for spring break. I touched the handle, tugged on it cautiously. It was unlocked. I fought to catch my breath, and opened the door.

The lobby was dark and empty, cool, the air conditioner thrumming. The plastic molded chairs were stacked along the walls, and the carpet was damp. The west dance floor was dark, I could see through the open viewing window. The east dance floor, the bigger room, the one from Archie's vision, was lit. But the blinds were closed on the window.

Terror seized me so strongly that I was literally trapped by it. I couldn't make my feet move forward.

And then my mom's voice called for me.

"Beau? Beau?" That same tone of hysterical panic. I sprinted to the door, to the sound of her voice.

"Beau, you scared me! Don't you ever do that to me again!" Her voice continued as I ran into the long, high-ceilinged room.

I stared around me, trying to find where her voice was coming from. I heard her laugh, and I spun toward the sound.

There she was, on the TV screen, mussing my hair in relief. It was Thanksgiving, and I was twelve. We'd gone to see my grandmother in California, the last year before she died. We went to the beach one day, and I'd leaned

too far over the edge of the pier. Mom had seen my feet flailing, trying to reclaim my balance. "Beau? Beau?" she'd cried out in panic.

And then the TV screen was blue.

I turned slowly. The tracker was standing very still by the back exit, so still I hadn't noticed her at first. In her hand was a remote control. We stared at each other for a long moment, and then she smiled.

She walked toward me, got just a few feet away, and then passed me to put the remote down next to the VCR. I pivoted carefully to watch her.

"Sorry about that, Beau, but isn't it better that your mother didn't really have to be involved in all this?" Her voice was kind.

And suddenly it hit me. My mom was safe. She was still in Florida. She'd never gotten my message. She'd never been terrified by the dark red eyes staring at me now. She wasn't in pain. She was safe.

"Yes," I answered, my voice breaking with relief.

"You don't sound angry that I tricked you."

"I'm not." My sudden high made me brave. What did it matter now? It would be over soon. Charlie and Mom would never be hurt, would never have to be afraid. I felt almost dizzy from the relief. Some analytical part of my mind warned me that I was close to snapping from the stress, but then, losing my mind sounded like a decent option right now.

"How odd. You really mean it." Her dark eyes looked me up and down. The irises were nearly black, just a hint of ruby around the edges. Thirsty. "I will give your strange coven this much, you humans can be quite interesting. I guess I can see the draw of observing you more closely. It's amazing—some of you seem to have no sense of your own self-interest at all."

She was standing a few feet away from me, arms folded, looking at me curiously. There was no menace in her expression or stance. She was so average-looking, nothing remarkable about her face or body at all. Just the white skin, the circled eyes I was used to. She wore a pale blue, long-sleeved shirt and faded blue jeans.

"I suppose you're going to tell me that your friends will avenge you?" she asked—hopefully, I thought.

"I asked them not to."

"And what did your lover think of that?"

"I don't know." It was weird how easy it was to talk to her. "I left her a letter."

"How romantic, a last letter. And do you think she will honor it?" Her voice was just a little harder now, a hint of sarcasm marring her polite tone.

"I hope so."

"Hmmm. Well, our hopes differ then. You see, this was all just a little too easy, too quick. To be quite honest, I'm disappointed. I expected a much greater challenge. And, after all, I only needed a little luck."

I waited silently.

"When Victor couldn't get to your father, I had him learn more about you. What's the sense in running all over the planet chasing you down when I could comfortably wait for you in a place of my choosing? After Victor gave me the information I needed, I decided to come to Phoenix to pay your mother a visit. I'd heard you say you were going home. At first, I never dreamed you meant it. But then I wondered. Humans can be very predictable; they like to be somewhere familiar.

"And wouldn't it be the perfect ploy, to go to the last place you should be when you're hiding—the place that you said you'd be.

"But of course I wasn't sure, it was just a hunch. I usually get a feeling about the prey that I'm hunting, a sixth sense, if you will. I listened to your message when I got to your mother's house, but of course I couldn't be sure where you'd called from. It was very useful to have your number, but you could have been in Antarctica for all I knew, and the game wouldn't work unless you were close by.

"Then your friends got on a plane to Phoenix. Victor was monitoring them for me, naturally; in a game with this many players, I couldn't be working alone. And so they told me what I'd hoped—what I'd sensed—that you were here after all. I was prepared; I'd already been through your charming home movies. And then it was simply a matter of the bluff.

"Very easy, you know, not really up to my standards. So, you see, I'm hoping you're wrong about the girl. Edythe, isn't it?"

I didn't answer. My bravado was wearing off. I could tell she was coming to the end of her monologuing, which I didn't get the point of anyway. Why explain to me? Where was the glory in beating some weak human? I didn't feel the need to rub it in to every cheeseburger I conquered.

"Would you mind, very much, if I left a little letter of my own for Edythe?"

She took a step back and touched a palm-sized digital video camera balanced carefully on top of the stereo. A small red light indicated that it was already running. She adjusted it a few times, widened the frame.

"I don't think she'll be able to resist hunting me after she watches this."

So this explained the gloating. It wasn't for me.

I stared into the camera lens.

My mother was safe, but Edythe wasn't. I tried to think of anything I could do to stop this from happening, to keep that video out of her hands, but I knew I wasn't fast enough to get to the camera before the tracker stopped me.

"I could be wrong about her level of interest," Joss went on. "Obviously, you're not important enough for her to decide to *keep* you. So . . . I'll have to make this *really* offensive, won't I?" She smiled at me, then turned to smile at the camera.

She stepped toward me, still smiling. "Before we begin . . ."

I'd known I was going to die. I'd thought I was prepared for that. I hadn't considered any other version but this—she would kill me, drink my blood, and that would be the end.

There was a different version after all.

I felt numb, frozen.

"I'm going to tell you a story, Beau. Once, a long time ago, my prey escaped me. Shocking, I know! It only happened the one time, so you can imagine how it's haunted me. It was a similar situation in many ways. There was a delicious human boy—he smelled even better than you do, no offense—but only one vampire protected him. It should have been a very easy meal. However, I underestimated the boy's protector. When she knew I was after her little friend, she stole him from the asylum where she worked—can you imagine the degradation? Actually working a human job for your food?" She shook her head in disbelief. "As I was saying, she took him from the asylum, and once she freed him she made him safe. He was important enough to her, but then, *he* was special. A hundred years earlier he would have been burned at the stake for his visions. In the nineteen-twenties it was the asylum and the shock treatments. Poor boy—he didn't even seem to notice the pain of his transformation. When

he opened his eyes, it was like he'd never seen the sun before. The old vampire made him a strong new vampire, and there was no reason for me to touch him then, no blood to enjoy." She sighed. "I destroyed the old one in vengeance."

"Archie!" I breathed.

"Yes, your friend. I was *so* surprised to see him in the clearing. This is why I've told you my story—to bring them comfort. I get you, but they get him. My one lost quarry—quite an honor, actually.

"I still regret that I never got to taste . . ."

She took another step toward me. Now she was just inches away. She leaned her face in closer to me, stretching up on her toes so that her nose could skim up the side of my throat. The touch of her cold skin made me want to recoil, but I couldn't move.

"I suppose you'll do," she said. "But not quite yet. We'll have some fun first, and then I'll call your friends and tell them where to find you—and my little message."

I was still numb. The only thing I was starting to be able to feel was my stomach, rolling with nausea. I stared into the camera, and it was like Edythe was already watching.

The tracker stepped back and began to circle me casually, like she was trying to get a better view of a statue in a museum. Her face was still friendly as she decided where to start. And then her smile got wider and wider and wider till her mouth was just a gash full of teeth. She slumped forward into a crouch.

I didn't see what part of her hit me—it was too fast. She just blurred, there was a loud snap, and my right arm was suddenly hanging like it wasn't connected to my elbow anymore. The very last thing was the pain—it lanced up my arm a long second later.

The hunter was watching again now, but her face hadn't gone back to normal, it was still mostly teeth. She waited for the pain to hit me, watched as I gasped and curled in around my broken arm.

Before I could even feel all of the first pain, while it was still building, she blurred again, and with more snapping pops, something knocked me back against the wall—the bar buckled behind my back and the mirrors splintered.

A strange, animal-like whine escaped between my teeth. I tried to suck in another breath, and it was like a dozen knives were stabbing my lungs.

"That's a nice effect, don't you think?" she asked, her face friendly again. She touched one of the spiderweb lines running away from where I'd hit the wall. "As soon as I saw this place, I knew it was the right set for my little film. Visually dynamic. And so many angles—I wouldn't want Edythe to miss even one little thing."

I didn't see her move, but there was another tiny crunch, and a dull throbbing started in my left index finger.

"Still on his feet," she said, and then she laughed.

The next crack was much louder—like a muffled detonation. The room seemed to fly up past me, like I was dropping through a hole. The agony hit the same time I hit the floor.

I choked on the scream that was trying to rip out of my throat, fighting through the bile that flooded my esophagus. There wasn't enough air, I couldn't fill my lungs. A strange, smothered groan seemed to come from deep inside my torso.

My body automatically coughed out the vomit so I could breathe, even though breathing felt like it was tearing my insides apart. The pain from my broken arm was throbbing in the background now—my leg was center stage. That pain was still peaking. I was splayed awkwardly on the floor in a pool of my own vomit, but I couldn't move anything.

She was down on her knees by my head now, and the red light was flashing in her hand.

"Time for your close-up, Beau."

I coughed more acid from my throat, wheezing.

"Now, what I'd like here is a retraction. Can you do that for me? You do me a favor, I speed this up a little. Does that sound fair?"

My eyes couldn't focus on her face—the red flashing light seemed hazy.

"Just tell Edythe how much this all hurts," she coaxed. "Tell her that you want vengeance—you deserve it. She brought you into this. In a very real sense, she's the one who's hurting you here. Try to sell it."

My eyes closed.

She lifted my head with surprising gentleness—though the movement sent ricochets of torture through my arms and ribs.

"Beau," she said softly, like I was sleeping and she was trying to wake me. "Beau? You can do this. Tell Edythe to come after me."

She shook me lightly, and a sound like a sigh leaked out of my lungs.

"Beau dear, you have so many bones left—and the big ones can be broken in so *many* places. Do what I want, please."

I looked at her out-of-focus face. She wasn't making me a real offer. Nothing I said now would save me. And there was too much at stake.

Carefully, I shook my head once. Maybe Edythe would know what I meant.

"It doesn't want to scream," she said in a funny little singsong voice. "Should we *make* it scream?"

I waited for the next snap.

Instead, she gently lifted my good arm and held my hand to her lips. The next pain was hardly even pain, compared to the rest. She could have easily taken off my finger, but she just nipped it. Her teeth didn't even go that deep.

I barely reacted, but she jumped up and spun away. My head thumped against the ground, and my broken ribs screamed. I watched her, strangely detached as she paced the far end of the room, snarling and shaking her head back and forth. She'd left the camera by my head, still running.

The first hint of what she'd done was the heat—my finger was so hot. I was surprised I could even feel that over the bigger agonies. But I remembered Carine's story. I knew what had started. I didn't have much time.

She was still trying to calm herself—the blood, that was the problem. She'd gotten some of my blood in her mouth, but she didn't want to kill me yet, so she had to fight off the frenzy. She was distracted, but it wouldn't take much to catch her attention.

The heat was building fast. I tried to ignore that, to ignore the stabbing in my chest. My hand shot out and I had the camera. I raised it up as high as I could and smashed it back toward the ground.

And I was flying backward, into the broken mirrors. The glass punctured my shoulders, my scalp. The impact seemed to rebreak all of my broken bones. But that wasn't why I screamed.

Fire had ignited my bitten finger—flames exploded across my palm. Heat

was scorching up my wrist. It was fire that was more than fire—a pain that was more than pain.

The other agonies were nothing. Broken bones weren't pain. Not like this.

The screaming sounded like it was coming from someplace outside my body—it was an unbroken yowling that was like an animal again.

My eyes were fixed, staring, and I saw the red light flashing in the tracker's hand. She'd been too fast, and I'd failed.

But I didn't care anymore.

Blood was running down my arm, pooling under my elbow.

The tracker's nostrils were flared, her eyes wild, her teeth bared. The blood dripped onto the floor, but I couldn't hear it over the screaming. Here was my last shred of hope. She wouldn't be able to stop herself now. She would have to kill me. Finally.

Her mouth opened wide.

I waited, screaming.

23. THE CHOICE

ANOTHER SCREAM ON TOP OF MINE—A SHRIEK LIKE A CHAINSAW CUT-
ting through rebar.

The hunter lunged, but her teeth snapped closed an inch from my face as
something yanked her back, flung her out of my sight.

The fire pooled in the crease of my elbow, and I screamed.

I wasn't alone, there were others screaming—the metallic snarl was joined
by a high keening that bounced off the walls and then cut off suddenly. A
thrumming growl was grinding underneath the other sounds. More metal
tearing, shredding . . .

"No!" someone howled in an agony to match mine. "No, no, no, no!"

This voice meant something to me, even through the burning that was
so much more than that. Though the flames had reached my shoulder, this
voice still claimed my attention. Even screaming, she sounded like an angel.

"Beau, please," Edythe sobbed. "Please, please, please, Beau, please!"

I tried to answer, but my mouth was disconnected from the rest of me. My
screams were gone, but only because there was no more air.

"Carine!" Edythe shrieked. "*Help me!* Beau, please, please, Beau, please!"

She was cradling my head in her lap, and her fingers were pressing hard
against my scalp. Her face was unfocused, just like the hunter's. I was falling down a tunnel in my head. The fire was coming with me, though, just
as sharp as before.

Something cool blew into my mouth, filling my lungs. My lungs pushed back. Another cool breath.

Edythe came into focus, her perfect face twisted and tortured.

"Keep breathing, Beau. Breathe."

She put her lips against mine and filled my lungs again.

There was gold around the edges of my vision—another set of cold hands.

"Archie, make splints for his leg and arm. Edythe, straighten out his airways. Which is the worst bleed?"

"Here, Carine."

I stared at her face while the pressure against my head eased. My screams were just a broken whimper now. The pain wasn't any less—it was worse. But the screaming didn't help me, and it did hurt Edythe. As long as I kept my eyes on her face, I could remember something beyond the burning.

"My bag, please. Hold your breath, Archie, it will help. Thank you, Eleanor, now leave, please. He's lost blood, but the wounds aren't too deep. I think his ribs are the biggest problem now. Find me tape."

"Something for the pain," Edythe hissed.

"There—I don't have hands. Will you?"

"This will make it better," Edythe promised.

Someone was straightening my leg. Edythe was holding her breath, waiting, I think, for me to react. But it didn't hurt like my arm.

"Edythe—"

"Shhh, Beau, it's going to be okay. I swear, it's going to be fine."

"E—it's—not—"

Something was digging into my scalp and something else was yanking tight against my broken arm. This tweaked my ribs, and I lost my breath.

"Hold on, Beau," Edythe begged. *"Please* just hold on."

I labored to pull in another breath.

"Not—ribs," I choked. "Hand."

"Can you understand him?" Carine's voice was right next to my head.

"Just rest, Beau. Breathe."

"No—hand," I gasped out. "Edythe—right hand!"

I couldn't feel her cold hands on my skin—the fire was too hot. But I heard her gasp.

"No!"

"Edythe?" Carine asked, startled.

"She bit him." Edythe's voice had no volume, like she'd run out of air, too.

Carine caught her breath in horror.

"What do I do, Carine?" Edythe demanded.

No one answered her. The tugging continued on my scalp, but it didn't hurt.

"Yes," Edythe said through her teeth. "I can try. Archie—scalpel."

"There's a good chance you'll kill him yourself," Archie said.

"Give it to me," she snapped. "I can do this."

I didn't see what she did with the scalpel. I couldn't feel anything else in my body anymore—nothing but the fire in my arm. But I watched her raise my hand to her mouth, like the hunter had. Fresh blood was welling from the wound. She put her lips over it.

I screamed again, I couldn't help it. It was like she was pulling the fire back down my arm.

"Edythe," Archie said.

She didn't react, her lips still pressed to my hand. The fire warred up and down my arm, sawing back and forth. Moans escaped through my clenched teeth.

"Edythe," Archie shouted. *"Look."*

"What is it, Archie?" Carine asked.

Archie's hand shot out and slapped Edythe's cheek.

"Stop it, Edythe! Stop it now!"

My hand dropped away from her face. She looked at Archie with her eyes so wide they seemed like half her face. She gasped.

"Archie!" Carine barked.

"It's too late," Archie said. "We got here too late."

"You can see it?" Carine said in a more subdued voice.

"There are only two futures left, Carine. He survives as one of us, or Edythe kills him trying to stop it from happening."

"No," Edythe moaned.

Carine was quiet. The tugging against my scalp slowed.

Edythe dropped her face to mine. She kissed my eyelids, my cheeks, my lips. "I'm sorry, I'm so sorry."

"It doesn't need to be this slow," Archie complained. "Carine?"

"I made an oath, Archie."

"I didn't," he snarled.

"Wait, wait," Edythe said, her head snapping up. "He deserves a choice."

Her lips were at my ear. I clamped my teeth against the moaning, straining to listen.

"Beau? I won't make this decision for you. I won't take this away from you. And I'll understand, I promise, Beau. If you don't want to live like this, I won't fight you. I'll respect what you want. I know it's a horrible choice. I would give you any other option if I could. I would die if I could give your life back to you." Her voice broke. "But I can't make that trade. I can't do *anything*—except stop the pain. If that's what you want. You don't have to be *this*. I can let you go—if that's what you need." It sounded like she was sobbing again. "Tell me what you want, Beau. Anything."

"You," I spit through my teeth. "Just you."

"Are you *sure?*" she whispered.

I groaned. The fire was reaching its fingers into my chest. "Yes," I coughed out. "Just—let me stay—with you."

"Out of my way, Edythe," Archie growled.

Her voice lashed back like a whip. "I didn't make any oaths, either."

Her face was at my throat, and I couldn't feel anything besides the fire, but I could hear the quiet sound of her teeth cutting through my skin.

24. CHANGE

I ENDED UP CHANGING MY MIND.

The fire in my arm wasn't really so bad—the worst thing I'd ever felt up to that point, yes. But not the same as my entire body on fire.

I begged her to make it stop. I told her that this was really all I wanted. For the burning to stop. Nothing else.

I heard Archie telling her that everyone had said the same thing—reminding her that she'd begged Carine to kill her, too. Telling her my first decision was the one that counted.

I remember at one point screaming at him to shut up.

I think he apologized.

But mostly it was hard to pay attention to what was happening outside the fire. I know they moved me. It seemed like I was on the bloody, vomit-covered wood floor for a long time, but it was hard to judge how the minutes passed. Sometimes Carine would say something and it would feel like a year had passed before Archie answered her, but it was probably just the fire that made the seconds into years.

And then someone carried me. I saw the sun for another year-long second—it looked pale and cool. Then everything was dark. It was dark for a long time.

I could still see Edythe. She held me in her arms, my face near hers, one of her hands on my cheek. Archie was nearby, too. I think he had my legs.

When I screamed, she apologized, over and over again. I tried not to scream. It didn't do any good. There was no relief, no release in it. The fire didn't care what I did. It just burned.

When my eyes were in focus, I could see dim lights moving across Edythe's face, though all around her head it was just black. Aside from her voice and mine, the only sound was a deep, constant thrumming. Sometimes it got louder, and then it was quiet again.

I didn't realize I was back in the black car until it stopped. I didn't hear the door open, but the sudden flash of light was blinding. I must have recoiled from it, because Edythe crooned in my ear.

"We're just stopping to refill the gas tank. We'll be home soon, Beau. You're doing so well. This will be over soon. I am so sorry."

I couldn't feel her hand against my face—it should have been cool, but nothing was cool anymore. I tried to reach for it, but I couldn't exactly tell what my limbs were doing. I think I was thrashing some, but Edythe and Archie kept me contained. Edythe guessed what I wanted. She grabbed my hand and held it to her lips. I wished I could feel it. I tried to grip her hand without knowing how to make the muscles move, or being able to feel them. Maybe I got it right. She didn't let go.

It got darker. Eventually, I couldn't see her anymore. It was black as ink inside the car—there was no difference between having my eyes open or closed. I started to panic. The fire made the night like a sensory deprivation chamber; I couldn't feel anything but pain—not the seat beneath me, not Archie restraining my legs, not Edythe holding my head, my hand. I was all alone with the burning, and I was terrified.

I don't know what I must have gasped out—my voice was totally gone now, either raw from screaming or burned past usability, I couldn't gues which—but Edythe's voice was in my ear again.

"I'm right here, Beau. You're not alone. I won't leave you. I will be here. Listen to my voice. I'm here with you. . . ."

Her voice calmed me—made the panic go away, if not the pain. I listened, keeping my breathing shallow so I could hear her better. I didn't need to scream anymore. The burning only got more and never less, but I was adapting. It was all I could feel, but not all I could think about.

"I never wanted this for you, Beau," Edythe continued. "I would give anything to take this away. I've made so many mistakes. I should have stayed away from you, from the first day. I should never have come back again. I've destroyed your life, I've taken everything from you. . . ." It sounded like she was sobbing again.

"No," I tried to say, but I'm not sure if I even shaped the word with my mouth.

"He's probably far enough along that he'll remember this," Archie said softly.

"I hope so," Edythe said, her voice breaking.

"I'm just saying, you might use the time more productively. There is so much he doesn't know."

"You're right, you're right." She sighed. "Where do I begin?"

"You could explain about being thirsty," Archie suggested. "That was the hardest part, when I first woke up. And we'll be expecting a lot from him."

When Edythe answered, it was like she was spitting the words through her teeth. "I won't hold him to that. He didn't choose this. He's free to become whatever he wants to be."

"Hah," Archie said. "You know him better than that, Edythe. The other way won't be good enough for him. Do you see? He'll be fine."

It was quiet while she tuned in to whatever Archie was seeing inside his head. Though I understood the silence, it still left me alone in the fire. I started panicking again.

"I'm here, Beau, I'm here. Don't be afraid." She took a deep breath. "I'll keep talking. There are so many things to tell you. The first one is that when this passes, when you're . . . new, you won't be exactly the same as I am, not in the very beginning. Being a young vampire means certain things, and the hardest to ignore is the thirst. You'll be thirsty—all the time. You won't be able to think about much else for a while. Maybe a year, maybe two. It's different for everyone. As soon as this is over, I'll take you hunting. You wanted to see that, didn't you? We'll bring Eleanor so you can see her bear impression—" She laughed once, a damaged little sound. "If you decide—if you want to live like us, it will be hard. Especially in the beginning. It might be too hard, and I understand that. We all do. If you want to try it my way, I'll go with you. I can tell you who the human monsters are. There are options.

Whatever you want. If . . . if you don't want me with you, I'll understand that, too, Beau. I swear I won't follow you if you tell me not to—"

"No," I gasped. I heard myself that time, so I knew I'd done it right.

"You don't have to make any more decisions now. There's time for that. Just know that I will respect any decision you make." She took another deep breath. "I should probably warn you about your eyes. They won't be blue anymore." Another half-sob. "But don't let them frighten you. They won't stay so bright for long.

"I suppose that's a very small thing, though. . . . I should focus on the most important things. The hard things—the very worst thing. Oh, I'm so sorry, Beau. You can't see your father or mother again. It's not safe. You would hurt them—you wouldn't be able to help yourself. And . . . there are rules. Rules that, as your creator, I'm bound by. We'd both be held responsible if you ran out of control. Oh—" Her breath caught. "There's so much he doesn't know, Archie."

"We've got time, Edythe. Just relax. Take it slow."

I heard her inhale again.

"The rules," she said. "One rule with a thousand different permutations—the reality of vampires must be kept secret. That means newborn vampires must be controlled. I will teach you—I'll keep you safe, I promise." Another sigh. "And you can't tell anyone what you are. I broke that rule. I didn't think it could hurt you—that anyone would ever find out. I should have known that just being near you would eventually destroy you. I should have known I would ruin your life—that I was lying to myself about any other path being possible. I've done everything wrong—"

"You're letting self-castigation get in the way of information again, Edythe."

"Right, right." A deep breath. "Beau. Do you remember the painting in Carine's study—the nighttime patrons of the arts I told you about? They're called the Volturi—they are . . . for the lack of a better word, the police of our world. I'll tell you more about them in a bit—you just need to know that they exist, so that I can explain why you can't tell Charlie or your mother where you are. You can't talk to them again, Beau." Her voice was straining higher, like it was about to fracture. "It's best . . . we

don't have much choice but to let them think you're dead. I'm so sorry. You didn't even get to say goodbye. It's not fair!"

There was a long pause while I could hear her breath hitching.

"Why don't you go back to the Volturi?" Archie suggested. "Keep emotion out of it."

"You're right," she repeated in a whisper. "Ready to learn a new world history, Beau?"

She talked all night without a break, until the sun came up and I could see her face again. She told me stories that sounded like dark fairy tales. I was beginning to grasp the edges of how big this world was, but I knew it would be a long time before I totally comprehended the size of it.

She told me about the people I'd seen in the painting with Carine—the Volturi. How they'd joined forces during the Mycenaean age, and begun a millennia-long campaign to create peace and order in the vampire world. How there had been six of them in the beginning. How betrayal and murder had cut them in half. Someone named Aro had murdered his sister—his best friend's wife. The best friend was Marcus—he was the man I'd seen standing with Carine. Aro's own wife—Sulpicia, the one with all the masses of dark hair in the painting—had been the only witness. She'd turned him over to Marcus and their soldiers. There had been some question of what to do—Aro had a very powerful extra gift, like what Edythe had, but *more*, she said—and the Volturi weren't sure they'd be able to succeed without him. But Sulpicia searched out a young girl—Mele, the one Edythe had called a servant and a thief—who had a gift of her own. She could absorb another vampire's gift. She couldn't use that stolen gift herself, but she *could* give it to someone else who she was touching. Sulpicia had Mele take Aro's gift, and then Marcus executed him. Once she had her husband's gift, Sulpicia found out that the third man in their group was in on the plot. He was executed, too, and his wife—Athenodora—joined with Sulpicia and Marcus to lead their soldiers. They overthrew the vampires who terrorized Europe, and then the ones who enslaved Egypt. Once they were in charge, they made regulations that kept the vampire world hidden and safe.

I listened as much as I could. It wasn't a distraction from the pain—there was no escape. But it was better to think about than the fire.

Edythe said the Volturi were the ones who'd made up all the stories about

crosses and holy water and mirrors. Over the centuries, they made all reports of vampires into myth. And now they continued to keep it that way. Vampires would stay in the shadows . . . or there would be consequences.

So I couldn't go to my dad's house and let him see the eyes that Edythe said would be *bright*. I couldn't drive to Florida and hug my mom and let her know that I wasn't dead. I couldn't even call her and explain the confusing message I'd left on her answering machine. If there was anything in the news, if any rumor spread that something unnatural was involved, the Volturi soldiers might come to investigate.

I had to disappear *quietly*.

The fire hurt more than hearing these things. But I knew that wouldn't always be the way it was. Soon, this would hurt the most.

Edythe moved on quickly—telling me about their friends in Canada who lived the same way. Three blond Russian brothers and two Spanish vampires who were the Cullens' closest family. She told me that two of them had extra powers—Kirill could do something electrical, and Elena knew the talents of every vampire she met.

She told me about other friends, all over the world. In Ireland and Brazil and Egypt. So many names. Eventually Archie stepped in again and told her to prioritize.

Edythe told me that I would never age. That I would always be seventeen, like she was. That the world would change around me, and I would remember all of it, never forgetting one second.

She told me how the Cullens lived—how they moved from cloudy place to cloudy place. Earnest would restore a house for them. Archie would invest their assets with amazingly good returns. They would decide on a story to explain their relationships to each other, and Jessamine would create new names and new documented pasts for each of them. Carine would take a job in a hospital with her new credentials, or she'd return to school to study a new field. If the location looked promising, the younger Cullens would pretend to be even younger than they were, so they could stay longer.

After my time as a new vampire was up, I would be able to go back to school. But my education wouldn't have to wait. I had a lot of time ahead of me, and I would remember everything I read or heard.

I would never sleep again.

Food would be disgusting to me. I would never be hungry again, only thirsty.

I would never get sick. I would never feel tired.

I would be able to run faster than a race car. I'd be stronger than any other living species on the planet.

I wouldn't need to breathe.

I would be able to see more clearly, hear even the smallest sound.

My heart would finish beating tomorrow or the next day, and it would never beat again.

I would be a vampire.

One good thing about the burning—it let me hear all this with some distance. It let me process what she was telling me without emotion. I knew the emotion would come later.

When it was starting to get dark again, our journey was over. Edythe carried me into the house like I was a child, and sat with me in the big room. The background behind her face went from black to white. I could see her much more clearly now, and I didn't think it was just the light.

In her eyes, my face reflected back, and I was surprised to see that it looked like a face and not a charcoal briquette—though a face in anguish. Still, maybe I wasn't the pile of ash I felt like.

She told me stories to fill the time, and the others took turns helping her. Carine sat on the ground next to me and told me the most amazing story about Jules's family—that her great-grandmother had actually been a *werewolf*. All the things Jules had scoffed about were straight history. Carine told me she'd promised them she would never bite another human. It was part of the treaty between them, the treaty that meant the Cullens could never go due west to the ocean.

Jessamine told me her story after all. I guess she'd decided I was ready now. I was glad, when she did, that my emotions were mostly buried under the fire. She'd lost family, too, when the man who created her stole her without warning. She told me about the army she'd belonged to, a life of carnage and death, and then breaking free. She told me about the day Archie had let her find him.

Earnest told me how his life had ended before he'd killed himself, about his unstable, alcoholic wife and the daughter he'd loved more than his own

soul. He told me about the night when his wife, in a drunken rampage, had jumped off a cliff with his little daughter in her arms, and how he hadn't been able to do anything but follow after them. Then he told me how, after the pain, there had been the most beautiful woman in a nurse's uniform—a nurse he recognized from a happier time in another place when he was just a young man. A nurse who hadn't aged at all.

Eleanor told me about being attacked by a bear, and then seeing an angel who took her to Carine instead of to heaven. She told me how she'd thought at first she'd been sent to hell—justly, she admitted—and then how she got into heaven after all.

She was the one who told me that the redhead had gotten away. He'd never come near Charlie after the one time that he'd searched Charlie's house. When we'd all gotten back to Forks, she, Royal, and Jessamine had followed the man's trail as far as they could; it disappeared into the Salish Sea and they hadn't been able to find the place where he came back out. For all they knew, he'd swum straight out to the Pacific and on to another continent. He must have assumed that Joss had lost the fight and realized it was smarter to disappear.

Even Royal took a turn. He told me about a life consumed with vanity, with material things, with ambition. He told me about the only daughter of a powerful man—exactly what kind of power this man wielded, Royal hadn't entirely understood—and how Royal had planned to marry her and become heir to the dynasty. How the beautiful daughter pretended to love him to please her father, and then how she had watched when her lover from a rival criminal syndicate had Royal beaten to death, how she'd laughed aloud the whole time. He told me about the revenge he'd gotten. Royal was the least careful with his words. He told me about losing his family, and how none of this was worth what he'd lost.

Edythe had whispered Eleanor's name; he'd growled once and left.

I think it must have been while Royal or Eleanor was talking that Archie watched Joss's video from the dance studio. When Royal was gone, Archie took his spot. At first I wasn't sure what they were talking about, because only Edythe was speaking out loud, but eventually I caught up. Archie was searching right there on his laptop, trying to narrow down the options of where he'd been kept in his human life. I was glad he didn't seem to

mention anything else about the tape—the focus was all on his past. I was trying to remember how to use my voice so that I could stop him if he tried to say anything about the rest of it. I hoped Archie was smart enough to have destroyed the tape before Edythe could watch.

The stories helped me think of other things, prepare myself, while the fire burned, but I was only able to pay partial attention. My mind was cataloguing the fire, experiencing it in new ways. It was amazing how each inch of my skin, each millimeter, was so distinct. It was like I could feel all my cells burning individually. I could feel the difference between the pain in the walls of my lungs, and the way the fire felt in the soles of my feet, inside my eyeballs, and down my spine. All the different agonies clearly separated.

I could hear my heart thudding—it seemed so loud. Like it had been hooked to an amp. I could hear other things, too. Mostly Edythe's voice, sometimes the others talking—though I couldn't see them. I heard music once, but I didn't know where it was coming from.

It seemed like I was on the couch, my head in Edythe's lap, for several years. The lights stayed bright, so I didn't know if it was night or day. But Edythe's eyes were always gold, so I guessed that the fire was lying about the time again.

I was so aware of every nerve ending in my body that I knew it immediately when something changed.

It started with my toes. I couldn't feel them. It seemed like the fire had finally won, that it had started burning off pieces of me. Edythe had said I was changing, not dying, but in this moment of panic I thought she'd gotten it wrong. Maybe this vampire thing wouldn't work on me. Maybe all this burning had been just a slow way to die. The worst way.

Edythe felt me freaking out again, and she started humming in my ear. I tried to look at the positives. If it was killing me, at least it would be over. And if it was going to end, at least I was in Edythe's arms for the rest of my life.

And then I realized that my toes were still there, they just weren't burning anymore. In fact, the fire was pulling out of the soles of my feet, too. I was glad I'd made sense of what was happening, because my fingertips were next. No need for more panic, maybe a reason for hope. The fire was leaving.

Only it seemed to be doing more than leaving—it was . . . moving. All

the fire that receded from my extremities seemed to be draining into the center of my body, stoking the blaze there so that it was hotter than before.

I couldn't believe there was such a thing as *hotter*.

My heart—already so loud—starting beating faster. The core of the fire seemed to be centered there. It was sucking the flames in from my hands and my ankles, leaving them pain-free, but multiplying the heat and pain in my heart.

"Carine," Edythe called.

Carine walked into the room, and the amazing part about that was that I *heard* her. Edythe and her family never made any noise when they moved. But now, if I listened, I could hear the low sound of Carine's lips brushing together as she spoke.

"Ah. It's almost over."

I wanted to be relieved, but the growing agony in my chest made it impossible to feel anything else. I stared up at Edythe's face. She was more beautiful than she had ever been, because I could see her better than I ever had. But I couldn't really appreciate her. So much pain.

"Edythe?" I gasped.

"You're all right, Beau. It's ending. I'm sorry, I know. I remember."

The fire ripped hotter through my heart, dragging the flames up from my elbows and knees. I thought about Edythe going through this, suffering this way, and it put a different perspective on my pain. She didn't even know Carine then. She didn't know what was happening to her. She hadn't been held the whole time in the arms of someone she loved.

The pain was almost gone from everywhere but my chest. The only left-over was my throat, but it was a different kind of burn now . . . drier . . . irritating. . . .

I heard more footsteps, and I was pretty sure I could tell the difference between them. The decisive, confident step was Eleanor, I was positive. Archie was the quicker, more rhythmic motion. Earnest was a little slower, thoughtful. Jessamine was the one who stopped by the door. I thought I heard Royal breathing behind her.

And then—

"Aaah!"

My heart took off, beating like helicopter blades, the sound almost a single

sustained note. It felt like it would grind through my ribs. The fire flared up in the center of my chest, sucking all the flames from the rest of my body to fuel the most painful burn yet. It was enough to stun me. My body bowed like the fire was dragging me upward by my heart.

It felt like a war inside me—my racing heart blitzing against the raging fire. They were both losing.

The fire constricted tighter, concentrating into one fist-sized ball of pain with a final, unbearable surge. The surge was answered by a deep, hollow-sounding thud. My heart stuttered twice, then thudded quietly again one more time.

There was no sound. No breathing. Not even mine.

For a second, all I could process was the absence of pain. The dull, dry afterburn in my throat was easy to ignore, because every other part of me felt amazing. The release was an incredible high.

I stared up at Edythe in wonder. I felt like I'd taken off a blindfold I'd been wearing all my life. What a view.

"Beau?" she asked. Now that I could really concentrate on it, the beauty of her voice was unreal.

"It's disorienting, I know. You get used to it."

Could you get used to hearing a voice like this? Seeing a face like that?

"Edythe," I said, and the sound of my own voice jolted me. Was that me? It didn't sound like me. It didn't sound . . . human.

Unnerved, I reached out to touch her cheek. In the same instant that the desire to touch her entered my mind, my hand was cradling the side of her face. There was no in-between—no process of lifting my hand, watching it move to its destination. It was just there.

"Huh."

She leaned into my touch, put her hand over mine, and held it against her face. It was strange because it was familiar—I'd always loved it when she'd done that, to see that she so obviously liked it when I touched her that way, that it meant something to her. But it was also nothing the same. Her face wasn't cold anymore. Her hand felt right against mine. There was no difference between us now.

I stared into her eyes, then looked closer at the picture reflected in them.

"Ahh . . ." A little gasp escaped my throat by accident, and I felt my body

lock down in surprise. It was weird—it felt like the natural thing to do, to be a statue because I was shocked.

"What is it, Beau?" She leaned closer, concerned, but that just brought the reflection closer.

"The eyes?" I breathed.

She sighed, and wrinkled her nose. "It goes away," she promised. "I terrified myself every time I looked in a mirror for six months."

"Six months," I murmured. "And then they'll be gold like yours?"

She looked away, over the back of the couch, to someone standing there behind us where I couldn't see. I wanted to sit up and look around, but I was a little afraid to move. My body felt so strange.

"That depends on your diet, Beau," Carine said calmly. "If you hunt like we do, your eyes will eventually turn this color. If not, your eyes will look like Lauren's did."

I decided to try sitting up.

And like before, thinking was doing. Without any movement, I was upright. Edythe kept my hand in hers as it left her face.

Behind the sofa, they were all there, watching. I'd been one hundred percent with my guesses—Carine closest, then Eleanor, Archie, and Earnest. Jessamine in the doorway to another room with Royal watching over her shoulder.

I looked at their faces, shocked again. If my brain hadn't been so much . . . roomier than before, I would have forgotten what I was about to say. As it was, I recovered pretty fast.

"No, I want to do it your way," I said to Carine. "That's the right thing to do."

Carine smiled. It would have knocked the breath out of me if I'd had to breathe.

"If only it were so easy. But that's a noble choice. We'll help you all we can."

Edythe touched my arm. "We should hunt now, Beau. It will make your throat hurt less."

When she mentioned my throat, the dry burn there was suddenly at the forefront of my mind. I swallowed. But . . .

"Hunt?" my new voice asked. "I, uh, well, I've never been hunting before.

Not even like normal hunting with rifles, so I don't really think I could . . . I mean, I have no idea how. . . ."

Eleanor chuckled under her breath.

Edythe smiled. "I'll show you. It's very easy, very natural. Didn't you want to see me hunt?"

"Just us?" I checked.

She looked confused for a fraction of a second, and then her face was smooth. "Of course. Whatever you want. Come with me, Beau."

And she was on her feet, still holding my hand. Then I was on my feet, too, and it was so simple to move, I wondered why I'd been afraid to try. Anything I wanted this body to do, it did.

She darted to the back wall of the big room—the glass wall that was a mirror now because it was night outside. I saw the two pale figures flashing by and I stopped. The strange thing was that when I stopped, it was so sudden that Edythe kept going, still holding my hand, and though she was still pulling, I didn't move. My grip on her hand pulled *her* back. Like it was nothing.

But I was only noticing that with part of my brain. Mostly I was looking at my reflection.

I'd seen my face warped around the convex shape of her eyes, just the center, lacking the edges. I'd only really seen my eyes—brilliant, almost glowing *red*—and that had been enough to pull my focus. Now I saw my whole face—my neck, my arms.

If someone had cut an outline of my human self, this version would still fit into that space. But though I took up the same volume, all the angles were different. Harder, more pronounced. Like someone had made an ice sculpture of me and left the edges sharp.

My eyes—it was hard to look around the color, but the shape of them, too, seemed different. So vaguely, like I was remembering something I'd seen only through muddy water—I remembered how my eyes used to look. Undecided. Like I was never sure who I was. Then, after Edythe—still so hard to see in my memory, uncomfortable to try—they were suddenly more resolved.

These eyes had gone one step further than resolved—they were *savage*. If I walked into this self in a dark alley, I would be terrified of me.

Which was the point, I guess. People were supposed to be afraid of me now.

I still wore my bloodstained jeans, but I had an unfamiliar, pale blue shirt on. I didn't remember that happening, but I could understand; vampire or human, no one wanted to hang around with someone drenched in vomit.

"Whoa," I said. I locked eyes with Edythe in the reflection.

This was strange, too. Because the Beau in the mirror looked . . . *right* next to Edythe. Like he belonged. Not like before, when people could only imagine that she was taking pity on me.

"It's a lot," she said.

I took a deep breath and nodded. "Okay."

She pulled on my hand again, and I followed. Before a fourth of a second had passed, we were through the glass doors behind the stairs and on the back lawn.

There were no moon and no stars—the clouds were too thick. It should have been pitch-black outside the rectangle of light shining through the glass wall, but it wasn't. I could see *everything*.

"*Whoa*," I said again. "That is *so* cool."

Edythe looked at me like she was surprised by my reaction. Had she forgotten what it was like the first time she saw the world through vampire eyes? I thought she'd said I wouldn't forget things anymore.

"We're going to have to go a ways out into the woods," she told me. "Just in case."

I remembered the gist of what she'd told me about hunting. "Right. So there aren't any people around. Got it."

Again—that same surprised look flashed across her face and then was gone.

"Follow me," she said.

She whipped down the lawn so fast that I knew she would have been invisible to my old eyes. Then, at the edge of the river, she launched herself into a high arc that spun her over the river and into the trees beyond.

"Really?" I called after her.

I heard her laugh. "I promise, it's easy."

Great.

I sighed, then started running.

Running had never been my forte. I was all right on a flat track, if I was paying enough attention and I kept my eyes on my feet. Okay, honestly, even then I was still able to tangle my feet up and go down.

This was so different. I was flying—*flying* down the lawn, faster than I'd ever moved, but it was only too simple to put my feet exactly where they were supposed to go. I could feel all of my muscles, almost see the connections as they worked together, will them to do exactly what I needed. When I got to the edge of the river I didn't even pause. I pushed off the same rock she'd used, and then I was *really* flying. The river slipped away behind me as I rocketed through the air. I passed where she'd landed and then fell down into the wood.

I felt an instant of panic when I realized I hadn't even considered the landing, but then my hand already seemed to know how to catch a thick branch and angle my body so that my feet hit the ground with barely a sound.

"Holy crow," I breathed in total disbelief.

I heard Edythe running through the trees, and already her gait was as familiar to me as the sound of my own breathing. I was sure I could tell the difference between the sound of her footfalls and anyone else's.

"We have to do that again!" I said as soon as I saw her.

She paused a few feet away from me, and a frustrated expression that I knew well crossed her face.

I laughed. "What do you want to know? I'll tell you what I'm thinking."

She frowned. "I don't understand. You're . . . in a very good mood."

"Oh. Is that wrong?"

"Aren't you incredibly thirsty?"

I swallowed against the burn. It was bad, but not as bad as the rest of the fire I'd just left behind. The thirst-burn was always there, and it got worse when I focused on it, but there were so many other things to focus on. "Yes, when I think about it."

Edythe squared her shoulders. "If you want to do this first, that's fine, too."

I looked at her. I was obviously missing something. "Do this? Do what?"

She stared at me for a second, her eyes doubtful. Suddenly she threw her hands up. "You know, I really thought that when your mind was more similar to mine, I'd be able to hear it. I guess that's never going to happen."

"Sorry."

She laughed, but there was an unhappy note in the sound. "Honestly, Beau."

"Can you please give me a clue as to what we're talking about?"

"You wanted us to be alone," she said, like this was an explanation.

"Uh, yeah."

"Because you had some things you wanted to say to me?" She braced her shoulders again, tensing like she was expecting something bad.

"Oh. Well, I guess there are things to say. I mean, there's one important thing, but I wasn't thinking about that." Seeing how frustrated she was by whatever misunderstanding was happening, I was totally honest. "I wanted to be alone with you because . . . well, I didn't want to be rude, but I also didn't want to do this hunting thing in front of Eleanor," I confessed. "I figured there was a good chance I would screw something up, and I don't know Eleanor all that well yet, but I have a feeling she would find that pretty funny."

Her eyes got wide. "You were afraid Eleanor would laugh at you? Really, that's all?"

"Really. Your turn, Edythe. What did you think was happening?"

She hesitated. "I thought you were being a gentleman. I thought you preferred to yell at me alone rather than in front of my family."

I froze up again. I wondered if that was going to happen every time I was surprised. It took me a second to thaw out.

"Yell at you?" I repeated. "Edythe—oh! You're talking about all that stuff you were saying in the car, right? Sorry about that, I—"

"*Sorry?* What *on earth* are you apologizing for now, Beau Swan?"

She looked angry. Angry and so beautiful. I couldn't guess why she was worked up. I shrugged. "I wanted to tell you then, but I couldn't. I mean, I couldn't even really concentrate—"

"Of *course* you couldn't concentrate—"

"Edythe!" I crossed the space between us in one invisibly fast stride and put my hands on her shoulders. "You'll never know what I'm thinking if you keep interrupting me."

The anger on her face faded as she deliberately calmed herself. Then she nodded.

"Okay," I said. "In the car—I wanted to tell you then that you didn't need to apologize, I felt horrible that you were so sad. This isn't your fault—"

She started to say something, so I put my finger over her lips.

"And it isn't all bad," I continued. "I'm . . . well, my head is still spinning and I know there are a million things to think about and I'm sad, of course, but I'm also good, Edythe. I'm always good when I'm with you."

She stared at me for a long minute. Slowly, she raised her hand to pull my finger away from her mouth. I didn't stop her.

"You aren't angry at me for what I've done to you?" she asked quietly.

"Edythe, you saved my life! Again. Why would I be angry? Because of the *way* you saved it? What else could you have done?"

She exhaled, almost like she was mad again. "How can you . . . ? Beau, you *have* to see that this is all my fault. I haven't saved your life, I've taken it from you. Charlie—Renée—"

I put my finger over her mouth again, and then took a deep breath. "Yes. It's hard, and it's going to be hard for a long time. Maybe forever, right? But why would I put that on you? Joss is the one who . . . well, who killed me. You brought me back to life."

She pushed my hand down. "If I hadn't involved you in my world—"

I laughed, and she looked up at me like I'd lost my mind. "Edythe—if you hadn't involved me in your world, Charlie and Renée would have lost me three months earlier."

She stared, frowning. It was obvious she wasn't accepting any of this.

"Do you remember what I said when you saved my life in Port Angeles? The second time, or third." I barely did. The words were easier to bring back than the images. I knew it went something like this. "That you were messing with fate because my number was up? Well . . . if I *had* to die, Edythe . . . isn't this the most amazing way to do it?"

A long minute passed while she stared at me, and then she shook her head. "Beau, *you* are amazing."

"I guess I am now."

"You always have been."

I didn't say anything, and my face gave me away. Or she was just that good. She knew my face so well, she spent so much time trying so hard to understand me, that she knew immediately when there was something I wasn't saying.

"What is it, Beau?"

"Just . . . something Joss said." I winced. Though it was hard to see things in my old memory, the dance studio was the most recent, the most vivid.

Edythe's jaw got hard. "She said a lot of things," she hissed.

"Oh." Suddenly I wanted to punch something. But I also didn't want to let go of Edythe to do that. "You saw the tape."

Her face was totally white. Furious and agonized at the same time. "Yes, I saw the tape."

"When? I didn't hear—"

"Headphones."

"I wish you hadn't—"

She shook her head. "I had to. But forget that now. Which lie were you thinking of?" She spit the words through her teeth.

It took me a minute. "You didn't want me to be a vampire."

"No, I absolutely did not."

"So that part wasn't a lie. And you've been so upset. . . . I know you feel bad about Charlie and my mom, but I guess I'm worried that part of it is because, well, you didn't expect to have me around very long, you weren't planning for that—" Her mouth flew open so fast that I put my whole hand over it. "Because if that's what it is, don't worry. If you want me to go away after a while, I can. You can show me what to do so I won't get either of us in trouble. I don't expect you to put up with me forever. You didn't choose this any more than I did. I want you to know that I'm aware of that."

She waited for me to move my hand. I did it slowly. I wasn't sure I wanted to hear what was next.

She growled softly and flashed her teeth at me—*not* in a smile.

"You're lucky I didn't bite you," she said. "The next time you put your hand on my mouth to say something so completely idiotic—and *insulting*—I *will*."

"Sorry."

She closed her eyes. Her arms wrapped around my waist and she leaned her head against my chest. My arms wound around her automatically. She tilted her face up so that she could look at me.

"I want you to listen to me very carefully, Beau. This—having you with me, getting to keep you here—it's like I've been granted every selfish wish I've ever had. But the price for everything I want was to take the exact same thing away from you. All of your life. I'm angry with myself, I'm

disappointed in myself. And I wish so much that I could bring that tracker back to life so that I could kill her myself, over and over and over again. . . .

"The reason I didn't want you to be a vampire wasn't because you weren't *special* enough—it was because you are too special and you deserve more. I wanted you to have what we all miss—a human life. But you have to know, if it were only about me, if there were no price for you to pay, then tonight would be the best night of my life. I've been staring forever in the face for a century, and tonight is the very first time it's looked beautiful to me. Because of you.

"Don't you ever again think that I don't want you. I will always want you. I don't deserve you, but I will always love you. Are we clear?"

It was obvious that she was being totally sincere. Truth echoed in every word.

A huge grin spread across my new face. "So that's okay, then."

She smiled back. "I'd say so."

"That was the one important thing I wanted to say—just, I love you. I always will. I knew that from pretty early in. So, with that being how things are, I think we can work the rest out."

I held her face in my hands and bent down to kiss her. Like everything else, this was so easy now. Nothing to worry about, no hesitation.

It felt strange, though, that my heart wasn't beating out a crazy drum solo, that the blood wasn't stampeding through my veins. But *something* was zinging through me like electricity, every nerve in my body alive. More than alive—like all of my cells were rejoicing. I only wanted to hold her like this and I would need nothing else for the next hundred years.

But she broke away, and she was laughing. This time her laugh was full of joy. It sounded like singing.

"How are you *doing* this?" she laughed. "You're supposed to be a newborn vampire and here you are, discussing the future calmly with me, smiling at me, *kissing* me! You're supposed to be thirsty and nothing else."

"I'm a lot of *else*," I said. "But I am pretty thirsty, now that you mention it."

She leaned up on her toes and kissed me once, hard. "I love you. Let's go hunt."

We ran together into the darkness that wasn't dark, and I was unafraid. This would be easy, I knew, just like everything else.

EPILOGUE: AN OCCASION

"ARE YOU SURE THIS WAS A GOOD IDEA?" SHE ASKED.

"I should be here."

"Tell me if it gets to be too much."

I nodded.

We were a hundred feet up in the branches of a tall hemlock, sitting side by side on a thick bough. I had my arm around her and she held my other hand in both of hers. I could feel her eyes on my face. Worried.

The branch swayed under us in the wind.

About two miles away, a caravan of cars was driving up Calawah Way with all their headlights on, though it was daytime. We were southeast and upwind, carefully situated so that we wouldn't be close to any people. It was too far for Edythe to be able to hear much of what anyone was thinking, but that was okay. I was sure I'd be able to guess most of it.

The first car was the hearse. Right behind it was the familiar cruiser. My mom was in the passenger seat, and Phil was in the back. I recognized almost everyone in the cars that followed.

I couldn't watch the actual funeral—it had been held inside a church building. The graveside service would have to be enough.

The hearse was overkill. There hadn't been enough of the body that they'd found inside the burned-out shell of my truck to need a casket. If I'd been able to consult with my parents, I would have told them not to waste the

money and just get an urn. But I guess if it made them feel better . . . Maybe they really wanted a grave to visit.

I'd seen where they were putting me—or what they thought was me. The hole was dug yesterday, right beside Grandma and Grandpa Swan. They'd both died when I was little, so I hadn't known them well. I hoped they didn't mind having a stranger next to them.

I didn't know the stranger's name. I hadn't wanted to know every detail about how Archie and Eleanor had faked my death. I just knew that someone roughly my size who had been recently interred had taken one last trip. I assumed that all the identifiers had been destroyed—teeth, prints, etc. I felt pretty bad for the guy, but I suppose he didn't mind. He hadn't felt anything when the truck veered into a ravine somewhere in Nevada and burst into flames. His family had already mourned. They had a tombstone with his name on it. Like my parents had now.

Charlie and my mom were both pallbearers. Even from this distance, I could see that Charlie looked twenty years older and my mom moved like she was sleepwalking. If she hadn't had the casket to hold on to, I'm not sure she would have been able to walk in a straight line across the cemetery lawn. I recognized the black dress she was wearing—she'd bought it for a formal party and then decided it aged her; she'd ended up going to the party in red. Charlie wore a suit I'd never seen before. I would guess it was old rather than new—it didn't look like it would button, and his tie was a little too wide.

Phil helped, too, and Allen and his dad, Reverend Weber. Jeremy walked behind Allen. Even Bonnie Black held on to one of the brass handles while Jules pushed her chair.

In the crowd, I saw almost every person I knew from school. Most were in black, and lots of them were holding each other and crying. It kind of surprised me—I didn't know many of them very well. I guessed they were just crying because it was sad in general, someone dying when they were only seventeen. It probably made them think about their own mortality and all of that.

One group of people stood out—Carine, Earnest, Archie, Jessamine, Royal, and Eleanor, all in light gray. They held themselves straighter than anyone else, and even from a distance their skin was obviously different . . . at least to a vampire's eyes.

It all seemed to take a really long time. Lowering the casket, the reverend giving some kind of speech—a sermon?—my mom and dad each throwing a flower into the hole after the casket, everyone awkwardly forming the obligatory line to speak to my parents. I wished they would let my mom leave. She was sagging into Phil, and I knew she needed to lie down. Charlie was holding up better, but he looked brittle. Jules wheeled Bonnie over so that she was behind him, a little to the side. Bonnie reached forward and took Charlie's hand. It looked like that helped some. This put Jules in a position where I could see her face really well, and I kind of wished I couldn't.

Carine and the rest of the Cullens were near the end of the line. We watched as they made their way slowly to the front. They were quick with my mom—they'd never met her before. Archie brought a chair up for my mom to sit in, and Phil thanked him; I wondered if Archie had seen that she was going to fall.

Carine spent more time with Charlie. I knew she was apologizing for Edythe's absence, explaining that she'd been too distraught to come. This was more than just an excuse for Edythe to be with me today, it was laying groundwork for the next school year, when Edythe would continue to be so distraught that Earnest would decide to homeschool her.

I watched as Bonnie and Jules left while Charlie was still talking to Carine. Bonnie threw a dark glance back at the Cullens, then suddenly stared in my direction.

Of course she couldn't see us. I glanced around, trying to figure out what she was looking at. I realized that Eleanor was looking at us, too—she had no trouble spotting us, and she was trying very hard not to smile; Eleanor never took anything seriously. Bonnie must have wondered what Eleanor was staring at.

Bonnie looked away after a few seconds. She said something to Jules. They continued out to their car.

The Cullens left after the Blacks. The line dwindled, and finally my parents were free. Phil took my mom away quickly; the reverend gave them a ride. Charlie stayed alone while the funeral home employees filled the hole in. He didn't watch. He sat in the chair that my mom had used and stared away to the north.

I felt my face working, trying to find the expression that went with my grief. My eyes were too dry; I blinked against the uncomfortable feeling. When I took my next breath, the air hitched out of my throat, like I was choking on it.

Edythe's arms wrapped tight around my waist. I buried my face in her hair.

"I'm so sorry, Beau. I never wanted this for you."

I just nodded.

We sat like that for a long time.

She nudged me when Charlie left, so I could watch him drive away.

"Do you want to go home?" she asked.

"Maybe in a little while."

"All right."

We stared at the mostly empty cemetery. It was starting to get darker. A few employees were cleaning up chairs and trash. One of them took away the big picture of me—my school picture from the beginning of junior year, back in Phoenix. I'd never liked that one much. I hardly recognized the boy with the uncertain blue eyes and the halfhearted smile. It was difficult to remember being him. Hard to imagine how he must have looked to Edythe, back in the beginning.

"You never wanted this for me," I said slowly. "What did you want? How did you see things happening—going with the fact that I was always going to be in love with you?"

She sighed. "Best-case scenario? I hoped that . . . I would get strong enough that we could be together while you were human. That we could be . . . something more than just boyfriend and girlfriend. Someday, if you didn't outgrow me, more than just husband and wife. We wouldn't be able to grow old together, but I would have stayed with you while you grew old. I would have been with you through all the years of your life." She paused for a second. "And then, when your life was over . . . I wouldn't have wanted to stay without you. I would have found a way to follow."

She looked startled when I laughed. It wasn't a very robust laugh, but I was surprised that it felt good.

"That was a really, really horrible idea," I told her. "Can you imagine? When people thought I was your dad? Your *granddad*? I'd probably get locked up."

She smiled hesitantly. "That wouldn't have bothered me. And if anyone had locked you up, I would have busted you out."

"But you would have married me?" I asked. "Really?"

Now she smiled wider. "I still will. Archie's seen it."

I blinked a few times. "Wow. I'm . . . super flattered. You would really marry *me*, Edythe?"

"Is that a proposal?"

I thought for half a second. "Sure. Sure it is. Will you?"

She threw her arms around me. "Of course I will. Whenever you want."

"Wow," I said again. I hugged her back, and kissed the top of her head. "I think I could have done better with the other version, though."

She leaned back to look at me, and her face was sad again. "Any other way ended here, too."

"But there could have been . . . a better goodbye." I didn't want to think about what my last words to Charlie were, but they were constantly on my mind. It was the biggest regret I had. I was glad the memory wasn't sharp, and I only hoped it would fade more with time. "What if we *had* gotten married? You know, graduated together, put in a few years at college, then had a great big wedding where we invited everyone we knew? Let them all see us happy together. Give really sappy speeches—have a reason to tell everyone how much we love them. Then go away again, back to school somewhere far away. . . ."

She sighed. "That sounds nice. But you end up with a double funeral in the end."

"Maybe. Maybe we'd be really busy for a year, and when I'm a mature vampire and all under control, I could see them again. . . ."

"Riiiight," she said, rolling her eyes. "And then all we have to worry about is never aging . . . and getting on the bad side of the Volturi. . . . I'm sure *that* would end well."

"Okay, okay, you're right. There's no other version."

"I'm sorry," she said quietly again.

"Either way, though, Edythe. If I hadn't been dumb enough to run off and meet that tracker"—she hissed, but I kept talking—"it would only have delayed things. We still end up here. *You're* the life I choose."

She smiled—slowly at first, but then suddenly her smile was huge and

dimpled. "It feels like my life never had a point until I found you. You're the life I was waiting for."

I took her face in my hands and kissed her while the branch swayed back and forth under us. I never could have imagined a life like this. There was a heavy price to pay, but one I would have chosen to pay even if I'd had all the time in the world to consider.

We both felt it when her phone vibrated in her pocket.

I figured it would be Eleanor, sarcastically wondering if we'd gotten lost on our way back, but then Edythe answered the phone, "Carine?"

She listened for just one second, her eyes flying open. I could hear Carine's voice trilling at top speed on the other end. Edythe shoved off the branch, phone still in hand.

"I'm coming," she promised as she fell toward the ground, breaking her fall with a branch here and there. I swung down quickly after her. She was already running when I hit the ground, and she didn't slow for me to catch up.

It must be really serious.

I ran flat out, using all the extra strength that I had because I was new. It was enough to keep her in sight as she sprinted across the most direct route back to the house. My strides were almost three times as long as hers, but still, chasing her was like chasing a bolt of lightning.

It was only when we were close to the house that she let me catch up.

"Be careful," she warned me. "We have visitors."

And then she was off again. I pushed myself even harder to try to match her. I didn't have a positive perception of *visitors*. I didn't want her to meet them without me next to her.

I could hear snarling before we were at the river. Edythe kept her leap low and straight, hurtling up the lawn. The metal shutters were down across the glass wall. She ran around the south end of the house. I was on her heels the whole way.

She darted over the railing onto the porch. All the Cullens were there, huddled into a tight, defensive cluster. Carine was a few steps in front of them, though I could tell no one was happy to have her there. She was leaning toward the steps, staring forward, a pleading look on her face. Edythe lunged to her side, and something snarled in the darkness in front of the house.

I launched myself onto the porch, and Eleanor yanked my arm back when I tried to go to Edythe.

"Let her translate," Eleanor murmured.

Ready to rip out of her hands—not even Eleanor was strong enough to stop me while I was so young—I looked out past Carine to see the vampires we were facing. I'm not sure what I was expecting. A large group, maybe, since the Cullens seemed so defensive.

I wasn't prepared to see three horse-sized *wolves*.

They weren't growling now—all of their massive heads were up, their noses pointing at me.

The one in the lead—pitch-black and larger than either of the others, though they were both three times bigger than I'd ever dreamed a wolf could get—took a step forward, his teeth bared.

"Sam," Edythe said sharply. The wolf's head swung around to face her. "You have no right to be here. We haven't broken the treaty."

The black monster-wolf snarled at her.

"They didn't attack," Carine said to Edythe. "I don't know what they want."

"They want us to leave. They were trying to drive you out."

"But *why?*" Carine asked.

The wolves seemed to be listening intently to every word. Could they understand?

"They thought we broke the treaty—that we killed Beau."

The big wolf growled, long and low. It sounded like a saw being dragged over chain-link.

"But—," Carine began.

"Obviously," Edythe answered before she could finish. "They still think we broke the treaty—that we chose to change him ourselves."

Carine looked at the wolves. "I can promise you, that's not how this happened."

The one Edythe called Sam kept up the long growl. Flecks of saliva dripped from his exposed fangs.

"Beau," Edythe murmured. "Can you tell them? They aren't going to believe us."

I'd been frozen solid this whole time. I tried to shake off the surprise as I moved to stand by Edythe.

"I don't understand. What are they? What treaty are you talking about?" I whispered the words fast, but it was obvious from the wolves' alert ears and watchful eyes that they were listening. Wolves that understood English? Eleanor had said Edythe was translating. Did she speak wolf?

"Beau," Edythe said in a louder voice. "These are the Quileute wolves. You remember the story?"

"The—" I stared at the massive animals. "They're *were*wolves?"

The black wolf growled louder, but the dark brown one in the back blew out a funny huff that sounded almost like a laugh.

"Not exactly," Edythe said. "A long time ago, we made a treaty with another pack leader. They think we've violated it. Can you tell them how you were transformed?"

"Uh, okay . . ." I looked at the black wolf, who seemed to be in charge. "I'm, uh, Beau Swan—"

"She knows who you are. You met Sam once—at the beach in La Push."

She. The cloudy human memories distracted me for a short second. I remembered the tall woman at La Push. And Jules saying that the wolves were her sisters. That her great-great-grandmother had made a treaty with the cold ones.

"Oh," I said.

"Just explain to her what happened."

"Right." I looked at the wolf again, trying to picture the tall woman somehow inside it. "Uh, a few weeks ago, there was a tracker—er, a vampire tracker—who came through here. She liked the way I smelled. The Cullens told her to back off. She left, but Edythe knew she was planning to try to kill me. I went back to Phoenix to hide out till the Cullens could . . . well, take care of her, you know. But the tracker figured out where I was and caught up to me. It was a game to her, a game with the Cullens—I was just a pawn. But she didn't want to just kill me. She . . . I guess you could say she was playing with her food. The Cullens found me before she could kill me, but she'd already bitten me. Hey—do we still have the video?" I glanced over at Edythe, who was staring at the wolves. She shook her head. I turned back to Sam. "That's too bad. The tracker was filming the whole thing. I could have shown you exactly what happened."

The wolves looked at each other. Edythe's eyes were narrowed as she

concentrated on what they were thinking. Suddenly the black wolf was staring at her again.

"That's acceptable," Edythe said. "Where?"

The black wolf huffed, and then all three were backing away from the house. When they got to the edge of the trees, they turned and ran into the forest.

The Cullens all converged on Edythe.

"What happened?" Carine asked.

"They aren't sure what to do," Edythe said. "They were asked to clear us out. Sam is the actual chief of the tribe, but only in secret. She's not a direct descendant of the chief we made a treaty with. They want us to talk to the acting chief, the true great-granddaughter of the last wolf-chief."

"But—wouldn't that be *Bonnie?*" I gasped.

Edythe looked at me. "Yes. They want to meet at a neutral location so that Bonnie can see you and make the call."

"*See* me? But I can't get that close. . . ."

"You can do it, Beau," Edythe said. "You're the most rational newborn I've ever seen."

"It's true," Carine agreed. "I've never seen someone adapt so easily. If I didn't know better, I'd say you were a decade old."

It wasn't that I thought they were lying—just that maybe they didn't get the magnitude of what they were proposing. "But it's *Bonnie*. She's my dad's best friend. What if I hurt her?"

"We'll be there," Eleanor said. "We won't let you do anything stupid."

"Actually . . . ," Edythe said.

Eleanor looked at her, shocked.

"They asked that we bring no more than their pack—only three. I already agreed. Beau has to be one, I have to be one, and the other needs to be Carine."

It was clear Eleanor was hurt.

"Is that safe?" Earnest asked.

Edythe shrugged. "It's not an ambush."

"Or they hadn't decided to make it one. Not yet," Jessamine said.

She was standing protectively by Archie, and there was something wrong with him. He looked a little dazed.

"Archie?" I asked. I'd never seen him look like . . . like he was behind things instead of ahead of them.

"I didn't see them," he whispered. "I didn't know they were coming. I can't see now—I can't see this meeting. It's like it doesn't exist."

I could see that this was news only to me. The others had heard it before we'd arrived, and Edythe had already picked it out of his head.

"What does that mean?" I asked.

"We don't know," Edythe answered sharply. "And we don't have time to figure it out now. We want to be there when they arrive. We don't want them to have a chance to change their minds."

"It will be fine," Carine said to the others, her eyes on Earnest. "The wolves are just trying to protect the people here. They're heroes, not villains."

"They think *we're* villains," Royal pointed out. "Heroes or not, Carine, we still have to accept that they're our enemies."

"It doesn't have to be that way," Carine whispered.

"And it doesn't matter either way tonight," Edythe said. "Tonight Beau needs to explain to Bonnie so that we don't have to make the choice between leaving Forks and raising suspicions, or getting into a fight with three barely legal wolves who are just trying to protect their tribe."

"Archie can't see if you'll be in danger," Jessamine reminded her.

"We'll be fine. Bonnie won't want to hurt Beau."

"I'm not sure that's true now. And I know she won't have any problem watching *you* get hurt."

"I can hear the wolves just fine. They won't take us by surprise."

"Tell us where to go," Eleanor said. "We'll keep our distance and only come in if you call."

"I promised. There's no reason to go back on my word. We need them to see that they can trust us, now more than ever. No!" Edythe said as Jessamine apparently thought of another argument. "We don't have time. We'll be back soon."

Eleanor grumbled, but Edythe ignored her.

"Beau, Carine, let's go."

I took off after her, and I could hear Carine do the same. Edythe didn't run as fast this time, and we both easily kept up.

"You seem very confident," Carine said to Edythe.

"I got a good look at their minds. They don't want this fight, either. There are eight of us. They know they won't win if it comes to actual bloodshed."

"It can't. I won't hurt them."

"I'm not in disagreement with that. But it would cause problems, if we left now."

"I know."

I listened, but my thoughts were far away, thinking about Bonnie and Charlie and the fact that I should be nowhere near human beings right now. I'd heard plenty from the others about the newborn years, especially Jessamine, and I wasn't ready to try to be the first exception to the rule. Sure, I hadn't had a hard time picking up most things, and everyone was surprised by how . . . *calm* I was, but this was different. Edythe had been very careful to make sure I was never tested when it came to the most important thing—not killing anyone. And if I screwed up tonight, not only would I destroy my father's world—he needed a friend now like he never had before—but I'd also ignite some kind of war between the Cullens and the giant werewolves.

I'd never felt clumsy in this new body, but suddenly that same sense of impending doom was hanging over me. Here was my chance to mess things up in a really spectacular way.

Edythe led us northeast. We crossed the freeway where it turned east toward Port Angeles and continued due north for a short time, following a smaller road. Edythe stopped in a wasteland on the side of the dark road, a large clearing recently made by loggers.

"Edythe, I don't think I can do this."

She took my hand. "We're upwind. Carine and I will try to stop you if something happens. Just remember not to fight us."

"What if I can't control it? What if I hurt *you*?"

"Don't panic, Beau, I know you can do this. Hold your breath. Run away if it gets bad."

"But Edythe—"

She put her finger to her lips and stared southward.

It wasn't long before a set of headlights turned into view.

I was expecting the car to pass. After all, the wolves wouldn't even fit inside the little sedan. But it slowly came to a stop not far from where

we waited, and I realized it was Bonnie inside, and someone else in the driver's seat.

Then two of the wolves were there, coming from the forest on the other side of the road. They split to move around the car on either side; it looked protective. The woman in the driver's seat got out and came around to get Bonnie. I was sure it wasn't Sam, though her hair was just as short. I stared at her, wondering if I'd met her on the beach, too, but she didn't look familiar. Like Sam, she was tall and looked strong.

Clearly she didn't just look strong. She picked Bonnie up in her arms and carried her like the older woman weighed nothing. Kind of like the way the Cullens had thrown me around as if I were a feather pillow. Maybe the wolves—because obviously this was the gray wolf who was missing from the original trio—were stronger than normal humans, too.

Sam and the dark brown wolf led the way as the tall woman carried Bonnie behind them. Sam stopped a good thirty yards away from where we stood.

"I can't see as well as you," I heard Bonnie say tartly. Sam prowled another ten yards forward.

"Hello, Bonnie," Carine said.

"I can't see, Paula," Bonnie complained again. Her voice sounded rough and weak to me; I'd been listening to no one but vampires for a month. The half-wolf, half-human pack moved slowly forward until they were only ten yards away. I held my breath, even though the light wind still blew from behind me.

"Carine Cullen," Bonnie said coldly. "I should have put it together sooner. It wasn't till I saw you at the funeral that I realized what had happened."

"But you were wrong," Edythe said.

"That's what Sam says," Bonnie answered. "I'm not sure she's right." Bonnie's eyes flickered to me, and she shuddered.

"All we have is Beau's word and our own. Will you believe either?" Edythe asked.

Bonnie harrumphed, but didn't answer.

"Please," Carine said, and her voice was much kinder than either of the others'. "We've never hurt anyone here. We won't start now. It would be better for us not to leave immediately, otherwise we would go without an argument."

"You don't want to look guilty," Bonnie agreed sarcastically.

"No, we would rather not," Carine said. "And in truth, we are not in breach."

Bonnie looked at me. "Then where is Beau? Do you expect me to believe he's inside that thing that bears some slight resemblance to him?" Hurt was strong in her voice, but so was hate. I was surprised by her reaction. Did I really seem so different? Like *I* wasn't even here?

"Bonnie, it's me," I said.

She winced at my voice.

I was out of air. I gripped Edythe's hand and took a shallow breath. Still upwind, it was okay.

"I know I look and sound a little different, but I'm still *me*, Bonnie."

"So you say."

I raised my free hand helplessly. "I don't know how to convince you. What I told Sam was true—another vampire bit me. She would have killed me, too, except that the Cullens got there in time. They didn't do anything wrong. They were always trying to protect me."

"If they hadn't gotten involved with you, this would never have happened! Charlie's life wouldn't be broken in pieces—you'd still be the boy I knew."

I'd had this argument before, and I was prepared. "Bonnie, there's something you didn't know about me. . . . I used to smell *really* good to vampires."

She flinched.

"If the Cullens hadn't been here, those other vampires would still have come to Forks. They might have killed more than me while they were here, but I can promise you, if Charlie had survived, he would be missing me just the same. And there would be nothing left of the boy you used to know. You might not be able to see it, but I'm still here, Bonnie."

Bonnie shook her head, less angry, though, I thought. More sad. She looked at Carine. "I'll concede that the treaty is intact. Will you tell me your plans?"

"We'll stay here another year. We'll leave after Edythe and Archie graduate. It will look natural that way."

Bonnie nodded. "All right. We'll wait. I apologize for our infraction tonight. I . . ." She sighed. "It was a mistake. I was . . . overwrought."

"We understand," Carine said softly. "There was no harm done. Maybe

even some good. It's better to understand each other as much as possible. Perhaps we could even talk again some—"

"The treaty is unbroken," Bonnie said in a hard voice. "Don't ask any more from us."

Carine nodded once.

Bonnie looked at me again and her face fell.

The breeze shifted.

Edythe and Carine both grabbed my arms at the same time. Bonnie's eyes went wide and then narrowed angrily. Sam snarled once.

"What are you doing to him?" Bonnie demanded.

"Protecting *you*," Edythe snapped.

The dark brown wolf took a half-step forward.

I took a quick breath, preparing myself to run if it was bad.

It was bad.

Bonnie's scent was like fire as it rushed down my throat, but it was more than just pain. It was a thousand times more appealing than any of the animals I'd hunted, not even in the same class. It was like someone waving a perfectly cooked filet mignon in front of me after I'd been living on stale crackers for a year. But more than that. I'd never tried drugs, but I thought Edythe's heroin comparison might be the closer version.

And yet, while I wanted to quench my thirst . . . badly . . . I knew instantly that I didn't *have* to. I wouldn't want to be any closer to her, no, but I was pretty sure I could handle it even then. I'd expected that when the newborn thing reared its ugly head, I wouldn't be able to think or decide. That I wouldn't be a person anymore, I'd be an animal.

I was still me. A very thirsty me, but me.

It only took half a second for me to figure all this out.

"No, don't worry, Bonnie," I said quickly. "I'm new to this, and they don't want me to . . . lose it, you know? But I'm okay."

Edythe slowly took her hand off my arm. Carine looked at me, her face kind of . . . awed.

Bonnie's eyes were still narrowed, but I could see she was confused, too. She hadn't expected me to act so much like myself, maybe. I decided to take advantage of the unexpected opportunity. I took another breath, and though it hurt just as badly, I knew I was fine.

"So it sounds like I won't have a chance to talk to you again," I said. "And I'm sorry it's that way. I guess I don't understand all the rules yet. But since you're here, if I could just ask one favor . . ."

Her face got hard again. "What?"

"My dad." My breath did that weird hitching thing again and I had to take a second before I could go on. Edythe put her hand on my back, but it was for comfort this time. "Please, just . . . take care of him? Don't let him be alone too much. I never wanted to do this to him . . . or my mom. That's the hardest part of all this. For me, it's fine. I'm good. If only there was any-thing I could do to make it better for them, I would, but I can't. Could you please watch out for him?"

Bonnie's face went blank for a minute. I couldn't read it. I wished I could hear like Edythe did.

"I would have done that regardless," Bonnie finally said.

"I know. I couldn't help asking, though. Do you think . . . you could let me know if there ever is something *I* can do? You know, from behind the scenes?"

She nodded slowly. "I suppose there may be some of Beau left after all."

I sighed. She was not going to believe it if I told her that all of me was left, that there was just more added on top.

"Is there anything else I can do for you?"

I froze for a tenth of a second, surprised by the offer. I could tell Edythe and Carine were surprised, too. But there *was* something more I wanted.

"If . . . ," I began. "Will you ever tell Jules about any of this?" I looked at the enormous wolves flanking Bonnie. "Or will it always be a secret?"

I didn't understand the look that crossed her face now. "Jules will know soon enough."

"Oh. Okay. Well, if she can know about me, can you tell her that I'm happy? It's not so bad, this whole vampire thing."

Bonnie shuddered. "I'll tell her what you said."

"Thanks, Bonnie."

She nodded, then she looked at the tall girl carrying her and jerked her chin back the way they'd come.

As they turned, I saw a tear escape the corner of her eye. The wolves backed away from us, too.

I hoped it wasn't the last time I would see Bonnie. I hoped that when Jules was in on the secret, I would be allowed to see her, too. Or at least talk to her again. I hoped that maybe someday the wolves would see that the Cullens were heroes, too.

Bonnie's car drove away. The wolves melted into the trees. I waited until Edythe was done listening to their departure.

"Tell me everything," I said.

She smiled. "I will when we get home—so I don't have to repeat all of it. There was a lot." She shook her head, like she was amazed.

We started running. Not so fast as before.

"Huh. Actual werewolves. This world is even weirder than I thought," I said.

"Agreed," Edythe said.

"That's right—you thought there weren't werewolves here anymore. That must have been kind of a shock."

"They weren't the most shocking thing I saw tonight."

I looked at her, then at Carine. Carine smiled like she was in on some joke.

"I mean, I knew you were special, Beau, but that was something else back there. Jessamine's not going to believe it."

"Oh. But . . ." I stared at her. "You said you knew I could do this."

She dimpled. "Well, I was pretty sure the wind would hold steady."

Carine laughed, then she exchanged a glance with Edythe. She sped up as Edythe slowed. In a second, we were alone.

I kept pace with Edythe, and stopped when she stopped. She put her hands on either side of my face.

"It's been a long day. A hard one. But I want you to know that you're extraordinary, and I love you."

I pulled her tight against me. "I can handle anything as long as you're with me."

She wrapped her arms around my neck. "Then here I will stay."

"Forever," I said.

"Forever," she agreed.

I leaned down until my lips found hers.

Forever was going to be amazing.

AFTERWORD

⤝ ⤞

We meet again, gentle reader.

I know it's a lot, to expect you to read both a foreword and an afterword, but there are a few things I wanted to say that I couldn't include in the beginning without spoiling the fun of your read.

So, obviously, I have cheated. I did not stay true to the original story in the conclusion of my swap, and I am not sorry. It was exciting, and I very much enjoyed writing the alternate ending.

But let me be quick to say, the fact that Beau becomes a vampire has nothing at all to do with the fact that he is a boy, not a girl. This change also does not mean that I prefer it to the original or think that the original was "wrong." This has always just been the big *what if?*, and I wanted to see what it would *feel* like if *Twilight* had been the end of the story. If, like Beau, Bella had left the airport just five minutes earlier.

There's a lot of happiness in Beau and Edythe coming together, in taking away the stumbling block between them, so much earlier. But there's also great sadness. As a human, Bella had to endure a lot more pain than Beau did, but in the end I know she would tell you it was all worth it. Beau will be fine—more than fine, he'll be very happy—but he'll always have the one big regret. Bella was able to put her house in order, and she's confident she got the best version of the story.

So that is the end of Beau and Edythe's story. You are free to imagine the rest—when, where, and how they get married . . . what Victor might try in order to get revenge . . . what Beau and Jules will say to each other when they meet again . . . if Beau and Royal ever become friends . . . whether the Volturi led by Sulpicia are a more benign, less corrupt organization (*I* think so). . . .

I hope you've enjoyed a different look at *Twilight* that really isn't very different at all (except for the end, which I don't apologize for).

Again, thank you for everything you've meant to me in the last ten years.

Thank you!
Stephenie

P.S. I didn't make a playlist for this one as I usually do, because the music I'm listening to now didn't exist in 2005, when the story begins, and that felt off. But if you are interested, the "sound track" inside my head for this one is basically three albums: *Royal Blood* by Royal Blood, *Seeds* by TV on the Radio, and *2.0* by Big Data.

STEPHENIE MEYER'S

the
twilight
saga

Twilight

New Moon

Twilight: The Graphic Novel
Volume 1

Twilight: The Graphic Novel
Volume 2

The Twilight Saga:
The Official Illustrated Guide

The Short Second
Life of Bree Tanner

Eclipse

Breaking Dawn

life and death

TWILIGHT REIMAGINED

STEPHENIE MEYER